Return to Budapest

Return to Budapest

a novel

*To Jake
our wonderful
"Friday Friends"
Thank you for
coming! I hope
you'll enjoy
the journey!*

Barbara E. Filo

Barbara E. Filo

SAN JUAN
PUBLISHING

SAN JUAN PUBLISHING
P.O. Box 923
Woodinville, WA 98072
425-485-2813
www.sanjuanbooks.com

© 2012 by Barbara E. Filo

Publisher: Michael D. McCloskey
Cover Design and Section Icons: Elizabeth Ward
Interior Design and Production, Cartography: Jennifer Shontz
Editor: Sherrill Carlson

Photo Credits: *Front cover composite photo—Hungarian Parliament Building; Palace; Chain Bridge; Lake Balaton; Back cover photo—Lake Balaton.* All by Elizabeth Ward.

All rights reserved. No part of this publication may be reproduced, stored in a retrieval system or on a computer disk, or transmitted in any form or by any means, mechanical, photocopying, recording, or otherwise, without written permission of the publisher. Permission is given for brief excerpts to be published with book reviews in newspapers, magazines, catalogs, and websites.

Library of Congress Control Number: 2012943898
ISBN: 978-0-9858897-0-8

First Printing 2012
10 9 8 7 6 5 4 3 2 1
Printed in United States of America

DEDICATION

—ɯ—

To
Robert
The best man I know

Wendy, Jessica, and Kate
Who read every word over and over from the beginning

And
Melinda Bodová
Who introduced me to Budapest

CONTENTS

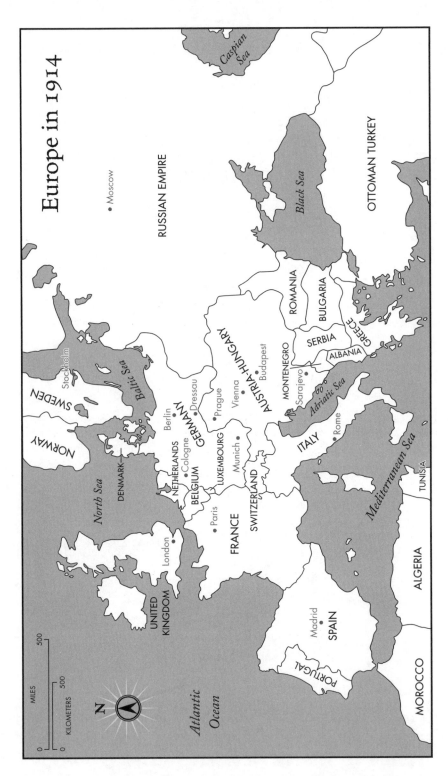

Europe in 1914

Europe in 1920

Atlantic Ocean

MILES
0   500
KILOMETERS
0   500

N

NORWAY
SWEDEN
FINLAND
Stockholm
Baltic Sea
ESTONIA
LATVIA
LITHUANIA

North Sea

UNITED KINGDOM
London

NETHERLANDS
DENMARK
Rostock
Berlin
EAST PRUSSIA
GERMANY
Cologne
BELGIUM
LUXEMBOURG
Dresbau
Prague
CZECHOSLOVAKIA
Dachau
Munich
Fürstenfeldbruck
SWITZERLAND
FRANCE
Paris

POLAND

SOVIET UNION
Moscow

Caspian Sea

Bratislava
Linz
Vienna
AUSTRIA
HUNGARY
Budapest

ROMANIA
BESSARABIA

Black Sea

YUGOSLAVIA
Adriatic Sea
ITALY
Rome

BULGARIA

ALBANIA
GREECE

TURKEY

Mediterranean Sea

PORTUGAL
SPAIN
Madrid

MOROCCO
ALGERIA
TUNISIA

9

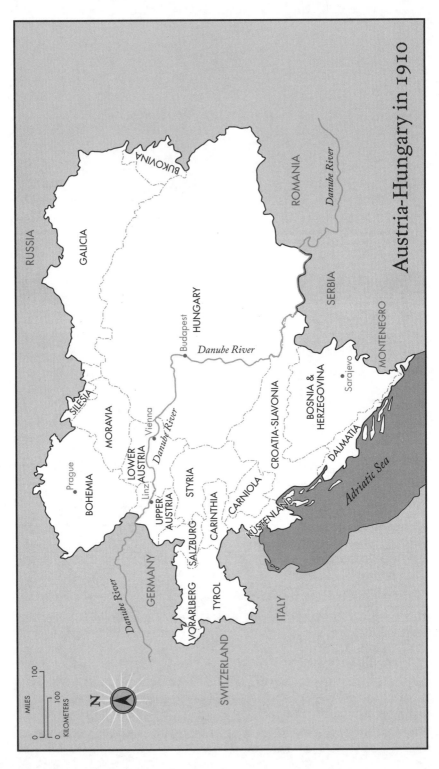

Austria-Hungary in 1910

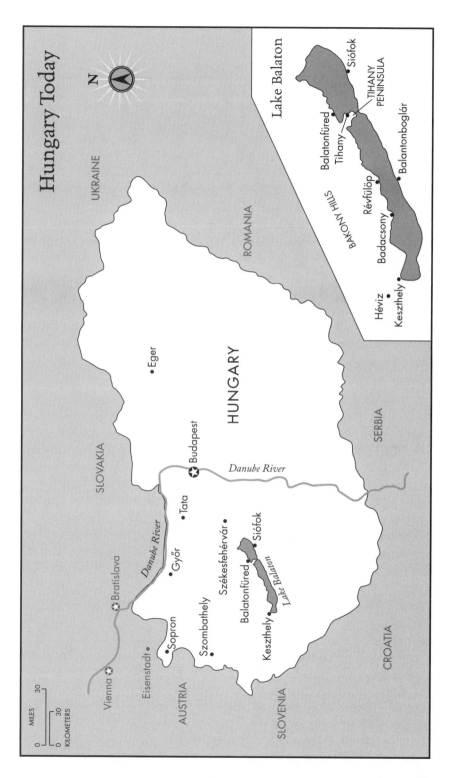

Hungary Today

N

Lake Balaton

Siófok
TIHANY PENINSULA
Balatonfüred
Tihany
Balatonboglár
BAKONY HILLS
Révfülöp
Badacsony
Héviz
Keszthely

UKRAINE

SLOVAKIA

ROMANIA

Vienna
Bratislava
Eisenstadt
Danube River
Győr
Tata
Eger
Budapest
Danube River

Sopron
Szombathely
Székesfehérvár
Balatonfüred
Siófok
Keszthely
Lake Balaton

AUSTRIA

SLOVENIA

CROATIA

SERBIA

HUNGARY

MILES
0   30
KILOMETERS
0   30

A LIST OF PRINCIPAL CHARACTERS

BOOK I

The von Esté Family

Leopold von Esté, *an Austro-Hungarian nobleman*

Tamás Tóth, *his valet and trusted friend*

Duke Louis von Esté and Duchess Maria, *Leopold's parents*

Princess Cili, *a member of the Austrian royal family, later Leopold's wife*

Stefan von Esté, *Leopold and Cili's son*

The von Házy Family

Christián von Házy, *Leopold's friend*

Count Francis von Házy and Countess Alexandra, *Christián's parents*

Countess Gabriele, *Cili's friend, later Christián's wife*

Rudolf von Házy, *Christián and Gabriele's son*

Emperor Franz Jószef, *the Hapsburg ruler of the Austro-Hungarian Empire*

Empress Elizabeth "Sisi," *married to Franz Jószef*

Other Characters:

Dr. Jakov Klein, *Visiting Professor at the Institute Pasteur in Paris*

Baron György Vadas, *a von Esté family friend*

Miguel Alejandro, *Napa Valley vintner*

Juanita Alejandro, *the vintner's daughter*

Elizabeth von Schrader, *Austrian noblewoman*

BOOK II

The von Esté Family

Duke Leopold von Esté, *Austro-Hungarian nobleman, head of family wine business*

Duchess Elizabeth "Betka" von Schrader, *Austrian noblewoman, Leopold's wife*

Baron Emmencht von Schrader and Baroness Beate, *Elizabeth's parents*

Stefan von Esté, *Leopold's son, an ardent supporter of King Karl*

Klára von Esté, *Leopold and Elizabeth's daughter, a pianist*

András von Werner, *Klára and Franz's son*

Marta Krause, *András's nanny*

Gita, *Klára's housekeeper and friend*

Hedy and Inge, *Klára's servants*

Tamás Tóth, *Leopold's valet and trusted friend*

Silva Marázova, *the von Esté's cook, married to Tamás Tóth*

Duchess Eugenia, *Leopold's older sister and a great writer of letters*

The von Házy Family

Count Christián von Házy, *Leopold's friend*

Count Francis von Házy and Countess Alexandra, *Christián's parents*

Countess Gabriele, *Christián's wife*

Count Rudolf "Dolf" von Házy, *Christián and Gabriele's son*

The Klein Family

Dr. Jakov Klein, *professor and Neolog Jew*

Mrs. Éva Klein, *pianist, also a Neolog Jew*

Magda, *the Klein's cook*

Sándor Klein, *the Klein's oldest son, a Hungarian soldier during the Great War*

Samuel Klein, *the Klein's second son, also a soldier in the Great War*

Ferenc and Abram Klein, *Jakov and Éva's sons, members of the resistance*

Eszter Klein, the Klein's older daughter, a Zionist

Rózsa Klein, *the youngest of six Klein children, a great friend of Klára's*

Pál Szabó, *Rózsa's boyfriend*

Other characters:
>   Baroness Renate von Werner, *Elizabeth's friend*
>>   Baron Franz von Werner, *Renate's son and later Klára's husband*
>   Baron György Vadas, *a von Esté family friend*
>>   Fábián Vadas, *the Baron's son*
>   King Karl (Charles IV), *monarch of Hungary*
>>   Queen Zita, *Karl's wife*
>   Admiral Miklós Horthy, *leader of the White Army, later Regent of Hungary*
>   Adolf Hitler, *Nazi leader, later German Chancellor*
>   Reinhard Heydrich, *S.S. officer*
>   Admiral Wilhelm Canaris, *German military intelligence director*
>   Hannelore Becker, *Klára's friend in Cologne*
>>   Max Segal, *Hannelore's boyfriend*
>   Countess Maria Maltzan, *member of the German resistance*
>   János Géza, *Rudolf's friend and fellow art student*
>   Yvette, *a Parisian girl*
>   Olivia Allen-Gainsborough, *member of the British secret intelligence service, MI6*
>   Clive Jeffreys, *also a member of MI6*

BOOK III

The von Esté Family
>   Duchess Elizabeth von Esté, *head of the family enterprise*
>   Tamás Tóth, *Elizabeth's associate in the business, in charge of von Esté household*
>>   Silva Tóth, *the von Esté's cook, married to Tamás Tóth*
>   Baroness Klára von Werner, *Elizabeth's daughter*
>   Baron Franz von Werner, *Nazi S.S. officer and Klára's husband*
>   András von Werner, *their son*
>>   Marta Krause, *András's nanny and a Nazi loyalist*
>   Hedy and Inge, *Klára's servants*
>   Duchess Eugenia, *Elizabeth's sister-in-law and a great writer of letters*

The von Házy Family
>   Count Rudolf von Házy, *a friend of the von Esté family and MI6 operative*
>   Countess Alexandra, *Rudolf's grandmother*

The Klein/Szabó Families

Rózsa Szabó, *Klára's childhood friend*

Pál Szabó, *Rózsa's husband*

József, Vera, and Sárika, *Rózsa and Pál's children*

Éva Klein (Mrs. Pap), *Rózsa's mother*

Magda, *the Klein family cook*

Ferenc and Abram Klein, *Rózsa's brothers, resistance fighters*

Other characters:

Clive Jeffreys, *Englishman and a member of MI6*

Olivia Allen-Gainsborough, *also a member of MI6*

János Géza, *Rudolf's friend in Paris, now in the French resistance*

Yvette, *Rudolf's friend in Paris, also in the resistance*

Joël Graund, *Yvette's boyfriend*

Countess Maria Maltzan, *member of the German resistance*

Fábián Vadas, *von Esté family friend, leader of a secret military unit*

Miklós Horthy, *Regent of Hungary*

Admiral Wilhelm Canaris, *German military intelligence director*

Reinhard Heydrich, *S.S. officer*

Adolf Hitler, *German chancellor*

Per Anger, *Swedish attaché in Berlin and later in Budapest*

Raoul Wallenberg, *also a Swedish diplomat*

Zsuzsanna Weisz, *Zionist and resistance fighter*

Theodore Rubin, *also a Zionist and resistance fighter*

Armin Stein, *another Zionist and resistance fighter*

BOOK I

Budapest, One Night in 1938

Early October, 1938

Thunderous explosions sent flames soaring into a fiery-orange sky. A deafening roar reverberated through his whole body. Black smoke choked the air. Flashes of red rose from the abyss surrounding him. A maze of brick walls stretched into the distance. He could see them through the smoke—Klára and András—standing atop one of those walls, the boy clinging to her. "Klára! András!" he called to them, "I'm here!" A feeling of panic rose inside his chest. He was breathless. She turned. He could see the terror in her green eyes. She and the boy moved toward him, but slowly, too slowly. He tried desperately to reach her. She stretched out her hand, but he felt frozen in place, his feet heavy, immobile. The boy slipped from the wall... she grabbed at the air to save him... but then the wall collapsed. They were gone.

Leopold awoke in a cold sweat, gasping for breath. Still gripped by the terrifying nightmare, he sat up in bed and took several deep breaths to calm his heart, beating so rapidly. He ran his fingers through his silvered hair and turned on the bedside lamp. He looked at the clock. *Not even nine o'clock... Elizabeth encouraged me to retire early. I was so tired then, but now I'm wide awake.*

Fejedelem raised his sleepy head and stared at Leopold.

"You have no trouble sleeping, do you old boy? No nightmares for you, only dreams of chasing rabbits in the old days. Let's you and I go down to the library. Perhaps I'll read awhile."

The handsome Vizsla hound rose, stretched, yawned, and followed at Leopold's heels, past Elizabeth's room, down the grand staircase, across the reception hall, through the parlor and into the library. Leopold turned on a single lamp, walked to the fireplace and used a poker to jab at the coals, even though no glimmer of heat remained. The room was chilly, so he wrapped a heavy shawl around his shoulders and poured himself a glass of *körtepálinka*, pear brandy, from an intricately carved crystal decanter. He moved from the fireplace to a window where he stood looking out toward Andrássy Avenue. By the street lamps he could see a light snow falling.

Leopold's thoughts turned to Klára and András and he spoke aloud to Fejedelem who sat nearby. "I must bring them back to Budapest as soon as possible, before that nightmare of mine becomes their reality. We'll encourage Rudolf to go to Berlin in my place to fetch them home. What terrible anxiety it is to have my daughter and grandson living in the midst of that evil muck! I should have done something about it years ago!"

Fejedelem rose from his spot and came to Leopold's side, seeming to sense his master's distress. Leopold stroked Fejedelem's smooth head and smiled down at him, "You're a good boy. You take such good care of me. I should think happier thoughts, remember better times."

"I can still envision Klára as a youngster, stretched out on the carpet in this very room looking at big picture books while her brother and Rudolf asked constant questions and spun that globe round and round."

Leopold moved from the window toward the shelves of books lining the room. His gaze fell upon several albums and an old memorabilia box sitting on a bottom shelf. He dragged a leather chair close to the shelf and pulled the oldest of the albums onto his lap.

Covered in burgundy velvet with brass hinges and a clasp, the album's big, heavy cover opened to reveal page after page of photographs, images on cabinet cards with names written in elegant script across the borders. He focused on three photographs—one of his parents, the Duke Louis von Esté and Duchess Maria of Moravia, sitting side by side in elaborately carved chairs; another of his dear sister, Eugenia, only eighteen years old, pictured with him, little Leopold, at age three leaning against her knee; and the third of their family castle, where he was born, with the town of Sopron spread out in the distance.

A flood of memories swept over Leopold as he held the three cards in his hands. He remembered his childhood spent in Sopron as the only child, since Eugenia was so much older. By the time he turned five she had married a German duke and moved to Cologne. Much of Leopold's time was spent with his Papa. He could still visualize standing beside Duke Louis on the castle wall as they surveyed the surrounding countryside. Far below stretched the von Esté vineyards, planted generations ago. Rows of vines followed the rolling landscape into the distance. Leopold could almost hear his father's voice addressing the vineyards as he stretched out his hand to the Kékfrankos and Traminer grapes, just beginning to ripen, and said, "These are the grapes that made the wines of Sopron famous."

As Leopold turned the album page he sighed at the image of a darling little boy dressed in a sailor suit, short pants with knee socks and shiny black shoes. The child stood beside a large carved wooden chair, his little hand on the chair's arm. In white ink and elaborate script, "Leopold 1879," was written across the bottom of the photograph. Surprisingly, Leopold had a very clear memory of that little boy and of that particular day.

Vienna, 1879

The little boy held his nanny's hand as they walked together in Hofburg Castle along a great hallway that seemed to stretch for miles. A wall of heavily draped windows lined one side of the hall; only a few opened draperies allowed him to see into the gardens where he would rather be. The other side presented deeply carved oak doors, one after another, the full length of the hall concealing…well, he had no idea what was behind them. His shoes squeaked as he walked on the shiny marble floor. Philomena jerked his arm, "Leopold, stop dragging your shoes. Pick up your feet, you are making unnecessary noise."

Philomena suddenly came to a stop across from one of those great floor-to-ceiling doors and told him to sit down. Leopold crawled up onto the velvet-cushioned bench and tried to be comfortable. Philomena sat next to him. They waited and watched the door across from them. Leopold tried to touch the floor with his toe, but even though he stretched his leg, his shoe would not quite reach. He slid off the cushion, making a tapping noise. Philomena frowned at him, "Stop fidgeting. Sit still."

He tried, but the wait seemed very long and she had to speak to him at least twice more. Suddenly the big door opened and it was his father who beckoned to him. Once again Leopold slid off the bench and walked to his father. Leopold stood as tall as a five year old could and looked up to his father's face. Duke Louis gave an encouraging smile to his son, put his finger to his lips, and ushered the child into the room.

Leopold was awestruck. There were many people in the darkened room, some he recognized and some he did not. They stood quietly, but smiled at him as he walked with his father across the carpeted floor. A beautiful basinet stood in a shaft of bright sunlight that streamed through an open drapery. Ruffles of taffeta, satin ribbons, lace, and rosettes covered the little bed. A canopy of netting fell in soft folds from a suspended golden crown. The Duke nudged Leopold toward the basinet. Leopold stood on tiptoe and peered into the mound of pink and white blankets. His father whispered to him, "Meet the Princess Cili, Leopold. When you grow up, she will be your wife."

The little boy was amazed. His father picked him up so he could see into the crib more easily. The baby looked up at him with her big blue eyes; her tiny bow-shaped lips blew little bubbles. Leopold thought she was beautiful; he smiled and said "pretty." Everyone in the room laughed and smiled and chatted quietly. Leopold stretched his hand toward Cili and touched her hand. She felt so soft. She curled her tiny fingers around his finger. Leopold made a small gasp and turned to the room of admirers with a big smile. He felt very proud.

—⚏—

Leopold still held the photograph, lost in memory, when the library door parted slightly and Tamás looked into the room through the opened door, "Is everything all right, Sir?"

"Yes, yes, Tamás, I just couldn't sleep…please, come in. I'm looking at our old photographs. Perhaps you can help me remember the stories that go with the pictures? I seem to be in a mood to remember the past."

"Of course, I would like very much to do that, but it's too cold in here for you. I'm going to get the fire going first. Go on with the pictures; just tell me about them while I work on this fire."

Tamás knelt at the fireplace as Leopold pointed to a photograph portraying a man and woman with a small child standing by a trellis of paprikas. They were dressed in traditional Hungarian costumes, including beautifully embroidered vests. "Here are your parents, Tamás." Leopold read their names reverently, "Gáspár and Ilonka Tóth. Ah, your good parents...greatly missed. They served our family well through all the years. I remember your Papa's paprikas strung on trellises to dry in the hot sun of late summer. Gáspár was famous in the region for those peppers."

Once the fire blazed again, Tamás pulled a big leather chair next to Leopold, "My mother used the brightest red ones in her recipes; especially in her famous *gulyás*, remember? Silva uses that recipe for her *gulyásleves*."

"Hmm, yes, delicious. Oh, Tamás, look at this one of us," Leopold smiled as he showed the *cabinet card* to Tamás. "Such handsome little boys we were!" He laughed, "How old do you think we are?"

Tamás looked at the photograph of himself and Leopold and smiled, "I think you must be about seven, making me eight or nine."

Leopold opened the memorabilia box and rummaged among the papers, "Here's an old hand-colored postcard of the lake." He read aloud the description on the card's back, "'Lake Balaton, the beautiful Hungarian Sea located approximately half the distance between Sopron and Budapest.' Remember those summers when we took the entire household from Sopron and moved to Balatonfüred? Of course in those early years, before our villa, we stayed in the old Promenade Hotel."

Tamás found another card and read from it, " 'Balatonfüred, Resort by the Lake—a charming little resort town on the northern bank of Lake Balaton, a favorite retreat for poets and writers, actors and musicians...offering every form of entertainment from concerts to dances to poetry readings...famous for its thermal mineral spring waters for drinking and for bathing to improve one's health.' Still all true," Tamás avowed as he picked up another postcard from the box depicting the tinted image of sailboats on the pale blue lake. "Of course, we cared little about the spa then. It was always the lake and surrounds that inspired us."

Leopold sighed once more as he turned the page to the next image. "A photograph of Rudolf's family," he announced as he read their names written around the margin, "the Count Francis and Countess Alexandra von Házy with Christián. Such a handsome family. Alexandra has always been an elegant woman—she is still."

"Yes, everyone thought so," Tamás agreed. "We were all quite young when we became friends—Christián, you, and I."

"We were the best of friends, loyal companions." Leopold's words had a far-away sound to them as he held a sepia photograph of three boys, all appearing to be around ten to twelve years old, arms draped over each others' shoulders. "We sailed and swam, we fished for *fogas* and *süllő*, we rode our ponies across the fields. Such bittersweet memories, Tamás, from so long ago."

Leopold rifled through images of Lake Balaton, letting some fall to the carpet. "Remember our excursions, exploring all those fantastic geological sites, our hikes on the trails, climbing the Badacsony rocks...exploring the caves, and the ancient Roman ruins near Veszprém? And those old castle ruins from the time of the Mongols? What fun we had! Oh, look at this: A photo of us after the Révfülöp to Balatonboglár swim race—so young and strong then."

On the next page appeared another handsome family—the Princess Cili and her parents, Prince Maximilian and Princess Margit, seated on throne-like chairs with pretty little Cili standing between them. Leopold thought about Cili's family also spending their summers at Lake Balaton, to escape the heat of Vienna. They, too, took suites of rooms at the Promenade Hotel.

Another album page held the image of Cili and her friend the Countess Gabriele standing outside the Promenade, dated 1889. Gabriele was Cili's dearest friend. The girls were much younger than the boys, so in those early days neither paid much attention to the other. Leopold smiled, thinking, *how much that lack of interest changed with time.*

From the memorabilia box, Tamás picked up an official looking *cabinet card*, the title written in an elegant script, "The Empress Elizabeth at Grassalkovich Mansion on her thirty-second birthday." "Ah, yes, the Empress Sisi," stated Tamás as he studied the photograph.

—✥—

Officially, Sisi was Empress Elizabeth, wife of Franz József, but to her friends and to subjects who loved her, she was Sisi, the extremely popular, beloved, and beautiful Empress of Austria. The Emperor Franz József met Sisi when she was only fifteen years old; he was supposed to marry her sister, but one look at the beautiful Sisi and he defied his family's wishes and became engaged to Sisi the very next day. The Emperor adored his wife and she him, but his mother, the Archduchess Sophie, never accepted Sisi, and made her life in the Viennese Court miserable. So, Sisi spent much of her time traveling to distant and exotic places. When she first accompanied Franz József on a spring retreat to the royal mansion in Gödöllő, she discovered a great love for all things Hungarian. From that time on, Empress Sisi made many visits to the mansion in Gödöllő and to Budapest.

On occasion, during the childhood of Leopold and Cili, they traveled with their mothers to Grassalkovich Mansion to visit the Empress for a week or so. Sisi's reputation as the most beautiful woman in the world was undisputed. Her voluptuous chestnut hair, particularly famous, fell in waves to her knees and required hours of work to arrange it in fashionable mounds and curls on her head. However, by the time the von Estés visited Gödöllő, Sisi was in her fifties and her famed beauty had begun to desert her. Fully aware of that fact, Sisi hid her face behind elegant fans or veils whenever she appeared in public. On her thirty-second birthday she declared no more portraits or photographs would be made of her.

—⚭—

"This image is the last one taken, the last official photograph," Tamás reminisced, "After this photograph, the world never saw her true image again. The myth of Sisi's beauty remains, almost a legend—*the Empress who never aged.*"

Leopold turned the album page to an image of his father, Duke Louis, who was standing beside his grape press at Sopron. Leopold remembered so clearly leaving the lake at each summer's end and returning to Sopron in time for the grape harvest and the winemaking process. *Then came the best times of all,* he thought, *hunting trips to the forests of the Burgenland. Trips planned by Papa and Count Francis to the von Házy manor house in Eisenstadt or to our castle at Sopron.*

"Remember the day this photo was taken?" Leopold ask as he showed Tamás the image, "Hunting Party with dogs at Eisenstadt Manor," depicting a large group of men with dogs and guns, their breath visible in the cold morning air.

"How could I ever forget?" Tamás exclaimed as he held the image, clearly recalling the day. "We were filled with excitement. Enormous breakfast of sausages and hams…dressed in layers against the cold mists of the forests…preparing our guns and ammunition…Duke Louis's Vizsla hounds prancing around anxiously. We were all nervous to get started!

"Here you are with Christián and me, just boys then." Tamás pointed to the figures in the photograph, "Count Francis and there's his faithful valet, László—still tending to the Countess after all these years—and my father next to yours."

"Look at this one of us." Leopold read the inscription, "'Leopold, Christián, and Tamás with their guns—Christián's twelfth birthday, 1886.' This is the very hunting trip when Christián lost his eye. Who could ever forget that day! This photograph was taken before the accident happened. See… Christián…no eye patch."

The two men shuddered with the memory.

"Here's another day I have always remembered," Leopold stated as he held another *cabinet card*. He read aloud the words written along the edge of the photograph, "Duke Louis and Leopold with the Emperor Franz József, August 1887, the Schönbrunn Summer Palace Gardens." Leopold let his mind embrace the memory of that day… *one of his life's favorite days.*

—⚭—

Every summer in August the von Estés returned to Vienna to celebrate the birthday of the Emperor, Franz József. Leopold always looked forward to the annual visit to Schönbrunn Palace for the parties, marvelous concerts, and breathtaking fireworks, all arranged to honor the Emperor.

Franz József became the Hapsburg Emperor in 1848 at the young age of eighteen. Just as emperors before him, Franz József faced great civil unrest from the Hapsburg province of Hungary. Many different ethnic groups clamored for equality; each one vying for its own national identity, language, and cultural traditions. Hungarians eager for their independence threatened revolution and demanded separation from Hapsburg Austria.

To settle the Hungarian problem, Franz József and the Hungarian leader, Ferenc Deák, arranged the complex Compromise of 1867, creating the Austro-Hungarian Empire, also called the Dual Monarchy. It made Franz József the Emperor of Austria and the Apostolic King of Hungary. The Emperor-King took great pride in the two capitals of his Austro-Hungarian Empire, Vienna and Budapest, both beautiful, vibrant, and progressive cities; each standing beside the magnificent Danube River.

The Compromise allowed Hungary to have an independent government and legislature in Budapest while Austria shared the management of Hungary's foreign affairs, defense, and financial matters. Although never perfect, the Compromise allowed for a peaceful period of co-existence between Austria and Hungary within a unified Empire.

August 1887

By 1887 Franz József still believed the Compromise to be his greatest accomplishment and he remained proud of his effort to bring peace and reconciliation between Austria and Hungary. Duke Louis von Esté, a true aristocrat and landowner with no particular occupation other than to serve his Emperor as confidant and advisor, admired Franz József, his ideals and accomplishments. In return, the Emperor valued Louis's counsel and friendship. Louie's close relationship with the Emperor filled Leopold with pride.

One hot August afternoon in the Schönbrunn Summer Palace Gardens, Leopold walked behind two powerful men, the Emperor and his father, at a respectful distance, but close enough to hear their conversation as they followed the graveled walkways around the vast formal gardens behind the palace. Leopold loved to listen to his father and the Emperor as they discussed politics and their progressive ideas.

On this particular day, the men were discussing Magyarization. Leopold was only thirteen, but he had heard his father discuss this subject many times and he knew by heart his father's philosophy in regard to Magyarization.

"When Count Széchényi first proposed the notion of Magyarization, nearly eighty years ago," stated Duke Louis, "he would not have imagined we would still be immersed in this debate and controversy."

"It seems the people will have to be dragged into the Modern Age," complained the Emperor. "I believe, as Széchényi did, that true liberty for the people will naturally follow economic progress and Magyarization seems to be the best path to that progress."

"Yes, common sense tells us that a nation is stronger if there is one official language—Hungarian—for all the peoples of Hungary! It is the logical thing to do, to demand that all peoples of Hungary—the Slavs, the Germans, the Armenians, the Transylvanians, the Romanians, the Serbs, the Jews, the Gypsies, the Turks—share one official language for all things—government, education, commerce, newspapers, geography, even religion," argued Louis, waving his arms.

"Hungary's minorities continue to desire self-determination, but, in my opinion, it is short-sighted to work against the Empire, against Magyarization," the Emperor said thoughtfully. "These malcontents cause nothing but disruption to progress."

"Magyarization has been working since 1867. Why do they want to destroy the progress we have made? I do not understand! So many have already assimilated, changed their personal and geographic names to reflect the Hungarian language. Why the resurgence of dissent?"

"The best thing about Széchényi's plan is its loyalty to the Hapsburgs," stated the Emperor. "He believed in the divine right of the king to retain power. Of course, I want fairness. I agree with the people that nobility should also pay taxes and even divest some of their land holdings—there *is* reason for that. The nobles have an obligation to serve as a model of justice," lamented the Emperor, "but the people must understand we can better rule if we are united as one. It is necessary for the rightful Hungarian King and Emperor to remain in power—I am the force of stability!"

"The purposes of Magyarization are righteous ones . . . to foster one national identity and to secure equal rights for all of Hungary's citizens," Louis stated firmly as he walked with determination at the side of the Emperor, "What can be the complaint?"

The Emperor paused, "Louis, you are a loyal friend and wise confidant." He stopped walking as he twisted a gold and sapphire ring from his finger. "I want you to have this as a symbol of our friendship." Franz József smiled, "Take it as a gift for you on my birthday."

Franz József turned toward Leopold, standing near the two great men; he winked at Leopold, "Someday, Louis, you may give this ring to Leopold when you tell him about our politics."

—⁓—

"Duke Louis knew history well. I remember on many occasions when we were children how the Duke enjoyed explaining his ideals to us," stated Tamás. "We listened carefully and believed the words he told us. It is a shame that Horthy and Imrédy were not listening. How they have corrupted the ideal of Magyarization," Tamás fretted.

"Yes, my father greatly admired the Emperor for his understanding and caring for *all* the people. It was always easy for me to understand the logic of Magyarization and now I wonder about our Regent and Prime Minister and their misunderstanding of its purpose. Magyarization unites us and, yet, allows us to be unique within the Empire. Magyarization is the way for each of us to distinguish ourselves. Now Horthy and Imrédy defile the ideal and use Magyarization to divide us! *Us*—the Magyars—and *them*, the others."

Tamás sadly agreed.

They turned their conversation from the heavy subject of Maygarization to a happier topic when Leopold picked up a beautifully decorated invitation and a hand-colored *cabinet card* depicting two lovely young girls dressed in stunning gowns: "Cili and Gabriele, the Anna Ball, July 27, 1895." The memory of that night so long ago brought a smile to Leopold as he began to reminisce.

1895

Every invitation included an explanation for the Anna Ball, Lake Balaton's most elegant event, held every July since the first, in 1825. The ball was hosted by the noble and devout Szentgyörgyi-Horváth family which originally presented the ball to honor St. Anna, the Blessed Mother of the Virgin Mary, for whom they named their daughter, Anna Krisztina. The ball is held on the Saturday closest to the feast day of St. Anna, always celebrated on July twenty-fourth.

The Ball provided the perfect event for aristocratic families summering at the lake to officially present their daughters for the first time. Since Cili and Gabriele both observed their sixteenth birthdays in 1895, they were eligible to attend. At last, something both of them had dreamt of since they were little girls. The two young women, Cili, the fair blonde, and Gabriele, the dark-haired one, made a spectacular impression on the guests who sat in the audience awaiting the grand promenade.

Cili wore a light blue gown of silk with matching dyed ostrich feathers in her hair while Gabriele's bejeweled gown was pink silk and lace. Stunning necklaces, birthday gifts from their fathers, encircled their throats—Cili's, brilliant blue sapphires arranged in flower shapes; Gabriele's, a threaded filigree design of dazzling green gems.

As Cili and Gabriele matured, they were both considered great beauties in turn-of-the-century Vienna. The two young women enjoyed a rich social life and could have chosen beaus from any of the many eligible European bachelors from fine houses. But both Cili and Gabriele had already found their mates— Leopold and Christián, their soul mates chosen for them by their parents. Fortunately for everyone, Leopold and Christián, both very handsome young men, were more than acceptable to Cili and Gabriele.

By 1895 Leopold and Christián were university students in Vienna, but they returned to Lake Balaton for the summer as usual. Tamás was absent from the lake that summer, traveling on his Grand Tour, a requirement for every gentleman's gentleman.

Leopold, tall, muscular, and athletic, wore his thick shock of black hair in the style of the day, smoothed straight back from his forehead, revealing deep-set green eyes shaded by dark expressive eyebrows. He had high cheekbones with deep, hollow-like clefts in his cheeks and a full black mustache over a broad smile. Leopold had worn that moustache since he was a teenager; it presented him as a much older, sophisticated man.

Leopold's love for the outdoors, particularly as a horseman, added to his healthy, robust appearance. With such a charming exterior and friendly smile, many expected a gregarious nature; however, Leopold was quite serious, observant, and thoughtful. He listened far more than he spoke. Though noted for his discrimination, Leopold was able to acquire a number of loyal friends; he never forgot a face or a name; he was known for his integrity, good judgment, and high ideals.

Next to Tamás, Leopold's closest friend was Christián von Házy. Christián always recognized his friendship with Leopold as an honor, although Leopold admonished him for saying such things. Of the three of them, Christián was considered the most handsome, exceptionally so by every young woman who happened into their presence. He was very tall, the tallest of the three, well over six feet, slender with dark brown hair that never stayed in place. Christián also wore a mustache although his was only a pencil-thin line across his upper lip. The most remarkable aspect of Christián's appearance was the black eye patch he wore over his right eye; it made him seem mysterious and a bit roguish, although in fact, he was a true gentleman with impeccable manners. The eye patch was usually a black one unless he was wearing a tuxedo, then Christián preferred to wear an emerald green satin patch. The emerald green color was Gabriele's favorite and whatever mattered to Gabriele mattered to Christián.

After several waltzes Christián and Gabriele walked from the ballroom out onto the terrace lit by Japanese lanterns. Christián kissed her hand and looked into her large brown eyes that engaged his so sincerely. He found Gabriele's beauty breathtaking; her long, thick hair, black as ebony, fell in deep waves onto her shoulders. She wore a lovely emerald and diamond necklace that her father had given her that afternoon for her sixteenth birthday. Christián's gaze followed his own fingers as they traced the delicate golden chain that lay against her skin. Their intimate moment was interrupted by Leopold and Cili who left the ball as well for a breath of fresh air. The four long-time friends shared their enthusiasm for the marvelous Anna Ball.

"Look, Cili…Leopold and Christián both have halos behind their heads," Gabriele laughed. The soft light from the Japanese lanterns created a radiant atmosphere. "It makes them look like angels, but we know what devils they really are!"

They all laughed as the boys twirled the girls around the terrace into the shadows, where they stole kisses and embraces just as Gabriele knew they would.

—⁂—

Leopold thought of his old friends and how over the years the families gathered for special occasions in Vienna, at Sopron and Eisenstadt, and of course, at Lake Balaton. They came to know each other so well. Their lives were good and carefree in the golden age of the Empire.

Tamás removed a gum band from around a packet of cabinet cards. The photograph on top, labeled "Leopold and Tamás in France, 1897–1898," showed two young men standing in a landscape of vineyards and distant hills. "Look at these memories, Leopold, of our adventures in France."

France, 1897–1898

After Leopold completed his university studies in Vienna, he and Tamás left Austria for the University of Paris where Leopold entered the Centre National de la Recherche Scientifique. It was there where they met Dr. Jakov Klein, a professor of chemistry at the Hungarian National Academy of Sciences in Budapest.

When Dr. Klein discovered Leopold's interest in viticulture, he encouraged Leopold to move from the Recherche Scientifique to the Institute Pasteur where Klein was teaching as a visiting professor. Professor Klein was engaged in experiments regarding viticulture methods of fermentation and pasteurization; experiments inherently interesting to Leopold. Any exploration that could enhance his knowledge of grapes and winemaking intrigued him. So, it was not difficult for Klein to convince Leopold to move to the Institute.

The Institute Pasteur was founded in honor of the Frenchman, Louis Pasteur, who studied the processes of the natural fermentation of wine in the 1850s. Of course, human beings had been engaged in winemaking since ancient times without knowing anything about the chemistry of fermentation or being aware of the need for pasteurization. However, Pasteur's discoveries of these processes were ultimately essential for the modern age of growing grapes and making wine. This was the science that truly fascinated Leopold and he was eager to learn as much as he could in preparation for taking over his father's vineyards.

"My father loves his vineyards and winemaking," Leopold informed Jakov Klein, "he is an expert vintner, but he approaches everything about the grapes and winemaking as more of a leisurely diversion than occupation. I see myself differently. I'm a modern man and I recognize that changes are occurring throughout Europe. The age of idle aristocracy is fast coming to a close and the time for the businessman is at hand.

"Those are the reasons I want a serious preparation as a vintner so I can take my father's hobby to a higher level." Leopold laughed, "Ultimately, I intend to become the consummate businessman who makes vast amounts of money bottling Hungarian wines that will be famous throughout Europe."

In the summer Leopold and Tamás accompanied Dr. Klein to Burgundy, southeast of Paris, to study the methods and styles of the French winemakers. The region had an ancient history of winemaking from pre-Roman times. Until the French Revolution, the Cistercian monks and French nobility owned the vineyards of Burgundy. After the revolution, according to the Napoleonic Code, all land holdings were divided equally among family heirs. By 1898 the vineyards of Burgundy were broken into small domains, each held by multiple owners.

The three men stood on the rise of a hill with a panoramic view of the French landscape behind them. They were dressed in similar fashion; slacks with white shirts, sleeves rolled up, ties blowing in the breeze, and straw hats. A farmer took their photograph with Leopold's camera. All three had broad smiles under various styles of mustaches.

The men traveled through the lovely Burgundy *terroir*—a vista of woodlands and green fields with sunflowers and red poppies, white Charolais cattle grazing in green pastures, and distinctively colored tiled rooftops on houses, churches, and châteaux of the villages. The vineyards spread across sloping hills, their vines leafy green and heavy with full clusters of grapes maturing in the warm sunshine.

They learned in great detail about the devastating disaster of the *Phylloxera* blight that nearly destroyed the vineyards of France; about the aphid that attacks the roots of the vine, destroying it and whole vineyards. A long trial and error process finally saved the French grapes shortly before their arrival in Burgundy.

Leopold, Tamás, and Dr. Klein formed a close friendship over shared suppers of Boeuf Bourguignon, delicious cheeses, mustards, and ginger breads.

Dr. Klein spoke often of the family he left in Budapest; he missed them very much. He described his wife Éva with pride as he explained how she had given up her career as a concert pianist with the Budapest Symphony to marry him and raise a family. Jakov proudly showed pictures of the beautiful Éva and their three children, Sándor, Samuel, and Ferenc.

Leopold was fascinated to learn that Dr. Klein, too, was a supporter of Magyarization. Being a Neolog Jew, Klein embraced the idea of Magyarization as a way for the Jewish community to assimilate into Hungarian life.

Dr. Klein said to his new friends, "Magyarization allows the Jew and all other ethnic groups to maintain their own religious practices and traditions, while one language unites us. I believe in the promise of Magyarization. If the Jews adopt the Hungarian language and culture they can be accepted as equal citizens of Hungary."

Leopold and Tamás agreed with him wholeheartedly.

In late August, Leopold received a letter from Cili:

Dearest Leopold: Mother and I will be in Geneva to visit the Empress for a few days and then we are staying for a while after... please join us for a holiday. You have been working so hard, darling, and you need to have some fun. Please make me the happiest girl at Lake Geneva and come as soon as you can. All my love, Cili

Leopold refolded the letter and announced that he and Támás would go to Geneva in early September. Tamás arranged rail passage for the two of them from Dijon to Geneva.

Switzerland, 1898

Leopold and Tamás arrived in Geneva on the eighth of September. The day, glorious with clear blue skies and a warm breeze, created a spectacular vision of Geneva, nestled on the banks of the lake. As the train pulled into the station, Leopold leaned out the window to catch a glimpse of Cili. He had not seen her since Christmas. When Leopold finally saw her on the platform, he shouted, "There she is! Look, she is like a bright light floating through the old gray station."

That is how Leopold always saw Cili—as an angel surrounded by an aura of light. Cili's blonde hair was so fair it appeared as if a halo glowed round her head. Bouncy curls framed her face and focused all attention on her sparkling blue eyes, the color of the summer sky. Petite in height and frame, she always had to look up to the tall, slender Leopold. But what she lacked in height was completely compensated for by her lively determination; Cili loved to laugh, to tease, especially Leopold.

He had been smitten by Cili since the first time he saw her in her basinet; he had never stopped being infatuated by her beauty and her sweet nature. He adored everything about her; the fact that she loved the outdoors more than the palaces in which she lived; that she was athletic and courageous; that she rode a horse like a man to the chagrin of her mother. Leopold's affection was completely embraced by Cili who loved and admired him fully in return. To Cili there had never been any other who could compare to Leopold. She teased him that she had fallen in love with him when she saw him peering over the edge of her basinet.

Leopold called to Cili from the train; at last she heard him and came toward their car waving and smiling. By the time the train had come to a complete stop, Leopold was already out onto the platform and had Cili lifted up into his arms. Tamás followed with their bags.

Cili could hardly contain her excitement, "I have a carriage waiting; the driver will take us to the hotel. Oh, Leopold, I'm so happy that you have come. It will be wonderful! It is good to see you, too, Tamás."

She reached out to squeeze Tamás's hand and then gave Leopold a big kiss. "I know I'm not being a proper lady, but I'm so happy to see you!"

Leopold and Tamás put their bags into the carriage, piled in with Cili, and the driver took them to the Hotel Beau-Rivage on Lake Geneva. Once settled into their rooms, Leopold and Tamás went down to the lobby to meet Cili and her mother, Princess Margit. Tamás greeted them and then left to join friends at a café near the hotel.

The ladies and Leopold had dinner that evening at the Les Armures restaurant where they enjoyed a typical Swiss peasant's meal beginning with a fondue of Emmenthaler and Gruyere cheeses mixed with cherry brandy followed by a *raclette*, a melted slab of salted cheese, with potatoes, pickled onions and thinly sliced *Bündnerfleisch*. They drank glasses of *Fendant*, a white wine from the Chasselas grape. They had a delightful time together.

Leopold talked of his and Tamás's adventures in France. He described the vineyards and winemaking methods; the vine diseases they had studied and told about their new friend, Dr. Klein from Budapest. Nineteen-year-old Cili blissfully hung onto Leopold's every word. She was so obviously thrilled to be with him once again and he, of course, was just as excited to be with her. Even in her mother's presence Cili was not hesitant to express her love for Leopold. She reached across the table to hold his hand and brought it to her lips as he brought hers to his. They gazed into each other's eyes and smiled happily.

Princess Margit finally brought the evening to a close, "We must go. It is getting late and I must meet the Empress Sisi tomorrow. Leopold, please, call a carriage for us."

As soon as Leopold was away from the table, Princess Margit admonished her daughter, "Cili, you are much too free with your affections for Leopold in public places. You should remember that you are a young lady of the Viennese court; you have the obligation to set a moral example."

Princess Magrit raised her eyebrows as she looked at Cili. Cili's cheeks flushed with red. She apologized, "I'm sorry, Mother, but I love Leopold so much and I have missed him so."

"I understand, Cili," Margit expressed a slight smile, "I think it is time to make definite plans for a wedding next summer, don't you?" Margit softened completely, giving Cili a smile and a wink, "After all, you will be twenty. I think the time will be right."

Leopold returned, "The carriage is here. What did I miss? You are both positively glowing, such happy smiles."

"Mother thinks we should make plans for our wedding next summer. What do you think?"

Without a word, Leopold leaned over to give Cili's mother a kiss on her cheek and smiled, "Thank you, Madam. I will do everything I can to make your daughter the happiest woman in the world."

They left the restaurant and returned to the Beau-Rivage.

The next day at one o'clock Cili and her mother walked along the quay to meet the Empress's boat as it drew into the harbor in front of the hotel. The Empress Sisi was traveling incognito under the name, Countess of Hohenembs, with her dear friend, the Countess Irma Sztaray. Sisi disliked having a procession of servants following her, so she sent most of them ahead by rail to the city of Territet on the far eastern end of Lake Geneva, her next destination. Only her closest friends were to accompany her in Geneva.

The four women, happy to see each other again, made a lovely quartet all dressed in the latest Parisian fashions as they strolled arm in arm along the quay stopping for ice cream. They laughed at each other as they tried to eat the ice cream without spoiling their gloves or beautiful dresses.

Each lady wore an extraordinary hat—large straw creations with silk flowers, veils of tulle, and yards of ribbon. Except for the Empress, who always wore black from head to toe since the death of her only son, the ladies wore dresses of pure white. All their dresses had variations of embroidery, lace, and pleated bodices, puffed and straight sleeves, pinched waistlines giving way to long flowing skirts that touched the ground. A photographer took a photograph of the four friends as they stood on the promenade with the lake behind them.

The day was still warm when the ladies made their way back to the hotel, so they met again on the luxurious balcony to enjoy the lake breezes. They lingered there for several hours reading, playing cards, just relaxing. Unfortunately, the Empress let down her guard and when a local newspaper reporter casually wandered onto the balcony, he overheard conversations that revealed her true identity. He wasted no time reporting the story that the Empress was present in Geneva and by the next morning Sisi's visit was widely publicized in the newspapers.

On September tenth Sisi awoke early. She ate a very small breakfast and then began her dressing ritual. Her personal maid laced her corset as tight as Sisi demanded until her waist was a scant eighteen inches which the maid measured every day. Next came stockings, chemise, petticoats and the dress, layer upon layer. The maids then turned to Sisi's hair, arranging it in voluminous swirls and curls. Sisi's hair was still her crowning glory, even at sixty years of age. And, finally, she wore a veil and carried a fan to carefully shield her face from public view; only her closest friends ever saw her true appearance.

By mid-morning Sisi invited her friends, the Countess Sztaray, Margit, and Cili to accompany her on a quick shopping trip to the rue Bonivard where she wanted to visit George Bäker's Music Shop. Cili found the little shop mesmerizing with its elegant cylinder music boxes in varying sizes, housed in an assortment of charming shapes with extraordinary decorations. An amazing myriad of musical melodies from every part of the shop inundated Cili's senses while the workings of the intricate music boxes fascinated her.

"This is a marvelous place, Empress," Cili laughed. "Thank you for bringing us here."

Cili found an ornately handsome box that she could not resist and bought it as a gift for Leopold. Much smaller than the one purchased by the Empress, Cili's music box was ceramic in an arch-shape. Pretty little ceramic birds of different sorts perched atop the gilded box decorated with delicate *scrafito*. The sides of the box held painted enamel panels that displayed fantastical landscape scenes. Cili delighted in the image of a handsome mustachioed man on a gray horse emerging from a misty forest and riding toward a beautiful princess standing atop a castle tower. She thought of the figures as representations of Leopold and herself at Sopron Castle.

Even though she was enamored by the paintings, she knew that Leopold would find much more intriguing the ornate crystal turn handle and the secret door that opened to reveal the intricate workings of the pinned cylinder and tooth comb. Cili bought rolls of waltz music for the box and imagined twirling around the floor in Leopold's arms. As the ladies left the shop, its owner promised to deliver the music boxes within the hour to their hotel.

After a very meager lunch, Sisi and the Countess prepared to leave the hotel for the boat to Territet; Sisi asked Margit to accompany them as they walked to the boat. Cili and Leopold bid the Empress farewell and safe journey and followed the trio to the front of the hotel where they remained watching the three ladies leave on foot for the short walk to the waiting boat. The three women, with Sisi in the middle and dressed in black, walked closely together along the quay.

Just as the ship's bells rang, announcing its departure, a man approached them; he stumbled and fell into the Empress, he raised his hand to her chest as though he was trying to steady himself and then he raced away. Sisi collapsed to her knees. Leopold, the hotel concierge, and a passing driver all saw the event and had already begun to run toward the Empress when they saw her fall. The driver arrived first and helped Sisi to her feet. Leopold, the concierge, and Cili all came to the Empress with great concern, but Sisi seemed completely unaffected by the circumstance. She waved them off, saying, "It was nothing. I must hurry so as not to miss the boat."

The concierge left them to speak with the *polizei* who arrived immediately after the occurrence. One of the policemen had also witnessed the scene and was far more concerned about the incident than the Empress seemed to be. A number of policemen pursued the unidentified man.

Leopold and Cili continued to walk along with the Empress who mused aloud, "Strange man. I wonder... do you think he was trying to steal my broach?"

Shortly after the little group boarded the boat, the concierge arrived to let the Empress know that the man had been apprehended. Sisi still seemed unconcerned with his news, but thanked him for his trouble. Leopold, Cili, and Margit said good-bye again and disembarked as the Captain began to move the boat out into the lake. Sisi and the Countess made their way toward her cabin when suddenly Sisi staggered and fainted. A woman passing by helped the Countess lift Sisi to her feet and into her cabin, but once inside the door, Sisi fainted again. The Countess spoke softly to the Empress, "I'm going to open your blouse, Madam. I think you need air."

As Sisi's blouse fell apart the Countess noticed a very small drop of blood on Sisi's chemise. Upon closer examination the Countess realized there was a minute piercing of the chemise. The Captain was notified immediately and turned the boat back to the landing dock in front of the Hotel Beau-Rivage. A makeshift gurney using a sail, oars, and cushions was prepared for the Empress and six boatmen carried her into the hotel.

Whispers of her identity spread quickly as hotel guests stared in stricken astonishment at the Empress's body being carried through the lobby, her hand dangling limply from the gurney. At one time such a beloved royal, so beautiful and grand and yet, she had suffered so many tragedies. Many wept as they watched her pass; they could hear the death rattle coming from the gurney. The Empress was taken to her suite where everyone waited for the doctor to arrive. At last Doctor Golay entered the room and hurried to her side, but it was too late, Sisi, the Empress, was dead.

When the doctor finally removed her clothing, including the tightly laced corset, he discovered a thin puncture wound at the fourth rib; the puncture had penetrated Sisi's breast, lung, and heart. The tight corset had kept outward bleeding very slight, but there had been heavy internal bleeding. The doctor offered one final consolation—*Sisi's death had been painless.*

While Sisi lay dying, her assassin was already in police custody. He was an Italian anarchist, Luigi Luccheni, who had been in Geneva since May. Luccheni was obsessed with his goal to abolish the Hapsburg State and to kill royals. He confessed that his intent had been to assassinate the Duke of Orléans, but the Duke had never come to Geneva that summer, so in pure frustration Luccheni quite randomly decided upon the Empress. She was an easy target; he stabbed her in the chest with a narrow file.

Cili, Leopold and, even more so, Margit, were devastated by the shock of Sisi's violent death. Tamás made immediate arrangements for their little group to leave Geneva for Vienna the next day. They were distraught with grief for the loss of a dear friend they had known all their lives, but the tragic event personally terrified each of them. For the first time in their lives they realized there were those who desired to kill members of the Hapsburg family, aristocrats like themselves, for reasons beyond their control. The assassination of the Empress resonated deeply in their hearts.

A small sense of relief swept over the little group as the train pulled into the Vienna station and they saw Duke Louis and Cili's father Prince Maximilian standing on the platform waiting for them.

—m—

The von Esté family and thousands of others spent two weeks in Vienna observing memorials for the beloved Empress. Finally, Leopold left Vienna for Sopron, finding it difficult to part from Cili, but promising to return as soon as he could.

As it turned out they saw each other much sooner than they imagined; within ten days of the family's return to Sopron Castle, Duke Louis suffered a severe heart attack. Louis lay in his bed, weak and failing, but he managed with great effort to speak with Gáspár as they tried to put the Duke's papers in order. His dear wife, the Duchess Maria, never left his bedside; she tried to make him rest, to stop fretting over papers, but it was as though he would not die until all things were in place and he said as much as he gasped for breath.

As the Duke weakened, he asked Leopold to come to him. With Gáspár's help Louis passed all his possessions, titles, and obligations on to Leopold. "You are the Duke von Esté of Sopron now—serve your family and your people well."

Louis choked as he tried to take a deep breath; he motioned to Tamás, calling his name weakly. Tamás answered, "Yes, Sir, I am here." He walked to Louis's bedside and touched his hand.

The Duke whispered, "Tamás, help Leopold whenever you can." Louis patted his hand, as Tamás choked back the sobs in his throat. "You are a good man, Tamás."

Duke Louis began to struggle with the ring on his finger; he could barely lift his hand. Gáspár helped him take it off, then Louis said, "Leopold, this is your ring now...it was a gift from the Emperor for our family's loyalty and steadfast support."

Leopold took the ring, speaking to his father in whispers, affirming that he would do his best...he would take care of his mother...he would be a good steward of all the von Esté family holdings. Leopold leaned over his father to kiss him and murmured, "You have been a good father to me and a great man. You are loved and respected by all people."

The Duke stared into his son's eyes and the slightest of smiles crossed his lips and then he was gone. The Duchess Maria sobbed uncontrollably and fell across her beloved husband. Leopold felt the loss profoundly, letting out his breath very slowly as he staggered from his father's bed. Tamás and Gáspár, standing nearby, did not conceal their grief at the loss of such a great man.

Cili and her family arrived in Sopron as soon as they could when they learned of the severity of Duke Louis's illness. Leopold's sister, the Duchess Eugenia, came by train from Cologne, but she arrived too late to see her father before his passing. With a castle full of visitors, Ilonka kept busy, making sure all had a comfortable place to stay, plenty of good food, and a well-managed house. She took pride in creating the right atmosphere for the solemn occasion.

Ilonka, Gáspár, and Tamás loved Duke Louis and the von Esté family with all their hearts. They took full responsibility to organize all the mundane tasks that would help the family celebrate and honor the life of the superb Duke, the brilliant master of the castle.

After Duke Louis's body was interred in the castle cemetery, the family and their friends traveled by train to Vienna where a final memorial service for the Duke took place. While Eugenia returned to Cologne, the Duchess Maria decided against going back to Sopron Castle, but instead to retire to the Viennese Court where she took residence in the family's apartments in the Hofburg Palace. Leopold's old nanny, Philomena, stayed with Maria as her personal companion. Gáspár and Ilonka remained at the castle as caretakers and overseers of the staff. By October Leopold and Tamás were back in the French Burgundy vineyards to complete Leopold's studies.

—❧—

Leopold took a handkerchief from his pocket and wiped tears from his eyes, sighing deeply as he remembered the vision of his dying father, so long ago, but still close in memory. "Please pardon my tears, Tamás, but thoughts of my dear father still cause much anxiety for me, even after all these years."

"I still miss Duke Louis, too," consoled Tamás. "Time cannot diminish memories of those who were dear to us. The Duke was kind and fair and cared deeply for all of us."

"You and I always understand each other so well, dear friend," Leopold took a deep breath. "Going through these old photographs is as though I'm living my life again. It's right that you are here with me tonight, Tamás. You've been with me all my life. You know these times as well as I."

"Here's a beautiful memory, Leopold." Tamás took a velvet-framed photograph from the box and handed it to Leopold—the wedding portrait of Leopold and Cili.

Vienna, May 1899

Nosegays of lily of the valley, tied with blue organza ribbons to every candlestick, allowed the sweet, subtle scent of lily to fill the medieval Gothic chapel, the *Augustinerkirche* of the Hofburg Palace; the chapel of urns in which the hearts of the Hapsburg family rest. Leopold could only hold his breath as Cili appeared at the chapel's door on her father's arm. She was a vision of light in a dress of cream *peau de soie* and *Gorizia lace* tatted by the nuns of the Ursuline Convent. The wedding dress was an heirloom worn by her mother, updated with ribbons, rosettes, and a special corset underneath that gave Cili's tiny figure an artificial hourglass shape, the fashion of the day. She carried a bouquet of her favorite wild alpine flowers picked fresh for her that very morning.

Cili kept her eyes on Leopold as she walked toward the altar. As he stood transfixed between the priest and Christián, he could not take his eyes from his beautiful bride. Cili thought her groom to be the most handsome of men. She handed her bouquet to Gabriele who stood on the other side of the priest. As Cili's father raised her veil she kissed him and tears of joy spilled from her sparkling blue eyes. She turned toward Leopold and reached for his hand that he gave willingly. They were both so ready to profess their love and make their promises before God.

Their complete happiness was evident to everyone present and it spread throughout the chapel. At the end of the ceremony the priest introduced them to their adoring guests as the Duke and Duchess von Esté of Sopron. They left Vienna for a month-long wedding trip to the Greek Islands, sailing from one island to another, reveling in the warm sun and blue Aegean Sea.

At the end of June the couple returned to Sopron Castle and began to make it their permanent residence with the help of Gáspár and Ilonka. Right away Leopold seriously considered the vineyards that fanned out from the castle. His vision of cultivating better, healthier varieties of grapes and becoming a prosperous professional vintner could finally begin.

In August, the Count Christián von Házy married Gabriele at Lake Balaton on the Tihany Peninsula. Leopold, Cili, and Tamás arrived at the von Házy villa about a week before the wedding and spent their time doing many of the things they had enjoyed as children at the lake, hiking to *Belső-tő*, Tihany's inner lake, up to *Visszhang-hegy*, Echo Hill, and to *Csúcs-hegy* for the view.

Tihany's eighteenth-century Benedictine church, *Ápátság Templom*, provided the wedding site. Christián, wearing a cool white cotton suit, stood with Leopold and the priest at the altar as Gabriele walked with her father toward him. She was a vision of beauty in a high-fashion summer dress of fine, white batiste. A high collar and delicate insets of eyelet, lace, and netting trimmed the camisole and elbow-length sleeves. A sash of green silk cinched her tiny waist even smaller and a fitted skirt of repeated insets of eyelet, lace, and netting flowed to the floor ending in a short train. Gabriele carried a bouquet of Tihany's summer flowers—butterfly orchids, larkspur, and fern.

After the wedding, Christián and Gabriele took their wedding trip to Odessa where they sailed the Black Sea. Afterwards the couple returned to Eisenstadt where they made their home at the manor. A few years earlier Christián's parents, Count Francis and Countess Alexandra, decided to leave the manor for Budapest. Buda had been Alexandra's childhood home and she had desired to return to Budapest for many years. Francis, who suffered poor health, agreed to leave Eisenstadt and turn over the management of the von Házy salt business to his son. The elder von Házys commissioned the building of a great mansion in the newer Pest area of Budapest, on a side street just off the elegant *Sugár út*, near the handsome *Városliget*, the millennium park at the northeast end of the Avenue. From the time of their move, Count Francis and Countess Alexandra spent the summer months at their Tihany villa on Lake Balaton and their winter months in Budapest.

Leopold took a folded paper and a sepia photograph, clipped together, from the memorabilia box. The unfolded paper revealed Cili's hand-drawn plans for their Lake Balaton villa while the photo showed Leopold and Cili standing amidst a construction site. Leopold considered his recollections about the villa.

Lake Balaton, Summer 1900

In late May, soon after Leopold and Cili arrived at the Promenade Hotel for their annual summer visit to Lake Balaton, they hired a horse-drawn carriage to take them from Balatonfüred out to their lakeside property. They surveyed the landscape, a lovely picturesque setting; the land, never cultivated, was covered with vetch and wildflowers. The property rose to the north from the little road that followed the lake's north shoreline from Balatonfüred to the Tihany Peninsula. About a mile north of the road Leopold and Cili discovered a natural spring that bubbled from an outcropping of sandstone formations and flowed downward to form a pond. Beyond the pond, in a meadow, longhaired sheep grazed oblivious to them. The meadow sloped upward toward a dense forest that continued up to the hilltop and as far as they could see toward the Bakony Hills. Barely visible at the edge of the forest were several humble cottages, dwellings for a family of shepherds.

"Those shepherds were serfs on this land for centuries," Leopold said as he pointed up to the cottages. "When they finally won their independence our family welcomed them to stay where they were as long as they wanted."

Leopold stretched his hand and gestured toward a rise in the property near the road and announced, "We'll build our summer villa right over there—that is, if you like the spot, Cili."

"Perfect!" She smiled and danced along the edge of the road, "We'll have windows all across the front, so that no matter where we are in the house we can see the lake and feel the breezes. I want the villa to be painted a mint green—to match your eyes, Leopold. Not the dark green when you are fussy or moody, but the light green they are right now when you're excited about something; then they sparkle mint green. Oh, Leopold, it will be lovely!" She threw her arms around his neck and kissed him, "We'll have such great fun here in the summers."

Cili made a plan for a large villa, not as grand as the von Házy mansion on Tihany, but large enough for the big family they planned to have, plus plenty of extra room for summertime guests. Cili drew rather rudimentary plans for the front and rear elevations of the villa and made sketches for the interior floors. The plans had an eclectic appearance—a bit Art Nouveau, a bit native Hungarian, a bit French Mansard. The drawings included a domed rotunda at the center of the house, a splayed flight of stairs leading up to a semi-circular veranda with wrought-iron railings and large double doors at the entry. Two wings projected at forty-five degree angles from the rotunda, one to the east and one to the west. A steeply gabled roof with wrought-iron cresting topped each wing. Six dormers projected from each wing's rooftop, three to the south and three to the north. Under all second floor windows were balconies with wrought-iron railings. From the front, the house appeared to have two floors while from the back, three. Leopold commissioned the construction to begin that summer.

As construction got under way, Gáspár and Tamás helped Leopold lay out the first rows of vines that stretched from behind the villa up toward the pond. Laborers also began construction on a number of outbuildings—the press, the cask cellar and bottling house, cottages for laborers, stables, and a carriage house.

While the men worked in the hot summer sun, Cili spent her time with her mother-in-law, the Duchess Maria, partaking of the thermal waters in

Balatonfüred. One afternoon, they ran into an old von Esté family friend, the Baron György Vadas. He had hunted with Duke Louis and Leopold for years in the Burgenland. The Baron excitedly shared news that his Vizsla bitch had had a litter of puppies and he was ready to find new homes for them.

"I know how much the von Estés admire their Vizsla hounds," the Baron stated. "It would delight me to give the young Duke a pup, as a gift. Come pick one out and take it to him."

"Oh, how generous you are, Baron. Leopold will be so pleased," Cili smiled, "but I dare not do the choosing. If I may, I will bring Leopold to visit and he can select the puppy he wants."

Arrangements were made and the following day Leopold went to receive his gift, a puppy he named Báró, in honor of the Baron's generosity. Báró looked up at Leopold with affectionate eyes while Leopold stroked the puppy's smooth golden coat. Leopold informed Cili, "*Vizsla* is Hungarian for alert. See, how intelligent our Báró is. Vizsla is the oldest breed in Hungary, brought to the Puszta plains by the Magyars a thousand years ago."

In mid-September the von Estés, including Leopold's mother, returned to Sopron Castle where Báró was introduced to Dörög, Duke Louis's old hound. Dörög's sensitive and gentle nature welcomed little Báró into his domain and tolerated well the puppy's annoying habits. Cili and Leopold spent the cold winter months in front of their warm fireplace watching the two dogs play and cuddle together as Báró especially enjoyed chewing on Dörög's long, smooth ears.

Leopold held Báró lovingly across his lap; the puppy made him think of the past, "My father usually kept two or three Vizsla hounds at a time. He often remarked that the Vizsla make excellent hunting dogs, obedient and smart, always eager to please their master."

Báró let his head fall backward from Leopold's lap and stretched his neck toward Cili's hand to give her several tender licks, making her squeal with delight. Cili nuzzled her face in Báró's neck. The puppy was instantly loved by all, even Duchess Maria who nodded her head at the puppy, "Báró reminds me of your father…always had a Vizsla by his side. Dörög will be happy to have a little one with him at the castle; he has missed his master."

1901

By the winter of 1901 Cili was with child; she could hardly wait for the spring and their return to the warmth of the lake. When May arrived she and Leopold left Sopron for Balaton and their lovely new villa, just recently completed. Once the villa's interior and furnishings were settled, with Ilonka's help, Cili and the Duchess oversaw an extensive landscaping plan that included graveled pathways and driveways, stone terraces, the building of a gazebo and grape arbor, the laying out of rose beds, and a beautiful kitchen garden.

Cili, under a wide-brimmed straw hat, spent all her days outdoors in the sunshine. She loved being in her garden getting her hands dirty. Leopold found her numerous times kneeling in the dirt beside the laborers, working the soil with her hands. More than once he took out his white handkerchief to wipe smudges of dirt from her beautiful face. Leopold was covered in soil, too, from working in the vineyards; neither of them had ever been happier in their lives.

They made plans for their little one. Cili decorated the nursery and embroidered tiny little clothes. She danced around holding up little dresses and bibs for Leopold to "Ooh" and "Ah" over. Leopold answered her every whim, every question, every anxiety; they were both overjoyed that they had made a new life and looked forward to a large family. All was well; there were no two people in the entire world more excited than Cili or Leopold with anticipation for the birth of their child. No child more loved than the one Cili carried. But, then, suddenly the pregnancy became difficult and in August they had to leave the lake and return to Sopron. Eventually, a doctor was called from Vienna; he insisted upon complete bed rest for Cili.

Leopold loved Cili more than life. He sat beside her as she slept in their great carved bed; Cili looked so small and so tired. Leopold could hardly believe the change in just a few weeks, everything so abruptly different. Sopron Castle dark and dismal compared to the bright and cheerful Balaton villa. By September Cili was so ill and weak that she could only smile feebly at him. Leopold felt devastated and angry and helpless; he could do nothing to make her well again. And, so every day, he and Báró waited by her bedside, praying that God would bring their child soon and Cili would be well again.

In the last two weeks of September, Cili became weaker and weaker. She complied with her doctor's dictate for complete bed rest, but she had only gotten worse despite the attendance of her doctor, nurses, and priest. Margit and Maximilian arrived from Vienna. Leopold would not leave her side; he held her hand and whispered to her words of encouragement and love. Eventually the nurses were as worried about him as her; he looked so ill and tired, but nothing could convince him to leave her side and he only slept with his head resting by her small, still body.

Labor finally began, but it was long and weakened her even more. They debated performing a Cesarean, but she was so weak. Everyone waited the long hours in agony. At last Leopold was forced to leave the room. He spent those hours pacing the hall outside her door, listening for any encouraging sound. Nurses seemingly always in a rush, ran in and out. Cili's room remained perfectly quiet; no sounds seeped out into the hall.

Finally, in the early hours of a September morning, the doctor did take the baby by Cesarean to save its life and Leopold heard the baby's hearty cry. The door opened and a nurse motioned for Leopold to enter. Except for one lamp lit near Cili's bed, the room was dark. A second nurse placed the tiny bundle next to Cili who lay limp, her eyes barely opened; Leopold knelt beside her and looked inside the swaddled blanket at his tiny son. He could hardly speak, but he forced himself to tell Cili how beautiful the little boy was and how well she had done to give him birth. Leopold tried to tilt the baby so that Cili could see him. She tried to raise her hand, but it was too difficult; Leopold helped her touch the little face. The smallest of smiles crossed her lips; she looked up at Leopold, and whispered so softly, "I love you, Leopold. I am sorry."

Leopold embraced them both; he touched his face to hers; his tears ran from his cheeks onto hers. And then she was gone. Leopold held onto Cili, rocking her back and forth to his chest. The nurse took the baby away. Leopold sobbed so deeply it sounded unnatural. The doctor and priest tried to pull him away from Cili, but he would not let go. He demanded that everyone leave the room. He held Cili and wept.

At last Tamás entered the room. He held firmly onto Leopold's shoulders and spoke calmly and softly, telling Leopold that he had to let Cili go, that she was gone. Támás assured him that Cili would want him to tend to their son. At last Leopold gave her up and fell exhausted onto the shoulders of Támás, his old friend.

Támás helped Leopold from the room as the doctor and nurses rushed in; Támás walked with Leopold down the hall to the nursery. Leopold looked down at his tiny son lying in his crib. The baby was wide awake making baby noises and seemed to look right at his father. Standing in darkness, Leopold stared down at his son and spoke without emotion to Tamás, "I feel nothing, nothing but an incredible emptiness."

Two days later Leopold found himself in the castle's chapel. His family, friends, and Cili's parents had gathered in the ancient space, the oldest and most original part of the castle. Cold stone walls with lancets of colored glass circled the apse while rounded arches formed the ceiling. Except for the sculpted capitals atop each column, the chapel was devoid of decoration or warmth. Cili, dressed in a white gown, lay in her coffin in front of the altar. Light reflected through the windows cast a mosaic of colored shapes across her form. Flower petals were strewn over her and the coffin. Leopold sat motionless with Tamás beside him. Cili's mother, Princess Margit, held the child.

The priest stood at the baptismal font and asked for the child to be brought forth. An exception had been made for such an early christening so the baby's mother's body could be present. And, so, beside his mother's coffin the child was christened Stefan József Leopold, Count Esté of Sopron. The baby slept peacefully through his christening.

After Cili's body was interred in the castle's cemetery, near that of Duke Louis, Leopold walked around the courtyard for hours. At last he came into the great hall and announced to everyone, "I have decided to leave Sopron, to travel and to investigate vineyards and wine-making techniques. Tamás will accompany me. I implore the child's grandparents to take him back to Vienna. I have no plan as to when I will return."

Christián and Gabriele tried to console Leopold by letting him know they, too, would take an interest in Stefan, but Leopold heard not a word from anyone.

Tamás made arrangements to retain the current manager of the vineyards and for the castle staff to remain under direction of his parents. The next morning Leopold and Tamás left Sopron; Leopold never held Stefan.

Tamás took two cards from the memorabilia box—the black-ribboned memorial card with Cili's likeness embossed on it and a white, cross-shaped christening card with the name *Stefan József Leopold, Count Esté of Sopron* engraved across the arms. The memory of that day and time still raw for Tamás, he wiped his eyes with his handkerchief and dropped the cards back into the box without passing them to Leopold. Tamás took out another card with a quite different memory—a hand-colored postcard depicting the S.S. *Umbria* with its two red funnels and three masts rigged for sails set against a blue sky.

1903

Leopold, with Tamás at his side, wandered aimlessly around Europe for nearly a year and a half. During that time Tamás remained responsible for all necessities, while Leopold indulged in a life of dissipation, completely unlike his former self. One spring day in 1903, quite suddenly, Leopold decided they should see America and within the week he and Tamás traveled by train back through Burgundy to LeHarve and from there sailed on the first of April to Liverpool, England. A few days later the two men boarded the S.S. *Umbria* for New York City, a passage lasting six days and nights. On board the *Umbria*, Leopold continued his wasteful, decadent pursuits, spending his nights gambling and drinking and his days sleeping. Tamás continued to serve as his protector, walking him back to their cabin suite in the early hours of every morning.

In the evenings Leopold emerged from his cabin dressed in tuxedo with boutonniere, looking extremely handsome and very suave; he instantly became the object of attention for women on board, both married and single. Leopold accepted their advances without discrimination, not knowing or caring who they were. One morning when Leopold awoke to find a beautiful stranger in his bed, Tamás scurried the lady out of the room as quickly as he could to keep any confrontation at bay. But despite Tamás's caution, Leopold continued to live dangerously aboard the *Umbria*. On the last night aboard ship, as Leopold stood against the deck railing smoking his pipe, he actually contemplated jumping into the swirling waters.

Leopold and Tamás arrived in New York City on the morning of April twelfth, 1903. They moved into the brand new Art Deco Washington Square Hotel, on Waverly Place. Their suite of rooms had an extraordinary view of the city's west side, including the park across the street and new skyscrapers under construction, taller than those already standing. They shared amazement for the soaring buildings and for the riveters who walked fearlessly on steel girders high above the city.

Sensationalized stories of Leopold's shipboard romances had been printed in the *New York Times* society pages, so by the time Leopold stepped on shore, his reputation was already set. Those stories, somewhat exaggerated, together with his title of Duke and romantic Hungarian accent made him very appealing to Americans, especially American women. As soon as Leopold's presence in New York was known, the city's high society involved him in their lives

Every afternoon Leopold and Tamás walked through Washington Square to improve Leopold's constitution, much needed after his nights on the town gambling, drinking, and womanizing. Leopold willingly took full advantage of New York's lively activity twenty-four hours a day.

By summer Leopold's rowdy behavior forced Tamás to make a change of address for them. He arranged their move to a suite of rooms in the new Dylan Hotel on 41st Street. However, the relocation did not have the effect Tamás hoped for; Leopold made no effort to adopt a new pattern of behavior, sinking further into a life of debauchery encouraged by his new, decadent society friends. To Tamás's way of thinking, they used Leopold's genteel and gentle nature terribly. Tamás understood his friend's misery; he knew that Leopold still suffered the devastating loss of his beloved Cili, but as the months passed, Tamás became more and more concerned that Leopold might be irretrievably lost.

A reminder of the past arrived one morning in the form of a letter from Eisenstadt. Tamás cheerfully handed the letter to Leopold, "Perhaps Christián has news to lift your spirits."

Leopold opened the letter, but he had no interest in hearing news from home, good or bad, "Tell me what he writes, Tamás."

"Christián begins with kind greetings. Best wishes for our health and regret that we are so far away. You and I are both missed. Ah, here is good news…Gabriele has given birth to a baby boy…Rudolf Nikolaus Francis Antal von Házy. They'll call him Dolf. There's a picture of the boy enclosed."

Támás offered the photograph to Leopold, but he only glanced at it. Támás continued, "Christián's pride is evident in the many superlatives he uses to describe his little Rudolf...Dolf. He promises that he and Gabriele will make certain Dolf and Stefan become acquainted and friends, just as you and Christián have always been."

Leopold made no comment, not a word, and walked from the room.

Tamás had very little respect for Leopold's new friends, a fast party crowd of gamblers and drinkers. He ran interference as best he could on behalf of Leopold, in particular where various women were concerned. Often showing up in the early morning hours just in time to intervene as Leopold might have stumbled from the gaming table into some compromising circumstance. Tamás tried to stay as close as possible while letting Leopold do as he wished as long as the jeopardy was not too great.

Leopold's crowd took to calling Tamás "the nanny" and many times Leopold rebuked him for hovering. However, Leopold was never too severe in his protestations, giving Tamás cause to believe there was still a part of Leopold that wanted some control, perhaps even protection from himself.

One cold November night Leopold's Park Avenue friends invited him to the theatre and then to a party. He had started drinking champagne during the afternoon and was quite tipsy by the time Tamás helped him into his tuxedo. Tamás reminded Leopold of the very compromising photograph that had appeared in yesterday's newspaper. The *Times* society page lay open on the dresser revealing a large black-and-white image of two rather unsavory women draped over Leopold's shoulders, all three of them appearing quite drunk.

"You may be treading on dangerous ground, Sir," Tamás warned. "Those women are not to be trusted."

"Do not scold me, Tamás," Leopold said, his face very close to that of Tamás, "I have nothing to lose to those women; they can have whatever they want."

Támás frowned and turned his face away from Leopold's foul breath. "There was a time, Sir, that you had everything to lose—your stellar reputation, your name, your good sense. I am obliged to look after you and you are making it very difficult."

Leopold patted Tamás's face and leaned into him, "I'm sorry, Old Man." He slurred his words, "I appreciate all that you do for me, really I do. I'll straighten up one day, I promise."

Then he staggered toward the table, pulled a red rose from the bouquet and struggled to fit it into his lapel. Tamás helped him, "Do you want me to go with you tonight?"

"No, no!" Leopold protested, "I promise I won't get into trouble. I'll be good." And out the door he went.

When would Leopold be able to shake off this cloud that enveloped him, changed him, and kept him from his true self?. . . Tamás wondered and shook his head.

He watched Leopold's dark eyes grow even darker and often stare blankly; the light, the spark, in them had gone. He knew that Leopold needed more time to reconcile his loss and find joy in life again, but Tamás missed his dear friend and he was worried, losing confidence that Leopold could overcome the obstacles that were intruding upon his life and making matters even worse.

Tamás had taken as much responsibility as possible for their lives in America. He kept close tabs on Leopold's whereabouts. He took care of Leopold's personal needs; put him to bed, made sure he ate something each day, and kept him looking as well groomed as possible. Since their crossing of the Atlantic, fortunately Leopold had let Tamás handle their finances. Each day Tamás made certain Leopold only had access to a small allowance, but still, Tamás was seriously concerned about Leopold's well-being.

The hotel doorman hailed a cab for Leopold and he was off to the theatre, but first he had the cab driver stop for another bottle of champagne. When he finally arrived at the theatre, stumbling drunk, he was met by a group of friends who were as wildly intoxicated as he. Dressed in tuxedos and lovely evening dresses, the boisterous group clicked champagne glasses, laughed loudly, and staggered into the theatre lobby. They were met by the theatre manager, who promptly tossed them all out onto the street.

The group of seven, unfazed, looked around for a place to continue their party. Arm-in-arm, the men and women made their way across the busy street dodging traffic, laughing all the way. They barged into a luxurious Broadway bar, found a large leather booth, slid in, and ordered a round of drinks. None of them paid any attention to the pianist as he played an enchanting, melancholy interpretation of "Melody of Love" that drifted throughout the bar under the chatter and clinking glasses.

Then he began to play for a stunning chanteuse whose voice filled the room with a sultry version of "I Can't Tell You Why I Love You, but I Do." Leopold quite suddenly began to hear the music despite the stupor he was floating through. He sat very still and stared at the singer. She was a platinum blond wearing a white sparkle-studded dress of slinky silk that clung to her slender form. Her voice was soft and smoky. If he closed his eyes he could imagine Cili standing at the piano singing a Gypsy ballad that she loved so much. Tears slipped from his eyes and he heard himself make a woeful sound. The woman sitting next to him, one of the same women in the newspaper photograph, took hold of his arm, "What's the matter Leo? Are you sick?"

He turned, looked up to the woman's face, and saw her grotesquely painted red lips and heavily black lined eyes staring at him. At that moment Leopold felt so overwhelmed by the clown-like woman and shrill voices hovering around him that he bolted from the booth, the bar, and out onto the wet street. A light rain was falling, making the night very dark.

Leopold's head swirled with booze and memories of Cili as he reeled along the sidewalk without a clue as to where he was or where he was going. Within only a few blocks he found himself completely lost and surrounded by three hooligans who began to push him back and forth between them. They shoved him into the brick wall of a building and then punched him until he fell to the sidewalk. They demanded money and his jeweled ring. He had no money to give them having spent it all in the bar on drinks for his friends.

One of the young thugs ripped Leopold's ring from his finger, even though Leopold protested, muttering, "The Emperor gave that ring to my father…it's centuries old." But they neither understood his words nor cared. They kicked him into the gutter and ran away. Leopold had no idea of how long he lay in the street, going in and out of consciousness. In the wee hours of the morning an old, toothless woman wrapped in rags startled him awake. "Wha' happen to ya?" she asked. "Are ya deed? Want me to call a copper for ya?"

Leopold could only groan and the old woman waddled off. Leopold passed out again.

Eventually, a policeman did find Leopold, soaking wet, lying in the gutter. Thinking he was probably sleeping off a bad drunk, the policeman roughly pushed Leopold over and realized the drunk was a gentleman. The cop nudged Leopold with his nightstick, "What's your name, Bub? Better move on now."

But when the policeman looked more closely, he saw Leopold's bloodied clothes, cuts and bruises, and hurried down the street to call an ambulance. Leopold was taken to Bellevue Hospital where the doctors found broken ribs, a broken nose, and a badly bruised face. Leopold's pockets were empty of any identification, so it was not until the next day when Leopold finally came to his senses that he could tell them who he was and ask them to call Tamás to come and fetch him home.

When Tamás entered the hospital room, he said nothing. Leopold hurt everywhere and could barely speak, but words were not necessary, he could read Tamás's mind and facial expressions. Leopold knew exactly what Tamás was thinking and he felt immense shame. He finally managed to speak, "Forgive me, Tamás, I am so sorry. Look at me. They found me in the street, in a gutter.

"What has happened to me?" He raised his hand, "As drunk as I was, I was sober enough to know when they took my ring. I thought they would take my life and I didn't care. I lay there all night in and out of consciousness until an old hag woke me going through my pockets."

Tamás, his face somber, his expression drawn, clutched Leopold's arm. Leopold went on, "I am done with New York for now; I want to find myself again. I have dishonored Cili, my father, you, all who are dear to me." Tears filled his eyes, "I regret these past months. It took this last debacle for me to feel so mortified that my only choice is to leave town. I must make amends."

The seriousness in Leopold's voice was palpable; Tamás knew that at last Leopold had returned to himself and could move through his grief to better times.

Two days later Leopold returned to their suite at the Dylan. Leopold had only to look in the mirror to remind him of his desire to live a better life. His broken nose was healing, but would forever have a bit of a bend on the bridge. He thought, *Serves me right.*

Leopold spent his time recuperating and reading as much information on America's vineyards and vintners as Tamás could supply. The seed of excitement beginning to grow within Leopold seemed to delight Tamás. Leopold's long-held interests in grapes and winemaking were rekindled. He began to talk about the subject enthusiastically; to think aloud about his own vineyards, about new lands and climate that might be good for grapes. Leopold began to look toward the future, even, perhaps, to a return to Austria-Hungary and Tamás felt very good about that.

The two men took daily walks down Broadway to Washington Square or uptown to Central Park. The brisk cold air of December sent snow swirling around them. Some days they rode in a Hansom cab through the park instead of walking. Christmastime in the city was exciting. As they rode past a frozen pond one afternoon, Leopold suddenly asked the cab driver to stop. Without speaking, Leopold gazed for a few moments at the children ice skating. It was the first time Tamás had witnessed Leopold's attention turning to children since leaving Sopron. Leopold said nothing, but clenched his jaw, narrowed his eyes, and then in a low voice ordered, "Drive on."

The Hudson River Valley, 1904

In the early spring of 1904, Leopold and Tamás packed their bags and left New York City by train. They traveled north into the Hudson River Valley. The valley's beauty was stunning; rolling hills like folds of green velvet lifted up against a bright blue sky filled with feathery clouds. Leopold and Tamás felt at peace in this familiar terrain that reminded them so much of their homeland. They rented a carriage and followed the ribbon of highway that hugged the winding Hudson, past Yonkers and White Plains all the way to West Point, before stopping at an inn for the night. Tamás enquired as to furnished cottages for rent along the river and found one to their liking near Poughkeepsie. He and Leopold took the cottage for the summer, moved in, and went fishing the same afternoon. The two men could have picked no better place for Leopold to rest and rediscover himself than this natural wild valley.

For the next year Leopold and Tamás spent their time traveling from vineyard to vineyard all the way to Lake George and ever further to the Finger Lakes region. In the village of Washingtonville they discovered the old Brotherhood Winery; Leopold was particularly interested in the network of subterranean caves under the winery, reminding him of similar regions in Hungary. The caves were filled with oak barrels of fermenting wine. Leopold enjoyed his long conversations with the master winemaker. They shared scientific information about fermentation, varieties of grapes, and unusual blends of grapes used to create various wines.

Leopold loved to walk through the rows of vines watching daily changes, from the first tiny green clusters to the plumping of the grapes. He took a job at harvest time picking grapes; good manual labor hauling baskets of grapes from field to carts to press. He loved the aromas; his mind was stimulated with images of his youth, of times when he and Cili participated with the workers laughing, tasting, dancing. Leopold had not noticed that his sadness for Cili had begun to dissipate, giving way to happier thoughts of her and, in time, he lost his ability to be sad; he was too content.

Leopold and Tamás enjoyed touring the new Bolognesi winery on the highland site of an old vineyard dating from pre-Revolutionary times. The view from the rocky bluff was spectacular, vistas of river and valley were spread out below the bluff, much like an Asher Durand painting Leopold had seen in a New York gallery. Although the Bolognesi fruity wines were pleasing to the palate, it was the claret from the winery near Pine Bush that most delighted Leopold's tastes.

California, 1905

By spring of 1905, Leopold grew restless; he and Tamás had been in the valley for a whole year. Leopold, lost in thought, stood by the cottage window early one morning, looking out toward the footbridge that swung across the river. Then rather absentmindedly he said, "Tamás, let's pack up and take the train to California. I think we should see the grapes in California."

And with that they packed, got back to the city, and bought tickets.

Their journey began in May. A great sense of adventure gripped the two friends as the steam locomotive pulled out of Central Station headed for Philadelphia and Pittsburgh. In Pittsburgh they left the train to spend a few days seeing the great steel mills along the Allegheny River. Thick yellowed-gray smoke billowed from tall stacks into the sky twenty-four hours a day, while fiery furnaces along the rivers glowed bright red through a smoky fog that covered the city day and night. The vigorous steel industry amazed the two Europeans.

Two days later Leopold and Tamás boarded a train for Chicago where they spent a week in awe of the vibrant city and its spectacular architecture. Sophisticated, beautifully designed buildings rose to great heights above

Michigan Avenue while people and vehicles crowded the street. The two men never expected to see such a modern, progressive city. To their thinking, Chicago was every bit as exciting and vigorous as New York City.

At the end of the week Leopold and Tamás boarded the daily Overland Limited, the most modern of trains, destined for Ogden, Utah. The Limited provided the ultimate in luxury—electric lights, an observation car with large windows, private sleeping compartments with their own drawing room, and an elegant dining car. Twelve hours later they arrived in Omaha where the two decided to visit the famous stockyards and have steaks for supper. Near midnight they re-boarded and by early morning the train was passing through the Great Platte Plains. The expansive country amazed them. Leopold and Támás sat in the observation car looking through extensive windows, hardly believing what they were seeing—herds of cattle, American bison and wild horses, cowboys on horseback, and occasionally Indians on their painted ponies. *A magnificent experience*, they agreed. From the conductor they purchased image cards of American Indians dressed in colorful attire; cards, too, of American cowboys in full costume on horseback.

The train steamed on and on toward Colorado, past panoramic views of snow-capped mountains, reminding Leopold and Tamás of their Austrian Alps. When the train pulled into Denver, they departed once again and spent several days there. A hired guide took them to Boulder and the Continental Divide; they hunted for deer near Lake Granby.

For the next leg of the trip the two men caught the train in Greely and headed north to Cheyenne, crossing the great plains of Wyoming through Rock Springs and, finally, on to Utah. They passed through fantastic basalt walls the color of desert rose into Echo Canyon and then steamed through the lush Weber River Valley and vast fields of alfalfa. Suddenly everyone rushed to the windows to get a better look at Devil's Slide, two light, cream-colored limestone ridges rising parallel to each other from the Weber River all the way to the top of the mountain.

Just a mile past Devil's Slide, the train entered Wilhelmina Pass where the conductor pointed out the "1,000 Mile Tree," a tree planted by the original builders of the railroad to mark the point of one thousand miles from Omaha.

"Can you imagine, Tamás! Just think! Budapest is less than a thousand miles from London, from Paris, Barcelona, Rome, even from Oslo, but in America, one thousand miles, two thousand miles, even three thousand miles are nothing! All this vast land united and everyone all the way speaks one language!" Leopold remarked in amazement, "Imagine! Americanization like Magyarization! What a wonder!"

After the 1,000 Mile Tree, the track passed through the breathtaking Devil's Gate, a rugged horseshoe-shaped gorge with steep canyon walls rising to thirteen thousand feet. At last the train pulled into Ogden. Leopold and

Tamás felt the need of a rest, so they hired a guide and stayed for a few days. They fished the Weber River for trout, rainbow and cutthroat. Their guide fried everything they caught on an outside fire at their campsite. Their shared opinion—*The Weber River must be close to heaven.*

From Ogden they boarded the Southern Pacific Line and crossed the Great Salt Lake into the desert. Neither Leopold nor Tamás had ever seen such desolation. Through Nevada, more barrenness, nothing but crusted salt residue, bleached animal bones, sagebrush, and miles of sand with no signs of human existence. To the Europeans, it was unearthly. The track followed the Humboldt River, until the river mysteriously disappeared into the Humboldt Sink near the Trinity Mountain range. After that the terrain had sporadic marshy wetlands with magnificent flocks of birds, every kind of bird. Leopold kept a list...warblers, ducks, orioles, sea gulls, black heron, pelicans, an occasional swan...and many, many more.

As the train chugged up the steep mountain toward the Truckee River Pass, Leopold spoke aloud about the great hunting he imagined when he saw pheasant, grouse, and partridge fly up from the tall grasses alongside the track. Very slowly the train wound its way through the pass and into the Sierra Nevada range with its steep, rugged palisades. When Leopold and Tamás looked out the window, the land fell away from the track's edge straight down for a mile.

As the train continued toward Donner Pass, the conductor related historic, gory tales about the pass. Finally, the train steamed through a narrow passage above Lake Tahoe and began to wind its way down into the beautiful country of California. Leopold and Tamás found the rolling green landscape of forested hills a visual relief from the arid bleakness of the last five hundred miles.

The whole experience of crossing the American landscape had been beyond imagination for the two men; the variety of terrain magnificent, the wildlife astounding, and the amount of empty space without human habitation almost unbelievable.

At seven twenty on a Thursday evening their train pulled into Oakland station. Leopold and Támás took a ferry across the bay to San Francisco, hailed a cab, and checked into a suite of rooms at the Palace Hotel on the corner of Market and Montgomery. Once again they were surprised by the elegance of the hotel and by other examples of classical architecture in San Francisco. They had not expected to find such world-class sophistication in the Wild, Wild West so far from the rest of civilization.

Their suite, on the seventh floor, had a large bay window overlooking the city and the busy streets below. The two men stood at the window in awe, surveying the expanse of the city as it stretched out toward the blue water only blocks away. The day was bright and cloudless.

After settling into their suite of rooms, Leopold and Tamás walked to the state-of-the-art hydraulic lift and descended with other guests to the Grand Court. They were told that at one time the Grand Court had been an open courtyard for carriages, but now it was a magnificent enclosed space with an elaborate skylight ceiling high overhead. Luxurious leather chairs and sofas, potted plants, gaming tables, a piano, and an ornate fountain filled the impressive lobby. Galleries supported by classical columns and balustrades rose around the court for each of the hotel's seven stories.

Sitting at the bar, they struck up a conversation with the bartender and other patrons who were very friendly and accommodating. Their new acquaintances suggested many sights for exploration, like Nob Hill and Telegraph Hill; all of San Francisco was built on hills with spectacular, panoramic views. For the real flavor of San Francisco, the famous wharf was also suggested. And when they learned of Leopold's interests in wine and grapes, everyone agreed the two Europeans must visit the wineries of Napa Valley north of the bay.

Leopold and Tamás dined in the fashionable Gentlemen's Grille where they ordered *cioppino*, a seafood stew made of shrimp, crab, and the fish of the day cooked with tomatoes, wine, and spices; a dish they had never had before. When Leopold and Tamás returned to their suite that evening and looked out of the windows, they were stunned by the beauty of the city, all lit up and spread out by the bay.

The next morning Leopold rose early. He drew open the draperies and got a surprise! The whole city was enveloped by a heavy fog. He could see nothing. It was as though the city had disappeared altogether.

After breakfast Leopold and Tamás went out onto the busy streets where the warmth of the mid-morning sun had begun to evaporate the fog. They were swept away by the sights of the city. Trolley tracks followed each side of the wide Market Street; such a busy street, they had rarely seen—cable cars, motor cars and vans, horse-drawn carts and wagons, men on bicycles and on horseback, hundreds of pedestrians, men, women, and children in a hurry, going in all directions. Chinamen with their single braids down their backs rushed along the streets while newspaper boys scurried by with stacks of papers. The two visitors were caught up in the movement of the city and surged along with the crowd toward the bay. A myriad of delightful aromas wafted through the air—grilled meats, Chinese spices, and the sea. The atmosphere was exhilarating!

Over the next two weeks they explored the fascinating city, riding cable cars to the end of the line and walking along the seacoast. They climbed to the top of every hill and spent time in the brand-new Golden Gate Park with its streams and rolling hills, a great respite from the bustle of the city, a peaceful place to relax. Some days they simply looked for fun and spent the day at the enormous water chutes on D Street.

Fall, Napa Valley, California

In September, Leopold decided to leave San Francisco and move to the Napa Valley. He purchased a 1905 Model C Buick from Rough Rider Charley's car dealership and then he and Tamás ferried across the bay and drove into Napa Valley. Once Leopold saw the beauty of the land and discovered the vitality of the vineyards, he was determined to stay for a while and make it a kind of laboratory for increasing his knowledge and experience.

The two men traveled throughout the valley and decided to stay in the Calistoga area because of its resort-like atmosphere. Warm and sunny with hot springs, everything about Calistoga reminded Leopold and Tamás of their beloved Lake Balaton in the summertime, its climate and geography. From a Spanish vintner, Señor Miguel Alejandro, they rented a log cabin that stood on the side of Mount St. Helena at the northern end of the valley.

Leopold and Tamás spent their time driving from one end of the valley to the other looking at vineyards, most of them owned by Europeans—Frenchmen, Italians, and Spaniards. They also noticed the abundant wildlife living in the valley—black bear, elk, and wildcats, once even a grizzly, but most of all they enjoyed fishing for salmon in the Napa River.

The Alejandro family, Spaniards from Old Mexico, were among the earliest vintners in the valley. In the mid-eighteen hundreds Alejandro's grandfather settled in the northern part of the valley and built a large ranchero. In early fall, Leopold asked Señor Alejandro if he could work in Alejandro's vineyard and study his wine-making methods. Alejandro was willing. Leopold discussed with him every phase of winemaking—from the vines to the grapes to the fermentation process to the bottling—and learned about the diseases and other problems that can destroy all the work at any phase. Alejandro's vines had suffered a severe attack of *phylloxera* before Leopold arrived. Leopold shared his French experiences with the blight while Alejandro told Leopold how he and another vintner, the Frenchman Georges de Latour, had responded to the aphids by importing hundreds of strong French grafted vines with a natural immunity to the disease. By the time Leopold arrived in the valley, the vines of Alejandro and the other vintners were much improved, strong and healthy.

One evening Señor Alejandro invited Leopold and Tamás for dinner at his hacienda where they joined Miguel's family outside on the patio around a warm fire. A small band, normally vineyard workers during the day, provided the entertainment—guitars and trumpets and wonderful, lively songs. Leopold and Tamás enjoyed the music very much; possibly because it reminded them of the joyous gypsy music of their homeland, a different meter, but similar. Tequila poured freely as they pulled delicious cornhusk-wrapped tamales from the fire.

As Tamás and Leopold sat with Alejandro listening to the music, suddenly a young woman began to dance around the fire. She wore colorful skirts and held castanets in the palms of her hands, clicking them rhythmically as she twirled in and out among the diners. As Tamás gazed at this vision of beauty, he was spellbound; he thought Juanita Alejandro was the most beautiful woman he had ever seen. Her long dark hair fell in silky waves across her bare shoulders as she undulated to the music; her large brown eyes flashed with the reflection of fire every time she looked in Tamás's direction.

Tamás was determined to know this woman and the very next day he went looking for her. He found Juanita in the stable brushing a handsome Appaloosa mare. Tamás complimented the horse and then introduced himself to Juanita. She seemed equally impressed with Tamás and immediately flattered him, referring to him as "a dashing, sophisticated gentleman" and noting that he had "a most unusual, charming accent."

From that first meeting Tamás and Juanita became known in the valley as a twosome, although Tamás was aware he was not alone in his attentions to Juanita. He heard there was another young man in the valley who also had dreams of the beautiful Juanita, Felix Rodrigus. Rodrigus and Juanita had long been thought of as a couple in the valley, at least until Tamás Tóth, the foreigner, had made his interest in Juanita known. Tamás could see that Juanita was flattered by his interest in her, she flaunted their attraction for each other in front of everyone, including Felix.

Throughout the winter months Tamás courted the beautiful Juanita. Falling in love with her was rather instant for him; he was convinced his passion for her was equaled in full by hers for him. He and Juanita took daily rides together, following trails by the river or going up into the hills. Juanita completely mesmerized Tamás and he could hardly imagine being apart from her for a moment, leading him seriously to contemplate marriage.

While Tamás was diverted by Juanita, Leopold was occupied by the grapes. He spent all of his time in some way or another working in the vineyards. One of the families who worked for Alejandro had a small child, Felipe, a boy of about five or six who took a liking to Leopold. Felipe followed Leopold everywhere around the vineyard causing Leopold to have restless feelings. Leopold began to wonder about his own son, Stefan. Perhaps it was the nearness in age of little Felipe to Stefan that made Leopold feel so agitated. Little Felipe seemed to inspire a change in Leopold and then one spring day a very serious Leopold felt it necessary to speak to Tamás.

"So much time and distance have passed between me and the son I don't know," Leopold agonized. "Tamás, I have made a terrible mistake leaving my son behind for so long. This little boy, Felipe, looks up to me, Tamás. I can tell that he thinks I'm special. I don't know why he does, but he does." Then Leopold hesitated and added, "Felipe makes me wonder who my boy is following around. He makes me wonder what Stefan is learning and from whom." Leopold hesitated again, "When I show Felipe how to graft the vines, I have this great urge to show Stefan about the vines."

"Is it too late for me to be a father to Stefan?" Leopold asked, "What must he think of me? I have deserted him all these years. Is it time for us to leave?" Leopold with tears in his eyes turned to Tamás for answers.

Tamás did not have time to answer before Leopold spoke again, "Time has come for me to go home, to return to Austria-Hungary, to once again embrace my father's vineyards as a serious business and to meet my son. I will find it most difficult to go without you, but I can see that you have found a new life for yourself in this valley," Leopold assured his friend, "You must know, Tamás, that you are completely free to decide your own future. Leave here with me or stay, but I have decided to go."

The next morning Tamás walked away from the vineyards toward the forest, up into the hills, intentionally alone; he had serious choices, decisions to make. Heaviness gripped his whole being and made his breathing labored as he climbed to the top of the hill. Tamás emerged from the forest to stand at a height far above the valley. He sat down on a large, flat rock and breathed in the warm pine-scented air. In the panoramic setting of vineyards far below him, row after row of vines undulating with the lay of the land, he began to contemplate his future.

I'm in a country where I can start from scratch; be my own man, make a completely different life...and, there is Juanita, a woman who seems to be in love with me. Tamás presented good arguments for himself. *I have met many beautiful women through the years in the places where I have traveled, but none as lovely as Juanita Alejandro. I enjoy being with her—our Spanish language lessons, riding on the trails, fishing, working together in the vineyard.*

Her father likes me. I know he would welcome me as his daughter's husband and even into the family's business. Tamás surveyed the beautiful landscape and thought, *How can I turn away from all this? Why should I?*

There was so much for Tamás to mull over in his mind. *I've known Leopold all my life...I can't remember a time when I have not known Leopold. My family—my dear father and my sweet mother—have been with Leopold's family for generations. Leopold and I were playmates from childhood, always the closest of friends.* With those memories of his life and relationship with Leopold, tears came to Tamás's eyes. *Like all best friends we have shared good times and bad. We know each others' strengths and weaknesses; we know we can always count on each other...and we trust each other completely.*

Tamás thought about the only time he had been away from the von Esté home and Leopold...*at age fourteen I left the duke's castle for five years to study in Vienna, but we were still together in the summers and for holidays...and then Leopold arrived in Vienna for university...our longest separation was the year of my Grand Tour. Since then I have been Leopold's valet, his best friend…I have been with him all his life.*

He wished he had brought pen and paper to the hilltop, so he could make a list of *pros* to stay and *cons* to go. *Certainly, the beautiful Juanita is at the top of the list to stay, but Leopold is at the top to go, especially in light of current happenings. Leopold has not mentioned his son, Stefan, in almost five years. Not since his birth have I heard Leopold say Stefan's name, but now suddenly he begins to speak of Stefan in conversations and wants to return home to meet him.*

Just the evening before, Leopold had mused about the little boy Felipe and how the child made him think of his own Stefan, Tamás recalled. *I listened to Leopold without interrupting him. I understood he was working through those questions on his own. He didn't need me to interject advice or opinion; he was coming to a conclusion on his own. It's clear to me that finally Leopold is ready to re-embrace his life, to go home to Europe, and to start life anew. The time has come for me to choose—to go or to stay.*

Well, in fact, the decision is not so hard after all. Of course, I will go with Leopold. I'll leave all that California has to offer, and Juanita, too. As much like heaven as all of this is, it isn't home. When I think of Austria and Hungary I can visualize the spectacular landscape, not so dissimilar from this valley. But place has a far greater meaning than just landscape or physical space. It's about place; knowing where my place is. I'll tell Juanita and her father that I must go. Támás felt relief; he no longer felt the stress of not knowing. *Going back to my homeland with Leopold is the right choice.*

The following evening, Tamás took Juanita for a walk in the moonlight through the vine-covered arbor, the vines just beginning to spring back to life. Telling Juanita good-bye was terribly difficult, but Tamás was convinced he had made the right decision. He hesitated to speak the words of good-bye to Juanita; instead he turned his attention to the tender green shoots of new life sprouting from the old vines. Finally, he spoke softly to her, "California is not my *place*," he told her, explaining as gently as he could, "I must leave; I must return to my home, my *place*."

She cried as he walked away, but Tamás knew she would not be alone for long. Certainly Felix would come to her rescue as soon as he heard the Europeans had left the valley. In fact, before Tamás and Leopold left the valley, Tamás spread the news that it was Juanita who had told him to go.

San Francisco–New York City, 1906

Together Tamás and Leopold moved back to San Francisco in April 1906. They resumed residence at the Palace Hotel on the seventh floor. On the morning of April fourteenth the two men were sitting in the Grand Court reading the newspaper when the hotel bellboy delivered a telegram to Leopold. The wire was from Cologne, Germany, from his sister, Eugenia.

Leopold read the telegram and handed it to Tamás, saying, "Well, Tamás, here we have another reason to leave this paradise as soon as possible."

Tamás read the telegram:

Dear Leopold Please rescue Elizabeth von Schrader daughter of my dear friend Baroness Beate Only eighteen her chaperone deserted her Her location the Martha Washington Hotel for Women Washington Square NYC Please hurry Eugenia

"We should get our tickets right away," Tamás suggested. "The express train will take three full days to get us back to New York City."

Leopold and Tamás made their way through the busy streets of San Francisco to the station to purchase tickets. Leopold sent a telegram to his sister, Eugenia, and one to Miss Schrader at the Martha Washington Hotel. Then they walked to the wharf for a last taste of fresh California sole. That afternoon Leopold sold the Buick, they packed their bags, settled their bill, had a last dinner of steak in the stunning white-and-gold American Dining Room, and called it a night.

Early the next morning Leopold and Tamás left San Francisco behind as they took a ferry for Oakland and from there boarded the express train for New York. They spent their days in the observation car watching the vast expanse of America disappear in the distance as they sped toward the East. Leopold felt he was speeding toward his future; he was hopeful, but anxious about what might be waiting ahead.

Somewhere between Cheyenne and Omaha, Leopold asked Tamás, "What made you decide to leave California, Tamás? I know Alejandro and America offered you a whole new kind of life. Why did you decide to leave?"

"Many reasons, but mainly California was simply not my place," Tamás answered. "I could never stop thinking of home—my paprikas," he laughed. "Maybe paprikas would grow in California, but it would never seem right; and my parents, I need to see them again."

Tamás looked at Leopold eye to eye and spoke in a serious tone, "I left California because I need to see you with your son. I need to meet Stefan. I need to see how that story goes."

"A good thing that you and I undertook this great adventure together. Tamás," Leopold responded thoughtfully. "You saved my life. I know that. You are my closest confidant, Tamás, like a brother to me and I am obliged to you for the rest of my life.

"My life in America, although brief, has changed me, Tamás," Leopold continued, "I see things differently now. I have new goals, new ambitions for the future and I hope that you will be part of my future. My desire is for you to stay with me and my family. I want you to be an associate in my business endeavors and the manager of my home. My intent is to make your decision to stay with me financially worthwhile for you."

"Of course, I'll continue to be with you, Leopold," Tamás laughed, "to continue doing exactly what I've been doing for the last twenty years and if you want to give me new duties and more money, then I believe I'll accept and thank you for it."

The two men shook hands across the table. Tamás smiled and added, "Let us have a glass of wine. I'll buy, now that I'm going to be a rich man."

After the seventy-two hour trip from California, they found themselves back in New York's Central Station. They checked into a Dylan Hotel suite on the evening of April eighteenth and slept soundly until early the next morning.

When Tamás opened the morning newspaper he experienced a great shock. He hurried into Leopold's room to deliver the dreadful news, "Look at this!" and held up the newspaper for Leopold to see the headline sprawled across the front page, "San Francisco destroyed by Earthquake!"

While Tamás read the horrific stories aloud, Leopold dressed quickly for the day. After breakfast they made their way to meet Elizabeth von Schrader at the Martha Washington Hotel for Women. They were the rare two gentlemen sitting in the hotel lobby waiting for her to appear. The lobby was comfortable, decorated in a fashionable Victorian style with heavy overstuffed furnishings, Persian carpets, and fringed velvet draperies.

Tamás continued to read the newspaper stories to Leopold, summarizing the articles for him, "Eyewitness reports of the devastating earthquake, thousands of lives lost, and millions of dollars in businesses and buildings gone!"

He showed the headlines to Leopold once more, "Horrible! We just missed being right there in the middle of it," Tamás shook his head. "The Palace Hotel burned to the ground. Today it is nothing more than a gutted-out shell."

Leopold observed the activities of the young ladies going and coming. Anxious to return to Europe, Leopold shifted on the settee; he was ready to begin his life anew. *There's so much to do*, he thought and said aloud to Tamás, "This rescue mission is a distraction."

While they waited the earthquake dominated their conversation. Tamás decided he should send a telegram to Señor Alejandro to enquire as to their well-being.

Then Leopold saw *her* or at least he surely hoped it was Elizabeth von Schrader. A stunning young woman dressed in a cream and pink lace dress seemed to float down the curved staircase. Leopold noticed her excellent posture as she walked with confidence toward him, her hand extended. Ash blonde hair piled atop her head with deep waves framed her beautiful face. "Duke von Esté?" she asked.

Leopold stood, took her hand, bowed and answered, "Miss von Schrader, I'm delighted to make your acquaintance." He looked into her clear blue eyes, much darker blue than Cili's, "You may call me Leopold." He smiled, "May I present my companion, Tamás Tóth."

Tamás stood, bowed, and invited her to sit with them.

"I am very grateful to you for coming to my rescue, sir. The situation has been extremely trying." She paused, took a breath, and added with deliberation, "I am perfectly capable of taking care of myself and I definitely could have booked my own passage home, but it would have been completely inappropriate for a lady to travel unescorted. My reputation would be in jeopardy and that is, of course unacceptable! So, I thank you for coming." She took another deep breath, "You may call me Elizabeth."

Leopold smiled, "We're very happy to be at your service, Elizabeth, and we can see that you are a very capable young woman." He added, "Perhaps it is Tamás and I who should thank you. It may be that you saved our lives; it appears we escaped San Francisco just in the nick of time."

She seemed suddenly shy and looked down, "Oh, yes, the earthquake. My troubles pale in comparison to those poor souls."

Leopold was impressed at her sense of propriety for one so young and by her gracious manner. Elizabeth's smile was most charming, but he noted that she remained reserved, even cool. She reminded him of the Viennese court expectations that he and Cili escaped as often as they could. In addition, she was beautiful and elegant and uncommonly self-assured for one so young, qualities he most certainly liked. Leopold affirmed to her that he and Tamás would make arrangements that afternoon for their passage to Europe as soon as possible and asked Elizabeth, "May we escort you to dinner this evening?"

She graciously accepted and the men took their leave. That evening at the Benjamin Steak House, only moments after they had taken their places at the table, Elizabeth felt compelled to further explain her situation. "My chaperone, a spinster aunt the Countess Mathilde, and I had been traveling for almost three months from city to city along America's east coast—Washington, Philadelphia, Baltimore, here to New York, and then to Boston."

Elizabeth described her aunt without mercy, "Mathilde is a silly, immature old maid without any sense of propriety." Elizabeth shook her head, "While we were in Baltimore Mathilde met a younger man who swept her off her feet. He turned out to be a ne'er-do-well gambler. He followed us to Boston and then suddenly one morning she was gone. She left a letter for me, writing that the two of them had run off to New Orleans together, leaving me alone, stranded, and unchaperoned."

"I was not frightened at all by this predicament," she looked from Leopold to Tamás for assurance that she had convinced them of her bravery. They were smiling and nodded to assure her. "I never minded being alone. Our hotel in

Boston was very fine, so I took the necessary steps to continue my accommodations there. But I am a proper young woman and I did not want to jeopardize my reputation, so I notified my mother in Linz, who contacted her friend, the Duchess Eugenia, who turned out to be your sister!"

She smiled broadly at Leopold. "I did take a risk by traveling alone to New York, but the concierge in Boston made arrangements for me at the Martha Washington Hotel…and then all I had to do was wait for you to appear! And now you have, and I will forever be in your debt. You are both very kind gentlemen."

For the next two weeks, Leopold occupied all of Elizabeth's time. They saw George M. Cohen's *Give My Regards to Broadway* one evening and another they attended a piano concert of Hungarian rhapsodies and mazurkas. On their last night in the city, a warm spring night, they took a Hansom cab ride through Central Park.

—⚹—

Leopold studied the *cabinet card* photograph of a young woman seated on a wicker sofa in front of a potted fern, "Elizabeth in New York, May 1906," was written across the corner. A second hand-colored postcard made him smile; a photograph of all three of them, Leopold, Elizabeth, and Tamás, standing by a ship's railing near a life preserver with "S.S. *Carpathia*" written on it. Leopold thought about meeting Elizabeth in America, in New York City, and about their homecoming sail on the *Carpathia*. Elizabeth was so young, so beautiful. No wonder he had fallen in love again.

There was a soft knock on the library door as it opened slightly allowing Silva to look into the room. She had on a robe and a nightcap on her head, "What are you two doing up so late? Do you know that it's past midnight?"

Tamás stretched and yawned, "Leopold and I have been reminiscing over all these old photographs and souvenirs, so many, many memories."

"Thank you, Silva, for coming to get us." Leopold stood up stretching. "We've been lost in the past. We should stop now. I am very tired." His legs were stiff. "Thank you, so much Tamás, for keeping me company and for helping me remember all our adventures."

Leopold put his arm over Tamás's shoulders and patted Silva's hand as well, "I'm so fortunate to have both of you with us. What would we do without you!"

The three, followed by Fejedelem, walked from the darkened room, leaving the albums and the memorabilia box on the floor. Photographs and other objects were scattered over the carpet. There were images of emperors and tsars…dashing soldiers and beautiful young women with bouquets of flowers in their arms…family groups and wedding portraits…babies in their christening clothes…little boys in sailor suits…little girls with big white bows in their hair…athletic boys and terribly injured ones…and many, more black memorial cards.

BOOK II

1906–1938

1906

On a spectacular morning in early May, Leopold, Tamás, and Elizabeth set sail on the Cunard Line S.S. *Carpathia*, a stunning ship of luxury, sleek and fast. Against the bright morning sky, white steam rolled up from a single red-and-black funnel standing at mid-ship. Four gigantic masts were located beside the funnel, two toward the bow and two toward the stern. The *Carpathia's* great black hull sliced through the water's surface, while its gleaming white bridge and cabin levels rose above the promenade deck

An air of excitement permeated the environment aboard ship; most of the first-class passengers were American tourists filled with anticipation for their grand adventures in old Europe. The presence of Tamás, Leopold, and Elizabeth among the passengers added an aura of the exotic for the Americans. The tourists were thrilled to have real Austro-Hungarian aristocracy in their midst. Although their anticipation was of a different sort, Tamás, Leopold, and Elizabeth experienced just as much excitement for going home as the Americans for going on their Grand Tour.

Standing by the railing of the ship's bow Leopold watched the skyline of New York and the Statue of Liberty recede as the ship steamed out into the open Atlantic. Six days and nights would pass before they would see land again. Leopold contemplated how differently he felt on this passage from how he had felt on his arrival three years ago. He remembered the desolation he suffered, as though there had been nothing to live for or hope for, only a gnawing emptiness. Cili's death had so destroyed him, he had not dreamt he would ever recover.

Now Leopold felt exhilarated as he looked down at the water. He let out a slow breath, grateful he had not succumbed to his darkest thoughts by jumping into the watery abyss that night years ago. The speed of the steamship cutting through the waves caused a great splashing of foam that sprayed across the bow. Leopold stood in the fine mist looking up at the bright, promising sky and felt joyful at the thought of his future, his home, and meeting Stefan, his son.

The image of Elizabeth came into Leopold's mind. He had not expected to ever again have an interest in any woman, believing there could be no other woman after Cili; but, he smiled to himself, and could not shake Elizabeth's image, her exquisite face, from his thoughts. He had to admit that since their first meeting Elizabeth had delighted him each day with her sense of optimism and curiosity, quite contagious.

Elizabeth asked question after question revealing her genuine interest in everything. She asked about Stefan and, without any hesitation, asked about

Cili, and about how his nose had been broken. When Leopold told Elizabeth the truth of it all, she kissed him gently on both cheeks and simply asked more questions. She asked about California and Sopron and Hungary, but she was most curious about his business interests. Elizabeth wanted to know his ideas for building a wine business and his plans for engaging in actual work to make money.

Leopold explained that he knew changes were coming to Europe. He believed that the life of privilege for the aristocracy without honest labor, or occupation, could no longer sustain itself. Elizabeth praised his dreams; she was impressed and seemed to share his sensibilities. Her mature and thoughtful questions, including detail about finance and structural procedures, astonished Leopoold.

"How can you know these questions? How do you know what to ask? You're so young."

"I am the only child of an entrepreneur, a capitalist who has invested in many ventures and dreams. My father told me many times, 'The way to real riches is through the dreamer.' "

Conversations with Elizabeth stimulated Leopold's own excitement to get home and to get started on his vines, on his dreams. Even though Leopold suspected his return to Sopron and Vienna would be agonizing in many ways, he remained hopeful for the possibilities despite the pain that might await.

His thoughts wandered once again to Cili; he could still *see* her; her delicate white form shining as an angelic light. He certainly had not forgotten her. No two women could be more different—Cili and Elizabeth, Cili warm and affectionate, Elizabeth cool and reserved. And in regard to business matters...business had never been a concern for Cili. The two women were completely opposite in personalities. What they shared in common was beauty, the kind of exceptional beauty that turned heads.

Very much the main attraction on board were Leopold and Elizabeth— he a handsome man of thirty-two and she, dazzling, at only nineteen. The passengers noticed the delightful couple as they strolled arm in arm on the promenade deck each afternoon and when they danced together in the ballroom each evening. Even though the days were few in number, Leopold and Elizabeth spent all of them together and time passed most pleasurably for both of them.

By the time the *Carpathia* sailed into Liverpool, the two were in love and Leopold planned to ask Elizabeth's father for her hand in marriage. Leopold had been so occupied on the Atlantic crossing he had not spent much time with Tamás, who spent his hours on board relaxing and reading. On the last night before the *Carpathia* docked at the Liverpool pier, Leopold asked Tamás to walk with him on deck; the two men walked together in silence, until Leopold finally spoke.

"What I am about to say will come as a shock to you, Tamás." Leopold cleared his throat, stopped walking, and looked directly at his oldest friend, "I never imagined I could feel love again." Leopold quickly added, "Not at all the same as it was with Cili, she was my soul mate, my life, but I do feel strongly for Elizabeth and she has fallen in love with me, so, Tamás, we will be married next year."

Tamás lit his pipe and took several puffs, "Neither I nor anyone else on this ship would be surprised by that news, Leopold." He laughed, "I think it is the best news. She is good for you…she will be good for young Stefan, too," Tamás puffed on his pipe, "and she will be good for business."

The next morning Leopold, Tamás, and Elizabeth were packed and ready to leave the *Carpathia* and all the wonderful memories of the Atlantic crossing. After a few days rest in Liverpool, they sailed away to Le Havre, then boarded a train for Vienna.

Vienna and Linz

After the train pulled into the *Hauptbahnhof* in Vienna, Tamás took his leave to travel on to Sopron while Leopold and Elizabeth immediately boarded a steamboat going to Linz via the Danube. Within only a few hours Leopold and Elizabeth arrived in her home town where a carriage awaited them. They were driven to an impressive five-storied Baroque mansion on the Promenade near Linz's finest square. Leopold delivered Elizabeth safely to her parents, the Baron and Baroness, Emmencht and Béate von Schrader.

"We are very grateful to you, sir, for your protection of our daughter and her safe delivery home. We are forever in your debt," promised the Baron.

Shortly after their arrival Elizabeth and her mother excused themselves to the upstairs. Leopold took the opportunity to declare his intentions to the Baron and ask for his blessing. Baron von Schrader was quite pleased that Elizabeth had made such a good match, as was Elizabeth's mother upon hearing the news; she also happily approved the pair. Over a lunch of *tafelspitz mit g'röste erdäpfel*, sliced beef with fried potatoes and applesauce, and glasses of pale beer Elizabeth proudly told her father about Leopold's dream to become a successful vintner; his ambition to become a businessman.

The Baron, a successful industrialist and very wealthy businessman himself, assured Leopold, "As I have told you, I am in your debt. I will help you and Elizabeth attain your goals in any way I can; only ask and it will be yours.

"You must realize your future bride has a man's mind when it comes to business," the Baron added with a smile. "She will be your equal in making the right financial choices and in understanding the market. You will be a wise man to trust her opinions and take her advice."

Then the Baron paused and rose from the table.

"Let us toast the returned travelers!" With a boisterous laugh and animated gestures, characteristic of the Baron, he held his glass high, "Welcome home to our lovely daughter and her excellent Duke! At last, her mother can get some rest."

They clinked their glasses together and launched into lively conversation, filled with questions about their American adventures and answers long and colorful. Their stories thrilled the Baron and Baroness.

Eventually the talk turned to Leopold's life and to his son. Leopold explained, "When I leave Linz, I'll return to Vienna and finally meet my son, Stefan. My hope is that he will be willing to go with me to Sopron where we can begin a new life together." Leopold took a nervous breath, then smiled at the von Schraders and said, "Please, all of you come to Sopron Castle so that you, too, can meet Stefan and see Elizabeth's future home."

The von Schraders happily accepted the invitation and assured him they would count the days until they could visit Sopron.

The following morning Leopold said good-bye and took the boat back to Vienna. After arriving at Hofburg Palace his first visit was to the apartments of his mother, the Duchess Maria. He was surprised at how frail she had become during his absence. Despite her physical state, however, her mind was sharp and she wanted to know all about America and then, once she heard of Elizabeth, she wanted to know about her.

Maria patted Leopold's hand that she held in hers, "I am happy for little Stefan. At last he will have his Papa again and a mother, too. I agree with your plan to take him back to Sopron. Sopron is a good place for a boy to grow."

"We want you to come home with us, too, Mother." Leopold kissed his mother's hand, "It would be good for Stefan to have his grandmother there. Your presence would give him some continuity. Will you consider coming with us?"

"Perhaps I shall visit, but this is my home now, Leopold," Maria seemed reflective. "You must go now to meet your son. They are expecting you."

Leopold kissed his mother good-bye and left. He walked quickly to another part of the palace to the apartments of Cili's mother. Sadly, while Leopold was in America, Cili's father had passed away. Before Leopold knocked on the door, he took a deep breath and tried to shake away his nerves. The maid led him to the reception room where Princess Margit greeted him warmly with an embrace, shared kisses and an invitation to sit down. Margit spoke sincerely, "I am so happy that you have returned at last; you have been away too long. Your son needs you."

"It took a long time for me to find myself. I would have been no good for Stefan or anyone during that dark time. But, then, at last, I began to remember the happy times with Cili; I could focus my thoughts on all that she loved about life...in particular, Stefan. I began to wonder about my son. I wanted to know Stefan. I wanted to know who was teaching him the things I should be teaching him. Who was he looking up to? I knew I had to come home. I missed my son."

"Good. He wants his father desperately." Margit pulled the servant's bell. The maid appeared instantly. "Lisa, please bring Stefan."

"One more thing that you must know, Madam—I am planning to marry again, next spring. I never thought I would ever again meet someone I could care for, but I have met someone. Of course, there is no comparison to Cili. Cili will forever be the love of my life, but Elizabeth is good for me and she will be good for Stefan, too."

Margit simply nodded her head, acknowledging that she had heard him, but made no comment. At that moment the door opened and the little boy, almost five years old, walked into the room. Leopold nearly gasped aloud when he saw Stefan. The little boy was the image of Cili. Like her, light blond curls circled his sweet face with a halo of sunlight and his eyes were the sky blue color of his mother's. Stefan remained standing by the open door, shifting his weight from one foot to the other.

"Come here to me, Stefan," Margit said. The child walked obediently to his grandmother's side. "This is your father. He has come home from America to meet you. Say hello to your father, Stefan."

Stefan scrutinized the man sitting across from him; he said "Hello" and walked across the carpet to Leopold. Stefan took Leopold's extended hand, exchanged kisses on both cheeks, and asked, "Are you going away again?"

"No, Stefan. I'm going to stay with you." Leopold did not let go of Stefan's hand, "Will you take a walk with me in the garden?"

Leopold and his son took their leave of Margit and made their way to the gardens outside. They walked along the graveled pathway, the day was gray and cloudy; a storm seemed imminent. Stefan looked up at his father; he was very glad to be holding Leopold's hand.

"I have a picture of you in my room," Stefan told Leopold. "I have a picture of my mother, too. I look like my mother."

"Yes, Stefan, you do. She was very beautiful and you are quite a handsome boy."

"Did you see cowboys in America?" Stefan asked, "Did you see Indians?"

"Yes, I did Stefan. I saw many cowboys riding their horses and roping cattle. I saw Indians, too, riding their painted ponies across the prairie. They are a handsome people, the Indians, with their long black hair and they are excellent horsemen, too. I think much like our own Magyars." Leopold smiled at Stefan, "America is a very exciting place. I have many stories to tell you, Stefan, about America and about your mother."

Stefan liked hearing his father speak; he felt good walking beside Leopold.

"Grandmother told me that you went away because you were sad. Are you still sad?"

"No, Stefan, I do not feel sad any more. I felt deep despair, because I loved your mother very much and it was hard for me when she had to leave me."

"You should not be worried, Papa." Stefan looked up to Leopold quite seriously, "she is happy, because she is in heaven with grandfather."

"That is true, Stefan," Leopold could see that Stefan was a compassionate little boy, "I am not worried any longer. I'm happy now, because I'm back home with you. I have missed you very much."

As big drops of rain began to fall, Leopold bent over to pick up Stefan and hold him in his arms, "I hope you will come with me to our castle in Sopron. I want you to meet my friends, Tamás and Gáspár and Ilonka. We have dogs and horses for you to meet at the castle, too. Would you like to live there with us?"

"Oh, yes, Papa, I would. Will Grandmother Margit live there, too?"

"No, she will stay here, but she and your Grandmother Maria will come to visit as often as they can."

After a few days in Vienna, Leopold and Stefan traveled to Sopron. Tamás met their train with great excitement; he could hardly wait to meet young Stefan. As the little boy stepped off the train, Tamás, too, was taken aback by his appearance. Tamás looked at Leopold, who nodded to him, "He looks just like her."

The two men embraced and Leopold introduced Tamás to Stefan.

"I'm your father's friend and I would like to be yours, too. You appear to be a fine young man just like your father."

As the three climbed into a horse-drawn coach, Stefan's trunks were taken to a waiting wagon. Stefan sat close to the coach's window watching the horse-drawn carriages, wagons, and motorized vehicles going and coming from the station. As they withdrew from the town to the countryside, Leopold said reflectively to Tamás, "I expected this meeting with my son to be difficult. I never thought he would be so accepting, so forgiving."

"Little Stefan not only looks like his mother, he has his mother's heart," said Tamás. "It is quite obvious there is no animosity in his little being. Stefan will be very happy at the castle; I'm sure of it."

—◊◊◊—

Leopold had great pride for his ancestral home. He was eager to return and to introduce all the castle's history and stories to his son. In the tenth century, when marauding tribal barbarians migrated through Eastern Europe, Leopold's von Esté ancestors built the castle atop a rocky crag in the cool, green Lövér Hills near Sopron, Hungary's westernmost city. In the sixteenth century the Esté castle, as protector of Sopron, stood in the path of Ottoman Turks who swept across Hungary on their way to the West. The town of Sopron, an ancient site with roots from Roman times, gained fame for its pleasant climate and picturesque location. By the eighteenth century, Sopron became quite popular for both Austrian and Hungarian aristocrats as an escape from the stifling summers of Vienna. Those aristocrats built many fine Baroque palaces, churches, and public buildings along the streets and squares of the town, making it a perfect retreat for the Viennese Court.

From the walls of the castle, the city of Sopron could be seen in the distance, with its great *Tűztorony* Firewatch Tower and many Old Town church spires. Even farther in the distance lay the Burgenland, Austria, and Eisenstadt, and farther beyond lay the *Neusiedlersee*, a shallow swampy lake.

As the coach approached the castle, its landscape of vineyards, forests, hills, and ponds intrigued Stefan; he was thrilled to see horses grazing in the meadow along with sheep and cattle. He smiled broadly when he noticed the large group of people standing outside the castle entrance; Stefan knew they were awaiting his arrival.

When the coach stopped, Leopold and Stefan stepped out to a vigorous welcome of applause and shouts of greeting from Gáspár, Ilonka, and the castle staff. After introductions were made all around, Ilonka announced, "Lunch has been prepared, all of the Duke Leopold's special favorites. I will serve you as soon as you have rested from your journey."

Leopold led Stefan up the grand staircase to his room where he immediately climbed onto a window seat from which he had a view of horses in the meadow just beyond the front lawn. Stefan laughed with joy as he used the little stair to get up onto his huge bed. He nestled into the downy comforter and pillows and then pointed to a beautiful box that stood in the center of a finely carved wooden dresser.

"What is that?" he asked.

"Your mother gave this to me." Leopold said as he walked over to the box and turned the crystal handle; a lovely melody drifted through the room. "She loved to hear the music; it made her very happy. Now the music box is yours."

At that moment servants delivered Stefan's trunks and Leopold said, "Ilonka will help you unpack your things later. We should go down for lunch now. Katalin, our cook, will have something very special for us."

Ilonka had arranged for lunch to be served outside on the loggia shaded by a grape arbor. She served Katalin's *Vadas hús kenyér gombóccal*, venison with bread dumplings, *csirke paprikás*, chicken paprika, *burgonya lángos*, fried potato cake, and for dessert, *Meggyleves*, sour cherry soup. Tamás ate with Leopold and Stefan until they could eat no more.

"Oh, Ilonka, please tell Katalin that I have missed her cooking!" Leopold exclaimed. "It is good to be home again!"

"Yes, it is good for all of us to be together again," echoed Tamás. Turning to Stefan, he asked, "Well, what did you think of your lunch, young man?"

"Hmmm…Good! Everything is my favorite, too, like my Papa." Stefan added with one of his big smiles, "Thank you, Katalin, you are a very good cook!"

After lunch the men led Stefan on a tour of the castle grounds. When Gáspár joined them, he brought Báró with him to meet Stefan. Only slightly older than Stefan, Báró took to the young boy instantly and followed him faithfully from that day forward.

Stefan asked, "Is Báró my dog now?"

"Absolutely!" Gáspár answered, "It appears Báró has decided he is yours."

Stefan looked very pleased and stroked Báró's head.

"I think Báró has been waiting for you all these years. He is ready for a youngster to go running with him." Gáspár added, "There is a pony out there in the meadow for you, too, Stefan. Tomorrow morning we will pick out the one you like."

These new circumstances completely delighted Stefan. He held tightly to his father's hand as they turned their attention to the vineyards. "Your grandfather loved these vines, Stefan. He taught me about the vines and the grapes and now I will teach you all that I know. Perhaps you will come to love them, too."

Stefan looked down the rows of vines that followed the land for as far as he could see. He felt a sense of pride and he was sure that one day he, too, would love these vines, although at the moment he had no idea why.

One afternoon, later that summer, while Leopold and Stefan were sitting under the grape arbor, Leopold spoke carefully to Stefan. "I have a very special friend, Stefan, whom I want you to meet. She is coming to visit us here in a few days. She is excited to meet you. She is a nice lady and very pretty, too. I think you will like her. Her name is Elizabeth."

"Will she be my new mother?"

Leopold was surprised by Stefan's insight and answered him honestly, "I would like that, Stefan. If you and Elizabeth become good friends it will make me very happy."

On a hot August afternoon from his window seat Stefan impatiently watched the long driveway leading up to the castle. At last, he saw a motor car coming toward the castle. He ran down the stairs, arriving at the entrance to join Leopold just as the automobile stopped. Leopold opened the car door and offered his hand to the lady inside. Stefan was breathless as he waited to see her. He expected her to be pretty, but when he saw her, he thought she was beautiful. Elizabeth smiled at him and knelt down to his level at once.

"How do you do, Stefan? I am Elizabeth."

At that very moment Báró gave Elizabeth a lick on the cheek, knocking her over. Although Elizabeth laughed, Stefan hurried to her aid and scolded Báró for being too rough.

"I'm all right, Stefan. We'll just think Báró is saying hello in his own special way," Elizabeth laughed and patted Báró on the head, still laughing as Leopold helped her to her feet.

Leopold escorted her parents, the Baron and Baroness, Emmencht and Béate von Schrader into the castle, while Elizabeth took Stefan's hand, "Will you show me all the castle's special places, Stefan?"

Stefan proudly promised he would and decided right then that he liked Elizabeth very much.

The von Schraders stayed at the Esté castle for two weeks. They explored every part of the castle ruins and were very interested in the renovations of the modern wing. The Baron enjoyed touring the vineyards in the summer sun to the sound of cicadas while discussing Leopold's business plans. Béate and Elizabeth preferred the cool beauty of the gardens and the house interior. Elizabeth and Stefan spent time together reading, playing card games, and telling stories to each other. Stefan told her about Vienna and Elizabeth told him about the cities she had visited in America. Ilonka and Katalin delighted everyone with delicious meals and Gáspár opened aged Sopron wines, wines that convinced the Baron that the Duke Leopold von Esté and his venture could become quite successful in the business world. With Stefan's approval the wedding date was set for the spring in Linz. When the von Schraders left Sopron, the sadness felt by everyone was genuine. The house seemed very quiet.

—⁂—

Leopold had been thinking of Lake Balaton all summer, but he dreaded going back to the place that held so many memories of Cili. He walked through the vineyard alone with his thoughts... *It was hard enough to return here... the site of Cili's terrible death. Only Stefan's presence made it possible. His joy and curiosity push every dark thought from my mind until only good memories of Cili and Lake Balaton remain.* Leopold wiped tears from his eyes; he was convinced that Cili's angelic aura had passed directly into little Stefan's heart. In such a brief time, Stefan was loved by everyone, just as his mother had been. *I am delighted that Stefan and Elizabeth formed such a strong bond so quickly.*

The memory of Elizabeth and Stefan, both claiming "broken hearts" when the von Schraders left Sopron, made Leopold smile. His smile widened as he thought of Stefan asking several times a day, "What do you think Elizabeth is doing now?"

One evening during dinner Leopold seemed distant and contemplative, "Tamás, do you think we should take young Stefan to Lake Balaton before the summer is over? There are a few weeks of summer left. We could look in on the grapes. What do you think?"

"An excellent idea, Leopold! When should we go?"

Stefan slid up to the edge of his chair, "What is Lake Balaton?"

"A most wonderful place," answered Tamás excitedly, "the place where your father and I spent all our summers when we were children. You, too, will have wonderful adventures there," Tamás said with a big smile.

"I think we should leave the day after tomorrow," Leopold said; he felt far more excited about going back to the lake than he had imagined he would. Once Leopold had said the words aloud, he could hardly wait to go. "Our very good friends, Christián and Gabriele, will be there. It will be good to see them after all these years and to meet their little son, Rudolf."

Two days later the von Estés arrived at their Lake Balaton villa; neither Leopold nor Tamás had been there since leaving with Cili almost five years ago to the day. Leopold held Stefan's hand, Tamás stood at his shoulder. Gáspár and Ilonka hesitated for only a moment before they hurried to the entrance. Gáspár opened the door, calling to the caretaker that they had arrived. Ilonka went straight to the kitchen. Over the years Gáspár and Ilonka had visited regularly to meet with the overseer of the grapes and to check on the condition of the house. Each year the overseer sold the grapes on market; no wine had been pressed or bottled on the property, but the grapevines continued to mature and produce exceptionally well. Ilonka returned to the entrance where Leopold still stood motionless.

"Come in and I will have supper ready by the time all of you are ready for it."

Finally, Leopold forced himself to move forward, "I'm all right now, Tamás...I just...I could see her standing there so clearly," Leopold held Stefan's hand tightly and looked to Tamás for reassurance, "Perhaps Cili was there...saying she is glad we have come back." Leopold looked down at Stefan, "Your mother loved this villa very much."

The three climbed the stairs together and entered the rotunda. Leopold and Stefan went up the staircase to the second floor to his new room. Once again Stefan's room had a window seat, but this time the beautiful, sparkling Lake Balaton was his view. He could see sailboats with colorful sails skimming through the milky, yellow-green water, a sight that enthralled him. Leopold leaned over his son's shoulder, "We'll go sailing after supper."

The next day Leopold and Tamás took Stefan to the von Házy villa on Tihany Peninsula. The Count and Countess, Christián and Gabriele, welcomed them with great excitement. They heartily embraced Leopold and Tamás, "We have missed you! We are overjoyed to have you back in our lives!"

"Leopold, you look wonderful, happy...you have taken good care of him, Tamás. Thank you for bringing him back to us," gushed Gabriele, "but we suspect this young man is the reason for your happiness, Leopold."

Gabriele and Christián turned their attention to Stefan, immediately remarking on his resemblance to Cili. The gregarious couple had Stefan smiling and laughing when their nanny entered the room holding the hand of an adorable toddler.

"Here's our boy, Rudolf...Dolf, meet our very dear friends, the Duke von

Esté and Tamás and Stefan. From now on we will be together often and you boys can become very good friends."

The last few weeks of summer passed by in a swirl of activity, just as in their youth. The days were filled with sailing and swimming and treks into the countryside, dinners in Balatonfüred and picnics and parties. Leopold spent much of his time walking through the vineyards and the press house. He was glad they had come back to the lake and to the villa; his family's life at the lake meant a great deal to him. Leopold was never more content than when he was at Lake Balaton. As he sat in an old wicker chair in the kitchen garden, he studied the back of the villa, painted a light mint green... *it is a handsome house... Elizabeth will be happy here in the summer...* of that he was certain.

1907

A week before the April wedding, Leopold and Stefan along with Tamás arrived by boat in Linz from Vienna and soon afterwards the von Házy family followed. They were all settled into the elegant Wolfinger Hotel, formerly a monastery, located on the *Hauptplatz* only a short distance from the von Schraders's townhouse. Even though the von Schrader home was a very busy place before the wedding day, all of the out-of-town guests were made welcome and entertained often.

Somewhat apprehensive about Leopold's intended, Christián and Gabriele were anxious about meeting Elizabeth, due primarily to her youthful age, just barely twenty. However, when they met her, all doubts were erased. Her mature sensibilities and no-nonsense manner complimented Leopold so well; it was quite obvious to them that Elizabeth cared deeply for Leopold.

Elizabeth's dear childhood friend, the Baroness Renate von Werner, arrived from Bavaria to stand with Elizabeth as her Matron of Honor. Elizabeth was thrilled to introduce her beloved Leopold to her dearest friend, Renate, who approved of Leopold at once and raved about his handsome little boy. Already mother of two children, Renate had married very young to the Baron Hoffman von Werner, owner of a vast German railroad empire. Renate immediately decided that Stefan and his little friend, Rudolf, could entertain her little baby girls, even though the two boys were not so enthusiastic to do so.

On the wedding day everyone boarded the new electric train that wound its way up to the top of *Postlingberg*; they exited the train and followed a pathway to the eighteenth century Pilgrimage church, *Wallfahrtskirche zu den Sieben Schmerzen Mariens*, Our Lady of the Seven Sorrows. The church's tall twin spires rose above the trees and served as a guide for the wedding party as they walked toward the church. The guests admired the spectacular views of Linz and the countryside made possible by the height of *Postlingberg*. One could hear exclamations, "We can see why Elizabeth chose this particular church for her wedding! It is spectacular up here!"

Once inside the church everyone took their places and awaited the arrival of Elizabeth and her father. Leopold stood with Tamás at his side and Stefan at his knee. The Baroness Renate stood across from them holding a bouquet of yellow buttercups. At last, the door opened and Elizabeth appeared on her father's arm. She was a vision of beauty in a wedding dress of the latest Parisian fashion that she and her mother had purchased on an earlier trip to Paris. White ostrich feathers decorated her hair which was arranged in a chignon with diamond clips. A short, light veil fell across her face. Her French couture dress was *la belle époque*; the S-shaped corset forced her bosom forward, cinched her waist, and accentuated her derriere, a look considered quite fashionable, feminine, and appealing.

Elizabeth was breathtaking. The low *décolletage* neckline of the dress exposed her long slender neck around which she wore the wedding gift given her by Leopold, a gold filigree chain with a delicate arrangement of Baroque pearls and diamonds in the likeness of a gardenia. Lavender ribbons held softly draped tulle at the shoulders of the sleeveless dress. She, like Renate, carried a bouquet of buttercups, but with the addition of white spiraea and ivy.

As Elizabeth walked toward the altar, little Stefan looked up to his father and whispered, "Elizabeth is very pretty, isn't she Papa?"

Leopold and Elizabeth returned to Sopron Castle after a wedding trip to Italy. A few days later, they traveled the short distance to Eisenstadt to the von Házy estate. The von Házys had entertained Stefan while Leopold and Elizabeth were on their month-long trip. By the time Leopold and Elizabeth returned, Stefan at six and Rudolf at four, had become very close. The younger Rudolf admired Stefan and followed him everywhere while Stefan watched over Rudolf as he would a little brother.

Fall

After a lovely summer spent at Lake Balaton, Leopold seemed restless. He had spent much of his time preparing the press and bottling processes at the Balaton villa; in another year or two the villa would be ready to begin bottling wine for market. During the summer Leopold and Elizabeth traveled to all their land holdings in Hungary and Austria. Leopold wanted to establish clear directions for his managers in regard to moving the vineyards from a hobby-oriented operation toward a true money-making business.

No longer would the grapes from his vineyards be sold on the market, now the grapes would begin the fermentation process on various von Esté properties. Leopold knew it would take time and skilled managers to run his wide-spread holdings, but, eventually, he hoped his vineyards would produce bottles of fine wine desired throughout Europe.

Now that fall had come, Leopold sat in the study of his castle looking out at the mist rising from the wide lawn. An idea had been nagging at him, an idea he wanted to embrace, but he was worried about Elizabeth accepting his new plan. He rose from his chair and walked out of the study toward Elizabeth's breakfast room where he found her finishing her tea and preparing to begin a morning of letter writing.

"Betka, I have an important question to ask you."

She looked up at him with a furrowed brow, he sounded so serious, "What is it, dear? You may ask me anything."

"I am thinking that I would like to move from the castle to Budapest. I want to establish my company headquarters in Budapest. I own property in the city where we could build a house...a house of your dreams, Elizabeth." He took a breath, "I know this is a surprise, but I think it is the right thing to do."

Elizabeth was surprised, but it was such an exciting proposal she smiled at him and answered, "If that is what you wish, then I say we shall do it. I would be very happy to plan a fine house...a house of my dreams. When will all of this begin?"

Within the week Leopold and Elizabeth traveled to Budapest where they had an invitation to stay with Christián von Házy's parents, the Count Francis and Countess Alexandra. Their grand mansion stood just around the corner from the undeveloped von Esté property on Andrássy Avenue, formerly known as Sugár út. From the train station Leopold and Elizabeth took the The Metro, continental Europe's first underground railway, all the way down the Avenue to a stop across from their property. The little train traveled back and forth from the heart of Pest to the end of the Avenue where *Városliget City Park*, the site of the great Millennial Exhibition of 1896, was located. Since the 1896 Exhibition, the avenue had become very popular as a residential area for wealthy Budapest citizens. Among the older mansions, many splendid new houses were under construction on both sides of the wide avenue.

Leopold and Elizabeth commissioned the well-respected Budapest architect, Alajos Hauszmann, to begin drawing plans for an impressive Italianate style house. They also contacted Karoly Lotz for the *Szecesszió*, Art Nouveau, interior decorations and the famous Czech artist, Alphons Mucha, for stained glass.

While Elizabeth was fully involved in plans for her new home, Leopold traveled into the city of Pest to find a place for his new business. He arranged to tour a building on *Hercegprimás Street* near a bank on *Kiss út*. Leopold admired the exterior appearance of the narrow, four-storied building; its architectural details were impressive. The building rose from a rusticated stone ground floor and had a stair of five steps leading to double oak doors with beveled glass windows and large brass door handles. Each of the three floors that rose above the entrance had three large windows across the front; each oriel window was framed by fluted Corinthian columns and a decorative spandrel. Two magnificent, crouched, muscle-bound stone Atlases supported the building's cornice on their shoulders. The interior space also met Leopold's needs, so he proceeded to the Árpád Bank and purchased the building that afternoon.

To celebrate the building's purchase and the beginning of his new life, Leopold called Dr. Jakov Klein. An hour later they met at the *Gerbeaud* pastry shop in *Vörösmarty Square*. Leopold conveyed his happiness that they could resume their personal friendship now that they lived in the same city. He gave Dr. Klein greetings from Tamás who would also be moving to Budapest in the spring. They discussed Leopold's plans for the new von Esté Wine Company and Leopold expressed his hope that Dr. Klein would be willing to share his expertise on the fermentation and aging processes.

Leopold walked all the way from *Vörösmarty Square* along Andrássy Avenue past his future homesite and on to the von Házy home, just a bit farther than a mile and a half. He breathed in the aromas of Budapest. He noticed the exquisite architecture, beautiful sycamore trees, and lovely gardens as he walked along and he felt exhilarated by the vigor of the bustling city full of prosperity and promise. Leopold was completely satisfied with his life and he counted his many blessings as night began to fall. By the time he made his way up the steps to the von Házy's front door, he was met by Elizabeth who admonished him for being gone so long and setting her to worry. He apologized immediately and with great enthusiasm began to tell her about his day and his new building.

1908

By the spring of 1908 the von Esté house was complete and the family made their move to Budapest. The picturesque mansion on Andrássy Avenue was spectacular! Architect Hauszmann designed an Italian-style villa inspired by the northern Italian Renaissance houses he had seen on his many travels to Italy. The style of the house was a blend of romantic and classical detail. Rising from a rusticated stone foundation, the charming three-storied, stone-block house had a center campanile-like tower that enclosed an elaborate entrance. A splayed stair led to beautifully carved double oak doors. Numerous tall, round-headed windows marched around the first and second floors, six across the front on the first floor and eight across the front of the second. Elaborate decorative brackets supported a low-pitched, lid-like roof; rectangular windows were nestled between each of the brackets, marking the attic.

Hauszmann's answer for the hot summer weather of Budapest was a shady loggia and terrace that spanned the back of the house. On the first floor, instead of windows across the back of the house, a string of windowed garden doors opened onto the terrace from the summer dining room, a small sitting room, Tamás's apartment and offices, and the kitchen. The terrace was interrupted by a conservatory that projected from the center rear of the house; the conservatory was constructed of an iron skeleton with glass panels.

The kitchen was spacious and well-lit with a large oak table in the center. A kitchen garden designed by Ilonka spread out from the kitchen's garden doors. Ilonka and Gáspár remained at the Sopron castle as caretaker and head of housekeeping while Katalin, long-time cook at the castle, moved with the family to the new residence in Budapest. Katalin had a small private room next to the kitchen.

The entrance to the house opened into a great wood-paneled reception hall. Directly across from the entrance was a wide, curved staircase rising to the upper floors and behind the staircase was the entrance to the conservatory. Doorways on the right of the reception hall led to the principal parlor and Leopold's library and near the terrace side, a sitting room and small summer dining room. To the left of the hall was the grand dining room and on the terrace side a hallway leading to Tamás's apartment, offices and the kitchen. Tamás had his own suite of rooms near the kitchen that included a garden door that opened onto his own private terrace adjacent to the kitchen garden.

The grand staircase rose from the entrance hall to a landing where large Mucha stained-glass windows brilliantly lit the entire space. The windows depicted lovely Hungarian maidens sitting beneath a grape arbor; plump, deep-purple grapes and peacocks were intertwined within the arbor while a rising sun illuminated a distant landscape of blue lake and green hills. Beneath the windows the grand staircase divided into two separate staircases, one to the left and one to the right, both leading up to the open, balconied second floor. Eight bedrooms were located on the second floor along with Elizabeth's breakfast room in the campanile.

Other than Tamás and Katalin, the cook, the rest of the household staff lived in the roomy dormitory-style space on the third floor. The attic was encircled by windows between the brackets supporting the roof. At the center of the third-floor servants' quarters was a community room located at the top of the campanile, above Elizabeth's breakfast room. The staff's tower room included an outdoor balcony.

The house also boasted several modern bathrooms, pantries, and fireplaces; a full cellar housed various rooms for cold storage, laundry, ironing, coal and ice deliveries, wine cellar, and a hallway from which a series of obscure staircases rose all the way to the third floor providing access to the first and second floors along the way.

Standing to the rear of the house was a large garage with room for a carriage and two new motor cars, a sporty two-seater Renault and a larger family car, the Lancia Alpha. An apartment of rooms over the garage provided living spaces for the chauffeur, gardener, and general caretaker. At the back of the house a six-foot-high stone wall wrapped around three sides of the expansive garden.

Even before the house was completed, Elizabeth and the gardener began to set out a charming arrangement of trees and shrubbery, roses, hydrangea and fuscia; a small grape arbor and hedge rows gave added definition to the garden's plan. Along the garden walls Elizabeth planted ivy, wisteria, clematis, and honeysuckle. An arched doorway was built into the garden's left wall, the wall shared by the von Esté and von Házy gardens. The gate opened into the back of the von Házy grounds.

By the time the von Esté family moved into their new home, Leopold's business endeavor was well under way. Elizabeth and Tamás shared completely Leopold's enthusiasm for the grapes, for his many vineyards, and now for his fine office building. They wanted to know all the details of the business that kept Leopold so excited.

"I have found a barrel maker, Miklós Szabó, from the town of Eger," Leopold announced to Elizabeth and Tamás, "We have arranged a contract for a large supply of barrels to be made of French oak, ideal for fermentation. We'll use Szabó barrels at all of our vineyards!"

"I look forward to the day when I can hold one of my bottles, uncork it, and drink the first von Esté fine wine!" Leopold smiled.

"That will be an exciting day," Elizabeth and Tamás agreed.

—ɯɯ—

Leopold felt fully involved in the thriving business atmosphere of Budapest— new building construction, new shops, entrepreneurs, a feeling of optimism everywhere. But beyond this hope-filled environment and the establishment of his new business, Leopold had additional challenges as a new citizen living in prosperous Pest. He had always been interested in politics and politics in Budapest was particularly challenging, always in some kind of unrestful flux.

Since the Compromise of 1867 Hungary had maintained some autonomy within the Austro-Hungarian Empire. The Compromise allowed the Hungarian Council to retain the right to agree or disagree with Vienna. Too often, however, Vienna made decisions that left Leopold and the Hungarians dissatisfied. As a member of the Hungarian Parliament, Leopold regularly spoke out vehemently against the Austro-Hungarian foreign minister, Duke von Aehrenthal, who at that particular moment was an ardent proponent for the Austrian annexation of Bosnia-Herzegovina.

"Austria's determination to acquire Bosnia-Herzegovina will have tragic results for Hungary," declared a distraught Leopold to a gathering of old friends who shared his views.

The men met in Leopold's library to draft a letter of opposition to their own Hungarian leaders who seemed determined to go along with the Emperor and von Aehrenthal in a dash to annex the Balkan countries. The letter they prepared warned the Council, *Aehrenthal has a great influence over the Emperor and the agenda Aehrenthal supports is ill-conceived. That agenda will once again lead Hungary into disaster if we follow Austria in this Balkan endeavor!*

Stefan sat on the floor listening to his father argue his opinions. When Stefan saw the other men nodding their heads in agreement, he felt very proud.

"It is unbelievable to me that Aehrenthal has made a deal with Russia's foreign minister," Leopold shared his recently acquired information with the men, "The Russians have promised support for Austria's annexation plan *if* Austria agrees to allow Russian warships to use the Dardanelles." In a lowered voice, Leopold added, "It is possible that the Kaiser has encouraged our Emperor to pursue the Balkan annexation."

One of the men sneered, *"Lay with curs and their mange will become yours."*

"The Austrians are dupes to trust the Russians," another muttered. "If disturbed, the 'Bear' will rise to the aid of their Slavic friends in the Balkans."

After the men had left the von Esté home, Stefan asked his father, "Why shouldn't we trust the Russians? I thought the Tsar was our friend."

"In 1849 Hungarians rose up in a fight for independence from Austria— almost sixty years ago," explained Leopold, "Lajos Kossuth, the great Hungarian hero, led the Hungarians in their struggle against Austria, but it was ill-fated from the beginning. Our Emperor Franz József put down the rebellion with help from his friend and cousin, Nicholas I. The Tsar sent his Russian troops into Hungary to annihilate the rebels, including thirteen Hungarian generals who were executed in the town of Arad. Their martyrdom is still celebrated to this very day by the people of Hungary."

Leopold looked seriously at Stefan, "Also to this day the Hungarian people have a deep distrust of the Russians, because of the brutality used against the Hungarians."

"But, Papa, why does Hungary want to be separate from Austria?"

"From my youth I have considered myself to be a progressive thinker... dedicated to the liberal movements within Hungary, but we are aristocrats and remain loyal to the Emperor. I will always be a loyal Monarchist! But I am an advocate for more shared government between Hungary and Austria—more independence for Hungary. Because of the Great Compromise, Austria has dominance over Hungary in all national matters, including this annexation idea. That means Hungary will be obligated to share in the consequences of this action by the Austrians, even if it leads to war with Russia." Leopold stated firmly, "In my opinion, there should be more attention paid to the will of the Hungarian people. And, yes, I am a friend of the Russian Tsar Nicholas. He is a good, gentle man, but, like our Emperor, some of his advisors have ideas that may lead Niki in a wrong direction."

Seven year-old Stefan listened intently to his father's every word; although he did not always understand completely the politics, he did take to heart his father's passions.

"Emperor Franz József shares my belief in equality and freedom for all of Hungary's citizens, Magyarization," stated Leopold. "Our Emperor's support for Magyarization is reason enough for me to continue my respect and loyalty for him. He has favored Magyarization since it was first conceived. Many times I heard the Emperor and my father discuss the positive character of Magyarization—the fair and equal treatment for all Hungary's citizens."

Leopold thought about his own employees, many of whom were of different ethnicities. "Magyarization works well in our company. Everyone speaks the Magyar's language and shares Hungarian culture...we can understand each other and run our country in the best way for everyone...and, yet, each person can remain true to their own religion and traditions...they are free to practice in any way they wish."

The *Roma*, Gypsies, came to Leopold's mind. He was especially fond of the Gypsy music that often drifted up to his office windows from *Hercegprimás Street*. Then he thought again of von Aehrenthal and his determination to annex Bosnia-Herzegovina.

"But this annexation idea is another matter; one in which I do not agree with the Emperor. I am certain he is being misguided by those who are more interested in power and greed. They have turned the Emperor from his true interests, peace and fairness for his people."

A serious look of concern across his face, Leopold said, "Hungary is an important part of the Austro-Hungarian Empire, Stefan, but we do not always want to go in the same direction as Austria. The Austrians often insist on taking us where we do not want to go and we should have the right to object. In this case, moving into the Balkans is a terrible mistake," Leopold spoke emphatically. "We can only hope that Vienna will listen to our objections."

Stefan looked at his father so intently it made Leopold smile down at him and pat his blond hair. Leopold did not dare frighten the little boy with his true fears that Vienna would not listen, but would drag Hungary into a violent conflict.

—ᵐ—

Although Elizabeth kept very busy with her new home, she remained interested in Leopold's business. Every evening when he returned from his office she asked many questions; she had a goal to know all aspects of the wine business. She began to keep a close eye on the business accounts.

Elizabeth realized early on that Leopold was fiercely determined to be fair; therefore, she became very protective of her husband, fearing that one day some unscrupulous person could take advantage of his more positive view of humanity. With help from Tamás, she studied Leopold's business relationships carefully and advised him on whom she thought trustworthy and whom she did not. She often called upon Tamás, whom she completely trusted, to agree with her when she found herself in some debate with Leopold. Elizabeth believed that Tamás, always the diplomat, served both Leopold and her as a valued confidant.

Leopold grew to trust Elizabeth's opinions on business and politics. Agreeing with her father's words about her head for business, Leopold often referred to Elizabeth *as a better businessman than he.*

1909

For Tamás, Thursdays were days of leisure. On a particular day in April, he rose at his usual early time, while it was still dark, and dressed as impeccably as he did every day. Tamás entered the kitchen, took his place at the large oak table, drank his coffee, ate his toast and sliced an apple. He plucked a sprig of stephanotis from the vase, slid it into his lapel, tucked a fresh handkerchief square into his breast pocket, put on his hat, took the umbrella from its holder, said farewell to Katalin and the kitchen staff and left the house by the kitchen door. He walked through the kitchen garden to the driveway and out onto Andrássy Avenue.

Since the day was unexpectedly warm and sunny he decided to forego the Metro and walk to town. It was a long walk down the Avenue, but he walked briskly past Mansion Row, past the Opera House, and on toward Váci Street and the Danube.

Tamás did some personal shopping, bought a newspaper, a new book at the bookstore, and went to his favorite restaurant, *Nagykövetséghház*. He greeted the hostess who welcomed him by name and seated him at his usual table in a corner by the window. Seeming pleased to see him, the waitress conversed a bit. Tamás lit his pipe, ordered coffee and *gombaleves*, mushroom soup, and *szilvás gomboc*, prune dumplings, the same as always. He opened his newspaper. The waitress brought his soup. He began to absentmindedly sip the soup.

Tamás looked up, motioned to the waitress.

"Is something wrong?" she asked.

"No, not at all. I've had soup here for almost two years and today it is different! It has always been tasty, good, but today, it is superb! What has happened since last Thursday?"

"We have a new cook in the kitchen."

"Please give him my compliments. The soup is delicious."

"I will, sir, be happy to give *her* your compliments."

Without fail, every Thursday whenever Tamás was in Budapest, he ate his lunch at the *Nagykövetségház*.

1910

One mid-March afternoon there was a soft rap on the library door. Leopold was not certain that he had heard anything at first; then he heard it again. "Enter," he said unsure if anyone was really there.

The door opened slowly and the cook, Katalin, walked in with her hands folded and her head down. She shyly approached his great desk and in a very soft voice said, "Sir, I am sorry to bother you, but I wish to speak with you."

"Yes, Katalin, what do you need?"

"Well, Sir, I have been with your family for many, many years. I was very happy to come here to Pest to serve your family. I thank you for bringing me to such a fine house and kitchen. I am truly grateful."

"You are very welcome, Katalin. You are an excellent cook."

"Oh, thank you, Sir. Your compliments make my words very difficult," she twisted her apron as she spoke, "You see, Sir, I am growing much older now and I see that there will soon be a little one in the house and I think it is time for you and the Duchess to find a new cook."

She took a deep breath, "I think that it is time for me to leave the service. I will leave Pest and return to Sopron to live with my daughter. I would like to leave by the end of April, before the family leaves here for Lake Balaton, that is, of course, if you can find a new cook by then."

"We will miss you greatly, Katalin, but if you must go, we accept your separation from us. We will help you with your move back to Sopron. You will be missed." Leopold stood, walked around his desk and placed his hand on her shoulder, "I will tell Elizabeth and Tamás to begin solicitation for a new cook. Thank you for giving us ample notice, Katalin. It will be a difficult task to find a new cook with your skill and talent."

Katalin began to weep, "You have always been a fair and kind master, Duke Esté. I will miss working for this family. I will miss the young master. I pray for the Duchess's good health and a healthy baby."

She wiped away tears with her apron as she backed away from the desk and out of the library, whispering as she went, "Thank you, thank you, Sir."

Leopold informed Elizabeth and Tamás that they must begin their search for a new cook. Elizabeth completely entrusted the task to Tamás.

Early the next morning, Tamás began his Thursday morning ritual even though the day was a Tuesday. He went straightaway to the *Nagykövetségház* restaurant. The hostess and waitresses were quite surprised to see him on a Tuesday. As soon as he was seated at his Thursday table, he asked to see the cook.

Shortly afterwards out of the kitchen came a woman clearly curious about being interrupted from her preparations for the mid-day customers. She wiped her hands on her clean white apron and with her arm pushed back a curl of hair that fell across her forehead. She had a wonderful jovial look about her, bright blue eyes, rosy cheeks, and an infectious smile with exceptionally white teeth. She was plump and healthy in appearance.

Tamás liked what he saw immediately; he rose to take her hand and asked her to sit at his table. She was hesitant, but sat down, still feeling a bit apprehensive. He introduced himself, "My name is Tamás Tóth. I am the gentleman's gentleman for the Duke von Esté and house administrator for the Duchess von Esté."

She responded, "I am Silva Marázova, a Slovak from Rimavská Sobota."

Tamás questioned her about her background, questions she answered with straightforward responses, "I learned to cook from my mother and grand-mother. My love for cooking became obvious to everyone and my willingness to experiment and discover delicious new recipes convinced my family that I should pursue this vocation, so I left home to become a cook."

Silva did not seem at all nervous, but kept her eyes lowered and treated Tamás with the utmost deference. Tamás could see that Miss Marázova was a well-mannered, respectable young woman. He already knew that she was a marvelous cook from his own experience enjoying her splendid dishes at the *Nagykövetségház* over the past year.

"Would you be willing to think about leaving *Nagykövetségház* to work for the von Esté family as their cook and head of housekeeping?" Tamás asked while trying to make eye contact with her. "I would like for you to come to the Andrássy Avenue house with your references for an interview with the Duchess, if you are willing."

"I would be interested in taking a look at the kitchen, sir."

Silva Marázova glanced up for only a second or two, just to get a better look at his face. A feeling of excitement made her shiver and she hoped that he had not noticed. He was a very handsome man. She estimated him to be in his late thirties—tall, erect, nice smooth hands, impeccably dressed. Threads of premature silver streaked through his dark hair and while his face was deeply lined, his tanned skin appeared soft; his dark eyes shaded by heavy black brows were kind, even gentle. She liked him. He asked her to come to the mansion the next afternoon and gave her a card with the address. He stood, bowed to her, took his hat and left.

The next afternoon Silva arrived. She was instantly impressed with the exterior appearance of the house and looked forward to seeing Tamás again. He met her in the entrance hall after Leona, the maid, had taken her coat. He took Silva directly through the great dining room and into the kitchen for a thorough tour of the cabinets, pantry, utensils and appliances. Tamás showed her the kitchen garden just beyond the rear garden door and the cook's accommodations, a small room just off the kitchen. Then Tamás took Silva to his office next to the kitchen where they found the Duchess von Esté seated at his desk. He introduced the two women.

The Duchess greeted Silva warmly and then smiled at her because no one could look at Silva without returning her great smile. Elizabeth went over the duties and benefits of the position while very clearly expressing her high standards and expectations. Silva presented her letters of introduction and after an exchange of questions and answers Elizabeth was quite satisfied that the family needed Silva; she was young, respectable, creative and cheerful.

"I realize events have moved quickly, Silva, but Tamás and I agree that you are what our family needs. Will you consider accepting the position?"

"Certainly I will accept and I can begin the middle of April. I look forward to serving your family, Madam." Silva stood up from the desk, "The kitchen garden has a good start, it is promising, but I would like to expand its size and variety with your approval," she smiled, "I would like to include medicinal herbs and a bee hive or two."

"Delightful, Silva, of course you may. Please think of it as your garden to do with as you wish. I believe you will find our villa garden at Lake Balaton more mature and interesting."

Just at that moment, Stefan looked into the office, his handsome face quite serious, "I just want to know if you can make *meggyleves*, cold cherry soup, *makós rétes*, poppy seed strudel, and *mézeskalács*, honey cake, and will you make *kolache*, cakes, for me?"

"And just who might you be, young man?"

"This is the young master of the house, Stefan." Elizabeth motioned for Stefan to come into the room. She held his shoulders, "He seems to be more interested in his stomach than in his good manners. Please greet Miss Silva Marázova, Stefan. She will be our cook from now on."

Stefan bowed properly to Silva as she answered him, "I can make *meggyleves*, *makós rétes* and *mézeskalács*, and I promise to make plenty of *kolache*, especially for you."

They shook hands and Stefan decided that very moment that he and Silva would become great friends.

Silva arrived on the fifteenth of April as she had promised. Within the week she had quickly made the kitchen and, in fact, the whole house her own. Tamás shared his housekeeping duties with Silva and put her in charge of all the staff. She helped with the housekeeping decisions and worked with

Elizabeth on day-to-day necessities, such as menus and staff assignments. Silva quickly followed her plan to expand the herb garden to include more medicinal plants and she added several hives of bees. Her cooking began to fill the house with delicious aromas from breads to stews to *kolache*. With Silva's influence the whole house embodied a fresh and cheerful atmosphere.

For the first time in his life Tamás felt that he had a helpmate in his day-to-day life. After only one week, since Silva's arrival, on the Thursday, Tamás rose at his usual early hour of the morning, dressed and entered the kitchen. Silva was sitting at the table. It was her day off as well. She smiled, rose from the table and poured a cup of coffee for him.

"You don't need to do that, Silva. It's your day off, too."

He thanked her as he took the cup. Blowing across the steaming brew and looking down into the dark swirling coffee, he asked, "May I ask if you have plans for your day?"

"I'm thinking of walking in the park this morning and then taking myself to lunch," she paused, "What are you planning for the day, Mr. Tóth?"

"Much the same," he answered still looking down into his cup. Then after an elongated silence, he asked, "Would you allow me to take you to supper this evening?"

Silva studied Tamás. She knew the invitation he extended to her was a serious one with many implications. She realized that her pause was a long one. Tamás looked up and stopped stirring his coffee; he seemed to hold his breath waiting for her answer. Silva smiled at him, "Yes, Mr. Tóth, I would like that very much."

"Fine," he nodded, "I'll meet you in front of the *New York Café* in Erzsébet Square at six o'clock. You know this restaurant?"

Silva nodded her head that she did and answered, "I know it. I look forward to seeing you there at six."

Summer

In early May the family, including Tamás and Silva, left Budapest for their Lake Balaton villa. Elizabeth was determined to avoid the stifling heat of Budapest; she wanted her baby to be born at the lake. Her personal maid, Ana, also accompanied the family. Left back at the Andrássy house for the summer were Leona and several other maids who remained to look after the house and Leopold. On weekends Leopold and Tamás were always at the lake, but come Mondays Leopold returned to Budapest, sometimes with Tamás, for work at the von Esté Fine Wine Company. The von Házys, all of them, were there, too, at their summer place on Tihany.

Elizabeth spent her time out-of-doors in the shade of the grape arbor or in her bedroom with all the windows wide open allowing the lake breezes to cool the interior, or in the music room playing the piano she loved. Music by Chopin was her favorite, but she also played Brahms and Liszt, Beethoven and the romantic Hungarian, Bartok. As the summer dragged on Elizabeth became more and more miserable; she was quite anxious for the birth of her child. Only Silva, with her special herbal remedies like feverfew, rosemary, and lavender teas over crushed ice, could soothe Elizabeth's discomfort against the oppressive heat.

Gabriele and her mother-in-law, Countess Alexandra, visited often, bringing Rudolf to play with Stefan. Just as their families had hoped and expected, the boys had become good friends. Summers at the lake and numerous visits between Eisenstadt and Sopron and Budapest gave the boys many opportunities to know each other well, so they were very happy to be together again.

Stefan, almost nine and Rudolf, seven, spent their days exploring every inch of the Tihany peninsula, the Bakony Hills, the northern shore of Lake Balaton, and Balatonfüred, usually with Tamás or with their fathers, but sometimes on their own. The boys especially enjoyed spending time with the family of shepherds who lived at the edge of the woods on the hill above the Esté villa.

Old Milan, the patriarch of the shepherd family, spent his time with his Puli dogs walking through the forests and fields looking for lost sheep. On many occasions Stefan and Rudolf accompanied him and his dogs on long treks through the countryside. Milan had many stories to tell and was quite pleased to have Stefan and Rudolf as listeners, since his own family had heard the tales far too many times.

In July the von Schraders arrived at the lake to await the birth of their grandchild. Elizabeth and her mother began with great anticipation to count the days. Elizabeth's greatest fear was that Leopold would be in Budapest and miss the birth, so as time drew nearer she insisted that he return each evening from Pest. Early one Sunday morning Doctor Nagy from Balatonfüred was summoned; he stayed all day and at last around seven o'clock in the evening the von Esté baby daughter was born.

They named her Klára Elizabeth Maria Beate in honor of her mother and grandmothers. She was a beautiful baby with her father's coloring, a head of black hair and unusual blue eyes that turned green within a few weeks. Hopeful for a baby girl, Leopold was smitten at first sight. He held tiny Klára in his arms and talked to her gently while thanking Elizabeth profusely for giving him such a lovely daughter. Stefan and Rudolf were equally infatuated by the little princess who had entered their lives. They felt very proud and protective of her from the first moment they saw her.

August

In early August while Leopold and Elizabeth were sitting in the garden gazebo playing with Baby Klára, as she lay cooing in her cradle, Tamás approached. He seemed uncharacteristically nervous. Leopold was puzzled by his mood.

"Yes, Tamás, what is it?"

"I know this is quite sudden, unexpected, but I have asked Silva to be my wife and we would like very much to marry here in the garden on Sunday morning."

Before Tamás could continue, Leopold had jumped to his feet and embraced Tamás, "Wonderful news, Tamás! Silva is delightful."

Tamás smiled broadly.

"We are happy for both of you!" Elizabeth's enthusiasm was evident, "Where is Silva? We must give her our best wishes."

"She's here," Tamás answered as he turned toward the arbor and motioned to Silva to come out of the shadows and into the gazebo. Although suddenly very shy, she was glowing with happiness. Both Leopold and Elizabeth embraced her warmly, congratulated Tamás and offered Silva, "every happiness to you with our kindest regards."

Elizabeth promised to help Silva create a beautiful wedding day.

The following Sunday, Tamás and Silva were married in the garden. The priest and happy couple stood in the gazebo to exchange their vows. The event was witnessed by a small party of guests including Gáspár and Ilonka, Leopold's sister Eugenia and her gentleman attendant Konrad, the von Schraders, the von Házy family, all the household staff and other friends from the lake.

Silva wore a white blouson dress of gossamer lace, with a dropped waist, and a ringlet of garden flowers in her hair. Tamás looked very handsome in a light summer linen suit. After lunch, a lovely buffet, the couple left for a wedding trip to Silva's home, Rimavská Sobota, in a Slovak region of northern Hungary.

Gáspár and Ilonka stayed at Lake Balaton for the rest of the summer to help run the estate—the vineyards, the orchards, the flower beds, the vegetable garden, and, especially, to help Elizabeth with her new baby. While Elizabeth and Ilonka placed most of their attention on Klára, Gáspár and Leopold concentrated on the vineyards. The vines and grapes were healthy and the press was made ready.

At the end of August the tempered and charred oak barrels arrived from the Szabó barrel makers in Eger. As soon as the grapes were harvested in the early fall, all was ready to begin the fermentation process. Leopold felt a sense of exhilaration; his business was under way at last.

Fall

In September Tamás and Silva returned to Andrássy Avenue, where Silva moved into Tamás's apartment, just a few steps from the kitchen. Soon after, the family returned to Budapest and Nanny Irén was hired to care for Klára. Irén enjoyed taking Klára into the warmth of Silva's kitchen, particularly when the weather began to cool. Silva loved having the baby nearby; from the beginning she took Klára to her heart. She and Tamás invested all their time and care and love in Stefan and Klára.

Leopold and Dr. Klein met regularly, at least once or twice a month, where their discussions over lunch focused on wine making. They talked about new blends of grapes, new processes, and possibilities for new kinds of barrels, old brandied or sherried wood often used for French barrels. Leopold wanted to experiment with processes that might make his wines unique, but he also remained committed to producing *különleges minőségű bor*, premium quality wine, and relied on the sound advice of his old friend, Dr. Klein. Especially when Leopold wanted to venture into new, unproven processes he trusted Dr. Klein's encouragement or caution.

By October Dr. Klein had good news to share. He announced to Leopold that Mrs. Klein had given birth to their sixth child, whom they named Rózsa. *At last, a sister for Eszter!* Leopold was very happy for Dr. Klein; they both had new baby daughters to celebrate.

1911

Leopold wore a wide-brimmed straw hat, loose shirt, wide-legged linen pants and sandals as he walked with Stefan and Rudolf through the Balaton villa vineyard. A loud chorus of cicadas added background music for the hot summer day. This was his favorite part of summer—the time he spent with the children in the vineyards. He wanted to share with them his passion about the vines and the grapes and the making of wine with them. He wanted the children to love the earth, the vines, and the grapes as much as he did.

"This extreme hot weather could be bad for the white grapes," Leopold said to the boys, "it could make their acidity too high, but as for the reds this year...they will be excellent."

With Klára in his arms Leopold walked along the dusty furrows between the vines. Stefan and Rudolf followed in single file, "Wine has been made here for thousands of years. First the Romans brought the vines to this land and then Christian monks from France came in medieval times. They brought a new kind of grape—the *Rieslings*."

"If the weather cools a bit we will have a very good harvest this year," Leopold said as he held up a cluster of tightly bunched small round green grapes and smiled. "The Rieslings, the white ones, especially love our rich volcanic soil."

He pointed toward the rising hills to the north, "Those on the hill are the cabernet and growing on Tihany are the Merlot grapes. We have vineyards in Austria and all over Hungary. In Sopron we have the *Kékfrankos*, near Szekszárd the *Kadarka*, from the three vineyards in Balaton and Badacsony come the *Olaszrizling, Chardonnay* and *Szürkebarát*; other vineyards in Hajos-Baha and Mor have the *Kékfrankos* and *Cabernets, Ezerjó* and *Leányka* and in Eger we have the *Kékfrankos* and *Kékoportó*. Grapes will come from the vineyards in all those places to our Balatonfüred presses and cellars."

Reciting the names of his vineyards and their grapes for the boys thoroughly delighted Leopold. But the boys especially liked hearing Leopold's stories about his and Tamás's grand adventures in exotic America. They asked Leopold to tell them over and over again about the long train trip across America, about the vast territories, amazing cities, and strange peoples.

The boys also wanted to hear Leopold's stories about his youth spent at Lake Balaton, about the adventures he and Christián and Tamás had shared. His stories filled the children with anticipation for the adventures they would have.

In July, just as they had in their youth, Leopold and Christián once again swam in the annual race across Lake Balaton from Révfülöp to Balatonboglár. Tamás rowed across the lake near the two swimmers while Stefan and Rudolf rode in the boat, cheering on their fathers. Christián promised the boys, "As soon as each of you turns twelve, you can join Leopold and me in the race."

Elizabeth and Gabriele watched the race from the stern of Leopold's yacht, moored at the Balatonboglár pier. As Leopold and Christián emerged from the waters, the women—holding bottles of sparkling wine—clapped and cheered for their husbands. They shouted for everyone to hurry aboard so the celebration could begin. Wrapped in blankets, Leopold and Christián led the way onto the boat, followed by Tamás, Stefan and Rudolf.

Leopold's sister, Eugenia and her companion Konrad, who had been her deceased husband's valet, were aboard. Nanny Irén held baby Klára in her arms while Silva stayed busy in the galley preparing a feast. The joyous occasion put everyone in good spirits. With everyone aboard, Leopold set sail for Siófok.

—⚒—

The Duchess Eugenia and Konrad came from Cologne to Lake Balaton every summer just as the von Estés had done in her youth. However, Eugenia and

Konrad disliked the northern side of the lake, the Balatonfüred side, site of the von Esté villa. To them, the Balatonfüred side seemed quiet, slow, even boring. The north side was where the regulars spent their whole summers in elegant villas while the men traveled back and forth between the lake and Budapest. Instead they preferred Siófok on the southern side, the side that drew tourists. The two always stayed at the luxurious Nagy Strand Hotel where they loved to watch from the hotel veranda the constant flow of people. It was their favorite pastime

Eugenia often said, "The *northside* regulars move through their daily routines like the ticking of a clock until the end of September, so often without emotion or surprise. Whereas, the *southside* Siófok people, the tourists, arrive for only a brief moment in the summer…they live in a hurry for sun, fun, adventure, and romance…each vignette lived out in only a few days or few weeks."

She and Konrad enjoyed watching those tourists from their comfortable veranda. The two found great pleasure in the anonymous stories that unfolded before them in the hotel or on the beach or on the promenade. Eugenia loved sharing these embellished accounts, whether fact or fiction, with any audience in her presence. She inevitably had her listeners rolling with laughter or sobbing in their lace handkerchiefs by the tale's end. Everyone seemed to thoroughly enjoy her charming stories.

—⁙—

On the afternoon of the race when the family gathered on the Siófok hotel veranda, Eugenia wanted to tell them about hers and Konrad's most recent adventure in Egypt, but she began laughing so hard she could barely speak. Her story describing herself—a rather robust woman dressed in a very fancy dress and big hat holding a parasol—being tossed about quite vigorously atop a camel as it bounded at breakneck speed over the dunes toward a distant oasis while several Egyptian servants ran behind yelling and trying to corral the camel had everyone falling out of their chairs with laughter, even the stoic Konrad.

Leopold wiped away the tears running down his face and kissed his sister on her bright red cheeks, "We must go, Eugenia, although we hate to leave such a happy time. You have the gift of a story teller!"

"Please come for tea at the villa next week, Eugenia," invited Elizabeth.

Eugenia and Konrad stood on the veranda and watched the yacht sail from the harbor toward Balatonfüred. The two looked forward to more family gatherings during the weeks ahead—the Anna Ball, concerts, hot mineral baths, parties at the von Esté villa or at their Siófok hotel. Even as dusk began to fall they could still make out the yacht as it sailed toward the distant lights of the northern shore.

October

In early October the von Házys invited the von Estés to accompany them on a trip to the spectacular alpine Styria region of Austria to visit their salt mines. The von Házy family had owned salt mines and distilleries in the region for centuries. While Elizabeth and Gabriele toured the spas, castle ruins, and Rococo churches, Count Francis and Christián took Leopold, Stefan, and Rudolf to the mines.

None of them would ever forget the experience made even more memorable by Count Francis. He had a passionate fascination for his mines and passed on to all his respect for the value of salt and necessity of mining. His deep, resonating voice enhanced every story with an air of excitement as he told the boys everything he knew about salt.

"Salt, white gold, the subterranean treasure... a symbol of faith in Biblical times... a medium for commercial exchange—the very basis of *salary* for centuries... a necessity for life itself!"

When they entered the cave-like mine of the great salt mountain, Stefan and Rudolf felt a bit of terror along with fascination, just as their fathers had felt when they visited the mine as boys.

"Men have mined salt from these mountains for thousands of years," the Count said. In the depths of the cave his powerful voice made his stories all the more chilling. "Just a few years ago, one of those ancient men was found in a mine near here... he was perfectly preserved in salt for a thousand years... just as he was—body, clothes, and tools—all mummified."

As their fathers before them, Stefan and Rudolf looked around their ominous surroundings and hoped they would never be trapped underground and preserved in salt forever in such a dark place. Despite his fears, Rudolf felt a sense of pride about his family's long history and important livelihood while Stefan simply felt awestruck about the work going on so deep beneath the ground.

—⁓—

From Styria, the von Esté and von Házy families traveled by train to the Schwarzau Castle in Lower Austria for the wedding of the Emperor's grand nephew, Karl and his lovely bride, Zita von Bourbon-Parma. Since Karl and Zita were themselves cousins, most of the aristocratic guests were related to each other and to the Emperor in some way. The wedding took place on the morning of October twenty-first, 1911. After a grand post-wedding breakfast the wedding party and all their many relatives were organized for a photograph.

Emperor Franz József proudly posed for the photograph at the center of his large family, the bride and groom stood beside him. Far to the Emperor's left stood Leopold just behind Elizabeth, who was the only other seated person. She held the baby Klára, only fifteen months old, on her lap. Klára wore her christening dress. Stefan and Rudolf stood together near Christián who constantly had to correct their behavior because they were unable to stand still.

1913
Summer

Every summer Elizabeth took Stefan and Klára to visit their grandparents in Linz, a visit they always found pleasurable. The Baron and Baroness von Schrader doted on the children, treating them to every child's fondest dream. A bicycle for Stefan that he rode as fast as the wind around Linz, through the busy *Hauptplatz*, on the pathways by the Danube, and as high up the *Postlingberg* as he could go. And a playhouse constructed in the garden for Klára where she had dolls and toys enough for many children.

Some summers at the end of their visit to Linz, Elizabeth and the children said their farewells to the von Schraders and then traveled north by train to Fürstenfeldbruck in Bavaria for a visit with Elizabeth's childhood friend, the Baroness Renate von Werner. The Baroness and her family lived on a large estate, in a grand manor house that had been greatly expanded since its medieval beginnings. By the summer of 1913, Renate had four children, three girls and a son, Franz. Every afternoon Elizabeth and the Baroness sat in wicker chairs in the garden, sipping lemonade and watching the children as they played on the lawn.

One afternoon Stefan, the oldest of the children, sat alone on a stone wall reading. He was distracted by the children and began to closely observe them...the girls, all dressed in white dresses with sashes and big bows in their hair...and the boy, Franz, a most unusual child, in both appearance and personality. His hair so blond it appeared almost as white as the little girls' dresses and his eyes so blue they were almost colorless, too. Stefan noticed that Franz, only five, but strong and athletic, bullied his own sisters as well as little Klára, only three years old. Franz teased the girls, hid their toys, pulled their hair, and knocked them down as he ran wild through their playhouse. The little boy's behavior annoyed Stefan, in particular, because Stefan noticed that whenever Franz was near the Baroness or Elizabeth, he was all smiles, charming and polite, but behind their backs he was a terror. Stefan saw in him a cunning nature, one not to be trusted.

Stefan also could see that Elizabeth, like her friend the Baroness, was fooled by Franz's perfect manners and lively personality. His baby face and big smile charmed both women, but out of their sight he purposely made evil faces at the little girls that sent them shrieking to their mothers' skirts. Stefan witnessed Franz in acts of great disrespect for everyone, adults and children. Even the servants were aware of Franz's true nature and did what they could to shield the little girls from his mischief.

During their visits Elizabeth and Renate joyfully rediscovered their youthful memories; they shared secrets and gossip, even giggled over old romances from their school days. In the mood of reminiscing about the past, they began to romanticize about the future.

"Klára is a lovely little girl," Renate mused, "I think Franz has taken to her…see how he teases her."

"He is such a handsome boy."

"Would it not be marvelous if they married someday?" Renate exclaimed, "I think Franz and Klára will make a perfect match when they are grown!"

Both women laughed as they watched the children play. Renate smiled, her eyes wide as she gushed, "We must find a way to pair them up when the time is right."

"What fun we will have putting them together, planning their wedding and then we will be related in fact!" Elizabeth laughed, "How wonderful it will be."

Elizabeth and Renate clicked their lemonade glasses to seal the bargain.

On their train back to Budapest, Stefan confided in Elizabeth, "I did not like the way Franz treated the girls. He's a bully around the little girls."

Elizabeth dismissed his concerns, "Franz is an adorable little boy with such an effervescent personality." She teased Stefan, "I think you may be a bit jealous of the attention Franz showed Klára."

"I'm not jealous, Elizabeth. Franz shows you and his mother one side and then another side to the children. He's cunning and a deceiver."

"Stefan! Those are very harsh words for a little boy." Elizabeth did not like to hear Stefan's accusations against Franz. She had never heard Stefan be so condemning of anyone, ever before. She frowned at him, "I never noticed any such behavior."

"I know," Stefan answered, "he's very clever. His bad behavior only happens behind his mother's back and yours."

"Well, if that is so, it's because he's young. I'm sure he will improve with age."

Stefan looked at Elizabeth skeptically; he suspected Franz's character was already sealed. "I don't think he will improve, Elizabeth." Then Stefan promised aloud, "I'll keep an eye on him whenever he's near Klára from now on."

The promise was more to himself than to Elizabeth. As the train steamed toward Budapest, Stefan kept his thoughts to himself. *With no male influence to curb Franz's wild nature, he is spoiled by a silly mother.* Stefan was certain of the reason for Franz's ill manner—*his father's absence. . . the Baron was rarely home.*

Baron von Werner owned a massive rail empire headquartered in Cologne and only visited his family once or twice a month. The Baroness, happiest in her Bavarian home with her children, had no intention of moving to Cologne. *Whatever the reason*, Stefan thought, *I do not like or trust Franz von Werner.*

1914
Late Spring, Budapest

In late April, Rudolf and his parents arrived in Budapest to visit the Countess Alexandra. The von Házys found the house dark with heavy draperies at the windows and the electric lights dimmed. Alexandra had become a widow during the winter when her beloved Francis passed away. Although she chose to live a secluded life from that terrible time on, she welcomed the visit of her beloved son and his family as a respite from her solitude. They had come to encourage her to travel with them back to Lake Balaton for the summer; however, she was reluctant to leave her Budapest house of memories.

Rudolf gave his grandmother kisses on both cheeks and then left to see his friends; he could hardly wait to see Stefan again. He crossed his grandmother's garden to its back wall where he found the arched garden gate almost completely obscured by honeysuckle vines. He pushed them aside, shoved open the gate into the von Esté garden and ran to enter Silva's bright, friendly kitchen where he was happily welcomed.

"You've come just in time to go with us to Városliget City Park," Stefan said. "Papa is taking us."

Only a short walk from the von Esté home, the park began at the end of Andrássy Avenue, across *Dózsa György Boulevard*. Leopold held Klára's hand as the boys ran ahead. A beautiful spring day awaited them; the almond trees were in full bloom as well as fuchsia, lilac, and hydrangea. Papa named each of the flowers they passed for Klára as well as the birds that twittered in the branches overhead. Klára loved to hold hands and walk with her Papa. They crossed the busy boulevard and entered *Hősök tere*, Heroes' Square. Leopold was anxious to conduct an on-site lesson in history for the children.

"In May of 1896, everyone, including the Emperor, was here in the park to celebrate Hungary's thousand years of history," Leopold said. "Rudolf, your father and I with our families rode on the brand new Metro, the little underground railway, all the way under *Sugár út*, now known as Andrássy Avenue, from *Gizella tér*, now called *Vörösmarty tér*, to Városliget City Park. We were all so proud of the Franz József Underground Electric Railway, the very first one on the continent! And then, when we came up from below ground, we were amazed!"

"There it was." Leopold made a broad gesture with his hand, "the Millennial Exhibition. Hundreds and hundreds of people were here, many more than today!"

Leopold and the children walked into the busy square. "This is *Hősök tere*, Heroes Square, he announced. "Here stands the history of Hungary…your history. Tell me, boys, who are these men? These great warriors?"

Klára held Leopold's hand while Stefan and Rudolf ran toward the monuments.

A semi-circular colonnade curved outward like two great arms embracing the square while in the center a single column over one hundred feet high rose from a pedestal. That pedestal also supported a sculpture of seven fierce men on horseback, encircling the column. Klára recoiled when she saw their faces, they were so wild and fierce, but she proudly pointed to the column.

In her sweet, little, almost four-year-old pronunciation she said, "I know who that is!" She pointed to the top of the column. "That is the angel Gabriel holding the cross and crown of Hungary."

"That's right, Klára." Leopold smiled at her, "Good for you! You remembered the angel gave the cross and crown to our king, Saint Stephen! Come, let's see if the boys know their history."

Leopold began to walk toward the warriors on horseback, but Klára pulled back; those Magyar faces always frightened her. "There's nothing to fear, Klára, these men are the great heroes of Hungary! The courageous Magyars who settled this land more than a thousand years ago."

Klára reluctantly followed her Papa to the foot of the great pedestal and looked up at the flaring nostrils of the horses, their flying manes of bronze, and the darkly cloaked faces of the Magyars staring down at her. Leopold tried to reassure her, "You shouldn't fear the Magyars, Klára, they are only made of metal and stone—here for us to admire."

"What is a Magyar, Papa?"

"Long ago the Magyar came from the Steppes of Russia, Klára. They were the earliest inhabitants of Hungary. From across the mountains, they wandered for many years and finally settled in the Carpathian Basin. The tribes and their chieftains were led by the great military ruler, Árpád—that one Klára—the one most brave and fierce. Árpád was the great-great-grandfather of Hungary's first Christian King, Stephen. "

Klára's brother and Rudolf shouted as they ran around the base of the sculpture, "That's Árpád and the others are his six brave chieftains who came here and founded Hungary!"

Then the boys turned toward the bronze statues standing in the niches between the columns of the semi-circular structures. Rudolf ran to the right while Stefan ran to the left. They began to shout the names of each man captured in bronze.

"This one is Saint Stephen, the first Christian king of Hungary...this one is King Bela, he defended Hungary against the Mongols and here is King Matthias, Hungary's Renaissance king. This one is Lajos Kossuth, leader of Hungary's War of Independence and this one is...." until they had named them all.

Leopold laughed at their enthusiasm, but he was also impressed by their interest and knowledge of Hungary's history. They all stood together looking at the four sculptures atop the cornices of the colonnades.

"What can you tell me about those figures?" Leopold proded.

Stefan answered first, "That's harder, because they are symbols. I know that one stands for *War* and that one must be *Peace.*"

Rudolf thoughtfully pointed toward the first figure on the far left, "*Work and Fortune* and the last one on the end is *Knowledge and Glory.*"

"Good." Leopold was pleased. He made certain the boys understood the sculptures' meaning and importance and then finally Leopold suggested, "Should we visit the Vajadahunyad Castle now?"

Klára loved the Vajadahunyad Castle. Although not a real castle, but only a fairy tale construction of blended Hungarian architectural styles from history—Gothic to Baroque to Romantic—it was always a favorite of children since its architect Alpár created it.

"After the castle, can we take a rowboat on the lake?" pleaded Stefan.

"Of course, and then we'll go to Gundel's for dessert—*palacsinta*, thin pancakes with sweet filling!"

The boys cheered!

—w—

Little Klára adored her Papa and looked forward to any time spent with him. An outing for a day at Millennial Park with Papa was the kind of day that brought Klára ultimate joy. Klára, tall and thin for her age, felt especially proud when people told her that she favored her father in appearance. Klára's light olive complexion, thick, straight black hair and green eyes were much like her Papa's, although her green eyes were a much deeper, richer shade of green than his. Her eyes, in fact, were quite spectacular, her most striking feature, sometimes grey-green, sometimes amber-green, and sometimes deep emerald green.

Klára's hair on the other hand, as black as Leopold's, was particularly difficult to manage, to her mother's great dismay. Regardless of any fashionable hairstyle popular for children, Klára's hair was impossible! With Nanny Irén's help, Elizabeth could sometimes get a big bow to stay in place for a bit of time, but most often the bow slid to the hair's end within moments. Braids or straight seemed the only answer.

Looking nothing like her mother, the only thing Klára shared in common with her mother was music. They both loved music, especially piano music.

Klára often sat beside her mother on the piano bench while Elizabeth mesmerized little Klára with beautiful melodies.

June, Lake Balaton

An unusually hot June day found the family gathered for supper in the dining room. All the windows on both sides of the room were opened and the lace curtains were pulled back to allow what little breeze there was to blow through the house. Silva had prepared a cold cucumber soup, cabbage slaw, and fish as a refreshing respite from the warm day.

Just as Leopold finished grace there was a loud knock at the door. A moment later Tamás presented a telegram to Leopold. As soon as Leopold opened it and scanned the words, his face became ashen; he gasped, stood up, and announced, "Franz Ferdinand, the Archduke, has been assassinated in Sarajevo by a Serbian student.

"I knew there would be trouble when Austria expanded into the Balkans and just arbitrarily took over Bosnia-Herzegovina!" Leopold paced at the end of the table; he held the telegram over his head, crushing it in his fist, "I advised against it! The Council and I told the Emperor it would be a grave mistake!"

Elizabeth, Stefan, and Klára sat in silence watching Leopold breathe heavily as he paced across the end of the dining room. Finally, Elizabeth asked, "What will his death mean? What will happen now?"

Leopold leaned toward the table and pounded his fist next to his soup bowl. He looked at each of them with a tense expression, "War."

Leopold spent the rest of the afternoon in his study. After a while Tamás joined him to mull over all the facts that led to this terrible day. Stefan came, too, to hear his father's opinions. They all knew this event was significant for the fate of the Empire and for everyone who lived within its borders. Leopold felt the traumatic event personally.

"What has happened, Papa?" Stefan asked.

"My warnings sent to the Emperor and to the Hungarian Council were never taken seriously. Hungary, by association with Austria, shares blame for this disastrous assassination!" Leopold could not sit still; he paced from one side of the room to the other, "As early as 1908, landlocked Serbia wanted access to the sea, to the Adriatic Sea. My compatriots and I warned the Emperor against expansion!"

Tamás and Stefan listened to Leopold; the sadness and disappointment were evident in his voice.

"Despite our warnings...when Serbia made its move toward the Adriatic, our Emperor chose to annex the former Turkish province, Bosnia-Herzegovina, putting an immediate barrier to the Serbs' march to the sea. Of course, they saw the Austrian action as an act of aggression and we knew there would be severe ramifications! And more will come if Serbia feels threatened... Russia will come to Serbia's aid! Many Hungarian members of the Council disagree with Austria's action, but Austria is not deterred by our warnings. Austria is determined to demonstrate its muscle to the Serbs," Leopold rubbed his brow and sighed deeply, "For six years bitterness and aggression have continued to build between the Slavic region and Austria, and now all of that turmoil, quite unnecessary to my thinking, has climaxed in the assassination of the Archduke!"

A few weeks later, Leopold learned the details of the assassination when he received an official letter from a Councilman who had accompanied the Archduke on his journey. The letter contained the newspaper account from Sarajevo.

The Archduke Franz Ferdinand, heir to the Austro-Hungarian throne, insisted on making a state visit to the Balkans even though he had been warned against traveling to the region.

Franz Ferdinand and his wife, Sophie, the Duchess of Hohenberg, arrived in the Bosnian capital, Sarajevo, to attend the five hundred and sixty-fifth anniversary of the Battle of Kosovo, a battle in which the Ottoman Turks handed a disastrous defeat to the Serbs. Even though five centuries have passed, the Serbs retain their deep feelings of humiliation suffered from that loss to the Turks. When the Austrian Archduke, already unpopular in the Balkans, arrived in Bosnia to recognize and celebrate the Kosovo Battle, he instantly became a hated and marked man by the Serbs.

The Archduke's visit was of particular interest to the terrorist group, Black Hand. Members of the group, mostly young idealists and students trained and armed in Serbia, often chose violence rather than words to make known their underlying principle—the fight for freedom from Austrian tyranny, freedom for the Balkans from the Austro-Hungarian Empire. Black Hand adamantly opposed the Archduke's visit to the Balkans.

Shortly after Franz Ferdinand's arrival in Sarajevo, as his motorcade made its way toward the City Hall, a member of Black Hand tossed a bomb at his car. The bomb exploded, but missed its target completely, so Franz Ferdinand decided the attack was not a serious one and insisted on continuing to the ceremony. He and the Duchess made a regal appearance. The Archduke was dressed in his full military uniform, plumed hat, gold braid and buttons, chest of medals and sword while his lady wore a lightweight dress of white batiste and lace. A bouquet of silk flowers at her waist was held in place by a wide blue silk sash. Silk flowers also decorated

*the crown of her wide-brimmed straw hat. She carried a parasol for shade
against the hot Bosnian sun.*

*After the official ceremony ended, the Archduke Franz Ferdinand
and his wife returned to their open-topped car. Their driver sped away
from the City Hall and began to maneuver through the ancient winding
streets of Sarajevo. Quite suddenly the driver realized he had lost his way;
he had taken a wrong turn down a dead-end street. As the driver tried to
turn the car around in the narrow street, simply by chance, one of the Black
Hand freedom fighters found himself standing within feet of the Archduke.
The nineteen-year-old Bosnian student, Gavrilo Princip, pulled his pistol
from his pocket and began firing. Within seconds both the Archduke Franz
Ferdinand and the Duchess lay in pools of their own blood.*

The Councilman added to the account, "They are dead and the world has
changed!"

Within days of this news Leopold met with the Hungarian Prime Minister,
Count István Tisza, to find out what kind of response Austria would make.

"Kaiser Wilhelm II has informed the Austro-Hungarian cabinet that
Germany will support an attack on Serbia." Tisza looked at Leopold very seriously, "In fact, the Kaiser encourages Austria to attack as soon as possible."

Count Tisza shook his head, "I do not support an attack, Leopold. I
believe other avenues of retribution must be considered. I am certain we will
awaken *the sleeping bear* if Austria goes into the Balkans. Russia will surely
come to the aid of the Serbs and who can say what will happen next? We need
cool heads, Leopold, to think this matter through."

July

By the next week secret discussions began in Vienna. A great debate ensued
over when and how to respond to the Serbs. Count Tisza and Leopold made
their opinions of opposition known, in particular, their fear of Russian involvement. Toward the end of July the Austro-Hungarian Council of Ministers
delivered an ultimatum to government officials in Belgrade, Serbia. The ultimatum contained fifteen demands, including a Serbian condemnation of the
Archduke's murder; a promise to thoroughly investigate the assassination; a
demand that Bosnia cease any acts of intrigue against Austria and the termina-
tion of all anti-Austrian propaganda in Serbia. In addition, Austria insisted on
a role in the judicial process of those involved in the assassination.

The ultimatum was delivered on the twenty-third of July and a response
from Serbia was expected within forty-eight hours.

On the twenty-eighth of July, Elizabeth and Tamás sat together quietly in the library waiting for Leopold to return from Parliament. As he entered the library, he appeared very solemn. Elizabeth and Tamás anxiously implored him to tell them the latest news.

"Serbia responded to the ultimatum on July twenty-fifth and agreed to most of the demands, but added one suggestion, that The Hague's International Tribunal be in charge of all judicial procedures rather than Austria. Unbiased diplomats from other countries agreed that Serbia responded to the ultimatum in a timely and positive manner. It appeared to all that Serbia's intentions were to pacify Austria, even if it meant further humiliation. Both Britain and Russia attempted to intervene on behalf of Serbia to avert conflict, but Vienna rejected all attempts to avoid the unthinkable." Leopold shook his head in resignation, "Vienna seems bent on marching to a glorious war. Count Tisza and I suspect that Germany is behind Austria's confidence and is eagerly supporting Austria's blind ambition against Serbia."

"Tisza is mystified," Leopold added. "He said to me, 'The Austrians are joyful about the prospect of war!'

"When I spoke before the Parliament, I made a plea for our beloved Hungary, I told them my greatest fear, that we will be drawn into it . . . A war— what a catastrophe! Late today we learned that Emperor Franz József neither read the ultimatum nor the Serbian response, but decided to proceed with Austria's attack on Serbia."

Exactly one month after the Archduke's assassination on June twenty-eighth, Austria declared war on Serbia. Bombardment of Belgrade began on July thirtieth and immediately thereafter the Russian Tsar, Nicholas II, called for full mobilization of the Russian armies to defend her Balkan friends. Russia's entry into the conflict brought her natural enemy, the German Empire, into the war as an eager ally of the Austro-Hungarian Empire. France, already angry with Germany over their annexation of two French territories—Alsace and Lorraine—joined the fight. The war—*the Great War to end all wars*—was under way. In time, the rest of the world, including Britain and the United States, entered the war.

Well into the throes of war Leopold learned that when an advisor eventually encouraged Franz József to read the ultimatum and the Serbian response, the Emperor realized war could have been avoided . . . but it was too late.

Lake Balaton

While countries all around Hungary were entering into the war, life for the children at Lake Balaton seemed the same, serene and innocent. As every

July at the lake, the children loved to stand outside the great house of Ádám Horváth Pálóczi to watch the exciting festivities and dancers at the annual Anna Ball. Just as Leopold, Christián, Cili, and Gabriele had stood in the garden to watch until they came of age to join in the dance, now it was Stefan, Rudolf, and Klára who watched with dreamy expressions, imagining their own times to twirl around the ballroom. Stefan held Klára on his shoulders and promised he would take her to the ball when she turned sixteen. She laughed and reminded him she had just turned four last week. He looked up at her perched on his shoulder and replied, "Only twelve years to go, little princess."

Klára adored her handsome brother. She could imagine twirling around the dance floor with Stefan. On the exterior she and Stefan could not have been more opposite. He resembled his mother, Cili, with his blond hair and eyes blue as a summer sky. Stefan always wore a broad smile and had a hearty laugh ready at any moment; he seemed to find humor in everything. Energetic, even reckless at times, whenever Stefan entered a room, it came to life with him at the center of attention, especially with girls.

Klára also imagined dancing with Rudolf, *her almost brother*. He, like her, was an opposite of Stefan, much taller, dark and slender...always pushing his black disheveled hair from his deep brown eyes, eyes that had a sleepy look. Even though quiet, observant, and shy, his face could become quite animated whenever Stefan made him laugh, which was often. Then suddenly a full, wide smile appeared that made dimple-like creases in Rudolf's cheeks and to Klára he became incredibly handsome.

That summer, as usual, Rudolf and Stefan set about their annual exploration of Lake Balaton to old and new places, always so much to do at the lake—swimming, sailing, hiking, cycling, caving, and their new activity, chasing girls. Stefan, at thirteen, was very good at attracting girls. He learned fairly quickly that one flash of his handsome smile worked like a magnet. As soon as he was noticed, he was surrounded by girls, girls who spent their summers on the lake's south side looking for romance. Rudolf, on the other hand, was the shy one who stood quietly by while Stefan did all the talking. However, Rudolf did find that plenty of the girls liked the shy type, too, so both boys enjoyed getting to know many young girls that summer, a summer of first kisses and broken hearts all around. But, of course, it was Klára both boys loved the most.

—⚏—

An enormous wooden table stood in Silva's kitchen in the villa; a table even greater in size than the one in her Andrássy kitchen. Silva often said that *a big wooden table right in the center of the kitchen* was all she needed to make the delicious Hungarian and Slovak foods that she created for the family she so dearly loved. Next to her Papa's library, Klára's favorite place in both houses was sitting at those tables where she could watch Silva cook. Silva sometimes let her help and always let her have tastes and samples. Klára and Silva spent countless hours together cooking and talking about things, everything.

A summer morning like all others found four-year-old Klára curled up on the big bench with her elbows on the table. Silva was making her special *ischler* and Klára was helping by dipping the apricot-filled shortbread in dark melted chocolate. They had already made *mézeskalács*, honey cake, and *gombaleves*, a mushroom soup that bubbled on the stove. Delicious aromas filled the kitchen.

Suddenly the garden door flew open and in came the noisy pair, Stefan and Rudolf. They were excited, hot and sweaty, pushing each other, laughing and talking loudly. The two boys fell upon the table and asked Silva for something cold to drink. She laughed at their exuberance, wiped her hands on her apron and left the kitchen for the cold cellar. Klára continued dipping the little cakes, "No! You can't eat them until supper," she scolded as Stefan smiled at her and reached for a cake.

"Oh, please Klára, give us just one or two apiece," they teased her. "We need sweets for our adventure."

Silva returned to the kitchen with cold fizzy cider just as Klára asked them where they were going. The boys guzzled down the cider, "We're going caving and no, you can't go with us. You're too little."

"I am not too little. I've been caving with Papa," she protested firmly. "Take me with you."

"You boys shouldn't tease Klára," admonished Silva. Then she asked a continuous string of questions, "Who is going with you? Which cave are you exploring? Does the Duke know where you're going? Perhaps you should take Milan with you."

"Aw, Silva, don't worry. We've been there before. Papa knows we know what we're doing. We're only going to *Köves Só barlang*," Stefan grabbed two little *ischler* cakes, "Klára can't go with us 'cause we're riding our bikes and besides that her legs aren't long enough for the rope ladder."

Stefan's cool demeanor faded away when he noticed the sad little face that looked up at him.

"Sorry, Klára, we'll take you swimming with us after supper. Will that be all right?"

Klára smiled, "All right, that's good. I'll save a whole plate of *ischler* just for the two of you."

Both boys gave Klára a hug and pulled her braids. She smiled, but pretended to ignore them. Stefan and Rudolf filled their knapsacks with salami, buttered bread, and apples. They laughed and waved as they went out the door. Silva and Klára heard their raucous voices until their bikes disappeared into the vineyards.

—⚏—

Stefan and Rudolf raced their bikes through the vineyards and up into the hills north of the villa. It took them less than an hour to reach the foothills of the

Bakony range that ran north above Balatonfüred. The town spread to the south below them all the way down to the edges of Lake Balaton. *Köves Só* cave was one of many caves in the Bakony. The boys left their bikes in the quarry of stones that led to the cave's entrance. Anxious to begin their adventure, they hurried to put on sweaters and heavy jackets. Their knapsacks went on their shoulders along with canteens and ropes; they tested their electric hand torches one more time.

As they entered the gaping hole of the cave they noticed the drop in temperature immediately. They followed the entrance tunnel as it made a steady decline toward darkness. Like all caves in the region, *Köves Só barlang* was formed by thermal springs.

Rudolf shined his light on the wall, "Look at nature's mural, Stefan!"

Stefan's hand followed the thin strata of colored limestone as it spread across the walls, "So, what do you think of this artwork, Dolf? Spectacular colors, huh! I've always loved this cave."

The two boys followed the natural trail of an expansive open ridge as it wound deep into the earth. *Köves Só* was miles long and deep. The cave had been discovered at least twenty years before this particular time by salt miners, but it had never been mapped or excavated. Nothing had been done to the natural interior of the cave to make their exploration easy; massive boulders and rubble lay unmoved in great piles over the cave floor. A labyrinth of limestone tunnels awaited them. The boys had been into the cave once before with Leopold and his friend, the famous geologist, Lajos Lóczy, but this time the boys wanted to go deeper and stay longer.

"Look at those stalactites and stalagmites!"

The deeper Stefan and Rudolf trekked into the cave the more frequently *dripstones* appeared, some hung from the ceiling, some grew from the floor, and some were joined together. The boys argued as they inspected the stones that varied in mass and extension, *Calcium carbonate or maybe calcite or calcareous? Or sodium chloride?* Neither could remember exactly.

"If you touch your tongue to this rock, it tastes like salt," Stefan said, as he licked the rock.

After walking upright for an hour or longer, they came to an intersection of tunnels going in different directions. Their first choice, a narrow tunnel, forced the boys to crawl on their hands and knees. The ceiling became lower and lower until Rudolf called back to Stefan, "This one is no good, Stefan, back out. Let's try another tunnel."

They crawled back to the intersection and choose another direction. Stefan left his red handkerchief as a marker for the way out at the intersection. Their new choice led them to an immense cavernous gallery with a natural ledge that fell away to a great depth shrouded in darkness. Rudolf held his electric torch out past the edge; the light illuminated many different levels within the room.

The glimmer of an aqua-green pool just below them caught the light.

The boys discovered an old rope ladder hanging over the precipice, secured some time before by earlier spelunkers. They decided to climb down the ladder to a lower ledge in the room and eat their lunch by the pool. They sat on large flat boulders that encircled the pool of salty water.

While they ate their lunch they played a game of turning out their torches just to see how truly dark the cave was. Each boy turned out his torch and sat in total darkness, listening to dripping water from various directions within the cave. The blackness was overwhelming. "Put your hand right up to your face. Can you see it? Or anything?"

"Nothing. There isn't a speck of light anywhere."

Stefan shuddered and turned his torch on again and then Rudolf relit his. They decided to explore one more tunnel that led from the great room. The tunnel led them in a twisted, gradual downward direction. After walking for several minutes, Stefan said, "Let's not go down any further. It will take too long to walk back up."

The boys agreed to go back to the pool and rest for a bit. Although they had lost all sense of time, they agreed it had to be getting late and time to start back for the villa.

Rudolf sat down on a boulder that was quite unsteady and wobbly. He stood up on the rock, shifting his weight vigorously back and forth. Stefan laughed at him, but joined in the fun by rocking another boulder. Rudolf was laughing, too, as he swung his electric torch over his head. The moving light cast strange shadows across the cave walls.

Suddenly a resounding crack reverberated through the air and Rudolf went over backwards along with the boulder and his torch into a dark crevasse that neither boy had noticed. Stefan, in complete disbelief, cried out Dolf's name and lunged forward to the edge of the crevasse. He shined his light down into the hole. There lay Rudolf in a crumpled state about ten feet below on a narrow ledge, the boulder on top of him; his torch smashed to bits. He was completely still and made no sound. Stefan felt terror welling up in his chest, thinking his dearest friend was dead. Stefan called down to him, "Dolf, Dolf, Dolf...."

Finally, Rudolf stirred and moaned with pain. Stefan shouted down to him, "Can you push off the stone? Can you move?" With each question Stefan knew his voice was filled with dread, that he sounded so frightened, "Are you all right? Dolf?"

Stefan felt panic. What could he do? He couldn't reach the ledge; even if he could, it was too small for the both of them. He knew he had to get help. He called to Rudolf again. "Can you hear me, Dolf? ... Dolf!"

Rudolf moved his arm a little, "Stefan," he moaned, "I can't move...oh, my leg is stuck...too heavy...it hurts bad."

"I have to get help, Dolf. I have to leave you."

Stefan felt a great urgency to go, but a tremendous guilt at the thought of leaving his friend. He had to encourage Rudolf, "I'm going to drop down my coat, put it over your head and shoulders. Here's my canteen, too," Stefan needed Rudolf to give him permission to leave, "Dolf, can I leave you here alone? I have to go get help!"

"Go Stefan. I can't move...you have to go. I'll be all right here...just hurry."

Stefan stood up from the ledge and immediately noticed how the light shifted away from the ledge, leaving Rudolf in dark shadows, "I have to take the torch with me, Dolf; that means you'll be in the dark. Can you stand it?"

"I can, Stefan, don't worry about that. I've been in the salt mines, remember. I'm not afraid of the dark. Just hurry, Stefan. I think I'm hurt real bad."

"I'll be back as fast as I can. Be brave, Dolf," and with that Stefan moved to the rope ladder and climbed up as quickly as he could. He called out to Rudolf, "I'm in the big room, going for the ridge."

Rudolf pulled Stefan's coat as close as he could. The cave was cold and damp and he was already shivering. He heard Stefan call out again, words he couldn't quite understand. Moments later he heard the faint sound of Stefan's voice once more and then finally nothing, nothing but dripping water. Rudolf lay with his eyes closed, because it was more terrifying to open his eyes and see nothing. Eventually he passed out due to the excruciating pain.

When he came to, there was no way to know how long he had lain there nor how long Stefan had been gone. It could have been minutes or hours...time did not exist in the darkness. Rudolf had lied to Stefan about having no fear of the darkness. Despite his experiences in the salt mines, he hated the darkness.

He let his mind wander to thoughts of his family's business, salt. He tried to remember every word his grandfather ever said to him. Salt had been their family business since the beginning of time. They had owned salt mines in Austria forever. Rudolf thought about the many times he had gone to the mines with his father and grandfather. Sliding down the slick chutes into the profound darkness deep within the earth. Going from room to room to watch the miners extract the mineral from rock. Rowing across the subterranean salt lake and hearing the eerie sounds bubble up from the depths.

Drifting between sleep and consciousness, Rudolf felt wet and feverish; he shivered with cold. His body wanted to toss and turn, but he was pinned under the rock without any space, without any forgiveness. He thought he heard his grandfather's booming voice call out to him, *Rudolf...remember...Salt...the subterranean treasure...a symbol of faith...Rudolf...a necessity for life itself.*

Expecting to see his grandfather, Rudolf opened his eyes, but there was only the oppressive blackness all around him. His thoughts continued to wander back to the salt mines. He imagined his father standing by the massive kettles where water evaporated from the mineral, leaving the salt. In a fit of delirium he called to his father, *Papa, Papa, save me*, and then sunk back into unconsciousness.

Stefan moved back through the winding passageways as quickly as he could, but the massive piles of boulders frustrated his efforts to move with any momentum. Fear possessed him. He imagined that he would return too late and Rudolf would be dead by the time he brought help, but he trudged on and on until he saw a faint light in the distance. The light inspired a renewed energy to push on faster. Finally, Stefan emerged breathless from the cave into the fading light of day. He paused only long enough to catch his breath before running across the quarry for his bicycle. He thought, *should I go back to the villa or down the hill into Balatonfüred? It has to be Balatonfüred, help will be closer, faster.*

Stefan turned his bike south, found a footpath leading downward, and sped toward town. The footpath eventually turned into a roadway leading to a string of houses. Stefan jumped off his bike at the first house, ran to the door and pounded until a woman hesitantly opened just a crack. A stream of words came from Stefan, "There's been a terrible accident. We need help, please help me."

The woman opened the door widely and looked at the mud-covered frantic boy who stood apparently exhausted in front of her. "What has happened? How can I help?"

A man appeared from behind her, "What is this all about, boy?"

"My friend is trapped in *Köves Só barlang*. He fell and there's a huge stone on top of him," Stefan fought back sobs that rose from his throat, "We must hurry."

The man went back into the room to get his boots while the woman brought Stefan into the house. She sat him at the table and gave him a cup of water. She brought a basin of water and a towel so that he could wash his hands and face.

"I'll go down to the police station for help," the man said, "It's not far...help will be here soon. You wait for us here, so you can show the way inside the cave."

"Will there be a telephone at the station?" asked the frantic boy, "I need to call my father. He should know right away."

"Who is your father?"

"The Duke von Esté. He's at the Esté villa."

The man and Stefan hurried down the road to the station. There was a telephone and one of the policemen rang the operator. He told her to alert the Balatonfüred police about the accident and then asked her to connect them to the Esté villa. Within a moment someone answered and the man handed the phone to Stefan.

"Hello? Tamás...." Stefan felt a great relief to hear Tamás's voice, "There was an accident in the cave and Rudolf is hurt. There's a huge boulder on top of him," Stefan began to sob uncontrollably.

"I had to leave him in there, Tamás...in the dark. Tell Papa and Dolf's Papa, too. I will meet you at *Köves Só barlang*. Come soon."

After Stefan hung up the phone, he and the men walked back up the hill to the man's front gate. Soon neighborhood men began to gather and women brought out baskets of food and water and blankets for the men to take with them to the cave.

Stefan felt a strong need to return to the cave; he didn't want to wait for the rescue team to arrive. Some of the men decided to go on ahead with him. Shortly after they left, several trucks arrived from town, each one loaded with men who were anxious to participate in the rescue. The trucks caught up with Stefan and the other men at the end of the road. Together they left the trucks, took all of their equipment, and began the long trek up the hill to the quarry. Stefan ran ahead as much as he could, trying to get back as soon as he could to the suffering Rudolf. The men followed him.

By the time they stood in front of the cave the sun was starting to set and long shadows were falling across the terrain. Stefan led the men into the cave following the same route the boys had followed that morning. It took them almost an hour to arrive in the great gallery. Stefan called out immediately, "Dolf, we're here. We're here!"

As quickly as he could Stefan moved to the precipice and held out his electric torch. He leaned out as far as he could and called again, "Dolf, are you all right?" Stefan pleaded with him, "Talk to me, Dolf."

When finally Stefan saw Rudolf begin to move, he was elated. Rudolf pulled weakly at the coat over his face and opened his eyes. He thought he was dreaming when he saw an angel in a halo of light flying down to him. He took a breath and moaned with agony.

"He's alive!" shouted Stefan.

Both electric torches and flaming torches brought plenty of light into the darkness, making movement in the gallery much easier for the rescuers.

Two of the men were tied with ropes and let down over the precipice to the ledge where Rudolf lay trapped under the boulder. They wrapped him in blankets, gave him some water, and washed his face and hands. The men assessed the situation before one of them came back up to the gallery.

"The boy is in a dire situation. We don't know if we should try to move the boulder without a doctor here."

Stefan lay on his stomach looking down at Rudolf, continuous silent prayers for Rudolf on his lips. Rudolf felt a bit more coherent, "I thought you were an angel, Stefan...it looked like a halo round your head." Rudolf spoke softly through the agonizing throb of pain. "Thank you for bringing help. Is my Papa coming?"

Just as the rescue party of about twenty men began to discuss their next move, Leopold and Christián stumbled into the gallery. Christián saw Stefan and went directly to him.

"Where is Rudolf?" His face was stricken with fear, "What happened?"

"He fell...down there."

Christián crawled toward the edge and looked down into the abyss at his precious son, "Rudolf, it's Papa. We're here now. We'll get you out of there soon."

Christián sounded certain, reassuring, "Hold on Rudolf. You're being very brave. I'm proud of you."

Leopold spoke with the team of rescuers and introduced the doctor that he and Christián had brought with them. One of the rescuers asked the doctor if they could lower him down to the boy. "It looks bad. We're not sure of what will happen when we move the boulder."

Dr. Corvinus agreed. The men tied a harness around the doctor and lowered him down to Rudolf. He stayed in the harness, but moved onto the ledge beside the injured boy. He opened his medical bag and began to examine Rudolf, checking his vital signs. Two other men dangled in harnesses near him. The well-lit area allowed the doctor to see clearly the predicament that entrapped Rudolf. The doctor discovered that the boy lay in a twisted position, skewed to the left where his right leg, crossed over the left, seemed to bear the brunt of the stone. He gave Rudolf a small amount of morphine, saying to him, "You're in a bad place, young man, but there are many people here to help you. So hold on a bit longer. We'll get you free as soon as we can."

The men raised Dr. Corvinus back to the gallery where he spoke to Christián and the rescuers, "It looks like the one leg is crushed," he told them. "The only blessing in this miserable situation is that the boulder is probably acting as a tourniquet for the crushed leg. His left leg is pressed into a small gap depriving me of the ability to see or even estimate the damage, but I assume Dolf's left hip is broken since it appears he landed on it in the fall and cannot shift his position."

Moments later the rescuers tried to move the boulder to no avail; it would not move.

Outside the cave Tamás, Elizabeth, and Klára waited in the car with Gabriele. The darkness of the night embraced the little group, adding to their feelings of desolation. After more than two hours without any word, one of the rescuers came out of the cave with news for the boy's mother. Leopold had sent him out to relate as much as he could, in the most positive of terms... *the Duke wishes for all of you to return home... things will be better in the morning... the boy will be home by morning.* However, Gabriele refused to leave, only wanting to move closer to the cave's entrance.

She and the rest decided to walk up to the quarry to be closer for receiving news. Within the next hour, townspeople began to arrive at the quarry with bread and cheese and drink. They built a great fire and offered kind words of encouragement to the women. Together they waited through the night.

Ropes were tied around the boulder and levers were applied, but the position was too awkward, too difficult to get any leverage to move the enormous boulder; it would not budge. Many hours passed and Rudolf still remained entrapped, but through it all he slept unaware in a morphine dream. Finally, Dr. Corvinus felt they could wait no longer. Rudolf had to be released from the grasp of death that drew closer by the hour.

The doctor called to Christián who dangled in a harness nearby, "It seems that I can move his left leg slightly. I don't think it is caught under the boulder." His voice was low and very serious, "however, Christián, I am certain his lower right leg is crushed beyond saving." He looked to Christián for permission to do what had to be done. "I believe amputation is the only way to free Dolf from the stone. I must do it now…I fear he cannot live as he is very much longer."

"Do what you must, doctor. Save my son."

Dr. Corvinus severed the lower part of Rudolf's right leg just below the knee. They pulled him gently from the rock. As Dr. Corvinus suspected, Rudolf's hip was fractured, but his left leg was not broken, only badly bruised.

Finally, late in the afternoon, Rudolf was placed onto a gurney and carefully lifted to the ledge above, his severed, crushed leg forever left behind in the dark abyss. Christián wanted to remove the severed leg from the cave, but it was impossible. For the rescuers, freeing Rudolf was a great success, they congratulated each other and gave a cheer of happiness.

Rudolf partially opened his eyes to see Stefan hovering over him. He managed a small smile and raised his hand slightly. Stefan grabbed it and smiled at him; Stefan was so overjoyed he couldn't speak. As soon as the rescuers left the gallery, complete darkness instantly consumed the space. When the entourage reached the entrance and emerged into the light, cheers went up from the gathered people and Gabriele ran forward to the gurney. When his mother put her arms around him, Rudolf cried for the first time.

He was immediately taken back to his grandmother's villa on Tihany where he and his parents stayed for the rest of the summer. Rudolf was very ill at first with fever and pain, but he did begin to heal and by mid-September he could be taken outside into the sunshine in a movable bed with big wheels. His faithful friend, Stefan, spent every day by Rudolf's side. On many occasions he brought Klára with him. The three spent the hours as best friends reading or playing games or doing nothing, just being together. Rudolf never complained; he remained optimistic, determined to walk again.

—⁂—

One warm September afternoon Rudolf sat propped up in his portable bed in the shade of a great weeping willow. He watched Klára making a flower chain.

"Is that for you, Klára, or are you making it for me?" he asked.

"Oh, it's for you, Dolfie. I'm going to make you a knight and this is your crown."

"Do knights wear crowns?"

"I think so...they are like kings. I'm going to make one for Stefan, too."

"Klára, may I draw a picture of you on my paper?"

Klára looked at him seriously, "How can you do that?"

"Well, you sit still, just like you are now and I'll use this charcoal. You can see it when I'm finished."

"Will it be a good picture?"

"I think so, because you are so beautiful, the picture will have to be good."

Klára sat very still, only moving her eyes just a little. She held her breath.

"You don't need to hold your breath, Klára. Come see. It's done."

"Oh, Dolfie, that's a good drawing. Does it look like me?"

"Don't you think it does?"

"I don't know. It looks pretty. I like it. Can I have it?"

"Yes, you can have this one, if you will sit still while I draw another one."

Klára agreed and sat very still for several more drawings. Dolf was engrossed in drawing when Stefan walked up to them, "What are you doing?"

"Dolf is drawing my picture. See."

"These are good, Dolf. You really are an artist," Stefan looked through the drawings, then over Dolf's shoulder. Some of the drawings were of just Klára's head, but some included the setting and the flowers she was lacing together, "How did you get her to sit still for so long?"

"I'm making knight crowns for you and Dolf," she answered his question.

"Knight crowns? What are they for?"

"I'm going to knight you and Dolf." She stood up with the two flower circlets, "Put your head down, Dolf. This one is for you," she put the ring of flowers on top of his head and tapped his shoulders, "you are Sir Dolf from now on."

Then she turned to Stefan, "Bend over, Stefan. Now you are Sir Stefan."

"Silva's been reading to you..."Quest for the Holy Grail"...right?" Stefan smiled. Silva had read the stories of King Arthur's court to him years before as well. "Now what happens, Klára?"

She looked puzzled, "I don't know. What happens?"

"Dolf and I swear to protect you all your life from this day forward," he said and then knelt beside Dolf's bed, bowed his head, and placed his fist across his chest. Dolf emulated Stefan as best as he could and in unison they said, "We are forever your servants and protectors, Lady Klára."

Then Stefan directed Klára, "Now you touch our heads and say, 'Rise brave and true knights. I accept your pledge with gratitude.'"

Stefan helped Klára recite the words. She giggled and smiled at the play.

She loved how her brother and Dolf made her feel—important and loved—and she had such good fun with them.

By the end of September Rudolf could sit up in a wheelchair and Stefan pushed him all over Tihany, even up to the top of Echo Hill.

—◦◦◦—

When Rudolf's family finally left Tihany in the early fall, they traveled to Vienna first because his father had promised he would search for the very best prosthesis available. They met with one of the foremost doctors in Vienna who examined Rudolf's stump and confirmed that it was healing well. The doctor predicted that the boy could be fitted for his artificial leg with a foot by mid-winter.

After a visit with their relatives at the Hofburg Palace, the family traveled to Eisenstadt. Rudolf began immediately to practice with his crutches; he worked hard to stand, to walk, to build his upper body strength so that he could support his weight with his arms. He had a great desire to do everything he had done before.

One night as Rudolf prepared for sleep, still suffering the pains of healing, his father entered his room and sat down on the edge of his bed.

"Rudolf, you cannot give up, ever," Christián's voice was deep and certain, "You must make the very best with what you have. I'm speaking from the experience of loss myself.

"I have met a number of people who believe that I can't see because I have only one good eye...because I wear a patch on one eye they think I'm blind. Some even think I'm not intelligent...that I'm not as smart as they are. I suppose it to be some strange quirk in human understanding," he mused, "that if a person appears outwardly, physically incomplete, then to others that person is also lacking inside, not as intelligent or as clever.

"In business dealings those people sometimes try to cheat me," Christián continued thoughtfully, "because they think I won't *see* it or catch on.

"So, this is my point," Christián looked directly at his son, "I sometimes use their faulty impressions to my own benefit. Sometimes if I'm dealing with an unscrupulous person in business, I use my loss to take advantage of him. My advantage is always completely unexpected and usually quite successful."

Christián smiled as he spoke, "It can be the same for you, Rudolf, but you must learn to use your loss as a special gift, make it serve you in whatever way gives you the best outcome. You have to learn to do as much as you can, as though it—*the prosthesis*—is your leg, a part of you, not an alien thing. You must make it serve you.

"This is the most important thing, Rudolf. Learn to walk as well as possible without the hint of a limp, but remember how to limp and use it if you must."

Rudolf felt comforted by his father's words; he knew that his father was proud of his efforts and he wanted to accomplish great things to honor his father. As Christián leaned toward him to kiss his forehead, Dolf asked, "Papa will you tell me once again the story of how you lost your eye?"

"Aren't you tired of that story?" Christián smiled.

Rudolf shook his head in the negative, "I'll fall asleep much quicker if you tell me one more time." He loved his father's story.

"Well, I was near your age. It happened on my twelfth birthday." Christián leaned back and began to let the memory flow back into his consciousness. Such a long time ago, but still he could visualize the details as though they had happened only yesterday.

"On many occasions Leopold, along with Tamás, came to Eisenstadt with Duke Louis on hunting trips to our forests here in the Burgenland. Sometimes my father and I went to their forests in Sopron to hunt. On this hunting trip Leopold's mother came as well to visit with my mother. They spent their time walking through the manor house gardens and having tea. I remember hearing my mother say how much she disliked the garden in the fall when the early chill first nipped the tender flowers and the garden's beauty began to fade. She said it gave her a melancholy feeling and made her wish for her childhood in Budapest.

"A few days before their arrival my father gave me a new gun, a trim, sporty Mauser hunting rifle. I was never so proud of a birthday present. I felt very grown up; I could hardly wait to show it to Leopold and Tamás. They were quite impressed and we could hardly sleep for anticipation of our first day of hunting to see how well it would fire. We rose early on my birthday while it was still dark to prepare for our day of hunting. All the men with their guns and dogs posed for a photograph and then, at last, we tramped into the forests looking for the trail of deer.

"By mid-morning we were in pursuit of our first trophy. Leopold, Tamás, and I were following deer tracks as quietly as possible through a wooded hollow when Leopold spoke softly, 'It's a big one, Christián. Can you see it?'

" 'Yes, there it is, an eight-pointer,' I whispered as I slowly crept forward to find a better position.

"Just as I felt that I had found a good spot, the deer bolted in terror. I was surprised because we were down wind and I was certain the deer had not heard me. I stood up and at the same moment I heard a low growl come from my left side."

Christián's low voice built the suspense, "I turned my head toward the sound and before I could move or even think, a giant paw slashed across my face knocking me backward. As I lay helpless I saw the giant form of a brown bear rise up over me. I thought my life was over.

"Suddenly Duke Louis's Vizsla hounds were barking ferociously at the legs of the beast…and then two shots rang out. The bear roared with agony and fell. By that time, I could barely see what was happening because blood was pouring from my head over my eyes.

"Leopold and Tamás burst breathless from the trees, they shouted at me, 'Christián, are you all right?' They tried to console me, but I heard the terror in their voices when they said, 'Oh, my God, you are terribly injured!'

"Almost at the same moment Duke Louis and my father and the rest of the hunting party arrived and began to attend to me. By then I was in a state of shock, so my memory is very vague. My father used water from his canteen and torn strips of cloth to bandage my face."

Christián made a motion across the right side of his face, "There were four slashes, two across my scalp and two across my forehead, one of them took my right eye. I guess it was a horrible sight. My father could hardly contain his sorrow to see me. Many times he would say, 'My beautiful son, so damaged.'

"My father also told everyone how astonished he was at the scene...his son so severely wounded lying beside the slain bear. '*Who shot the bear?*' my father asked.

"A very excited Leopold answered, '*We both did—Tamás and me!*' as they waved their Mannlicher rifles over their heads.

"I remember hearing Leopold's words, 'Is Christián going to be all right? His eye is gone.'

"That was when I knew. I tried to touch my face, my eye, but my father would not let me. He directed the men in the party to make a litter for me and they carried me out of the forest while others in the party stayed behind to tend to the dead bear."

Christián smiled at his son who lay in rapture at his father's story, "You know, Rudolf, that bear's fur hide hangs on the wall in my study, your grandfather's study back then.

"I was put into a horse-drawn cart and brought with great haste back to the estate," Christián continued. "My mother became hysterical when she saw me being carried from the cart across the lawn toward the house. She ran to meet us. My head and half of my face were wrapped in bloody strips of cloth making it impossible for your grandmother to see the extent of my injuries. They sent for the doctor and shortly afterwards he arrived.

"So, you see, the slashes on my scalp can be concealed by my thick black hair, but the two slashes on my face," Christián indicated the one across his forehead and the other across his eye socket and down the cheek, "are still visible and," at this point in the story Christián always smiled widely, "only add to my handsome good looks. Your beautiful mother always tells me the scars give me a rugged kind of wild appeal. See, Rudolf, you can make tragedies work for you."

Rudolf smiled and closed his eyes. He loved his father's story. Christián was his hero. Rudolf was determined to be as brave as his father had been.

Although the hard work and endurance were his own, Rudolf gave much credit to his dear father for the optimistic attitude Christián helped him develop about his disability.

1915

In the beginning, in 1914, when the declaration of war was first pronounced, every country celebrated with parades and a shared romantic notion that the conflict would be short and victorious, "*over by Christmas.*" However, by 1915 all the participants, *the Central Powers*—Germany and the Austro-Hungarian Empire—and *the Great Entente* or *the Allies*—France, Britain, Russia, and Italy—understood they were into something much different from their initial expectations.

All sides realized this war, like all wars, would be much more difficult to end than it was to start. The horrors of trench warfare, the use of unthinkable lethal weapons, the introduction of war machines—the tank, the airplane, the machine gun—brought a war like no other, so horrific they called it "*the war to end all wars.*"

Lake Balaton

Although the terrors of war raged all around Hungary, Hungary itself remained relatively free of battle, allowing the von Esté family and others to go on living their lives as usual. Leopold paid sustained attention to the war and to Hungary's war involvements, but he was too old to go to war and Stefan was too young. War seemed only on the periphery of their lives. As in all other years, the families, the von Estés and the von Házys, spent the summer months at Lake Balaton.

Much later than usual, Rudolf and his family arrived at the lake; he was already strong and able to use his new artificial leg. The prosthesis, made of wood with a leather-covered foot that could support a shoe, was attached to his leg just above his knee. Rudolf used a cane to steady himself, but his determination to walk, to run, and even to climb astonished his parents. By the time the von Házys arrived at the lake Rudolf was able to walk without a noticeable limp, unless he was very tired. He could hardly wait to impress his old friends, Stefan and Klára, with his awesome accomplishments.

He had been greatly missed. Stefan and Klára had not seen him since the fall and they were concerned about him, about what he could do, about what they should say to him, about how they should treat him. Klára paced around the veranda at the front of the villa waiting impatiently for the von Házys to arrive for her birthday party. She kept asking Stefan, "When will they come?"

"Be patient, Klára, they're on their way," he answered, but in truth, he was as eager to see Rudolf as she was.

Finally, the von Hazy's motor car turned into the drive, pulled up to the stair, and stopped. The chauffeur opened the door for Christián and Gabriele who stepped out into the welcoming arms of Leopold, Elizabeth, and Aunt Eugenia. They all turned toward Rudolf as he began to emerge from the car. The chauffeur handed him an ornately carved cane and when he stepped from the car, he was standing on two feet. Brown shoes protruded from the bottom of his tan trousers. And then, to everyone's amazement, he walked with the aid of his cane.

Stefan ran down the steps to embrace him, Klára followed. They could not believe their eyes. Rudolf raised the right leg of his trousers. "*Wood,*" he said as he tapped on the prosthesis with his cane. Stefan was greatly impressed.

The chauffeur helped Rudolf up the flight of steps, but once inside he got around quite well. Silva invited everyone into the dining room where she was ready to serve Klára's birthday dinner. Klára felt very grown up turning five; she got to sit in Papa's chair at the head of the table. She looked around the table at her family and dear friends who were like family...they were all smiling at her. Tamás and Silva stood close by. Silva had made all of Klára's favorite dishes. Papa stood up with his glass of wine and invited everyone to stand as he lifted his glass to Klára, "Here are best wishes to the lovely Klára who is five today! We wish for her many, many more birthdays and may God bless you always."

Papa kissed her on the forehead; they all cheered and sipped from their glasses. Klára laughed, she was thrilled to be at the center of attention. She looked around the table again and asked with great anticipation, "Will everyone come back for my *Saint's Name Day* party in August? That's the real party...when you must bring presents and candy for me."

Gabriele laughed at her innocence and answered, "Of course we will! We will celebrate your birthday again with lots of presents and especially, candy."

"And we'll pull your ears for good luck, too," laughed Stefan.

From the dining room the family moved into the large reception hall where Elizabeth sat down at the piano. As she played, Gabriele began to sing Hungarian folk songs beginning with "*Kedves kis bajos leany,*" "My little graceful girl." Then Elizabeth played a military *verbunko* tune that had Leopold and Christián along with Stefan on their feet marching around the room clicking their heels. Rudolf laughed at their dance and vowed to himself that he too, one day, would join in the dance. He was determined to do everything he had done before his accident.

Klára wanted to stay awake with the guests, but she fell asleep in the midst of the party while her mother filled the room with the lovely music of Liszt. Elizabeth played beautifully the romantic "Liebestraum" and "Rhapsody Number Two." Leopold carried the sleeping child up to her bed where Nanny Irén tucked her in. When he returned to the hall, their guests were preparing to leave. Rudolf and Stefan agreed to spend the following day at the *Kisfaludy Strand*, the best beach in Balatonfüred.

Silva packed a lunch for the children to take with them to the strand. She smiled at the thought of Stefan and Rudolf willing to take Klára with them for the day. *What good boys they were to treat Klára so well.* Silva decided she would make *meggyleves* for the evening dinner dessert, because Stefan liked it so much. As she sang to herself, she spread butter on bread to make bear grass sandwiches, carefully wrapped a dozen *Plnene Trubky*, Lady Locks, in a little tin, washed three apples and filled canteens with honey-sweetened cold water. She opened a knapsack and arranged all the goodies inside, then she called to Stefan, "Lunch is ready to take to the strand. Come and get it!"

The three children left the big house and walked down to the roadway that followed along the shoreline of the lake. Klára was feeling quite grown up having just turned five and being invited to accompany Stefan and Rudolf for the day. As they waited for the local *autóbusz* to come along to take them into Balatonfüred, Stefan laid back on the grass and yawned, "You're amazing Dolf!" he stated, as casually as possible. "You have a better tan than I have."

Rudolf laughed and hit Stefan on the shoulder with his fist. He knew Stefan was quite astonished by his ease of movement, but was avoiding mentioning the actual *loss*. "Yeah, I'm tanning quite well, aren't I! Much better than you ever thought I would, huh? You thought I'd be up in my room hiding from the sun, didn't you!"

Stefan leaned on his elbow, "No, really I just didn't think you'd be this far along so soon. It's fantastic."

"Well, I'm lucky that I kept my knee." Rudolf confessed, "It makes movement much easier." He looked a bit wistful when he added, "I'm still working to conquer the balance part, but I'm getting the hang of it."

The bus arrived and the three boarded; Stefan lifted Klára up to the steps and hesitantly offered a hand to Rudolf who declined with a smile. Rudolf used his cane only for balance and then bounded up the steps. Once they arrived at *Kisfaludy Strand*, they found a good place on the grass near the water to lay out their blankets and set up beach chairs. They slipped out of their clothes having their bathing clothes underneath. Rudolf removed his prosthesis and laid it on the blanket under his clothes.

The swim attire for both Stefan and Rudolf was a dark blue wool jersey sleeveless shirt that hung to the hips over knee-length dark blue wool jersey pants. Klára wore a lighter blue wool jersey sleeveless dress with bloomers underneath. Rudolf's stump was visible just barely below the hem of his pants as he stood on the grass leaning on his cane.

This time Rudolf allowed Stefan to help him make his way to the lapping water along the lake's edge. The three children lowered themselves into the warm milky-blue water. Rudolf swam out several yards; he felt buoyant and completely normal; the water felt good, enabling. The missing lower leg did not hamper his movement in the water at all. He liked the added strength in his shoulders and upper arms that had not been there last summer. As he swam back toward the shore he felt a renewed confidence.

Klára was getting a ride on Stefan's shoulders as he paddled around in the shallow water. He remarked, "So, Dolf, still a strong swimmer...we'll do the race together in July, if you want."

The rest of the day was spent in the water and in the sun, building sand castles and napping. Stefan noticed some people on the beach stared at Rudolf's stump; a few asked him what had happened and a couple of young boys blatantly pointed, laughed, and whispered. Rudolf didn't seem disturbed by their attention and remained in good spirits.

Stefan finally remarked, "Aren't you bothered by those nitwits, Dolf?" he looked directly at his friend, "Are you really all right? You seem to be taking all this so well. I'm amazed."

"This is what life has given me, Stefan." Rudolf said as he lifted his stump into the air. "This is the way it is, so I have to deal with it the best way I can," he shrugged his shoulders and smiled, "people will think whatever they will. I can't control that. I can only know who I am and do my best with what I have just like everyone else."

—⁂—

During the next few weeks Rudolf began to swim every day in Lake Balaton. Christián proudly rowed a little dinghy alongside his son, offering words of encouragement. Swimming in the brilliant summer sun helped Rudolf regain his full strength and inspired a deep confidence within him. By the end of July he was ready to enter the great race of the summer; Stefan agreed to enter as well.

The famous swimming race across Lake Balaton began at Révfülöp on the north side of the lake and ended at Balatonboglár on the south side, a distance of a little more than five miles. The boys had entered before, but neither had ever made it all the way across the lake. Every year large groups of people of all ages entered the race. This year Rudolf was determined to go the distance.

The boys' families gathered at Révfülöp's shore and cheered enthusiastically for Rudolf and Stefan as they jumped into the water with hundreds of swimmers. Christián and László rowed alongside the swimmers at a safe distance, just in case Rudolf or Stefan needed to quit the race. Leopold and the rest of the families sailed the yacht toward Balatonboglár. Very quickly the lead swimmers in the race stretched far ahead of the splashing throng. As hard as they tried there was no way anyone in the families could spot Rudolf or Stefan among the moving, splashing mass.

Tacking far to the east, Leopold steered his yacht wide of the swimmers and made it to the lake's south shore just behind the lead swimmers. Rudolf and Stefan reached the beach at Balatonboglár within a decent time. They were joyously greeted as they came ashore; Rudolf with his arm draped over Stefan's shoulders for support, hopped vigorously toward the yacht.

Holding Klára on his shoulders, Leopold cheered the boys with great excitement, along with other family members. Two deck hands steered the boat into a slip on the dock. Christián's rowboat pulled alongside as the boys climbed into the yacht. Everyone gathered on the deck to toast the boys with sparkling wine. Silva appeared from below with trays of food for the hungry boys as Tamás brought towels and Rudolf's prosthesis.

Stefan bragged loudly about Rudolf's great feat, "He was far ahead of me…I was worn out, but he kept calling to me, *'You can do it, Stefan, come on!'* He was fantastic! He even treaded water waiting for me to catch up! He's a superman!"

"It's the weights I've been lifting," Rudolf offered shyly, but with a laugh. "You had better start lifting some pounds, too, if you want to keep up with me."

August

Only those families whose men were involved as soldiers seemed to suffer the effects of war, families like that of Dr. Klein. The Klein's two oldest sons, Sándor and Samuel, were both fighting in the Great War as Hungarian soldiers under the command of Austrian officers. The Kleins only knew that Samuel was somewhere on the Eastern Front and that Sándor was to the west, perhaps in Italy. Letters were rare and arrived long past the time they were written, so Dr. Klein relied on the Budapest newspaper for information that might possibly concern his sons.

Éva Klein and Magda, the Klein's cook, were making jam on a warm August afternoon while Dr. Klein sat at the kitchen table reading the afternoon newspaper. He read with passion the day's editorial:

> *Formal complaint has been lodged by the Prime Minister to the Austrian War Office regarding the poorly equipped Hungarian soldier. Hungarians will not tolerate the deficit of resources for our sons; we cannot allow improper uniforms, ill-fitting boots, inferior weapons, or lack of ammunition! Our sons cannot abide this neglect!*

The two women shook their heads and wiped their eyes with their aprons; they both felt the suffering of Sándor and Samuel in their hearts and would have given anything to bring comfort to the sons of the Klein house.

Dr. Klein began to read aloud an article with a detailed account of a battle in some distant place, but Éva interrupted him, "Please, Jakov, stop. I cannot bear to hear those horrible things, not knowing if my own sons might be among those who are suffering so. It is too much for me; it is almost unbearable. When will this nightmare end?"

"I remember when we all dressed in our finest and went down to the station to send our boys off," Magda said. "They were so handsome in their uniforms. Remember we gave them bouquets of flowers and said that we would see them soon."

Somewhere in Poland

While the Kleins spoke in Budapest of their sons, Samuel was marching toward Warsaw, Poland. He was part of a successful German-Austrian offensive that sent the Russians into retreat. Samuel thought about his family at home and yearned for the day he would be there again, playing his balalaika with his brothers and sisters while his mother played the piano. He longed to hear his father discuss politics and religion while Eszter argued with him. He smiled to himself as he adjusted the load on his back and wiped the dripping sweat from his face. It was a hot summer.

The German army had control of Warsaw by August and Samuel's unit was sent south along the Galicia Front. He began a letter to his mother. He wrote a little every day, but it was hard to find time to write very much and he didn't want to tell her what it was really like on the front. So, he wrote about the flowers—poppies and sunflowers, the birds—many different songbirds and falcons and grouse—and about the kinds of dinners he would like to have when he returned to Budapest.

September

By the fall of 1915, after a series of Austrian invasion attempts, the Central Powers launched a massive bombardment of Serbia and, finally, Serbia fell to the combined forces of Austria, Germany, and Bulgaria. Dr. Klein continued to track the progress of the war through the newspaper. He read aloud to Éva that Serbian troops had fled into Greece and Albania where the *Entente* forces joined them. On the Western Front, terrible trench warfare had begun with the Germans entrenched from the Flemish coast to Lorraine. Austrian-Hungarian forces were involved in Italy and on the Eastern Front in the conflict with the Russians.

War dragged on and on across Europe, bringing devastation to vast stretches of land from Belgium and France to the Mediterranean to the Baltic Sea to Galicia to the northern shores of the Black Sea and, yet, except for the thousands of young men gone from their Hungarian homes, the war seemed distant.

In late September Samuel Klein marched through the Pripet Marshes and was nearing the Dniester River on the Rumanian frontier. Austrian Galicia had been retaken from the Russians by the German-Austrian-Hungarian soldiers; the Russian armies had been decimated. Men lost were in the millions. Samuel was on the winning side at the moment, but he felt no joy and wondered, *Why am I here? What gain will there be for my family, for my people, the Jews?*

Somewhere in Italy

While Samuel languished on the Romanian front, Sándor Klein marched with an Austrian-Hungarian unit through the Julian Alps south toward Italy. He found himself stagnated atop Mount San Michele near the Isonzo River. Sándor's unit was completely outnumbered by Italian forces; artillery constantly pounded their position. Through the turmoil, at intervals, things grew quiet and Sándor played the violin he carried; he played soulful Bartok melodies that floated through the thin air over the mayhem. His music settled the nerves of his anxious companions as they hid in their trenches waiting for the next round of fire and explosion. The familiar music allowed the men to lean back and to breathe normally again; they could let their thoughts drift back to home, hoping they would be there soon.

One night Sándor contemplated his situation on top of the mount: He could not descend, he could only wait for salvation or death. In a moment of complete bewilderment and anxiety, Sándor decided to write a letter to his father. He hurriedly scribbled the words on a small piece of paper torn from a book of poems he carried in his pack. When he finished his words, he folded the paper, wrote "*Papa*" on the outside and put it in a small tin box that he kept in his shirt pocket.

Budapest

In late September, soon after the von Esté family returned from Lake Balaton to Andrássy Avenue, Elizabeth asked Klára to sit with her for tea in the conservatory. Elizabeth poured a cup of tea for her five-year-old daughter and smiled as Klára struggled to sit on the edge of her seat and reach for the cup.

"Careful dear, it's still a bit warm," Elizabeth warned. She observed Klára as she began to sip her tea.

"You're getting to be a very big girl now and I was wondering if you might like to begin piano lessons?"

Klára looked up at her mother with a wide-eyed expression of surprise, "Oh yes, Mommy, I would love to play the piano. I love the music so much."

"I know that you do, Klára, and you already show a talent for it. So, Papa and I think you may be ready for lessons... Papa knows of a very good music teacher. Tomorrow you and I will go together to meet Mrs. Klein to see if she will take you as a student."

Klára was thrilled and smiled broadly as she sipped her tea and reached for another of Silva's delicious *ischler*.

The following day, just after lunch, Elizabeth and Klára put on their hats and went out the front door to the great touring car waiting in the driveway. The chauffeur, Auguste, opened the door for them and they climbed into the back seat. Klára sat close to the window and watched the houses and streets as they passed by; she was very excited to meet her music teacher. The car traveled on Andrássy Avenue toward town, passed the Opera House as though they were going to Papa's office, but instead of turning right the car turned left into an area Klára had never seen before. The streets were narrow and twisting with tall skinny buildings, little shops and restaurants, and many people walking in all directions.

At last, their chauffeur stopped the car in front of a formidable structure, a three-storied brick building. The Klein townhouse stood just a few blocks east of the great Synagogue on Dohány Street. An iron railing followed the edge of the sidewalk, protecting the pedestrian from the deep open space next to the exposed basement below the sidewalk. The railing continued up both sides of a stone staircase that bridged the space between the sidewalk and grand entrance. A pair of carved oak doors with beveled glass windows let any visitor know the inhabitants who lived here were of some importance and wealth.

A servant greeted them and ushered Elizabeth and Klára into the grand entrance foyer. As they passed an open door they could see into the music room where several pianos stood. Klára observed carefully her surroundings—a staircase with an oak banister that curved around the wall and up to balconied second and third floors, and the oval skylight that formed the ceiling above the stairs. She noticed the open door straight back from the entrance beyond the foyer that appeared to lead into the kitchen. The servant led Elizabeth and Klára into the parlor where she asked them to be seated. Soon afterwards Mrs. Klein entered the room, warmly welcomed them, and offered them tea.

Éva Klein, an elegant woman, not very tall, but slender, had dressed in a starched white blouse tucked into a long black skirt. Older than Elizabeth by more than ten years, her silver-streaked black hair was piled high on her head and held in place by ebony clasps. Crinkly lines around her warm brown eyes deepened when she smiled sweetly at her guests. Klára noticed her beautiful hands with long fingers and short nails adorned by several sparkling diamond rings. Mrs. Klein's lavender-scented skin appeared soft and youthful. Klára thought she was quite beautiful.

Elizabeth and Mrs. Klein began their acquaintance with friendly recognition of their husbands' long professional friendship and commented that it was too bad they had never met, although Elizabeth was familiar with Mrs. Klein's immense talent as a former pianist with the Budapest Symphony.

Mrs. Klein had played with the symphony in her younger days, becoming a rather well-known concert pianist in Vienna as well. Mrs. Klein responded that Elizabeth was kind to remember because she had not played with the symphony for many years. She referred to her six children as her reason for retiring from the symphony and the reason she began to take on students.

With that last comment she turned toward Klára who was sitting very lady-like on a velvet-covered chair. Mrs. Klein asked if she could see Klára's hands and then held them with her own and studied Klára's fingers.

"She has beautiful hands. Long fingers and a good span. Do you like music, Klára?"

Klára nodded her head in the affirmative.

"Can you hum a little tune for me, Klára?"

Klára looked shyly at Elizabeth who encouraged her and then she sang a little lullaby, quite tuneful with appropriate intonation.

"Very nice, Klára," exclaimed Mrs. Klein, "I think we can turn you into a lovely pianist. Would you like to see the music room?"

Mrs. Klein led Elizabeth and Klára across the entry hall into the music room where three pianos—two grand pianos and one smaller upright—stood on the highly polished dark wood floor with several Persian rugs strewn in random places. Velvet curtains with lace sheers hung over the great windows. Between the windows several delicate chairs stood against the dark-paneled walls. Various musical instrument cases leaned against a group of chairs arranged among the pianos.

"The instruments are those of our children. We have a brief concert for Dr.

Klein each evening after supper." As she took her seat at the grandest of the pianos, she said, "Sit here, Klára, by me."

After their initial meeting, Klára began her piano lessons every Wednesday afternoon at three o'clock. Sometimes, Auguste drove Klára and Elizabeth to Mrs. Klein's, but other times Elizabeth and Klára walked across Andrássy Avenue to the Metro stop in front of their house and took the Metro to the Opera House stop. From there they walked to Paulay Street and into the Jewish District. As they walked south on Kazinczy Street they passed well-known delicatessens with windows full of delicious smelling Kosher sausages and cheeses and bakeries with the best of Jewish breads and sweets; sometimes they stopped on their way home to buy special treats. From the corner of Dohány Street they walked to the Klein's townhouse, only a few blocks from the Great Synagogue.

Elizabeth enjoyed her afternoons in the Klein's parlor where she could nestle into the tufted cushions of the settee, read, or just close her eyes and listen to the beautiful music that drifted into the room from across the hall. Elizabeth recognized that Klára, even at her young age, had a natural ability for creating music. It seemed Klára could hear the notes in her head and reproduce the melodies easily. Mrs. Klein had a reputation as an excellent teacher, but Elizabeth imagined that Klára was a most pliable student with an innate ability and willing attitude. Elizabeth looked forward to these peaceful afternoons as a welcome respite from her routine.

One particular afternoon Elizabeth had another engagement and sent Klára by car with Tamás to the Klein's. Klára arrived about fifteen minutes early and was escorted into the parlor by the maid. After only a few moments Mrs. Klein appeared with her daughter Rózsa, who had also recently turned five years old; Klára in July and Rózsa in September. Mrs. Klein introduced the two girls who were instantly interested in each other.

Rózsa Klein, the youngest of the six Klein children, was a cheerful, lively little girl who loved to laugh. Although she could be somewhat shy, she was fun-loving and full of mischief. Her curly crimson hair, the color of rubies, threatened a temper, but her deep, blue eyes, the color of blueberries, promised a good nature. With a face the image of her mother's, petite Rózsa Klein was a charming, pretty little girl.

She took Klára upstairs to her room to see her wonderful dollhouse and other treasures and then back down to the kitchen to meet the cook, Magda, who gave the girls glasses of cider and pieces of *torta*, layered cake with filling.

"Come to the music room, girls," Mrs. Klein called, "you can learn to play a duet today."

The girls were very happy to play together; they shared a love of music. Over time the girls discovered many other common interests and pastimes, like reading, cards, and outdoor games. From that day forward Rózsa and

Klára became the dearest and most loyal of friends; true kindred spirits who shared all of their most intimate dreams.

1916

By May all the families were at Lake Balaton as in summers past, but this year Klára brought her new dearest friend, Rózsa Klein. She would stay for two weeks in May and then return for another two weeks in July for Klára's birthday. Klára was very proud to have her own personal friend to show all around her favorite places... Silva's kitchen, the grounds of the villa, the shepherds' cottages and Milan's Puli dogs, the vineyards and the gardens, the spring and pool of deep water beyond the villa, the town of Balatonfüred and—of course—the lake. Stefan and Rudolf were happy to take Klára and Rózsa sailing and swimming and they included the girls on hikes and picnics on Tihany Peninsula.

That summer at Lake Balaton, the war still seemed very far away. They rarely saw soldiers or any vestiges of war. Except for Rózsa's two older brothers who were soldiers, it was easy for the children to forget there was a war, a horrible war, raging so near.

While the children enjoyed their days in the sun, Rózsa's brother Samuel was sitting near the Dniester River on the Romanian border as part of a large division of the Austrian-Hungarian Army. His division's duty was to hold the front line against the Russians, but quite suddenly, on the fourth of June, the Russians launched a surprise attack.

Samuel wrote his thoughts in his diary... *The weather is terrible... the mud so deep that when I walk it takes everything I have to keep my boots on my feet. Bombs are exploding all around us. The enemy is everywhere... the Cossacks are coming.*

Oblivious to the war, the children could completely immerse themselves in summertime at the lake. Stefan and the girls often took the ferry from Balatonfüred to visit Rudolf at his family villa on the Tihany Peninsula. Rudolf's grandmother, the Countess Alexandra, had always fascinated Klára; the countess seemed very mysterious to her.

Ever since the Countess had lost her husband she wore only black. Even inside her apartments, she wore a black, gossamer veil pulled across her face. The Countess kept all the draperies drawn tightly, so it seemed like night all the time inside her rooms. Despite those morbid appearances, she was kind and generous to the children and seemed cheered by their visits. She always called to her faithful companion, Lázslo, to bring sweets for her special guests.

Rudolf's parents, Christián and Gabriele, enjoyed an opposite atmosphere in their section of the great Tihany villa. Their draperies were pulled back from the windows to allow the light and lake breezes to bathe the rooms with sunshine and fresh air while Gabriele's gramophone filled the space with her favorite operas. A party atmosphere prevailed when the children were present. They practiced Hungarian folk dances and sang traditional songs; they played popular games and cards and put together jigsaw puzzles. Christián and Gabriele were great fun.

During one of those afternoons, Stefan and Rudolf noticed the sunlight shining directly on Rózsa, on her very curly, red hair which glowed like gold. Both boys decided to call her *Arany*, golden-red, from that day on. They meant the nickname as a compliment, agreeing that she had the most beautiful hair. Klára agreed completely; she, too, admired Rózsa's crowning glory of bright red.

Christián enjoyed taking the children on explorations of Tihany Peninsula. They often spent entire days on adventurous hikes. The children loved the lakes, *Belső-tő* and *Kulső-tő,* where they could watch abundant birdlife. They used their binoculars and recorded the names of the birds they saw—white egrets, herons, cormorants, spoonbills, falcons, terns, and warblers. All summer long they returned to add new sightings to their lists.

Lunchtime was usually spent atop Echo Hill where they could see a panoramic view of Lake Balaton, including a view of Balatonfüred. For great fun they could face the wall of the Benedictine monastery and shout out words that came echoing back to them. After lunch Christián took the children into the cool interior of the *Apátság Templom* to escape the afternoon's stifling heat. The *Templom* was a very special place to the von Hazy's, having been the wedding site for Christián and Gabriele. Amazing art filled the church from ceiling frescoes to altarpieces to carved wooden screens. King Andrew's sarcophagus lying in the crypt put the boys in awe, especially the sword-like cross carved on the cover.

From the church the hikers followed a long path to an old castle ruin and to the ancient cells hollowed into the walls of basalt by hermit monks. Christián told the children a legend from olden times about a beautiful, heartbroken princess whose silky tears first formed the lake, "Lake Balaton will exist as long as the maiden continues to weep," he told them.

Klára and Arany did not like the story, "It makes the lake seem sad…we don't want her to keep crying, but we don't want the lake to go away."

Other days the children enjoyed playing on the beaches of velvety sand and swimming in the smooth, warm waters of the lake. There were occasions when Rudolf's grandmother, the Countess, dressed in black, requested her grandson and Stefan accompany her to the resort spa at Hévíz, the place of hot water. Klára and Rósza were too young to go to the spa; the waters were almost bottomless and too warm for them. Rudolf and Stefan enjoyed going with the Countess on the steamboat to Keszthely, then the *autóbusz* to Hévíz. While Countess Alexandra enjoyed hot water treatments for her rheumatism, the boys swam among the lily pads that covered a large part of the warm water.

Every August, Elizabeth, Stefan, and Klára took their annual trip to Vienna and Linz and then in September, the von Estés held a big goulash party at the villa to mark the waning days of summer. Tamás stirred Silva's delicious concoction in a huge black iron cauldron over an outdoor fire while the many guests shared memories of the summer. Thoughts turned to the coming of fall and places far from Lake Balaton. By the end of September, summer life came to an end and the von Estés returned home to Budapest where their normal routine of city life resumed.

The wine business occupied Leopold, while Elizabeth divided her time between helping her husband in his business and running her household. Stefan turned fifteen and began his scientific studies at university and Klára returned to her piano lessons with Mrs. Klein.

Late September

Concerned about his sons, Dr. Klein read from the newspaper about the offensive drive of the Russian general and how his armies had overrun the Austrian-Hungarian units near the Dniester River on the Romanian border. Jakov Klein knew Samuel was somewhere on the Eastern Front and wondered if this battle might be one that involved him.

In fact, the conflict did involve Samuel. It had begun in June. First the Russians came from the north, bombarding the city of Lutsk. Lutsk fell within two days. Secondly, the Russians came from the south, routing the Austrian-Hungarian armies at the Dniester River. The Russian onslaught devastated confidence and caused great loss of life.

Samuel continued his written thoughts... *The Russians came at us with so many soldiers... by the end of the month thousands of us were dead or taken prisoner. A German general tried to take control of our troops here in Galicia, but we were demoralized when they brought a bunch of Turks into our ranks. There was nothing the Germans could do to save us... the Russians just kept coming... there were so many of them.*

In late September the Russian offensive ended as suddenly as it had begun. By then the Austrian-Hungarian armies had lost almost half a million dead and wounded and hundreds of thousands had been taken prisoner. Samuel was one of those prisoners.

Once again he wrote in his diary ... *They carried me away from the dead and dying to a medical wagon. Conditions were miserable, too few nurses, only one doctor, no medications...and so many wounded soldiers...the Russians could not manage so many...I was moved to a tent pitched in the mud where I shared a bed with another poor carcass worse off than I.*

After a few days of lying in that bed head to toe with another wounded soul, Samuel Klein got up, packed his gear, and started walking home.

Budapest

Stefan admired his father and treasured the times he and Leopold spent together in the Andrássy house library. Sometimes Rudolf was there and he, too, cherished the hours spent listening to Leopold talk about his beliefs and ideals. Leopold encouraged the boys to read history and philosophy. Especially fond of the Greeks, Stefan studied their mythology and philosophy, in particular, Plato's discussions on Beauty and Truth. Even as a youth, Stefan developed a sensitive eye for the beauties he found in nature and in finely made objects. He contemplated the detail of things more seriously than anyone Leopold had seen at such a young age.

Leopold's discussions of American ideals—equality, opportunity, individual rights—fascinated Stefan and Rudolf. Leopold's ability to intertwine American goals with his long-held ideal, Magyarization, intrigued the boys.

"There are many ethnic groups who make up the population of America, but everyone speaks English," Leopold pointed out. "I'm convinced the adoption of a single language helped unify America...actually holds it together."

"All the different ethnic groups that inhabit Hungary can assimilate to create a unified Hungary. My friend, Dr. Klein, is the perfect example of Magyarization. A strong proponent of Magyarization, he tells me that for the Jewish people, Magyarization has been a way to incorporate themselves into Hungarian society and culture without losing their religion. Dr. Klein considers himself a Magyar. He says that his religion is Judaism, but he is a Hungarian. This is the attitude of our Emperor who has always advocated the emancipation of the Jew and their equal citizenship in the Empire."

Stefan and Rudolf loved to hear Leopold speak of his progressive ideals of fairness and equality for all Hungarians and both boys adopted Leopold's philosophies as their own. As the boys listened to Leopold they looked through their favorite books or studied the large globe that stood by Leopold's desk. Anytime Papa and the boys were in the library Klára wanted to be there, too. She lay on the thick carpet looking at the atlas or the big book of watercolored images depicting birds and flowers. She listened to Leopold and the boys talk about things she did not understand, but which were fascinating nonetheless. She turned the pages quietly so she could hear every word spoken by those she adored. Klára knew their talk was of *big* ideas, she could tell by the excitement in their voices.

October

One very cold afternoon at the end of October, a freezing wind blew into the Klein's kitchen from the sudden opening of the front door. Éva Klein and Magda both rushed from the kitchen into the hallway to see who the unexpected arrival could be. Both recoiled from the sinister, filthy, ragged hulk that stood in the lighted doorway and then in the next instant ran toward the figure whose eyes they knew so well. Éva wrapped her arms around Samuel, crying out his name over and over, while Magda shut the door behind him. The two women guided Samuel into the warm kitchen and started to care for him.

They removed the threadbare coat from his shoulders; unwrapped the scarves from his head and neck, and took off his straw-lined boots. Magda exclaimed over his blistered and bloodied feet and made him put them into a pan of warm water as she poured salts and herbs into the water. Éva washed his face and hands and then went upstairs to fill a tub of hot water for him. Magda gave him a bowl of hot *zöldségleves*, vegetable soup, and *csirke*, chicken, with a glass of *körtepálinka*, pear brandy. He ate so quickly Magda refilled his bowl and plate and glass three times before he sat back and smiled. Big tears rolled down his face, "There were many times I thought I would never sit at this table again," he sobbed.

Éva and Magda wept, too as they helped Samuel up the stairs. He had always been the largest of the Klein sons, the tallest, the heaviest; now he was stoop shouldered and only skin and bone. There were wounds from which they removed dirty bandages, shaking their heads, certain that infection was surely present. They helped him undress and slip into the warm, scented bath. He slid down into the water's depth up to his chin and closed his eyes. The two women bathed the grime and blood from his body. Finally, they helped him dress in a clean, white nightshirt and tucked him into his own bed which Magda had warmed with a long-handled copper pan filled with glowing coals. Samuel fell asleep within moments. Éva stayed by his bed watching him sleep while Magda went downstairs to call the family doctor to come tend to his injuries.

Dr. Klein arrived home that evening just as the doctor was leaving. Jakov Klein could hardly believe his precious son was upstairs in his own bed.

"Samuel received several gunshot wounds," Dr. Weisz told Jakov. "Fortunately three bullets completely passed through his body. A fourth lodged in the ribs on his right side.... the bullet was removed while he was a prisoner in Romania. I've cleaned all the wounds and given Éva strong medicines to administer. I am amazed that Samuel walked so far in his condition, filled with infection." The doctor sounded confident, "That determination is a good sign he will recover."

Jakov Klein's eyes filled with tears as he thanked the doctor, then turned toward the stairs and went up to his son. He found Éva sitting by Samuel's bed in the darkened room lit only by the hallway light. They embraced each other before Jakov leaned over to kiss his sleeping son. Such a deep sigh of relief had not left Jakov for years, not since the war began and his sons had gone off marching behind the Hungarian flag.

Éva whispered to Jakov, "We should call Rachael Lévi to let her know that Samuel is home. I think it would be good for Samuel to have her here when he awakens."

Jakov agreed and Rachael was called. Within the hour she was sitting by Samuel's bed, holding his hand and whispering his name.

—⁓—

The von Estés were elated to hear of Samuel Klein's return home. Samuel's terrible ordeal suffered during what Leopold believed to be an ill-conceived war simply added to Leopold's adamant opposition to Austria's arrogant march to war over a year ago. Leopold often shook his head, "Poor Hungary...Austria dragged us into this world-wide conflict that has no end in sight. What has it brought Austria? Only humiliation...and, worst of all, German dominance. Tizsa and I warned them Russia would enter the war...not to mention Britain and France! The Emperor was misled by those who wanted war!"

"Why do some men want war, Papa?" Stefan asked his father

"Power, greed, resources, revenge, more land, more money—who knows the reason?" said an agitated Leopold. "They tout other reasons to the people—noble causes, freedom perhaps, fear maybe, otherwise they could never raise an army. What soldier would give his blood for some other man to gain power or riches?

"It is true that some causes are worth fighting for, like freedom, but in our modern age why can we not simply demand our freedom?" Leopold continued. "It is the reasonable thing for all men to be free. It is good for business. At the end of this terrible conflict—when one side runs out of money or the war becomes too unpopular—it will end. Men will sit down and talk and bring an end to it. We pray that when that day finally comes, reason and fairness will guide their negotiations. I believe the Emperor realizes all of this must come to an end as soon as he can end it!"

November

On the twenty-first of November at nine o'clock in the evening, after a sixty-eight year reign, the beloved Emperor Franz József died in Vienna. He was eighty-six years old. Word of the Emperor's death spread quickly throughout Budapest. Kind words came easily to describe the old man and his many years as the Emperor of Austria and King of Hungary. The people of Budapest filled to capacity St. Stephen's Basilica for the Emperor's special memorial service.

The von Esté and von Házy families found themselves standing near the Chapel of the Holy Right. One of Hungary's most sacred relics, the Holy Right, referred to the severed, withered hand of Hungary's beloved first Christian king, St. Stephen. The Holy Right resided in its own reliquary, a miniature jewel-encrusted cathedral made of gold and silver. The mummified right hand could be seen vaguely through the reliquary's glass windows.

Before the service began, Stefan lifted up Klára so she could see the holy relic through the reliquary's smoke-stained glass. The boys had already told her stories of *the hand* with all its gory details and now, they reminded her of the horrors, making *the holy hand* seem all the more gruesome and frightening. Even after the choir began to sing Klára had a creepy feeling up her spine.

"Klára…Klára," Stefan whispered in a strangely eerie voice just behind her ear, "*the hand* is coming…coming for you."

Klára shrugged him off and turned to make a face at him, "Leave me alone, Stefan."

"I see *the hand*…it's creeping out of its box…it's coming," whispered Rudolf as he walked his fingers up her back.

"Mommy, the boys are bothering me. They're trying to scare me."

"Stefan…Rudolf, behave yourselves. This is a solemn occasion…have some respect for your Emperor." Elizabeth gave them a stern look with her reprimand, "Leave Klára alone."

Klára smiled smugly at them and turned away.

When Franz József died he left no immediate heirs. His son had committed suicide and his nephew, Franz Ferdinand, had been assassinated, so the crown went to his grand nephew, Karl. Known as a benevolent, simple man, Karl was an unlikely ruler. Still, he found himself next in line for the Hapsburg throne to become Emperor of Austria and King of Hungary; Karl was crowned *Emperor Charles IV* in Vienna.

In December, Karl (Charles IV) and his wife, Zita, traveled to Budapest for Karl's coronation as King of Hungary, according to the expectations of the Austro-Hungarian Dual Monarchy. A regal coronation service held in Buda's

Matthias Church of Our Lady was attended by the von Esté and von Házy families. The families of Leopold and Christián had attended the wedding of Karl and Zita and now they happily anticipated sharing this grand occasion with the handsome couple.

The young royals wore splendid ancestral robes of white and gold for the ceremony. Karl was crowned with the ancient Hungarian coronation regalia of the Árpáds dating back to St. Stephen. The sacred coronation continued the apostolic, divine rule of Hungarian kings, since Pope Sylvester II crowned Stephen King in the year one thousand one.

The ancient crown, made of gold, combined a magnificent Byzantine diadem and a Latin crown with a tilted cross. Set with precious jewels, pearls, and enameled scenes of Christ and Holy Saints, four pendants of braided gold dangled from the diadem. As the crown was placed upon Karl's head, the many guests who filled the nave of Matthias Church held their breath for a moment, knowing he was the new Apostolic King of Hungary, Charles IV, but to those who knew him best, he would remain *Karl*.

After the ceremony the King and Queen rode in an elegant carriage the short distance to Buda Palace for a gala celebration. The guests followed, some by carriage, most on foot. The adults were served a grand supper in the great hall while the children enjoyed their own special supper in one of the banquet halls.

After Stefan and Klára had finished their supper, Rudolf whispered to Stefan, "Let's go, I'll take you down into the labyrinth. I know where the secret doors are hidden."

Stefan stood up from the table, "Come on, Klára, Dolf is taking us on an adventure."

Klára was thrilled to be included in the adventure with the big boys, even though she had no idea where she was going. No one paid any attention to them as the three left the banquet hall. Rudolf led his companions down the hallway to one seemingly random room. He tried the doorknob and opened the door, "We could actually go into almost any of these rooms and find a secret entrance into the labyrinth, but this is one I know best."

The room was dark, but Rudolf found the light switch and punched it on. The room was quite large with an enormous wall-sized fireplace at the opposite end from where they were standing. Rudolf moved to a large tapestry that hung on one wall by a built-in bookcase. He stepped on a particular spot on the floor and almost immediately there was a low click sound and the bookcase moved, only slightly.

Stefan and Klára were astonished, "How did you know how to do that?" Stefan asked.

"My father showed me when we were visiting the palace last summer. The labyrinth is lit by oil lamps. You'll see. Follow me. You'll be amazed!"

Rudolf opened the bookcase wider for all of them to enter.

The three children passed through the opening into the labyrinth below the palace. Truly, they were astonished at the cave-like tunnels with smooth concrete floors that ran in several directions. Bulbous rock formations projected from the walls and ceiling of the cave. They spiraled down a concrete staircase that led to a large passageway in which they could see random tables and chairs.

Stefan looked around, "I'm most amazed that you would come down here, Dolf! It looks so much like *Köves Só barlang*. I would expect you to hate it down here."

"That's the reason Father brought me. When we came down the stairs, into the dark, he told me to face my fears. He told me not to fear the cave; that I would not die in a cave, certainly not this one."

Rudolf led the way. Stefan held Klára's hand.

"This labyrinth was formed a million years ago by hot water running through the tufa rock," Rudolf informed them. "The labyrinth goes all the way to Matthais Church and then under Old Town with secret doors into restaurants and courtyards all along the way. Some day we should explore the whole labyrinth, all the way to its end."

From the network of large tunnels, staircases at regular intervals led to doors high above their heads. Showing Stefan and Klára the labyrinth was very exciting for Rudolf. He asked them, "Do you want to try sneaking back into the banquet room where we had supper without anyone catching us?"

A challenge, they all agreed, would be the best fun. Rudolf led them back through the tunnels until he recognized the correct staircase. They climbed to the top of the stairs and then Rudolf opened the door, only slightly. He peered out furtively, pushing the door just wide enough for each of them to squeeze through. They found themselves behind a tapestry that hung against an ordinary paneled wall, revealing no secrets. They could hear the voices of the diners and the tinkling of glass and silver against china. Each one, Stefan, Klára, and Rudolf, slipped from behind the tapestry unnoticed; they resumed their seats at the table just in time for dessert. They looked at each other with wide, knowing smiles, very proud of their caper. They had accomplished a secret mission with no discoverers.

A Wedding

A week before the Kleins began their celebration of *Hanukkah*, the Festival of Lights, Samuel married Rachael Lévi. Dancing, singing, and good food—*kreplach, kugel, blintzes*, and *challah*—prepared by Magda and Éva, delighted all the guests. At the end of the evening, the Kleins took up their instruments—Éva and Rózsa on pianos, Ferenc, Abram, and Eszter, violins, and Samuel, his *balalaika*, the twelve-stringed harp—and played *Hinay Ma Tov*, "How Good It Is To Be Together," and their absent brother, Sándor's favorite, *Hava Nagila*, "Come Let Us Rejoice!" Complete happiness would have embraced the Klein household if only Sándor had been with them to share the joyous event.

1917

Spring came to Budapest in gusts of warm winds and daily showers. Violets and the waxy, yellow flowers of the dolomite flax sprung up in unexpected places. The refreshing scent of spring brought a sigh of relief... glad for winter's passing and hopeful that war's end would come soon.

One afternoon, Elizabeth and Klára visited Leopold's office on Hércegprimás Street to celebrate the tenth anniversary of Papa's von Esté Fine Wine Company. Klára loved to go into town with her mother to visit Papa's office. They took the Metro from the stop in front of their home and were in Papa's square within minutes. Papa's beautiful building was sandwiched between the Árpád Bank owned by an old Magyar family and the Löwy Fine Fabrics and Lace Company owned by a Jewish family.

Klára looked up to admire the magnificent muscled Atlases crouched under the cornice far above her head. She eagerly bounded up the stairs to the impressive entrance where a shiny brass plaque, bearing the words "The von Esté House of Fine Wine," was attached to the rusticated stone. Once inside the cool interior Klára felt chilled and excited. Large slabs of marble covered the floor, the walls were paneled in dark wood with insets of rich green velvet. A shiny brass elevator cage stood in one corner while a staircase wound upward around the walls behind the cage. A wrought-iron railing followed the curve of the stairs. Zol, the old gentleman who operated the elevator, greeted Klára and her mother warmly and allowed Klára to operate the elevator. He always let her run the elevator on her visits.

On the first floor sat the receptionist, Judit, at a massive oak desk just beyond the elevator and staircase. Behind Judit sat the switchboard operator, who sometimes let Klára try on her earphones, and beyond her were several men busy at their desks. All the workers looked up from their work to greet Klára and her mother. A tasting room and more offices were on the second floor. On the third floor, the top floor, was Papa's fine office of dark wood and brass, plush carpets, and two big oriel windows. Klára loved to look through the windows down onto the street with so many busy people hurrying along in all directions.

When the big clock chimed five o'clock, Leopold, Elizabeth, and Klára walked to Vaci Street where they entered the elegant Nádor Hotel for their celebratory supper. Tamás met them at their table and shortly after, Stefan joined them, coming from his day of studies at the Hungarian Academy of Sciences. They began their dinner with a hearty toast, "*To the von Esté House of Fine Wine, Egészségére!*" Despite the war, Leopold's wine had found great success. The von Esté wines had gained a good reputation and sales were strong.

Summer at Lake Balaton

Rudolf and Stefan had been working in the vineyard with Tamás all morning; it was an exceptionally hot day. When noontime arrived, Silva called them into the kitchen for cold cider and *nyit-szembenéz szendvics*, open-face sandwiches of radishes and cheese on buns. When Rudolf walked out of the villa and through the kitchen garden on his way back to the vineyard, he saw Klára sitting on a high branch of the cherry tree just beyond the kitchen garden. He walked nonchalantly as though he had not seen her and stopped just under the branch where she was sitting. He waited for her to make her presence known.

In a moment or two leaves began to flutter around him and then a few cherries landed on his head. He looked up acting very surprised. Klára's smile widened as she laughed, very pleased with herself that she had hidden so well.

"What are you doing up there, Klára?" He feigned a very disapproving tone and frowned up at her, "Your mother would not approve of a young lady such as yourself climbing trees."

"I'm spying," she declared proudly.

"On whom?"

"You and Stefan."

"Well, the purpose of spying is to learn something you don't know. Stefan and I aren't doing anything."

"I know. Spying on you and Stefan is boring. I'm ready to come down now."

"Then come on. I'll help you, so that you won't fall and break your silly neck."

Klára began to inch her way down. She was higher than she had realized. It was much scarier coming down than going up. "I'm afraid, Dolfie."

"Just a little further and I can reach your shoe. Careful."

She stretched her foot as far down the trunk as possible, just barely touching another branch with her toe. Rudolf took hold of her foot. "I've got you. You won't fall. Just a little more…kneel down and lean toward me…I'll catch you."

She followed his instructions, trusting Rudolf completely. She leaned out from the tree and fell toward him. He caught her and swung her around until they both fell to the ground.

"You saved me, Dolfie!" She kissed him on the cheek.

"No more spying and no more climbing trees. We don't want you to end up a cripple like me."

"Dolfie, don't say that, you're wonderful."

"You know that I'll always be here for you. Stefan and I swore to be your protectors for ever and ever. Remember?"

As they stood up, Rudolf tousled her hair, "Silva was just making *mákos rétes*, poppy seed cakes. Let's go see if they're ready and have one before Stefan eats them all."

The boys spent most of their days working in the vineyards, rather than exploring as they had done in their younger years. Now they were more interested in earning money, so they could spend their evenings in Balatonfüred or across the lake in Aunt Eugenia's Siófok, with its tourist hotels. Adventures of the old kind the boys had shared with Klára were now rare; she was far too young to be included in their teenaged escapades.

So, her summer days were spent playing the piano with her mother, helping Silva in the kitchen, following Tamás around, spending time with Papa on the weekends, or just daydreaming. She waited impatiently for Rósza's annual visits and was very happy when her dear companion arrived at last.

Leopold directed the workmen to take time to build a fantastic playhouse under the cherry tree for the girls, a wonderful house with a gabled roof, a little door, and three shuttered windows. Klára and Arany painted it a creamy yellow with mint-green shutters and door. They also painted a sign, *Klára és Arany Kiss Villa*, Little Villa, which they hung above the door.

The girls had to stoop over to enter the house, but once inside they could stand upright. Inside, the house had a wooden floor and plenty of room for a table with chairs, boxes for a pretend kitchen, and little beds for their dolls. Elizabeth and Ana made lace curtains for the windows and a little tablecloth. Silva let them have some dishes for their kitchen and provided treats every day for their little table. The boys often poked their heads through the windows to tease them. It was another glorious summer at the lake.

Fall

The fall brought turmoil to Hungary on many fronts. More than a million Hungarian soldiers had been killed in the war; a war that had become very unpopular. Word of the Bolsheviks' Glorious Revolution in Russia inspired the workers of Hungary to take their cause to the streets. In late November, over one hundred thousand workers marched through the streets of Budapest to protest the war with a call for an immediate peace and a complaint about their economic plight. The marchers also celebrated their support for the Bolshevik victory over the Russian Tsar.

When Leopold and Dr. Klein met for coffee at Gerbeaud's and discussed the newspaper articles and editorials, they discovered their reactions were similar. The two men agreed that the rise of disgruntled workers was not a good thing, knowing the result could be revolution within Hungary itself—a problem that would certainly lead to total disruption and chaos. Both men were hopeful the monarchy of King Karl might calm the situation.

"In fact, I have heard," Leopold said, "that the Emperor Karl has made overtures to the *Entente*. Word comes to me that he has suggested a break with Germany and is likely to agree to an arrangement between the Austro-Hungarian Empire and the *Entente* for a separate peace. I have also heard, unfortunately, that France, in response to Karl's overtures, has proposed the total dissolution of the Austro-Hungarian Empire and the monarchy. On the other hand, I hear that Britain and America continue to support the monarchy, recognizing that the monarchy is *the* stabilizing force in the region, a safeguard for the rest of Europe, a bulwark against German and Bolshevik advances toward the West."

"My hope is that the *Entente* sees how the Bolshevik movement in Russia has influenced and motivated Hungarian workers," lamented Dr. Klein. "The workers' unrest has grown, in part, because of the dire situation throughout Hungary...caused by the war—food shortages, low wages, and high inflation. The *Entente* must intervene. Peace is the only answer. You've heard, I'm sure, that the Russian Commissars have called for all proletarians of the world to unite and rise up against the oppression of the ruling class. This is a cause for concern far beyond Hungary's borders."

"Tamás believes the words of the American President Wilson also inspired this revolution in the making," Leopold offered. "The Wilsonian doctrine calls for national self-determination and equality for all citizens. I believe his is a doctrine we basically support, but I also believe it is our king who can make these ideals work for our people.

"I share Tamás's fear," Leopold had a worried expression as he sipped his coffee, "that a Wilson-like doctrine could eventually bring an end to the monarchy in Hungary."

The year ended in tension with Bolshevik influences growing at a rapid, unstoppable rate throughout Hungary.

1918

By spring the "war to end all wars" was drawing to a close. However, the waning war did not ease the apprehension felt by the *Entente* countries—France, Britain, and now America; they continued to dread German and Bolshevik expansion into Austro-Hungarian territories. Everywhere in Eastern Europe, the *Entente* saw fertile ground for the spread of Bolshevism, a movement they feared more than any other. The continuing conflict brought a devastation of spirit that swept across Europe.

As spring breezes began to warm Budapest, revolution blew in the wind as well. Groups of university students with strong socialist sensibilities formed alliances with trade unions and dissatisfied minorities. They marched in mass protests through the center of Budapest shouting anti-military slogans, demanding peace and an end to the war. In unity, they voiced their desire for freedom from oppression and for better lives. Strikes and demonstrations spread through the city, causing disruption and confusion.

The von Estés, like most Budapest citizens, went on living their lives as normally as they could, avoiding the disgruntled masses, following their ordinary routines. Stefan's group of university friends remained apolitical. Although they enjoyed discussing philosophical ideals and arguing about Hungary's current situation, the young aristocrats were content to spend their time in cafés drinking coffee. They seemed unconcerned, even disinterested, in protests or marches or radical ideals.

—�∿—

Elizabeth continued to take her nearly eight-year-old daughter to the home of Mrs. Klein for her weekly piano lesson. If there was a Metro strike, then Auguste simply drove them where they needed to go. One particular day Elizabeth had a headache and asked Stefan if he could take Klára to her piano lesson at the Kleins' that afternoon.

Klára felt very grown up with Stefan's dependence upon her to tell him the way to the Klein's townhouse. They began their short journey at the Metro stop just across the avenue, got off the Metro at the Opera House stop, and then crossed Andrássy to Paulay Street into the Jewish District. From there they wound through the narrow streets, south onto Kazincy Street to Dohány Avenue. Rain had begun to fall while they were still on Paulay Street and by the time they got to Dohány it was pouring. When they rang the bell next to the grand entrance door, they were soaked to the skin. The servant girl, Zeát, opened the door, quickly let them in, ushered them into the parlor, and took their wet wraps.

When Mrs. Klein and Rózsa came into the room, Mrs. Klein became very animated, giving directions and exclaiming, "Oh, you're both so wet you'll catch your death. Rózsa take Klára up to your room, dry her off and give her something dry to wear. Zeát, take the young man to the kitchen, put him near the oven. Ask Magda to put his feet in a tub of hot water and give him tea to drink."

Everyone moved quickly according to her orders. In no time Klára and Rózsa hurried up the stairs and Stefan found himself at the kitchen table. Before he could protest the attention, his shoes were off, feet in hot water, a blanket on his shoulders, and a cup of spiced tea in his hand. He had planned to meet friends at a coffee house on Károly Street, but decided one just did not protest the ideas of Mrs. Klein and besides the kitchen was warm and comfortable.

Low rumbles of thunder from outside could be heard in the kitchen while the cook stood by the great stove stirring steaming pots that were filling the kitchen with delicious aromas. Stefan expressed his thoughts aloud, "I think here in this fine kitchen is someone who can rival our great cook, Silva!"

In only moments Stefan's big smile and jovial personality had Magda and her helpers all blushing and giggling. Magda kept offering him tastes of her delectable recipes from a big wooden spoon. Stefan held the warm cup in his hands and blew across it sending swirls of steam outward. He turned toward a squeak he heard on the servant stairs that led from the kitchen to other parts of the house.

At that very moment, a young woman leapt from the stair into the kitchen and Stefan saw a bright flash of lightning and heard a loud clap of thunder. At least he was certain a thunderbolt had hit him when he saw her for the first time. Stefan found himself standing up in the tub of water, starring at the most beautiful girl he had ever seen. She walked over to the stove and dipped a spoon into the boiling pot without looking at him.

"Mmm, Magda, this is yummy." The girl completely ignored the young man standing by the table, but he could not take his eyes off her. She was tall and thin; her long black curly hair fell in a tangle down her back. Finally, she turned toward him. Dark brown eyes like pools of velvet looked boldly at him, "Who are you? Why are you in my kitchen?"

"Stefan von Esté," he stammered his name and added, "I...I'm Klára's brother."

"Oh, so you're the young Count. You've never been here before; are you anti-Semite?"

The cook cleared her throat and gave the girl a raised eyebrow, obviously disapproving of her rude behavior.

"No, no, I'm not, not at all. My mother usually comes with Klára. She enjoys her visits so much, listening to Mrs. Klein's music. Only today she had a headache, so I brought Klára instead."

He stopped himself, feeling embarrassed by such a long protestation. He was certain his face was flushed, he could feel the heat; a nervous laugh produced a broad smile and gave him more confidence. Stefan could usually disarm any adversary with his charm. He asked, "Who are you?"

"I'm Rózsa's sister, Eszter."

She poured herself a cup of tea from the kettle and sat down at the table across from Stefan. He resumed his seat. She was smiling now, but retained a skeptical air as she surveyed this good-looking young man. "What do you do?"

They began to exchange information, discovering they were both seventeen and third-year university students, he Chemistry and she History. Stefan told her that he admired her father and looked forward to studying with him in later years. He wanted to become a vintner as his father. Eszter, interested in politics, began to ask him pointed questions about his politics.

"You seem so informed," Stefan complimented her. "I'm grateful that I have been so attentive to my father's many political discussions." He thought she might be impressed if he mentioned, "My father and I are quintessential proponents of Magyarization. We believe the strength of Hungary can be found in its diversity of citizens. All Hungary's people are important in the building of our great nation." Stefan wanted to be convincing. "Everyone...the Slavs, the Serbs, the Austrians, the Slovaks...the Jews...everyone."

Eszter appreciated Stefan's progressive views and his passionate expression of those views. They talked with animation, loud inflection, argued and laughed. The hour passed very quickly and when Mrs. Klein and Klára appeared in the kitchen, Stefan was not ready to leave. He put on his shoes, gathered his things, and said his good-byes to all in the kitchen. He shook Eszter's hand and said he hoped they could meet for further discussions. She only smiled.

Stefan and Klára emerged from the Kleins' into a sunny afternoon. Stefan looked up at the bright blue sky; life had changed in that brief encounter, he was in love with Eszter Klein. As Stefan and Klára walked down Dohány Street, Eszter and Rózsa watched them from an upstairs window until they disappeared around a corner. Eszter smiled and thought to herself, *I want to know that handsome gentile boy a lot better.*

—m—

Stefan and Eszter did meet again, two days later at his favorite café on Zrinyi Street near his university. They sat in a booth on leather-covered benches and had coffee. At first Stefan felt tongue-tied and awkward, a very unusual feeling for him. Eszter immediately realized that she had caused this effect, so she flirted with him without mercy, telling him he need not be shy with her. Finally, she relented, smiled at him and touched his hand gently.

"I have never been shy in my life," Stefan blushed. "You have a devastating effect on me Eszter Klein."

After coffee they walked along the Danube embankment, talking non-stop all the way. Politics and the law were the primary topics. Eszter revealed her plan to become a lawyer and represent labor. They decided to meet again the next afternoon. Stefan wanted to take her to meet some of his friends at an apartment soirée. "There will be Gypsy music and dancing. Do you like to dance?"

The next afternoon when Eszter entered the apartment beside Stefan, she made an instant impression on everyone. Certainly, it was not unusual to see the prettiest girl in the room on Stefan's arm, but everyone agreed this girl was exceptional. He proudly introduced her, got drinks and then the twosome settled close together on a sofa. Loud conversation, boisterous laughing, and gypsy music filled the room; the mood was jovial.

"Is this typical of your gatherings, Stefan?" Eszter asked, "Is there ever any serious discussion?"

"Of course, we get serious over coffee, but this is pure relaxation…just for music and laughs," he nuzzled Eszter, "don't you ever relax? Are you always so serious? Don't you like to have a little fun now and again?"

She looked into his lovely blue eyes, "You can make me smile, Stefan, when no one else can."

A few days later Eszter took Stefan to meet her Jewish friends. She warned him that some of her friends were communists. They arrived at her friend's apartment in time for a meeting of the *Makkabeas*, a Zionist organization. Heated, passionate discussions—ranging from arguments over adopting communism to leaving Hungary for Palestine to Magyarization to anti-Semitism—filled the dimly lit, smoky apartment. Stefan had never heard such dialogue, such debate from different points of view. He had not realized until that day how deeply rooted anti-Semitist feelings were in Hungarian attitudes. He had never experienced those kinds of feelings in his own family…he was completely unaware.

A strong argument ensued that their group should join with the new Hungarian Communist Party. *There would be strength in numbers to voice our demand for equality.* Others wanted to organize immigration for a great number of Jews… *We must leave Hungary, all together, for Palestine! We want to create our own nation in the land of our ancestors, the land given to the Jews by YHWH.*

Stefan had always believed in his father's explanation of Magyarization. It had always seemed fair and reasonable to him, but now in the midst of these young people, he began to have second thoughts. One young man, who did not in the least look Jewish, stood in a dark corner of the apartment. Eszter said his name was Theodore Rubin. Rubin suddenly stepped from the shadows and began a long harangue, "Magyarization is a farce. It makes fools of us! Oh yes, we speak their language, we dress like them, we fight in their wars, we are patriotic in every way, but we remain *other*, always! NEVER one of them! Neither the Catholic nor the Protestant Magyars accept us as equals. We face discrimination every day—unequal wages, unequal work, no admittance, no membership! Inequality!"

"Even our own people rile against us, against the Zionists. We scare the Neologs and the Orthodox," said another young man, Imre Löwy, thin with a beard and glasses. "Look at this article in the *Egyenlőség*." He held up a newspaper, shaking it at everyone, "This Jewish newspaper calls *us*, the Zionists, perverse and evil because we see the truth of Magyarization and because we want to form our own nation."

Stefan recognized Imre Löwy, because his parents owned the lace shop next to Papa's von Este Fine Wine Company. He didn't know him, but he had seen him in the shop many times through the years. Stefan realized, now, how strange it seemed that he had never actually met or spoken to Imre, never known that he had these thoughts about Magyarization. Stefan had met Mr. and Mrs. Löwy; he found them to be friendly and he knew that Leopold thought Mr. Löwy was an honest, hard-working businessman. But Stefan had to admit he did not *know* them.

"All of you should be reading our own *Zsidó Szemle*," responded a young woman named Zsuzsanna Weisz. "We write articles every week to counter the *Egyenlőség* propaganda. We explain how unfavorable a choice Magyarization is for the Jewish people. It means dissolution! It is the ultimate of *syncretism*...it dilutes us until the Jew is crushed!"

She spoke of trends in the government of Hungary, "The Hungarian People's Party and the Christian Socialist Party have merged into the new Christian Socialist People's Party. We expect those parties will intensify anti-Jewish legislation. Their Christian press and some of our own university professors are determined to annihilate the Jews...or at the least drive us out of *their country*."

"Then there our own people like József Patai and his Zionist journal, *Mult és jövő*, that receive attack from both sides. From the anti-Semitic Magyars and the anti-Zionist Jews, the Neologs in particular," stated another young man named Armin Stein, who, Stefan noticed, seemed to know Eszter very well.

"Patai is pro-Magyarization. He sends his own children to Hungarian-speaking school, yet, for the Magyars he is not Hungarian enough. Jews never quite meet the requirements to be a full citizen or, perhaps, even to be fully human."

Anger permeated Armin's voice as he continued, "Patai exposes our enemies' ridiculous accusations against Jews and makes a mockery of their false claims. We have never wanted to add the Star of David to the Hungarian flag as our enemies say we do...our interest in a Palestine State is not treason against Hungary as our enemies say...we do not and never have conspired against our king! None of it is fact! But the truth does not stop the propagandists from spewing their hatred for us, even the Neologs, every day."

Stefan sat quietly in the apartment listening and mulling over what he heard. Ideals and recriminations that he had never heard before; he was surprised, even shocked, by the words and emotions expressed by Eszter's friends. They were zealots, so different from his own fun-loving, not-so-serious friends. He had been so certain of his beliefs until this afternoon and now he felt confused, at least about some of what he had thought for his whole life to be true.

As he and Eszter emerged from the apartment into an early evening mist, Stefan put his arm around her shoulder, "Let's get something to eat before I take you home. I need to think about what I heard in there—so much passion and anger in that room. Is it that way every time you get together? Is that how you feel? What you believe? There was so much about which I knew nothing. You must help me understand, if you will."

Eszter stopped on the sidewalk under a street light and looked up at Stefan, at his handsome face. They embraced each other and shared a long, adoring kiss. She felt so content in his arms, so glad that he cared about her and her life. From that afternoon on, Stefan continued to go to meetings with Eszter. Some meetings focused on immigration to Palestine; some concentrated on organized approaches to the government to ensure equal rights for Jews; and some argued the ethics of Magyarization and the immorality of anti-Semitism. He was determined to know everything about Eszter Klein, even if it meant finding out things about himself and his country that would be difficult to know.

—⚉—

Since fall, Rudolf was a student at the Hungarian Drawing Academy and lived in the home of his grandmother, the Countess Alexandra. He and Stefan, although busy students, took advantage of living in the same city and got to together as often as they could. The two young men also made special time for Klára—times she treasured—desserts at the New York Palace Hotel, swimming at the Margit Island Baths, operettas at the Orfeum Theatre, walks along Fishermen's Bastion at Buda Castle, visits to the National Art Gallery in Városliget City Park and very special evenings at the Royal Opera.

One afternoon, Stefan and Rudolf decided to meet for coffee at Gerbeaud's in Vörösmarty Square. Over cups of lemon espresso and plum pies they caught up on the happenings that kept their lives so busy. Rudolf was surprised to see how agitated Stefan seemed, not his usual happy-go-lucky self.

"What's going on? You seem very distracted."

"I'm amazed, Dolf, at how little I knew of my city and its attitudes," Stefan jabbed his cigarette in the ash tray and took another from its pack. He had an effortless way of lighting a match with one hand. He held the match book, flicked out the match, bent it over, struck it and lit the cigarette. Rudolf always marveled at the ease of it.

"You still aren't smoking?" Stefan took a long drag as he looked Rudolf in the eye, "How can you resist it?"

"What attitudes are bothering you?" Rudolf asked.

"Are you aware of the abhorrent anti-Semitism movements all over this city? Have you read the articles written by *seemingly reputable* journalists that describe Jews in despicable ways? Jews serve Hungary bravely as soldiers in the War! Many die as heroes!" Again Stefan looked directly at Rudolf, "Jews have contributed to Hungary's society in many ways...economically, socially, intellectually, not to mention artistically."

"I agree, Stefan. I have no problem or prejudice against our Jewish citizens. Why are you caring about all this? I've never heard you address Jewish concerns before. What is all this about?"

And then Rudolf answered his own question, "It's about a girl, isn't it."

"It's much more than that." Stefan got defensive, "I've just become aware of deep-rooted prejudices in our society that I never knew existed. It's all terribly unfair, misplaced." He paused, "Did you know there are those, even high in our government, who actually believe Jews are not patriotic...that they care nothing for Hungary...that they are actually responsible for all the economic problems plaguing Hungary?"

"All right, I agree, you're right. There is injustice, but I still want to know, who is she?"

"You know me well, my friend, I have met someone. She is the most beautiful, smartest, most exciting girl. Eszter...isn't that an incredible name! We've been seeing each other for a few weeks. I want you to meet her...soon."

Stefan twirled the coffee spoon in his hand, staring beyond the present moment. Then he looked back to Rudolf, smiled broadly, and in a teasing voice, nudged his friend, "I saw you with a very cute blonde. Is she your model?"

"You know the only girl for me is Klára."

"Oh yeah, I forgot...let's take Klára to the operetta tonight."

Summer at Lake Balaton

The von Házys and the von Estés made their usual trek to the lake in early May—Rudolf and Stefan remained in Budapest at their university studies for several more weeks. As usual, Klára invited Rósza to come for a visit. She came for two weeks in May and then returned with her sister, Eszter, for the whole month of July.

May was quiet and slow-paced for the girls, but when Rózsa returned with Eszter in July the days were filled with exciting adventures thanks to Stefan and Rudolf. Although the boys spent much of their time working in the vineyards there was still plenty of daylight for fun times together. One weekend when they were not working, Rudolf asked Stefan to bring the girls to his grandmother's villa on Tihany for lunch and for an afternoon of exploring. The von Estés and their guests could have walked to Tihany, but they took the ferry from Balatonfüred and Rudolf met the excited foursome at the pier. They all hurried off to his grandmother's villa.

The Countess and László were happy to have the voices of young people in the house even though their part of the house remained dark as night. Christián and Gabriele joined the party for a lovely lunch of *gyümölosleves*, fruit soup, *sajtos kenyér*, cheese bread, and *diós palacsinta*, thin pancakes with sweet, nutty filling.

The five—Stefan, Rudolf, Klára, Rózsa, and Eszter—spent the afternoon exploring the Tihany Peninsula. Having never been there, Eszter had much to see. Countess Alexandra's cook prepared a picnic snack with canteens of cold lemonade for them to take on their excursion. It was an unusually hot, but brilliant day to explore the old village of Tihany and the peninsula. They walked past the Abbey church and along the promenade for panoramic views of Lake Balaton, its surface shimmering as though covered by millions of sparkling diamonds. They passed the open farmers' market and the Paprika House with its trellis of peppers drying in the sun. Rudolf called to them, "Let's race to the top of Echo Hill."

They all took off running along the winding path up Echo Hill, falling onto the grass panting once they reached the top. Then suddenly, they noticed Stefan and Eszter had not followed them.

Rudolf and the girls ran to the bluff; they could see the town of Tihany, its Abbey church and the lake spread out below them. Neither Stefan nor Eszter were anywhere to be seen. The children faced the Abbey Church and called out, "Stefan…Eszter," as loudly as they could. They counted the number of times each syllable bounced back at them and rolled on the grass with laughter. Still Stefan and Eszter did not appear.

"Let's eat without them!" Rózsa said.

"Good idea," they agreed and spread a blanket on the ground. Klára took fresh, soft buns filled with apricot and honey from Rudolf's backpack. His grandmother's cook was famous for her sweet-smelling breads. Klára rose from the grass and walked to a stone wall. She stood on the wall and scanned the woods below for her brother. At last she spotted him far below walking in the trees, hand in hand with Eszter. Klára's eyes followed them and she saw the pair stop and kiss. She started to say, *there they are, kissing in the trees*, but instead she remained silent and watched them.

After that day, with its revelation, Klára observed the two of them, Stefan and Eszter, more closely. She watched them share secret glances, touches, and suddenly disappear when no one else noticed. A few days later Klára decided to confront Stefan about Eszter, "I saw you kiss Eszter one time on Tihany and you hold hands with her."

"So, you are a little spy!" Stefan laughed, but he seemed surprised and somewhat evasive as he looked at her seriously, "Klára, please keep this a secret between just you and me. Don't tell anyone about Eszter and me."

"Not even Papa?"

"Especially not Papa!"

"Why? Papa loves Professor Klein. He would be happy for you to like Eszter…to be special friends."

"Yes, they would think it is fine for Eszter and me to be friends, Klára, but they will not think it is fine for us to be in love and we do love each other."

Stefan took a deep breath and looked kindly at his little sister. "Eszter is a Jewess, Klára…Jews marry Jews and Catholics marry Catholics. A marriage between Eszter and me is completely unacceptable."

He thought to himself, but did not say it, *and even worse, she is a communist.* Again, he looked at Klára in a very serious manner.

"I do plan to marry Eszter. Someday soon, I hope, but we will have to go away, perhaps to America or maybe, even, to Palestine."

Klára felt a terrible pain in her chest. She wondered at the cause. Was it because she dreaded a time when Stefan would go away from Budapest, from Lake Balaton, or was it because he was in love with someone other than his little sister?

There was so much to keep the youngsters busy at the lake, so much to show Eszter. After finishing their work in the vineyards, Stefan and Rudolf took the girls with them everywhere. Ferry trips to the town of Keszthely to the Festetics Palace for an early evening concert and to Héviz Spa where they all swam among the pink and white lily pads while Rudolf's grandmother took hot spa treatments for her rheumatism.

Rock-climbing expeditions filled their days with adventures—to the basalt columns of *Fekete-hegy*, the Black Mount, to the bizarre wind-eroded stones of *Szentbékkálla* and *Kővágóörs* and to *Rózsakő*, the Red Stone, near Badacsony. They took the autóbusz to the *Kál Basin* region and to *Kékkút* for Theodora, the famous bottled mineral water, supposedly good for one's health. Each one took a taste, but spit out the strong-tasting liquid immediately, wondering how their parents could drink Theodora every day.

Christián and Leopold took the girls sailing on Little Balaton Lake where they saw beautiful birds—white heron, spoonbills, and cormorants. Once again Stefan and Rudolf swam across Lake Balaton in the annual race. The hot summer days passed quickly—sailing, swimming, hiking—even though at times the children simply lazed away the days under the shade of the cherry tree. Through it all, day by day, Klára kept an eye on Stefan and Eszter, while suffering conflicted feelings.

July, Budapest

Leopold prepared to leave his Pest office early one Thursday afternoon; he was looking forward to his weekend at the lake where many festivities were planned, the Anna Ball and a regatta. His secretary opened the office door gently, "Sir, a special-delivery letter has arrived for you."

She crossed the room with the brown envelope extended toward him. Leopold took the envelope, thanked her and sliced it open with a letter opener. Quite surprised, he recognized the elaborate insignia at the top of the linen paper and knew the letter came from the Dowager Empress Maria Feodorovna, the widow of Tsar Alexander III of Russia. The very sight of her name brought memories of his youth when he and his family often joined the Romanovs in Odessa. He remembered boarding the Romanovs' luxurious yacht, the *Alexandria*, and sailing the Black Sea. The return address on the envelope indicated the Dowager was writing from her villa in the Crimea.

The Dowager began her letter with kindest regards for Leopold and his family and reminisced about his parents, *my dear friends*. Her words changed—

> *With deepest regret I have a story of tragedy to tell. All of this was told to me by a servant who witnessed the events.*

In her narration the Dowager wrote that she had left St. Petersburg in early 1917,

> *. . . due to the immoral behavior of the monstrous, inhumane Bolsheviks who stirred severe unrest among the Russian people.*

The Tsarina's great disdain for the ruthless Bolsheviks became evident to Leopold.

> *I implored the Tsar Nicholas II, my adored son Nicki, to leave with his family, but he would not abandon his beloved Russian people. In March of 1917 poor Nicki was forced to abdicate his throne and replaced by a provisional government, but they had no power. In October when that Bolshevik, Vladimir Lenin, sneaked back into Russia from exile he led the Workers' Soviets to overthrow the government in a full revolution. By November Lenin and his Bolsheviks went to St. Petersburg where they engaged the White Army in civil war.*
> *Immediately after the defeat of the White Russians in St. Petersburg the Bolsheviks arrested the Tsar, my dearest Nicki, and his wife Alexandra*

Feodorova and each one of their precious children, Olga, Tatiana, Maria,
Anastasis and little Alexi. The family was held near St. Petersburg until
April, but then the whole family was transported by train to the Ural
Mountains of Siberia. They were imprisoned in a small house near the
village of Ekaterinburg. As the White Army neared the village to rescue
them, the Bolsheviks herded the Tsar and his family along with their doctor
and three servants into the basement of the house and murdered every one
of them. Their precious bodies were carried from the house into woods and
buried in unmarked graves.

Leopold held his breath as he read the letter. The Dowager's devastating words were very disturbing. He thought of his sister, Eugenia and her lifelong friendship with Alexandra, the Tsarina. He thought of the handsome Nicki standing at the helm of the *Alexandria* alongside his father, Tsar Alexander. Leopold shook his head thinking of Nicki, the deeply religious royal who often worried about the souls of his people and prayed for them, now gone and lost…and his children…all of them gone.

Leopold shared the Dowager's disdain for the heartless, godless Bolsheviks. He sat at his desk a long time before he took pen and paper and wrote a heartfelt letter of sympathy to the Dowager; he lovingly addressed her as his mother had, *My Dearest Tsarina Dagmar.*

That afternoon Leopold left his office feeling greatly saddened by the terrible unfolding of events in Russia. The Romanovs were aristocrats and they were murdered simply because of who they were…reminding him of his feelings at times of other senseless assassinations…the Archduke…the Empress Sisi so long ago. He wiped tears from his eyes as he walked toward Andrássy Avenue.

The Dowager's news troubled Leopold on a personal level, because he knew…*the long tentacles of the Bolsheviks are here in Budapest.* Activities of the Hungarian Communist Party were becoming obvious in his own city and it gave him pause to wonder if they would come for all the Hapsburgs, all the aristocrats, one day. Leopold was glad to have the weekend at the lake with his family to look forward to; the lake, always a place where he could find relief from his heavy thoughts.

Lake Balaton

The annual Anna Ball was held on the last Saturday night of July; the weekend before Rózsa and Eszter were to leave the lake for Budapest. The girls were estatic and could hardly wait to watch the elegant event. Stefan would be one of the dancers again this year at age seventeen. Handsomely dressed in a Huszar uniform, Stefan wore a white military jacket with gold braid and buttons, black pants and black shiny boots with jingling spurs. Rudolf would have to wait one more year, until he turned sixteen, before he could attend.

Rudolf, Klára, Rózsa, and Eszter sat outside on a stone wall watching the elegant dancers from the dark. They exclaimed over the spectacular costumes, decorations, and chandeliers that made the Anna Ball so splendid. They could see their parents and Aunt Eugenia seated at a table near the dance floor; Leopold and Elizabeth stood and applauded when they saw Stefan and his lovely partner appear.

Klára watched Eszter as she sat nearby on the wall; she seemed to glow with pride as she stared in Stefan's direction. Klára saw Eszter make a slight wave to Stefan and noticed that he seemed to respond. Klára realized: *He can see us. The light from the room shines on our faces here in the dark.*

"I'll have to dance next year," Rudolf said thoughtfully. "I'm not such a good dancer at the moment...I doubt I'll be expected to join in every dance...I'll have to practice...I'll get better," he said with determination. Then Rudolf turned toward Klára, "I promise I'll dance with you at your Anna Ball, Klára."

Klára leaned over to kiss him on the cheek, "Oh, you must, you and Stefan, because I'll be too afraid to dance in front of all these people without you."

Stefan left the dance as soon as he could and approached Eszter. He lifted her from the wall and spun her around in the moonlight. He danced with Klára and Rózsa, too, but Klára could see it was Eszter who kept his attention; he held her especially tight and stared into her velvet brown eyes. Rudolf sat on the wall watching Klára and Rózsa spin around until the two girls forced him down from the wall and made him dance with them.

"Dolf, you can dance! You're very good at waltzing," they flattered him.

Fall

At the end of September the von Estés returned home, Christián and Gabriele went back to Eisenstadt, and Rudolf returned to Budapest with his grandmother. Everyone resumed their normal routines. Stefan entered his fourth year at university and Rudolf continued to learn all that he could from the master artists who taught his classes at the Drawing Academy.

October

On the seventeenth of October, Hungary declared its independence from Austria and formed the First Republic, ruled by a National Council with representatives from the Independent, Radical, and Social Democratic parties, and Leopold's Progressive minority. The council appointed liberal politician Count Mihaly Károlyi, as Prime Minister. In opposition to the war and with complete disregard for the Austrians, Károlyi immediately demanded a separate peace neogiation for Hungary with the *Entente*.

Károlyi recognized the difficult struggle endured by the diverse nationalities and minorities living within Hungary's borders. He knew that each minority wanted independence from Austria. He encouraged the new National Council to issue a manifesto advocating that each nationality within Hungary should have the right of self-determination. The intent of the manifesto, clearly nationalistic and anti-Magyarization, was designed to appease minorities who wanted more regional independence within Hungary and threated severe unrest. The council optimistically expected that giving self-determination to each ethnic group would halt the anxiety growing within Hungary's borders.

Leopold sat behind his grand desk in the library while absentmindedly stroking the sleek head of Herceg, son of Báró. Tamás entered the library, sat down across from Leopold, and began to light his pipe. Leopold, preferring a cigar, poured glasses of *körtepálinka*, pear brandy, for Tamás and himself. The two men sat in silence for a few moments enjoying the brandy and the tobacco as they had done together for many years.

Finally Leopold spoke, "Károlyi's manifesto will destroy Hungary. He hopes it will bring Hungary's mishmash of nationalities to unite as one, but once he gives autonomy to each region...how can the country be united if everyone is speaking a different language...electing their own ministers and making their own laws?"

"Have you heard the rumors that he's going to call on our king to abdicate?"

"It's the end of Hungary! A move toward radical nationalism! The Bolsheviks will profit from this."

October 31

It was a crisp cold day, the last day of October, when Eszter pulled Stefan along the street toward the Vadászkürt Hotel where a large group of students were gathered to cheer on dissident Hungarian soldiers and Romanian freedom fighters. Brightly colored aster blooms decorated many of the soldiers' caps. Eszter reached out to catch a flower from the bouquets being thrown out into the crowd. She proudly stuck the aster into her beret and then reached to catch another one for Stefan.

Eszter felt exhilarated, "Oh Stefan! This is so exciting, to be a part of such an important day for Hungary."

Eszter and Stefan stood arm in arm listening to the speakers who were standing on the stone walls that ringed the trees of the square. The two responded with shouts of agreement and cheered along with the crowd that surrounded them.

Stefan wished his father could hear the speeches. He wondered what Leopold would think of this revolutionary talk that seemed the direct antithesis to Leopold's long-held dreams of Magyarization. Stefan remembered well when his father and Tamás shared its progressive ideals with Rudolf and him. He wondered what Leopold might think of the opinions being shouted by the speaker with the megaphone and the crowd's response.

"We agree with the American President Wilson who calls for national self-determination!"

"We want a Democratic Hungary! Individual rights! Equality for all!"

Cheers rang out from the people.

Stefan stood near the stone wall in the midst of hundreds of enthusiastic supporters who shouted in response, "We call for an end to the Austro-Hungarian Monarchy! An end to the Dual Monarchy! Karl must abdicate!"

Eszter felt chills run through her spine, "What a grand day, Stefan!" She kissed him fully on the lips in front of everyone. She felt liberated. Stefan could understand the first part of the rebels' words about a Democratic Hungary, self-determination, but he was much less certain about getting rid of the king.

Since his childhood, Stefan had held practically sacred the words of his father... *You boys must know your history! It is true that you are Austrian by birth and ancestry, but Hungary is our homeland. Sopron has always stood on land that alternates at any given time between Austria and Hungary! We are as Hungarian as any other, because we have all come here from another place and it is together that we can make Hungary great.*

Stefan knew his father believed in the Emperor/King. Stefan's ears rang with memory of Leopold's words... *the king makes all progress possible... the king supports equality and freedom for all of Hungary's people.* Stefan thought of rainy days spent in the library and walks through the vineyards with his father; he could picture his father moving through the rows of vines, brushing the grape leaves with his hand as he passed by them. Stefan knew his father loved the land and wanted Hungary to become a great and independent country. His father's words, so familiar, came to mind again...

This land has always been a home to diverse peoples—the Slavs, the Germanic tribes, the Romans, the Huns led by Attila, the Avars, the Moravians, the Byzantines, the Gypsies, the Jews, and even the Turks. Coming and going and coming back again; always leaving something behind of themselves, including their diverse seed that remains in the faces of the people for ever. Look at us. How can we say that we are pure Austrian or pure Hungarian? We are all the people who have inhabited this land. Although we take the Magyar name— Hungary, as title for this collective nation of ours, there is little of the original Magyar race left, only bits and pieces of their culture remain.

After the rally Stefan walked beside Eszter to her home. She skipped up the stairs, still exhilarated by the day's events. She turned back to him expecting a kiss. Stefan held her shoulders, looked into her unfathomable brown eyes, he was much more reserved than she, rarely showing his passion in public places. On the other hand, Eszter was not one to rein in her emotions, she fell fully onto his chest, wrapping her arms around him and kissing him with abandon. Uncontrolled, involuntary feelings swept over his body; he could hardly stand. He could feel his body respond to hers with an equal lack of restraint. Finally, they separated, stared at each other, flushed and breathless.

"When can I see you again, Eszter? Make it soon."

"Tomorrow, Stefan. Tomorrow." She kissed him again.

"I have a friend who has a flat near the university," he looked down at their intertwined hands, then up to her face, "We could be alone there, if you want."

"I want," she said as she took a deep breath, "tomorrow."

And she went into the house.

Fortunately for Eszter, no one in the house had observed her reckless behavior on the front stairs. She would not have cared if they had, but at least there was no admonishment or accusation with which to deal. She smiled to herself; she felt very warm and thought of the next day with great anticipation. She started to walk up the stairs when her father called to her.

"Eszter, what is that in your hat?" Professor Klein knew very well the symbolism of the aster that protruded from her beret. "Politics! You should stay out of politics, Eszter! Nothing good can come of it."

Professor Klein shook his head and walked toward the parlor before turning back to her, "We are Neolog Jews, Eszter, and Magyars, citizens of Hungary who happen to be Jewish by religion. We have spent many years assimilating into the Hungarian population. We are considered equal citizens! We are prosperous and free to practice our faith." Jakov Klein could not conceal his anger, "You...the youth...should leave well enough alone!"

Eszter had very different opinions, but she was in no mood to argue with him at that moment. She simply smiled at him and walked up to him. "We can discuss it at supper, if you wish," she said and kissed him on the cheek. She went up to her room and laid across her bed. She wrapped her arms around her chest and inhaled deeply; she could still breathe in Stefan's scent on her sweater. She loved him with all her being. She wanted to be with him completely and thought about the next day and how it might be to share a bed with Stefan. The thought gave her chills, made her roll over and bury her face in the covers. It would be almost impossible to wait for him to come for her tomorrow.

The next afternoon Stefan and Eszter walked through the city holding hands. They were oblivious to the weather, to the people; they heard none of the sounds of the street. Neither spoke. The usually exuberant, talkative, strong-willed Eszter was uncharacteristically silent. They climbed the building's stone stairs all the way to the attic rooms of Stefan's friend. Stefan unlocked the door and pulled her gently into the room. Muslin curtains fluttered at the window allowing shafts of soft golden light into the room, much of which still remained in shadow. A bouquet of fall asters filled a vase on the table in the center of the room. Eszter walked to the vase, "How beautiful."

"I brought them this morning with the wine and bread and cheese," he whispered.

To Stefan, the moment and the place seemed almost sacred. He stepped behind her and put his arms around her waist. She did not turn toward him. He turned her chin slightly. Tears trickled down her face.

"I love you Eszter." Stefan held her very close, "This is not just for today, Eszter, but forever."

November

Leopold and Tamás sat by the warmth of a roaring fire in the library, sipping a superb brandy from cut crystal snifters, discussing the news of the day as they stared at the burning embers. Leopold puffed on his cigar and mused thoughtfully, "So many disasters for the Hungarian soldiers as this war draws to a close; so many lost."

"We knew from the start that joining with the Kaiser was a mistake," Tamás stated. "When has throwing in with Germany ever been good for Hungary? Now there is only animosity for the Kaiser." Tamás showed Leopold a newspaper cartoon depicting an obese Kaiser in a trench being blown to bits. "The people have no sympathy for him."

"Well, he has abdicated now and slinked off into exile." Leopold stroked Herceg's head as it lay across his knee, "Perhaps, at last, the new German Republic will be willing to negotiate peace with the West . . . then we'll find out what will happen to us . . . to Hungary. I fear nothing good will come our way."

In fact, the Armistice was signed on the eleventh of November at five o'clock in the morning in a railroad car parked on a track in a forest on the Western front in France. The results of that Armistice greatly affected the once powerful Austro-Hungarian Empire, in existence since 1867. The Empire completely collapsed, bringing an end to the Dual Monarchy. Many in Hungary were exhilarated by these results.

On the same day in November, the Emperor Charles IV, Karl, was forced to renounce the Austrian throne as Emperor and on the thirteenth of the month renounce the Hungarian throne; both considered a sacrilege by the Empress Zita. She denied the state had any right to demand that her husband reject his Divine Right to rule. She believed that God alone had ordained Karl to be Emperor and King. The future of their oldest son, Otto, also concerned Zita, who believed that Otto, by divine birthright of ascension, ought one day to sit on the thrones of Austria and Hungary.

Certainly not everyone in Hungary saw this turn of events as a good thing. In particular, Leopold, Christián von Házy, and their extended Hapsburg family shared the concerns of Empress Zita. They were unified in the belief that their Emperor, the benevolent Karl, could have been a positive force for his people through the period of transition. Now, it seemed, only disaster lay ahead for Hungary.

After the Armistice went into effect, the Hungarian Republic National Council reaffirmed its appointment of the liberal Count Károlyi as prime minister and on November sixteenth, Hungary officially declared its independence from Austria and pronounced the right of self-determination for all minorities, including the Jews.

Although Leopold agreed that Hungary should be an independent nation and that all of its citizens should have equality, he continued to be a Monarchist, who honored his king. Leopold felt in the depths of his soul that Karl was the rightful monarch and would be the right person to lead Hungary into a united, progressive future. He believed that Karl, like his uncle, Franz József, embraced the ideals of Magyarization and Leopold also continued to believe in Magyarization as the only way to unite a diverse people. Leopold proudly and openly advocated for the return of the king to the throne of Hungary.

—⁂—

One cold afternoon as Rudolf sat in his room at his drawing table in his grandmother's house, László knocked softly at his door and opened it. He announced, "Master Rudolf, your grandmother wishes for you to come to the drawing room at once." And then he closed the door.

Rudolf put away his pencils and walked downstairs to the parlor. He thought it was an unusual request. His grandmother had never asked an audience in such a formal manner. He opened the door and knew instantly that something was very wrong. Two strange men stood by the window.

"What is the matter, Grandmother? Are you all right?"

Alexandra started to say something to him, but sobbed into her lace handkerchief instead.

One of the men turned toward Rudolf, walked to him with an outstretched hand and grasped his hand, "Count von Házy. I am the Duke Albrecht Baden and this is Solicitor Ingel. We are from Vienna. I fear that we have shocking news for you, young man. Your father the Count Christián von Házy and your mother have been killed in a terrible car crash near their home, near your home in Eisenstadt. They were both killed instantly. I am so sorry to be the bearer of such dreadful news."

"What happened?" Rudolf was in a deep state of shock; he sat down, his head spinning, his mouth completely dry, "How could this happen?"

Rudolf could picture so clearly his magnificent father and beautiful mother, Gabriele. *They were just here in Budapest,* he thought. *How can I face this tragedy? How can I face anything without the guidance of my father, the gentle love of my mother?* He felt completely overwhelmed. Tragedy seemed to stalk him. He could hear Baden's words, but was not making any sense of them.

"They were driving much too fast...it was raining...the car flew from the road on a rather sharp curve. We are not sure who was driving at the time. We know that your father had been teaching your mother to drive."

Rudolf looked off into space and sighed. He only answered, "Yes."

Then he stood, walked to his grandmother, knelt at her knees and put his head on her lap; he was well aware of how much she loved his father. Alexandra smoothed his unruly hair, but said nothing.

The next afternoon Leopold, Elizabeth, Stefan, and Tamás accompanied the Countess Alexandra, László, and Rudolf by train to Eisenstadt. There was much to be done to settle the affairs of the Count Christián and Countess Gabriele von Házy. Their deaths, so unexpected, left unfinished business. Rudolf, grateful for Leopold's help and business acumen, found himself to be a very wealthy young man, the owner of several salt mines and mining equipment, but he was a devastated young man, too. He believed himself to be the most unfortunate of human beings. Pessimistic and miserable, Rudolf sat quietly and alone in the chapel of his family's manor house. Leopold found him there in the most ancient part of the house; he slid into a chair beside Rudolf.

"This is much worse than losing my leg, Duke. I never imagined feeling a greater loss than that." Rudolf's voice sounded so lifeless and resigned to sorrow, "What do I do now?"

"You get up and go to work, Rudolf. You are the Count von Házy now and you have obligations, not only to yourself, but to others."

"It is the only way...work through the sorrow, the loss, the grief...the darkness," Leopold's hand gripped Rudolf's shoulder, "the only way to the other side is work and thinking of others.

"I, too, loved your sweet mother and father and I will miss them." Leopold wiped tears from his own eyes, "I understand how difficult their loss will be for you, but you know that your father would tell you to be strong, to be the great man you are meant to be.

"I will help you in any way I can," Leopold patted Rudolf on the back. "Know that you can count on me and, of course, Stefan and Tamás. Whenever you need us, we will be there for you."

A small intimate service was held in the tiny chapel for Rudolf's parents. Rudolf attended to his grandmother faithfully; he seemed sensitive to her every need and she came to depend upon him. Together, they managed to walk through this darkest hour arm in arm.

When all matters of the estate were settled at last, Rudolf, Alexandra, and their Budapest friends left Eisenstadt and returned home. Rudolf resumed his studies at the Drawing Academy and life continued, although for him, life would never again have the same comfort. He worked even harder and regarded his obligations with reverence.

December

A cold wind blew snowflakes in drifts along Dohány Street as a young Austrian soldier darted between cars making his way toward the Klein house. He tugged at the collar of his wool coat to cover his ears from the biting wind. He climbed the stairs and rang the bell. The maid, Zeát, opened the door and led him to the parlor. He asked to see Dr. Klein, but since he was not at home, it was Éva who came to the parlor entrance.

When Éva saw the young man in uniform, she hesitated to enter; a sudden chill made her shudder as she imagined why he had come. He stood, took her extended hand and bowed as she addressed him, "Please sit... Zeát, bring tea and torta, please."

Éva sat down, taking a deep breath, almost holding it, dreading the news he had come to tell her. He said, "I am Lieutenant Péter Eberle. I was commanding officer for your son, Sándor." Péter looked directly at Éva, "I have news of your son. Would you rather wait until your husband is home with you?"

"No, please continue. My husband is not entirely well. I would rather prepare him, if your news is bad."

"I regret to inform you, Madam, that the news is of the worst kind. Your son was killed on October twenty-fifth near the Italian Piave River. I have just recently been able to make my way to Budapest to give you this news. I wanted to tell you of Sándor's death, because he was a good soldier and my friend. Sándor brought much joy to our unit through his humor and his music. He cared about his fellow compatriots and fought bravely alongside them. I felt his loss most profoundly."

Éva had only half listened to Péter's words after he had said her beloved son was dead. She sat numb and emotionless…picturing Sándor when he took his first steps in this very room…when he carried his little brother, Ferenc, home with a broken arm…when he played his violin so beautifully. She said nothing but tears began to roll down her cheeks. She dabbed her eyes with a lace handkerchief, "Please stay for dinner with us, so that you might repeat to Dr. Klein what you have told me about our lovely son, Sándor." Éva stood, Péter as well; she spoke quietly, "Please excuse me now…I must see to dinner."

Within the hour Dr. Klein arrived home. Éva met him at the door, "We have a visitor, Jakov." Éva held his arm tightly and looked directly into his eyes, "Lieutenant Péter Eberle, Sándor's commanding officer. He has come to tell us of Sándor's death."

This news was not a shock to Jakov; he and Éva suspected that Sándor had been killed in the horrible war. The family had heard nothing from him, even though the Armistice had been signed on the eleventh of November. Jakov and Éva noticed that a few Hungarian soldiers had begun to return to Budapest in the last months, but so many had not, so many were lost forever. He kissed Éva, embraced her, whispered into her ear, "God's will," and walked into the parlor. Lieutenant Eberle rose to introduce himself as Jakov closed the parlor doors.

When the Lieutenant told Jakov where Sándor had died on the road from the Piave River, Jakov instantly recalled the story of the disastrous Piave River battle from what he had read in newspaper accounts. Jakov remembered the disturbing details from the article and the images that had come into his mind at the time… *completely exhausted, decimated Hungarian and Austrian troops in Italy… their Austrian officers refusing to fight any longer… all of them begging their leaders to sign an armistice.*

According to the newspaper, on October twenty-fifth the Hungarian troops, under the command of Austrian officers, began to retreat across the Piave River. The report described a long column of men, vehicles, guns, and horses stretched out along the winding road when quite suddenly Allied forces appeared overhead. The troops were caught out in the open with no cover…no place to hide or to escape…it was a slaughter…after the bombs stopped there was nothing left. Jakov shuddered at the thought of his precious son dying in such a brutal way. He focused again on the young man who sat before him.

Lieutenant Eberle took a small box from his pocket. He held it in his hand looking down at it with personal thoughts of his own. When he and his fellow soldiers saw the Caproni airplanes swoop down upon them and bombs began to burst over their heads and all around them, Péter Eberle, like many others froze in his steps. At that moment every image before his eyes seemed to move in slow motion as though he was only an observer of something happening somewhere else...but then came the noise, the noise that still rang in his ears, the loud explosions, the agonizing cries of the pitiful horses, the excruciating screams coming from his soldiers and friends, all torn to shreds by metal and fire.

Péter had miraculously stood in the midst of horror unscathed for what seemed like endless time before he was pushed down behind a mangled *Junovicz*, an Austrian armored car. As he gasped for breath, he looked at the one who had pulled him back into reality. It was Sándor Klein.

Sándor had been injured, blood streamed from his dark hair and from another wound somewhere under his shirt, but even so, he had reached out and pulled Lieutenant Eberle, his officer and friend, to relative safety, at least out of plain sight of the planes with their machine guns. Péter and Sándor laid crammed together against the *Junovicz*, sunk deeply in a crater.

They spoke softly to each other, Sándor because he had such little breath and Péter out of reverence, because he could tell that Sándor would not be alive much longer. Sándor struggled to take a small tin box and a handkerchief from his jacket; he passed the objects to Péter's hand; then feebly reached for the chains around his neck. He asked Péter if he would take these things to his family in Budapest. Péter promised that he would and tried to make Sándor more comfortable. Sándor began to talk of his beloved mother, the father he admired, his brothers and sisters. With a slow rattled exhale of breath Sándor died in Péter's arms.

Lieutenant Eberle handed the small box to Dr. Klein, "These are Sándor's things...he wanted me to bring them to you. He spoke of you and Mrs. Klein often with great admiration and love."

Jakov opened the box. Inside he found a small folded paper with the word "Papa" handwritten on it, Sándor's dog tags, a chain with the Star of David, and a handkerchief with embroidered almond flowers sewn by Eszter. Jakov held in his hands the handkerchief spotted with large browned areas he knew were his son's blood. Tears welled in his eyes. There is nothing more devastating for a parent than losing a child.

The Lieutenant stayed for dinner that night and as the family sat together he told them stories of better times in Italy, of Sándor playing an old fiddle in the quiet nights, stories of the men in their unit and of the adventures they had had together. The Lieutenant even made them laugh.

After Lieutenant Eberle had gone, Dr. Klein returned to his study and laid the little tin box on his desk. He opened it and looked at the contents again. He unfolded the little paper that had "Papa" written on the outside. He read his son's words.

Dearest Papa, When you hear them say that war is glorious and noble, a grand endeavor...tell them, Papa, that those on the Front only feel the futility of it. We see only the cruelty borne by the innocent...the horrifying injury, death and devastation. Where are the wise men of reason who see the future? They must know where the road to war leads. Why in God's name can they not demand peace? Why are there men who want war? Why were their negotiations so useless? War is failure. War is never the answer! It is a loss of life and art, property and nature, commerce and education. Only the arms merchants benefit, no one else. Some day men will sit down together, they will talk and they will bring all of this evilness to an end. Why does it take so long? So many years of death and destruction before they can use reason? Will it be too late? Too late for me?

I think only of home, of Mama and Eszter and little Rózsa, Samuel and Ferenc and Abram and Magda and her gulyásleves… and most of all, you, Papa. Your loving son, Sándor

1919

The Monarchists of Hungary were not content with the plight of their beloved sovereign, the exiled Karl, who as the deposed monarch was living in Switzerland with his wife and children. Many Hungarians wanted Prime Minister Károlyi to call Karl back to power. In fact, many factions throughout Hungary were unhappy for various reasons with Károlyi's government. Not only had Károlyi lost all credibility, his government's popular support had also disappeared because it failed to address severe domestic and military problems that were destroying Hungary. And then to make a bad situation even worse, the *Great Entente* of France, Britain, and America decided to punish Hungary for being Germany's ally in the Great War by demanding that Hungary withdraw its troops from its own borders. Such humiliation devastated the Hungarian people; they blamed Károlyi and forced him to resign.

On the twenty-first of March, the event that Leopold feared most happened. The Communist Party led by an unknown, Béla Kun, took control of Hungary's National Council. Kun and the council created the new Hungarian Soviet Republic and promised equality and social justice for all. The Soviets nationalized all industry and property throughout Hungary, including Leopold's lands.

Leopold had great disdain for the Soviets, whom he continued to call Bolsheviks. He laughed at their incompetence. Although the Bolsheviks had stolen his lands, they realized early on they had no idea of how to run vineyards or wineries. So, in their desperation, they put Leopold back in charge of his own land and company. Leopold could, with Elizabeth's help, run things his own way, right under their noses.

"Who is this man, Kun?" Elizabeth asked.

"A Hungarian Jew, a ne'er-do-well, who served in the Hungarian army during the war," Tamás answered. He had heard plenty of gossip about Kun, the rogue politician. "He was captured, taken to Russia and while a prisoner of war became a communist. Last year he formed the Hungarian Communist Party here in Budapest. After that, all the Bolsheviks had to do was wait for a weakness to let them in. Well, they're in; we have them now!"

"I am terribly disappointed that some of our Hungarian Jewish people, particularly the young, seem so enthusiastic about the ideals of communism," Leopold said, shaking his head in wonderment. "I have never understood why Jewish youth rejected Magyarization and, yet, seem to embrace communism so enthusiastically."

Eszter and many of her Jewish friends became avid supporters of the communists and many of them obtained jobs in Kun's government, including Eszter who worked for a few hours in the afternoons as a receptionist for the Department of the Interior. She was proud to work for the Party.

But Stefan, never sure about communism, certainly did not approve of the nationalization of land, in particular his father's land, nor did he find the Soviets honorable or restrained. His father called them heartless Bolsheviks and Stefan trusted his father's opinions.

April

Eszter ducked into a café on the Promenade as a light rain fell in the early evening. She sat at a small table by a window and looked through the rain-streaked glass to watch for Stefan. She saw him approaching by the light of the street lamp and could hardly wait to see his handsome face across from her. He kissed her on the cheek, briskly shook the rain from his coat and cap, and sat down at the table. His brilliant smile made her blush. The warm golden light from the candle on their table reflected in their eyes as they held hands and stared at each other.

For over a year Stefan had been going with Eszter to her weekly meetings for both the Zionists and the Communists. The two young lovers agreed on many aspects of radical thinking—a free Hungary, equality for her citizens, nationalism to a point, but they argued about Magyarization and on that particular point, they disagreed fervently.

"I am a Monarchist, Eszter. I will forever remain in favor of the king's return. The king will treat all of Hungary's citizens fairly and assure equality for Jews as well. Karl is a compassionate king who cares for his people, *all* the people."

"I have a father, Stefan, a kind one. I do not need another father figure to take care of me. The one I have is quite enough. A king is patronizing, as though people cannot take care of themselves or make their own decisions. The thought of a king is demeaning to intelligent people."

Eszter made Stefan smile every time they argued. She was so certain about her opinions, so stern in her expression; he could not help but laugh which, of course, made her very angry with him. So far in their relationship, Stefan had not found any problem arguing with Eszter, even if he made her angry, because making up with her was always a worthwhile experience. He adored Eszter; everything about her, her tangled hair, her velvet eyes, her extraordinary mind with all of its complexities and her exquisite body that he had come to know quite well.

—∞—

Leopold had his suspicions of the new Kun government as did many Hungarians who began to protest his radical communist ideas and actions. Eventually a coup was attempted. Although Leopold and Tamás knew about the coup, Elizabeth forbade them to participate, at least in any outward, recognizable way.

"Remember those Bolsheviks killed the Tsar and women and children." She warned them, "They won't hesitate for a moment to do away with either of you."

Kun's government reacted to the coup quickly and severely with a rogue militaristic group, the Lenin Boys. The Lenin Boys immediately began violent reprisals and conducted a purge against all those unwilling to conform to communist ideals. Called "The Red Terror," their rampage of arrests and executions without trial created a reign of fear through every part of Hungary.

Summer

When the von Estés returned to Lake Balaton for the summer, Leopold discovered that his long-time friend, the Baron György Vadas, was under arrest in Balatonfüred. Leopold and Tamás went straightaway to the police station to investigate the situation, to see if they could be of help. They discovered the Bolsheviks in control of the station. With no written warrant, no formal accusation, the Baron was simply arrested as an enemy of the State.

"What has this man done? He is eighty years old. What threat can he possibly be?" Leopold argued with the local commissar, whom he did not know. "Will you let him go into my custody? I will make sure he causes no harm."

Without any emotion, the administrator answered, "I do not have the authority to release the old man."

After another twenty minutes of trying in vain to free the Baron, Tamás finally pulled Leopold back. "This is going nowhere, Leopold. Nowhere, except to make you a target of the Lenin Boys. We should leave and try another approach tomorrow."

Leopold and Tamás returned to the villa where Elizabeth was trying to console the Baron's wife. The Baroness, like her beloved husband, was in her eighties and, although before that night was considered hearty, she now appeared frail and disoriented. Terribly upset, she told over and over the story of how the thugs had come in the night and taken the Baron.

"They knocked me to the floor when I protested. They disallowed any of our servants to help me. They told our servants that they owned the land now and were no longer required to serve me."

"What is wrong with these heartless Bolsheviks?" Leopold became uncontrollably angry.

"Leopold, you must not let your anger or disgust get the better of you," Elizabeth warned. "These fiends arrest for no reason but to rid themselves of problem-makers. I do not want them coming for you."

Ana interrupted their discussion, "The Baroness's son, Fábián Vadas, is here. May I bring him to his mother?"

"Of course, Ana," replied Leopold and Elizabeth as they immediately went downstairs to the reception hall to welcome him.

They escorted the younger Vadas upstairs to a guest room where his mother was resting. After a tender greeting and reassurance that his mother was comfortable, Fábián turned to Leopold, "I was just in Balatonfüred…I learned that you tried to rescue my father…unfortunately soon after you left, they removed him from the town. I have not yet learned where they've taken him."

"I'm so sorry to hear that…I should not have made them angry," Leopold was terribly distraught. "I fear that I may have caused your father damage, perhaps they would have released him if I had not interfered."

"You need never consider that, my dear Duke, you have nothing to do with their barbarous acts against humanity. They do whatever they want, regardless of anyone's plea for conscience or compassion. I have eyes that will tell me where they have taken my father. There is still a chance to bring him home to my mother."

Leopold and Tamás both considered his words carefully, "You have eyes?"

"Is there some kind of active resistance under way?" asked Tamás.

"Yes, on two fronts. The *Entente* is very opposed to Soviet control of Hungary and our own Admiral Miklós Horthy is in Vienna raising an army to rise against the Reds." A militaristic edge was evident in Fábián's words, "and, of course we have our own spies right here. Change is coming, if we can only endure until it arrives."

"Any way that we can help, we will," Leopold and Tamás offered.

Fábián Vadas, the Baron's youngest son, assured them that they would be called upon. As Fábián said his farewells to Elizabeth and thanked her for tending to his mother's needs, Leopold placed a large sum of money in Fábián's hand.

"For the resistance," he said and Fábián Vadas was gone.

No one ever saw or heard of the elder Baron Vadas again and within a month his dear wife died of a broken heart. The Red Terror was responsible for hundreds of deaths that summer.

—⚬⚬—

Stefan finished his scientific studies at university that spring and planned to continue master studies at university in Vienna come fall. Rudolf had also completed his training at the Drawing Academy in Budapest and in late September planned to enter the Fine Art Academy in Prague. Klára could hardly bear the thought of summer's end when both of her dearest boys would leave Budapest for distant places. The passing of summer days seemed terribly bittersweet to the ten-year-old. Silva was the only one who could bring her some cheer.

"This summer seems so awfully sad, Silva," Klára complained. "Stefan and Dolf will both be gone when it ends. Mommy and Papa seem so gloomy. We are not going anywhere, not to Linz or to Vienna or even back to Budapest for a weekend. Aunt Eugenia is not coming this summer and Papa never goes back to his office in the city. Everything seems wrong."

"Be grateful for what you have, young lady," Silva scolded. "You have bright, sunny days to enjoy, plenty of good food to eat, the lake to swim. The boys are here right now for you to tease and dear Rózsa will be arriving next week. What more could any young girl want!"

"I'm sorry, Silva." Klára felt great chagrin, "You're right." Klára slid off the bench and stretched, "I'll go find Dolf; he's never sad."

"Here, Miss Klára, take him a plate of *ischler*; he loves them."

"Me, too," Klára smiled as she stuffed a whole one in her mouth, "Thank you Silva."

Klára wiped her mouth as she left the kitchen while Silva laughed to herself at Klára's dramatics. Klára found Rudolf sitting in the garden gazebo; he had just finished his work in the vineyard for the day. Klára noticed the object of his attention—a fuzzy caterpillar inching up the stem of a hollyhock. With one hand, Rudolf turned the stem to keep the caterpillar in view while he drew the flower and insect with the other.

"Oh, Klára, you're just in time to hold this stem for me. See, keep turning it to keep the caterpillar crawling on it. He seems to like going up, see?"

"Okay, like this?" she held the flower upside down, then right side up and the little bug just kept creeping along.

"Let me see your drawing. Umm, that's really good. It really looks fuzzy," she said, and then sighed.

"What's the matter with you?"

"I've been feeling sorry for myself. Silva scolded me for it. I know I should only think of the good things I have, but I'm just feeling sad today."

"Well, think about me. I have to go to dancing practice. My first Anna Ball is in two weeks and I have to dance in front of everyone! How sad do you think I am?"

Klára laughed, "Oh, Dolf, you're a good dancer. You'll be fine. All the girls will want to dance with you. You're very handsome, especially when you smile."

Rudolf blushed, "Hey, where did my caterpillar go?"

They looked into the blooms of the hollyhock, but couldn't find it.

"That's all right. I would rather draw you, anyway. Sit still, Klára."

"Rózsa will be here this weekend. I'm glad, because you and Stefan work all the time and I don't have anyone to explore with when you're so busy."

"Is Eszter coming with her?"

"No, she's got a job in the city now, so she can't come this summer."

Rudolf noticed there were tears rolling down Klára's cheeks, "What's bothering you today, Klára?"

"I keep thinking about you and Stefan going so far away when summer is over…the very thought of it has just ruined the whole summer."

"Klára, how silly is that? To let the future ruin the present? That makes no sense! Live the days as they come. If you're sad thinking about the future, then your past will be filled with regret. Next fall, do you want to look back to this summer and see only days of sadness or do you want to see days filled with joyful memories, like right now? Is not this a great moment? Holding hollyhocks and caterpillars for a handsome boy like me! What can be happier than that?"

"I knew you could make me smile, Dolfie. I love you."

"I love you, too, little Klára. What do you think of this?" He showed her the drawing he had made of her, complete with a caterpillar on her shoulder. She made a quick glance to her shoulder.

"No, it isn't really there, Klára, just a bit of artistic license."

When Rózsa arrived at last, she helped Klára forget the blues she'd been feeling. The two girls easily found plenty to do and spent hours laughing together. Silva found real joy to see Klára smiling again. But for everyone that summer, feelings of regret and sadness hovered near the surface as the Anna Ball drew near. Christián and Gabriele were greatly missed, especially at the lake where the merry couple had been such an integral part of every activity for so many years.

All the von Estés gathered for the Anna Ball to support Rudolf. Even his reclusive grandmother, the Countess Alexandra, arrived at the ball. She radiated a sincere enthusiasm to see her grandson participate in the grand event.

Although Rudolf carried a cane, most people rarely noticed, because he carried it in such a way that it simply appeared to be a debonair decoration. But for the ball, he left his cane behind. There he was standing at the ballroom entrance with a very pretty young lady on his arm. He was sharply dressed in the white and gold Huszar uniform complete with shiny black boots and spurs. Alexandra's pride was obvious and she expressed it with tears, applause, and even a cheer when he and his partner were introduced.

"Rudolf is by far the most handsome. Isn't he? Just like his father," the Countess insisted to all who could hear her.

Just as Stefan had done at his Anna Ball, Rudolf came out onto the terrace and danced with Klára and with Rózsa, both of whom felt thrilled to be dancing with one so gallant and handsome. Stefan complimented Rudolf, "Well done, Sir. You accomplished the *Palotás* perfectly and not bad on the *cszárdás* either. I'm proud of you, Old Man."

Obvious to all, Rudolf took pride in his accomplishment, but despite his broad smile there was a melancholy in his brown eyes that revealed his profound sorrow. If only his beloved parents could share the joyful moment they had always wanted for their son. However, not one to wallow in self-pity, he twirled Klára around the terrace until they both felt dizzy and collapsed onto a wrought-iron settee beside his grandmother. A laughing Klára, absolutely thrilled, kissed Rudolf on both cheeks and complimented his dancing skills profusely before he twirled her away again.

Alexandra looked at the two young people and thought, *how well they suit each other.* She smiled to herself and thought, *they're already in love with each other... they just don't know it yet.* She motioned for them to come back to her. She held their hands together in hers and gave both of them kisses, "You have made an old lady very happy tonight. Thank you."

August

Shortly after Rózsa left the lake for Budapest, the unbelievable happened. The Romanian army, encouraged and supported by the *Great Entente*, marched into southern Hungary and all the way to Budapest where they drove the Red government out. The Romanians occupied the city and sent Béla Kun into exile. With this change of events, Leopold decided the family should travel by train for a visit to Vienna. While Leopold and Stefan tended to business, Elizabeth and Klára went on to Linz. Silva and Tamás took their vacation to Sopron to visit Gáspár and Ilonka.

Leopold and Stefan, accompanied by Fábián Vadas, met with Admiral Miklós Horthy. Horthy's plan to take Budapest from the Romanians and restore the kingdom greatly impressed Leopold. Horthy believed in the monarchy, too. After their meeting, Leopold and Stefan walked along the *Rotenturmstrasse* together. Leopold expressed his pleasure at hearing that Horthy would provide the force needed to rid Hungary of the communists and restore Karl to the throne of Hungary. Leopold felt relieved; at last he could imagine a brighter future. He and Stefan stopped at a small outdoor café for supper.

Over a platter of *Bauernschmaus*, meats with sauerkraut and dumplings, Stefan hesitated, cleared his throat, looked down at the wine stain on the tablecloth and said, "Papa, I have something to discuss with you."

He spoke rapidly, without taking a breath, "I have made a decision. I have decided to not come to the university here in Vienna," he took a breath, "I prefer to stay in Budapest. I wish to work in the Budapest office with you so I may learn the wine business." He looked up, eye to eye with his father, "I hope you will honor my wishes."

Leopold appeared stunned at first, reconsidered, then raised his shoulders in a gesture of acceptance, "I think we can work that out. You should learn the business first hand. Yes, Stefan, we can do that for you." Leopold smiled proudly at his son, "It will be good to have you in the office.

"And you cannot imagine how happy your little sister will be when she hears that you are staying in Budapest…and for that matter, Elizabeth, too…well, the whole household will stop making gloomy faces."

September

The Romanians were still in charge when the von Estés returned to Budapest in late September. Even though the actions of the communist government had been reversed, anxiety still hung in the air. Leopold and Elizabeth spent many hours in the office undoing the damage done during the nationalization of industry and land. Although hopeful for the return of Horthy and, eventually, the king, they remained concerned about what might happen next. Uncertainty reigned throughout Budapest.

Despite the uncertainty, Leopold had a surprise for Stefan for his birthday—an Alfa Romeo sports car. Stefan was euphoric, exclaiming disbelief over and over. Tamás and Auguste had taught him to drive several years before and he had driven one of the family's cars now and then, but to have his own car was simply beyond belief. He swore eternal gratitude and left immediately to "show his friends." Of course he drove straight to his and Eszter's favorite café and telephoned her to meet him there.

Within the hour, Eszter arrived. Stefan's joy was met with Eszter's despair. She no longer had her job at the Department of the Interior and she was fearful of what might happen to those who supported Kun's government. Stefan tried to soothe her fears.

"Marry me, Eszter, I'll protect you." He kept smiling at her.

"Why are you so happy, Stefan?"

"Come outside. I'll show you."

Once outside he told her to cover her eyes; he guided her to the curb. "All right, open your eyes."

She could not believe the bright red roadster standing by the curb. She was speechless, but climbed into the two seater beside Stefan and they sped away into the night.

—m—

A week later the time had arrived for Rudolf to leave Budapest for the Academy of Fine Art in Prague. Stefan insisted he drive Rudolf to *Déli pályaudvar*, the train station just west of the Castle Hill. Of course, Klára wanted to go along, too. She squeezed in between the two boys and held Rudolf's bag across her lap. She put her hand on Rudolf's shoulder, "Dolfie, why do you have to go so far away? Why can't you stay with us?"

He turned to face her. She looked so woebegone. "I'll be coming home to see you. It's not so far away, just a few hours by train." He tousled her hair, because he knew she hated for anyone to muss her hair. "Perhaps you and Stefan can visit me in Prague."

Klára slipped her arm around Rudolf's neck. At this moment she wasn't bothered by his teasing, "I wish we were all going to Balaton instead."

"This is a good move for Dolf, Klára. He's going to study with the best artists and someday he'll be famous, too!" Stefan reached across Klára and fisted Rudolf on the shoulder, smiling his radiant smile at Rudolf, "But you can't forget us! You have to come back to Budapest one day! You know we can't get along without you!"

Stefan parked the Alfa Romeo; the three got out and walked arm in arm to the station platform. Rudolf carried one small suitcase and a portfolio. They stopped under the placard that read "Trains to Praha" by a long track of seemingly impatient cars, waiting, puffing heavily, and emitting big gusts of steam. Klára held Rudolf's hand tightly; she looked at the train and sniffled, "Will you forget me, Dolfie?"

"Of course not, Klára! You'll always be my special girl. I could never forget you. Give me a kiss."

He bent down and kissed her cheeks; she kissed his, then the three friends gave each other vigorous hugs and Rudolf stepped up into the car. He felt a moment of regret at leaving, but made his way to his compartment. He sat down by the window and looked out at Stefan and Klára standing side by side waving to him. Klára wiped tears from her eyes and blew kisses to him. Rudolf smiled at them, touched his fingers to his lips and slowly waved good-bye as the train pulled forward with a great surge of energy.

Prague

Rudolf enjoyed traveling through the Carpathian landscape along the Danube from Hungary into Czechoslovakia. As the train steamed through the landscape he took great pleasure watching the picturesque villages and distant snowcapped High Tatra Mountains stream past. Finally, nine hours later, he arrived at *Hlavní nádezí*, Prague's New Town rail station. He disembarked from the train and walked toward the city, past the Opera House, around the incomplete St. Wenceslas Monument, and down *Václavské námĕstí* past the Hotel Europa. While he walked briskly along the busy sidewalks, he noticed the beauty of the architecture and the park-like green space separating the two sides of wide Václavské Avenue.

Like much of Pest, Prague's New Town was modern, bustling with commercial energy and a sense of optimism. Rudolf breathed in the feeling and smiled to himself. He felt older, independent and eager to begin this new phase of his life, although he instantly remembered Klára and knew he would be happy to return to Budapest in the future. For now he intended to embrace this adventure wholeheartedly.

Rudolf stayed with the wide Václavské Avenue until it gave way to the narrow winding streets of Old Town which he followed as one would follow a hedge maze in his search for Karlova Street. At last he came to a "Y" with Seminářská Street to the left and Karlova to the right. As he looked for the correct house number a familiar voice shouted down to him from an open window. Rudolf looked up and waved to his friend János Géza whom he had known at the Hungarian Drawing Academy. János called to him, "You're here! Great to see you! I'll be right down!"

A charming Renaissance period house stood as Rudolf's destination. Painted a pale pink, the stucco facade held colorful fresco paintings of maidens and youths frolicking among flowers while sculpted figures of stone crouched under each window sill. János came bounding down the stairs and gave Rudolf a hearty handshake, a kiss on each cheek, and a slap on the back. He was a good-natured fellow and Rudolf was glad to have such a friend in the strange city. János explained that the four-storied structure was divided into flats for students and assured Rudolf that he would appreciate the abundant good fellowship and intellectual stimulation. János showed him the small dining room on the ground floor where breakfast was served every morning and took him down the stairs to the Gothic-period wine cellar, telling him, "This is where all the students relax."

Then János took Rudolf's bag and led him up the winding staircase to the fourth floor to his flat, across the hall from that of János. Rudolf's window opened onto a view of the courtyard below and beyond to the city with its many spires of every description—tall slender finials, bulbous Eastern-style domes, colorful cupolas, and double towers topped by Christian crosses. He thought to himself, *It's magnificent... who could not love this city... this ancient city of universities and churches and romance? I do hope Klára and Stefan will come to visit me here.*

Rudolf had barely unpacked his belongings when János knocked at his door, "Come, we're going across the alley to a wonderful little restaurant for dinner... you can meet some of your housemates and *Praha pivo* is especially good."

The camaraderie was instant and easy. After all, these men had much in common... they were students, they were on their own in an exciting city, and they were young! They laughed loudly, sang several beer drinking songs with many dissonant notes and argued over who could drink the most Pilsner.

"You have arrived in Praha at the perfect moment," János proclaimed loudly, "So much is happening! We are part of the avant-garde. Down with the old and on to the future!"

In the midst of this raucous setting, Rudolf suddenly realized he was famished; it was almost nine o'clock. János offered to order for Rudolf and soon he was wolfing down *houskové knedliky* with *hovezi*, bread dumplings with beef, and *jablkový,* strudel, with a *velké,* clear and golden Pilsner.

When Rudolf got back to his flat late in the night, he felt good knowing he'd chosen the right place to study. He was excited to see where this adventure would take him, to begin his studies at the Academy, to find out what kind of art he would make and, most of all, to find answers to the questions that filled his mind. *Who am I? What is my purpose in this world? Where do I fit?*

Although Rudolf began his course of study at the Academy of Fine Arts in drawing and painting with Josef Čapek, after the first few weeks, he became more interested in the School of Printmaking, directed by the famous master printmaker, Max Švakinsky. Based upon Rudolf's excellent drawing skills, Švakinsky admitted him into the prestigious graphic arts program. The young, impressionable Rudolf was amazed by Švakinsky's talent and influenced by his unrelenting advocacy for modern art and belief in the power of contemporary art to change the world. Very early in his training, Rudolf began to hold Švakinsky, three times his age, in great esteem as the ideal example of a true artist—one he desired to emulate.

Švakinsky rejected all traditional classical approaches to art. He rebuffed conventional expectations of realistic, representational imagery, inspired by the Greco-Roman and Renaissance methods, preferring instead the new modern styles of Symbolism and turn-of-the-century Art Nouveau for ways to visually express ideas. With great expertise, Švakinsky passed on to his students his knowledge of all printing methods, among them etching, mezzotint, and woodblock. He encouraged Rudolf to study calligraphy and typography.

Eventually Rudolf studied under Academy professors František Kupka and Karel Teige, who introduced him to commercial design, a field of art that greatly piqued his curiosity.

Karel Teige was one of the founders of *Devétsil*, or Nine Forces, the avant-garde association of artists—men and women visual artists, poets, architects, musicians, photographers, actors, film makers, directors, and writers. Teige invited Rudolf to join *Devétsil*. Rudolf felt quite honored to be part of the group, an active association that organized exhibitions of work, published art magazines, and sponsored impressive guest lecturers, including Modern Expressionists from Paris, Munich, and Vienna. Teige, also the editor and graphic designer for *ReD*, the *Revue Devétsil* magazine, hired Rudolf to create graphic designs for the magazine.

His many new friends, young Academy students, men and women, seemed just as passionate as he. They were painters, printmakers, and journalists, but many were also political activists with avid opinions, usually anti-establishment. Rudolf began a network of acquaintances he suspected would be very useful in his future.

Several of the *Devétsil* activists were also members of the Czechoslovak Social Democratic Workers' Party, Communists. Their enthusiasm reminded Rudolf of the Zionist gatherings and Party meetings he had attended with Stefan and Eszter in Budapest. Regardless of his new-found Academy friends and his shared interests with them in art, Rudolf's mind remained unchanged about the communists—he neither trusted them nor believed in their philosophies. He and Stefan agreed with Eszter that the Zionists had the right to advocate for a homeland in Palestine, but they completely disagreed with her when it came to communist ideology; neither of them would ever trust a Bolshevik. Nor would either of the two friends ever consider communism as the answer to Hungary's problems. Stefan and Rudolf, both avowed Monarchists, believed the return of the king to Budapest was the best solution for Hungary's peaceful future.

"The Hungarian people have rejected communism with the help of the Romanians," Rudolf argued with his fellow Czech students. "Hungarians still love their benevolent King Karl and I'm sure will someday support his return." He added, quite convincingly he thought, "Many Hungarians still believe the ancient assumption that the king is given absolute authority to rule by God himself and that no mere mortal can take that right away from the king."

Rudolf could see his new friends remained unswayed, so he continued, "I have many strong objections to the communists and their goals—land redistribution and a cooperative labor system to name two ill-conceived ideas that do not work. The Bolsheviks are a ruthless mob who murder women and children. I would never trust a Bolshevik...there is always the possibility of a purge by the Reds...their ultimate intent is to sweep away the educated, the intelligentsia and, certainly the art students." Rudolf warned, "They would definitely come for us...the elite, they call us...we make art and art has power...it is dangerous!"

Well aware that most simply shrugged off his views as those of a youth inexperienced in the real world, Rudolf persisted in his judgment of the Reds and despite the differences of opinion, Rudolf earned respect and even admiration from both faculty and students for his intelligent arguments. He recognized Leopold as the greatest influence on the formulation of his ideas, his opinions. From a very young age, he and Stefan, at Leopold's insistence, studied history and philosophy and then engaged in long discussions and debates in defense of their positions.

Although well prepared for arguments about many subjects, Rudolf found, after his arrival at the Academy, he had new questions, new searches of a personal nature: self identity, purpose, goals. Through his professors and fellow students, Rudolf discovered a new culture of artistic values based upon a familiar, conservative classical foundation, but with an expanded appreciation for contemporary artistic movements. He realized he must find an artistic language to express his own points of view and define personal meaning in the creation of his art. Rudolf identified the power of symbolism in graphic design and determined printmaking would become his medium of self-expression.

November, Hungary

For several months Admiral Miklós Horthy and István Bethlen planned the Hungarian response to both the communist Red Terror that swept over Hungary and the Romanian occupation of Budapest, their beloved capital. Unaware that Horthy and Bethlen had organized an extremely conservative right-wing White Army as a counter-revolutionary movement to the communists, Leopold and most Hungarians anxiously anticipated the liberating invasion of Horthy's forces. Neither Leopold nor most Hungarians suspected that Horthy not only intended to rid Hungary of the communists, but also *all* their sympathizers, in particular, their Jewish supporters.

The White Army first crossed into Hungary from the west. Bent on revenge, their retaliation, known as the White Terror, was as severe as the Red Terror had been. Horthy's army struck with a violent vengeance all communists still in the country and all Jews who supported the Kun government. As the White Army made its way toward Budapest, arrests and executions without trial ensued against all those they considered enemies of Hungary.

Horthy's White Army marched into Budapest on the sixteenth day of November, drove out the Romanians and established a new government.

Horthy restored security within the city and imprisoned thousands of sup-porters of both Károlyi and Kun. All radical movements were suppressed by official bans on newspapers, literature, and group meetings. Based upon a right-wing belief that Jews caused all of Hungary's problems, conservatives within Hungary's Parliament began a campaign of anti-Semitism through a series of sanctioned pogroms of wide-spread economic and social persecution of Jews. Despite this surge of reprisals, winter snows brought calm to the city and life seemingly preceded normally.

—⁂—

Strange, Leopold thought when he read the long letter from his sister, Eugenia, postmarked Cologne... *happenings in Hungary seem strangely similar to those in Germany.*

> *Eugenia wrote... an odd little man with a mustache and charismatic personality seems to have mesmerized the citizens of Germany. I would think it humorous, if his ideas and words were not so serious. He is a part of the German Workers' Party, founded in Munich. The Party's agenda is downright terrifying. They have extreme ideas of nationalism... contempt for parliamentary democracy... and actually advocate for a dictatorship. Worst of all they are unashamed racists and anti-Semites.*
>
> > *The only good thing about these fools is their hatred of the Bolshe-viks, but then even their hatred is corrupted! They have the twisted idea that the Bolsheviks are somehow manipulated by International Jewish financiers... so they say that even Bolshevik atrocities are caused by Jews. Unbelievably unfair!*
> >
> > *Oh well, what can I do? Konrad and I are leaving next week for South America. We will be back to Europe by summer. We shall see you in Siófok this year.*
> >
> > *Your loving sister, Eugenia*

1920

In January Hungary held its first free elections and elected a new National Assembly with a right-wing majority. In February Leopold read aloud to Elizabeth an article in his newspaper about Germany, "The German Workers' Party changed its name to the National Socialist German Workers' Party. Members call themselves the Nazi Party."

"This is certainly troubling," Leopold read further, "the party advocates violence, if necessary, to achieve their goals. They have organized an armed force, called the *Sturmabteilung*, storm troopers, to apply that force with Ernst

Röhm as their designated leader. And there's more…the Nazis have a list of enemies…communists, socialists, trade unionists, and Jews."

"Since the article indicates the Nazi Party originated in Bavaria," Elizabeth interjected, "I wonder if Renate knows anything about them. I'll write to her and ask."

"I wonder why the Nazis believe they need violence to enforce their policies. I cannot fathom a government that would act with cruelty and violence against its own citizens. What kind of policies are they making that would require armed enforcers? Why the obsession with unfounded prejudices?

"Well, I'm glad that Eugenia is away from Germany for a while," Leopold sighed. "I must agree with her…this new Nazi Party cannot possibly last long nor have much effect, surely the intelligent people of Germany will put a stop to it."

—⁓—

In March the new Hungarian Parliament agreed to restore the monarchy to Hungary. However, Miklós Horthy realized that Western Europe, the *Great Entente*, did not favor the king's return. Fearful that the king's return might lead more easily to a reconstitution of the Austro-Hungary Empire, the *Great Entente* definitely opposed *that* re-unification. Horthy cleverly influenced the parliament to delay the election of Karl as king and instead to elect Horthy as regent—to rule until the return of the king. Horthy received significant powers from the parliament, powers even greater than those of the parliament itself—the parliament could act only at Horthy's will. Parliament's conservatives appreciated Horthy's advocacy for Hungary's traditional values of family, state, and religion and welcomed his inclination to ignore the plight of the peasants and the working class.

Summer, Lake Balaton

At the villa, Klára sat in Stefan's window seat all afternoon waiting for Stefan and Rudolf to appear on the lakeside road. When the family left Budapest for the lake, Stefan stayed behind to work at the von Esté Fine Wine Company. This summer he would only come to the lake on weekends. And Klára could hardly wait for this particular weekend, because Stefan was to pick up Rudolf at the train station in the morning and bring him to the lake in the afternoon. Klára couldn't take her eyes from the road; she strained to see the Alfa Romeo…and finally, there it was! She raced down the stairs, shouting to everyone, "They're here, they're here at last!"

Klára ran outside to the gravel drive and almost all the way to the road before the red car reached the drive. Stefan stopped the car to let Klára climb inside. Stefan and Rudolf were just as happy to see her. In a spirit of great happiness the summer routine of work and play began once again.

June

On the fourth of June in France, the *Great Entente* met to decide the fate of Hungary. The *Entente* had little sympathy for Hungary and wanted to punish the country for its involvement with Germany in the Great War. The *Entente* demanded the signature of Hungary on the Treaty of Trianon, a document that devastated Hungary, spiritually and geographically.

At the moment of signing, the treaty created new international borders for Hungary that immediately separated millions of ethnic Hungarians from their homeland, divested Hungary of more than two-thirds of its territory and three-fifths of its population. Every country on Hungary's borders increased in size—Slovakia, Romania, Croatia, and Serbia. Hungary lost many of its natural resources—timber, iron, and farmlands. For Hungarians, the Treaty of Trianon was an absolute disaster.

News of the treaty and its details spread quickly throughout Hungary. Hungarians instantly despised the document, cursed the fourth day of June, and became obsessed from that date on to restore all of Hungary's lands lost through the treaty.

In an effort to form a new Hungarian government, Horthy and the National Assembly rejected some members' push for a military dictatorship and briefly adopted a democratic model of reform. However, the assembly—inspired by the great successes of Adolf Hitler in Bavaria—decided to make a move to the far conservative right. Horthy based his move on economics, believing Hungary must prepare for eventual war by using finances to build the country's military defenses. Horthy knew arms preparation would keep his country economically sound. He had no doubt of another war in the future, a war the people wanted, a war to reclaim lost Hungarian territories.

July

In July, Horthy appointed the right-wing conservative Count Pál Teleki, a man Leopold never trusted, as Prime Minister.

"Teleki represents an extreme Conservative-Christian political right," worried Leopold, "he's strongly opposed to Magyarization and now he's beginning to undo all assimilation policies, adopting harsh nationalistic laws against religious and ethnic minorities…the Gypsies, the Jews, and the Slavs!"

"Hungary has not been in a tolerant mood since the war," observed Tamás.

"Teleki's motto, 'Family, State, Religion,' sounds good," interjected Stefan, "It's hard to argue."

"Yes, it sounds good," agreed Leopold. "Who can deny the moral value of honoring one's family, country, or faith? But it's all code, Stefan, for a non-inclusive, intolerant government without compassion for any diversity within Hungary's own borders. It's a way to justify prejudice against equality for all of Hungary's citizens. In fact, it's a way to legally deny equality. Teleki is a very dangerous man!"

"But Teleki is a pro-monarchist," offered Stefan who listened carefully to his father.

"True, but that doesn't mean he's pro-Karl," stated Leopold. "He's in full support of Horthy, because Horthy, at the moment anyway, is omnipotent."

—⁂—

Under Horthy Hungary's Jewish population had lived in relative safety, but now under Teleki, the nature of their existence immediately changed. Teleki imposed a *numerus clausus* policy that applied a Jewish quota limiting the number of Jewish students allowed to study at university. Jewish students within the total student population could not exceed the same percentage of Jews within the general population. The *numerus clausus* also affected professionals in many occupations in addition to education.

Early October

Dr. Klein opened the front door and stood still for a moment surveying his entry hall, the carpet, the wallpaper, the staircase. He sighed heavily, stepped into the house, and in a kind of slow motion, set down his briefcase, took off his coat and hat, and hung them on the coat rack.

Éva Klein walked into the hallway, drying her hands on her apron, "Jakov, what are you doing home?"

It was not even noon and, yet, here he was.

"I no longer have a position at the Institute. I have been dismissed."

"What?" her voice betrayed her shock and disbelief, "Why? What has happened?"

"There is a purge, a pogrom against the Jews. All the Jews at the Institute, the faculty, the students, everyone lost their places today."

Éva stood looking at her husband, the brilliant and beloved Professor Klein, now bent with age and devastated.

At that very moment Eszter and Ferenc arrived home. Eszter was furious,

"I was sitting in my classroom and the professor walked into the room and said, 'All Jews in this class are dismissed. Leave now and do not return.' Just like that; we are out! I ran into Ferenc at the Metro station. The same thing happened at his university. All the Jews are out!"

She threw her coat at the coat rack, her face flushed red. "They call it *numerus clausus*—a Jewish quota to keep enrollments and jobs *fair*. Fair they say because we are taking more than our share. *We* are taking away *their* places."

Hot tears streamed down her cheeks.

Ferenc agreed with her, nodding his head, but seemingly more resigned and less angry than she.

Eszter started up the stair, "We need another change of government. See, Father, I told you the communists were better...more interested in equality for all!"

"Eszter! Politics is politics. It is better to remain quiet, at the edges, tending to one's own business. You know it is because of Jewish involvement in Kun's Red government that these harsh recriminations have fallen upon us!"

"It is Teleki and Horthy policies that have done this," ventured Ferenc. "What can we do now?"

"Wait. We wait, Ferenc, change always comes. We stay the same and wait." Jakov Klein's voice sounded wistful as he added, "Perhaps, when the king returns, he will bring sanity and things will return to normal. The Hapsburgs have always been fair to the Jews."

With great melancholy Jakov reflected, "They have forgotten their Jewish soldiers who have always fought bravely for Hungary. Our own Sándor gave his life for the Empire and now they have turned their backs on us."

"And you are surprised, Father? Don't they always turn against us? They blame us for the war, for the bad economy, for every problem!" Eszter turned on the stair, grabbed her coat, "I'm going out."

Dr. Klein and Éva went to the kitchen. He sat at the table as Magda poured a cup of tea. He drank the tea slowly, looked up to Éva, his eyes welled with tears, "My students said nothing when the Dean told me to leave. No one protested or rose to my defense. A few even shouted obscenities and called out '*Jude*'!"

Éva put her arms around him and held him close, letting her tears drop into his silver hair. She knew how much he loved his students and how painful their betrayal was for him. "Maybe Duke Esté can help in some way. Will you ask him?"

"We will see, Éva, don't worry. We will be all right."

Eszter left the house, hurrying along Dohány Street toward the *Hungária* coffee house on Körut Street where she hoped to find Stefan. As she passed in front of the restaurant she looked through the big glass window to see if Stefan was there. He was not at their usual spot, but she went in, ordered a Turkish coffee and scooted into the red leather booth. The restaurant was crowded and noisy; everyone talking with an air of excitement. She imagined they were all expressing their anti-Semitic views. Her cheeks were burning; she wanted to stand on the table and curse them all. She stared at her coffee cup and wondered if they knew there was a Jewess in their midst.

Suddenly Stefan slid into the booth beside her, "I heard. Are you all right? I'm so sorry, Eszter."

"I went by your house." He hugged her and kissed her, "Rósza said you were very angry and ran out. I thought you might be here. I'm glad that I found you."

Eszter restated all the feelings and thoughts that she had expressed to her father. She cried very hard, but silently.

"Father is such an idealist! He believes that because the Neologs adopted the Hungarian language and Magyarized themselves that they are truly equal...equal citizens just like everyone else." There was great skepticism in her voice; then she continued, "He thinks that because the Hungarian Jews embraced Magyarization and actively assimilated that they are irrevocably part of Hungarian society. And just because he and all the other Jews—Orthodox and Neolog—are allowed to retain their faith...they must think that Hungary is an ideal world!"

She rocked back and forth in the booth, so angry, "But the truth. . .the truth is that the Jews...no matter how rich, no matter how remarkable...are never thought of as equal, never fully accepted by the *real* Magyars.

"And worst of all, because he is so progressive and so determined to be a good Magyarized citizen, he has no tolerance or understanding for the Zionists!" She shook with anger and tears streamed down her cheeks, "His Neologs hate us because they think we're going to upset the fragile tightrope they are walking on...between who they are and who they're trying to be."

"You're right, Eszter," Stefan stirred his coffee, quietly contemplating Eszter's point of view, "but your father is also right."

He ventured further in an attempt to calm her anger, "You know my father is a great advocate of Magyarization, because he believes it's the only way to bring about a civil society within Hungary. With so many different peoples living together in Hungary, seeking national unity is a good thing. It's not the *idea*, Eszter, that is the evil thing. It's the men who govern us who have turned the ideas of ethnic assimilation into something alien, something to fear, to hate. It's Horthy and his right-wing pawns that have made these abhorrent policies."

Eszter nodded her head, "Your words help, Stefan, but I still feel terrible about everything that is happening to us."

"I do believe that restoration of the monarchy is the way. Karl is a reasonable man, kind and wise," Stefan stated convincingly, "if we bring Karl back to Budapest as our king, I'm certain he would bring justice. He would abolish these absurd policies and rule with an open mind and fairness. The king would enact the true purpose of Magyarization—a democracy within Hungary where all peoples must be treated equally.

"Karl has never expressed any anti-Semite feelings," Stefan tried to console Eszter as he looked into her red, swollen eyes.

"My gentle Stefan." Eszter ran her fingers across Stefan's furrowed brow, brushing away strands of blond curls that fell into his eyes, "How can you still love me if the world hates me?"

"Eszter, I will always love you. It is evil that hates a beautiful, intelligent human being, not the world. Remember, you and I believe the world a beautiful place. Only those who see darkness and fear the world hate goodness and purity. How could anyone hate you, Eszter Klein? Or your brilliant father? Or anyone in your lovely family?"

"Thank you, Stefan," Eszter sighed and sank deeper into Stefan's chest. "You are so dear to me, Stefan; so good to me. I will love you forever."

—◆—

A few days later Dr. Klein went to Leopold's von Esté Fine Wine Company on Hércegprimas Street. He opened the great oak door, took the lift up to the first floor, gave his name to the receptionist, and asked if he might see the Duke. The receptionist, Judit, asked him to take a seat and turned to the telephone. In a few moments Dr. Klein noticed that the lift moved upward and then back down again. The Duke came out of the brass cage with his hand extended, "Professor Klein, so good to see you. Please come up to my office."

They entered the lift and Zol took them to the third floor. Leopold asked his secretary to bring coffee and ushered Dr. Klein into his office. They sat in leather chairs by the bay window. "What brings you here, Jakov?"

"Perhaps you have heard of Teleki's *numerous clausus*?" Leopold frowned and nodded in the affirmative. "I've lost my position at the Institute, Leopold, my position of almost thirty years," Jakov took a deep breath, "I thought, perhaps, there might be a place for me in your wine-making business...until things change and hopefully settle down a bit."

"I'm so sorry, Jakov. Teleki is a serious problem. Horthy will have to calm this disastrous situation." Leopold spoke with conviction, his anger unchecked, "We as Hungarians cannot discriminate against our own citizens, nor can we legally deprive them of their rights."

The secretary knocked and brought in the coffee.

"Of course, Jakov, there is a place for you here. We will find something and you can stay as long as you want or until you can go back to the Institute."

They sipped their hot coffees and Jakov smiled, "It is good to know such a fine man as you, Leopold. My faith in human beings has already been restored."

"Come Jakov," Leopold stood, "I will show you the operations on the first floor. They went down on the lift and Leopold introduced Dr. Klein to his staff. An empty desk by a window instantly became Dr. Klein's desk. Leopold and Jakov spoke with one of the technicians and decided to put Dr. Klein in charge of the maturation of selected wines and blends. Jakov was very pleased.

When Jakov walked out of the von Esté Fine Wine Company, he took a deep breath and looked up to the sky, thinking to himself... *things are not so dismal after all... things could be worse .. look at this beautiful day.* He walked all the way back to the Jewish Quarter to Dohány Street, past the Great Synagogue, and up the stairs of his home. He opened his door and called out, "Éva, I'm home from my new job at the von Esté Fine Wine Company."

1921
Late Winter, Budapest

Leopold received a letter from Eugenia informing him that she and Konrad were in India. She wrote of Calcutta and Chowringhee Avenue and the Hooghly River, Delhi and Agra with its Taj Mahal and of Madras on the Bay of Bengal and how they planned to sail to Ceylon within the month. Such exotic names and places, Leopold was filled with wonder and looked forward to hearing her stories in the summer in Siófok. She had written she and Konrad would return to Cologne in early spring

Eugenia's tone turned serious when she warned Leopold about the Nazi Party, *growing in strength and popularity in Germany* and her fear that *the movement would likely spread throughout Europe. It is an ugly group... they are filled with hatred and revenge for Germany's loss in the Great War. A party such as this one has no place in a civilized country like Germany.*

Leopold refolded the letter and slid it into the top drawer of his desk. As he pushed the drawer closed, he smiled as he thought of his exotic sister and her companion... their fantastic stories of distant places and their embellished tales of characters they met along the way. Letters from Eugenia were sporadic at best and he enjoyed rereading them as a way to connect with her.

Although Leopold did consider Eugenia's worries about a workers' movement, that problem did not concern him so much at the moment. His concern was his king, Leopold was still very hopeful that Hungary would bring the king back to his throne. Karl, the good man that he was, would bring peace and equality to all the people of Hungary; of that Leopold was certain.

Spring, Switzerland

As spring came to Switzerland the deposed King Karl felt restless; he sensed his life was languishing away. With prodding from Zita, he began to seriously consider reclaiming his Hungarian throne. In secret negotiations with the French Prime Minister, Aristide Briand, Karl became convinced the French and the other royals of Europe would support his return to the Hungarian throne. Karl was also convinced that none of Hungary's neighboring countries, the *Little Entente*, would interfere with his return.

Karl was an optimist. He loved the Hungarian people and knew they loved him. Karl was certain once they heard of his return, they would be overjoyed to have their rightful king on the throne once again. Karl and a small cadre of supporters decided to return to Hungary on Easter weekend, a time when most of Hungary's government was on holiday. By shaving his mustache, traveling in inconspicuous clothing, and carrying a fake Portuguese passport, Karl entered Hungary undetected. He traveled directly to the Hungarian town of Szombathely, home of Count János Mikes, a loyal monarchist and long-time friend.

In the early hours of Easter morning many of Karl's supporters gathered in Szombathely at the palace of Count Mikes. Very quickly Karl realized opinions varied; there were those who encouraged his return and those, like the Duke Leopold von Esté, who warned, "the time is not right."

"Horthy is too powerful at the moment. It is not likely he will give up his power easily." Leopold implored the king, "A period of negotiation would serve you better, a compromise of some sort, perhaps, that might allow Horthy to retain some importance."

"The National Assembly is dominated by conservative right-wing groups," warned another supporter, the Baron Balazs. "The Christian Union members are primarily monarchists. They believe in your legitimate claim as the ordained monarch and favor your return, but then there are the free-electors who favor electing a king of their choice, creating a kind of democratic monarchy."

"Since you do not have the support of the assembly's majority, I cannot see how you can push Horthy out," argued Count Andrássy. "Horthy has the support of all minority factions within the assembly."

Several members of Horthy's government shared even more negative opinions with Karl. Only Colonel Antal Lehár, an avid supporter, promised an army for Karl's protection. But even Lehár warned Karl, "A return to Budapest at this time would be a dangerous undertaking."

At last Karl decided he must speak directly with Prime Minister Teleki who just happened to be on retreat near Szombathely. A meeting was quickly arranged.

"The whole idea of your restoration is preposterous!" Teleki declared. "I have the utmost respect for you, Your Majesty," Teleki asserted forcefully, "but it is far too soon for you to attempt a return. In fact, for your safety you should leave Hungary immediately."

Teleki paced the room as he tried to convince Karl his attempt at restoration would bring chaos, "The countries on Hungary's borders, the *Little Entente*, will attack if you try to retake the throne. Civil war will certainly erupt throughout Hungary. It will be nothing short of another disaster for Hungary! Please reconsider!"

"I have obviously wasted my time here, Teleki." Karl appeared quite disturbed, "I should have spoken with Horthy in the first place." He straightened himself, engaged Teleki eye to eye, and pronounced, "I demand an immediate audience with Horthy. Inform him I am on my way to the palace. He should prepare for my imminent return to Budapest."

Even though Teleki left for Budapest at that moment, he arrived there long after Karl, due to some sort of car trouble...he said. So, when Karl arrived at the Buda Palace unannounced, he interrupted the surprised Horthy at his Easter lunch—an extremely awkward situation for both men. They spoke privately in the regent's office, which only a short time before had been Karl's official office in the Buda Palace.

Karl simply informed Horthy, "I have returned for my throne and you must give up your power at once."

Horthy, quite astonished, declared, "Your Majesty, you must return to Switzerland at once, before the *Little Entente* realizes that you are here! They will attack Hungary if we allow a Hapsburg back on the throne...at least at this time!"

"I have assurances from France," Karl declared, "that neither the *Great Entente* nor the *Little Entente* will interfere in my resumption of the throne."

Horthy doubted Karl's claim and the two men argued; each presenting reasons in support of their positions.

"You must acknowledge that in 1918 at the Schönbrunn Palace you swore allegiance to me as your Hapsburg monarch!" Karl reminded Horthy. "I am the Apostolic King of Hungary!"

Finally, the two men agreed to a three-weeks truce. Unfortunately for Karl his understanding of the truce was not the same as Horthy's. Karl believed the three weeks provided a time of preparation for his return to the throne, but Horthy considered the three weeks as time to remove any possibility for Karl's return to Hungary. Horthy encouraged Karl to leave the palace by a discreet rear exit. Horthy wanted him out of Budapest as soon and as quietly as possible. Karl returned to Szombathely naively feeling positive about the future.

On the Monday after Easter, representatives from the countries within the *Little Entente* arrived in Budapest to declare that, in fact, had Karl been allowed to return to the Hungarian throne, they would have declared war. On April first the National Assembly resolved to re-endorse Horthy as regent and to maintain the status quo in Hungary. The assembly also issued an arrest warrant for Karl. On April third the French denied any official agreement to support Karl's restoration to the throne. On April fifth Karl, disappointed and disillusioned, left Hungary by train for Switzerland. The Easter Crisis came to a quiet end.

—⁓—

The non-actions of Teleki during the Easter Crisis upset Horthy. Horthy perceived that Teleki had deserted him without warning to deal with Karl, so Horthy demanded Teleki's resignation as prime minister. Horthy then immediately appointed Count István Bethlen to the position. Bethlen designated the major goal of his new government, the Party of Unity, as bringing peace to Hungary by calming all tensions between factions within and outside the country.

Bethlen, determined to stop the disruptive activities of the Social Democrats and trade unions, promised to legalize their activities if they would stop organizing peasants, stop their call for strikes, and stop spreading anti-Hungarian and anti-Jewish propaganda. Unknown to most Hungarians, Bethlen actually paid the radical conservatives with money and government jobs to stop their harmful campaigns against his government and Hungary's minorities.

Summer

Throughout the summer an undercurrent of debate, optimism tainted with pessimism, colored every conversation. *Was the king coming back? Would Horthy stop his return? Would there be war? Could good King Karl bring peace and prosperity to the people of Hungary?*

Leopold and Tamás, advocates for the return of the king, were aware of a militant group of legitimists who were uniting behind a call for Karl's immediate return to the throne.

"Karl, as the *legitimate* monarch, is entitled by God to sit upon the Hungarian throne! We *legitimists* believe it is important to diminish the power and prestige of Horthy. We see Horthy as the major obstacle to the king's return.

"But we know a confrontation with Horthy will mean trouble." Leopold and Tamás were monarchists, but never militant in their support of Karl. They would try to remain optimistic, although cautious.

Stefan and Rudolf listened carefully to the discussions Leopold and Tamás engaged in with each other and with their friends. Stefan, in particular, seemed more interested in politics than ever before. He wanted to know his father's opinion about the treatment of the Jews and asked Leopold, "Do you believe the king will bring tolerance, fairness to the Jewish people?"

When Leopold affirmed that the king had benevolent feelings for Hungarian Jews and would bring relief to their situation, Stefan became convinced that the king's return would provide the best solution for the Jews.

Stefan spent most of the summer in Budapest working in the office and seeing Eszter as often as possible, but when he was at the lake, he and Rudolf engaged in all their usual pastimes. Rudolf, almost eighteen, had returned to Lake Balaton from Prague for the whole summer. He spent his time working in Leopold's vineyards and helping his grandmother. By now Rudolf could do anything he wanted without calling attention to his missing lower leg. Both he and Stefan enjoyed the quiet respite offered by the lake, finding the atmosphere a relief from the heated political conversations in Budapest and Prague.

Klára and Rózsa were, of course, oblivious to any politics of the day. Especially when away from Budapest, the troubled times seemed very distant to their lives. The two young girls spent their summer days happily engaged in the normal, lazy activities they loved so much. The special times spent with Stefan and Rudolf when they weren't busy were the best, especially those days when they all piled into Stefan's Alfa Romeo and drove for miles. Rudolf flattered the two eleven-year-olds by drawing their portraits. His pastel drawings were sensitive and revealed as much of the girls' personalities as they did their outer appearance. Laughing Rózsa, her blueberry blue eyes peeking mischievously from under a halo of golden-red hair and serious Klára, her striking green eyes, shy and mysterious, always concealing her true feelings.

One afternoon as they sailed lazily across the lake in a small skiff Stefan asked, "What do you think of Hungarian politics at the moment, Dolf? In particular, what do you think of the king's possible return to Hungary's throne? Where do you stand? I support the king's return enthusiastically. He would likely bring a bit of common sense back to the government. What do you think?"

"It's possible that the king could put a stop to the oppression and discrimination. I would like to see his return. In my opinion, Horthy tolerates anti-Semites and now he's leaning too far right. I'm concerned."

"Father agrees with you. He's leery of Horthy's positioning. Horthy speaks well of the king and even suggests the king is welcome to return, but then he and his assembly seem to move in an opposite direction, perhaps even toward a dictatorship."

"In Prague there's uncertainty as well," Rudolf offered his perspective. "Instead of moving right as the Germans and Horthy seem to be doing, the Czechs are moving left. The Czechoslovakia Social Democratic Workers'

Party just formed the Communists Party of Czechoslovakia."

"At the very least I give Horthy credit for his staunch stand against communism and the Bolsheviks," reflected Stefan. "Although I don't like everything he's doing, he did drive out the Reds and most of us are relieved by his disdain for communism."

"Men are always talking about politics," yawned Klára, "I think politics is boring to girls."

"Not to my sister," denied Rózsa, "that's all Eszter ever thinks about or talks about."

In August, Horthy released official word to the governments of the *Great* and *Little Ententes* that preparations were under way for the king's return to Hungary's throne. "It is the desire of the Hungarian people," justified Horthy, "that we prepare for the return of their king."

Leopold remained skeptical about Horthy's sincerity and wrote to the king in Switzerland, warning him and his supporters. *Your majesty must be aware that Horthy's actions may not match his words.*

"I doubt that Horthy will ever allow Karl to return to the throne of Hungary," Leopold said sorrowfully. "Horthy has too much power now. Just tell me the name of one powerful man who has given up his power willingly!"

September

Stefan traveled back and forth between the lake and Budapest all summer. He worked in both the vineyards and in his father's office, learning all that he could about the grapes. Although Stefan and Eszter spent as much time together as possible, he never went to the Klein's home, instead always meeting her at cafés or at the apartments of friends.

Eszter's brothers had seen her with Stefan on occasion, but no one acknowledged the possibility of a relationship, since the very thought of any attachment between the two would be completely unacceptable. Based purely on religious grounds, a Jew and a Gentile Catholic could not possibly form a lasting union. Their families were aware the two young people had a fascination for each other, but everyone chose to ignore that fact, believing their infatuation would eventually pass, as young people naturally lose interest.

For months Stefan attended Zionist meetings with Eszter. His feelings remained mixed about the movement. He understood their passion in wanting to immigrate to Palestine, to their *promised land*, but he did not understand why the Zionists felt so compelled to leave their homes in Hungary. In his opinion, there should be no acceptable reason for Jews to feel so unwelcomed in their own homeland.

"Your father has made a good life for himself and his family here in Budapest." Stefan argued with Eszter, "He, like my father, believes all minorities can live together peacefully and successfully. Why must you leave Hungary for a place so far away?"

"Because, Stefan, regardless of how it may seem at the moment, Christian Magyars have never and will never truly accept us. We live in a constant precarious situation. At any moment, at the government's whim, we can lose our jobs, be dismissed from our classes, or unfairly taxed for ordinary services. You've seen it happen, it will happen again. That's why Jews want their own nation so desperately.

"My own father, the Neolog Magyar, is simply hopeful." Eszter could be so firm, so determined when making her point, "Father always wants to trust those in charge who, he believes, care about his interests. But I know prejudice is deeply ingrained, Stefan."

Eszter's tone became angrier as she spoke, "Dressing in Hungarian fashion or speaking perfect Hungarian or—worst of all—fighting in their wars, none of it matters! We are still considered *others*! Not *true* Hungarians!"

—⁕—

While Stefan sat waiting for Eszter in a Váci Street sidewalk café one late September afternoon, he noticed Efrem Meyer engaged in a heated conversation with another young man. Efrem worked in the accounting office of the von Esté Fine Wine Company. Stefan had known of him for a number of years, purely on a professional basis. With no effort on his part, Stefan could hear clearly their argument.

The two men were debating an article in the Jewish newspaper, *Egyenlőség*. Stefan heard Meyer say rather emphatically, "The *Egyenlőség* is an anti-Zionists newspaper! Here is the evidence that there are Jews who despise the Zionists! Listen to this. '*Zionism is a perverse manifestation of religious fanaticism, the bastard of evil parents!*'"

"So, what is your point, Efrem?" posed the second man. "What you have read is true! The Zionists make trouble for all of us. Zionists are unpatriotic! They put all of the Hungarian Jews in jeopardy! The authorities should be notified...Zionists may be engaged in illegal activities. Perhaps, all active Zionists in Budapest should be charged with treason!"

"Absalom, your attitude is insane!" Efrem was quite heated, "Here, I have an old issue of *Mult és Jövő*. You must read Patai's words!"

Efrem handed a folded and worn paper to Absalom.

"Patai's argument on behalf of Zionism makes your anti-Zionism reasons fall apart as quickly as this *keksz*." Efrem crushed a cookie in his hand as he stood up and shook the crumbs onto the table. He left the café quickly in a huff.

Stefan sipped his coffee and contemplated what he had heard. *Danger*, he thought, *yet another reason to encourage Eszter to withdraw from the Zionists. If*

Jews are against the Zionists and threaten to inform on them to the government, Eszter could be arrested!

He was deep in thought when she arrived, gave him a kiss on the cheek and sat down, smiling and cheerful. Stefan decided to wait until a later time to bring up Zionism. He knew his views on the subject would only upset her and he wanted no arguments with Eszter tonight. He only wanted to hold her safely in his arms.

October

Stefan burst into his father's library without knocking, "Papa! Have you heard the rumors? Karl is coming back...the king will return!"

"Yes, Stefan, we have heard. Tamás and I are in the midst of discussing this letter I received this morning."

"I just ran into Fábián Vadas in town, Papa. Fábián is on his way to Sopron. That's where the king will enter Hungary...at Sopron," Stefan was so excited, he was nearly breathless, "I told Fábián I would meet him there."

"Stefan, slow down. I'm sending my response to the king to let him know his timing is wrong. Bethlen is much opposed to the king's return and General Gömbös will raise an army against the king. Karl must approach this crucial decision with great caution and, above all, diplomacy."

"Papa, what are you saying? The sooner the king comes to power again the sooner our people can receive fairness, equality," Stefan was very frustrated. "I thought you fully supported the king's return."

"I do, Stefan, but Karl's position, coming from outside, is not tenable. He must be invited back by Horthy and the assembly. Otherwise, it appears that his entry into Hungary is a putsch and Karl is not strong enough to support a coup."

Leopold seemed very worried, "It would be better, Stefan, if you stay out of it."

"But, I feel strongly, Papa. I want to be there to welcome the king."

"I advise against it, Son. There will be trouble if Karl does not stay in Switzerland. I am hopeful he will not come," Leopold put his hand on Stefan's shoulder, "Please, Stefan, heed my advice and do not go to Sopron."

"Perhaps I should go." Stefan was restless, "If the king does come, I could convey your warning to him."

Stefan felt totally deflated, quite the opposite of his feeling of exhilaration when he had entered the library.

"I'll pour a brandy for all of us," said Tamás, sensing Stefan's profound disappointment. "We share your love for our king, Stefan," Tamás tried to be convincing, "We, too, believe in him. We want his return, but we are concerned about his well-being."

The three men raised their glasses and toasted to the health of the king and then spontaneously gave each other a vigorous embrace.

Leopold spoke to Stefan again, "We may be headed toward tumultuous days, Stefan. Stay here in Budapest…promise me, Stefan…attend to the wine business and let politics spin to its own will. At this moment, there is little we can do."

—⁓—

The rumors were true. Karl had decided to make a second attempt to regain the throne of Hungary. He felt time was running out, partly because his Swiss visa was going to expire on the thirty-first of October.

"My family and I have been living in exile in Switzerland long enough!" Karl stated his feelings aloud, "Where are we to go? The time has come for us to return to our home in Hungary!"

Eager to return to Hungary, Zita agreed with her husband wholeheartedly. Her primary goal, her ambition for Karl, had always been for him to once again secure his rightful place as the King of Hungary and, thereby, assure their son, Otto, his divine right of succession to his father's throne. Zita herself began to make contacts with powerful Hungarian businessmen who she believed would help Karl with the details of his imminent return.

In October Karl and Zita left their children at their Swiss chalet near Lake Lucerne and flew from Switzerland to the Cziráky estate near Sopron.

Stefan von Esté was waiting there for his king with more than twenty former Austro-Hungarian dignitaries gathered at the hilltop Czíráky estate—aristocrats, industrialists, and liberal thinkers, all legitimists, loyal to the king, anxious for the restoration of Karl to the throne of Hungary.

Stefan paced back and forth across the stones of the Czíráky castle terrace smoking one cigarette after another. It seemed they would never come. The day was gray and cool. His breath and smoke swirled around him as he moved back and forth across the veranda. Finally, he heard the buzz of a low-flying plane. All the men came together at the balustrade and gave a cheer. The king was here at last. The plane emerged from the low clouds and then disappeared again behind the trees along the horizon.

The men left the veranda, passed through the great hall and gathered on the gravel drive at the front of the house. Their conversation was sparse. A morning mist rose from the lawn that stretched out in front of them. All eyes scanned the forest below for signs of the approaching king. At last several cars emerged from the forest and followed the driveway leading to the house from the distant landing field.

Count Gyula Andrássy stamped out his cigarette and said in a deep, low voice, "I just swore an oath before Bethlen and the whole parliament that there would be no attempt at restoration by the king until Hungary was ready for it," he laughed, "so, why am I here waiting for my king?"

"Because Hungary is ready for the return of her legitimate sovereign, Karl the Fourth! He has the royal ancestral right, the God-given right! We *are* ready for him!"

A cheer went up from the men as they moved into a respectful formation to welcome the king. When the black touring car stopped in the graveled drive, two of the Cziráky servants opened the car door and stood at attention as King Karl, dressed in full military uniform, stepped out onto Hungarian soil, followed by his beautiful queen, Zita. Clearly, from their broad smiles, the couple was thrilled to be in Hungary standing among dear and loyal friends, many of whom they had known all their lives.

Count József Cziráky guided the king and queen into the grand house where servants showed them to rooms where they could freshen themselves before lunch. When the king and queen returned to the dining room they were seated at opposite ends of the table. The other guests took their places around the dining table set for twenty-four.

Over a lunch, including *vadas* and *fácán*, cold game and wine, the conversation grew animated and optimistic. Stefan had brought wine from his father's cellars and he rose to give a toast, "My father, the Duke Leopold, who deeply regrets his absence on this auspicious occasion, sends his heartfelt good wishes and support for the return of our King and Queen! *Egészségére!* To your health!"

Stefan bowed to the royal couple as the others jumped to their feet and responded loudly and positively. Stefan continued, impulsively, "He and my mother extend to Your Majesty and your queen an invitation to be guests in their Pest home within the month!"

Again cheers rose from the men standing around the table. The king stood and raised his glass, "We accept your dear father's invitation. Now, on to Budapest!"

And once again, cheers.

In an effort to justify his lie to himself, Stefan rationalized the evidence. Convinced by the outpouring of support for the king's return, Stefan had no doubt of success. He imagined when the king marched successfully into Budapest his father would be one of the first to welcome the royal couple and the king would thank him for his support and kind words. His falsehood—on behalf of his father—made sense, it was perfectly logical. Stefan ceased to feel any guilt.

Servants brought in course after course while the king and his guests discussed the restoration. Colonel Antal Lehár related the latest information regarding Sopron, "The city itself is primarily a Magyar-speaking stronghold for pro-monarchists. The ranks of soldiers are, to the man, legitimists, loyal to Your Majesty's legitimate claim to the throne."

"My Huszars will support Your Majesty's return to Budapest," proclaimed Pál Hegedüs, "They are prepared to storm the parliament with sabers drawn, if necessary."

Everyone shook their heads in agreement as Lehár added, "But there are concerns. We know the *Great Entente* has spies in Sopron and rumors have spread already about Your Majesty's arrival in Hungary."

"Times have changed in Budapest. Horthy has replaced our friend, the pro-monarchist Teleki with the very conservative, anti-Hapsburg István Bethlen," observed Fábián Vadas. "This change is not in our favor and may cause more trouble than we want or expect. And then, of course, there is General Gömbös to consider.

"Gömbös, supreme commander of the *Honvéd*," Vadas continued his point, "has threatened to use violence against the king if your majesty should return to Budapest."

No one present at the king's table on this day at the Cziráky estate thought Gömbös would dare act against the king. All in agreement, they reassured Karl of his righteous mission.

"I do not expect resistance upon my return to the throne." Karl stated, "The people are on our side."

"His Majesty has Divine authority to reclaim his throne." Zita interjected, "He holds the scepter of St. Stephen. Karl is our rightful king."

All the men leapt to their feet, raised their glasses once again and in unison shouted, "Long Live Karl, King of Hungary!"

At the close of lunch, the king promoted Colonel Lehár to the rank of General and made Count Stefan von Rákovszky the Prime Minister of Hungary, thereby negating the right of Bethlen to legitimately hold that position. Karl appointed others at the table to positions in his provisional cabinet. After all, Karl announced to everyone, since he was once again present in Hungary there was no longer any need for Horthy to hold the position of regent.

General Lehár announced the cars were ready to take the king to Sopron where he planned to meet the troops and view the trains for his glorious Budapest homecoming. The king and queen settled back into the car's smooth leather seats and watched the vibrant fall colors stream by the windows as the car made its way to Sopron through the Lőver hills and forests. The king had decided Zita would stay at the Hotel Pannonia, while he preferred to stay in camp with his troops.

Stefan rode in the automobile that followed behind the king into the city. When the king's entourage reached the hotel, it was Stefan who helped Zita to her accommodations while Lehár escorted Karl to the military camp at the edge of the city. Afterwards Stefan traveled to the von Esté family castle. He and old Gáspár sat by the fire in the great reception room and spoke of days past and of new days in the future, a future they expected to be brighter with the return of their king.

Although Stefan feared the severe anti-Semitic leanings of Horthy and Bethlen, he had no doubt that King Karl would hold no such prejudices against his Jewish subjects. Stefan determined he would try to speak with the king during their journey to Budapest to discern the king's true feelings toward Jews.

By the next morning, word had spread, "*The king is in Sopron!*" Sopron's citizenry lined the town's streets to welcome their king. They waved banners, threw flowers, and shouted, "*Karl! King of Hungary!*" and "*Zita! Our Queen!*" These sincere expressions of loyalty greatly moved Karl and Zita. They felt reaffirmed by the outpouring of support, an exuberant confirmation for the Hapsburg restoration. General Lehár, watching the crowd surge toward the king's car as it made its way slowly through the town square, spotted several *Entente* spies despite their attempt to blend into the masses. The general sent two of his lieutenants to follow their movements.

As the king's parade began to subside, Lehár's informers returned to relate that the *Entente* spies were at the train station waiting for a train to Vienna. Convinced the king needed to arrive in Budapest as soon as possible, Lehár wasted no time organizing his troops and supplies for their train to the capital.

By mid-morning hundreds of volunteer soldiers made their way into Sopron from villages and farms to become a part of Karl's glorious restoration. They were anxious to rid Hungary of the Regent Horthy, believing restoration of the king would also restore Hungary's golden era of prosperity enjoyed during the great Hapsburg Empire.

Late in the evening hours of October twenty-seventh Lehár's military train, filled with the fearsome Huszars and their leader, Pál Hegedüs, finally pulled out of the Sopron station. Almost fourteen hours later the royal train carrying Karl and Zita, their royal soldiers, many Austro-Hungarian dignitaries, and Stefan left Sopron. When the Huszars reached the pro-monarchist city of Győr, the decision was made to wait for the royal train to catch up. Meanwhile the Győr city commander, General Lőrinczy, surrendered to Hegedüs without any confrontation, but confessed he had contacted Horthy about the arrival of the Huszars in Győr.

Lőrinczy also informed Hegedüs that a message from Horthy had been received. As soon as the king arrived in Győr, he was given the message. Karl read aloud the straight-forward pronouncement from Horthy: "The Great Entente protests fervently the restoration of the Hapsburg king and will respond with a violent reaction if Karl should pursue this folly."

Stunned, the king wondered...*Am I mistaken to believe that I still have the French Premier Briand's assurances? I am certain that I have the Great Entente's support! Neither France nor England nor Russia will interfere in my reclamation of the Hungarian throne*...so he decided to ignore Horthy's warning and stated aloud, "We must proceed to Budapest!"

Zita pointed out to her husband, "Listen, Dearest, the people are calling out to you. Their king! They are calling you their savior. They expect your restoration will restore Hungary's Golden Age."

Hundreds of enthusiastic men and boys, desiring to be a part of the king's jubilant return, eagerly jumped onto the trains as they rolled through the countryside. Karl felt a great sense of optimism, Confidence swept through the trains, affecting everyone. Both Karl and Zita began to anticipate their regal lives beginning anew in the Hungarian court.

As the fast-moving trains steamed closer to Budapest, the forward locomotive abruptly stopped, forcing the royal train to a standstill as well. Pro-Horthy forces from the nearby town of Komárom had blown up a section of track. Lehár's monarchist troops moved into action immediately; some to guard the trains while a larger contingent repaired the track. As the wait for repairs dragged on, a nervous tension grabbed both troops and royals. The dramatic change of mood from assurance to anxiety spread quickly.

Lehár thought the town of Komárom should be destroyed for this treason against the king, but Karl refused any kind of revenge against the town, defending the villagers as his beloved subjects. The townspeople affirmed Karl's optimistic view of their town when they gathered around his train and shouted their support for the king.

While the trains remained stalled—only one hour away from Budapest—Karl began to initiate new action. He ordered his Premier Stefan von Rákovszky to telephone the "Pretender" Premier Bethlen and deliver the king's message to him.

When Bethlen answered, Rákovszky informed him that he was no longer the legitimate premier and that the tracks to Budapest must remain clear for the royal train. Bethlen found Rákovszky's words laughable and simply answered, "Please call back in fifteen minutes."

Unable to further contact Bethlen for more than an hour, an infuriated Rákovszky called Bethlen at his home and shouted into the phone, "As of this moment, Sir, you are court-martialed! If King Karl is not allowed to return to Budapest, you will be hanged!"

Lehár's goal to reach the Sandberg tunnel under the Danube River by dawn was delayed once again just beyond Komárom. An official government automobile sent by Horthy pulled alongside the military train and signaled for it to stop. General Lehár and Premier Rákovszky got off the train and approached the car. The passenger inside was one of Horthy's ministers, Dr. József Vass who, on foot, met Lehár and Rákovszky beside the tracks.

"I have a letter for His Majesty from the Hungarian Regent Horthy," Vass announced.

"Inform Horthy that any future letters he may write to His Majesty should be delivered to the king at his palace in Budapest." With a click of his heels and a cursory bow, Rákovszky dismissed Vass without looking at him.

Arrogant prig, Vass muttered under his breath as he turned from Rákovszky and walked briskly back to his car and sped away.

The moment Rákovszky returned to the train, he ordered the engineer to proceed, walked straight to Karl's private car and informed the king that Horthy had sent yet another warning. Rather than show Horthy's letter to the king, Rákovszky shared its implication...*stop your misguided mission to reclaim Budapest.* Rákovszky added, "But I implore Your Majesty to disregard any advocacy on the part of Horthy to convince you to disengage in your quest." Rákovszky's voice was filled with anger as he addressed his king, "In my opinion, Your Majesty's mission to regain your ordained role as the King of Hungary is a righteous one."

The king decided to take Rákovszky's advice and proceed to Budapest.

When Dr. Vass returned to the Buda Palace, he went directly to Horthy to report the results of his mission, "I personally never met with nor saw the king." Vass added with some hesitation, "The king's *premier*, Rákovszky, took the letter from me with great disrespect. I dare surmise that, in fact, the king may never see your letter. And, even further, my skepticism leads me to believe that even if His Majesty does read your letter he will be advised to ignore your demands."

Horthy shook his head, partly for what he believed to be the king's naïveté and partly for the personal sorrow he felt for Karl, a man he knew to be kind and sincere. Horthy met with his ministers to relay the newest information regarding the king's progress toward Budapest.

"I begged the king to abandon his advance on Budapest," Horthy stated passionately as he conveyed to his ministers the contents of the letter he had send by Vass to the king. "I told him that the *Little Entente* would surely invade Hungary if a Hapsburg king returned to the throne. Where is his good sense, that he cannot see the disastrous result of this folly? Who knows what the outcome could be...*civil war...a Bolshevik coup...anarchy?* I am most distraught! I even promised a safe exit from Hungary for him and his queen...yet he comes!"

Soon afterwards Horthy ordered General Gömbös to call together all government forces, including Gömbös's own cavalry units, to defend the capital. By the morning of October twenty-ninth, Gömbös had rallied a great contingent of regular government troops. Armed with information from Colonel Perczel and other spies, Gömbös was fully aware of the king's location. Gömbös harbored a deep hatred for all royals, including the Regent Horthy and his ilk.

Without Horthy's knowledge, Gömbös extended his own authority to recruit irregular bands of rebels and students, particularly students with

Bolshevik leanings who naturally hated royals. Gömbös led his army of regulars and irregulars out of the city and up into a high terrain called Türkensprung, *the Turk's Jump*. Gömbös and his army lay in wait in the Türkensprung Hills high above the railway line between the ancient Hapsburg ancestral city of Tata and Budapest.

The king's forward military train, loaded with fearsome Huszars, sped toward Budapest. The royal train stopped in the Tata Station to meet with Prince Ferenc Esterházy, the king's dear friend. The prince welcomed Karl and Zita to Tata and pledged his allegiance to their restoration. After all, Prince Esterházy represented the ancient Hapsburg family in the region, they were related. Although their reunion was warm and genuine, Esterházy warned the king that General Gömbös and his armies, including Bolsheviks, were waiting in the nearby Türkensprung Hills. Karl was disturbed by the news and decided his train must speed ahead to catch up with his military. They bid Esterházy farewell and implored him to visit them soon at their Buda Palace.

As Karl's train pulled away from the station, the people of Tata crowded around the royal cars and shouted cheers of encouragement and adoration. The royal train steamed on toward Budapest as quickly as possible, but as it neared the town of Budaörs, a suburb of Budapest, artillery fire could be heard. The royal train slowed and finally stopped before crossing the viaduct into Budaörs, waiting to proceed until Lehár's troops could take control of the situation ahead.

Karl and Zita used the delay to disembark from the train and stroll along the tracks. Soldiers took the time to relax by lounging in the grass, playing cards, talking of Budapest. Since it was Sunday, Zita decided the priests who were in their company should conduct the celebration of Holy Mass. A table with chalice and paten was arranged in an open field alongside the tracks and communion was given to all passengers, soldiers, dignitaries and aristocrats on the train, including Stefan. During the Eucharist celebration, gunshots could be heard sporadically, but by the end of the service the sounds had grown to a barrage of artillery fire. Strengthened by the priests' blessings, the legitimist–monarchist soldiers formed their ranks and rushed across the viaduct into Budaörs with no idea of the severity of the conflict that lay ahead.

Stefan and Fábián Vadas ran with the soldiers, guns in hand, across the bridge. Stefan's heart pounded in his throat, beads of perspiration formed on his upper lip and brow, even though the air was cool. Surrounded by uniformed regulars and volunteers in all manner of dress from the finest gentleman to the peasant, Stefan still wore the suit and tie he had worn in Sopron. He noticed the faces of those around him, some were smiling broadly, others looked serious, and still others had tears running down their cheeks.

Stefan's compatriots enthusiastically shouted slogans of support for the king as they ran toward Budaörs. Stefan felt neither joy nor fear at this moment on the bridge; he only knew that he believed completely in the restoration of the king. His thoughts were of a king who would unite the people and put an end to discrimination against ethnic citizens of Hungary, especially the Jews. He believed Karl's cause was right and that victory would be theirs in the end.

Even before the legitimists and Stefan reached the end of the viaduct, bullets were whistling past their ears and quite suddenly several young men dropped in pools of blood. But still following the royal brigade Stefan and Fábián ran on together into the city of Budaörs.

The king and his queen stood in front of the royal train's engine and watched their men running to the viaduct, into the gunfire. Karl reached out for Zita's hand, "I never wanted war," he said. "I had not imagined that Magyar brother would ever rise up against Magyar brother."

"You are their rightful king!" Zita, her eyes filled with tears, repeated her conviction once again, as though she needed to reassure herself and Karl, "You were crowned with the regalia of St. Stephen. The throne is your apostolic right."

"I made it perfectly clear to everyone from the start that no blood should be spilt," he said in a whisper as the words caught in his throat.

Karl had believed with his whole heart that the people of Budapest would cheer his return and all would be as it should be. The two stood together staring into the distance as the sounds of artillery fire came closer.

Several hours earlier General Gömbös had watched Lehár's military train reach Budaörs. Gömbös's armies allowed the train to enter a very vulnerable space within the Budaörs train yards before they opened fire, stopping the train. Completely surprised to find the city so heavily fortified, Lehár's legitimists did not expect to become engaged in a full-fledged battle, but that is exactly what they got. The legitimist soldiers were caught in their locomotive cars strung out along the track surrounded by the enemy. The violent battle raged from the highlands of the Türkensprung into the center of Budaörs. Even though their position was at a great disadvantage, the legitimists continued their courageous fight despite the many quickly wounded or killed. The legitimists' situation deteriorated rapidly. Gömbös quickly encircled the forward cars, preventing any possibility of the train reversing to rejoin the royal train.

Once across the viaduct Stefan and Fábián along with their fellow soldiers found themselves in the midst of chaos. They ran in all directions to find cover from the onslaught of Gömbös's cavalry who brandished saber and gun. In the confusion Stefan, Fábián and their compatriots found themselves separated from one another and alone, crouching behind whatever they could find available in the train yards of Budaörs. Stefan could see the last car of Lehár's train in the distance, but to get there, they would have to run the gantlet of Gömbös's soldiers.

By late afternoon Stefan and Fábián had maneuvered their way to Lehár's train. Armed legitimists lay atop every car while others leveled their guns out the windows. When they saw Stefan and Fábián approaching, the legitimists fired relentlessly at the enemy to cover the run of Stefan and Fábián across the yard, allowing them to board the last car. As the two men walked through the heavily damaged cars, they were discouraged to find so many wounded and dying soldiers. Very little ammunition remained. Reports from the front of the train described the engine as too badly damaged to move either forward or backward. The train was immovable; they were trapped. Stefan and Fábián agreed they had to inform the king about this dire situation. Stefan expected that the legitimists would raise the white flag of surrender with the morning sun and he preferred to be with his king at that moment.

A group of nine, including Stefan and Fábián, agreed to leave the train and make their way back to the king as quickly as possible. Fortunately for the group their escape was aided by the weather, a dismal day with heavy gray clouds. Stefan, Fábián and their new allies lowered themselves down between the cars and crawled on their bellies under the cars over the tracks until they reached terrain more conducive to escape. A sharp vertical rise only a few yards from the track marked the landscape and included several large boulders that jutted upward into the gray sky. The small group inched their way one at a time over the tracks and onto the gravel berm separating the track from the rocky incline. Stefan slipped into the crevice and climbed the rocky surface upward, away from the tracks and eventually into golden leafy branches that covered the hills.

Their group moved northward toward the viaduct, timing their movements in accordance with clouds that darkened the sky. At last the little group reached the bridge at the very place where, mere hours before, Stefan and Fábián had eagerly run toward Budaörs. Now they had to make their way back across the viaduct under the watchful eyes of the enemy. Stefan and Fábián, followed by the others, moved out onto the bridge. They hunkered down against the iron railings and girders, cautiously making their way. Suddenly, about a third of the way across the bridge, shots rang out from behind them. Four of their group were shot immediately, two killed on the spot, and two wounded, including Stefan.

Stefan felt the burning pain of the bullet pass through his back and into his gut. He stumbled to his knees, thinking he was killed, but Fábián reached out to help him and Stefan responded with pure desire to keep moving away from Budaörs. Another of the non-wounded did the same for the other injured man while Fábián and another of their party turned to fire upon the advancing enemy. Stefan felt himself being lifted off his feet and carried. Shots continued back and forth until his rescuer was shot in the leg and Stefan was hit in the back a second time. At that moment it was Fábián who picked him up and carried him forward. As the small wounded group reached the midway point on the bridge, they were met by an onslaught of monarchist troops from the king's train who ran past them, firing at the enemy who retreated from the bridge at once. The monarchists turned back to help the wounded. Only three of Stefan's group of nine were left, including Stefan and Fábián Vadas.

Karl, frantic to know what was happening in Budaörs, had sent his own personal guards to advance across the viaduct and return with news from the forward train. It was that force of soldiers who ran into Stefan and his fellow retreating soldiers. With great haste they took Stefan and their report to the royal train. Karl recognized Stefan at once and had him brought into the king's private car where he was laid on a velvet sofa. Fábián stayed by Stefan's side. Karl felt miserable—here before him lay the battered son of one of Hungary's most loyal monarchist families. The king leaned over the young man and asked in genuine concern, "How are you? Is it bad?"

"I'm all right, Your Majesty," even in extreme pain Stefan managed one of his famous smiles for Karl and Zita, "I'm sorry the day did not go better. We'll try again tomorrow."

"Well, we'll make sure that you are back in your father's house by tomorrow. You are a brave soldier, Stefan. I am honored to have men like you with me."

"My surgeon is here," the king held Stefan's hand and stroked his bloodied blond hair as he spoke softly with compassion. "He will take care of you until you are safely home."

Fábián Vadas leaned close to Stefan and whispered, "I'm leaving now, Stefan. Things are going from bad to worse very quickly. I'm going back to Balatonfüred. The king will make certain you get back home to your father. Give my best to the duke."

Stefan managed to lift his hand to touch Fábián's shoulder, "Thank you, Fábián, for dragging me across that bridge."

Karl and Zita stepped outside the car to receive the report from their soldiers returning from Budaörs. The news they brought to the young pacifist king was devastating. One lieutenant exclaimed in rapid, almost breathless detail, "The legitimists…monarchists are surrounded and disabled. Their train can neither go forward nor backward. Many have been wounded and killed. Some brave souls fight on and are holding against Horthy's forces, but they have little hope without reinforcements or ammunition and," he took a deep breath and added with quiet resignation, "morning's light may bring a bloody slaughter, Your Majesty."

A late afternoon darkness seemed to cast a shroud of gloom as Karl looked into the eyes of the desperate soldiers who stood around him. The king paced back and forth beside the train. He could hardly think—his mind so burdened with pain and loss. *Events are not at all as I expected them to be. I believed my return would bring glory and goodness to the Hungarian people. This is turning out to be a horrible nightmare and my goals have been terribly misunderstood. Now what can I do to make things right?*

Karl turned abruptly, boarded the train and ordered the engineer, "Take the train full-speed across the viaduct into Budaörs and then, straight on to Budapest."

Surrounded by his wife, ministers, and generals, Karl stood in his private car and declared, "We will proceed to Budaörs, seek an armistice with Gömbös, and then on to Budapest where I will negotiate with Horthy for an end to this violence."

Both Zita and Pál Hegedüs strongly objected to the king's plan. "We cannot trust Gömbös!" Hegedüs hotly protested, "He believes we are conspirators against the regent's government! We will all be court-martialed, possibly hanged on the spot!"

Nothing they said could change the king's resolve to proceed on to Budaörs and Budapest. "I am determined to stop the killing, to stop this indefensible violence. It is my ultimate goal to stop this hostility before it is too late."

Before the train began to move forward, Karl was joined by Zita in the locomotive's engine. He looked at her with vacant eyes, "Stopping this bloodshed has usurped my dream of the throne. Peace is a higher purpose."

In silence they waited together as the train made its way across the viaduct and into Budaörs. Government soldiers and artillery fire surrounded them as soon as they crossed the bridge. In the last hour of daylight as the royal train drew closer to the train yard, the engineer stopped the train. He turned to the king, "Your Majesty, I can take you no further into harm's way. The battle is too fierce! Your life and that of the queen are in danger!"

Karl felt a heavy weight—the dilemma, the choice. Then suddenly he saw monarchist soldiers running toward his train, many carrying the wounded with them. His choice was made. The enemy ceased fire, allowing fleeing soldiers to climb onto the king's train, while the wounded were put inside the cars. Karl realized that he had, even by accident, provided an escape for his troops and that gave him some solace. He nodded to the engineer in agreement that they should leave at once. The engineer threw the throttle into reverse and steamed out of Budaörs as fast as possible with soldiers clinging to the sides and tops of every car. Once across the viaduct, the engineer steamed backwards toward Tata, stopping along the way to pick up bands of retreating soldiers, many severely wounded.

The king's surgeon did all he could for Stefan. The second bullet had passed completely through Stefan's side and the wound was not serious, but the first bullet had lodged in Stefan's gut and the surgeon feared that wound was a fatal one. The surgeon said nothing of the severity of the wound to the king or to Stefan, but asked one of the queen's maids to tend Stefan. "Make him as comfortable as possible. He is feverish, so he may say nonsense. His name is Stefan."

While the train steamed on toward Tata, Stefan slipped in and out of consciousness. He had visions of Eszter's cool hand on his forehead and felt comforted knowing she was near. He said her name and tried to open his eyes to see Eszter's beautiful face. He dreamt he heard her voice, saying, *Shhhh, sleep now, Stefan. You'll be better in the morning.*

By dawn, the royal train pulled into Tata Station where Prince Esterházy arrived with news for the king. The prince was escorted to Karl's private car, served coffee by the king's valet, and then the prince spoke quietly, but forcefully, "Gömbös' troops are camped between here and Györ. They have severed the tracks farther to the west." He hesitated to give Karl the worst part, "I fear that you can proceed no farther. Gömbös is arresting everyone—everyone associated with *this*...what they are calling *a revolution against the legitimate government.*"

The prince looked upon his dear friend and king with compassion. He waited for Karl's response, but the king said nothing for a long moment. Then with his head lowered and in a quiet voice, the king said, "There are many wounded. There is one wounded man in the next car, the son of Duke von Esté. Is there a way we can send him safely home to his father?"

Prince Esterházy affirmed that it was possible. "I will arrange a car for him, but there are other pressing concerns, Your Majesty. You and your queen must become guests at my estate. I will do my best to give you a safe refuge until we can find a reasonable solution for this situation."

Karl acquiesced to the prince's suggestions without any resistance. He knew that he was finished.

After arriving in Tata, the prince immediately moved the heavily medicated Stefan to a private automobile, accompanied by two servants. The driver used less-traveled back roads for the sixty kilometers that separated Stefan from his home. Although several truckloads of Horthy's soldiers passed their car, they were not stopped or even noticed. At last the car sped into the Buda District, crossed the Chain Bridge, maneuvered through Pest and drove onto Andrássy Avenue. The driver parked the car in the entrance drive and then the two servants helped Stefan from the car. They knocked on the great door.

Tamás opened the door to find the servants standing with Stefan draped between them. Although an attempt had been made to clean Stefan's wounds and arrange his clothes more properly, the sight of him shook Tamás beyond words. Tamás brought the group into the foyer where Stefan slumped onto the stair and could go no further. A great commotion followed as the servant girls ran for Leopold and Elizabeth while Tamás directed Ana to call for the doctor at once.

When Leopold entered the foyer from his library the urgency did not seem clear, but when he realized Stefan was injured he hurried to his side. Leopold held his son's face in his hands and kissed his forehead. He pulled open Stefan's coat and gasped to see how much blood was lost. He realized at once his son's injuries were severe. Leopold motioned to all present, "Let us move him into the library. Ana, make a bed on the sofa. Silva, something warm to drink. Has someone sent for Dr. Kovács?"

Stefan held onto his father's hand and whispered, "We were not successful. Karl is not our king."

"It doesn't matter, Stefan. You are all that matters now."

At that moment Klára stood at the top of the stairs. She was terrified by the sight of her beloved brother lying motionless. She went down the stairs close to Leopold and leaned over Stefan. Her eyes filled with tears, she reached out for Stefan's hand. A grimace passed by his lips, but he looked at her and managed the faintest smile. Klára could barely hear him as he murmured, "Little Klára, my favorite girl, I love you always."

Stefan turned his eyes to his father. Leopold could see the light in Stefan's beautiful blue eyes beginning to dim. A sense of panic rose up in Leopold's chest, "Let's make him more comfortable in the library."

He helped the prince's servants lift and carry Stefan, "Dr. Kovács must be here soon."

Ana had blankets and pillows in place by the time the men carried Stefan to the library. Silva had a basin of water and towels to wash Stefan. She and Elizabeth carefully opened his shirt and cut away the bandages. They gently washed his face and body. Elizabeth applied a new bandage to his wound that continued to bleed profusely. Stefan, too weak to speak, touched Elizabeth's hand and she kissed him and held the cool cloth to his fevered brow.

At last Dr. Kovács arrived in the midst of the family tragedy. As soon as Tamás took the doctor's coat he walked directly to Leopold who met him at the library door. Dr. Kovács held Leopold's shoulders in an attempt to calm him, "Take me to Stefan, Leopold," and he entered the library.

Dr. Kovács examined Stefan's wounds and then quietly spoke to Leopold in a corner of the room. "My dear Duke, your son has a grave internal injury. His side wound is not serious, but there is a second bullet entry from the back with no exit. That bullet is lodged somewhere in his lower abdomen and it is that wound causing the fever and bleeding. There is nothing that can be done, this is a mortal wound."

Leopold wept with disbelief, "Surely there is something you can do."

"To be completely honest, Leopold, he should have died from this wound hours ago. I believe it may have been his sheer will to return home to you that allowed him to live."

"What can we do?" Leopold's words faltered as his hands trembled, "How much longer?"

"I will make him as comfortable as possible," consoled Dr. Kovács as he added, "Stay near him, Leopold, his time with us is short."

Klára came near to Elizabeth and Silva, "What can I do, Mommy?"

"Sit here by your brother, stroke his hand and talk to him."

Klára spoke softly to him, saying over and over, "You'll be all right; I know you'll be all right. I love you, Stefan."

Stefan's eyes flickered open for only a moment, "Little one," he murmured as he lightly tugged on her sleeve. He whispered, but she could not understand what he said, so she leaned closer to him.

Stefan whispered, "Eszter."

"Eszter? Did he say Eszter?" Elizabeth asked, but Klára answered that she was not sure.

Tamás and the entire household stayed near Stefan and the family for whom they all cared so deeply. Everyone wanted to help, but none knew what to do. Stefan had always been the joyful light within a very traditionally proper, somewhat staid family. Tamás had known Stefan nearly all his life; now at this moment Tamás felt the same devastation he had felt on that sad morning of Stefan's christening by Cili's coffin.

In the early evening, at the time for vespers, Leopold led the household in prayer. They knelt where they stood. Leopold began in his deep, powerful voice, "If it is not your will, Almighty Father, to heal Stefan of his injury, then we petition you through the mercy of your son Jesus Christ for an end to Stefan's pain, his deliverance from earthly bonds and peace for those who love him."

All answered "Amen" in unison. Some began to pray the rosary.

The hours of that evening passed slowly. Lights were kept low. Dr. Kovács administered morphine to ease Stefan's pain. Elizabeth and Silva continued to moisten Stefan's lips and cool his brow while he slept quietly, seemingly in peace. Leopold and Klára sat close to him and carried on a conversation of memories they supposed might bring him comfort. Only once when Klára mentioned Rudolf did Stefan seem to respond. In the hour past midnight Stefan's breath became irregular and a short time later they could no longer hear his breath at all.

Dr. Kovács listened with his stethoscope and then shook his head. Leopold let out a most excruciating moan. Klára hugged Stefan's legs and cried out, "Don't die, Stefan, don't leave us." Elizabeth fell back against the bookcase with her hand over her mouth to stifle the scream in her throat. Silva and Tamás held each other while the other servants hurried away from the foyer to their own private places to mourn the passing of their beautiful young master.

Meanwhile in Prague

An open window allowed a cold wind to fill Rudolf's flat with fresh air and aromas from the café across the alley. He sat at his desk working on a new placard for a graphic design project and thinking about going out to get an early supper when a classmate pushed open his door, "Hey, you got a telegram." Rudolf put down his drawing board and took the yellow envelope.

"I hope it's not bad news for you."

Rudolf tore open the envelope, unfolded the paper, and could not believe the words he read. *Dolf... Come home... Stefan is dead... We need you... Leopold.*

Completely inconceivable... he thought as he read the words again... *so few words. What possibly could have happened?* He stood, paced around his room. His mind void, he could muster no feeling. *Stefan dead? Incomprehensible!*

"Oh, it was bad news. I'm sorry."

"Yes, my friend has died. I must go to Budapest tonight." Rudolf grabbed his suitcase, packed absent-mindedly, descended the stair, and hailed a taxi for the station. He purchased a ticket for Budapest via Vienna, leaving at seven-thirty. He checked his watch, a little more than an hour to wait. He walked to the telegraph office and wired Leopold that he was coming by rail and would arrive at about two o'clock the next afternoon. He sent a second telegram to his grandmother informing her of his arrival. Finally Rudolf boarded the train. He went to his private sleeping compartment, anxious for darkness to surround him. He prepared for bed, pulled the shade, turned out the light, and slept fretfully most of the way.

After a fitful sleep Rudolf awoke early, dressed and made his way to the dining car for coffee. At the early hour he found the tables sparsely occupied. He chose a table, sat by the window and watched the approaching countryside speed toward him and pass in a blur. He admired the beauty of the landscape as the train followed the serpentine tracks through deep alpine valleys. High snow-capped peaks rose to the east and reminded him of ski trips with Stefan when they were boys and then he thought of all their adventures together.

In fact there were no memories from his youth that did not include Stefan. *Stefan... my handsome, fun-loving, loyal friend... the great athlete who swam across Lake Balaton, the faithful friend who pushed my wheelchair up Echo Hill on Tihany... Stefan... who encouraged me to be more extroverted... who praised me when I gave my opinions even if they differed from his own.* Rudolf smiled when he thought about their pranks and mischief and then he thought of Klára. *She must be devastated.* He could hardly wait to reassure her, to tell her that she had him, would always have him.

Rudolf stirred his coffee and noticed the elegant china cup and saucer. He observed the delicate lace tablecloth and curtains at the window. He knew Stefan would have noticed all the details of the dining car. Stefan would have commented on the fine intricacies of the wood carvings and moldings that gave the car its luxurious appeal. Stefan appreciated all fine things. How many times had he heard Stefan paraphrase Plato…

> *A contemplation of beauty brings something close to a divine experience…*
> *fine things and things of nature enhance life, raise expectations, and make*
> *savage destruction impossible.*

Stefan's convictions rang in Rudolf's memory and he shook his head at the loss of Stefan… *such a pure soul, so innocent as a youth, so passionate as an adult. And now he is dead. Something fine and beautiful destroyed.*

After about an hour's wait in Vienna, the train proceeded to Budapest, pulling into Keleti Station just after one-thirty. As he stepped from the train he was very happy to see Tamás coming toward him. They greeted each other warmly with an embrace. Rudolf asked immediately, "What happened to our dear Stefan?"

"I knew you would want information, so I asked your grandmother if it would be all right if I met your train."

As they walked together through the station toward the waiting auto, Tamás began his grave narrative, "A tragedy indeed has happened to all of us. The young count became a participant in the king's second attempt at restoration just last weekend. At Budaörs Horthy's government troops stopped the king's progress toward the capital. It was there in Budaörs where Stefan received his mortal wound. Prince Esterházy sent him home in a private car from Tata. Dr. Kovács attended to him, but there was nothing to be done. All the family was by his side when he passed away. Of course, you were thought of immediately by the duke."

"My deepest desire would to have been to be by his side. I cannot imagine life without Stefan. He was the catalyst for all of us," Rudolf responded pensively. "I read a small bit in the Prague newspaper on Monday about the king's venture, described as a fiasco, a catastrophe. Why was Stefan involved? I can only imagine as to his interest. I know he was convinced the king would bring a better Hungary for minorities, but I'm shocked that he involved himself in such danger!" And then Rudolf added, "and Horthy! Why such a severe response to a person like Karl? Well, perhaps Leopold will have some answers."

"I regret his questions are the same as yours."

After a short drive from the station the car pulled into the mansion's entrance drive. Wreaths of dyed black cedar boughs draped with black ribbons hung on the front doors. Tamás led Rudolf into the foyer. Leopold met them with a heartfelt embrace for Rudolf, "It is good that you are here, Dolf. Thank you for coming so quickly."

Rudolf was surprised to see how aged Leopold had become. His shoulders were uncharacteristically stooped, his walk slowed, his dark silver-streaked hair turned completely white, but most of all, his brilliant smile was gone. Leopold's dark eyes seemed deeper and his brow severely furrowed. Leopold put his arm over Rudolf's shoulders and guided him into the library, "Tamás, will you pour brandy for us, please, and one for yourself."

The three men sat together.

"You've been told what happened? How we lost our beloved son?" Rudolf nodded in the affirmative, as Leopold continued, "You know what a disaster the whole experience turned out to be. A waste of so many. The king, so ill-advised and naïve and it has only gotten worse."

"I know nothing of recent news, only what Tamás has told me and what I read in last Monday's paper."

"Our dear friend and cousin, Prince Esterházy, who graciously sent Stefan back to us, has given refuge to the king and queen. They stayed the first night in the Tata Palace as his guests. Horthy's government troops surrounded Tata and the king could neither escape to Budapest nor flee to the west. Esterházy only hopes he can safeguard the king until hostile feelings subside and a calm reason returns.

"By the next morning Gömbös' troops were camped in the town's rail station with arrest orders for Counts Rákovszky and Andrássy as well as many other nobles who supported Karl's *revolution*, at least as Horthy saw it."

Leopold paused briefly, "We understand that many are being hunted down as we speak. Court-martials have been prepared for all military involved, officers as well as the lowest ranks. Karl's reckless plan has become a total disaster!"

Rudolf sat in disbelief, "How could the king have led his loyal friends into such a situation? What will happen to him now?"

"We will have to wait and see. There is much at stake for everyone," lamented Leopold. "My greatest question…why was Stefan involved? I know his interest in politics increased in the last few years, but why did he take such a risk?"

"I only know that he was very distraught over many of Horthy's policies, particularly the strictness of policies toward Hungary's minorities," Rudolf informed them. "He discussed the matter with me rather dramatically on several occasions."

"I fear that all of this is my fault. I may have shaped his thinking over these many years. Ideas concerning Magyarization of all citizens, equality of all. I can never forgive myself for planting an idea of revolution in his head." Leopold sighed heavily. "I'm glad that you have come home to us, Dolf. You were Stefan's dearest friend, like a brother to him, like a second son to me."

"Please relieve yourself of any blame or guilt, Duke." Rudolf consoled as best he could. "Stefan loved and admired you above all, but he was his own man. We may never know why, but we can be sure that he had his own reasons for becoming involved." Rudolf stood, placed his hand on Leopold's shoulder, and asked, "May I see Klára now?"

Rudolf left the library and climbed the staircase to Klára's room. He knocked gently on her door, "Klára, it's me, Dolf."

He heard her from within move to the door quickly. She fell into his arms crying with a mix of despair and delight, "Oh, Dolf, I'm so glad that you're here...it's good to see you."

They walked together down the hallway to the landing of the great stair and sat down on the top stair below the Mucha stained glass. Rudolf held her close. At first they sat in silence; then she sighed as she leaned into him, "There's where I first saw Stefan, wounded and bleeding," she pointed down the stairs, "It was so sad, Dolf, there was nothing anyone could do for him and he was in such pain."

Rudolf kept his arm wrapped around her shoulders and pulled her closer to him. Klára continued, "When the doctor came, they carried him into the library. I went to him and held his hand. He could only whisper, 'Hello Little One. I love you.' Then he died."

Klára buried her face in Rudolf's jacket and sobbed, "I'm all alone now, Stefan is gone and so are you."

"No, no Klára, you're not alone. I'll come back to Budapest. I'll always come to you when you call me. Always. Remember I swore to be your protector when you made Stefan and me knights of your realm. Remember?"

Rudolf held up her chin to look into her eyes, those beautiful emerald green eyes that now looked like deep watery pools. He managed a smile and patted her cheeks with his handkerchief. Klára looked into his sincere brown eyes and for the first time since Stefan's death felt comforted as though this painful time might pass. She adored Rudolf.

From the bottom of the stairs, Elizabeth called to them, "Dolf, we want you to accompany the family when we take Stefan's body to Sopron. We all go by train tomorrow."

—⁂—

At Sopron Castle, after a moving service in the chapel, Stefan's body was interred next to his mother's tomb in the castle cemetery. Tombs of Leopold's parents, Duke Louis and Duchess Maria stood nearby. The following day, a courier arrived with a letter from the Regent Horthy requesting that Leopold...*travel immediately to Tata to receive the deposed king and queen, Karl and Zita. You must act as their escort along with Hungarian soldiers as they conduct the couple to the Abbey at Tihany where they will be detained for an indefinite period of time.*

Leopold responded in writing to Horthy's request and gave it to the courier to take back to Budapest. Leopold wrote that due to the recent death of his son, Stefan, he would be unable to leave his family or Sopron at this time. He wrote that Count Rudolf von Házy would go in his place to Tata and would serve as escort for the deposed king and queen.

The next morning Rudolf prepared to leave Sopron. He found Klára in the castle's courtyard. She walked toward him looking very dejected. Rudolf kissed her on the forehead, "Be brave, Little Princess. I promise to return soon; before I go back to Prague, I will come to see you."

Two weeks later the von Estés returned to Budapest from Sopron and began to resume their routines. As Rudolf promised, he came to visit before taking his train back to Prague. He sat quietly with Leopold and Tamás in the library as they contemplated the tragedy that had befallen them. Leopold asked if Dolf would return for Christmas and he affirmed that he would.

Eventually, the conversation turned to the king. Rudolf had escorted the royal couple to the Tihany Abbey where he left them with the Abbot and Horthy's soldiers. "The king believes Horthy's guards are there to protect him," related Rudolf, "but I cautioned him to beware of them. I'm certain the soldiers serve Horthy as spies on the king."

"Still the king is naïve!" Leopold shook his head, "Horthy is being pressured by the *Little Entente*. Particularly by the Czechoslovak premier who demands that Karl renounce his claim to the Crown of St. Stephen and the thrones of Austria and Bohemia."

Rudolf offered his perspective, "Prague is obsessed with fear that the Hapsburgs are going to reclaim all of Central Europe. They have threatened Horthy with invasion if he does not remove Karl from any possibility of restoration."

"Yes, but Karl continues to rebuff abdication. I'm told he refused to sign the document of abdication presented to him at Tihany." Leopold spoke in a solemn tone, "I understand Karl...I even agree with him to deny abdication. His sacred oath and divine inheritance bind him to the throne." Leopold wiped his wet eyes, "Why did he place himself in this hopeless situation?" Leopold cleared his throat, "He could have been king in exile and negotiated through diplomacy and conciliation. Eventually, Horthy, who is ultimately a monarchist, would have found a way for his return without this disastrous turn of events, without the loss of our beloved Stefan."

Klára knocked at the library door before entering. She went straight to Rudolf, kissed him, nestled beside him in the big leather chair and listened to the men's discussion of past and the future. When Rudolf stood to go, Klára could not hold back her tears. In fact, all four of them shared a tearful farewell as he took his leave of the von Estés.

Rudolf stepped out into the cold November wind, raised his collar and ducked into the von Esté car that would take him to the train station. He had very mixed feelings...ready to return to his studies in Prague, but yearning to stay in Budapest with his dearest friends, especially little Klára.

—✲—

Hungary's Premier Bethlen did not support a return of the monarchy; he wanted to rid Hungary of Karl's influence as soon as possible. So, Bethlen introduced to the National Assembly an edict ordering the deportation of Karl and Zita. With no opposition, the edict passed immediately. Once again, Karl chose to defy any such order, insisting that he alone was the rightful ruler of Hungary and would never renounce the holy Crown of St. Stephen.

Hoping to bring the matter to a calm and quick closure, Britain, of the *Great Entente,* entered the situation. A British flotilla of gunboats steamed up the Danube and moored in Budapest, while a fleet of armored cars drove to the Tihany Abbey. In the early morning hours, the Abbot awoke the royal couple, fed them breakfast, and handed them over to their British escort. Karl and Zita were driven to Budapest where they boarded a British ship and left Hungary for an unknown destination. A number of Hungarians, including some soldiers, stood on the river's bank waving a nostalgic farewell to the king.

In early November, the British transferred Karl and Zita from their exile in Romania to the *Cardiff,* an ocean-going vessel. The *Cardiff* sailed from the Black Sea, through the straits into the Mediterranean, past Gibraltar, to their final destination, the sub-tropical isle of Funchal in the Atlantic Madeiras. Once settled in their new home, Karl and Zita were anxious to bring their children, who were still in Switzerland, to Funchal.

Zita left the isle alone, traveling to Switzerland to collect her four children. Zita's presence in Switzerland put her in great peril, because Karl's enemies wanted to retain her and the children in Europe, believing that a permanent separation from Karl would end all possibilities of his restoration. British influence prevailed and Zita, with her children, was allowed to return to Funchal. The reunited royal family lived on a pension provided by the *Great Entente* in a rather humble villa, *Capo do Monte.*

Early December

A month had passed since Stefan's death and yet the draperies remained drawn over the windows, black cloths still covered the mirrors and portraits, and the scent of incense was still in the air. The house remained eerily quiet, except for the cautious steps of servants scurrying up and down the stairs on their way to Elizabeth's breakfast room where she stayed most of the day. Leopold rarely left the library. Klára whiled away the days in her bedroom sitting on the window seat. This evening she stared into the empty garden below as a dusting of snow began to cover neglected piles of autumn leaves. She looked toward the darkened windows across the back of Dolf's house. The thought of him and Stefan brought a smile to her lips.

A soft rap at her door drew her back from memories of happier times to the despair of the present. The door opened slightly and Leona looked into the darkened room, "Miss Klára, there's a young woman asking to see you."

"Who is it? Did she say?"

"It's Miss Eszter Klein. She says she is very sorry to disturb you, but it is very important that she speak with you."

Klára followed Leona down the stairs into the foyer. Eszter stood facing the door; she was wrapped in a hooded cape that obscured her face from view. In a voice barely audible Eszter asked Klára if they could walk together outside. The two stood in awkward silence until Klára put on her coat and they walked from the reception hall out into the night.

A light snow fell around them. Eszter led Klára to the sidewalk along Andrássy Avenue. She turned her face toward Klára and then, by the light of the streetlamp, Klára could see Eszter's red and swollen eyes. Eszter pressed a handkerchief to her face and finally spoke, "You are very young, Klára, but I know Stefan trusted you with secrets. I want to trust you, too, with my secret. I must tell someone and I have decided that it must be you."

As Eszter inhaled and exhaled deeply her steamy breath mixed with the swirling snowflakes. "I'm leaving Budapest tomorrow with friends. We're going to Palestine. My family doesn't know, no one knows, except now you."

Eszter stopped walking. "I'm going to have a baby. Stefan's baby."

She sobbed until her shoulders shook. She was so distraught that Klára feared she might faint onto the sidewalk. Klára reached out for Eszter and embraced her. Eszter leaned on Klára and in broken words declared that she and Stefan loved each other and planned to marry.

"Please tell my Papa," Klára implored her. "Your news of Stefan's baby will make him very happy."

"No, Klára, you mustn't ever tell him or anyone." Then she hugged Klára once more, tightly, and hurried away toward the Metro stop.

Klára stood alone on the sidewalk watching Eszter walk away. Klára was only eleven, but she did grasp some of what Eszter had said, although she wasn't sure of all its meaning. Klára remembered a hot summer day three years ago when Rózsa and Eszter were visiting their Lake Balaton villa. All the children had gone together by ferry to Tihany to visit Rudolf and his family for the day. Klára remembered she had seen Stefan kiss Eszter and when she asked him about the kiss, he told her that he loved Eszter and they would marry some day. Klára remembered, too, the pain she felt when he told her to keep it a secret, to tell no one. Klára had felt a strange stab in her chest when she heard his words. *He loved someone else.* Klára realized she was losing her beloved brother and for the first time she felt a bit of jealousy.

On this night when Klára heard the words from Eszter, *Stefan and I loved each other,* Klára knew it was true. Pain stabbed at her chest again, only this time Stefan had gone away forever. Their secret still troubled Klára. She couldn't understand why neither Stefan nor Eszter trusted Papa. *Surely, Papa would have been happy to learn of their love and, of course, he would be happy to know there was a baby coming.* Tears began to stream down Klára's face as she watched Eszter walk away until she disappeared in the snowy darkness.

—⁓—

A week later, Klára sat at the top of the stairs waiting for Rudolf; he was to arrive at any moment. She peered down from her vantage spot through the balcony railing into the reception hall below. Usually the house was decorated with many candles and red and gold ribbons, but this year because the family was still in mourning for the loss of Stefan Christmas would be more somber, without its usual gaiety.

Of course the Advent wreath, a necessary part of Christmas, had its usual place of importance in the middle of the great dining room sideboard, but Elizabeth and Leopold had not decided, yet, whether *the angels* would or would not bring the Christmas tree on Holy Night.

Papa reminded everyone, "Christmas for Hungarians is a time to be with loved ones, those closest to one's heart."

That sentiment seemed more profound than ever this year thought Klára. *Oh, how I wish Dolf would hurry home. I miss him so!*

When the doorbell rang Klára flew down the stairs, getting to the door before Tamás. She opened it, threw her arms around Dolf, and exclaimed her joy at seeing him. He returned her smile and greeted Tamás with hearty enthusiasm.

"Welcome, Count, it is good to have you here again."

"We have all been waiting for your arrival," said Leopold as he crossed the hall from the library. "Klára has been counting the days, more for your arrival than for that of the Christmas angels."

"We are glad that you've come at last," Leopold gave Rudolf a robust embrace.

Klára held Rudolf's hand and didn't let go of it, even when the others embraced and kissed him.

"Silva has prepared a dinner for you," said Leopold, "but first come have an aperitif in the library. I want to hear of your studies. Tamás, please let Silva and Elizabeth know that Dolf has arrived."

Still holding Dolf's hand, Klára followed her Papa to the library.

"So, Klára, did Mikulás fill your shoes with lots of goodies?" Rudolf teased her, "certainly, I suspect there were no switches?"

"I decided not to put out my shoes this year," answered Klára as she smiled at Leopold, "but he left candies and a new book on my pillow."

According to Hungarian tradition, children leave their shoes on the window sill on St. Mikulás Day, the sixth of December, in hopes that Mikulás will leave candies and small gifts for them, if they're good children. If naughty, Mikulás might leave a switch with a little devil attached to it.

"I know you've been a very worthy young lady this year, Klára," smiled Rudolf as he kissed her on the forehead. "Did you throw pieces of lead in the garden on St. Luca Day?"

Klára laughed, "Of course I did and I saw the little pieces form into the shape of a paint brush."

The three of them laughed heartily. According to tradition, young single girls throw pieces of lead in their gardens on Saint Luca's Day, December thirteenth, to see the occupation of their future love.

After a brief time, Tamás entered the library to announce supper. As Rudolf entered the dining room, Elizabeth embraced him warmly and welcomed him with kisses on both cheeks. Silva happily guided him to a chair and the family sat down to the feast prepared by Silva and her staff. Leopold said a blessing over the meal, raised a toast to those present and to those who were not, and then invited everyone to enjoy the good food blessed by God.

A few days later Rudolf and his grandmother returned to the von Esté home for dinner on Christmas Eve. A beautifully embroidered Christmas cloth spread over the dining table symbolized health and abundance while straw strewn under the table reminded everyone of Jesus' humble birth in a Bethlehem manger. Silva served all the traditional Christmas dishes—turkey with cabbage and *beigli*, fried *fogas*, *torta* with poppy seed and walnuts, and gingerbread. Leopold's excellent wines complemented every course.

After everyone had eaten their fill, they heard the ringing of tiny bells from the reception hall. Excitement swept around the table and the diners adjourned to the hall where, with great surprise, the von Estés and their guests found a wondrous Christmas tree. Just as when Klára and Stefan were young children, the tree miraculously appeared by the staircase while the family and their guests dined. Lighted candles and ribbons adorned the tree while piles of small packages lay beneath. Obviously, Elizabeth and Leopold had decided the *angels* should bring a tree, after all.

"In our hearts we know that Stefan certainly approves," Elizabeth said to all, "In fact, we know he would admonish us, if we did not have a tree on his account."

Elizabeth sat down at the piano and everyone joined in singing Christmas songs while Klára passed out the gifts. Each gift was something special for the recipient. Klára gave her mother a lace handkerchief; Silva had helped her tat the edges. To Rudolf's grandmother Klára gave a vial of lavender water she and Silva had made last fall and to Silva a pair of gloves and to Tamás a woolen scarf Klára had purchased on a shopping trip to Vienna with her mother. Klára's gift for Papa was a sheet of his favorite music decorated with pressed flowers. She told him she would play the music for him on Christmas Day. And for Rudolf, Klára embroidered a fine linen handkerchief. His initials intertwined with cherry blossoms and little brown sparrows filled one corner.

"Every knight should carry his lady's handkerchief, Klára, thank you. It's a lovely gift."

Then Rudolf took from his pocket five small packages; he gave one each to Leopold, Elizabeth, Klára, Silva, and Tamás. Inside each box was a miniature watercolor painting of Stefan, the perfect size for a man's pocket watch or a lady's locket. They all agreed that the paintings were a perfect likeness and were quite taken by Rudolf's artistic ability and thoughtfulness.

Tamás poured glasses of plum brandy and Silva passed around more gingerbread. Klára sat beside Rudolf. She looked around at her family and friends; she was so proud of them all. She knew everyone missed Stefan, but they were not miserable, because they shared their sorrow of his loss with each other and they also shared their joyful memories of him. It seemed to Klára that as long as they all remembered Stefan, he was there with them and it made her Christmas very special.

1922

Toward the end of April, Leopold received a letter from a mutual friend of the exiled King Karl.

In March a wintery freeze still gripped Madeira. The gray, bitter winds further depressed our dear Karl. His already weakened constitution, plus his dire mental attitude, could not shake off the recurring fevers and chills that plagued him. A terrible cough developed into severe pneumonia that sent Zita into a panic. She demanded that Austrian doctors be brought to the isle, but by the time two specialists arrived it was too late. Karl died with his young son, Otto, as a witness. Karl wanted his son to know the reality of a king's obligation, how one must conduct himself with dignity and bravery as a Catholic and as a king even at the hour of death. Our beloved Karl died on the first of April during the night. He was only thirty-four years old.

Leopold wept.

May

In May when Klára's family left Budapest for their villa at Lake Balaton they took Rózsa with them; she would stay until mid-July. One afternoon in late June the girls were sitting in the garden helping Silva shell peas and sipping minted tea when the postman arrived. Silva offered him a glass of tea as he left the post on the table. Klára noticed a letter right on top of the pile, "It's for you, Rózsa!"

"It's from my mother," Rózsa said as she opened it and began to read, "Oh, my goodness...oh my goodness."

"What is it, Rózsa ... what has happened?"

"Well, you know that Eszter left us last winter and since then Mama and Father have had no idea where she'd gone...after all this time."

Rózsa looked up from the letter with an anxious expression, "They were so worried they didn't know what to do. Now Mama writes that Eszter went to Palestine with Mrs. Löwy's son...and a number of others. Mama says they can hardly believe it...Father keeps saying...'a daughter of mine in Palestine.'"

"What else does the letter say?"

"I can hardly believe this...my mother writes that Eszter married Imre Löwy!

"I didn't think she even liked him." Rózsa frowned, "She always said he looked like a scarecrow."

"What else does the letter say?" asked Klára again anxiously.

"Eszter wrote to Mama that they live on a *kibbutz*, whatever that is, and that they have a baby! A girl! They named her Stefánia." Rózsa looked up again. "I'm an aunt with a little niece!...hmmm, but I doubt I'll ever see her unless they come back to Budapest someday."

Klára sat quietly, feeling an overwhelming sadness. She was thinking...*I, too, am an aunt. Stefánia is my niece, too. She's Stefan's baby.* Her eyes filled with tears as she thought... *my Papa will never see his grandchild.*

"Why are you crying, Klára?"

"It's sad that your mother and father will not get to see their grandchild. I hope Eszter will send a picture someday and that you'll let me see Stefánia, too."

"I will, if she does, but I doubt Eszter will think of it."

August

Rudolf didn't come to Lake Balaton until August. He stayed in Prague for the summer to work with his master teacher, Max Švakinsky. When he finally did come to the lake he told Klára, with great excitement, that he would stay in Prague at the academy for only one more year and then he would go to Paris with Švakinsky to study at *Academie Julian.*

Klára just stared at him. She found it difficult to share his enthusiasm, "But Paris is even farther away than Prague, Dolf."

"It is, Klára," he answered, "but I'll visit as often as I can and I'll always think of you." He tousled her hair to tease her and smiled at her, "and I promise that one day I'll come back to Budapest for good… never to move away again."

Klára smiled back at him, but remained unconvinced, "How long will you be here at the lake now?"

"Two weeks, Klára, and I'll spend every day with you." He looked at her most sincerely, "What should we do today?"

"Let's sail, just like we did with Stefan."

—⁓—

The September afternoon was hot; a smothering kind of heat that made everyone lethargic. Cicadas were making their usual racket while dragonflies buzzed around the bougainvillea-covered gazebo. When Klára entered the heavily shaded gazebo she found her mother and Silva lounging lazily in their wicker chairs, eyes closed, fanning themselves with big woven straw fans. Klára flopped down on a padded settee, looking very bored and hot.

Elizabeth barely spoke, but managed to correct her daughter, "Ladies do not flop, Klára, no matter how hot the day."

Klára breathed in and out very slowly while watching bumblebees disappear and reappear in the blue blossoms of the bougainvillea. "I miss Rózsa and Papa and Dolf… there is no one here to have fun with."

"When did Dolf go back to town?"

"This morning."

"No," said an unexpected voice from the steps of the gazebo, "I didn't leave as planned. I've decided to stay a bit longer."

There stood Rudolf dressed in all white, wearing a straw bowler and carrying an ornate cane of brass and carved brown wood.

"Oh, Dolfie, you're still here," cried Klára, as she leapt from her chair and ran toward him, just as Elizabeth reminded her with a firm, "Klára, show a bit of restraint."

But Klára flung her arms around Rudolf's neck and kissed him on both cheeks. "How long will you stay? I've been so blue today...with nothing to do. I missed you so...already."

"I've decided to stay until my grandmother leaves for Budapest."

"I'm so happy, Dolfie."

"I thought, perhaps, we could go into Balatonfüred this afternoon for ice cream, if it's all right with you, Duchess?"

"Of course, go...she's been miserable all day."

Arm in arm, Rudolf and Klára walked away from the gazebo. Rudolf's grandmother's chauffeur drove them into Balatonfüred, letting them out of the car near the strand. They laughed and teased each other as they walked along the promenade in the shade of sycamore trees watching swooping gulls and elegant swans along the shore. They stopped at a shoreline restaurant, the Veranda, famous for its panoramic view of the lake and its southern shore.

They sat down at a table by the railing and ordered two extravagant ice cream desserts. Even though the late afternoon was still quite warm, the veranda was cooled by lake breezes and the ice cream tasted marvelous.

Klára drew each ice cream-filled spoon slowly through her lips several times before the ice cream completely disappeared, "ummm...good, Dolfie. I love it here. Thank you for bringing me."

"You're very welcome, Klára. Are you feeling better now?"

"Yes, of course I am." Klára frowned and looked away thoughtfully.

"Is there a problem, Klára? You seem to have some serious thoughts in your head."

"Well," she was conflicted. "What if you had a secret that you were not supposed to tell anyone, but you never actually promised not to tell?"

"It would depend, Klára, on what kind of secret...if it would harm someone to tell it, then I would not tell it, but if not telling it could bring harm, then I might tell someone, a person who could stop the harm. Did that make any sense to you? Does that help?"

"Well, I don't think that the secret really harms anyone, but I don't know. I want to tell you so badly, because I have not told anyone and I think about it all the time and it makes me very sad."

"You made no promise not to tell it?" Rudolf asked with a very serious expression. "So, you only feel obliged not to tell, because the teller told you not to tell anyone, right?"

"Yes, that's right." Klára took a deep breath and bit her bottom lip as she always did when bothered. "The most important part of what is in my head is not even a secret...people know...even the people who are not supposed to know the secret know that part."

"Now I'm confused," confessed Rudolf. "What should we do? Well, you can tell me the part everyone knows and then, perhaps, I can guess the secret. Would that work?"

"While Rózsa was here in May she got a letter from her mother." Klára felt great relief just saying that much to him. "Mrs. Klein wrote that she had gotten a letter from Eszter...did you know that Eszter is in Palestine? Or that she married Imre Löwy?"

"No, I've heard nothing of Eszter Klein in a very long time," Rudolf frowned as he listened to Klára's words.

"Well, Mrs. Klein wrote in Rózsa's letter that Eszter had a baby, a baby girl." Klára took a deep breath, "Eszter named her Stefánia." Tears began to slip from Klára's eyes, "That is the part that everyone knows."

Rudolf reached across the table and grasped Klára's hands as she twisted at her napkin, "Who told you the secret, Klára? Stefan or Eszter?" He knew the truth the moment he heard that Eszter had a baby. The baby's name confirmed it.

"Eszter...the night before she left Budapest. I wanted to tell Papa, but she didn't want me to tell him." Klára cried more openly, "It's too late to tell him now, isn't it?"

"You knew this at Christmastime, didn't you?"

"Yes, I knew the secret then."

"Poor little Klára, you kept this burden a long time. It was very grown-up of you to keep it all to yourself, but it wasn't very fair of Eszter. She wanted you to know, because you are Stefan's family." Rudolf frowned, "Poor Eszter. I know she and Stefan loved each other very much. She had no choice but to leave. I also know that Imre is a good man. I'm sure he must care deeply for Eszter and her baby. He's Stefánia's father now and for that reason, Klára, you and I both must keep Eszter's secret.

"Will it help to know that your secret is shared, will it relieve your sadness?" Rudolf continued to hold Klára's hand, "I don't want you to worry about it anymore. Someday, perhaps, you can share it with your Papa, but I don't know if this is the right time. It may bring him joy or it may bring him even more pain."

Rudolf suspected that if Leopold realized how close Stefan and Eszter had been, he would also understand the reason Stefan became so involved with the king's ill-fated restoration attempt. At last an explanation for Stefan's obsession to bring about a more just atmosphere in Hungary for Jewish citizens could be understood. Rudolf also supposed that Leopold would only feel more regret to know that Stefan's child was in the world, but so far away her grandfather would never know her.

"I'm certain, Klára, Eszter's secret should be kept between just you and me...at least for now."

Klára agreed and did feel much better.

1923

In November Leopold received a letter from Eugenia.

Things are very bad here in Germany. We have severe inflation. The middle class has been destroyed. So many are completely impoverished and filled with despair. I fear the masses will become vulnerable to radical politics. It makes me very nervous. Konrad and I are going to visit Canada in North America.

You have probably heard that the National Socialists German Workers' Party is gaining power. They elected that charismatic man about whom I have written to you in the past...Adolf Hitler. He is chair of the party now and has started a daily newspaper, Volkischer Beobachter, *to spread his obscene propaganda.*

Last week Hitler and about six hundred of his thugs, called Brownshirts, stormed into the Bürgerbraukeller in Munich intending to take Gustav von Kahr prisoner! The audacity! Von Kahr is head of the provincial Bavarian government! General Erich Ludendorff was at Hitler's side. Ludendorff's presence indicates to all of us how serious this situation has become. They took Kahr and his associates as prisoners right in front of everyone...at a public meeting.

Thank God...the very next day Hitler and Ludendorff were arrested. Hitler received a five-year sentence!

Konrad and I are praying that will be the end of it. The Nazis have been verboten! We are very glad, because we are convinced this Hitler is a dangerous man with dangerous ideas. Well, enough of that. We shall see you in Siófok in the summer.

Love to all, Eugenia

Professor Klein took the lift up to the top floor of the von Esté Fine Wine Company and asked Judit if the Duke might have a minute to see him. Within moments Leopold opened the door for his old friend, "Come in. Come in, Jakov."

Leopold offered him a chair and Doctor Klein sat down, "Thank you for seeing me. I know you are a very busy man."

"I always have time for you, Jakov. What can I do for you?"

"As you know, the Regent Horthy and Bethlen have begun to relax restrictions imposed against Hungary's Jewish community."

"Yes, it seems they may have come at last to their senses!" smiled Leopold.

"Some professorships have been restored in strategic areas, so I have been asked to return to my position at the National Academy of Sciences. Therefore, I will need to resign from my work here. I do not know how my family can ever thank you for your kindness and generosity."

"You've been a long-time and dear friend, Jakov. You would do the same for me," Leopold rose from his chair and shook hands with Doctor Klein. "This is very good news, Jakov! Let's hope those in power have finally realized the futility of discrimination against our own citizens. How could they have ever justified curtailing the productivity of such a large and industrious segment of Hungary's population?"

The two old friends shared a heartfelt embrace.

"Let's go to Gerbeaud's for coffee and *körtepálinka* to celebrate."

As they passed Judit's desk, Leopold said, "Please telephone my home and ask Tamás to meet us at Gerbeaud's. I'll be gone for the rest of the afternoon. Thank you, Judit."

1924

Rudolf left Prague in mid-May, exhausted from his studies and traveled directly to Lake Balaton where he moved into his grandmother's villa for the summer. He wanted to use the summer to refresh and reflect on his last three years in Prague at university. Rudolf's experience at the academy had opened his eyes to the power of art, in particular, to the persuasive tools of graphic design and industrial arts. Rudolf realized that the visual image could be used to create change in people's thinking and, even, perhaps, their hearts. While in Prague, Rudolf witnessed the dramatic influence far-leftist propaganda had on visual expression and the effect those leftist visual messages had on the masses. Rudolf determined that his artistic abilities must be used for good purposes.

Some of Rudolf's associates at the university shared their interests and research in the study of psychology with him. His friends enjoyed discussing symbolism and hidden meanings that filled contemporary artworks exhibited in Prague. Rudolf began to see how art could challenge the mind as well as the eye. The modern art he saw explored the subconscious, memories, dreams, and nightmares common to every human being.

Rudolf spent hours standing before the art creations of many different artists in various styles, works of art that deliberately broke all rules, classical conventions, and expectations. Often the artworks visually broke apart reality, on purpose, because *since the Great War…what is reality?*

He remembered reading Kandinsky's words...*he could never again paint a lovely field of red poppies swaying in gentle breezes after he had seen the horrors of Flanders' fields.*

Works by cubist painters and sculptors, Picasso and Arp completely engaged Rudolf's interest. The Dadaists—Duchamp and Man Ray—seemed curious, but he got their point of deliberate devaluation of valued icons. Rudolf found the surrealists'—DeChirico, Klee, and Ernst—embrace of psychological proclivities disturbing and thrilling at the same time. But the works that intrigued Rudolf most were the Expressionists—the Germans—Grosz, Beckmann, and printmaker Kolwitz. Rudolf admired their works that bravely ridiculed and admonished their own governments.

How could that visual power not be admired? Rudolf wondered, as he hoped he could find the energy and voice within the depth of his own artistic talent to make a worthwhile difference in the world.

Good wine, good friends, and the sun and water of Lake Balaton revitalized Rudolf quickly. He escorted his grandmother to Hévíz many times, worked long hours in Leopold's vineyards, and spent much of his time entertaining Klára, or perhaps, it was Klára who entertained him. At fourteen, Klára's ebony hair and emerald eyes were striking. Rudolf drew her portrait many times through the summer days. Together they did all the usual lake things, swimming, sailing across the lake to Siófok, participating in all the traditional festivities.

August

Rudolf and Klára strolled through the booths at the annual Balatonfüred wine festival, tasting wines and testing their palates. "This one is a bit too dry for my taste"..."This *Riezling* lacks crispness, not enough acidity"..."I like the fruity aroma and taste of this one"..."The tannin is too heavy for me in this one; it leaves my mouth so dry"..."Try this red, the tannin is rich and toasty."

"Perhaps we should go to supper," Rudolf suggested, "I think we've had enough wine for today."

"Let's go back to the Veranda. The setting is so divine at sunset." Klára looped her arm through Rudolf's as they left the festival. Even though Klára drank wine as a matter of course, she was feeling a bit tipsy.

The two sat at the same table where they had sat before and Rudolf ordered fried *fogas* and iced coffees.

"As lovely as the evening is, I feel it's bittersweet," Klára lamented. "It's been a perfect day, Dolf, but it will be our last together for a long time. You leave tomorrow...for Paris...so far away. I'm happy for you, Dolf, really I am. I know it's a wonderful opportunity for you to study in Paris. But I'm very selfish...I don't want you to go."

"I know, but soon you'll be back in Budapest with all the things that keep you busy and before you know it, it will be summer again," consoled Rudolf, "and we'll come here again for supper." He smiled at her.

"I love you, Dolfie," Klára declared. She knew he thought she meant it as a friend, a sister, but that was not how she felt about him any longer.

"I love you, too, Klára."

Paris

At the end of summer Rudolf, at twenty-one years of age, traveled to Paris to begin his grand adventure. His old friend, János Géza, met him at the station. János, who had left Prague the year before, worked in the restoration department of the Louvre. He invited Rudolf to stay in his flat until Rudolf could find a flat of his own. In the meantime János showed him all around Paris.

They took a cruise on the Seine from which János pointed out the Eiffel Tower, Tuileries Gardens, the Left Bank where he lived, and Notre Dame. János also gave Rudolf an extensive tour of the unseen workrooms of the Louvre and then left him to walk through the galleries on his own. Rudolf spent so much time in the galleries and seeing the sights that he had no time for flat hunting.

Evenings were just as full for Rudolf, because János took him to all the best cafés, the ballet, art galleries, and the very popular avant-garde theatre. On one particular evening the two young men accompanied a group of art friends to a soiree at 27 Rue de Fleurus, the salon of Gertrude Stein and her friend, Alice B. Toklas.

The Steins were prolific art collectors. Paintings by the most avant-garde artists...Matisse, Picasso, Braque, Cezanne, and some artists unknown to Rudolf...covered the walls of their flat. The eloquent and charming Miss Stein captivated Rudolf. Her words of encouragement and advice for artists, writers, and musicians were taken quite seriously. Every Stein soiree was crowded with talkative, animated people engaged in lively conversation and to Rudolf's great delight every person passionately discussed art. He could see that Miss Stein clearly commanded great respect from her cultured audience and he felt great joy being part of that audience. *What an environment. I love Paris!*

Finally, Rudolf did find a reasonable flat in the Latin Quarter. Though very small and four stories up a spiraling stone staircase, he was very happy with its location. He began his studies and apprenticeship in the atelier of Max

Seltzer, the famous avant-garde German printmaker. Both János and Rudolf took classes at the Academie Julian. They spent their afternoons roaming the galleries of the Louvre and their Sundays searching *les bouquinistes*, the old green booths that lined the banks of the Seine, looking for second-hand treasures. Often with bread and cheese, some fruit, and a bottle of wine, Rudolf found a bench in Jardin du Luxembourg and spent time reading or sketching.

In the evenings the two young men fully participated in Parisian nightlife at favored night spots like Aux Deux Magots or Café de Flore, frequented by artists. It was Café de Flore where Rudolf first saw *the tiny blonde*. She was one of many pretty girls who hung around the artists. Most of the girls were in the ballet and posed as models for the artists in their off-hours. One evening Rudolf found himself across the table from her. She flirted with him, telling him that he had magnificent eyes. Flattered by her attention, but fully aware she flirted with every man in their midst, Rudolf only smiled at her compliments and didn't take them too seriously.

A few weeks later at one of Gertrude Stein's soirees, once again Rudolf met the pretty little blonde who had flirted with him at the café. Yvette was her name and, indeed, she was a ballerina and model for artists. Rudolf and Yvette stood by an open window allowing a cool breeze to blow past them into the smoky room while they looked at the sparkling lights of Paris in the distance. Aromas of cinnamon drifted up to them from the *patisserie* below while low conversations throughout the room served as a kind of background music.

Rudolf and Yvette shared their histories. Yvette was from Montmartre, her mother, a Russian, had been a ballerina, too, one who posed for Edgar Degas and Auguste Renoir. Yvette imagined her father to be a famous sculptor, but wasn't certain and she had one sister, Monique, also a model. Yvette told Rudolf all about her part in Fernand Leger's film, *Ballet mecanque*, and about the artist's avant-garde experimental cinema.

Yvette's interest in art and associations with artists quite impressed Rudolf. He asked how long she had been dancing and she answered since thirteen, but would not confess her age at the moment. Rudolf surmised Yvette to be around twenty, more or less.

Always introduced to the soirée guests as the Count von Házy from Budapest, Rudolf told Yvette little about himself, only that he studied art in Budapest and Prague and, now, studied in Paris. He supplied the minimum about his past or person.

However, *the count* completely fascinated Yvette. She had never met an exotic Hungarian count before and this one was so handsome and charming, mysterious and romantic, too. She judged him to be a true gentleman, because he treated her like a lady. She imagined becoming his model and hoped they would form a romantic relationship.

After another hour of mingling with the other guests, Rudolf suggested to

Yvette they go to a nearby café for coffee. Delighted, she accepted at once. They said their good-byes and left the flat. They walked from the Stein apartment on the Rue de Fleurus along the west side of the Jardin du Luxembourg all the way to St. Germaine-Des-Pres. Yvette noticed Rudolf had the slightest limp and carried a cane, although he didn't seem to be dependent upon the cane.

Being a very straightforward, blunt person, she asked, "What's wrong with your leg?"

"I lost half of it."

"No kidding." She was amazed, "Half of it?" She stopped walking, "What happened?"

"I was just a boy crawling around in a cave and got caught under a big rock," Rudolf knew he was talking to someone who liked the facts, even if a bit gory, "A doctor had to cut it off just below the knee to save my life." He knocked on his shin, "Wood."

Yvette was almost gleeful, "You seem to handle it quite well. Your limp is hardly noticeable at all."

"It was a long time ago."

They arrived at their destination, Aux Deux Magots, and entered into a perfect artsy atmosphere, dark and smoky with glowing table lights, clinking glasses and everyone talking at once. Picasso sat in a round booth with several other men and women. Yvette waved to him and he returned a nod.

"You know Picasso?" Rudolf asked her.

"Sure, I've posed for him."

Yvette and Rudolf sat at a table near the window and ordered coffees. They continued their conversation mostly about Rudolf's accident and Budapest. He asked her if she would like to spend some time with him at the Louvre and she agreed most eagerly to meet him there.

The next afternoon, Rudolf and Yvette spent a couple of hours together walking through ancient sculpture. She was excited to show Rudolf her favorite piece, the *Nike of Samothrace*, a sculpture that equally impressed him. As they walked on the stone floor of the museum, Yvette noticed the sound of Rudolf's footsteps, the rather uneven rhythm in his step that heightened her curiosity. After their excursion through just a small part of the galleries, time had escaped them, the hour was late, and the closing bell rang. They decided to go for supper at a little brasserie near the Louvre where they ordered a *pichet* of wine and *blanquette de veau* with *pommes frites*.

"This cuisine reminds me of Budapest," he said.

"Your limp is more noticeable today."

Rudolf looked down at his right foot, the one made of wood. "When I'm tired or walk a lot, it's harder to conceal the limp."

Sympathetic, but also morbidly curious, Yvette teased, "Don't you want to take me home with you tonight? Haven't you known me long enough?"

As they walked out into the night, a light mist enveloped them. They crossed the bridge over the Seine and began to follow the Rue Mazarine.

"Is it much further? You've walked quite a bit." Yvette asked, "Should we hail a taxi?"

"It isn't much further now. I'm fine…only a few blocks more once we get to Rue Monsieur Le Prince."

Yvette realized Rudolf had a great deal of pride, but also great strength. She especially loved holding onto his arm. She could feel his powerful muscles through his jacket and imagined the beauty of his body. She smiled at the thought. Finally they reached the little alley where Rudolf's flat was located. They entered the building and Yvette followed him up the spiraling stair to the atelier. She marveled at his agility as he maneuvered up the stairs, quite amazed by his wooden leg.

He took his key from the molding above the door. She laughed, "Why do you hide your key in such an obvious place?"

"So when I've had too much wine, I'll still know where to find it."

"But now I'll know where to find it, too," she cooed. "I can come in when- ever I want to."

Rudolf smiled a mischievous grin, thinking how pretty she was, and answered, "Any time." He pushed open the somewhat warped door and turned on a lamp.

So, here they were in his apartment after several meetings at the café, lunch that noon in Jardin du Luxembourg and a few hours in the Louvre. Rudolf crossed the room and turned on another lamp by the small settee. Yvette looked around the very compact apartment with little sets of steps everywhere.

"That is where I have my morning coffee," he pointed to the tiny kitchen, "and my lunch and where I drink at night." Pointing to the alcove, two steps up from the entry door, "That's where I sleep."

"Where do you work?" Yvette asked.

"Right here," he said and walked to a table between two windows. There were drawings pinned to the wall and stacks of papers with drawings on the table.

"Oh, you're really good. These are wonderful." She studied each drawing and then focused on one image of a beautiful young girl.

"Who is she? She's lovely."

Rudolf gazed at the image while the hint of a smile crossed his lips, "That's Klára from my home."

"She's very pretty. Is she the one you love?"

"Oh, no," he answered too quickly. "She's only my dear friend's little sister."

Two steps led up to each of the four windows in the flat; each window was a French door that opened onto a narrow wrought-iron balcony. Yvette walked across the room to the tiny kitchen and its window. She opened it and stepped out onto the balcony. She looked over the rooftops of the nearby flats and then leaned to the left just a bit to see the lights of St. Germaine shining down the dark alley leading to Rudolf's flat. A small wrought-iron table and two chairs were squeezed onto the balcony.

Rudolf stepped out onto the balcony with a bottle of wine and two glasses. "This is wine I brought from Hungary." He poured the wine and toasted in Hungarian, *"Egészségedre! To your health!"*

Yvette downed the wine in one big gulp, put the glass on the table and said in a very seductive voice, "I'm ready to see that leg of yours, if you're ready to show me."

That night Rudolf and Yvette did become lovers, although neither of them assumed it would be a lasting relationship. In fact, within a few months Yvette had moved on to another artist for intimacy, but she and Rudolf remained close friends and on occasion she modeled for him. Yvette knew there was no future in a relationship with Rudolf, because it was obvious to her his heart belonged to the young girl in the many drawings he had pinned to the wall.

Sometimes Yvette was smart, she had experienced hopelessness in love before and she would not allow herself to fall for Rudolf, even though he was the kindest, most sensitive, exotic and handsome man she had ever known. She loved to tease him about the girl named Klára. Depending on his mood, he either blushed, denying any feelings, or he became very irritated and flustered. Either way Yvette could get under his skin, but she could make him laugh, too, and Rudolf enjoyed her company. He didn't mind her frequent visits to his flat. He had a new friend.

November

In early November, Rudolf received a letter from Klára. It was written on lavender paper.

> *Dearest Dolfie, I'm looking at an enormous full, golden moon in the October sky. I'm thinking of you and wondering if you are looking at it, too.*
> *Love, Klára*

Rudolf smiled to think that he, too, a week or so before, had stared at the same huge ball of golden light shining over Paris. The memory of it made him feel closer to Budapest and to those he loved who were there. He pinned the folded lavender paper to the wall beside his drawings of Klára.

1925
Budapest

A cold and snowy January cloaked Budapest, compelling Leopold and Tamás to spend much of their time in front of a warm fire in the library, Tamás with his pipe and Leopold with a cigar. One particular morning, the mail occupied Leopold's attention.

"Well, Tamás, I must say that I'm very proud of our Sopron," Leopold announced aloud as he read from a letter from Sopron's *polgármester*—

Despite Horthy's severe inspection of Sopron's loyalties after the Budaörs catastrophe of 1921, Sopron's citizens voted to separate from Burgenland, Austria, and return as part of Hungary. The citizens also voted to change their city's name from the German, Ödenburg, back to its ancient Hungarian name, Sopron.

Leopold continued to read, "Of course, we never called our home 'Ödenburg'... it has always been Sopron to us. *'Sopron has been designated Hungary's Most Loyal Town'...* is not that amazing?"

Holding the letter in his hand, Leopold thought...*remarkable, the government turning in Sopron without much noise or resistance. The alterations, monumental as they are, have come about so easily. Hungary is so calm at the moment.* He shook his head and sighed.

"The ebb and flow of events can move in a single day from great turmoil, commotion, anxiety and then quite suddenly, without notice, the moment turns to order, peace and hopeful assurance. How incredible. . . how painful when one is caught up on the day of the former rather than the latter."

Leopold still remembered so clearly his feelings the day Stefan had come into the house wounded...*a hurricane had swept through the house. Everything went askew and, then the very next day, so quiet, so ordinary. Leopold remembered that quiet day, seeing a house martin. . . the pretty little black and white bird... sitting on a tree branch outside the library window puffing out his breast and singing his song as though the day was the very same as the day before, but it was not the same... not at all. Stefan loved birds...he kept lists of the birds he had seen and tried to emulate their songs, just as Leopold had as a boy.* Leopold looked out the same window. The tree branch was heavy with snow; the martins had all gone far away.

Summer

As they did every summer, Elizabeth and Klára traveled by train to Linz to visit the von Schraders. This summer Elizabeth wanted to travel on to Bavaria to visit her friend, the Baroness Renate von Werner. The three von Werner girls were always pleasant companions for Klára. By this summer, only one of the girls, Greta, remained unmarried and at home. The two girls spent their days together quietly, reading, writing letters, or making music. Klára played the piano while Greta played her violin.

Over afternoon *kaffee* and *lebkuchen* Elizabeth and Renate spent their time talking and laughing together. Franz, now seventeen, was absent from Furstenfeldbruck during their visit; he was spending the summer in Cologne with his father learning the family rail business.

On several occasions the ladies were driven into Munich, less than twenty miles from the von Werner manor. Elizabeth and Klára enjoyed being tourists while the von Werner ladies guided them through historical sites, the *Frauenkirche* and the *Alte Pinakothek*. They all took great pleasure visiting the fabulous seventeenth century palace, *Schloss Nymphenburg*, its galleries, beautiful grounds, and china factory. In the evening they attended a concert celebrating Mozart in the famous rococo-style *Cuvilliís Theatre* at the *Royal Residenz*.

As they passed by, Renate pointed out the *Burgerbraukeller*, "There is the place you may have read about a couple of years ago…the place where Adolf Hitler and his *Sturmabteilungen* or Brownshirts staged a putsch. Did you hear of it?"

"Oh, yes, there was an article in our newspaper."

"Hitler tried to arrest the Bavarian governor, von Kahr." Renate shared her opinions in a flippant manner, "The German government is so weak. I will not be surprised if Hitler tries again. The Weimar Republic is very vulnerable to any stronger will that comes along."

"That Hitler was arrested though. Was he not?" asked Elizabeth.

"He was in jail for less than a year and while he was there he wrote a book about his life. The Baron has read it and said he was intrigued by it."

Another day they were all driven to the very pleasant little nearby village, Dachau, nestled in the picturesque Bavarian countryside. The ladies had tea in the garden of the *Schloss Dachau*, once the elegant summer palace of the Wittelsbach Dynasty, now the site of an artist colony.

Renate took the von Estés to the von Werner's lake cottage on the lovely Lake Ammersee where Klára was instantly reminded of Lake Balaton. In all, the visit was quite relaxing. Elizabeth and Renate renewed their friendship and their determination to make a match between Klára and Franz as soon as they came of age.

Upon their return to Budapest, fifteen-year-old Klára entered the College of Music, the *Zeneakadémia* of the Royal National Hungarian Academy of Music on Király Street in Ferenc Liszt Square. Originally named the Franz Liszt Academy of Music, the college had an excellent reputation. She studied piano under the direction of the great Béla Bartók. Bartók inspired her interest in Hungarian folk music; music he referred to as "old Magyar melodies."

Late September, Paris

"You must come, Rudolf," invited Yvette, "it will be at the Theatre des Champs-Elysées. I'm only in the chorus," she shrugged her shoulders, "but perhaps you can find me." Then she added with great excitement, "Last summer in Monte Carlo was marvelous! I modeled for Picasso again."

Very impressed, Rudolf wondered if he would recognize Yvette in Picasso's paintings and his mind wandered to the Picasso paintings of women he had seen in Paris.

"I was in Monte Carlo with Diaghilev's Ballet Company, of course. We were rehearsing for Cocteau's ballet, *Train Bleu*." Yvette mused about her summer, "Picasso designed the curtain and Coco Chanel designed the costumes. We modeled for Picasso between rehearsals." Yvette smiled at Rudolf, "Are you listening to me?"

Rudolf did go to the Theatre des Champs-Elysées to see the ballet, *Train Bleu*. He found the ballet tolerable, could never be sure that he found Yvette in the chorus, but was completely enthralled by Picasso's curtain. While the ballet portrayed happy people in a summer reverie, Picasso's curtain design depicted enormous, voluptuous females, certainly not Yvette, frolicking on the beach. A vision of pure sensual pleasure in brilliant colors and flowing curved lines filled the fabric. Rudolf found the images breathtaking and took the opportunity to compliment Picasso himself who was there in attendance with his wife, Olga. The critics panned the ballet as decadent and bourgeois, but like Rudolf, the critic Andre Breton hailed Picasso's curtain design as genius.

Rudolf and János took Yvette with them to the first surrealist exhibition of art at the *Galerie Pierre*. The works astonished them all, so classically realistic and yet so haunting, provocative in subject matter. The opening was a major event with Picasso, Man Ray, Jean Arp, and Max Ernst all represented. The strange works intrigued Yvette, because she had worked with Leger on his film, *Ballet Mecanque*, and clearly understood avant-garde experimental cinema. However, the two-dimensional paintings and strange three-dimensional objects were far more challenging.

In particular, Yvette and Rudolf stood for a long time in front of Man Ray's *Object*, an actual metronome, including its hammer. Attached to the hammer was the photograph of an eye. The eye and eyebrow were clearly that of Man Ray's lover Kiki, a beautiful woman, who stood only a few feet from Yvette. Man Ray had meticulously cut from a black and white photograph the eye and perfectly arched eyebrow and then he attached the eye to the very tip of the hammer with a paper clip. The metronome set in motion sent the eye tick-tocking back and forth, back and forth. The relentless eye, never blinking, back and forth, watched Yvette and Rudolf.

The two were completely captivated by the eye, unable to turn their own eyes away. Feeling judged, scrutinized, disciplined like children forced to sit at the piano for hours, the object exasperated them. Rudolf understood why Man Ray had named the art piece, *Object to be Destroyed*. It demanded destruction.

The hypnotic *Object* held viewers prisoner with its staring, irritating tick-tock. All who saw it felt compelled to smash it to bits, just to be free of the infuriating thing. Respecters of art, of course, resisted the primitive urge to destroy, even though Man Ray himself said that some day it was his intention to physically and violently annihilate the *Object*.

1926
Summer

The summer of 1926 began as all other summers. In May the family and staff packed and left the city to spend the summer months at the lake. Leopold spent weekdays in Pest at his office and the weekends at the villa. He traveled by train or on some days Tamás drove him back and forth.

Klára loved to see the Lake Balaton villa come to life when everyone moved back in. Silva and her staff removed the covers from all the furniture, untied the draperies from their dust sacks, and aired the comforters and pillows. She directed the maids to sweep the floors with bundled branches of lavender interwoven with rosemary and Ana put sachets of rose petals, honeysuckle, and peppermint in the linen closets. Klára wanted to do something useful, so Silva suggested she open windows, seemingly hundreds of windows throughout the villa. A job Klára loved.

Klára opened all the first floor windows and then went up to the second floor, into her room. She thought her villa room was perfectly lovely with its pale yellow plastered walls and the rolled white flower designs that covered them. A tall yellow ceramic stove stood in the corner. Of course the warm

May days made the stove's use rare. When she opened the windows the lace curtains blew out onto the balcony and then back again into the room. Klára looked out toward the hills north of the villa to the east and west of the great meadow that stretched up the hill toward the shepherds' cottages and to the vineyards where rows and rows of vines followed the lay of the land as far as she could see. Klára inhaled deeply, smiled, and thought, *this is the place where I was born and it is beautiful.*

After a while Klára crossed the hall to Stefan's room, dark and musty. She pushed back the heavy draperies and opened the windows allowing shafts of bright sunshine to extend across the room. From Stefan's balcony Lake Balaton glistened in the distance. Leaning against the balustrade she thought of Stefan swimming across the lake, sailing in races, or just fishing. Her brother was such fun; the lake, the villa, summer, nothing was the same since he was gone. She missed him terribly.

She walked around Stefan's room running her hand along the edges of the furnishings, collecting dust on the tips of her fingers. Stefan would never be forgotten. She lay down on his bed and stared at the model airplane hanging from the ceiling; tears ran from the corners of her eyes, down into her hair. Klára remembered well the days her father and Stefan built the model and hung it over the bed. She walked over to his beautiful music box, turned the crystal handle, and listened to the lovely melody that began to drift into the air. Along with the airplane and the music box were all sorts of objects that belonged to Stefan—paddles, walking sticks, fishing poles—all evidence of the full life he lived at the lake.

When Klára returned to her room, she began to open drawers filled with odds and ends—old photos and souvenirs from the past. Just as she began to reminisce, Ana pushed open the door and looked in, "Supper's served, Miss Klára."

The two followed the winding servants' stair to the dining room. Ana continued down to the cellar while Klára kissed her father and took her place at the middle of the long table, her mother at the opposite end. Returning to Lake Balaton was always a pleasant experience, their conversation light and cheerful, even though a profound sadness still lingered under their happiness.

Most of the month of May Klára spent on her bicycle riding into Balatonfüred or up into the hills north of the lake or all the way to Tihany where she visited Dolf's grandmother. She swam in the lake on hot days and walked through the vineyards with her father whenever he was at the villa. Klára took the ferry with her mother to Siófok for tea with Aunt Eugenia. Sometimes she simply followed the flocks of sheep as they wandered the valleys beyond the villa. Shepherd Milan's grandchildren, much younger than Klára, loved to accompany her on walks. They eagerly showed her the new litter of Puli puppies born shortly before the von Estés' arrival. Klára found plenty to do to keep busy, never missed the city, but she could hardly wait for Rózsa to come in August for a few weeks.

In the meantime, she spent much of her time with Silva in the kitchen. If Klára could find nothing to do, she climbed the old cherry tree, up to a special branch just the right shape for a big pillow. She could lean on the pillow and read for a whole afternoon. One of those afternoons she was interrupted by Ana who stood under the tree, shouting up to her in a voice filled with excitement, "Miss Klára, you have a telegram!"

Ana stretched up as far as she could holding the telegram high. Klára reached down for it and ripped it open. It was her first telegram. Black type on yellow paper.

> *So you will be sixteen in July... I will be at Tihany Villa... I will be your escort for the Anna Ball as promised... Your liege... Dolf*

Thrilled, Klára slid from the tree and ran to the kitchen, "Silva, Silva, he didn't forget, he's coming! He's going to take me to the Anna Ball."

She twirled around the kitchen clutching the telegram, "He sent a telegram. Isn't it wonderful!"

Elizabeth entered the kitchen. Klára gave the telegram to her to read. Elizabeth smiled at Klára, "How nice of Rudolf to remember. You and I should take the train to Vienna for a shopping trip. You'll need a special dress."

Klára was happier than she had ever been in her whole life. When Leopold arrived he arranged to send Rudolf a telegraph of greeting and an affirmative reply.

In late June Klára and her mother made a trip to Linz and a successful side trip to the couture shops of Vienna. The shop ladies enjoyed dressing Klára in the latest Parisian fashions, even though Elizabeth cautioned Klára that just the right fit and fashion might be difficult to find. After all, Klára was tall and thin, actually rather skinny with few curves.

"A dress for a very special occasion that must flatter the young lady's figure on the verge of becoming a woman," said the shop owner, "I understand perfectly... not too low cut, not too sophisticated, not too grown up... but something lovely that will make the young lady feel very beautiful."

Even though Elizabeth kept complete control over Klára's choices, the final choice completely satisfied Klára and her mother. The perfect dress turned out to be one designed by the famous Parisian designer, Jeanne Lanvin.

On the afternoon of the Anna Ball, Elizabeth, Silva, and Ana gathered in Klára's room to help her dress. In addition to the Lanvin dress, Klára would wear several different Hungarian costumes required for the ball. The contemporary Anna Ball still honored its roots with young boys and girls singing and dancing to Hungarian folk songs in traditional costumes. A program of folk dances filled the first half of the ball and then waltzes the second half when the girls could wear their own choices of gowns.

Ana styled Klára's unruly hair with many hairpins while Silva captured it in a white lace and pearl band. Klára stood up and turned to face the three women. She wore her first folk costume—an ankle-length white dress with a lace blouse, full ruffled sleeves, and a gathered skirt with a decorative woven band at the hem. A ruffled lace apron over the skirt and a beautifully embroidered brown vest with golden threads completed the costume. Silva and Elizabeth began to cry as they praised her beauty, "You've grown into such a lovely young woman, Klára." And, "We're very proud of you, Klára."

The chauffeur drove the von Estés into Balatonfüred to the elegant lakeside Ádám Horváth Palace for the one hundred and first anniversary of the Anna Ball. Klára got out of the car and joined a group of enthusiastic friends dressed exactly as she. Nearby stood a group of young men dressed in Hungarian Huszar tunics, formal military white jackets with gold trim and buttons, pressed black slacks and spurred cavalry boots that jingled when they walked. Seeing Klára engaged with so many young people pleased Elizabeth and Leopold. She had gotten to know them over the last year at dancing classes where they learned the traditional folk dances.

Elizabeth and Leopold chose a good spot to see the opening ceremonies. In the meantime Tamás arrived with Silva and Ana who positioned themselves where they could see the activities from a good vantage point in the garden, the same spot from which Klára, as a child, had watched the ball with Stefan, Rudolf, and Rósza and the same spot from which Leopold, Christián, and Tamás had watched when they were children.

When Rudolf arrived he joined Elizabeth and Leopold at their table near the dance floor. Events began with a parade of dancers, each young woman escorted by a young man; two by two they walked into the palace ballroom. The crowd of viewers clapped as each couple was introduced and took their place in a circle, the ladies on the inside facing the young men on the outside. The orchestra began to play music for the *palotás*, the traditional opening dance. Folk dances proceeded for nearly a half hour.

After a brief intermission the dancers reappeared; this time the ladies were dressed in full red skirts with black laced vests over blouses with white ruffled sleeves, white aprons, and headdresses of pearls and flowing ribbons. Music for the *csárdás* began. Each couple started with two steps to the right and two to the left and then the young man spun the lady around his raised hand as the couples moved around the circle repeating the steps. Twirling red skirts, streaks of gold, and jingling spurs were exhilarating under the sparkling chandeliers. As Klára spun round and round she caught a glimpse of Rudolf sitting at her parents' table.

When the folk dances were over, Elizabeth met Klára in the dressing room to help her change into her new Lanvin dress. The light mint-green silk chiffon gown was charming, delicate and feminine, yet sophisticated enough for Klára to appear very grown up. A graceful neckline curved over her tanned shoulders while the softly draped bodice flattered her boyish shape. Silk ribbons of light green laced around the dropped waistline and embroidered flowers embellished the lush full skirt of tulle.

"You look so beautiful, Klára." Elizabeth put her hand to her lips, "Your father will see his little girl has become a beautiful young lady." Her compliments continued, "The dances were delightful, so well done. You accomplished the *csárdás* expertly. We are proud of you, Klára. This is such an exciting night for all of us."

Delighted by her mother's praise Klára felt radiant and very grown up. "I saw Dolf sitting at your table. I'm so happy that he's come. This is the most wonderful night of my life."

As Klára walked to the entrance with the other girls, Elizabeth gave her daughter a kiss and returned to the ballroom. All of the young men had changed from their folk costumes into tuxedos. One more variation of a *csárdás* to perform brought the couples to their places in a circle and then a Bartók Magyar melody began. After the dance, Klára went straight to her parents' table. Leopold proudly met her with an embrace and several kisses, his delight obvious as he wiped tears from his eyes. Rudolf embraced and kissed her as well, while Leopold patted his back. Klára beamed as she thought, *this is a glorious night.*

After Klára and Rudolf danced several waltzes together, he guided her out onto the terrace, into a spectacular night. A million stars twinkled overhead.

"You have grown taller, Klára. You've become a beautiful young woman. I think I've lost the little girl I knew so well."

"You've been away too long, Dolf. I haven't been a little girl for a long time."

"You do look very grown up tonight. That is a beautiful dress." Rudolf smiled as he took a velvet box from his pocket. He opened the box and took from it a necklace, slipping the box back into his pocket. "This was my mother's necklace, Klára. My grandfather gave it to her for her sixteenth birthday. I want you to have it for your birthday. I know she would want you to have it. Will you wear it tonight?"

"It's lovely, Dolf. Thank you. I would be honored to wear it." She turned her back to him, "Will you fasten it for me?"

Rudolf slipped the delicate gold chain with its cluster of petite green emeralds and diamonds around her throat and clasped it. She turned, touching the stones, her smile glowing, "I love it, Dolf. Thank you so very much" and she kissed him on both cheeks.

"You should always wear emeralds, Klára. They reflect the color of your eyes perfectly."

Suddenly, shaken by her beauty and maturity, Rudolf thought of Stefan and the many times Stefan had teased him about being in love with Klára. Rudolf remembered his adamant protests. But now, at this moment, he realized Stefan had been right all along, he had always loved Klára. No other woman would ever compare to her and he knew that he would wait for as long as it took to make her his own.

He held her hands, stared into her lovely green eyes, and felt himself sinking into the abyss. He cleared his throat, "We should go back inside…there's more dancing to be done. I've been practicing for months, so I won't embarrass you."

"Dolf, you could never embarrass me." Klára protested, "I think you're a marvelous dancer." She spoke with such conviction, such sincerity to convince him, Rudolf had to smile as she continued, "I'm having a wonderful time and I thank you so much for coming all the way from Paris as you promised. This is the most special night of my whole life."

Rudolf guided her back to the dance floor where Klára danced a few dances with Leopold and a few with her Balaton friends, but for all the rest it was Rudolf who led her across the floor through waltz after waltz until midnight brought an end to the ball. He walked Klára and her parents to their car and gave Klára a kiss on the forehead. She looked at him seriously and gave him a soft kiss on his cheek. She could hardly sleep that night, thinking of the wonderful things that had happened, but most of all she thought of Dolf and how wonderful he had been to her. She felt the necklace at her throat and finally fell asleep.

The next day Elizabeth studied the necklace Rudolf had given Klára, still around her daughter's neck. The little green emeralds and diamonds, set in gold, formed three small flower shapes clustered together in an asymmetrical design that fit perfectly in the hollow of Klára's throat.

"That is a precious gift, Klára," Elizabeth stated. "Rudolf asked your father for permission to give it to you." Elizabeth took a deep breath, "You should know that I did not approve. I believe the necklace too intimate a gift for him to give. However, your father considered our close family connections reason enough to make the gift appropriate."

Sunday afternoon, a gorgeous summer day, Klára went sailing with Rudolf. He sailed the small boat out into the silky yellow-green water of their "Hungarian Sea." Klára dragged her hand in the warm water as the boat glided through the lapping waves. She spent most of the afternoon studying Dolf, his movements, the details of his face and his body. Klára teased him about his skill at sailing the boat and how muscular he had become. She asked him relentless questions about Paris. She especially wanted to know all about his girlfriends. But he provided few answers to her questions. Then he asked about her life.

"So, do you have a crush on that boy you danced with for the *palotás*…the tall one?

"I definitely have a crush on someone...not him...but someone very wonderful. It's a secret. I can't tell who it is, yet."

"Well, I hope he's worthy of you. You know how very special you are, don't you?"

"I can assure you that I'm certain he knows how special I am," she said in a sassy tone with a coquettish smile. "I think he loves me, too, but I don't think he knows it yet."

They both laughed. "I'm sure he does Klára. How could he not."

The breeze picked up, sending the boat tacking far to the left and ending their conversation. Klára and Rudolf shifted their attention to the sails, working together to bring the craft back to shore. Rudolf returned to Paris the next week.

September, Paris

Rudolf and his crowd were kept very busy by a full calendar of Parisian cultural and intellectual events, including Yvette's new ballet, Sergei Diaghilev's *Romeo and Juliet* and an opening for Picasso's one-man exhibit at Paul Rosenberg's gallery, featuring Picasso's *de femme* series from the summer in Monte Carlo. Oil paintings of his son Palo and his analytical *Guitare* collage series also astounded Rudolf. Picasso's free-flowing india ink drawings, diversity of thought and style greatly impressed Rudolf.

More astonishing to Rudolf than Yvette's ballet itself, were the set designs and costumes created by Joan Miró and Max Ernst, two fantastical expressionists. Since first attending the *Ballet Russe*, Rudolf noticed that all the greatest contemporary artists in Paris seemed to be involved in ballet productions.

"Yvette, could you arrange an introduction to Diaghilev for me? I want to apply for a set construction job. Maybe he'll let me use my graphic design skills for the next ballet."

"I'll introduce you to Diaghilev's secretary, Boris," Yvette frowned. "Diaghilev is a marvelous teacher, but he scares me. I never speak directly to him; he's so harsh. When he gets really angry, he pounds the bar or the floor with his cane and then he gives us one of his looks. It makes me shake in my shoes. So, we'll start with Boris. He's much nicer. I'm sure he'll agree to connect you with the next set designer."

Leopold received a letter from his sister, Eugenia. He understood that his sister felt strongly she should keep him informed about the German government situation. They often discussed how disgruntled the German people were by the 1920 Treaty of Versailles, feelings shared by many Hungarians who despised the Treaty of Trianon. Eugenia shared her worries about the weak

Weimar government and the threats against it by certain factions, the Nazis in particular. Eugenia wrote that she and Konrad had visited friends in Munich recently and were shocked by activities they witnessed. She feared their spread to Berlin. She also wrote...

Adolf Hitler was released from prison in early 1924. His National Socialist Party, the Nazi Party, had been outlawed throughout Germany, but now he has begun to rebuild the party over the past two years. The German people are suffering severely from wretched conditions, so many are dealing with abject poverty. We fear the times are ripe for Hitler and his party's return. He has established himself as the leader of the party... he calls himself Führer.

Konrad says that Führer Hitler uses Ernest Röhm's Sturmabteilungen, the brownshirted storm troopers, to defend, disrupt, and persecute.

The Brownshirts defend Nazi meetings, disrupt every other organization's meetings—like the liberal democrats, the communists, and the trade unions—but worst of all they persecute the Jews and the Gypsies and even the disabled. The Brownshirts are nothing but thugs who go around harassing innocent people and destroying property and businesses. Many former German soldiers who have been disillusioned by the failures of the Weimar government have joined the S.A.

This Hitler evidently believes he needs a personal protective force, so he organized a special elite guard, the Blackshirted Schutzstaffeln, the S.S. Now we see these troops everywhere. The S.S. seems to be more of a spy or informative unit, very intimidating, rude, and never smiling. They are forever checking papers, even mine and Konrad's. Hitler is making Germany intolerable. Konrad and I think that this little man, Hitler, wants to take Germany into another war some day in our future. If only the good German people would awaken! We are thankful that these interferences have not made their way to Cologne, but we fear they are coming our way.

Your faithful sister, Eugenia

—〰—

On the evening of October sixteenth, Leopold, Elizabeth, and Klára dressed in their finest formal wear for the premier of Zoltán Kodály's comic opera, *Háry János*, at the Royal Hungarian Opera House on Andrássy Avenue. Kodály spent a lifetime researching Hungarian folk music and in the folk opera, *Háry János*, Kodály told the story of a Huszar soldier in the Austrian army who tells all who will listen the extraordinary tale of his adventures of love and riches while he sits in a village inn. Although the hit of the evening was the baritone, Palló, it was Sebeöl's sweet songs as the Empress, object of János's affections, that moved Klára to tears. Klára felt proud to be Kodály's student.

1927

Rudolf decided he could not visit Hungary or the lake during the summer of 1927, but he did write letters to Klára.

I will not be coming back to Hungary this summer... it will be the first time in my life that I have not come to Lake Balaton in the summer. I will miss you, Little Klára.

I have taken a job in Monte Carlo for the whole summer. I will be working with a great Russian artist, Naum Gabo, to create stage sets for Diaghilev's new ballet. The ballet, La Chatte, is about a young man who has a little kitten. One day the kitten is transformed into a beautiful young woman, but she pays little attention to the man, because she is too busy chasing mice.

Gabo invented the constructivist style of art—he has inspired many followers of his style here in Paris. I like the forms Gabo makes very much. He has broken with traditional sculpting methods and materials to make something very new. Instead of using the expected, he constructs his forms by adding industrial materials together to build up non-representational structures. Although the structures do not appear as recognizable objects, they seem familiar, as though they have some purpose, even though they do not.

A second letter came to Klára in mid-June...

I went back to Paris a few days ago to see a new ballet, Le Pas d'acier. It opened as a sensational success at the Théâtre Sarah Bernhardt. I had never seen anything like it. The ballet, based upon an opera, The Flaming Angel, has two acts. The first takes place in rural Russia during a famine and the second takes place in a factory. The theme addresses the revolutionary ideal of transformation from an agrarian to an industrial society that glorifies the machine and ennobles the laborer.

You know, I am suspicious of Russian thinking... too often the laborer is thought of as a continuation of the machine, part of a mechanical move-ment, important to the whole, but void of individuality. The Bolsheviks embrace that ideal.

It was not the theme of the ballet that excited me... it was the stage set created by the Russian constructivist, Georgi Yakoulov! As a follower of Gabo, Yakoulov made a set of cogs and pulleys, wheels and conveyor belts to create a whole new world. He took the interworkings of the machine

and made a vision of metal and color and movement into something quite
beautiful to see. The dancers were choreographed to move as if they, too,
were machines and the music emulated the sounds of a factory. It was a
most spectacular performance! My only regret is that you were not with me
to see such a fabulous ballet!

In late July, Rózsa arrived at the lake for only a week's stay. The two young
women spent their days in the sun, swimming, sailing, or riding their bicycles.
They talked of their plans for the future. While Klára continued her studies at
the Music Academy, Rózsa had decided not to pursue university. She instead
preferred to enter the work force and planned to look for a job in September.
They also spoke of their hopes to find interesting young men in their futures,
although Rózsa doubted Klára would ever think of anyone other than Rudolf.

Rózsa had comforting words for Klára when she lamented Rudolf's
absence, "Just wait, I bet he'll show up before the summer's over. He's in love
with you, you know."

Klára just laughed and shook her head, "He is not! He's just my friend, my
brother."

"You can say that, Klára, if you want, but I know he loves you and you love
him...always have," Rózsa teased her, "Now, if I can find my own beau that
would be lovely."

That evening Leopold arrived by train from Budapest. He entered the
gazebo where Elizabeth was sitting with the girls; they were enjoying the
warm evening while sipping cold minted tea. Silva had a glass for him as soon
as he sat down. They shared the news of the day from the lake and the city.
Then Leopold engaged Rózsa, "I hear from your father that you are not interested in university, Rózsa. What are you planning to do?"

"I'm not sure, but I will be looking next week."

"Well perhaps you should come round the von Esté Fine Wine Company.
We may have a place for you there, if you have an interest in the wine business."

"I would like that, Sir, very much. Thank you"

August

Late August arrived, only a few weeks of summer were left. Rózsa had gone
back to town weeks before and Klára had to search for things to keep herself
busy. Standing in the shade of the old cherry tree, Klára stood painting her old
playhouse, now serving as a potting shed. She moved the paint brush over the
old boards with very little regard—her thoughts were on days past when she
and Rózsa played inside while Stefan and Rudolf teased them from outside,

pelting the roof with old apples or sticking their heads in the windows. Klára smiled at the thought...*how quiet the days are now.* Suddenly two large hands went across her eyes and a very familiar voice asked, "Guess who?"

"Oh, Dolf, you have come! I was so hoping that you would!"

They embraced and shared kisses and laughed. It was a wonderful homecoming.

"I could stay away no longer ... a summer without Lake Balaton just would not be summer," teased Rudolf, "not to mention a summer without Klára."

The two spent every day of the following week visiting all their favorite places, renewing all their old memories. He told her about his summer in Monte Carlo with the ballet company and about his new friends. Klára told him about her year at the academy and about Rózsa who was perhaps going to work for her father's company in Budapest.

Rudolf proudly informed Klára that when he returned to Paris, he would be leaving his position at the Academie Julian for a new teaching position at the Ecole des Beaux Arts.

1928
April, Budapest

Pál Szabó left the elevator and walked toward the reception desk of the von Esté Fine Wine Company. He informed the woman behind the desk that he had arrived for his appointment with Duke von Esté. She asked him to be seated and rang Leopold's office. After a few moments a young woman entered the reception room, pressed the elevator up button, and with a pleasant smile asked Pál to follow her. He rose from his chair thinking that he would follow her anywhere. She was the most enchanting girl he had ever seen; her red hair framing her pretty face like a halo of golden light.

In the elevator he introduced himself, "My name is Pál Szabó and you are?"

"I know who you are, Mr. Szabó. The Duke is looking forward to his meeting with you."

The old operator, Zol, opened the door and the beautiful young woman led Pál to a closed door; she knocked, opened it, and ushered him into the office.

"Thank you, Rózsa," said Leopold as he walked toward Pál extending his hand, "Come in, Pál. I'm happy to see you! Sit."

Leopold designated a large leather chair by a table; Pál took his seat. Leopold's new Vizsla puppy, Fejedelem, moved alongside Leopold, settled down by his feet, licked his hand, and gave Pál a dubious look.

"Beautiful dog, Sir. Is he a good hunter?"

"I don't hunt any longer, poor puppy. He won't have that purpose," said

Leopold as he gently stroked the pup's head as he gazed up at his master adoringly, "In this life he's meant only to be my companion and so far he's very faithful."

"So...your father has given the rights of contract negotiations to you! That speaks well of you. Your father is a very respected businessman...a man of his word and a trusted associate in my business. We have worked together for many years. So, what have you to say for Miklós Szabó and his barrels?"

Pál leaned forward, putting his briefcase on the table and pulling out a stack of papers. He began with a deep, clear, and confident voice, "This is what we're thinking about for next year's harvest...."

After almost an hour, Pál and Leopold emerged from the office in good humor, laughing, each absentmindedly giving Fejedelem pats on the head. Leopold escorted Pál to the elevator and pressed the button, but just as the elevator arrived, Pál hesitated. He looked back at the gorgeous red-haired girl standing in the doorway. He smiled directly at her as Leopold said good-bye and Zol slid shut the door.

Pál looked at his wrist watch—four-thirty. He asked the receptionist when the office closed and she answered five o'clock. Pál walked outside. He breathed in the warm April air and glanced around the street at the row of trees just beginning to spring back to life. Tiny pale green leaves like lace appeared at the ends of the gray limbs. Puddles of newly collected rainwater nestled in the cobblestones. He suddenly realized Hércegprimas was the most extraordinary street he had ever seen. He walked across the street, sat on a low stone wall with a clear view of the von Esté Fine Wine Company's front door, and waited.

As bells tolled five times from someplace in the distance, the employees began to descend the stairs one by one. He saw Leopold and Fejedelem exit the building and get into a dark green car and move away down the avenue. Finally, the red-haired girl appeared with a group of young women. He stood up, walked to the middle of the street, and called her name, "Rózsa!"

The whole group stopped and stared at him. He walked toward her, "Rózsa...see I know your name, too."

She smiled at him and sent her giggling friends along.

"Aren't you the clever one finding out my name!" she said teasingly. "So, if you are so clever why are you sitting out here in the rain?"

"It's not raining...just misting...worth getting a little damp, if you'll let me walk you home," he reached for her hand, "It's very nice to meet you, Rózsa...?"

"Klein," she answered and shook his hand. Clearly, he was a gentile boy. "Nice to meet you as well, Mr. Szabó," responded Rózsa as she studied his face, his extremely good-looking face. She liked his thick sandy hair and steely gray eyes. He was tanned and a bit rugged, quite unlike any of the boys she knew in Budapest. "All right, let's walk. My home is not too far away...in the Jewish Quarter."

They began talking instantly, finding out all the facts about each other. He from Eger, she in Budapest all her life, details about their families, and discovering that neither was attached to anyone. As they walked down Hércegprimas Street they passed a coffee shop and stepped in to warm up with a cup of strong Turkish coffee. They sat in a corner booth, laughed and talked until it grew dark outside.

"Oh, it's late. My mother will be worried. I should go. You don't have to come with me, I'll catch a tram."

"No, no. I'll come with you. It's my fault you're not on time." Pál asked very seriously, "Is it too soon for me to meet your mother?"

Rózsa laughed, "My mother will think you're a very handsome gentile boy, but she'll wonder why I'm bringing you home. What should I tell her?"

"You can tell her she'll have to get use to having a gentile boy for supper whenever I'm in Pest." Pál smiled broadly.

Rózsa tilted her head and twisted her hair around her fingers, typical of her when serious thoughts were stewing in her head. She smiled at him, raised her chin with confidence, fully aware that taking him to her home would surely bring controversy. She replied jokingly, "Sounds good to me. You're lucky my family are Neolog Jews; if we were Orthodox, there would be no suppers for you!"

Rózsa studied his face again, "My parents will adore you."

He paid the bill and they went out onto the street where the lamplights had come on. A tram appeared from around the corner; they ran for it and rode to Dohány Street, getting off near the synagogue. The two walked to the Klein home, climbed the stairs, and went inside.

"I'm home," Rózsa called from the hallway. "Sorry to be so late. I brought a guest."

Suddenly everyone appeared—her mother, Dr. Klein, her brothers Ferenc and Abram, all coming from the dining room and even Magda came from the kitchen. Éva would have scolded Rózsa for her lateness, but that was impossible in front of a guest. And what a guest! Everyone was astonished…a gentile boy none of them had ever seen before and knew nothing about.

Rózsa introduced everyone to everyone and added that Pál was from Eger and in town on business with the Duke. That bit of information seemed to clarify the questions they had about why Rózsa was bringing this particular boy home. *New in town with nowhere to go* and it turned out that Dr. Klein had met Pál's father during the time he had worked for the Duke.

Within moments Rózsa's family happily welcomed Pál as their guest and swept him into the dining room where Magda had already set a place for him. Pál eagerly engaged in conversation. He delighted them all with stories of Eger and his family and listened to their stories with equal interest.

After dinner, the Klein family retired to the music room as usual for a private concert. Rózsa and Éva on the pianos, Ferenc the violin, and Abram the viola. Dr. Klein sat in his chair while Pál sat comfortably on the sofa. After several pieces of music, Mrs. Klein announced, "That will do for this evening. We hope you have enjoyed our music and please come back to visit us when you are in the neighborhood, Mr. Szabó."

"It's truly been an honor to be in your home," Pál rose from the sofa. "Thank you for dinner and for the delightful concert. I do hope that I may accept your invitation on my next visit to Budapest."

Rózsa led him to the front door and opened it for him. "Well, that turned out much better than I expected, actually quite enjoyable. Thank you for walking me home."

She followed him out onto the stair and offered her hand. He took it, held it for a moment and then raised it to his lips.

"Rózsa…Rózsa. I'll find many reasons to come to this neighborhood."

"Pál, I must be honest. There's no reason for you to come back here." Rózsa looked down when she said the words; she couldn't look at him. "I could never let myself be interested in a gentile…my family would not allow it…I must marry a Jew."

She said the words, but her feelings of sadness surprised her. Again she tilted her head and twisted her hair in her fingers.

"I have known you for less than a day, Rózsa," Pál lifted her chin upward and looked into her eyes, "but I know I will see you again and again until you're mine forever. Send me away if you don't feel the same, but I know you feel the same as I do…we'll find a way."

He kissed her gently on the forehead, the nose, and the lips and then he was down the stairs, waving to her and shouting that he would be back soon.

Unbelievable. . . what has happened in the last few hours, Rózsa thought. Such a short time before she had never even seen this young man and now she knew in her heart she would love him for her whole life…*and he's not a Jew… what can be done?* What a strange dichotomy of feelings…extreme elation experienced through the thought of this truly lovely young man caring for her… contradicted by the knowledge any relationship was completely impossible.

Rózsa stepped into the hall and closed the door behind her. Her cheeks were hot to the touch and she knew her blush would betray her thoughts. She called good-night to her family and hurried up the stairs to her room. As she prepared for bed she wished she could talk with Klára; she needed to tell someone about this miracle and about the doubt that weighted so heavily upon her. She knew Klára would be as thrilled as she and would give her encouragement. Rózsa snuggled under her covers and decided to telephone Klára in the morning. She turned out the light and hoped she would dream of Pál and she did.

—ᘛ—

The next afternoon after work Rózsa hurried to the Gundel restaurant on Allatkerti Street near the Museum of Fine Arts and waited impatiently for

Klára to arrive. Klára worked part time at the museum playing the piano for art exhibits. After an exchange of greetings, settling in at their table and ordering coffees, Klára confronted Rózsa, "This must be really important for you to want to meet here...so posh. What's happening?"

With gypsy music playing in the background Rózsa took a deep breath and smiled widely, "Well, I thought Gundel's would be the most convenient for you. How is the piano playing going? Still having fun?"

"Come on, Rózsa," Klára was skeptical, "we're not here to talk about me...hmmm...it must be love we're here to talk about...so out with it! I haven't heard about anyone before this. How can you be so secretive?"

"I just met him yesterday...and it's real and wonderful and terrible at the same time. That's why I had to talk to you today!"

Rózsa recited all the facts and details, meeting Pál, the coffee, the dinner...what he said...*the kiss*...what she felt and that he was not a Jew. Klára instantly thought of Stefan and Eszter and what a disaster their love had turned out to be. She didn't mention those thoughts aloud, but they made her feel more compassion for Rózsa.

"I'm so happy for you, Rózsa. It's just like Silva always says, *One day you do not know your love and then the next day there he is*. It's so romantic, Rózsa. Just as it should be. I can hardly wait to meet him. When do you think he'll come back to Budapest?"

"I don't even know, but I think soon. At least I hope so." Rózsa's smile faded to a vacant resigned look; her head tilted, "But my parents...they won't approve. They're not Orthodox Jews; they're Neologs who supposedly believe in modern ways and change. They call themselves reformers, but they won't go along with this. They would never approve a marriage with a non-Jew." She sighed, "Well, these worries are very premature, aren't they? Maybe I won't even like him if I get to know him better."

Klára looked at her friend with great sympathy, "It's amazing to me that so much feeling passed between the two of you in such a short span of time. I think that means something...like destiny or maybe even something divine. So who are your parents or anyone to deny the two of you your fate?" Klára held Rózsa's hand, "Let's see what happens. It's quite exciting, isn't it?"

"Oh, yes, it is, Klára. I knew that you would say what I needed to hear." Tears filled Rózsa's deep blue eyes. "You are such a dear friend."

—☿—

Only eight days later, Rózsa left work to find Pál sitting on the stair, the first of many times Pál would come as he promised. On this first return visit, the two avoided dinner at the Kleins and instead met Klára at a little café in Vörösmarty Square for dinner topped off with Viennese-style cappuccinos and a luscious chocolate torta. Klára and Pál became instant friends; after all they shared a great love for Rózsa.

Sipping his hot coffee through a mound of whipped cream, Pál asked Klára, "So, who is the lucky man in your life, Klára?"

Rózsa looked at Klára and wondered if she would confess, at last, her love for Dolf. She nudged Klára, teasing her, "Go ahead, tell him whom you've dreamt about all your life."

Klára blushed and looked down.

"So, I've stumbled onto a secret." Pál joined the teasing, "There is someone."

"No, no, not really. Just my silly childhood fantasy. He's my friend, more like my brother. He's older and he lives in Paris. It's nothing…really."

"Whoa! Too many protestations! It must be real. So who is he?"

"Dolf!" Rózsa blurted out with a big smile, "and he loves her, too, but neither will tell the other."

"Rózsa, you don't know that," Klára frowned at her. "I haven't even seen Dolf since August of last year."

"Who's Dolf?"

"Dolf is a family friend, the Count Rudolf von Házy. I've known him all my life. He was my brother Stefan's dearest friend. Dolf has always been there when I've needed him, but to him I'm still a child, a little sister. I think he can't think of me in any other way." She smiled, "Only Rózsa knows I've had a huge crush on him…I guess forever."

Pál studied the two young women sitting across from him. They were both stunning beauties…Rózsa's sweet face framed by her halo of red gold and in contrast the striking Klára with her sleek black hair and brilliant eyes. He reached for Rózsa's hand, "We're lucky, aren't we, to have found each other and to know it?"

He turned to Klára, "I would like to meet your Dolf someday."

Pál continued to make regular trips to Budapest from Eger throughout the summer and one weekend in August Klára invited the couple to come to Lake Balaton. Klára and Tamás met their train at the Balatonfüred station. Klára was thrilled to host Rózsa once again and to introduce Pál to the lake. Klára planned activities for their entire visit—swimming, sailing, hiking, riding, sight-seeing the countryside.

Back at the villa, Silva served apricot and cherry strudel with glasses of cold cider. She loved having young people in the villa again reminding her of so many past happy summers.

Klára led Rózsa and Pál outside to the garden where Elizabeth welcomed them. They avoided the hot sun by sitting in the shade of the old cherry tree at the corner of the kitchen. Elizabeth liked Pál and in her very forthright manner told him so; as well, she informed Rózsa that she had made a good choice. Elizabeth believed wholeheartedly in her own opinions and never had a problem expressing them openly. Klára didn't always appreciate her mother's opinions or openness, but in this particular case agreed with her completely, so the afternoon was spent congenially.

The next morning after breakfast Klára took Rózsa and Pál on a tour of the villa grounds. First a walk through the vineyards and the pasture where several horses grazed and switched their tails lazily. Then up the hill to the shepherds' cottages to meet a particular Puli, *Fekete*, Blackie. Klára explained, while scratching the Puli's neck deep within its curls, "He and I have taken a liking to each other. It would be too lonely for him at the villa, but when I'm here, we go for long walks together."

Fekete followed behind Klára as they started back down the hill. They stopped at the winery to see where the grapes from the villa's vineyard were pressed and stored in barrels and then to the building for bottling next door. The large size of the operation surprised Pál.

"We've made many barrels for the Duke over the years, but I've visited only a few of the larger wineries." Pál asked, "How many of these small wineries does the Duke operate?"

"Most of Papa's wineries are much larger, like the one in Balatonfüred. The press here is just for Papa, the villa and our home in Budapest."

"Impressive," whistled Pál. "Will the Duke be here sometime this week? I would like very much to visit with him again."

"He'll be home tomorrow evening." Klára led them out of the complex onto the driveway and passed the open carriage house.

Pál noticed a car-like object covered in canvas, "What's that?"

"That was my brother's car." Klára walked into the garage and began to roll back the canvas cover. "He left it in Sopron before he was killed. Papa and Tamás just brought it back to the villa about a year ago. No one has driven it since."

"It's fantastic. What is it?"

A deep voice answered, "It's a 1920 Alfa Romeo Torpedo 20-30 HP."

The three instantly turned toward the strange voice. A tall, dark silhouette stood against the doorway, backlit by the sun. Klára recognized him instantly, "Dolf!"

She ran toward him and he swept her up, kissing her on both cheeks.

"Your Papa thinks I should teach you to drive. What do you think?"

Klára shrieked with delight, but it wasn't the thought of driving that thrilled her, it was Dolf! She could hardly believe it... *Dolf here! Nothing compares to that.*

Rudolf turned to Rózsa, "Hello *Little Arany*, beautiful as ever."

They exchanged an embrace and kisses on the cheeks. Rózsa quickly introduced Pál to Rudolf. They moved toward the car, took off the canvas to have a better look at the wheels, the engine, and all the brilliant Merosi details.

"What a machine! A few years old, but still incredible!" Pál was clearly impressed, "It sure beats my little truck. How lucky you are, Klára!"

They pulled the canvas back over the car and left the garage. Silva saw them coming from her herb garden and called to them, "How many for dinner? We're having *silurus* and *burgonya lángos*, fish and deep-fried potato cakes, with *mákos rétes*, poppy seed strudel. I know it's your favorite, Count."

"We'll all be there, Silva, Thank you," Rudolf answered.

The next afternoon, the four rode horses up into the Badacsony Hills. They took a picnic packed by Silva with them. While Rózsa and Klára collected wildflowers, Rudolf and Pál relaxed against some logs watching their horses graze nearby.

"So, Count, what's your story?" Pál motioned toward Rudolf's leg.

"My leg?" Rudolf laughed, "I lost it in a cave not too far from here when I was twelve." He looked at Pál, "What about you? What are you doing with a nice Jewish girl like Rózsa?"

"I'm going to marry Rózsa...in September a year from now."

"How is that going to happen? Is she going to stop being Jewish?"

"No, never. It has to be me. I'll convert, but she doesn't know that yet."

"So, will your conversion set well with your family?" Rudolf voiced his assumption, "They're Catholic, aren't they?"

"Yes, Catholic, but I love Rózsa and I'm going to be her husband, so like it or not, they'll have to accept us."

"Oh, Pál, well, you know your family, I don't. But they could throw you out, disown you, who knows? I doubt it will be easy, but I admire your determination."

Pál shrugged his shoulders, "I could never walk away from Rózsa. Who else could compare to her? Neither of us would ever come close to happiness again."

Then Pál leaned on one elbow and engaged Rudolf, "You've given me the right to ask about your intentions for Klára."

"Klára? She's my little sister," Rudolf shifted his weight and stood up. "I've known Klára since she was in the cradle."

"She's not your sister. I've seen how you look at her. It's not in a brotherly way."

Rudolf became defensive, "She's only eighteen; I'm twenty-five." He walked toward the horses, feeling the sting of this stranger's intrusion. He liked Pál very much, but he just didn't think it was the right time to let Klára know how he felt about her. *I'm certainly aware that I love Klára*, but, he thought to himself, and then almost inaudibly said, "she's so young, only eighteen. She's had so few experiences. I promised myself I would wait until she's older, at least twenty, before I tell her how I feel. It's the reason I stay so far away."

"Sorry, Dolf, I apologize for asking questions." Pál stood by the horses with his hands in his pockets. "It's apparent to me that you know better than I your relationship with Klára. It's none of my business. I apologize for intruding." He took a step forward and offered his hand to Rudolf. They shook hands and laughed, "Our secret."

After Rózsa and Pál returned to Budapest, Klára's driving lessons began. She and Rudolf sped in Stefan's old Alfa Romeo around the north side of the lake, onto Tihany Peninsula, and up into the Badacsony. They had great fun together, even though Rudolf continued to be somewhat aloof. Although he could hardly keep his eyes from staring at her lovely face, he remained determined to check his feelings. He truly believed her to be too young, too inexperienced. He honestly wanted her to have a chance to discover things about the world beyond Budapest and the lake and, even, about herself before he confessed his love for her. And, perhaps worst of all, he harbored a deep fear that Klára would rebuff his feelings and tell him she only thought of him as a brother.

Rudolf did share a bit of news with Klára, "I'm considering leaving my teaching post at the Ecole des Beaux Arts. I received a letter from a friend, László Móholy-Nagy, who teaches at the Bauhaus in Dressau, Germany. He inquired if I would be interested in a teaching position there.

"The Bauhaus philosophy on art is quite compatible to my way of thinking…that art must be integrated into contemporary life through modern technology. If I choose to go, I will teach typography and basic design courses, possibly calligraphy, too. Great artists—printmakers, painters, sculptors, and architects—teach there. It would be a fantastic environment. I'm seriously considering leaving Paris. What do you think, Klára?"

"Well, it sounds like a grand opportunity, but you know I'm very selfish. I only want you to come back to Budapest," Klára pouted, but embraced him.

"I will, Klára. I will someday soon."

December, Budapest

By December snow covered the streets and squares, but nothing stopped Pál's visits. Everyone could clearly see the deep affection Pál and Rózsa had for each other. Many suppers were consumed in the Klein home. Éva had spoken to her daughter an equal number of times warning her… *friendship is perfectly acceptable, Rózsa, but nothing more can be tolerated.*

Rózsa answered each of her mother's admonitions very simply, "I understand, Mama."

Dr. Klein spoke to Pál as well, allowing that Pál would always be welcome as a guest, but never as a son-in-law. The Kleins were concerned; they considered denying their daughter's friendship with Pál altogether; they even considered sending Rózsa to Palestine to live with Eszter and her family.

1929

In February Rudolf attended a soiree at the famous Madame Fauchon's salon on the Boulevard St. Germaine near Aux Deux Magots Café. He had been invited by a young Englishwoman, Olivia Allen-Gainsborough whom he had met at the opening of a gallery exhibition of surrealist painters René Magritte, Paul Eluard, and Max Ernst.

While Rudolf stared, somewhat perplexed, at the surreal juxtaposition of objects in Magritte's *L'Idée fixe*, a stunning young woman had approached him. She commented on the painting and they began a discussion of Magritte's unique interpretation of reality. They both admired Magritte's superior polished draftsmanship and ability to render technically realistic images. And they agreed the recognizable objects set in Magritte's bizarre reality must make some profound revelation, but Magritte's meaning eluded both of them. Rudolf and the Miss Allen-Gainsborough shared more conversation over a glass of wine and rather spontaneously she asked him if he would consider joining her for an evening of intellectual stimulation at a friend's apartment.

And now here he was at Madame Fauchon's salon in the midst of an interesting mix of guests—students, artists, poets, musicians, authors, and politicos—who smoked cigars and drank very good brandy. Rudolf enjoyed the variety of conversations he heard, but he rarely participated, rarely spoke, preferring to stay on the edges and listen. Finally, he did ask one question of the rather pro-socialist crowd, "As artists and intellectuals, should we consider how a socialist regime might react toward individualism? Should we expect a lenient or severe response?"

The guests turned toward him and immediately engaged enthusiastically in the argument.

One serious-looking young man asked Rudolf, "Your accent? I don't recognize it."

"Austrian... Hungarian, not so rare," answered Rudolf.

A stimulating discussion about art ensued, prompting Rudolf to willingly share his opinions, but when the conversation turned to politics, he decided to share none of his private thoughts. After the engaging conversation began to wane, Olivia and Rudolf moved to the bar where Olivia ran into a friend, Clive Jeffreys, an Englishman, whom she introduced to Rudolf.

The friendly and talkative Jeffreys, seeming to assume right away Olivia and Rudolf a couple, invited them for a weekend at the Lafayette Chateau in the Fontainebleau Forest, assuring them, "It isn't far from Paris."

Laughing at the assumption, Olivia addressed Rudolf, "A weekend away sounds wonderful... I think we should accept," and boldly added, "I think I like very much the thought of being coupled with a dashing Hungarian count."

The chill of the night air sent shivers down their spines as Rudolf and Olivia left Madame Fauchon's salon and walked arm-in-arm along the Boulevard St. Germaine.

"Did you mind my accepting Clive's invitation for the weekend? It should be fun. Did you mind his thinking we're a couple?"

Rudolf smiled as he looked down upon the pretty brunette, "No, I didn't mind at all...I look forward to spending the weekend with you, and getting to know you."

"Here's my flat. Would you like to come up for a nightcap?" She stood very close to him, "to warm you up a bit before walking home?"

"It is cold tonight...I could use a warming up."

The two entered the chic building, much grander than his humble flat, crossed the marble floor and went up the lift to the top floor. Once inside the luxurious apartment, Olivia left him in the large living room while she went to get drinks. She invited him to look around and make himself comfortable, explaining that her maid had already gone to bed. When Olivia returned, dressed in a satin and lace negligee, she offered him a dry martini, "I hope this suits your taste. I've been told I make a luscious martini."

Rudolf took the drink, sipped from the glass, raised his eyebrow and licked his lip, "Yes, Olivia, *luscious*...it suits my taste perfectly."

Late the next Friday afternoon, Olivia called for Rudolf at his flat and drove the two of them in her Renault to the Lafayette Chateau. They arrived late in the evening; it was already quite dark. As Olivia drove along the wide avenue leading to the house, the number of glowing windows allowed Rudolf to make an assessment of its grand nature and scale. The chateau's opulence and enormity were impressive. When they neared the entrance he noticed a great number of cars parked in the driveway. A servant met them, took their bags, and escorted them into the main entrance where Clive Jeffreys met them with a friendly smile.

Many guests, both English and French, men and women, filled the reception rooms. Good food and drink were served as some guests played cards, some stood in groups talking, while others relaxed. Clive asked Rudolf to join him in the library while Olivia excused herself, saying she would change into a bathing suit and join other guests for a swim in the elegant indoor pool. Through glass doors Rudolf could see the chateau's pool lit by strings of lanterns.

When he and Clive entered the library, Rudolf was surprised to see three men seated around a table apparently waiting for him. Clive steered him toward an armed leather chair and introduced him to only one of the gentlemen, Sir George Narberth.

"This may surprise you, Count Házy, but we have had our eye on you for some time now. We are interested in your points of view," Narberth said. "It appears to us that you have little interest in government or politics."

"I am aware, Sir, that the world turns," Rudolf felt quite uncomfortable.

"We appreciate that you keep your opinions close. I wonder if you are concerned at all for the future of Europe."

"I am."

"Have you felt the winds of war swirling around you?"

"I am a very busy man, Sir, but I do have the good sense to watch the weather."

"Have you an opinion regarding Germany?"

"I have."

"Your answers do not reveal a great deal. That is an admirable quality."

Another gentleman, unnamed, began to address Rudolf, "Let me give you some information. We are part of a group who cares deeply about the welfare of Europe, France and Britain in particular. Our aim is to avoid another disastrous war. We are gravely concerned about the direction of German policies and this upstart politician, Hitler. We need more information and we are thinking that you, Count Házy, could become a valuable friend. If you are interested in joining our cause, we invite you to come to London for some training. We know that you have been offered a teaching position in Germany. If you could take that position at a later date, if possible, it would be advantageous to us."

"Two questions...," Rudolf looked directly at the gentleman whose name he did not know, "Was the offer of a position at the Bauhaus arranged by you and is Miss Allen-Gainsborough part of this organization?"

"We have nothing to do with the Bauhaus, but we heard about their offer to you and decided that if you should accept our offer, your position at the Bauhaus would be a fortuitous move for our organization as well." He paused. "Miss Allen-Gainsborough is an associate."

"I am interested. I will do whatever I can to help Europe avoid a war."

A few weeks later Rudolf and Olivia left Paris for London. They crossed the Channel, landing at Dover where Olivia picked up her car, a Rolls-Royce Phantom 1, and drove them to London. She dropped him at the Ritz Hotel in Piccadilly; they would meet later for dinner. After getting settled at the Ritz, Rudolf took a taxi to Whitehall for an appointment in the Old War Office on Horse Guards Avenue. He went up to the seventh floor and walked down the long corridor to a door marked "M.I." The door was locked; he knocked and to his surprise, it was Olivia who opened the door and invited him into an immense complex of cubicles where seemingly hundreds were deeply absorbed in work.

"Welcome to SIS Headquarters," she smiled, "British Secret Intelligence Service."

Rudolf walked with Olivia to a large office; she knocked on the door. A secretary invited them in and guided them to padded leather chairs where they waited. After a few minutes, they were ushered into the plush office of the director, Admiral Sir Hugh Quex Sinclair…"Q." Olivia introduced Rudolf.

"The mission of MI6 is to ensure national security through counter-espionage," Q. explained to Rudolf. "In particular, MI6 is interested in your artistic skills—calligraphy, printmaking, even drawing. We foresee the use of your skills in a wide variety of ways—forgeries, false communiqués, diplomatic documents and letters, as well as your expertise in advertising propaganda."

Q. cautioned, "This is not a simple task to be taken lightly, Count Házy. What we are asking you to do is fraught with danger. You need extensive training for this mission. Everything is top secret, of course. You may not divulge anything to anyone…your mission…your schedule…even that you work for MI6. Are you still interested in working with us?"

Rudolf affirmed that, indeed, he was.

Olivia and Rudolf left England the following day for their return trip to Paris.

In May Rudolf took a three-month summer leave from his position at the Ecole des Beaux Arts and began three months of training at SIS-MI6 in London. Assuming Rudolf was in Hungary, Yvette was happy to have his flat while he was out of town for the summer. He only told her he would return to Paris in the fall and would resume his teaching position at the Ecole des Beaux Arts.

Spring in Hungary

In the early spring of 1929, Pál Szabó decided to visit Rabbi Sofer at the synagogue in his hometown of Eger to discuss his love for Rózsa Klein and his intention to marry her. The rabbi greeted Pál amiably and listened to the young man's ideas and then questioned him with sensitivity. Pál left the synagogue very discouraged by the rabbi who doubted that Pál could ever truly leave his own Catholic Church or receive his family's approval for a marriage with a Jewess.

A few days later Pál asked his parents to sit with him at the family dining table. Miklós and Borbála took their places and studied Pál, knowing their son had something serious to say. He began by pacing at the end of the table. Finally Miklós poured three glasses of *barackpálinka*, apricot brandy, raised a toast to their health and they all drank from the heirloom glasses.

Pál sat down at the table and began, "I'm in love with a girl who lives in Budapest. I've been seeing her for almost a year. I want to marry her in September. Her name is Rózsa Klein. She is Jewish."

Miklós and Borbála looked at each other, but said nothing.

"I can't marry Rózsa unless I become a Jew." Pál continued cautiously, "I've spoken to the rabbi here in Eger, but he's skeptical that I'll go through with the process. I want your support so I can do this."

His parents continued their silence.

Their silence surprised Pál; he had actually expected hysteria.

"Her family does not know of our intentions. They do not know I'm willing to convert to Judaism. I want you to meet Rózsa and her family."

Now their silence was eerie. "Why aren't you saying something? Are you going to disown me or what? Say something."

"We've known about Rózsa for some time," Miklós began slowly. "Your brother saw you with her in Budapest months ago and told us. Then we received a letter from Dr. Klein, a very kind letter. We've been waiting for you to talk to us."

"A letter from Dr. Klein?" Pál was shocked, "What did he write in his letter?"

Borbála answered, "Only that he was concerned that our son and his daughter were involved in an impossible relationship and he was worried that one or both of you would be deeply hurt."

"So what is your response?" Pál sighed heavily.

"You may become a Jew if that is what you want. We will not disown you and we will be very happy to meet Rózsa," Miklós added, "István told us that she is a beautiful girl with red hair."

"I don't understand. You're both so calm, too calm."

Borbála rose from the table and walked to the great sideboard that had been in her family for generations. She dug deeply into one of the drawers and brought out a leather pouch tied with leather thongs. She returned to the table and began to unwrap the contents.

"Your father and I decided to give you this information only if you ever told us what you have told us tonight."

From the pouch she withdrew very old yellowed papers with strange writings. "My great grandparents came here to Hungary from the Steppes of Russia many years ago. There were many immigrants from many different places who settled here in this valley. According to our family stories and recorded in these letters is a family secret. My great-grandfather, Antal, fell in love with a Jewish woman, Rachel. They married. Do you know what that means, Pál? It means that all of her descendants are Jewish, even though we have all been Catholic by faith, never practiced the Jewish faith. So, here we are in a circle. How can we tell you that you cannot become a Jew, when by their law you are already a Jew?"

"But Pál, you do understand that this is a serious family secret?" Miklós cautioned as he looked at Pál with a certain severity. "Eger's rabbi does not know; our priest does not know; no one knows except, now, the three of us. You do understand why it is important that this information remain concealed?

You also realize the peril that you may be entering by becoming a Jew? I'm not concerned about you from the aspects of religion or faith; I am concerned about you and Rózsa from the aspect of politics. Do you understand these things I am saying?"

Pál did understand and it gave him pause to think of anyone ever treating Rózsa unfairly.

"If you pursue Judaism we will support you and Rózsa. We will build a house here for you, if you want."

On Pál's next visit to Budapest he met Rózsa at the Central Café on *Ferenciek tere*. He related his family's secret to Rózsa, that by heritage he was already Jewish, he would formally convert to Judaism, and his parents would not oppose them. Rózsa could hardly believe it; she had been prepared to leave her faith for him.

She stood up, walked away from him, then returned to the table, "How ironic! You are Jewish by accident, not even knowing until now, but you are a Catholic in your heart."

"It's true, I'm Catholic by faith, but you're my heart." Pál protested, "I can change my religion."

"No, Pal, you cannot. I won't ask you to do that. You can no more follow Judaism than I can become Catholic," Rózsa sounded firm, immoveable. "It's more important that we each remain who we are and make our lives together a mix of our heritage. How does that sound? I hope it's a good argument, because that's what I'm going to tell my father."

Pál laughed, "Well, if anyone can convince him, it will be you."

"Well, after all, he's been preaching Magyarization all my life and now here we are, a perfect example of ethnically different Hungarians wanting to unite. I know that no Catholic priest will agree, but surely there is some progressive Neolog rabbi who will marry us."

Now they were both laughing. They walked from the café out into the cool evening air. Pál threw his arms around her waist, picked her up and spun her around in the middle of the sidewalk. Then they walked toward Rózsa's home on Dohány Street, holding hands and smiling with confidence at each other, even though their nervous giggles betrayed that confidence.

"You know that speaking with your father is to meet your wishes for tradition," Pál declared. "If your father doesn't give us his blessing, we leave Budapest and marry anyway. Don't try to leave me for some little Jewish boy."

Rózsa smiled and kissed him on the nose, "Sit here and don't get into any trouble. It may take a while, be patient."

Pál sat on a stone wall around one of the big sycamore trees on Dohány Street across from the Klein's home while Rózsa ran up the stairs and into the house. First she went into the kitchen, "Mama, I want to talk to you in the parlor with Father."

Her mother, involved in dinner-making with Magda, washed her hands and removed her apron. She stared at Rózsa with an expression of concern. *What has happened?...*she wondered...*something serious?* She followed Rózsa to the parlor.

Rózsa approached her father as he sat in his big leather chair writing on some papers, deeply engaged in his favorite pastime, his hobby, writing a thorough family history. Rózsa cleared her throat to get his attention. He looked up over the top of his glasses, magnifying glass in one hand, pen in the other. She announced to him she wanted to speak with him as her mother entered the room and sat down. Her father sat back in his chair and sighed.

"I have something to say." Rózsa paused, and took a deep breath, "Pál and I love each other and we want to marry in September, in just a few weeks. Pál will not convert to Judaism and I will not become a Catholic. We'll remain who we are. We want your blessing and we want you to help find a rabbi who will marry us."

Dr. Klein stood up and slammed the book he was reading onto the table.

"Jakov!" quietly cautioned Éva.

He had known for many months this day was coming. He knew that if he had any chance to stop it, he should have acted months ago. Éva patted his hand and spoke softly, "What can we do, Jakov? It seems she has already decided. If we stand in their way we will lose our Rózsa."

A long-ago sister returned to his thoughts...*dead*...his favorite sister, the beautiful red-headed Júlia. He studied Rózsa's face...*she looks so much like the aunt she has never known.* Jakov sat down in his chair, but remained silent letting his thoughts wander back in time. *I was so young, only seven, but I can still see her beautiful face leaning toward me that night...kissing my face through her tears. 'I love you Little Jakov. Don't forget me. Good-bye.'*

Jakov never knew what happened to Júlia or where she had gone, nothing except his father declaring, "She is dead to this family." Jakov asked his mother, but she only said, "We cannot say her name in this house ever again." But when his mother died he found a little box among her things. When he opened it he found an old darkened tintype of the beautiful Júlia as a young girl and one newer photograph of her with a young man in a uniform. On the back of the photo was written, in an unfamiliar hand, *Sig. e Sig.ra Michele Giordano...Montepescali.*

His eyes filled with tears, *What to do? Times are changing. Young people choose their own way these days. Rózsa is a good person. She wants to remain Jewish. Pál is a good person. He wants to remain Catholic. This is the dream of Hungary...every individual has the right to be who he is. That right is the basis for the philosophy for true unity...Magyarization. What can I say against them?*

Finally, her father spoke, "Rózsa, ask your young man to come visit me," he smiled gently.

Rózsa burst into tears. She fell upon her father's neck, "Oh, Father, thank you. I love you. Oh, Mama, I love you."

"Is it too old-fashioned for me to expect Pál to ask for your hand?"

Rózsa kissed her father's forehead, "I don't know what I would have done if you had said no to us. He is here, just outside, will you see him now?"

Éva rose from the sofa, "Of course, bring him in. He must stay for supper."

September

Rózsa could hardly wait to tell Klára her news. They met at two o'clock in the afternoon at Gerbeaud's. Rózsa insisted they order *kávés* and *kirsch*. As they drank their *kirsch*, through a broad smile, Rózsa began, "Pál and I are going to be married September seventeenth at my parent's home."

Klára was thrilled. She jumped up from the table, embraced Rózsa, and they kissed each other's cheeks.

"Father and Mama and I traveled by train to Eger to meet Pál's parents. They are Catholic, you know, but they have no objection to our marriage and they want to participate as much as they can. Pál's whole family met us at the station. My parents rode in the car with his parents, Miklós and Borbála, while Pál and I rode in a horse-drawn cart. Eger is a beautiful city—the countryside is lovely, green rolling hills with vineyards and forests. The Szabós live a few miles from town in a large complex of buildings—a barrel factory and sawmill, a blacksmith shop, barns, and other shops. Their house is quite nice, large and comfortable. The family is going to build a house for Pál and me right there on the grounds. Can you imagine? My own house?"

"Father asked a Neolog rabbi, Béla Steiner, from here in Budapest to meet us there. We had a light supper in their garden with wine including *Egri bika-vér*, "Bull's Blood," and then we moved into their home to the family dining table, Pál's table. That's a Jewish custom to go to the groom's table. Rabbi Steiner took out the *Tena'im*, the official document of engagement, like a contract, and then he read it in Aramaic. Mama and Mrs. Szabó each broke a china plate. Mama brought one of her special plates from home. I couldn't stop crying, tears were streaming down my cheeks. Pál kept his arm around me for support. It was all so beautiful," Rózsa was breathless.

"Then our parents discussed the wedding arrangements and the date that Pál and I had agreed upon with the rabbi. Our wedding will be Tuesday, September seventeenth, at our house on Dohány Street," Rózsa took a deep breath. "Tuesday, because it was the third day of Creation and God said it was good. Then we had a big engagement party with Pál's family."

Rózsa was so happy. She gave Klára a beautiful invitation to the wedding for her and her parents, "I have sent one to Dolf, too. I hope that he'll come.

"Oh, and some of my neighborhood friends are arranging a *Shabbet Kallah* for me, a party, and I want you to be there."

September 17, 1929, a Tuesday, the Hebrew month of Elul the 12ᵗʰ day, Year 5689

According to custom, Pál and Rózsa saw each other for the last time before their wedding on Tuesday the tenth. On the wedding day, beginning at dawn, each in their own separate places, Pál and Rózsa began their fast and the saying of special prayers, prayers for forgiveness for their wrongdoings as a kind of atonement for their sins, much like a personal *Yom Kippur*. Only with renewed and pure souls, could they stand together under the *Chupah* for their wedding ceremony.

When Pál arrived at the Klein's home, he was sequestered in his own private room where he dressed for the *Chupah* ceremony. In a different room Rózsa's girlfriends, including Klára, helped her slip into a beautiful white satin wedding dress with long sleeves down to her fingertips and a band of lace at the neck. The girls giggled as they buttoned more than a dozen pearl buttons down the back. With tear-filled eyes, Éva kissed her daughter's forehead, cheeks, and nose. "You are a beautiful bride, Rózsa. Your father and I are very happy for you to find such a fine young man."

The sound of music from the Klezmer band drifted closer to Rózsa's room. "They're coming," Rózsa cried. "My heart is beating so fast. Can you hear it, Klára? Oh, Mama, I'm so happy and so excited."

Suddenly there was a knock at the door. Klára opened it to find Pál, Dr. Klein, and Mr. Szabó in the hallway, a band of musicians stood behind them.

"May I come in?" Pál asked shyly. He had his first glimpse of Rózsa and smiled broadly at her. She looked so beautiful he felt somewhat faint, but the two fathers held him steady. As he walked toward Rózsa, Éva took her own mother's veil from a satin-covered box and handed it to Pál, giving him a kiss on the cheek. Pál gently placed the veil atop Rózsa's beautifully arranged red hair, looked deeply into her blue eyes, and let the veil fall over her face.

"This ritual in the wedding rites is inspired by the Genesis story of Jakov," Éva explained to Klára. "Remember the deception Jakov suffered? When he raised his first bride's veil he discovered the bride to be Leah rather than his expected Rachel. So, tradition allows Pál, the groom, to see his bride before they enter the *Chupah*. No deception here!" Éva laughed. "The veil also symbolizes Rózsa's dignity and modesty."

A voice singing a wedding song rose from the hallway while the trill of a twelve-stringed balalaika, strummed by her brother Samuel, filled the air. Led by the musicians and surrounded by their parents, Rózsa and Pál walked out of the room into the hallway and down the staircase. Pál waited at the doorway of the large music room, site of the wedding ceremony. Along with his father and Dr. Klein, Pál entered the *Chupah*, the four-posted canopy symbolizing God's protection and blessings for the home the young couple would share.

Rózsa entered the music room with her mother Éva, Klára, and the other girls. They circled around the *Chupah* seven times, signifying the seven days of creation and the bride's journey from her parents' home to her new home with her husband. Two married couples, friends of the Kleins, serving as witnesses, led Rózsa into the *Chupah* to stand at Pál's right side. Each of the four witnesses carried a lighted candle representing a joyful light in the world's darkness.

Rabbi Steiner welcomed the bride and groom; he blessed a cup of wine to signify the holiness of the marriage and the personal relationship of Pál and Rózsa; they each sipped from the same cup. The rabbi then recited seven blessings... *Praising God as Creator of all things; Praising God for creating mankind in His own image and giving man the ability to recreate, in particular Pál and Rósza; Thanking God for creating the world and blessing the wedding party; Rejoicing for the happiness of the bride and groom; Praying for the restoration of Jerusalem and the rebuilding of the Temple; Hoping for love to grow between the young bride and groom;* and finally *a Plea for redemption and peace for all the world.*

After these blessings Pál and Rózsa drank wine from a second glass. Wrapped in a white cloth, that glass was broken by Pál who stomped on it. Everyone present shouted *Mazel tov!* Rabbi Steiner spoke of the obligations, joys, and burdens of married life and asked Pál and Rózsa if they truly loved each other. A resounding *yes!* was their answer. Then the rabbi summoned the four witnesses, "Come near to observe and validate this ceremony."

The witnesses observed Pál as he placed the solid gold unadorned band on Rózsa's right index finger. The witnesses confirmed that the ring met the standards of value commanded by the Torah. Next the rabbi read the marriage contract, signed by Pál and Rózsa at the time of their engagement in Eger, describing their commitment to each other. The rabbi gave the contract to Rósza to keep forever.

At this point the wedding ceremony was over, except for the *being together time*. Pál and Rózsa retreated from the *Chupah* to the parlor, followed by the four witnesses. A silver spoon was laid across the threshold of the parlor. Pál and Rózsa, both laughing, hopped over it and entered into the parlor where they would sit alone together for a brief time. Rózsa's brothers and the witnesses guarded the entry from the outside and let no one disturb them. At last, the newlyweds could break their fast, sharing a single bowl of chicken soup and soda cookies, provided by Magda.

When Rózsa and Pál emerged from the parlor, the music and dancing began. Their strong brothers hoisted Rózsa and Pál seated in chairs onto their shoulders and carried them around the music room. Their guests shouted enthusiastically with great joy and happiness in celebration for the young couple. In a short speech Pál expressed his gratitude to all present and then surprised Rózsa by singing a Gypsy love song. Great cheers and loud shouts of *Mazel tov! Mazel tov!* rang out. Pál's efforts were greatly appreciated by everyone.

Rózsa's brothers Abram and Ferenc played in the traditional Klezmer band along with five other musicians, three of whom were Gypsies; they played together often for Jewish celebrations, especially weddings. Klezmer music was an ancient mix of ethnic melodies, blended sounds and styles of Gypsy, Romanian, Polish, traditional Hungarian, a bit from the Russian Steppes, and even a sound or two from Turkish music. Ferenc played the violin and Abram the viola; the other band members played clarinet, drums, guitar, cimbalom, and trumpet, and other instruments, too, like the saxophone and xylophone.

The music was exuberant, filled with joyful trills and modified rhythms. At the beginning of most tunes the whole ensemble built to a dramatic crescendo, then each instrument became quite independent from the others. Constant fluctuations in tone occurred throughout the music, building in volume toward the end. Each musician played his instrument to respond or to imitate or to complement another instrumental sound. The wedding guests expressed their excitement for the happy couple by clapping their hands, dancing and singing along with the familiar lyrics and Klezmer beat.

At an Orthodox wedding, men and women could not dance together, but at the Neolog wedding that rule did not exist, so couples joined the bride and groom in a marathon of joyful, traditional dances—the Hungarian folk *csárdás*, the strenuous *freylachs*, and the *sirba* circle dances. Many of the dances involved circles of men on the outside and women on the inside while some dances allowed men and women to dance together.

Klára danced with her father and with Rózsa's brothers, but for most dances she preferred Rudolf, who surprised them all by arriving from Paris the previous evening. He guided her through the intricate dances with confidence, although he avoided more difficult steps by spinning Klára round and round the dance floor while he stood in one place. Finally, the two collapsed onto chairs standing against the wall. Breathless, Klára slid down into her chair exclaiming, "The music is so good. I have never had such fun!"

Rudolf kept his arm around her shoulder, "Weddings are good for us all. We'll be dancing all night!"

After another hour of music, the wedding feast was served. Magda outdid herself. Mounds of beautiful food emitting delicious aromas filled the tables. *Knaidlach, csirkeleves, zöldbableves, sálata, gombócsult, palacsinta, gulyás, borju süsavalt gombával, csirke paprikás, roston sült bárány, dinsztelt savanyukaposzta, diós torta,* and Rósza's favorite, *mogyorós kifli.* Silva contributed *plnene trubky,* a Slovak favorite, and Duke von Esté provided all the wine as a wedding gift.

The wedding festivities did not end until the following morning. The Duke and Duchess von Esté left just after midnight, but Klára and Rudolf stayed until the very end. When they walked out of the Klein's house into the morning light, a night rain had fallen, leaving puddles on the street, refreshing the morning air and making them shiver. Fall was in the air. Feeling extremely light-hearted and a bit light-headed, Klára and Rudolf decided to walk all the way back home. They splashed through puddles, chased each other, got the giggles, and held hands as they walked without speaking. When they reached Klára's door, Rudolf looked into her eyes without any inhibitions. He hugged her and came very close to kissing her lips, but with all his strength he resisted his own desire and gently held her beautiful face, flush with excitement, in his hands. He kissed her on the forehead and nose, said "Good Morning" and left.

Fall

By November all of Europe realized they were in the grip of an economic crisis. A terrible period of unemployment, labor strikes, and poverty stifled the people of Europe and caused great suffering.

Aunt Eugenia wrote of the dire situation in Germany:

Dear Brother, The parliamentary democracy of the Weimar Republic has come under political attack from the communists on the left and the Nazis on the right. The poor German people have never fully recovered from the devastating loss of the Great War, but now the situation has become desperate. Despite Chancellor Brüning's efforts and decrees, foreign trade continues to decline, industry has slowed, and unemployment soars.

We fear that the Weimar government has been weakened to the point it may not survive. Wealthy industrialists are so fearful of the trade unions and communists that they have thrown in with the Nazis. Their financial support has allowed the Nazis to gain strength in every general election. Konrad and I are much more concerned about these Nazis than we are about unions!

How is Hungary coping with this economic disaster? How is the wine business? Konrad and I leave for the Congo at the end of the month. We will return to Cologne in April and then on to Siófok.

Your adoring sister, Eugenia.

Leopold thought about his sister's words. They concerned him deeply. His knowledge of history told him that events in Germany had a way of adversely affecting Hungary and Austria. If Eugenia feared for the future of Germany, then he should fear for Hungary as well. Although well aware of the economic crisis in Europe, Leopold believed Hungary remained somewhat stable, at least at the moment. The Bethlen government had initiated specific financial policies to shore up agriculture and those policies certainly helped Leopold's personal business.

Still, many of Bethlen's political and social policies led Leopold, like his sister, to fear the inclination of Hungary's impoverished and disillusioned masses to embrace the severe ideology of the extreme right or the communist left. Then he thought again of Eugenia's smiling face. He admired her ability to leave any unpleasant situation at any moment for more exotic places.

1930
Late April, Paris

Even though spring in Paris was as lovely as ever, a terrible economic depression spread its misery throughout Europe, sparing none. Rudolf's tenure at the Ecole des Beaux Arts had come to an end, so he spent an afternoon packing his things in a bag when there was a knock at his door.

"Come in," he called out and looked around the drapery to see who entered. Yvette. He was glad to see her since she had been gone from Paris for several months with the ballet company.

"Where are you off to?" She walked to him, gave him kisses on both cheeks and dropped her suitcase. "I was hoping you'd let me stay for a while until I find a new place."

"Your timing is perfect. I'm off for Budapest, so you can have the place all to yourself." He buckled his case shut, "I'll be gone for the entire summer."

"Great!" She smiled as she fell across the bed. "I just want to sleep all summer. Now that Diaghilev is dead, nothing is the same with the ballet! Our new director, Balanchine, is a taskmaster. I think too difficult for me.

"What are you going to do in Budapest?," she asked, "see that little girl you draw year after year?"

"I hope so," Rudolf blushed as he hoisted his bag and smiled broadly. He made his way down the spiraling stairs, landing to landing, to the front door where he was met by Madame Deverau.

"Off on another trip?" she asked him.

"Yes, I'm on my way to Budapest. I'll be gone for several months. Yvette will take care of things while I'm gone." He gave Madame Deverau money for the flat and hurried out into the street, hailed a taxi, and headed for Gare du Nord The taxi followed St. Michel, went across the Seine and Ile de la Cité to Rue d'Hauteville and finally to the station. Rudolf purchased his ticket for London.

After crossing the Channel, Rudolf boarded a train for London, settled back and thought about his future, a future he hoped would be spent with Klára in Budapest. The train pulled into Victoria Station and he walked the distance to the War Office in Whitehall. *London is quite nice in spring*, he thought as he made his way to the MI6 office where he was met by Olivia and Clive Jeffreys.

"So we have you at last!" smiled Jeffreys. Olivia set Rudolf's bag aside and led him to one of the cubicles. The three sat down while Jeffreys poured a round of scotch from a silver flask and then raised his glass, "Here's to MI6 and the defeat of all enemies of the crown!"

They clicked their glasses as Jeffreys added, "We're putting you to work straightaway. Your training will begin today. We want to keep our eye on the 'Jerries.' Something is afoot there and we need to be a step ahead of them. This is your desk, Count Házy, so Olivia, get him started."

Jeffreys left them to it. Olivia explained to Rudolf his role within the organization, "Basically MI6 expects your artistic skills to be used for forgeries and false documents and your personal connections in Europe to be useful for counter-intelligence operations."

Several weeks later, Rudolf traveled to Amsterdam, Stockholm, and Berlin where he established a network of communication contacts and safe houses. After Berlin he made a side trip to the Bauhaus in Dressau where he met its Director, Hannes Meyer, and an old Hungarian friend, László Moholy-Nagy, instructor. Rudolf confirmed to Meyer that he would accept the offer of an instructor position at the Bauhaus beginning in October. He returned to London for debriefing.

September, Lake Balaton

Klára sat at Silva's table in the villa kitchen, concentrating on peeling apples, trying to peel one long continuous spiral of yellow. She looked up at Silva, "Now that I've completed my studies at the Music Academy, Mother wants me to go to Cologne to live with Aunt Eugenia for a year." Klára sighed, "I don't feel that I know Aunt Eugenia that well...to live with her for a year."

Clearly Klára didn't want to go. "Even though I've seen Aunt Eugenia every summer, she spends most of the time talking with Mother and Papa. I never pay much attention."

"Your mother thinks it's important for you to have new experiences away from home. You've not traveled much, Klára. She wants you to see something of the world beyond the lake and Budapest."

"I suppose, but I can hardly bear to think of being away from everyone. I'll be so homesick."

The postman knocked at the kitchen door. Silva greeted him and invited him in for a cold drink. He tipped his hat to Klára, gave the mail to Silva and said, "This one is for you, Miss Klára."

"Oh, it's from Rózsa!" Klára ripped open the envelope, pulled out the folded paper and scanned the words, "She wants me to come to Eger for a visit. Oh, she wants me to meet her new baby, József." Klára smiled broadly, "I want to go! How wonderful to see Rózsa and Pál and their little baby!"

Klára wrote to Rózsa immediately to say that she would be there in two weeks. A week later she went back to Budapest to get ready for the trip.

—ᴍ—

After London, Rudolf returned to Paris and visited his flat where he found Yvette. "This is only a quick stop and then I'm off again. You can stay another month at least."

Rudolf hurried off to the station where he purchased a ticket on the Orient Express, leaving at seven thirty that evening and traveling through Strasbourg and Vienna on its way to Budapest. Rudolf boarded the train and went to his private sleeping compartment. Checking his watch, he still had a little more than an hour before departure, so he settled into the comforts of his compartment and waited for the porter to take his order for a late night snack. Finally, the Express began its journey east, steaming through the French countryside into the falling darkness. He stared out the window at the glittering lights from each little village that passed by his window and thought of home and of Klára.

Over the last year he felt the tenor of their letters had changed...*I'm convinced my lifelong friendship with Klára has begun to move toward something different...deeper. I've known Klára was the only one for me since she was sixteen, but still I must keep distance between us.* Dolf felt terribly conflicted...*I want to find out where I stand with her, but at the moment I'm inextricably involved in such complex entanglements. She's twenty, old enough at last, but now the timing is off.*

Questions and thoughts of Klára kept him tossing all night. *Well, she probably doesn't even feel as I do. So, what does the timing matter? Perhaps she never remembers me or thinks of me the way I think of her. Maybe I'm still a brother to her. Maybe even a replacement brother? Perhaps she only considers me a dear friend as I have always been. I have no idea how she really feels about me. At the moment I'm not free to pursue the relationship I want to have with Klára. The timing is bad.* He sighed; he could not stop his thoughts. *Now I'm immersed in obligations to MI6. My work is important, necessary. The things I have learned... the imminent danger Europe is facing, the inevitability of war. I can't walk away from my part.*

I can't put my personal desire above the good I may be able to do for my country. I still have dreams that one day I'll return to Budapest, accept a professorship at the Hungarian Drawing School and marry Klára . . . but not now . . . not until Europe is free of this Hitler.

Imagining a life with Klára in Budapest and at Lake Balaton and the family they would have brought comfort to Rudolf . . . *such a pleasing dream* . . . he thought. Finally, he pulled the shade, turned his face from the window, and slept until morning light began to filter into his compartment.

Only a few hours after settling in at his grandmother's, Rudolf walked across the back garden to the von Esté's, anticipating his reunion with Klára. He had not been in Budapest since Rózsa's wedding, so everyone greeted him with warm excitement. But he met disappointment when he learned that Klára planned to leave town within the hour to catch a train for Eger.

Leopold noted Rudolf's disappointment and proposed, "Why don't the two of you travel to Eger? I'm sure Rózsa would enjoy showing off her family to you as well. You can act as Klára's chaperone."

More than happy to do so, Rudolf turned to Klára, "Would you mind having me trail along with you?"

She was inwardly thrilled, but calmly smiled, "Of course you'll come. Hurry, pack your things. Tamás and I will pick you up in twenty minutes. Will that give you enough time?"

Rudolf left immediately, grabbed his valise, and they were off to the Keleti Rail Station barely in time to make the train. The trip to Eger took two hours through forested rolling hills and plateaus. Klára could hardly wait to see her old friend and her family, since she had not seen Rózsa since her wedding.

As the train steamed through the countryside, Rudolf gazed at Klára. Flashes of sunlight illuminated her face. Thoughts crowded his head . . . *I've loved you for so long. You're a young woman now . . . should I reveal my true feelings for you? Would that be fair at this particular time? How do you feel? I know you love me, but as a brother? Will you laugh at me? You always seem so careful around me. You're still so young. I'm so involved, the time is wrong. I must keep my feelings in check. I can't enter into your life now . . . war is on the horizon . . . do you even know what is happening in Europe?*

"You look so serious. What are you thinking about?"

"You. You have become a very beautiful woman, Klára. I've been away so much of the time you've been growing up. I didn't realize."

"I know, Dolfie. I think it's time you stop thinking of me as that little girl."

Pál and Rózsa, holding their bundled baby, József, stood on the platform as the train pulled into the station. Pleasantly surprised to see Rudolf arrive with Klára, Pál eagerly took their bags to his truck. Rudolf got into the back while the others squeezed inside the cab. Pál drove them northeast of Eger along Dűlő Road, a winding road through lush green hills of beech trees and vineyards.

They arrived at the Szabó property to find a complex of buildings much as Klára expected from Rózsa's description. The large Szabó family home, the barrel factory, sawmill, blacksmith shop, and a new cottage Pál's family had constructed near the edge of the property. Rózsa loved showing Klára her home—lace curtains at all the windows, a piano in the parlor, the nursery next to their bedroom, and the gabled loft upstairs where Klára would stay. Rudolf would be staying in town in a small *panzió*.

Pál's parents were quite thrilled to entertain the Budapest guests at a large family dinner in the main house. A gregarious Miklós stood with his glass of "Bull's Blood" and spoke with gusto, "We insist that tomorrow Rózsa and Pál show you every bit of our beautiful city! We are very proud of Eger, 'the baroque pearl of Europe!' Our city is an ancient one with history dating back to the Stone Age. There's much for you to see!"

After an exhilarating evening of good wine, stories, music, and laughter, Pál drove Dolf to his hotel on Érsek Street just off Dobó István Square in the heart of Old Eger.

The next morning, right after breakfast, Pál, Rózsa with József, and Klára arrived at the first of Eger's historic sites, the needle-shaped minaret built by the Turks in the sixteenth century. Rudolf walked from his hotel to meet them. They all entered the narrow cylinder and started to climb the steps that spiraled against the stone wall upward into the darkness. After only a few moments, Rudolf felt claustrophobic in the dark, enclosed space and decided to forego the ninety-seven steps to the top. He started back down, with Pál, carrying little József, behind him. Rózsa and Klára continued to the top while Rudolf and Pál stretched out on benches at the base of the minaret. Eventually the young women called and waved to them from the iron-railed balcony high above their heads. Rózsa could see the sleeping baby wrapped in Pál's arms.

From the minaret the four followed the winding cobblestone streets to Dobó István Square where many townspeople criss-crossed the square's busy marketplace. The beauty of the baroque architecture and sculptures surrounding the square impressed the visitors. The pink- and cream-colored Minorite Church stood across from them. As they entered the church, their footsteps echoed in the quiet spaciousness; the walls and ceiling provided a visual feast of baroque gold in frescoes and sculpture. Even Rózsa joined the others as they lit candles before the altarpiece of the Virgin Mary with St. Anthony.

Pál greeted several elderly women who sat prayerfully in the pews. They were eager to see the baby he carried in his arms. One of them, dressed in black from head to toe, walked over to Pál, embraced him, and spoke with animated gestures. She gave him a pat on the back before leaving. Pál informed his little group that he had known the ladies since his youth, "The old woman in black…she's the widow Madách. She told me, 'You have a beautiful wife' and congratulated me on my fine son." Pál smiled at Rózsa, "See, you've made an impression on these old ladies of Eger. They approve my choice. I have excellent taste!"

They left the cool interior for the heat of the square. They crossed Eger Brook by a picturesque bridge where vines and flowers covered the stone walls that channeled the stream through the city. A tree-lined street up to Dózsa György Square led them to the base of Castle Hill where the famous twelfth century Eger Castle rose intrepidly above them and the city. A steep walk up to the fortress, built to defend the city from the fearsome Turks, gave Rudolf a sense of the fortress's awesome power. He and Klára stood on the outer edges of the ramparts while Rózsa sat with József on a large pile of stones. Her red hair, backlit by the hot summer sun, glowed as brilliantly as a golden halo. She avowed, "It's breathtaking up here, isn't it?"

Pál stood above her shielding his eyes as he surveyed the complete circle of the city below them. He pointed out into the distance, "The Turks, all 80,000 of them, were camped out there." He turned toward Rudolf, "Did you read Gárdonyi's *Egri Csillagok?*"

"Of course!" Rudolf answered with a broad smile. "Klára's father, the Duke, made us all read it, but I didn't mind, I loved it. A magnificent story! Captain István Dobó was a brilliant leader."

"Imagine, only two thousand Hungarian soldiers, women and children were right here behind these walls," Pál said proudly. Klára looked over the edge of the wall thinking about the women who poured hot oil over their attackers. "They defended Eger for thirty-eight days against the siege of those terrifying Turks."

Rudolf patted the perspiration from his brow, "I would like to have some of that *Egri bikavér* right now!"

Only about ten years old when he read Gárdonyi's novel, Rudolf thought Dobó was the cleverest of men. The part about the red wine, *Egri bikavér,* or "Bull's Blood," was always his favorite part. Whether by plan or accident, Dobó gave each of his men a cup of the rich red regional wine as reward for their bravery and the wine worked perfectly to defeat the Turks. As the men drank the wine, it ran down from their lips onto their beards. So, when the Turks saw the Hungarians standing atop the ramparts with their red-stained beards they were convinced the Hungarians were drinking the blood of the mighty bull, the ancient symbol of invincible masculine strength. The Turks were so frightened by the powerful image of the red beards they gave up the siege and left. The defense of Eger Castle remains one of Hungary's most honored moments from history, Dobó István one of Hungary's greatest heroes, and *bikavér,* a blend of cabernet and merlot grapes, the nationally treasured wine.

By the time the four had come down from the castle they were ready for dinner. Rudolf suggested the restaurant in his little *panzió*. They settled at a lace-covered table near a window that opened onto a lovely interior courtyard with a fountain and urns of flowers. While baby József slept soundly in Rózsa's lap, the four enjoyed glasses of *bikavér* and delicious trout with fried potatoes and *palacsinta* stuffed with apples and cream. The foursome genuinely enjoyed each others' company. Klára and Rudolf shared stories with Pál about Rózsa and themselves as children at Balaton. They laughed until their cheeks ached. The hour grew late and Rózsa and Pál had to return home with little József. Rudolf held Klára's hand as they walked to Pál's truck. Good-night embraces and kisses on the cheeks, including kisses for little József, were shared by all.

The next day they met in the morning at Rudolf's hotel. Klára wore a white masculine-style shirt with a stiff standing collar, her sleeves rolled up to the elbow and a high-waisted gray, gabardine gored skirt with a double row of four buttons and flat black shoes. Rudolf came out of the hotel wearing a white shirt with sleeves rolled up and gray slacks. Rózsa and Pál teased them about being dressed alike. He and Klára laughingly protested. . . *pure coincidence, quite by accident. . .* but they knew they looked striking together for their second day of Eger exploration with Rózsa, Pál, and little József.

First they walked to Eszterházy Square and made a quick tour of the spectacular neo-classical basilica with its ornate altars, domed ceilings, and frescoes. Next they visited the Lyceum with its *camera obscura.* They climbed the stairs to the ninth floor for a panoramic view of the city. Rózsa nudged everyone along, "I can hardly wait for you to see the next great place! It's my favorite!"

A twenty minute walk took them south toward Béla Square, along Király Street to the top of a hill where they could look into the valley below. "See!" Rózsa declared, "It's called *Szépasszony-völgy* . . . the 'Valley of Beautiful Women' or by some, 'Valley of the Sirens.' Look at all the little wine cellars!"

A narrow street wound through the valley passing dozens of little wine bars. "Each wine cellar is built into a natural cave," Pál explained.

"Some are standing bars only," added Rózsa, "while others have large restaurants with tables and waiters who wear little black bow ties. I think it's very romantic."

Stopping for a taste now and then, they walked from cellar to cellar. Suddenly a clap of thunder sounded. None of them had noticed the dark clouds gathering overhead. Rain poured down almost instantly sending them running for cover in opposite directions. Rósza and Pál with little József ended up in one cellar and Rudolf and Klára in another.

Rudolf and Klára found themselves in a quaint little cellar. The wine keeper invited them to sit at a table with a lit candle that glowed in the darkness of the cellar. Rudolf ordered a glass of *Egri bikavér* for himself, a glass of *hárslevelű*, white wine, for Klára and a tray of cheese and bread. While they sipped their wine, they talked of home, Stefan, and Paris. Rudolf continued to refer to Klára in careful, brotherly terms.

Klára touched Rudolf s hand and looked at him shyly. He said nothing, but took her hands within both of his, staring downward. Klára felt emboldened, "I do not think of you as a brother, Dolf. It's true that I did when I was small, but no more, not for a long time. I'm not your sister. I don't want to be your sister. I want something more from you, Dolf."

When their eyes met, Rudolf hesitated, released her hand, and stood up, stammering, "I'm sorry, Klára, I feel awkward." He walked out into the pouring rain. Klára followed him outside. Flashes of lightning and thunder roared all around them. Rudolf stood sopping wet under a tree. Klára walked straight to him, "Awkward? Awkward with me? Why would you ever feel awkward with me?"

"Your father, Klára." Rudolf held her at arms length, "Your father asked me to be your chaperone. Now I feel that I may be the very reason you need a chaperone." He turned from her, "I've waited for a moment with you like this for a very long time and now I feel I'm tied by honor to your father. I can't act on desire with such a trust, such a responsibility given to me by Leopold."

"My Papa is very clever, Dolf. Perhaps he asked you to come with me so that we would have a moment like this."

"Perhaps," Rudolf smiled.

"I love you, Dolf. I have loved you for as long as I can remember. I know you have some silly notion that you're too old for me, but I'm twenty years old, certainly old enough! I'm not a child. I know *who* I want."

Rudolf moved toward her, took her in his arms and kissed her. "You know that I have always loved you, Klára. I realized you were the only one for me years ago…at the Anna Ball, but you were only sixteen, so young. I couldn't allow myself to confess it until you were grown. I've tried to stay away until you were old enough. And still, Klára, I don't know if you are really ready. You've had so few experiences away from Budapest or your parents, so few adventures."

"I've had experiences," she smiled. "A few boyfriends—all insignificant. I've had disappointments; certainly. I have witnessed death. It's true I've traveled little, but regardless of all that, what does it matter? I have dreamt of you. There is no one else anywhere but you. Why should I go off on adventures without you?"

"Klára," he breathed a deep sigh, "at last I can kiss your lips and get lost in those incredible eyes of yours." He couldn't stop kissing her, "I've waited too long to have you in my arms. And now, at last, I have you, the woman I've been waiting for."

Amidst the flashes of lightning and tremendous thunder, they embraced and kissed with all the passion of lovers who discover each other for the first time. Eventually common sense interrupted them and Rudolf pulled her back into the little cellar out of the lightning's danger. They were breathless and soaking wet. He asked the waiter, "Is there a way we can get a car back to town?"

"I'll take you in my truck."

They agreed. Rudolf wanted to look for Pál and Rózsa, but he had no idea into which cellar they had run, so he asked the waiter to bring his friends and their baby to town as soon as the rain stopped; the waiter agreed. Rudolf and Klára ran out to the truck and climbed inside. They could barely see beyond the hood, the rain was so heavy on the windshield. The bumpy ride over the rutted, mud-covered road to Rudolf's hotel took about twenty minutes.

"Thank you for the ride. We appreciate it." Rudolf handed the driver several folded bills. "There's extra money to bring our friends here when the rain stops. You won't miss them—she has red hair and a baby."

Rudolf and Klára ducked out of the rain into the hotel as the concierge held open the door. The *panzió* was small and Madame Gregora noticed the pair immediately. Rudolf addressed her, "We're going up to my room just to dry off; then we'll be back down for hot soup and tea. Two friends and their baby will be joining us." He took his key and the two went up the stairs to his room. He opened the door and drew Klára inside, into his arms. They were both so wet. She shivered.

Klára took off her wet clothes down to her chemise and Rudolf to his shorts. He grabbed a blanket from the bed, wrapped it around her while enveloping her in his arms. He dried her hair and face, kissing her all the while. She opened her arms wrapping the blanket around him, too, and they fell onto the bed. Rudolf experienced a great release of pent-up emotions and wondered how he could ever stop embracing her.

They lay against each other; their fingers intertwined, their eyes studied every detail of the other's face, even though they knew each other so well. They whispered how much they loved each other as their lips touched softly. Suddenly, Rudolf could hardly breathe, he rolled off the bed, "Madame Gregora will be pounding on the door any minute to save you. To be honest, she should hurry."

"Here put this on." He took a clean starched shirt from the wardrobe, "I don't know what to do for a skirt." He took out a shirt and slacks for himself. They dressed. His shirt was long on her, but not long enough. They finally decided his pajama pants would do. With a belt around her waist, she actually looked very modern, like in American cinema. Klára gathered her wet clothes; one more kiss and they left his room, down the stairs and into the dining room. Madame Gregora looked at the two with a raised eyebrow and pursed lips, "Your friends arrived twenty minutes ago."

The two scooted into chairs at the table. Neither Rózsa nor Pál were wet, little József slept peacefully in Rózsa's arms. Pál laughed at them, "What happened to you two? You were in front of us and then you were gone! New clothes! I guess you two got wet!"

The glowing couple shrugged their shoulders and smiled. They were changed and both Rózsa and Pál could see it right away. "What's going on? You're both too happy!"

"We finally admitted to each other that we love each other. Dolf wanted to wait until I grew up. Well, finally he sees that I have!"

"You said you were going to wait until she turned twenty."

Everyone immediately turned toward Pál.

"You told Pál that you loved me before you told me!"

They laughed heartily as the waiter brought their soup.

"I'm starving," said Rudolf.

After dinner the four walked to Pál's truck and drove back home leaving Rudolf behind.

Only one day more in Eger before it was time to take the train back to Budapest. They spent the last day touring the Szabós' barrel works and enjoying the countryside. Rudolf returned to his *panzió* late in the evening.

On the train back to Budapest, Klára snuggled into Rudolf's chest. He was very quiet. Unknown to Klára, he was terribly conflicted. Questions filled his head... *Why have I let myself become so involved in matters of the world when I only want to be here holding Klára in my arms?* Finally he spoke, "Klára, I must go back to Paris by the end of the week. I'm not sure when I can return to Budapest."

Klára looked up at him, "Please, Dolf, don't go. After all these years we're finally together. I can't imagine being apart now."

"I'm sorry, but I've got to go," he held her tightly to his chest. "I would marry you right now, if I could, but I have obligations."

Klára sat straighter and looked at him seriously. "I could go back to Paris with you. It would be wonderful to be there together. We can ask Papa tonight. I know he'll say yes. He'll be thrilled."

"I can't Klára," Rudolf held her, kissed her, but insisted, "The timing isn't right. I really can't explain it, except that I've made commitments I can't quit." He had a faraway look in his eyes. "I can't even say how long we'll have to wait to marry, Klára."

"Are you saying that you don't want to speak to Papa about us? Have you changed your mind about your feelings for me?"

"Of course not, Klára, I love you, that is certain, forever," Rudolf said the words firmly, but without looking at her. He spoke thoughtfully, "But I don't think it's fair for me to ask for any commitments from you or to ask your father for your hand until I know for certain when we can marry. I'm sorry, so sorry."

"What are you so committed to that it's in the way of your commitment to me?"

"My work, my art." Rudolf sighed heavily and uttered a lie, but the truth was impossible to tell.

"I believe in your work, Dolf, I know it's important, but it should not be something that you feel you can't share with me. I think I don't understand."

Rudolf hugged her again, "I'm sorry, Klára."

They sat in silence as the train pulled into the station where Tamás was waiting. When the car pulled into the drive of the Esté home, Rudolf gave Klára a kiss, got out, and walked home. Klára went inside and straight to her room, completely confused. *What happened? I know he loves me and he knows I wouldn't mind waiting longer for him. I've waited half my life for him... a few more months wouldn't change anything. But not knowing why... knowing he has some sort of reason he can't share with me... makes me both sad and a bit angry.*

When Rudolf walked into his grandmother's front door Lázsló met him with a silver tray holding a telegram, "This arrived for you yesterday."

Before he opened it, he knew what it was. *"Return London as soon as possible. Urgent. Olivia."*

After greeting his grandmother and sitting with her for supper, Rudolf went upstairs, sat down at his desk and tried to write a letter to Klára. He had several false starts... wadding each paper and tossing it in the waste bin. He had to write to her, because if he tried to explain to her in person, the words would not come to him. Finally, he only wrote that he had been called back to Paris on urgent business and did not know when he would return. He encouraged her to go to Cologne as her mother wanted her to do.

The next morning Rudolf delivered the letter himself. It was very early; he wanted to catch the first train to Vienna. He went through the gardens and knocked at the kitchen door; Tamás met him. Rudolf asked if he had seen Klára yet. He had not.

"Please give this letter to her. I'm off to the station. I must return to Paris as soon as possible. Please tell her good-bye for me."

Klára rose early. She'd had a restless night and still felt confused by Dolf's sudden coolness at the end of their wonderful time in Eger. She walked downstairs, entered the kitchen, and slid onto a stool by the big oak table. She yawned, "Good morning, Silva. May I have a cup of tea this morning? I feel tired and achy."

Silva poured boiling water over a mixture of dried, crushed rosemary, marjoram, and verbena leaves. "Tell me about Rózsa's baby and your trip."

Klára held the hot cup in both hands breathing in the aroma of the steeping tea.

"József is adorable, all pudgy and sweet. Rózsa is a wonderful little mother and Pál is wonderful, too. The home Pál's family built for them is lovely. Eger is beautiful... everything was perfect. Dolf told me that he loved me."

"What?" Silva gasped, stopped peeling carrots, and stared at Klára, "Oh, Tamás, did you hear? The young Count finally said the word! And what did you say?"

"That I loved him, too. I have loved Dolf forever," glowed Klára.

Silva smiled broadly, wiped her hands on her apron, and hurried to give Klára a hug.

Tamás had been standing by the garden door with a quite serious expression, "The Count came by earlier this morning. He was on his way to the station. He left this for you." Tamás handed the envelope to Klára.

"You mean he's gone?"

Tamás nodded in the affirmative, "Vienna, Paris I think."

Klára opened the envelope; only a few lines were written across the paper.

Dearest Klára, I have been called back to Paris on urgent business. I could not say good-bye. I do not know when I will return to Budapest. Go on with your life. Your devoted liege. My love, Dolf

"Oh, Silva, I'm confused. Our time together was good. I know that he loves me, but he's been so strange since telling me. Saying that he has obligations, commitments, that the timing is not good. We must wait. I should '*go on with my life!*'" Tears streamed down her cheeks, "Now he's gone without saying good-bye. What has happened?" She sobbed.

Silva hugged Klára to her breast and smoothed her hair from her face, "Of course you love each other. Tamás and I have known that for years. You must trust Rudolf. There must be a good reason why he has gone so suddenly. He'll explain and all will be as it should be. Don't cry, Miss Klára. It will be all right."

Paris

When Rudolf arrived in Paris he hurried to his flat to gather his things for a return trip to London. As he was packing, Yvette showed up. He was happy to see her. Always so petite, cheerful and light-hearted, like a little elf flitting around the flat, making humorous comments about everything. But now she came into the flat appearing quite distraught with swollen eyes and a red nose.

"Yvette, what's wrong... what has happened?" He walked to her, embraced her, and offered a handkerchief. "Tell me, what's wrong?"

"I'm going to have a baby, Rudolf. I can't dance. I can't model. What will I do?"

"Yvette, poor, poor, little Yvette," he gently wiped the tears from her cheeks. "Who is the father? Can he help you?"

"Joël... Joël Graund," she sighed. "He can't help. He's in the ballet company, too. He has no money," she sobbed. "I loved him, Rudolf, but it was stupid. He's nobody."

"Does he know, Yvette? Perhaps he can do more than you think."

"No, he doesn't know. He might care, but it would only be a disaster."

"I'm leaving Paris right away, so you can stay here for as long as you need. I'll pay the rent. You don't need to worry about that," Rudolf held her shoulders.

"Perhaps I can find something to do that will help me with the rest," she mused. "I could sew for the ballet company, perhaps. Enough to pay for food, maybe."

Things seemed brighter, "Thank you, Rudolf. You're always so kind to me. That's why I came here. Thank you." She kissed him on both cheeks.

"Well, the place is yours, Yvette." And with that Rudolf was gone and on his way to London.

Budapest

Dolf's absence and the mystery of it all continued to cause Klára great anxiety. Only Silva could make her feel better. Klára believed Silva's words were true…*Dolf has his reasons, you must trust him and everything will turn out just as you hope it will.* Dolf loved her, of that Klára was certain. *It's just so hard knowing there's a reason for his going and he won't tell me what it is.* Klára felt sad, devastated, and angry all at once. She wrote a letter to Dolf at his Paris address, but she heard nothing for several weeks and then only the same kind of generalizations. He continued to write, sending a letter or a postcard every few weeks, but there were no promises, no explanations, no particulars. Klára wrote back to him, but her questions and invitations went unanswered.

Klára confided in her mother that she and Dolf were in love and would marry in the future. Klára remained as unemotional as she could when she explained that Dolf had obligations in Paris and that no particular date for an engagement was set. Klára assured her mother that Dolf would ask Papa for permission to marry her as soon as he could. Klára had never felt comfortable sharing her feelings with her mother. And now Klára felt insecure, sensing very little support from Elizabeth for any relationship with Dolf.

Elizabeth listened to Klára's news with trepidation. This was not the news Elizabeth wanted to hear. Elizabeth felt great anxiety. After all she had plans for her daughter and Rudolf was not part of those plans.

"Perhaps you are mistaken, Klára. Dolf has always thought of you as a sister." Elizabeth spoke in a convincing tone. "He has always loved you as Stefan's little sister."

Klára argued amidst tears, but it was futile; she could see her mother was against them. At that moment Klára decided she would never again share her feelings about Dolf with her mother, never again!

The following afternoon Klára went into her Papa's library to find Leopold sitting behind his desk, "Come in, Klára. Sit here." He pulled a padded chair close to his. "You appear very sad, Dearest," Leopold held her hands in his and leaned toward her, "What's wrong, Klára? Where's your beautiful smile? Tell Papa."

"I'm sad, Papa, because I'm in love. I love Dolf and he loves me. But I'm confused. I have always dreamt of loving Dolf and I thought it would be the happiest time of my life when we finally told each other, but instead it's miserable."

Klára related most of their Eger conversation, trying to convince Leopold as well as herself that it was all real. She described how distant he was on the train, about *the obligations*, *the bad timing*, and now his abrupt departure.

"What do you think it means, Papa? Did he change his mind? What happened?"

"Well, of course, we have no way to know the whys of Dolf's actions, Klára, but I know that Dolf loves you. He is an honorable man and if he has told you that he loves you then it is true. Perhaps I am wrong, Klára, but I think Dolf has some business that he must complete before he can commit to you. I also believe him when he tells you that you must go on enjoying life. I know he doesn't want your tears. He wants you to embrace your life. It will all end well, my darling, you will see."

Leopold kissed her on the forehead. They stood by his desk and he embraced her as they walked toward the door, "Let's go see what Silva has in her pantry. Perhaps she has something filled with chocolate. That should make us happy again. Don't you agree?"

Klára laughed. She adored her Papa, he could always make her forget the dark and look to the light. He had a way of lifting her spirits. She embraced him as they walked through the dining room toward the kitchen. Leopold thought about Rudolf—he knew that his love for Klára had begun as a brother, but others, including Stefan, had realized long ago that Rudolf and Klára were destined for each other. Leopold had especially noticed Rudolf's obvious love for Klára during the Anna Ball when Klára turned sixteen—he had looked at her in such an adoring way. Leopold smiled when remembering how flustered Rudolf had been as he watched her twirling around the ballroom.

Leopold admired Rudolf for keeping his distance while Klára grew into the lovely young woman she was today. He suspected that Rudolf had not decided, as yet, if Klára was truly old enough for him. Leopold surmised he might be waiting a bit longer for that reason, perhaps after her year in Cologne.

After Klára's confession of love, Elizabeth began in earnest to encourage her to leave Budapest as soon as possible for Cologne, "Klára, you must take advantage of your Aunt Eugenia's invitation to visit her in Cologne." Elizabeth showed Klára the written invitation, waving it in the air. "You can enroll in the

Cologne Conservatory. Immerse yourself in music and in the social life Aunt Eugenia will introduce to you. We should leave within the week. It's not too late to enter the conservatory for the fall term."

Now Elizabeth had an additional motive for sending Klára to Cologne, a far more urgent reason than mere music or a new social life. Elizabeth was terribly anxious about Klára's presumed love for Rudolf. She knew it would be difficult to sway Klára's devotion to Rudolf, so she began to consider how she would go about convincing Klára to go to Cologne and to forget about Rudolf as someone who only confused her.

Previously, in letters from her friend the Baroness Renate, Elizabeth had learned that Renate's husband, the Baron Hoffman von Werner, died in October of 1928. In November of that year the young Baron Franz von Werner became the new president and director of his father's massive rail empire in Germany. During the winter of 1929, Franz had moved to Cologne, the company headquarters, and taken charge of the business. Since Klára's confession of love to her mother, letters between Elizabeth and Renate had flown back and forth. Letters filled with plans to send Klára to Cologne to live with her aunt, study at the Cologne Conservatory, and meet the young baron once again. After all, Elizabeth and her friend had plans, old plans and dreams for Klára and Franz.

In late September, Elizabeth finally convinced Klára that she should go to Cologne.

Germany

Just as Aunt Eugenia predicted, the world-wide depression hit Germany hard. By the fall of 1930, Germans, suffering widespread feelings of anxiety, turned to the extreme right for answers to their plight and membership in the Nazi party grew rapidly. The party's ranks filled with unemployed civil servants, bankrupt shopkeepers, impoverished farmers, and disillusioned youth. Union-led strikes and work disruptions infuriated wealthy industrialists, in particular the steelworks owners. Those industrialists poured money into the Nazi party because the party had a serious interest in rebuilding Germany's military war machine and also promised to crush labor unionists. It was obvious to the industrialists that money could be made, lots of money.

Germany's government, a democratic parliament, was ruled by a sovereign legislative assembly, the *Reichstag*. The *Reichstag* occupied an impressive building by the same name in Berlin. Election results from the fourteenth of September kept the social democrats in the majority with one hundred forty-three seats, but the Nazis won one hundred and seven seats and the communists received seventy-seven seats. The Nazis gained more power every day within the Reichstag. Eugenia wrote Leopold that she and Konrad were very concerned... *Chancellor Brüning's government is failing... so vulnerable. If either party, the Nazis or the communists, wins a majority, it will be our end.*

Cologne

During the last week of September Klára and Elizabeth boarded the night train to Cologne. Once they settled into their private car, Klára prepared for bed, pulled the sheets over her head, and slept almost all the way to Cologne. As they neared the city just past noon Elizabeth woke her with a croissant and coffee. Klára, having had a fretful night, felt no excitement for Cologne or the Music Conservatory or any of it. She washed in the basin provided and finished dressing just as the train pulled into the station. Aunt Eugenia's elderly gentleman companion, Konrad Gerr, familiar to the ladies, met their train. Klára and Elizabeth greeted Herr Gerr warmly as he smiled in delight at their arrival. "The Duchess is thrilled at your coming. She has been looking forward to this day with great anticipation!"

Konrad directed a young man to gather their bags and take them to the van waiting at the station's entrance. Elizabeth walked briskly alongside Konrad while Klára followed. They all got into a large Rolls-Royce Phantom Town Car waiting by the curb.

As the driver sped through broad avenues, over bridges, and around parks, Klára remained oblivious to the city's details. Klára did not want to think of anything other than Dolf. *What wrong had she done? What had happened?* She could not erase him from her thoughts.

Finally, the Rolls-Royce turned onto Frankenwerft Street, passed through an open iron grille, drove along a graveled drive that wound behind a row of tall trimmed hedges and stopped at the grand entrance of an elegant town house. A small van with their luggage pulled in behind the Rolls.

The Duchess emerged from the house with loud cheerful hellos, arms outstretched in welcome. Elizabeth and Klára left the car and walked up the stairs into the arms of the exuberant Aunt Eugenia, in her seventies, but still able and young at heart.

"I'm overjoyed to have you both come visit at last!" Aunt Eugenia exclaimed. "It will be wonderful for us to have a young woman living in our home. Welcome! Welcome!"

They all entered into an opulent display of a vast variety of textures and colors, everything from Belgium carpets to Chinese vases to colorful leaded glass to profusely patterned fabrics to mounted animal head trophies. Klára was spellbound; it was like walking into a very crowded antique shop on Falk Miksa Street in Buda and for the first time in a month, Dolf slipped from her thoughts.

Aunt Eugenia ushered the ladies into the parlor where a high tea had been arranged for them. Two maids quietly shuffled around the ladies pouring tea, offering sugar, milk, and lemon in the English style, serving petite sandwiches and scones with jam and cream. Even before they had finished these treats the maids returned with sweets, chocolate tortes, cream pies, sugared fruits, and marzipan.

"Oh my, Eugenia, if Klára eats like this too often, she will have real problems with the piano bench."

Aunt Eugenia laughed, "At my age I have discovered the true pleasure of life, delicious food." She smiled broadly, "My dear Duke died so many years ago. I've been a widow for more than fifty years. Just me and Konrad and the servants rummaging around this big house. Of course, we have traveled some, to England and to India and Africa, China and South America, even as Leopold to the great American West. I have my clubs and cards, but I would say that life is just now beginning to get interesting again...with our dear Klára come to live with us."

Elizabeth and Klára hardly said a word while Aunt Eugenia continued long narratives about everything—her travels, her city, the conservatory, the social life she hoped Klára would find entertaining. After more than an hour, the housekeeper entered the room and Aunt Eugenia made introductions, "This is my invaluable housekeeper, Gita. She reminds me that you may both be tired and want to rest and I agree! So, please follow Gita to your rooms. Your luggage is waiting for you there. After your rest please come back down to join me for supper."

After thanking Eugenia for her kindness and cheerful conversation, Elizabeth and Klára followed Gita up the grand staircase to the second floor. Elizabeth's room was at the front of the house with a balcony overlooking the home's entrance and the tall spires of *Kölner Dom*, a few blocks away. On the opposite side of the hallway was Klára's room with a balcony overlooking a large formal garden and the *Rhein* just beyond the garden wall.

The next week Klára entered the Conservatory of Music to study piano. One morning while Klára was away, Elizabeth took the opportunity during morning tea to tell Aunt Eugenia about Klára's romantic interest in Count Rudolf von Házy.

"Rudolf has broken her heart, Eugenia. Klára has completely misinterpreted his affections. He only thinks of her as a little sister...the little sister of Stefan, his dearest friend. Rudolf has no intention of forming a serious relationship with Klára. It has been a most upsetting situation for all of us. Removing her to Cologne has been a godsend. Leopold and I are so grateful that you have invited her."

"Such a shame, Elizabeth. I remember the Count as a very fine young man," Aunt Eugenia had a worried expression.

"Oh, Rudolf is a fine gentleman. I am saying nothing against him, Eugenia. I'm certain that he has been made quite uncomfortable by this circumstance. Klára declared her feelings to him causing him to leave Budapest immediately. She, of course, was devastated."

"A young first love can be so hurtful." Eugenia shook her head sadly. "I feel great affection for dear little Klára."

"Please, do not mention any of this to Klára. She would be terribly embarrassed if she knew that I had shared these details with you. I implore you to interfere if you sense that Klára is corresponding with the Count."

Eugenia frowned at Elizabeth's suggestion, but Elizabeth continued, "I think it is best, if Klára does not make a fool of herself chasing after him." Elizabeth sipped her tea, "I hope that you will encourage Klára to enter into a full social calendar here in Cologne."

"Certainly. I will," replied Eugenia. "We will entertain the sadness right out of her, I promise."

"I know of a young man here in Cologne. He is the son of my dearest childhood friend. I'm sure you have met . . . the Baroness Renate von Werner?"

Eugenia nodded her head in the affirmative. "Only once," she whispered.

"Her son is the Baron Franz von Werner, president of the von Werner Railway conglomerate," Elizabeth continued. "He is quite young, near Klára's age, but he is mature and responsible. They have met in their youth. Perhaps you could arrange for them to meet again?"

This prospect quite thrilled Eugenia. "Oh, what fun Konrad and I will have playing cupid. We can be wonderful matchmakers! The young baron will surely sweep away any thoughts of the heartbreaking Count von Házy!" Eugenia giggled at the thought.

After two weeks passed, being assured that Klára was settled, Elizabeth left for Budapest.

In early October Klára sat with Aunt Eugenia and Konrad in the breakfast room. As they were reading the newspaper over their tea and toast, Aunt Eugenia referred to an article, "Look Konrad, that Hitler advocates ripping up the Treaty of Versailles and refusing to pay war reparations."

"How monstrously clever he is," answered Konrad. "That move should make him even more popular with the masses."

"Listen to this . . . *the Nazis elected to the Reichstag marched into the hall together . . . each one shouted 'Heil Hitler!' in answer to the roll call.* The Op Ed says that the Nazis have no intention of supporting the democratic Weimar government. The Nazis have announced their desire for the social democrats to fail. The Nazis know if the social democrats fail and the German people become completely miserable they will turn to the Nazi Party and Hitler."

"The Nazi S.A., storm troopers, went on another rampage of violence to celebrate their victory in the *Reichstag*." Konrad commented on the article he was reading, "They've smashed windows of Jewish-owned businesses, including restaurants and department stores."

What a shame! Klára thought to herself, *Politics again. It's all anyone talks about.*

Despite her despair, Klára did become engaged in her classes and lessons at the conservatory and found herself quite busy. Klára began to breathe more easily as she rationalized Dolf's inaction and convinced herself that everything would make sense eventually once she found herself in his arms again. *Dolf loves me... he will explain and everything will be all right.*

Klára met another piano student, a lovely and talented young woman, Hannelore Becker, who had come to Cologne from Munich. Almost as tall as Klára, but opposite in coloring, Hannelore was very blonde and blue eyed. She had a serious boyfriend, the very good-looking Max Segal who played wind instruments, including the clarinet.

Hannelore introduced Klára to many other students including a very funny Ruthie Katz, Hannelore's close friend from Munich. Hannelore, Max, and Ruthie ran with a crowd of musicians, all students at the conservatory. They were a close group who played music together and had great fun together. As soon as Klára was introduced to them she became a part of the "gang" that included Lars Krause, Manfred "Freddy" Hoffmann, Oskar Müller, Mose Kohn, Viktor Veicht, Trude Meyer, and Pia Herman.

At the conservatory these students studied serious classical music. They appreciated classical music, but they loved American jazz. After their studies the group gathered regularly to listen to jazz on the radio or go to jazz clubs for dancing. Other times they met in their flats for jam sessions where they could listen to American records, imitate the music, or dance. The group especially praised Klára for her skill at improvisation and syncopation. She seemed to have an innate sense of when to shift the accent to the weak beat of the bar—an intuitive trait of jazz's rhythmic sounds.

With Aunt Eugenia's encouragement, Klára invited the group to come to her aunt's home for their jam sessions. The group found the Duchess's enormous music room, with its raised stage, the perfect location for their sessions. But the main reason the students loved going to Aunt Eugenia's was the great spread of food her servants laid out for them. Klára's aunt loved having the energetic young people around and she often sat in the room listening to their music which she also liked very much. When Freddy called her "cool," Aunt Eugenia was delighted!

Each one of the group played a variety of instruments in addition to their specialty. Max the clarinet, Lars on trumpet, Freddy saxophone, Oskar on drums, Mose guitar, Viktor on base, and Trude on flute. Pia and Ruthie, voice students, sang. Of course, Hannelore and Klára played piano, often improvised duets.

Their afternoons and evenings were spent together as friends sharing a love of music and good times. Aunt Eugenia had never had more fun.

The Jewish boys, Max, Freddy, and Mose added their expert knowledge of Klezmer music to enhance the jazz style for the group, just as it had helped American musicians develop jazz. The group felt very fortunate to have Mose Kohn because he had relatives in New York City who regularly sent him packages of popular American sheet music, records, and magazines. The magazines used jazz lingo and described the latest styles of dress, allowing them to become the *hep cats* of Cologne.

Budapest

As the term neared its end, Klára said good-bye to her new friends and returned to Budapest for Christmas. Her train traveled through snow-covered countryside to Vienna and on to Budapest. She was happy to be home again...to be in Silva's warm kitchen, to drive around the city with Tamás, to sit with her father in his library.

Tamás asked if she was corresponding with Count Rudolf and when she answered no, he only responded with "hmmm...."

Klára and the household staff put cedar boughs with red and gold ribbons over the doorways, an advent wreath on the dining room table, straw under the table, and a crèche on the sideboard while Silva's baking filled the house with scents of cinnamon and nutmeg. Klára visited Rudolf's grandmother seeking information, but the Countess Alexandra knew nothing, except that this year Rudolf was not coming home to Budapest for Christmas.

Klára got her hair bobbed, the newest, most modern style. Her black hair naturally resisted the popular pasted finger waves and spit-curls, so the new bob—a severely cut bang above her eyebrows and straight shingles at the sides and back—fit her perfectly. When Elizabeth saw Klára, she exclaimed, "At last you have a cut that compliments that hair of yours! It looks quite nice, very grown-up, and flatters your eyes."

1931
January

Just after New Year, Klára returned to Cologne and very deep snow. Time in Budapest with her family had been wonderful, but she had been deeply disappointed by Rudolf's absence. She had not seen Rósza either. Mrs. Klein traveled to Eger and invited Klára to accompany her, but Klára declined. She could not bring herself to revisit Eger; the memories of summer were still too confusing and sad. So, the holidays were quiet and slow-paced, very different from the joyful noise and frantic pace Cologne had been with her new friends. The depth of happiness Klára felt upon her return to Aunt Eugenia's surprised her. She was far more content to be back in Cologne than she had ever expected to be.

Shortly after Klára's return, Aunt Eugenia invited Franz von Werner to come enjoy an afternoon of music. To Klára's surprise, Franz arrived in the music room in the middle of a jam session. Aunt Eugenia rose to welcome him, then guided him toward Klára. His presence caused quite a stir.

"Oh, my God, he's movie-star gorgeous!" Ruthie exclaimed. "I mean I've seen good-looking guys, but this guy is spectacular!"

"Shhh, he'll hear you, Ruthie," Hannelore scolded her, "but you're right; he is marvelous."

Franz was blond. In fact his thick hair was so bleached by the sun, it appeared almost colorless as it fell onto his tanned forehead and across his eyes. His eyes were such a light blue they reminded Klára of the milky waters of Lake Balaton. Having spent the holidays skiing in the Bavarian Alps, Franz's tanned skin stretched taut over well-defined cheek bones, a long straight nose, and a strong angular jaw. A definite brow with heavy blond eyebrows and a wide smile displaying straight white teeth gave him the look of a Nordic god. Dressed casually in a sweater and shirt with rolled-up sleeves and dark wool slacks, Franz stood just under six feet tall.

Klára had not seen Franz since they were much younger; a time when she paid very little attention to him. Franz gave her a vigorous embrace and noted, "You've changed since I saw you last. What were you then…about ten? My mother sends greetings."

Klára introduced him all around, "We're all students at the conservatory, but we really like to play jazz. You're welcome to listen or join us, if you play."

"I play the piano a bit, but certainly not as well as you. I could never improvise like that," Franz confessed, "but I like what I've heard so far. Please, don't let me interrupt, continue. I'll just sit here by the Duchess and listen."

Franz and Aunt Eugenia sat together keeping time and smiling while quietly whispering comments about the lively music. They clapped enthusiastically when they heard Ruthie sing "Black Water Blues" in the style of Bessie Smith. Klára and Hannelore played a duet on the piano while the rest of the group accompanied them and Pia sang along with Ruthie.

"You're all so good!" exclaimed Aunt Eugenia. "I think you should play for a club. More people should hear your music."

Franz clapped loudly, "Very good. I'm glad to be here. Play more, please."

The group eagerly agreed and looked to Oskar to start a beat and then they all joined in on Duke Ellington's "St. Louis Toodle-Oo" and then a Louis Armstrong bluesy piece. Pia sang a couple of Josephine Baker songs, "After I Say I'm Sorry" and "I Love Dancing," from the sheet music Mose received from New York. Freddy had actually seen Baker at the Folies Bergère last spring when he visited Paris. He purchased sheet music and as many recordings as he could find.

"I know one," Franz ventured. "Do you know Ma Rainey's 'Blame It on the Blues?' I can sing the words."

"Yeah, we know it," answered a surprised Max. "How do you know it?"

"I told the Duchess that I liked blues when she asked me to come today. I've gone to the Excelsior Club in Berlin a few times and I heard Dajos Bélas Odeon Five play there. I picked up some records. 'Blame It on the Blues' is the only song I know all the words for."

Franz started to sing and the group improvised behind him. Ruthie and Pia sang as backup for him. Aunt Eugenia smiled and clapped for them. After more than an hour had passed, Franz learned some new songs and played the piano with Klára. With enthusiasm he joined the vigorous conversation and lively music.

Gita interrupted them, announcing, "Dinner is served."

The whole gang left their instruments and walked into the dining room where they found an immense spread of delights. Cold meats and sausages, cheeses, mustards, flatbreads, potato salads, and apple strudel. Of course there was plenty of beer and red wine to go along with the feast. The young people filled their plates and sat around the large table sharing stories, singing bits of songs, and laughing. They were animated, full of life, happy, and Klára felt happy, too. *It's good to be with these fun-loving friends,* she thought.

When everyone gathered up their instruments and said good-bye, Franz stayed. He and Klára lingered at the front entrance. Franz complimented Klára on her musical abilities and stood staring at her until she blushed and turned her eyes away from him.

"I can't help but stare at you. I apologize. It's just that you've become such a beauty."

He leaned against the wall with his arms folded, "I remember pulling your braids. I was a rotten child." He laughed, "Again, I apologize. I would like to see you again, Klára, if that would be all right with you?" Franz smiled broadly, "I know it would make our mothers very happy."

Klára leaned on the opposite door jamb, "I think that would be all right. We should try to make our mothers happy."

The two of them, Klára and Franz, made a handsome couple, he so blond and she so dark. Both were slender and tall, Franz just a few inches taller than she. Even though they both had instant broad smiles, he was outgoing, gregarious, while she was more reserved, even shy at times. Franz talked a lot, was opinionated, while Klára was observant, more of a listener and expressed her opinions rarely.

As the weeks went by she saw Franz more and more; their friends laughingly referred to them as the hare and the tortoise. Franz always eager, quick to jump into things, seeking out adventure, going places, while Klára seemed reticent, slow to follow him. Eventually, however, she usually came around and kept up with him quite well.

At the end of January Klára received a letter from Rózsa; *Oh how she wished Rózsa was here with her in Cologne.* Hannelore was a wonderful new friend, but they had not shared any history and Klára longed for Rózsa's perspective to help her understand why Dolf had disappeared from her life. Rózsa wrote that she and Pál had traveled to Budapest at the end of January for a special ceremony at the new Heroes Temple constructed next to the Great Synagogue on Dohány Street. The domed Heroes Temple was built to honor Jewish soldiers killed in the Great War fighting for Hungary. Rózsa's beloved brother Sándor, the Klein's oldest son, was listed among the names etched in stone. Rózsa wrote that her father was so proud and that her whole family appreciated so deeply Duke Leopold's presence at the dedication. Klára thought she should have been there, too. Then she thought about Dolf and how her pain of losing him paled in comparison to the loss of a precious son and brother and decided to stop wallowing in self-pity...to move on and forget Dolf.

March

With the arrival of spring Franz began to pressure Klára for a more intimate relationship, telling her that he loved her and then one night on the first of April he asked her to marry him. Franz argued that their families wanted their marriage and he proposed they plan a fall wedding. Klára liked Franz; he was entertaining, certainly handsome. She knew her parents would approve, but she could not get Dolf out of her thoughts and she knew her heart would never accept anyone but him. She still loved Dolf, but it seemed that he had changed his mind about her and didn't want a relationship. She remained very confused.

"I can't imagine why you're having such a hard time saying yes to Franz!" Hannelore shook her head, "he's gorgeous and so much fun!"

Reluctant to share her feelings for Dolf with her Cologne friends, Klára really did not know what to say, because she never understood what had happened. "You and Max...how long have you been together?"

"Since I came to Cologne two years ago, we saw each other in orchestra and started playing together. We fell in love. He says we'll marry as soon as he can afford a wife, but I think sooner."

"I've noticed Ruthie seems to have a huge crush on Oskar."

"Oh, yes. She does, poor Ruthie. She thinks she's in love with Oskar, even though we have all warned her against it for almost two years!"

"Why poor Ruthie?" Klára was puzzled. "Why discourage her? He's a great guy."

"Oskar?" Hannelore looked skeptically at Klára. "He's a great guy, but he doesn't dig girls. You know, he digs guys, but Ruthie thinks she can change him. We all tell her that's never going to happen. She'll just get her heart broken over and over."

"Oh," considered Klára; she had not been aware of Oskar's preferences. The revelation made her feel very naïve.

"Well, what about you and Franz? You've known him for a long time. Or do you have someone else in your head?" Klára looked at Hannelore as though she had discovered her deepest secret. Hannelore smiled, "That's it! *The reason.*"

"There was someone else I thought I loved. From the time I was just a child, it was always him." Klára decided to confide in Hannelore. "We confessed our feelings to each other last summer, but then it all fell apart." Tears began to stream down her cheeks, "I never knew why. He said he had obligations, commitments...the timing was wrong. He stopped writing to me."

"That's tragic, Klára!" Hannelore embraced her as she spoke, "What a mystery! He's terrible to treat you like that. I think you may be lucky, even though you're so tortured, to be rid of such a fellow."

Hannelore's words were exactly why Klára didn't like to share her feelings with someone who didn't know Dolf. Klára could hardly bear to hear Hannelore speak badly of him. Dolf's actions and words were so out of character for him; deep in her heart she knew they still loved each other, nothing had really changed. She could only ever truly love Dolf. Klára longed to talk to Rózsa, but that was impossible. And it was impossible to give Franz an answer.

Paris

In mid-March Aunt Eugenia asked Klára if she would like to take a trip to Paris to shop for spring fashions. Instantly Klára imagined the trip to be a chance to go where Rudolf would be. They boarded the train for the four-hour trip and arrived in Paris by mid-afternoon. Aunt Eugenia had many friends in Paris, one of them her long-time friend, the Austrian-Hungarian Princess Mimi Thököly. Madame Thököly along with her chauffeur, Louis, met them at the station and drove them to her townhouse on the Avenue de la Bourdonnaise.

After a week of afternoon teas, shopping at the best design houses, attending the ballet, the opera, and museum tours, Klára finally had an afternoon free to do what she wanted to do most…*find Dolf.* She asked Louis directions to Rudolf's address and was surprised to learn how near he was to Madame Thököly's town house. She walked all the way to the north end of Jardin du Luxembourg and wound around the alleyways until she stood in front of his flat.

She walked into the tall, narrow house and looked at the post boxes. Her heart pounded rapidly, hoping he would be home, but if not she had written a note to slip under his door telling him where she was staying in Paris. As Klára studied the boxes, a pretty petite blonde came skipping down the spiral stair, smiled at her, and went out the door, calling cheerfully, *"Au revoir, Madame Deverau."*

Klára realized at that moment that the landlady had appeared from her flat. She asked Klára, "Are you looking for someone?"

Klára moistened her lips, her mouth seemed terribly dry, and stammered, "I…I'm looking for the flat of Count von Házy?"

"He isn't here at the moment," said the landlady, "only Yvette."

"Yvette?"

"Yes, the woman who just ran past you. She's the only one in the flat."

"Oh," responded Klára, quite confused.

"Would you like to leave a message for the gentleman?"

"No, no, that's all right. I'm just in Paris for a short time." Klára wanted to run as fast as she could from the place.

"Do you want to leave your name for him? I'll tell him that you came by."

"No…no, don't do that. I'm just an old friend, he wouldn't remember me." Klára turned and was out the door, "I'm sorry to have bothered you… *Au revoir.*"

Once outside in the cobblestone alleyway, Klára saw the little blonde, Yvette, round the corner at the end of the alley. Klára walked briskly to catch up to her. Yvette walked along Rue Monsieur Le Prince, crossed Saint Germain, through a narrow alley onto Rue de Buci, and into the market. Klára had no problem keeping up with Yvette, because she stopped often to smell the flowers, look at various items, and buy grapes and cheeses, wine and paté. Finally, Yvette stopped at an outdoor café for coffee. She put her packages on the table. For a moment Klára thought about approaching her, introducing herself, and asking about Dolf, but then, just before Yvette sat down in the wrought-iron chair, she yawned and stretched, allowing her duster to fall open revealing a swollen, very pregnant belly beneath the flowered batiste dress she wore.

At the sight of Yvette's belly, Klára fell against one of the booths and gasped for breath; she was completely shaken. At last she understood Dolf's *obligation*, the *commitment*, and his reluctance to share the reasons with her. Klára was shocked, devastated, heart broken. *Dolf lied to me. It is this woman he loves, not me.* Klára suddenly realized that Dolf must care nothing for her. *I threw myself at him in Eger when all the time he obviously loved another woman… this woman.*

Klára turned from the market and fled down the street; through her tears Klára lost her way. The distance back to Princess Thököly's apartment seemed much farther. When Klára looked at the swirling waters of the Seine, she momentarily contemplated throwing herself into the abyss. Instead, she fell against a tree and sobbed freely until she realized that people on a passing barge were staring at her. Finally, she composed herself enough to remember the way to Madame Thököly's apartment. Once there, she hid herself in her room for the rest of the day and night. When she emerged, she begged Aunt Eugenia to take her home to Cologne as soon as possible.

Cologne

When Klára returned to Cologne, Franz met her at the station and swept her up in a warm embrace. "I'm so glad to have you back. How was your shopping trip? My life has been a bore without you. Let's never spend such a long time apart again!"

Klára returned his embrace and then a kiss, but it was difficult; she was in no mood to be cheerful yet. *Oh well*, Klára thought, *I'm willing to give Franz a chance to make me happy, but it will take time. Perhaps, Franz is my destiny after all. Perhaps Dolf was only a child's fantasy, an unrealistic dream, never meant to be.* Anyway, Klára knew now that Dolf was lost to her forever. Her heart still ached and she wondered if it would ever stop. The only thing left for her was to refocus on Franz who, at the moment, was chatting away without realizing she had heard nothing. Klára managed a smile and sighed deeply. *At least he's entertaining and seems to care for me. I'll try.*

Franz and Klára saw each other often over the next few months, sometimes double-dating with Hannelore and Max and continuing to participate with the gang in music sessions at the Kölner Jazz Haus café or at Aunt Eugenia's. Klára was having fun with Franz, almost in spite of herself, but she knew she would never completely forget Dolf and thoughts of him still made her very melancholy.

As the months passed, still no word came from Dolf and Klára wondered... *is he already a father? Has he married Yvette?* To Klára it seemed as though he had completely forgotten about her. Whenever thoughts of him crept into the moment, Klára shook her head and practiced thinking of other things.

July

Much to Aunt Eugenia's surprise, Klára showed no interest in returning to Lake Balaton or Budapest that summer. Eugenia noticed that Klára seemed very melancholy and so Eugenia became determined to fill Klára's summer months with travel and activities. In mid-July she and Klára sailed to the German port of Rostock on Mecklenburg Bay. They stayed in a lovely little hotel on Neuer Markt Street near the thirteenth-century St. Mary's Church. Klára enjoyed following her guide book as she walked around the town. She followed the book's directions down Kröpeliner Strasse to discover a lovely fountain in the middle of the street, the Brunnen der Lebensfreude, the fountain of happiness. Klára threw a silver coin into the fountain and made a wish. As hard as she tried, she found it impossible to erase her thoughts of Dolf.

She continued along the Promenade following the old city wall back to her hotel where Aunt Eugenia had evening plans for the theater. The next morning they took a steamship around the islands of the bay and another day they found themselves in the charming fishing village of Warnemünde where they spent the afternoon watching tall sailing ships tack with the wind. Klára's favorite time was spent lying in the warm summer sun on the lovely white sand beach that curved around the clear blue Baltic Sea. The trip was restful for Klára and she did feel better when they returned to Cologne.

Once again Franz was there at her arrival. He met their ship with flowers and showered her with words of love. Klára rather brushed off his syrupy words, but she did appreciate his seemingly sincere enthusiasm at her return. He had many plans for them to keep her busy for the next several weeks.

August

In late August, Franz insisted that Klára travel by train with him to Fürstenfeldbruck. He wanted to visit his mother and promised that Klára's mother would be there as well. Once Franz and Klára arrived at the great manor house, the two mothers, Renate and Elizabeth, put in place an overt plot to encourage the young couple toward the altar. The mothers laughed and teased and complimented them constantly.

Such a well-matched pair...such a handsome couple...so well-suited for each other...they will make us all so happy...just think of the beautiful children they will have.

Franz seemed to have no problem with their attention, but Klára found it annoying. She wished that her Papa had come.

Klára was happiest when she and Franz could disappear from the house and their mothers' presence. Klára and Franz climbed up Holy Mountain of the Andechs to visit the medieval Braüstüberl church where they sampled the monks' famous beer. They sailed on the sparkling Ammersee Lake; a beautiful lake that only made Klára miss her own Lake Balaton and all of its precious memories.

Eventually, persistence prevailed and when Franz asked Klára to marry him in front of their mothers, she answered "Yes." He placed a beautiful amethyst and diamond ring which had once belonged to his grandmother on her finger. The two mothers were thrilled, they wanted to begin planning the wedding that very instant. But Franz had railroad business in Africa that would take him away from Cologne for several months, so the mothers would be forced to wait until winter for the wedding to take place. The thought of delay deterred the mothers for only a moment before they were chatting away about *the where, the when, and the what to wear.*

Klára realized her own feelings were more of resignation than delight, but she sat with them and listened to her fate being laid out before her in every minute detail of expectation and spectacle. However, Franz and Klára did continue to insist their wedding be small and simple. When Klára and Franz returned to Cologne, Aunt Eugenia gave an engagement party for them that also served as a bon voyage party for Franz, since he was leaving for Africa the following week.

While Franz was away during the fall months, Klára concentrated on her music. She played with the Cologne Symphony Orchestra and with her jazz friends. Hannelore and Ruthie were far more excited about the approaching marriage than Klára, but their enthusiasm piqued her anticipation for the marriage with a bit more joy. Hannelore and Max announced they were going to elope, but had not set a date as yet. Always eager to interject more information about her love for Oskar, Ruthie contributed to every conversation. So, love and marriage were the main topics of the girls' talks throughout the fall.

Fall

Rudolf had spent very little time in Paris over the past year. He resigned his faculty position at the Ecole des Beaux Arts in the spring and spent most of the summer in London and elsewhere on special MI6 assignments. Travels to Amsterdam and Stockholm, to Spain and Germany, filled his summer months. He knew that Klára had gone to Cologne to study music and live with her aunt, but because his travels were top secret, he had not tried to visit her there. Rudolf knew if he had seen her, she would ask questions he could not answer, upsetting her all over again. Not wanting to cause more distress, he decided it would be better to simply avoid stopping in Cologne, but he did look forward to a day when he could tell her all about what he had been doing.

In fact Rudolf felt quite good about what he was doing; he was fully confident as to his capabilities to perform the tasks assigned him by MI6. Undermining the dangerous threat growing within Germany was an integral part of his assignments. No one in MI6 doubted that Germany wanted war. As he learned more about the approaching war and the ideology of the Nazi regime, he knew Klára's stay in Cologne would come to an end soon. Rudolf decided against pursuing the Bauhaus position and favored leaving Paris and London before a war might begin He was determined to return to Budapest where he could protect Klára and those he loved. If a war began, he was assured he could still serve MI6 in Budapest.

When Rudolf left Paris by train for Budapest he intended to stay there, to ask Leopold for Klára's hand, and then go to Cologne and bring her back to Budapest with him.

Late September, Budapest

A day and a half later Rudolf walked from his grandmother's front door, down the street, around the corner onto Andrássy and climbed the steps to the von Esté front door. He took a deep breath and knocked. After a few moments Tamás opened the door, smiled broadly, and exclaimed, "Good morning, Count, it's wonderful to see you! What brings you to the front door?"

"I've come to speak with the Duke. Is he here?" Rudolf suddenly realized he had not considered whether the Duke would be at home or not.

Tamás opened the door fully and invited him into the foyer, "He's in the conservatory. Won't you please wait for him in the library? I'll let him know that you are here."

Rudolf walked to the library feeling confident and excited; his thoughts were of Klára and he couldn't help but smile. He went straight to his favorite section of the library and perused the leather-bound books. Great atlases of exotic places, a book of Audubon's birds, mechanical drawings of machines, medieval illuminated manuscripts, and volumes of history. Rudolf's smile widened as he remembered many times as a boy when he and Stefan listened in awe as the Duke read passages about all sorts of exciting things and encouraged the boys to read on their own. Together they made astounding discoveries.

He could still recall Stefan's voice and the excitement they felt when Leopold read aloud about the great battles between the Hungarians and the Turks... *Hungary's terrible loss of men and objectives in the great battle of Mohács* and *the glorious victory of Buda's liberation from the Turks.* Rudolf walked along the walls of books, running his hand over the leather spines, trying to recapture the memories of his childhood. He heard the heavy door handle and the slide of the door across the carpet; he turned expecting to see Leopold standing in the doorway, but it was not Leopold, it was Elizabeth who entered the room.

As Elizabeth welcomed him, she seemed as gracious as ever, "It's so wonderful to see you again, Rudolf. I believe it's been more than a year. The Duke regrets that he is unable to meet with you. How are you? How is your dear grandmother? I haven't seen her in several weeks."

Rudolf crossed the room, took her extended hand, kissed it, and bowed deeply, "It's a delight to see you looking so well, Duchess. My dear grandmother is very well, thank you for your inquiry."

Without making eye contact, Elizabeth walked to her husband's great oak desk and sat down. She did not ask Rudolf to take a seat. He stood awkwardly, puzzled by her coolness. He decided to begin, "I have come today to ask the Duke... and you... for Klára's hand in marriage. We are very much in love, as I am sure she has told you after our time in Eger last summer."

Elizabeth smiled at him, but he sensed her control as she began to speak, "Rudolf, you are very dear to the Duke and to me. You have helped us through these many years to fill the void left by the death of our precious Stefan." Her words had a rehearsed sound to them, "Of course, Klára told us of your declarations of love during your short time in Eger last year."

She took a breath and forced a smile, "You have been a kind and sensitive brother to Klára. She loves you dearly, Rudolf, as do we all. You have been her friend all her life; however, I fear that you have mistaken Klára's feelings for something they are not. We believe that she was confused as to her true feelings for you."

Rudolf felt a rise of protest within, but stood quietly as Elizabeth continued, "Klára was a rather sheltered girl with few experiences that summer in Eger. She has enjoyed her life in Cologne and is more mature than when you last met. I understand that you have been absent from her life over the past year. I think you would find Klára very changed."

Elizabeth sat straighter and pressed her lips firmly together before continuing, "We assume you think we should approve your request to extend your relationship with Klára. However, the Duke and I find you unacceptable for Klára; you have no occupation, no business. You live off your inheritance with no means to replenish it. One day you may find yourself in great need. Klára cannot be expected to scrimp or go without. The monarchy is over, Rudolf. Your title is of no consequence in these modern times. You lead the life of an artist, a bohemian life...for all we know, you are a communist! What are you thinking? Do you plan to live with Klára in some garret?"

Elizabeth paused for a breath before going on without looking at him. "We have approved of something very different for Klára, a future that will allow her to continue to live as she has been accustomed."

Again she paused, but this time she looked directly at Rudolf as she rose from behind the desk. "There is no point in discussing this issue any further. The Duke and I neither give our blessing nor approval for you to pursue a personal, intimate relationship with Klára. We have already given our consent for her to marry someone else, so this matter is finished."

Then she added an afterthought, "Of course, you are always welcome here, but do not think of interfering in Klára's life. She has made a commitment to another."

As Elizabeth swept past him from the room, Rudolf stood in disbelief at her revelation of Klára's *commitment to another*, not to mention his sense of complete rejection by the Duke and his wife. Until only a few moments before he had thought the Duke, even Elizabeth, loved him as a son and would welcome him into their family as the husband of Klára, whom he loved beyond life itself.

Elizabeth left the library without giving Rudolf a chance to recover from her stunning blow to his feelings. He was shattered to his very being. He leaned against the shelves of books trying to make sense of what had just occurred, when Tamás entered the room.

"Are you all right, Count?" he asked, "You look ill. Can I help you?"

Rudolf quickly composed himself and left the room without responding, crossed the foyer, and escaped the house. He returned to his home as quickly as possible, went to his room and sat by his window looking toward Klára's window. The leafy branches of summer partly obscured his view. His raging thoughts crushed him. He was devastated, there were so many things to consider. *Klára marrying someone else! Impossible to fathom! I love her and I know she loves me.*

This is all my fault. Since last summer when we were so close I let too much time pass…I was not attentive enough to Klára. London, Stockholm, Spain have occupied far too much of my time! I thought she was occupied in Cologne with her studies. Rudolf paced across his room. *I intentionally stayed away to let her be on her own to have adventures. Even though I wrote to her, her letters stopped. How could she have fallen in love with someone else?*

But there was more. The disdain shown for him by Elizabeth, and even worse, by Leopold, who apparently had not even wanted to see him, left Rudolf astonished and broken. *What little regard the two of them obviously have for me. I thought they loved me, would be joyful for Klára to marry me. What have I done to lose such favor? Perhaps they despise me for the loss of my leg long ago and I never realized it?*

He took paper and pen and began a brief letter to Leopold apologizing for any wrong he had done and imploring Leopold to forgive him. He described to Leopold how he admired him and how devastated he was to have lost his favor and that he would do what he could to regain his love and respect.

After saying good-bye to his grandmother, Rudolf walked back to the von Estés' front door, and left the letter with the von Esté maid. He rushed immediately from the von Esté home for the train station and Paris.

The maid gave Rudolf's letter to Elizabeth who put it in her pocket without opening it and then went to her room where she took the letter from her pocket, studied it unopened, placed it in the waste bin and set fire to it. She placed a heavy tray on top to extinguish the flames and then opened the window to disperse the smoke. Elizabeth actually felt terrible remembering the horrified, stricken expression on Rudolf's face. She did have a sickening surge of guilt for taking such control of events, but she had convinced herself Klára would be much happier with Franz von Werner. She exhaled a deep sign.

After all, it had been our plan, mine and Renate's, for our children to marry since they were very young. My prime motivation against Rudolf is that he interfered in our plans for Klára. I am convinced that Klára does not know her own heart. Rudolf is like family, a brother to Klára and besides, Klára is so obviously happy to be with Franz.

When Elizabeth had observed the lovely couple in Furstenfeldbruck just a month ago, they were delightful! Elizabeth rationalized away all of her dark thoughts and felt much better. She freshened her face, smiled in her mirror, and went back downstairs to the conservatory where she found Leopold and Fejedelem napping.

Leopold stirred as she came near him, "Tamás told me that Rudolf was here. Why didn't you wake me? I would have loved a visit with him. It's been too long."

"He was only passing through and had a train to catch...he was in a terrible hurry...seemed very preoccupied...his mind elsewhere."

"Ummm...well, I'm sorry to have missed him."

—◠◠—

As quickly as he could, Rudolf was on the train back to France. He decided he would continue his work with MI6 and follow previously delayed plans to take the position at the Bauhaus. He tried not to think of Klára or her family; to forget Elizabeth's devastating words; to forget, to occupy his thoughts with other things. Rudolf took a taxi from the station to his flat, climbed the stairs, took the key from the door frame and opened the door. Yvette was obviously still living there. He had not thought of Yvette, but now he wondered what arrangement could be made for her now that he had returned.

Within the hour Yvette came through the door, "Hello, Count Rudolf. So you have returned." She tossed her things on a chair and moved toward him, giving him kisses on both cheeks, "Have you been to Budapest? Did you see your great love? What's her name?"

Without answering her questions, Rudolf returned her greeting, "How have you been?" He motioned to her flat belly, "You had your baby? Did things go well?"

"Oh, yes, a girl, Belle-Marie, she's with my sister, Monique, in Sévers. Monique has four children, so one more is no problem for her. I can visit Belle-Marie whenever I have the time." Yvette chattered on and on as she pulled her stockings and other clothes from chairs and hooks around the flat. "So, I suppose you want me out of here now. Well, don't worry. It's no problem. I just met a young American artist. He's fresh to Paris and wants me to model for him. I think he has lots of money."

"Careful, Yvette, what kind of fellow is he?" Rudolf smiled at her and shook his head. "What about Belle-Marie's papa? Is he completely out of the story now?"

"No, he's still around, but he's ballet, remember? No money there."

"Are you going to dance with the ballet again?"

"Of course, I will! The company is going to Marseilles for the winter to get ready for the spring program. I can't wait to go. Paris is so dreary in the winter." She smiled at Rudolf, "What are you up to?"

"I'm leaving Paris, too, in a few days. You can stay here, if you want. I'm going to keep the flat for a while longer. I'll probably be in and out of Paris for a while."

"So, you didn't say, what happened with that girl back home?" Yvette smiled at him.

"Just didn't turn out, that's all I can say," he answered and thought to himself, *I'm moving on, trying to forget.*

"Well, what about that Englishwoman?"

"Yes, I'll probably see her again," a hesitant Rudolf answered.

Rudolf left Paris that evening and traveled across the English Channel where Olivia met his boat. The two of them drove past Dover and further on to a secluded manor house near Sissinghurst. When Olivia pulled into the long graveled drive leading to the house's entrance, Rudolf sighed. *This must be my purpose,* he thought. *I'll once again throw myself into this work. I must remember it is for the greater good—a fight against an insidious evil that wants to create a new world order—an order that could destroy all that's good about Europe.* He stayed at the manor house for several weeks of training and then left England for Dressau, Germany and the Bauhaus.

Dressau, Germany

In 1930 Rudolf had been hired by the Bauhaus director, Hannes Meyer. At that time Rudolf's position was to be an instructor of typography and printmaking under the supervision of Herbert Bayer, graphic design master. Now, after a delay, Rudolf arrived at last at the Bauhaus located in the Törten District of Dressau. In the time lapsed, the art school had suffered some turmoil. In the fall of 1930, Meyer was dismissed as director due to his communist leanings, even though he had discouraged student involvement in leftist political demonstrations. Herbert Bayer resigned and left Germany for the United States. In the fall of 1930, the apolitical architect Ludwig Mies van der Rohe became the school's director.

Rudolf eagerly took up his position in the typography workshop run by the graphic design artist, Joost Schmidt, who told him, "This workshop emphasizes an avant-garde approach to advertising. We use clear, unadorned type, dramatic symbols and color only for emphasis. Simplification of design gives great power to advertising."

Schmidt pulled open the print drawers containing sheets of images, "These bold, clean, precise prints have become characteristic of the Bauhaus and have influenced graphic designers all over the world."

The images were familiar to Rudolf; he had seen similar artworks during the spring of 1930 in Paris at *The Bauhaus Exhibition— Société des artists décorateurs.* At that time he realized that graphic design could be a powerful tool of propaganda. Rudolf recognized how easily art could use that power for either good or evil, entirely dependent on the intent of the artist or the patron.

In the 1920s, Walter Gropius founded the Bauhaus with a vision for a school created as a utopian, socialist community where all art would be created for the good of society. Gropius said, "The purpose of industrial design is for a million unified, trained workers to construct the new ideal buildings of the future."

Van der Rohe continued the philosophical ideals of Groppius, who believed in the integration of art and technology and the combined roles of artist and craftsperson. Van der Rohe developed International style architecture, characterized by pure "skin and bones" structures in clear glass and elegant steel, and the clean, plain style spread around the world.

Thoughts of Eszter Klein and her communistic ideals came to Rudolf's mind... *how much she would appreciate the look and purpose of this place!* The whole complex, consisting of workshops, classrooms, a community dining room, theater, gymnasium, administrators' offices, and students' studio apartments, created a complete social, communal living and working environment.

The Bauhaus workshops housed the learning environment for architecture, interior design, sculpture, painting, graphic design, and advertising, all developed to complement and interrelate with each other. For Rudolf the academic year got under way quickly as he became completely immersed in his work, his teaching duties and various design projects, and, of course, his continued work for MI6.

November

In November the Dressau City Council held elections and the *Nationalsozialistische Deutsche Arberter Party*, the NSDAP or Nazi Party, gained a majority of members. Their first action was to immediately stop financial support for the Bauhaus because the NSDAP believed that the Bauhaus still harbored pro-communist leanings. The council also let it be known that their ultimate desire was to permanently end the school and demolish the complex. Several master artist instructors, Paul Klee and Rudolf's Hungarian friend, László Moholy-Nagy among them, resigned their positions at the school and left Germany.

Rudolf remained as an instructor at the school and spent much of his free time traveling to Munich and Berlin quietly gathering information and making connections. He maintained communication with MI6 in a variety of ways through his previously established network and new sources.

1932
January, Cologne

Klára wanted to marry at her Lake Balaton villa, but Franz insisted that he could not get away from Cologne until spring and he didn't want to delay any longer. Klára acquiesced to a January wedding even though the wind blew cold and snow piled from Budapest to Cologne. Leopold and Elizabeth along with Tamás and Silva made their way north by train across the frozen landscape. The Duchess Eugenia sent her drivers to the station to pick up the wedding guests. Eugenia was beside herself with excitement to have visitors coming to her home for such a festive occasion. When the von Estés arrived, Eugenia greeted them warmly and sent them in different directions to their accommodations.

Konrad led Tamás and Silva through several rooms to the kitchen where Gita waited to welcome them. Silva was anxious to see the kitchen and to meet the staff; she wanted to begin right away making all her special dishes for the wedding. Klára arrived from her orchestra rehearsal and went straight to the kitchen just as Tamás and Silva entered. Klára missed Silva so much and could hardly wait to see her and Tamás. They embraced heartily, all three of them. Klára felt great happiness to have her dear friends come so far for her wedding and she was happy Silva and Gita could finally meet. Klára left them chatting in the kitchen and ran upstairs to greet her beloved Papa and mother.

Three days later, Klára married Franz in the *Marienkapelle* of the Kölner Dom, Cologne's magnificent Gothic Cathedral, only a few blocks from Aunt Eugenia's great townhouse. The late afternoon light filtered through the spectacular stained glass windows creating a mosaic of colors that reflected across the walls and floor. Standing in that kaleidoscope of color, Klára's cream-colored suit took on an iridescent glow.

Leopold took her hand, "We've not had the chance to talk for so long it seems, Klára," he stared into her lovely eyes and smiled at her. "Are you certain this is the young man you want, Klára? If he is, then I am happy for you. The Baron does seem like a good match for you. It's just I thought you would marry and live close to me."

"I'm sorry, Papa. I would rather live in Budapest, if I could. I, too, am surprised by the way my life has turned out." Klára kissed her Papa. "I'm so pleased that you and mother are here with me today."

Klára was stunning in a Schiaparelli silk suit and stylish Dali-inspired hat with an angled crown and tulle netting that fell across her face. She held a bouquet of yew and holly with red berries. Leopold escorted his daughter to the chapel's altar where they met Franz, who appeared handsome as ever in a dark navy blue suit.

Although the little chapel was filled to capacity, Klára longed for her friends Rózsa and Pál to be there, but that was impossible. Instead, Renate and Elizabeth stood beside each other, congratulating themselves on their matchmaking. Franz's three sisters, Greta and the two married ones with their families were there. Hannelore and Max, as well as Ruthie and Oskar, and the others of Klára's jazz group attended, too. Tamás and Silva stood together glowing with joy for Klára. *Not perfect to our way of thinking, but it is as it is. We will never understand how the love shared by Klára and Dolf became so broken.*

After the wedding Aunt Eugenia held the wedding party at her home, elated to host such a grand event. Klára's jazz group provided the music with both Klára and Franz participating in some of the songs. Franz even sang to Klára an American ballad, "What Is This Thing Called Love?"

Silva and Gita beamed with pride as they set out the wedding feast they had so lovingly prepared. There were platters of *Martinsgans*, goose with crunchy skin, *Sauerbraten* and *Kartoffelklössen*, potato dumplings, *Schwartenbraten* with *Sauerkraut, Reibekuchen*, potato pancakes, sausages and cold meats. Silva offered a fine *Budapest Módra*, thinly sliced steak and *burgonya lángos*, deep fried potato cakes. Aunt Eugenia's cook made a spectacular Black Forest Cake, *Schwarzwalder Kirshtorte*, a chocolate gateau with a filling of whipped cream and cherries while Silva made Klára's favorite *Dobos Torta*, a sponge cake with whipped chocolate cream between the layers and iced with a rich caramel glaze. Everyone was delighted. Despite Klára's longing to stay with her beloved guests longer, she and Franz left the very next day for their wedding trip.

—⚛—

After their honeymoon trip to Spain and the island of Majorca, Franz and Klára returned home to the cold snows of Cologne. Franz immediately went back to his work at the Werner Railroad offices and Klára immersed herself in the moving process. Franz had purchased a four-storied townhouse on Kleine Budengrasse, a short walk from Aunt Eugenia's mansion. Aunt Eugenia sent her housekeeper, Gita, to help Klára establish her new home.

While Klára was living with Aunt Eugenia she and Gita had become well-acquainted. In fact, Klára had become very fond of Gita. There was much about Gita that reminded her of dear Silva. Klára trusted Gita's opinions and became rather dependent upon her good judgment in household matters. The mature, motherly Gita brought great comfort to Klára who missed her family exceedingly. Klára had no one to talk to about deeply personal things and in time Gita became more than a servant, she became a trusted and dependable friend. When Klára felt distressed or puzzled, it was to Gita she turned. Klára wanted to tell Gita about her honeymoon.

As Gita and Klára unwrapped her Herend porcelain plates and stacked them on the table, Klára began, "We had a marvelous time, Gita. First, we went to Spain, but we didn't stay there very long. Franz wanted to leave almost immediately and go to the island of Majorca." Klára moved the stack of plates to the cupboard. "It's so beautiful there. Warmer than Germany at this time of year, at least on the island's south side, but they do have snow-capped mountains in the Tramuntana range. We stayed in Palma, the capitol city. Shopping, music, the cathedral, castles, and beautiful walks along the sea, the usual touristy things. The food was delicious—a saffron rice with chicken and a sweet called *ensaïmada*." Klára looked up at Gita, her eyes were filled with tears.

"What is it, Baroness? Why the tears?" Gita asked with great concern as she put down the cups she was unwrapping.

"I don't know, Gita, but something is not right." Klára bit her lip and wiped the tears away, "I can't explain, but..." she hesitated and looked down, she couldn't look at Gita. She sat down at the table, "I...I thought love would be wonderful...you know...making love with your husband. I thought it would be tender and gentle. I thought that I would feel loved." Klára cried, "What's wrong with me, Gita. Why is it so difficult?"

Gita put her arms around Klára and held her until she stopped crying. Gita whispered questions to Klára, trying to discover her expectations and her responses to Franz, but Klára's answers revealed to Gita that Klára was a willing wife, although completely inexperienced. Gita shuddered to hear what Klára told her and knew the fault lay wholly with Franz. From Klára's words Gita learned that he had a distorted, even perverted view of love-making. Gita shuddered again to think of how he had degraded his relationship with his sweet, innocent wife. *Poor Klára.*

Now, Gita's eyes filled with tears as Klára continued, "I did love someone else once and he kissed me and he held me. He was so gentle, so loving, so different, exactly as beautiful as I imagined love to be." Klára sighed deeply, "Is it my fault? Does Franz know that I loved someone else once?"

"No, child, he doesn't know and you should never tell him." Gita thought to herself, *my poor little Baroness.* Gita never suspected Franz would be the kind of man to have these perversions; such twisted proclivities made her shiver. She now realized that Franz was a man to watch, to fear. She would tell the Duchess, but she knew there was very little either of them could do. "You know, Baroness, that your aunt will always welcome you to her home, if you become too unhappy."

"Oh, no, Gita, please don't tell my aunt or anyone what I have told you," Klára begged her. "I'll try to do all that I can do to be a good wife and to help Franz be a good husband. It'll be all right. I know it will. Thank you, dear Gita, for listening to my problems. You're so good to me."

That same afternoon, Franz stood at a large window in his office looking down at the vast train yards stretching out in all directions; he was proud of his rail empire. Tracks radiating outward to distant cities and foreign countries, powerful steam engines, thousands of cars of all descriptions, several great roundhouses, and a thousand workers or more. Franz silently thanked his father, the father he had rarely seen and barely knew, but greatly admired for his business acumen. Franz felt important and confident; he recognized that his inherited power and money brought him great influence and prestige.

As he stood admiring his domain, his secretary entered the room. "Your three o'clock appointment is here, Sir. Colonel Himmler and Major Heydrich." She turned toward the door and ushered the two men into the office. Heydrich and Himmler, both in black military uniforms, stopped at the entrance, clicked their heels, raised their right arms and shouted "Heil, Hitler."

Franz, still standing by the window, was somewhat startled; he had never before been addressed with such a ritual. He walked toward the men with enthusiasm, introduced himself, and shook hands with them. They in turn introduced themselves as Reinhard Heydrich and Heinrich Himmler, both S.S. Nazi officers. Franz invited them to sit down in comfortable leather armchairs and offered cigarettes and coffee. They declined the coffee, but took the cigarettes.

Himmler began the conversation. "We represent the German government. We are here to discuss the expansion of certain rail lines in Germany as well as the extension of lines into some eastern regions and into the far south. We are interested in very particular places. In addition to the lines we are also interested in contracting the use of numerous wagons, boxcars. If you are interested in working with us, we can be very specific on timing, locations, and numbers."

Franz was, of course, interested and delighted in answering, "I and my railroad are at your service."

Himmler continued to speak of details while Heydrich relaxed in his chair and blew smoke rings in the air.

Finally, Heydrich spoke, "Himmler, look at this young man. Is he not the perfect Aryan specimen?" Heydrich leaned forward, "Astounding good looks—blond, blue-eyed, chiseled bone structure, tall and strong."

"Baron von Werner, you should become the poster boy for the Third Reich," responded Himmler enthusiastically. "Mein Führer will be quite excited that we have come for trains and found Aryan perfection."

Most men would find this conversation unbearably embarrassing, but not Franz. Quite flattered, he succumbed quickly to their compliments. The three men continued their conversation over glasses of schnapps. Heydrich discovered that the Baron and his wife loved music.

"I'm thrilled to hear that you have an interest in music. Good classical German music, I hope. None of that detestable American noise that is infiltrating Germany, polluting the tastes of our young people." Heydrich sipped smugly from his glass. "You and your wife should have a concert at your home. There are many prominent officers in Cologne at the moment who would enjoy a musical evening."

"Excellent idea, Reinhard," bellowed Himmler. "Baron, you should inspire your wife to entertain. It would be delightful."

When the men stood to leave Reinhard Heydrich presented Franz with a copy of *Mein Kampf,* signed by Hitler himself and told Franz, "Read this and learn about our leader and his ideals for Germany and her people."

Franz could hardly contain his excitement. These men were so energetic and pleasant. He was flattered that they would include him in their social circle. Franz simply smiled his broad, handsome smile and agreed with the two on everything. He would tell Klára...*as soon as the household is unpacked and put in order, we must have a dinner party for these new acquaintances. It would be good for business.*

Reinhard Heydrich, a member of the Nazi Party since 1931, himself an excellent example of Aryan perfection, had risen quickly to the rank of major in the S.S. Called by some "the Blond Moses," Heydrich was tall, over six feet, athletic, with hard, sculpted features, and arrogant. Franz and Reinhard shared many traits in addition to their pure Aryan appearances, in particular their temperament and disarming personalities. The slightly older Reinhard greatly impressed the younger Franz who looked forward to a long relationship; they had recognized each other as kindred spirits instantly.

March

Franz, rarely home, spent his days at his office and his evenings with business acquaintances whom Klára had not met. She really didn't mind that he was never home. Franz had changed so much since their wedding she sometimes stared at him wondering who he really was. When Franz was at home he talked constantly with great enthusiasm about a fellow named Reinhard Heydrich; Franz was clearly in awe of this man. Klára knew very little except that Heydrich was a Nazi, interested in Franz's railroad and was going to make them very rich and from what Franz said, he must look like a Nordic god.

With Gita's part-time help Klára spent her days putting her house in order. Gita also helped Klára hire a household staff—Lisbeth as housekeeper, Trudi as cook, and a maid, Hedy. Having four capable women in the house to help, including Gita, gave Klára more confidence to set up her new home. Klára also spent time with Aunt Eugenia; tea at her mansion at least twice a week, shopping together on Fischmarkt, walking through a museum now and then, or attending mass together at the Dom or St. Martin's.

On occasion Aunt Eugenia invited Hannelore and Ruthie for tea as well. Eugenia adored the lively conversation of the three young women and loved hearing gossip and tales of romance they willingly shared with her. Aunt Eugenia did notice that Klára listened far more than she spoke. Eugenia sensed she either had nothing to share or did not want to reveal any information about hers and Franz's life together as newlyweds.

Gita shared part of Klára's woeful tale with Aunt Eugenia, but only to say that Klára had a disappointing wedding trip and that she could say no more. Gita encouraged the Duchess to be supportive of Klára and wait for her decision to confide.

After a day's outing with Aunt Eugenia including lunch at the Dom Hotel and an afternoon of shopping, Klára returned home to find Franz.

"Franz, I'm so glad that you're home. You will never guess who I ran into today!" Klára put down her packages and took off her coat and hat. Franz made no response. "I saw Mose Kohn! He's just come back to Cologne from America." Klára's smile revealed her excitement, "He's brought back a bunch of new jazz records…Louis Armstrong, Ethel Waters, Al Jolson, Duke Ellington. He invited us to come to a party at his flat tomorrow evening."

Klára prattled on even though Franz showed no sign of interest, "He says we'll push back the furniture, roll up the carpet and he said, 'cut a rug!' Isn't that funny? It means dance!"

"You'll have to tell him that we can't come," Franz stated calmly.

"We can't? Why not?"

"Klára, jazz music is completely unacceptable. Music made by Jews and Negroes! Just think about the names you listed—all Jews and Negroes." Franz stared at her intently. "Their music attempts to corrupt and distort legitimate German music. Major Heydrich disapproves of it completely. We want to focus our attention on putting forth German composers, classical and romantic music. Wagner, for instance."

Franz looked at her with his new stern face, "I do not want you to associate with those radical Jews any longer."

"But Franz, they're our friends." She was completely aghast. "How can you…?"

"They are not *my* friends, Klára. They were your friends, but no more. I've made new business associations now and your friends would be very bad for business."

Klára started to protest, but Franz put up his hand. "This matter is closed. There will be no more discussion. You're not to associate with those people…ever."

"Will you be home for dinner this evening?" Klára took her packages and turned away from him.

An already distracted Franz answered in the negative and went back to reading the stack of paperwork piled on the desk before him. Klára walked up the stairs to her bedroom, closed the door behind her and fell across her bed. She sobbed into the pillow, not wanting anyone to hear her. *This is the man who liked jazz music very much...sang songs and played the piano with me, laughed with our Jewish friends. What has happened? What have I done? He has such disdain for me. I can see it in his eyes. He is so cold, so rough. I thought I could love him. He begged me to love him, to marry him. He must know that I loved someone else.*

April

Franz paced across the reception room, looking at his watch. "They'll probably be early. Heydrich is always prompt or early. Is everything ready, Klára?"

Klára had thrown herself into preparing for the party; she enjoyed planning the menu, deciding on the dishes and glassware, setting the mood for the rooms. Her new staff had a great time sampling everything; they laughed and worked so well together.

By the time the evening arrived, Klára was certain she had done her best to create a lovely evening for Franz's new business friends. She looked into the mirror that hung near the entrance and tucked in some loose ends of her black hair. She thought...*perhaps I should have a short cut again.*

Just at that moment the doorbell rang. Klára moved toward Franz, while Hedy went to the door. Klára was proud of the women she had hired; Hedy was pleasant, well-groomed, exacting in her manner and very familiar with genteel protocol. Hedy opened the door, greeted the guests, took their hats and coats and quietly disappeared from the room.

Franz introduced his friends to Klára, all of them dressed in their black S.S. uniforms, Reinhard Heydrich, Jörg Müller, Fritz Lichtermann, and Rike Friedrich. They in turn introduced the women who had come with them, Lili, Thea, Gisela, and Katrina. Klára had thought they would bring their wives, but these women were obviously not their wives. All were blonde in varying tints, none natural...each one trying to be a Marlene Dietrich look-alike...platinum blonde hair, bright red lips and false eyelashes.

Hedy passed around a tray of hors d'oeuvres while Franz and Reinhard mixed drinks at the bar. Loud discussion and waves of raucous laughter ensued. Gisela sat on the lap of the obese little Lichtermann, exposing a great deal of her leg. Lili and Katrina stood at the bar with Reinhard and Franz clicking glasses and laughing loudly. The very flirtatious Thea was doing her best to entertain the other two men.

"I have heard that you are a virtuoso." Reinhard turned his attention toward Klára, insisting that she play the piano, "With your permission, I would like to play my violin along with you," he said, as he took a violin from the case he had brought with him.

He controlled the choices of music, each time choosing something very German, very traditional, and to Klára's taste rather gloomy, but he could actually play the violin very well and he was charming, speaking softly to her and smiling. His politeness seemed quite incongruent with the mood of the room or the company. While the two played rather somber music the others were dancing, even Franz. No jazz was played, although it might have been more appropriate for the women's behavior.

After almost two hours of music, boisterous activity, and drinking, Klára's head was spinning. She spoke to Franz, "We must eat, Trudi's dinner will be ruined and there's been too much drinking. No one will be able to taste her delicious dishes."

"If you aren't feeling well, Klára, you may go to your room. Don't spoil everyone's good time." Franz dismissed her.

Klára felt the heat rise in her cheeks. She only nodded to Reinhard Heydrich and left the room. Instead of going upstairs, she went into the kitchen where she found Hedy, Lisbeth, the housekeeper, and Trudi, stirring the soup, "I'm so sorry about dinner. Is it ruined?"

"No, no it's not ruined, Madam." Trudi saw how upset the Baroness had become. "You mustn't worry. That's my job to keep everything ready. It'll be fine."

"Well, I'm starved and I have no idea if they will ever eat, so may I have my dinner, now, in here with you?"

"Of course," said Lisbeth. "Here—sit. Hedy, set a place for the Baroness."

"Have you eaten?" Klára was very distraught, but she certainly did not want to cry in front of her new employees. "It's so late, come sit, eat with me, please."

Eventually, Klára went upstairs by way of the servant stair and to bed. She could hear music from the gramophone drifting upstairs from below. She took a deep breath and tried to think of better times and different places. When Klára awoke the next morning and went downstairs she learned that the party had ended very late. Hardly any of Trudi's delicious dinner had been eaten.

All of them, including Franz, had left the house together sometime past midnight. Franz had not returned. Klára's staff concealed their true opinions of the Baron and his guests from the young Baroness while maintaining cheerful expressions, but they did notice how tired and miserable she looked.

"Where do you want to have your breakfast this morning, Baroness?" Trudi asked. "I have oranges from the orangery and I could make crepes with jam for you, if you like. Whatever you want."

"I'm not very hungry this morning. I think just tea and toast in my morning room, thank you."

By early May, Reinhard Heydrich had rather easily seduced Franz into fully embracing Nazi philosophies. After enthusiastic encouragement by Heydrich, Franz joined the Nazi Party and became a lieutenant in the S.S. Although Franz continued to run the von Werner Railroads, he entrusted much of the day-to-day business to a fellow Nazi who served as manager in Franz's absence. Franz considered his new job as Heydrich's personal attaché and their work with the party more interesting and far more important than anything he had ever done.

Heydrich told Franz, "Hitler distrusts capitalists because they have a tendency to exploit the economically weak, but industrialists like you work for the good of the nation. You have shown true loyalty and responsibility to Germany." Heydrich continued, "You will gain the favor of Hitler himself when he learns how much you have contributed to the Reich."

When Franz made his first appearance in his new, black uniform, Klára was surprised. "What is this, Franz?" she asked, "You have joined the Nazi party? You have become part of the military? What of your company? I don't understand."

"My company is in good hands, in the service of Germany," he said matter of factly. "I have chosen to join a great movement that will bring long-deserved greatness to Germany. I want to be part of the Nazis' goal to bring forth a magnificent nation with a government that reflects the collective will of the people. The German people are tired of being downtrodden, oppressed, and broken by others from outside and enemies within. We are ready to become leaders of the world, to fulfill our destiny."

Klára thought his words and demeanor were almost otherworldly, as though he was perfectly programmed. She took a deep breath, "And the uniform? What have you joined? What does it mean?"

"This is the uniform of the S.S., the *Sicherheitsdienst*, the Secret Service, the most prestigious unit in the German military." Franz's expression and stance indicated a great sense of pride. "Adolf Hitler created the S.S. to serve him as his personal guard unit."

At this time, Klára knew very little about, nor had she paid any attention to, the Nazis or the S.S. or even Adolf Hitler, but she did know that Aunt Eugenia had no use for any of it. When reading the newspaper or speaking with Konrad, Eugenia grew very red in the face over stories about the Nazi political movement. Klára decided she should become more aware of this movement that infatuated Franz. She found Franz's copy of *Mein Kampf* and began to read Hitler's own words.

As Klára read Adolf Hitler's little book, she began to dismiss his philosophies as nonsense since Hitler's ideas were so utterly opposed to her Papa's philosophies and to her own personal experience. Her own informed opinions on diversity differed completely from this man's. *Hitler sees difference within populations of the Austro-Hungarian Empire as a weakening factor while Papa and I see differences as a strength.*

Klára found Hitler's ideas illogical. He accused Jews and communists of a conspiracy against Germany and all of Europe, believed the Aryans to be a "Master Race" and advocated that the Aryans/Germans had a God-given right to invade and expand their living space into any territory of their choosing.

When she finished reading *Mein Kampf,* Klára considered it nonsense, but Hitler's ideas obviously made sense to others and that made her agree with Aunt Eugenia...*this Adolf Hitler is a very dangerous man with heinous ideas.*

July

Since Franz was absent from their home most of the time, he had little time for Klára. His Nazi friends occupied his evenings and weekends, and when he was home he was too *busy* to bother with Klára's daily concerns. Klára simply discovered activities to keep herself engaged in useful endeavors, such as her work with the Ursuline nuns to aid Cologne's hungry children.

As an excuse for his absence, Franz told Klára, "My interest in the Nazi agenda will guarantee my place in Germany's new government." He seemed very proud as he added, "My place of prominence in the Third Reich will bring power, riches, and success to me; therefore, I must dedicate the majority of my time and energy to the party."

One mid-July evening Klára approached Franz in his study and as usual found him engaged with a large stack of documents piled on his desk. He did not like interruptions, but Klára had news she wanted to share with him.

Finally, Franz put down his papers and looked at her, "Well, what is it? What is so important?"

By then she had lost the joy of the moment, but announced to him, "We are going to have a baby, Franz, in the winter." She looked at him with expectation.

A big, wide, handsome smile glowed from his face, "Excellent, Klára! This is wonderful news! Hitler encourages his S.S. officers to marry and to have children. The Third Reich disapproves of Germany's low birth rate and high number of abortions."

Klára had no words in response to Franz. Her news seemed only to have significance due to what Hitler might think. Klára's disappointment was profound.

"This is a good thing, Klára." Franz's response was cool and impersonal; he continued speaking without direct connection to Klára. "The Nazis offer incentives for good Aryan mothers to have many babies. Jörg's wife just gave birth to her fourth child and she received a bronze medal from Hitler himself! I heard of another officer whose wife received a gold medal for having eight children, every one of them blond with blue-eyes."

When Franz had finished his string of thoughts, he returned to his papers. Klára's breath was hot, her expectations dashed, he had never risen from his desk. He had not even looked at her for more than a second. Her mouth suddenly filled with bile and she ran from the room. She wanted to run away to Aunt Eugenia's or even better, far away, all the way to Budapest.

—⁂—

Reinhard Heydrich summoned Franz to his office early one July morning. Heydrich had just been promoted to the rank of colonel and appointed Chief of Intelligence by Himmler. Himmler gave Heydrich a new assignment that he eagerly described to Franz.

"I am to create a highly secret counter-intelligence division, the S.D., *Sicherheitsdienst* or Security Service, within the S.S.," announced Heydrich proudly. "I have been given full control of the new S.D., including the Gestapo."

"Himmler recognizes that I'm the perfect choice for this assignment," Heydrich smiled at Franz. "He knows I'm willing to spy on everyone, including other Nazis." Heydrich took Franz into his confidence, "I've already designed a network of secret agents, paid informants, hidden cameras, and microphones."

"Let me show you what else I'm working on for the Führer." Heydrich said as he spread a stack of white cards across the table. "This is a top secret project for the S.D., a file card system that holds detailed information on everyone, even the most loyal members of the party." Heydrich smiled—a cunning smirk—as he added, "Even on you, Franz von Werner. I keep every tidbit of information—rumors, gossip, ancestry, proclivities, everything," he confessed to Franz.

"As a naval cadet, I served under Wilhelm Canaris. He was my neighbor and became my friend and mentor," Heydrich said as he turned a white card over and over in his hand. "Although he seems to support Hitler, he has never become a member of the Nazi Party nor has he sworn allegiance to Hitler."

Heydrich laid the card on the table. *WILHELM FRANZ CANARIS* was written across the top. "I'm suspicious of his loyalty to the Third Reich. So, we'll keep an eye on him for the S.D. You'll serve as my Adjunct Officer from now on, Franz."

Franz threw himself wholeheartedly into Heydrich's new project. From that day onward he spent hours helping Heydrich keep intricate files on fellow Nazis. Quite soon Franz became fully aware that Heydrich was just as charming and just as dangerous as he was.

Budapest

Financial disaster continued to plague the world causing personal and corporate losses of great proportion. Although not as devastating in some countries as in others, the world-wide depression spread by degrees everywhere.

"This weakened economy is causing Horthy to make very unwise choices," Leopold announced to Elizabeth and Tamás. "Choices that will come back to haunt us all without a doubt."

The three sat together in the von Esté wine office, going over the books, trying to make decisions that would keep production profitable in the future.

"So far in this disaster, the von Esté Company has suffered very little," Elizabeth stated wistfully, "but the depression continues year after year and Budapest is experiencing a significant drop in its standard of living."

"Harder times are expected," Tamás said. "You are wise to prepare for the worst."

"I'm certain Horthy's direction is very bad." Leopold had become completely disillusioned with the Horthy government. "It's difficult to remain confident when Horthy appoints Gyula Gömbös as the new prime minister."

Just saying Gömbös's name brought tears to Leopold's eyes. *Gömbös…the general and supreme commander of the Honvéd…the official Hungarian army…that met the king that fateful day in Budaörs.* Leopold always believed Gömbös severely over-reacted to the monarchists at the Battle of Budaörs, the battle in which his beloved son, Stefan, suffered his mortal wound.

"Horthy and Gömbös are moving Hungary closer and closer to Germany once again," said Tamás. "They've signed a trade agreement with Germany that, to a degree, relieves Hungary of financial woes, but makes Hungary far too dependent on Germany."

"I'm particularly concerned with Gömbös's new interest in Magyarization." Worry was evident in Leopold's voice; he said wistfully, "My dream of Magyarization for Hungary has always been one of unity for all ethnic minorities, but I fear Horthy's move to require Magyarization for Hungary is inspired by Germany's fascist right. I fear Horthy will use Magyarization to control or exclude our minorities."

October, Cologne

One afternoon as Franz read through his daily reports, one particular report concerning the Bauhaus came to his attention.

Dressau City Council, controlled by the Nazi Party, voted to close the Bauhaus and expel all instructors and students from the Dressau complex. Director Mies Van der Rohe moved the Bauhaus and its participants from Dressau to the Steglitz area of Berlin. Van der Rohe has transformed an abandoned telephone factory into a facility for the new Bauhaus.

Franz brought the information to Heydrich's attention; he found Rohe's response to saving the Bauhaus foolhardy. Convinced the school had communistic inclinations, Heydrich ordered Franz to keep a card in the file with all information gathered on the Bauhaus. Informants assured Franz the Bauhaus remained closely tied to its original utopian ideals. As Franz recorded the report onto the Bauhaus card, he made note of the school's socialist and communist ideals—its mission to integrate art into society and to unite industry, technology, and art.

Franz also made notes on the school's director, Van der Rohe, and its faculty. A few of the old faculty remained on staff in Berlin, including the Russian non-objective painter, Vassily Kandinsky, the German designer and painter, Josef Albers, the German photographer Walter Peterhans, and the printmaker, Rudolf von Házy. Franz never made a connection with Rudolf von Házy's name, because Klára had never used the name when speaking of her childhood friend to Franz; she had only used Dolf.

Even though only fourteen students continued their enrollment in Berlin, Heydrich and Franz considered the Bauhaus worth watching. The S.S. began a system of harassment and kept the school under constant scrutiny. Shortly after the school reopened, Hitler visited Berlin and declared the artwork coming out of the Bauhaus degenerate, unfit for the German populace to see. Almost immediately many instructors at the Bauhaus felt pressure to leave the school and Germany.

—⁂—

As she did every afternoon, when Franz was home, Klára brought a cup of coffee and the afternoon newspaper to him. In addition to reading reports, Franz studied stories and analyzed headlines in the Cologne newspaper, "Hitler loses presidential bid to Paul von Hindenburg," Franz read aloud, "but Hindenburg's Social Democrats lost their majority in the *Reichstag* to the Nazis. That's good.

"The Nazis don't trust parliamentary democracies," Franz stated confidently to Klára. "Democracy is a force that destabilizes the government, because it puts far too much power in the hands of minorities who have neither the ability nor the right to have any say in the running of our government. Democracy creates a divide against itself." He continued as though he was lecturing her, "Any country that embraces democracy is weak and doomed to fail."

Klára said nothing, but she remembered her Papa's stories of America and how he admired American ideals of democracy. She remembered well how Papa loved to tell the children about all the different ethnic groups who lived in America as he proudly related, "Everyone spoke English and they all came together to unite the vast American land! A perfect example of my dream for Hungary...Magyarization." Klára listened to Franz's rantings and decided his opinions and arrogant statements were foolish, based only upon nonsense and ignorance and prejudice.

December

The arrival of her parents in Cologne just before Christmas elated Klára. The von Estés wanted to be present for the birth of their grandchild. They stayed with Aunt Eugenia at her mansion on Frankenwerft, but spent their days and evenings at Klára's home on Kleine Budengrasse. Klára's housekeeper, Lisbeth, and Hedy decorated the von Werner home beautifully for the Christmas season with boughs of cedar and holly, a tall tree in the reception room decorated with colorful glass ornaments, and seemingly hundreds of candles.

The crisp aroma of spices and fir filtered through the house. Trudi, the cook, had baked for weeks in advance of their arrival—fruitcakes, candies, and *Lebkuchen*. Klára spent most of the holiday season reclining on a chaise lounge removed from her bedroom to the downstairs. Everyone waited on her every whim, treating her like a queen. After almost a year apart, having her parents in Cologne filled Klára with joy.

Soon after their arrival Elizabeth handed a wrapped box to Klára, "Silva sent this gift for your baby, Klára. She and Tamás send their love and hope that you will visit as soon as you can."

Klára opened the box to find a beautiful hand-knit ensemble of soft, white pieces, a sweater, hat, booties, and blanket. She clutched them to her breast, smiling and crying, saying, "I'll write to Silva right away. Aren't these so precious! Silva is such a dear to make them for my little one."

Leopold and Elizabeth passed the days quietly, but pleasantly, with Klára and Aunt Eugenia. Elizabeth played the piano while Leopold read the newspaper; they also talked of old times or read or played cards.

One evening after supper, as they rode back to Aunt Eugenia's, Leopold asked Elizabeth, "Why do you think Franz is absent so often? He's rarely home for a full evening and usually gone before we arrive in the morning; we have hardly seen him. Do you think he's displeased by our visit? Or might it be that he's truly busy?"

"Of course, he's busy, Leopold, with his important government job."

Elizabeth felt uncomfortable hearing Leopold's questions, because she, too, had noticed Franz's disengagement, not only with her and Leopold, but with Klára, too. "But when Franz is present, he's so attentive and pleasant, just as charming and effervescent as he was as a child."

Leopold thought differently from Elizabeth, but decided not to share his perceptions. To Leopold, Franz seemed cold, pre-occupied, and he made very strange comments that bothered Leopold deeply. Leopold recalled one rare evening when Franz was at home and asked Leopold, "Have you read the works of the Anglo-German writer H.S. Chamberlain... *Foundations of the Nineteenth Century?*"

As Leopold answered that he had not, he studied Franz carefully. Franz continued, "Chamberlain clearly believes in Teutonic supremacy. We, the German race, are the Master Race. Our race is destined to lead humanity and spread German culture all over the world." Franz leaned close to Leopold, "You, the Austrian, and I... we Germans are the true chosen people. You realize, of course, that Jews and other inferior races are our enemies, the destroyers of German blood. They assault the purity of our race."

Leopold feigned a mild interest, but decided to neither engage Franz in discussion nor argue against any of Franz's disjointed, bizarre statements, even though Franz's opinions appalled him. However, Franz continued to express his hatred for communists and Jews and paired the two in his rantings.

"The German people are under attack from a Jewish-Bolshevik conspiracy. Jewish financiers want to keep capitalism intact. You are aware that Jews control the banks?" Franz made direct eye-contact with Leopold, "The banks are the cause of the economic crisis that has so greatly afflicted Germany and her people. Jews are at the root of all our problems. Jews are the problem!"

Neither Leopold nor Elizabeth had sympathy for the communists, whom they always referred to as Bolsheviks, but Franz's harsh words regarding Jews bothered both of them. They had witnessed the devastating effect of anti-Semitism on individuals in Hungary.

As the evenings passed Leopold read article after article in the Nazi newspaper, *Der Stürmer*, articles written by Julius Streicher, the editor. At times Leopold shuddered at the harsh words he read. Streicher advocated the elimination of Jews and other minorities from Germany. His articles praised Nazi policy declaring minorities unworthy to be part of Germany, even undeserving to live. The newspaper's motto, *"Die Juden sind unser Unglück!* The Jews are our misfortune,"* spread across the front page every day. Leopold wadded the paper in front of Franz without a word, but making it clear he thought the paper nothing more than rubbish.

Franz's adulation for Adolf Hitler and his ideas for a New World Order particularly bothered Leopold. From his readings, Leopold found Hitler's ideas far too sinister. The ideology of the Aryan superman, accomplished through breeding, seemed too far-fetched for Leopold, but the words that stunned him most were those that glorified and idealized war. Leopold could hardly believe Franz as he boasted, "The Nazi Party is ready and willing to use violence to accomplish our goals." Obviously, Franz anticipated war with enthusiasm.

1933
January, Cologne

Franz spent New Years' Eve with his friends. Klára had no idea where he had gone. But to keep her parents unaware of the great rift between them, she told Leopold and Elizabeth that she had been invited, too, but, of course, could not go, insisting instead that Franz go without her.

Not until early the next morning did Franz return home and then he slept until mid-day. When he did finally rise, he dressed, came downstairs as affable as ever, and greeted everyone with *"Glückwunsch... Gutes Neues Jahr!"* He kissed Klára on top of her head most affectionately, then turned to everyone with a charming smile and began to engage in polite conversation. Elizabeth was especially pleased to see Franz so relaxed and absorbed in the moment.

Later in the day Elizabeth happily pointed out to Leopold, "See, he's a perfect fellow. It's just that his work is so demanding. After all, he's running a railroad and trying to serve his country at the same time."

Leopold nodded his head and smiled at Elizabeth, but he remained unconvinced and thought to himself, *Franz has become a Nazi with untenable positions, deplorable opinions, and a dangerous vision for Germany that will, in the long run, probably involve Hungary as well. Franz is not to be trusted.*

Worst of all, Leopold felt a heavy weight of guilt, because he implored God to sever his daughter's marriage and send her and her child out of her monstrous husband's grip. Leopold sincerely believed he sinned as he prayed for an end to a marriage blessed by God, but he had come to the conclusion Franz was a demon. Leopold noticed that whenever his daughter looked at Franz there was a terrified sadness in her eyes. Leopold was convinced there was no love between them, he was sure of it, even though Klára did everything she could to make him and Elizabeth think otherwise.

During the second week of January, while Franz was away from Cologne, Klára gave birth to a baby boy whom she named András. Leopold and Elizabeth were thrilled to have their first grandchild. They praised Klára for her superb job giving birth to such a handsome, healthy baby and lavished their love on both the new mother and baby.

Leopold held the tiny little being in his arms, rocking and cooing to András. Leopold felt an instant bond with the little boy. Holding András gave

Leopold a happiness he thought he would never feel again since the loss of his beloved Stefan, but one look into the face of András renewed in Leopold a great sense of life and hope for the future.

By the time Franz returned to Cologne the baby was over a week old. The nurse brought András wrapped in a soft blue blanket into Klára's bedroom. As Klára held the baby to her breast, she pulled the blanket away from his little face and body, so his father could have a first look at the tiny miracle. She introduced Franz to his little son. Franz looked at the baby and made a slight gasp, "He's dark like you, black hair. I don't know why I'm surprised. I had hoped he would be blond and blue-eyed, but how could that be with you as the mother."

Franz's disappointment was cruel and he did nothing to conceal it. Klára was heart-broken. To her, the angel she held in her arms was perfect and beautiful. *How could Franz feel nothing but disdain for his own son?*

"He's lovely, Franz, don't you see?" she pleaded.

"He looks nothing like an S.S. child should look," Franz answered. "He looks nothing like me," and with that, Franz turned and left the room without a single word of love or praise or gratitude.

Franz's dismissive attitude toward his own child did not really shock Klára, but she was surprised how he concealed his negative attitudes toward her and András from her parents. When Leopold and Elizabeth were present Franz was kind, even attentive to Klára and gave every outer sign of pride in his baby son.

Elizabeth and Klára met with Aunt Eugenia at her home to plan the baby's christening to be held in the *Marienkapelle* the following Friday evening. Aunt Eugenia, quite excited to have a party, encouraged Klára to invite all of her old friends for a dinner party the evening after the ceremony, but Klára declined.

"Let's keep it small, Aunt Eugenia. Franz no longer cares for our old friends and I don't care for his new ones, so it would be better to keep it very small."

On the Friday evening of the last week before Leopold and Elizabeth were to return to Budapest, they along with Franz and Klára and Aunt Eugenia arrived at the Dom. They walked to the *Marienkapelle* where they met the priest who had married Franz and Klára. To Klára's surprise Jörg Müller and his wife were also there. Franz and Jörg were dressed in their black S.S. uniforms. The baby was christened András Franz Stefan.

Afterwards the small group, including the Müllers, left the cathedral for a dinner party at Aunt Eugenia's home. The mood varied around the table from almost euphoric to incredulous to somber. Franz and Jörg monopolized the conversation with their admiration for Hitler. They raised their glasses in a toast... "To our new Chancellor, Adolf Hitler! Heil Hitler!" Everyone, forced to rise for the toast, offered only a weak "Heil Hitler!" in response.

"Hitler's great popularity forced Hindenburg to appoint him chancellor."

Jörg said proudly, then added more accolades, "Now, Hitler can officially create the national socialist state, the Third Reich, he desires for Germany. At last Germany's destiny to be a great nation with a pure Aryan population will be fulfilled."

"Did everyone hear about the fire in Berlin that burned the *Reichstag* to the ground? Of course the communists were responsible." Franz laughed, "Well, Röhm's Brownshirts will teach them a lesson. Communists and social democrats alike will face a wave of brutal violence at the hands of the Brownshirts. That should put an end to criticism of the Nazis! Soon, the only legal party in Germany will be the NSDAP!"

Leopold sat silently skeptical, listening to the views of Franz and Jörg, views Leopold found most improbable. Klára paid little attention to the political discourse and instead simply dreaded her parents' departure, allowing her mind to wander to happier places.

Aunt Eugenia, although finding it difficult to hold her tongue, hardly said a word through the entire dinner. She confided later to Konrad and Gita, "I felt most uncharitable toward my guests. I could hardly sit at my own table with those two Nazis and retain the semblance of a courteous hostess."

—⁕—

Franz was the most devious person Klára had ever known; she had no idea how to respond to him. She became secretive and deceptive herself, traits she detested in him and now found in herself. Once her parents returned to Budapest, Klára was alone. Only when Gita came to visit or when she saw Gita at Aunt Eugenia's, could she share her most intimate disappointments. Franz spent the majority of time away from home, often staying out well past midnight, actually allowing Klára some respite from dread. Some nights, when she was awakened by his hard boot steps on the tiled bathroom floor that separated their bedrooms, she lay frozen with fear that he might come to her in her bed, but since the birth of András, Franz rarely came into her bedroom. On the rare times that he did come, his breath was strong with alcohol, he was vulgar, and the experience was coarse and impersonal, leaving Klára completely demoralized.

One morning as Klára sat in her morning room feeding her cherished baby, Franz entered the room. She looked up at him with great disdain and courageously asked, "Why did you want to marry me, Franz? Why did you beg me to marry you?"

"You don't know, Klára?" He looked at her with a wicked smile, "Really? I've told you many times. Our mothers, Klára, they desired it since we were children." Franz walked to her and kissed her on the cheek, "I take great pleasure in making my mother happy."

When Franz left the room, Klára sank deeply into her chair; she looked at the little baby in her arms. Despite her revulsion for his father, she only felt the deepest love for András and was thankful for his existence. Klára sighed heavily and wondered about a different life that she might have had.

The servants in the von Werner house were fully aware of Franz's true nature. They knew more than Klára realized about her marriage, about his proclivities, and about his attitude toward little András, but, of course, there was nothing they could do about anything.

—m—

Franz could care less about Klára's thoughts or feelings; he was far more concerned about an unused munitions factory in the town of Dachau located near Furstenfeldbruck, his childhood home. Work to convert the factory into a labor camp had been completed and Franz was responsible for the new spur of track running to Dachau from Munich. That track had to be ready for prisoner transport to the new camp. Franz traveled back to Furstenfeldbruck for a couple of weeks to check on the track's progress and to make final arrangements for enough railcars to move Jews to the camp. Finally, when all was ready, Franz took a ride on the new track where he smiled to see the words, *"Arbeir macht Frei,* Work Sets You Free," written on the great arch over the entrance into the camp.

At the same moment, elsewhere in Germany, Reinhard Heydrich had begun a program of mass arrests of Jews, communists, trade unionists, Catholic politicians, and any other persons who spoke against the Nazis. As Dachau opened, other tracks and other camps—Buchenwald, Sachsenhausen. and Lichienburg—opened as well, all ready for the next step.

—m—

Shortly after Franz's return to Cologne, Heydrich informed Franz of his transfer to Berlin; he wanted Franz to go with him. Klára and little András visited Aunt Eugenia to share with her what Klára believed to be very bad news—the von Werners would move to Berlin by the end of March. Over tea, Klára confessed her sadness to leave Cologne, her friends, and especially Aunt Eugenia.

"This will surprise you, Klára," said Aunt Eugenia, "but Konrad and I, too, are leaving Cologne. We're moving to Quebec...in Canada. We doubt we'll ever return to Germany."

Klára was surprised. Her aunt's news troubled her. "I will miss you terribly. Just knowing that you are no longer in Germany will be very difficult for me."

"Konrad and I object vehemently to the strong-arm politics of that little monstrous Hitler. We abhor the arrival of the Gestapo in Cologne and Rohm's Brownshirts are nothing but unintelligent criminals. The S.S. is even worse." Eugenia's face grew red as her voice raised, "And Konrad suspects there will be war."

"Aunt Eugenia, you must be careful expressing your opinions outside of this house," Klára warned. "I'm genuinely worried for your safety."

"Another reason to leave this pitiful place," Eugenia said. "One can no longer speak one's mind. In my opinion, Klára, you should think about going back to Budapest as soon as possible."

"I can't do that," answered Klára, as she looked into her teacup rather than into Aunt Eugenia's eyes.

At that moment Eugenia's housekeeper, Gita, entered the room with hot water to refill the teapot.

"Well, Gita and I have a proposition for you, Klára." Aunt Eugenia passed a plate of sweets to Klára, "I would like for you to take Gita with you when you move to Berlin. She is a treasure, as you know, and she can help you set up your home in Berlin as she did here and now that you have a little one, you will need her help even more until you find a nanny. Gita's daughter lives in Berlin, so the move is good for her as well."

"I would be thrilled, Gita, if you would come with me. I have been feeling very alone lately and it will only be worse in Berlin. Will you come?"

"Of course, I will," answered Gita. "It will give me much pleasure to help you set up your home and to care for little András. My daughter, Bela, and her family live near Berlin. I can visit them on my days off."

Although Gita had happily served the Duchess for many years and was completely devoted to her, she was very happy for the opportunity to leave Cologne and move with Klára to Berlin. In these troubled times Gita had great concern for her family—being Jewish in Germany demanded a rather precarious walk. Klára knew that Gita was nervous for herself and her daughter's family and believed this new arrangement very good for both of them.

ℳarch, Berlin

In late March Franz and Klára moved to Berlin, Gita and Hedy with them. Franz had found a lovely townhouse on Ebertstrasse across from the Tiergarten, a four-storied stone building with a private walled garden at the rear of the house. The kitchen and dining room were on the ground floor; reception, Franz's study and Klára's morning room—the sunniest room—on the first floor; bedrooms for Franz and Klára, the nanny's rooms, and nursery on the second floor; and the servants' quarters in the attic. Klára loved the raised terrace and garden beyond the morning room. Gita helped Klára hire a new staff—Inge as cook and Liesel as a second maid. Hedy would continue as Klára's personal maid.

Heinrich Himmler recommended to Franz a superb nanny for András. Without any input from Klára, Franz brought Marta Krause home one afternoon and moved her into the small bedroom next to András.

Marta Krause, a small woman of about fifty, had a friendly face and a proper manner, but she was cold and distant. Marta watched everyone carefully and Klára suspected she reported to Franz anything she thought might be of interest to him. Marta was a woman of few words, but with strong opinions on everything—the spices Inge used, the way Liesel ironed the sheets, how Hedy answered the telephone and, in particular, on how Klára spoiled András.

Marta clearly admired Franz, as she constantly mentioned his handsome Aryan looks to Klára as though Klára may not have noticed. Marta spoke of Franz's dedication to the Reich with extravagant adjectives and she practically squealed with delight whenever she saw him in his S.S. uniform. Klára also noticed that Marta made a point of going into Franz's study to speak privately with him every afternoon. Klára realized early on that Marta could not be trusted.

April

Shortly after getting settled in their new house Franz wanted to host a small cocktail party prior to an evening at the Berlin Symphony. When Heinrich Himmler, Reinhard Heydrich and several other S.S. officers arrived with their wives and girlfriends, they were greeted by Gita who took their coats and hats and led them into the reception room. Liesel and Hedy served the guests drinks and canapés. The atmosphere was congenial and quite pleasant, thought Klára, much nicer than the horrible evening party in Cologne.

The female guests sat together in the alcove by the bay window immersed in their own light conversation of fashion and the weather while the men stood by the fireplace. Except for Klára the women paid little attention to the men, even though Heydrich and Himmler were speaking loudly. Anyone listening could hear most of what they were saying. The bits and pieces Klára heard shocked and even terrified her.

"The Aryan race is physically superior to all other races. Just look at Franz. Is he not a fine example? Franz will be our Aryan model for a series of new posters," Himmler announced. Himmler liked to think he was personally responsible for discovering Franz. "Perfect features and bone structure, that blond hair and blue eyes, what a handsome specimen he is."

"Much like you, Reinhard," teased Jörg Müller, their friend from Cologne who had also moved to Berlin.

"Yes, Franz is the perfect choice for the new propaganda program our Führer wants to launch," Himmler said. "Franz fits perfectly Rosenberg's formula for desired Aryan physical traits. Rosenberg based his formula on the ideals of H.S. Chamberlain, the renowned Anglo-German author."

"Our Master Race is superior over all others," stated another officer. "These posters will put forth a visual statement for those mongrel races, the Jews and Gypsies, and make it very clear just how inferior they are. One day soon we will rid our nation of these pollutants."

Gita glanced up from the tray of canapés she was serving, making eye contact with Klára. It was obvious to Klára that Gita heard their words and clearly understood their meaning. Klára, seeing the fear in her eyes, stood and took the tray from Gita, "Thank you, Gita. Please, return to the kitchen and ask Liesel to bring more wine."

Gita gladly left the room and did not return to the reception that evening. She missed hearing the rest of the evening's conversation that spiraled downward to more depraved talk about Jews and others these men believed unfit to live in Germany.

"The labor camps are ready for the Jews and other undesirables," offered Heydrich. "Plans are under way to increase the arrests and deportations. Everything is going quite smoothly."

After that evening, Gita grew more anxious. Although glad to be in Berlin, Gita worried more and more about her daughter and her family. On her days off, Gita traveled by bus to the northern edge of Berlin to visit her only daughter, Bela, a married woman with one son—Gita's beloved grandson, Lars. For years Bela's husband worked as a civil servant with the Postal Service, but recently Gita learned his job was in jeopardy. Gita witnessed bitterness and fear in poor Bela's home, causing thoughts of leaving Germany to enter their minds.

While Klára worked in her garden one May afternoon, she was approached by Nanny Marta who whispered, "Baroness, did you know that Gita is a Jewess?" and before Klára could answer, Marta asked, "Does the Baron know?"

"I suppose that everyone knows, Marta," Klára answered. "As yet there is no law against having Jews as servants."

At that moment Klára realized Marta was a dangerous woman and from that day forward whenever Klára wanted to speak with Gita alone, she sent Marta to the Tiergarten with András in his pram for a long walk.

Summer

During Rudolf's most recent travel to London he found things quite busy at British Intelligence, MI6. A rapid flow of information regarding Germany arrived almost daily—the labor camps were open and the arrests of German citizens had begun.

At the beginning of Berlin's new Bauhaus summer session, the S.S. arrived unexpectedly to search the building. The S.S. arrested thirty-two students as communist suspects, sealed the building, and warned the faculty to leave the city or face arrest themselves. Rudolf, just returned to Berlin from London, was not present for the search or arrests, but his position at the Bauhaus had come to an end. He would have to resort to other business reasons for his travels to Germany.

Klára answered a soft knock on her bedroom door, "Come in."

Hedy opened the door wide enough to look in, "There's a gentleman requesting to see you, Madam."

"Who is it?"

"He said to tell you that it's Dolf."

Klára gasped. Sitting at her dressing table, she saw her own expression reflected in the mirror, an expression of surprise and joy that she could not conceal. Klára had not seen Dolf since Eger, four years ago. She composed herself, "Please tell him I will see him, Hedy. Take him into the morning room."

Klára stared into the mirror. She opened her jewelry box and took the emerald necklace from its velvet cradle and fastened it around her throat. She stood and walked to the door, her heart pounding against the emeralds. Klára flew down the stairs and to the doors of the morning room. She stepped into the heavy air of the sunlit room.

Sanding by a tall palm near the panes of glass, Rudolf's smile conveyed pure joy at seeing her, but his stance showed an obvious restraint. Klára hurried to him and embraced him fully, she was breathless, and tears streamed down her cheeks.

"What are you doing here?" she sobbed. "How did you find me? It's so good to see you."

Rudolf held her gently in his arms and softly implored her not to cry. He spoke quietly, "Hitler has officially closed the Bauhaus. My teaching is over. I'm on my way out of Germany, but I wanted to see you before leaving. Tamás told me where to find you."

"Oh, Dolf, you've been here in Berlin all this time? I've missed you so. There's so much to say."

Wiping tears from her cheeks, Klára moved away from him. At that moment, a third person in the room cleared her throat, shifting Klára's attention to that person, Marta.

"It's time for the baby's outing," Marta said, "should I take him now?"

Klára knew Marta was spying on her and would report to the Baron the intimacy she had witnessed, but Klára felt no obligation to introduce Dolf, instead she straightened her shoulders and announced they would all go for a walk in the park. "I want my friend to meet little András. Prepare him for the walk and we will meet you in the foyer."

Marta hurried from the morning room.

"These are difficult times, are they not?" Klára nodded toward Marta, "She's not to be trusted."

"That is part of my purpose in coming here, Klára," Rudolf replied. "I'm concerned about your safety."

"How did we come to this?" Klára asked. "I thought my life would be so different."

Klára and Rudolf walked to the foyer where Marta appeared with András, dressed in a navy blue sailor suit, sitting up in her arms. "This is my beautiful little son, András," Klára said proudly, "almost six months old already."

Rudolf extended his hand toward the handsome little boy touching his dark hair. The baby smiled and wrapped his little hand around Rudolf's finger. Rudolf returned the smile, thinking how much the little fellow looked like his grandfather, the duke.

Even though the child could not understand her words, Klára said, "András, this is my dearest friend from when I was a little girl, Count Rudolf. He will be your dear friend, too"

Klára, Rudolf, Marta, and András left the house and were met on the sidewalk by the chauffeur who provided a rather elegant carriage for the child.

As Marta put András in the basket of the carriage, Klára said to her, "Go ahead, Marta, we'll follow."

They moved down the street to the intersection, crossing over to the Linden Avenue Promenade. Marta pushed the stroller ahead of them while Klára put her arm through Rudolf's arm and gave it a squeeze. She was so happy to be near him once again. As they walked together under the linden trees, Klára took a breath and asked, "How old is your baby now?"

"What? My baby? What are you talking about, Klára? I don't have a baby."

"Dolf, I saw her...your young woman, in Paris." Rudolf looked at her so strangely that she frowned and stammered, "At your flat, in April, two years ago. Are you married to her?"

"Yvette!" Rudolf stopped walking, "you're talking about Yvette. No, Klára," he laughed, "I'm not married to Yvette. Her baby is not my baby."

Then he stared intently at Klára, "You were in Paris? I never knew you were in Paris." His smile faded as he comprehended this revelation. "Klára, what you must have thought."

"I thought I had discovered your *obligation, the commitment* you couldn't tell me about." Her mind was racing, "I thought you were in love with another woman and that you were having a baby together."

Now she was doubtful, "Why did you stop writing to me?"

"I wrote to you, Klára, but you never answered."

"I never stopped writing, Dolf! Not until I married." Klára looked devastated, suddenly she realized someone had interfered in their lives... *Dolf's and mine... our lives were altered.* "And *the complicated thing*, Dolf, that thing you couldn't share with me?" Klára began to walk forward again.

"My job, Klára. Not teaching, not art, but another. I...I still can't...I've said too much already." Rudolf was thinking. . . *a disaster has happened to us... our lives have diverged in some ruthless way from what should have been.* "I never thought our lives would take a turn like this...away from each other."

"Nor did I, so unexpected." Klára let her eyes close as she walked with Rudolf, her arm through his.

"I must leave you now, Klára, and you must consider leaving Berlin as soon as possible. I fear Berlin will not remain safe for you and your little boy."

He said good-bye to her in the garden. She watched him walk away down the graveled pathway until he disappeared in the shadows cast by the linden trees. She sighed heavily, but she knew he would come again; someday soon, she hoped.

—⟁—

In late July Heydrich was promoted to the rank of brigadier general and to celebrate, his friends arranged a grand party at the Café Montbijou, the very famous Berlin cabaret with the equally popular host, Elow. Franz and Klára were, of course, invited. The party, on a Monday night, was the night of acts by the "Nameless" at the café. Fifteen acts, each one performed by a nameless person with no talent whatsoever, although each performer thought he or she was immensely talented. Females of all ages thought of themselves as show-girls, disillusioned men and women erroneously thought they could sing and other equally inept acts including jugglers, comics, and musicians, each one clueless as to their complete lack of talent. But the audience, keenly aware of the true situation, was in on the joke. Encouraged by Elow the performers put their whole hearts into their acts while at the same time Elow urged the audience to jeer and boo each of the actors without mercy.

The whole evening seemed cynical and cruel to Klára, but to Franz and his friends the so-called entertainment was hilarious. Franz roared with laughter until he cried. Some of the performers were obviously mentally disabled, but that didn't matter to Franz or his friends. They exhibited no compassion or mercy for any of the hopeless actors. Klára began to see a pattern of blind brutality and a complete lack of sensitivity in Franz and his friends.

On their drive home Franz directed the chauffeur to pass by Wittenburg Platz where he pointed out the boot whores and dominatrix to Klára and laughed at her disgust. He seemed to be quite familiar with the women who made obscene gestures at them and called his name as their car passed by the Platz.

"You know those women, Franz?"

"Of course I do, Klára. Does that surprise you?"

She sighed, thinking to herself... *no it does not surprise me.*

—⟁—

Franz came home one afternoon very excited, smiling his most enchanting smile, "Klára we have been invited to attend the opera with the Führer and I have invited him and the others for pre-opera drinks here in our home this Saturday...the Führer!"

Saturday evening Klára found herself face to face with Herr Führer, Hitler himself.

"What a pretty wife you have, Baron." Hitler held her hand, clicked his heels together, bowed and kissed her hand. "I'm so pleased to make your acquaintance at last. May I call you Klára? Klára is such a beautiful name—my beloved mother's name, my favorite." He smiled sweetly at her while still holding her hand.

Klára only nodded to him, stood very straight, keeping her eyes lowered. Her blood ran cold, but her cheeks flushed with heat. She felt as if the air was being sucked from the room.

"How charming, she blushes," Hitler gushed. "Your wife's shyness is delightful, Baron"

Klára withdrew her hand slowly and uttered a very quiet "Thank you, Sir."

"The baron tells me that you are a superb pianist. Perhaps you'll play something for us?"

Again, Klára nodded her head; she moved to the piano, relieved to be free of him. She sat down as Franz quickly moved behind her. He leaned over her, whispering into her ear, "Do not dare play jazz, Klára."

In a soft voice, she asked, "What would you like to hear, Herr Hitler?"

"Your choice, Madam," he answered, "something gay."

Klára glanced at Franz and began to play Bartók's Allegro Barbaro. She played loudly and hard the quick, energetic, repetitive piece while her guests continued their conversation using soft voices in respect for the music.

When Klára finished, Hitler commented, "Well, that was lively. I didn't recognize the piece. Who is the composer? It has a folk sound"

"Bartók...Béla Bartók, our premier Hungarian composer."

"Where is your home, Klára?" Hitler asked.

"Hungary, I am a Magyar," she answered strongly, knowing that Franz would have expected her to answer Austria. "I was born in Balatonfüred."

"You sound very proud, my dear. Proud to be Hungarian."

She smiled at the Führer, "Yes, very proud. I miss Budapest terribly."

Hitler raised his eyebrow, "Perhaps you should return there if Berlin does not suit you."

Franz suddenly swept into the conversation, "Don't take Klára too seriously, Mein Führer." Franz put his arm around Klára shoulder, smiled widely, even chuckled when he added, "She is simply a bit homesick for paprikas. Klára is as pure Austrian as I am. Her mother is from Linz, Mein Führer, your hometown...Baron von Schrader is her grandfather."

"Ah, the industrialist. Yes, I remember your family...their elegant house on the Promenade. So, you are Austrian after all. You should be more proud of your heritage, Baroness."

"Klára plays beautifully, doesn't she?" Heydrich interjected to calm the tenseness that had risen in the room. "Perhaps we can encourage her to play another one for us. What would you like to hear, Mein Führer?"

"Again, it is her choice; perhaps something German this time?" Hitler seemed to almost dare her to play another Hungarian piece.

Klára began to play, a rather dramatic piece, Version B In Hungarian Style from Bartok's *Mikrokosmos*...Gypsy music. Then she changed abruptly to Wagner's *Eine Faust Ouvertüre*. Then bits of another Bartok and another Wagner...*Fantasia Op. 3*. Klára played with a kind of frenzy and detachment from her guests. She completely disregarded Hitler and played as though entirely for herself.

Within the hour, Gita brought their guests' wraps. Franz brought Klára's coat to her at the piano, "It's time to go, Klára."

She could tell from his voice he was not pleased with her. They all left for the theater.

When the couple returned home, Klára went directly to András' room. She pulled his blanket up to his chin, kissed him on the forehead, and walked to her own room. In the midst of removing her jewelry, Franz entered her room without knocking.

"Klára, you embarrassed me this evening." Franz walked straight toward her. He took hold of her arm and squeezed it tightly. "How dare you be rude to the Führer? You led him to believe you're Hungarian. With your black hair, he may even think you're a Turk. Ridiculous! You're no more a Hungarian than I am. You act as though you're ashamed to be Austrian."

Franz let go of her arm, leaving a bruise, and turned to walk out of the room. He stopped at the door, turning back to her. The blue color of his eyes drained away to an icy white, "Be warned, Klára, you cannot play with this man. He is more powerful than you can imagine."

His voice was tightly controlled, but the anger underneath was obvious, "I will not protect you against him, nor will I tolerate your pointless insolence. Understand that the world is changing. Your thoughtless words can get you, and perhaps even me, into trouble. I won't allow it!" He pointed his finger at her, "Do you understand?"

"Yes, I understand completely, Franz," she answered. It was then she knew she hated him; that she had never known him; and worst of all, that she feared him.

—〰—

In late August, Franz and Klára attended the christening ceremony of a new baby born to a young S.S. officer in Franz's office. Franz introduced Klára to the couple, Lieutenant Gustav Brenner and his wife Astrid, a very young and very pretty, plumpish blonde with small features and small blue eyes. Astrid held her baby boy wrapped in a blanket close to her breast. She tugged at the blue folds, pulling them from the baby's face to show Klára. Astrid's baby was very fair. The ceremony, held in a small, plain Protestant church, was attended by both Himmler and Heydrich. All of the men wore their S.S. uniforms.

Everyone gathered near the baptismal font as the chaplain began the christening rite. As Astrid extended the baby out over the font, one of the S.S. officers held a black and silver dagger over the baby's chest and addressed the child.

"We take you into our community as an extension of ourselves. We will protect you as you grow. As a man you will bring honor to your father's name, pride to our brotherhood, and glory to your race."

Then little Astrid swore an oath, "I, Astrid Brenner, swear by God this sacred oath that I shall render unconditional obedience to Adolf Hitler, the Führer of Germany and the German people."

Everyone glowed with pride and congratulated each other. The petite Aryan, Astrid, seemed especially proud.

On their way home Franz could not stop talking about the glorious moment. He raved about Astrid and her devotion to the Führer and the dedication of her son to the Nazi Party. Then suddenly he said, "We must christen András again in the S.S. ritual. You must swear the sacred oath as Astrid did."

Appalled by the whole event, Klára knew she would never say those words or have a dagger held above her tiny son. *How have I come to such a terrible place?*

Events happening all around them seemed to predict disaster and inspired Klára and Gita to make some kind of plan of escape from these unknown disasters. The two women knew they lived in danger, but were at a loss to know what to do.

Fall

Franz informed Klára he had been asked to host a dinner to which women would not be invited. He exhibited great anxiety about the gathering. Klára assumed it was because the guests were important high-ups in the party, but in fact, Franz's nervousness came because even though he did not know these guests personally, he and Heydrich had *cards* on all of them. Franz simply knew too much.

The dinner happened on a Thursday evening, a cold and rainy night. Every man arrived wearing his S.S. uniform, each one of them fiercely dedicated to Adolf Hitler and the NSDAP.

The guests took their places at Franz's dining room table and began their discussion. Gita and Liesel served the dinner while Klára stayed as close outside the door as possible, she wanted to hear their conversation. From their exchange she realized the gathering addressed religion and the church in Germany. Agreement seemed unanimous among the men that both religion and the church posed a serious threat to the Nazi Party and to their future plans. The men concurred it was their duty to find a way to neutralize this threat.

Impressed by the philosophical discussion, Franz agreed with the ideas he heard. Since his childhood Franz had never embraced the teachings of his mother's church nor had he any use for the priests or nuns who constantly pointed out his mischievous ways to his mother. He greatly resented the priests and nuns for the countless penances they had required of him as atonement for the many sins of his youth. Franz was in full agreement with the anti-religious views discussed among his guests.

"Those who preach love and tolerance...preach a false religion. People who believe in this kind of false religion become slaves."

"The misguided emphasis on kindness, tolerance, and service creates a weak, spineless society."

"That kind of religion and its church hinders a strong national pride."

"Some religions even embrace the servant model for their great leaders...teaching leaders that they should be servants to their people...pure nonsense!"

"That kind of religious servitude cannot be allowed to exist in Germany. It must be wiped out. Priests who do not conform to the dictates of the NSDAP must suffer the consequences."

"Priests of all religions, Catholic and Protestant, must preach to the expectations of the party. The intent of their sermons is to keep their congregations in line...the party line!"

"The Nazis are willing to pay priests to do the right thing. Any clergy who object to our expectations will be arrested and sent to labor camps for readjustment. Any religious school or seminary that refuses to conform will be closed."

"The party will use the Gestapo and S.S. to harass all priests and institutions into conformity, but I suspect money in the right hands will bring about a willingness in most cases to follow our demands."

"We cannot ignore the atheists who take great pride as freethinkers. Completely unacceptable! Atheists as well could undermine our goals."

"The Third Reich must ban the German Freethinkers League as soon as possible! We can say their existence is forbidden, because they are a Godless movement. And, of course, God has ordained the Nazi movement and empowered our leader Adolf Hitler as ruler over all."

The men adjourned their dinner meeting with handshakes and a general sense of unity of thought and consensus of goals. They left the von Werner house quite pleased by their discussion and conclusion.

Klára sat in a dark corner near the dining room feeling that Satan himself had been at her table.

1934

Baron Emmencht von Schrader wrote a letter to his son-in-law in February to describe events in Linz.

My dear son, Leopold... The world is changing before our eyes. The Baroness and I have just witnessed days of bloody riots in our city. Our Chancellor Dollfuss is trying to keep a clear head in a terrible time, but there are the most evil of forces working against him. The nationalists have called for Austria to return to her German roots and unite with the Third Reich of Germany. Of course Dollfuss is against this union!

Dollfuss has used his power and the strong arm of the government to repress the social democrats. He banned the communist and the national socialist parties in Austria and has attempted to isolate those Nazis who have tried to infiltrate our Assembly.

Pray for us Leopold... if Austria fails against this onslaught of evilness, know that Hungary will be next.

Your faithful father-in-law, Emmencht

Berlin

Other events in February were just as ominous. Hitler met with Ernest Röhm to explain the change of role for the S.A. Brownshirts, "From this day forward, the primary function for the S.A. forces is to provide security at all political rallies."

Hitler's words shocked Röhm, but he realized immediately the meaning of those words. Röhm knew that he and his beloved S.A., the *Sturmabteilung*, were being pushed aside, stripped of all prestige and power.

The document Hitler presented to Röhm clearly stated the change in orders for his storm troopers. Röhm protested passionately, but eventually submitted and signed his name on the written orders. However in his mind and heart,

Röhm fully intended to ignore Hitler's command. Röhm felt anger rise in his chest... *How can Hitler treat me and the* Sturmabteilung *with so little respect after all we have done to bring him to power?*

Soon after the confrontation with Hitler, Röhm declared to his aides, "Rather than Hitler, the true agents of the national socialist revolution are the S.A. and me. After all, we are responsible for the rise against the old Weimar government. We are the true liberators of Germany... the releasers from old oppressors! My storm troopers and I are strong enough to defy Hitler's despicable order!"

By May, Hitler realized he had a serious problem with Röhm. Rumors spread of a military coup planned by Röhm to overthrow Hitler and his Nazi Party. On the night of June fourth, Hitler met once again with Röhm and they argued late into the night. Finally Hitler convinced Röhm to take a personal vacation and give his S.A. a month-long leave beginning the first day of July.

Röhm announced to his S.A. leaders that prior to their July leave a meeting would convene on the thirtieth of June at Bad Wiessee. Röhm announced that Hitler had promised he would appear at the meeting and address the S.A. troops. Röhm expected Hitler to reassure the S.A. troops with praise for their valued service to the Third Reich.

June

Reinhard Heydrich was a frequent visitor to the von Werner home. On many occasions he and Franz spoke freely in front of Klára, allowing everyone in the house to hear their conversations, conversations often filled with anti-Semitism. But on other visits the two men sequestered themselves in Franz's study and spoke so quietly that Klára could hear nothing. In mid-June Franz invited Heydrich and several other officers for dinner with Klára the only woman present. The men around the table spoke to each other as if Klára was not there, but in fact, she listened carefully to their every word.

"A problem has arisen between Röhm's *Sturmabteilung* and the Wehrmacht. The S.A. Brownshirts want equal social status with Germany's regular soldiers! For their own benefit they want a redistribution of estates and a nationalization of industry!" Heydrich complained. "They want the Wehrmacht officers from the upper classes replaced. They want a revolution against the elite, the capitalists. The S.A. openly oppose the conservatives."

"Röhm's Brownshirts are nothing but a rogue mob of thugs," stated Franz. "We should not be forced to worry about them. They are nothing. The S.A. are not as powerful as they think they are."

"Hitler needed them in the beginning," explained Heydrich. "They were the perfect sort, a force of street brawlers, used to get rid of those who stood in Hitler's way, but now they are too vulgar, too crude. The Wehrmacht elite see Röhm and the Brownshirts as riffraff."

"The German High Command thinks of Ernest Röhm as nothing more than a low-class boor. Röhm and his S.A. threaten German traditions of nobility and rank."

"Reliable sources have informed us that Röhm is threatening a military coup to overthrow Hitler," offered Jörg Müller. "Röhm is a Judas to Hitler."

"The Brownshirts have outlived their purpose, but there are at least four million members. What can we do about them?"

"Hitler is caught in a dilemma, because he recognizes Röhm's storm troopers as the force that brought him to power. The S.A.'s reign of terror stopped all opposition to the Nazi Party," noted Fritz Lichtermann. "They were key to breaking the Marxists."

"All true, but now the S.A. and Röhm have become more trouble than they are worth," declared Heydrich. "Their effectiveness is no longer a factor. The S.S. can handle any trouble that may occur. We no longer need the S.A."

None of the men seated at Klára's table had any respect for Ernst Röhm and they had already begun to plot his demise. Heydrich and his S.S. officers originated the rumors about Röhm and his S.A. planning a violent putsch against Hitler. The rumors were intended to reinforce the negative and frightening view of the S.A. already held by most German people. The S.S. made a secret arrangement with the Wehrmacht generals to support an end to Röhm and his storm troopers. Near the end of June Hitler put the German Wehrmacht on alert. Clearly, something was about to happen.

On the twenty-eighth of June Hitler traveled to Essen for a wedding. While there, his attaché received a telephone call from Heydrich who informed him that Röhm's putsch had begun, although in reality it had not. The following day, a Friday, while Hitler was in Bonn, he received another call from Himmler.

"I regret to inform Mein Führer that the Brownshirts are rioting in the streets of Munich." Himmler cleared his throat and spoke forcefully, "They're denying the rumor of a putsch. They say it's a trick to discredit them."

Before dawn on Saturday, the thirtieth of June, a furious Hitler arrived in Munich and ordered the arrest of all S.A. men in the Munich Nazi headquarters. Meanwhile, unaware of Hitler's actions in Munich, Röhm and his S.A. leaders gathered as previously planned at the resort town of Bad Wiessee, a short distance from Munich. In the early morning hours Hitler and his S.S. soldiers drove to Röhm's Bad Wiessee hotel where they immediately roused Röhm and all S.A. officers from their beds, arrested them, and took them to Stadelheim Prison where S.S. soldiers executed them all that same morning.

Saturday, June 30, Berlin

Franz had been in his study since before dawn. He left the study door slightly ajar and gave strict instructions to bring Heydrich to his study the moment he arrived. Klára could hear the ring of the telephone many times throughout the pre-dawn hours. When Heydrich finally arrived Hedy led him straight to the study. Both Hedy and Klára noticed that the men were highly agitated, excited. Klára listened as best she could to the conversation coming from the study. At about ten o'clock in the morning, the telephone rang once again. Franz lifted the receiver... said nothing... only listened. He hung up, looked at Heydrich, and said, *"Kolibri."*

Heydrich repeated, *"Kolibri,"* and the two men immediately left the study. Both carried revolvers. They hurried out the front door without saying a word to Klára or anyone, leaving Klára very puzzled. *Kolibri... hummingbird... what could that mean?*

Soon after Heydrich and Franz left, the haunting sound of police sirens seemed to come from every street near the von Werner house. The women of the house stopped what they were doing, their hearts in their throats. The sirens came to a stop very near. Klára went to the front door and cautiously opened it. Police cars and policemen swarmed on Unter den Linden and hurried towards Tiergartenstrasse.

That mysterious phone call originated with Hitler when he called his emissary in Berlin, Herman Göring, to let him know that Röhm had been arrested and executed. The next action taken by Göring was to telephone Heydrich and other S.S. officers to pass on the code word *kolibri*... that single word unleashed a wave of terror as S.S. troops began a murderous rampage in Berlin and throughout Germany. Over the next twenty-four hours all S.A. leaders—and anyone else deemed an enemy of the Nazi Party—were executed by the S.S. or the Gestapo on the spot without arrest or trial or a chance to protest. Heydrich's list, the "Reich List of Unwanted Persons," compiled by Franz, was used by the S.S. to target victims.

Hitler flew into Berlin that Saturday night and was shown the "Reich List of Unwanted Persons." He was quite pleased to hear that most persons on the list had been eliminated by his S.S. and Gestapo troops. By Sunday afternoon, July first, sporadic gunfire still could be heard near the von Werner house.

Klára and her household staff, completely unnerved by the continuous gun shots and sirens of the last two days, stayed indoors and away from the windows, gripped by fear. The radio informed them of a coup attempt by Röhm and his storm troopers. The announcer told the audience that Hitler and the

S.S. had taken quick and courageous action to save Germany from the S.A., "a known group of criminal thugs." Of course, knowing how Franz felt about the S.A., Klára assumed the entire report to be a lie. She was certain Franz had taken part in the bloody massacre.

When Franz finally returned home late Sunday afternoon, he astounded Klára by announcing, "Hurry, change into something nice. The Führer has invited us to a tea party at the Chancellery. Everyone will be there to celebrate our victory."

On Monday, the second of July, Klára and Gita listened to Hitler's speech given in the *Reichstag* and aired on the wireless. Hitler justified the purge of the S.A., declaring it to be a great success. He proudly proclaimed that the Nazi Party had gotten rid of its Röhm problem as well as many other voices of opposition. Hitler assured the people the purge ultimately protected them from the S.A., an illegitimate military force terrorizing good German citizens. He gave the official name, "The Night of the Long Knives," to the purge of June thirtieth.

Across the wireless came Hitler's praise for the S.S. actions and a warning to all who could hear his words…*anyone who speaks against the Third Reich or against me will be sought out, imprisoned, or executed.* He decreed…*I am solely responsible for Germany's future and I am the supreme judge of the German people.* Lastly, Hitler reminded the German people…*great nations are made by great homogeneous populations. I assure the good German people that I will cleanse Germany of those who would pollute the Aryan race.*

From the day of that speech, Hitler's word became law—his word was above any former German law. Klára had questions about the Night of the Long Knives. Even though she heard Hitler's own explanation on the radio, she knew that reason was untrue. Klára knew the true purpose for Hitler's purge was to inspire fear in good German people. She assumed that was the point…the violent purge would keep the people quiet and compliant to Hitler's will. In that sense, Klára agreed, the purge was hugely successful and set the future of Germany.

Summer, Beyond Berlin

From Linz and Budapest Baron von Schrader and Duke Leopold von Esté watched events unfold quickly around them. In their respective newspapers they read about the death of Germany's President Hindenburg and were appalled to read that Adolf Hitler became President of the Third Reich and Chancellor of Germany, a dual promotion supported and approved by a great majority of Germany's people. Hitler received full power over Germany as dictator. Both von Schrader and Leopold realized personal ramifications would come from these events.

In Austria there was a Nazi coup. Although the coup failed, Chancellor Dollfuss was assassinated and replaced by Chancellor Schuschnigg, far more accommodating to Hitler's desires for an Austrian–German unification. By mid-summer the national socialist party gained seats and power in the Austrian government. Soon afterward Nazi agents began to harass Baron von Schrader and other private industrialists in Linz.

In Hungary, despite Leopold's words of caution, Horthy's government resolved to appease the national socialists of Germany. As a progressive member in the minority of the Hungarian Parliament, Leopold recognized Horthy's growing tendency to move closer to Germany. Leopold and von Schrader continued to share letters about their growing apprehension of the sweeping threat of Nazism in both their countries.

September, Berlin

Klára could hear Franz and Reinhard Heydrich in Franz's study discussing the recent *Reichsparteitage*, the national party rally in Nuremberg. They had just returned from the week-long conference. Reinhard was speaking, "A great success! The conference clearly exhibited solidarity between our party and the German people. The people support us with such enthusiasm and they exhibit sincere love and adoration for Hitler! It's inspiring! I give the credit for all of it to Mein Führer. He has such a way with words, so convincing and inspiring!"

Franz had traveled to his first Nuremberg Rally with Heydrich where they stayed at Nuremburg's Deutscher Hof. Hitler stayed there, too. "I could hardly breathe when our Führer came out onto the hotel balcony to speak to the mass of people gathered in the square. There must have been a thousand or more cheering as if he was the Messiah. It became so clear to me that Röhm was his Judas and had to be destroyed. Hitler's speeches inspired all of us."

"When we all marched together as thousands into Zeppelin Air Field with the "Badenweiler March" blaring from the speakers, I felt a thrill surge through my veins," reminisced Reinhard. "There's nothing more invigorating than being a part of something greater than one's self!"

"I agree," Franz nodded his head. "Everyone felt it. Hitler's words were uplifting when he proclaimed, *'Germany has entered a new era, reclaimed its ancient heritage of leadership, and will last for a thousand years without revolution!'* I was awestruck. And then the voices of the people rose in a deafening roar of agreement."

"Ah, yes," concurred Reinhard. "The speeches of Rosenberg and Streicher were noteworthy as well." Reinhard blew smoke rings into the air. "It's fortunate that we have correct newspapers, like Streicher's *Der Stürmer* to record accurately the events and speeches. As the party insists, 'The press has an obligation to advocate for the policies of national socialism and to write favorably about our Führer and the Nazi Party.'"

Reinhard thoughtfully expanded on this point, "Old newspapers of the Weimar era lost their connection with the people. The old press focused on special interests of the church and corporations, economics, and all the differences within political parties. Never a focus on individual goodness or strength of community, only negativity. The old press led to nothing but moral corruption, religious agitation, social unrest, and class struggle."

"Streicher's *Der Stürmer*, on the other hand, is an excellent newspaper," interjected Franz. "Their articles represent Nazi ideals to the fullest, putting forth the right information so that our good German citizens can make correct decisions."

Klára listened to their long dialogue while pretending to read a book, but she had not turned a page since their conversation began. She looked down at the folded *Der Stürmer* lying on the table beside her. Her opinion was quite opposite from the positive opinion of Franz. Klára found the articles to be terribly biased and the cartoons obscene, in particular those depicting German Jews. From her line of sight, without unfolding the newspaper, she could read the paper's banner... *Die Juden sind unser Unglück!* Such tripe made Klára sick to her stomach. Article after article encouraged German citizens to act in violent ways to rid Germany of Jews and other undesirables. Streicher's paper, widely known to be gravely anti-communist, anti-capitalist, anti-Catholic, and of course, anti-Semitic, could, in fact, employ no non-Aryan in any capacity at the paper. Klára breathed in deeply to calm the anxiety she felt and continued to eavesdrop on her husband's conversation.

"I agree... I, too, admire Streicher's methods of humor and clever caricatures, such an effective way to influence outrage within the German people against the Jew. I have heard that the Führer finds Streicher's paper a valuable tool of propaganda. *Der Stürmer* reveals the *truth* about how dangerous the Jews actually are to German society."

Truth! Klára thought, *the Nazis neither know nor want to know the truth... none of them.*

London

Since the closing of the Bauhaus, Rudolf spent his time traveling to and from England on assignments for MI6. While he was sitting at his London desk one afternoon, Olivia handed a file to him, "Read this, Rudolf."

Rudolf opened the file labeled "Reich Chamber of Culture." Already aware that Hitler had appointed the faithful Nazi, Joseph Goebbels to form the Chamber of Culture, Rudolf scanned the information describing Goebbels's assignment—*to administer all artistic production and to require that all art must visually reflect Nazi goals.*

He had personally experienced the power of Goebbels as the Minister of Propaganda. Goebbels' campaign of censorship and harassment against the Bauhaus had been brutal. The names of those artists driven from the Bauhaus and Germany by Goebbels's henchmen passed through Rudolf's memory. He breathed deeply as he thought of Goebbels's viciousness.

Goebbels alone defined whether an artist was *acceptable* or *unacceptable* and applied the same designations to works of art. *Unacceptable* for an artist could mean execution or imprisonment, certainly eventual exile. *Unacceptable* for a work of art meant destruction. For the Nazis, every piece of art had to represent the party's noble ideals or it was considered degenerate, even pornographic. The MI6 file contained a list of the *unacceptable*, artists and art.

The *unacceptable* list—most of the artists had Jewish or Russian names— Kandinsky, Beckmann, Chagall, Grosz, Nolde, Dix, Barlach, Jewlensky. During Rudolf's time in Germany, he had met many of the artists listed. Since that time most had left Germany and much of their work had been destroyed or stolen by the S.S.

The MI6 file also contained a list of the *accepted* artists, those allowed to work in Germany because they conformed to Nazi ideology and created visual works conveying the prescribed Nazi message. Among those *accepted* artists were Breker, Hommel, Thorak, and Peiner.

The report included Goebbels's ominous edict… *any deviation from the strict expectations of the Nazi Party for art imagery will bring immediate harassment, condemnation, and ultimately destruction of both art work and artist.*

Attached to the report was a photograph of a Peiner poster, a Nazi propaganda poster. Rudolf recognized the man in the image. It was Franz von Werner. The poster depicted Franz as the model of Nordic beauty prescribed by Nazi propaganda…a super-human figure, against a background of lofty Alps, looking upward, his jaw firmly set…Franz…a perfect Aryan god, one to inspire the German masses. Across the lower portion of the poster was written: "The Pure Aryan—good health, intelligence, and courage—The Master Race will save us."

Rudolf read a note attached to the photograph's back: Hitler had made the final choice for this image and message and approved mass production.

October

British SIS became aware of Hitler's decision to ignore the Treaty of Versailles. The treaty, signed at the end of the Great War, placed strict economic and military restrictions on Germany. No secret to MI6, Hitler desired to redevelop Germany as a military power. To accomplish that goal, Hitler began to base the country's financial system on a war economy, alerting MI6 to the inherent dangers lurking in Hitler's plan.

By this time, the Third Reich had acquired ownership of all German companies, industries, and raw materials needed for Hitler's militaristic plan and as dictator, Hitler also controlled the work force of Germany. All workers were forced to become members of the German Labor Force, the state controlled *DAF, Deutsche Arbeitsfornt.*

In October MI6 learned that Hitler intended to withdraw Germany from the International Disarmament Conference and from the League of Nations. This isolationist move completed Germany's transformation into a totalitarian state. Only loyal Nazi Party members could hold a government office, regardless of level—national, regional, or local. Strict standards were required for membership in the Nazi Party. One had to be of pure German blood, at least eighteen years of age, and swear allegiance to the Führer.

MI6 Director Sinclair expressed pride in his agency's vision. From Hitler's beginning, MI6 had recognized him and Nazi ideology as an imminent threat to Britain and had begun surveillance and information collection. Quite early Sinclair began to inform Prime Minister Chamberlain of the agency's findings and warn him of the possible horrors that might lie ahead for Britain.

1935
January

Reinhard Heydrich and Franz continued to watch Wilhelm Canaris closely, especially after Hitler appointed Canaris director of *Abwehr*, the German Military Intelligence Agency, and promoted him to the rank of Rear Admiral. Heydrich appreciated Canaris's appointment, because in his new position Heydrich gained greater ability to scrutinize Canaris's actions. Heydrich noted in his file that Canaris, as head of *Abwehr*, encouraged Hitler to form a relationship with Francisco Franco of Spain, because Canaris believed an affiliation between Germany and Spain would benefit Germany in the future.

Heydrich, present for Canaris's conversation with Hitler, recorded his memory of Canaris's argument for an alliance....

> *Due to severe unrest in Spain, civil war could break out at any moment and such a war would be advantageous to Germany. The current republican government is supported by communists, the Soviets. Spain's government is under attack by the nacionales, a far-right fascist movement led by Franco. Germany and the nacionales share natural interests; therefore Germany should encourage and support the rebels as Italy currently supports them.*

Heydrich attached another card to the Canaris file—his vita: member of the Imperial Navy since age seventeen / served Germany with honors during the Great War / captured and imprisoned in Chile / fluent in Spanish. After the war, as naval officer, important influence in Weimar government / continues influence within the Nazi government / not a member of the Nazi Party / has not sworn allegiance to the Führer.

After the Third Reich agreed Canaris should make contact with Franco, Canaris traveled to Madrid for a meeting with Franco and Heydrich added "Spanish trip—Franco" to his *Canaris* card. Heydrich, however, was not privy to Canaris's entire Spanish agenda.

Madrid, Spain

In addition to meeting with Franco, Canaris also arranged a secret meeting with a British MI6 operative. The meeting took place in Parque del Retiro, by an extraordinary fountain.

"Interesting choice of meeting place...by the *Fountain of the Fallen Angel.* Is that your prediction for the future," Canaris asked the man who sat next to him on the bench, "hell on earth?"

"Could turn out that way unless men like you and me can redirect those in power," answered Count von Házy.

"I supported Hitler, at first. He seemed the best choice for Germany at the time, as a force against the communist influences gaining so much power in Germany." Canaris seemed reflective and conflicted. "Hitler has been incredibly successful, but, well, now, I'm feeling nothing but trepidation. That's why I'm here speaking to you."

"The British are well aware of Hitler's pros and cons," offered Rudolf.

"Hitler talks about national pride and unity, but his speeches and policies are quite fanatical in tone. Most of his ideas are nonsensical, based entirely upon hate. Ideas that I can neither support nor affirm, but that I can no longer ignore."

Having read Canaris's dossier, Rudolf knew that Canaris was a refined gentleman sincerely dedicated to Germany and to its great military tradition. The British saw Canaris as a disillusioned and disgruntled military officer who had genuine concern for the direction Hitler was taking his country. MI6 wanted to make contact with Canaris as soon as possible while he remained conflicted, knowing that a relationship with him could be quite fortuitous in the future. MI6 directed Rudolf to Spain.

After exchange of contacts and code names, Rudolf and Canaris stood, shook hands, and agreed to stay in contact. Canaris went in one direction, Rudolf in another. Rudolf left Madrid for London, then to Sweden, before returning to Paris for the summer.

Fall

In September Franz left Berlin for his second party rally in Nuremberg where Hitler arrived shortly afterward to attend the *Reichstag*, which assembled in the ancient city for a special meeting. Hitler wanted to make his position on the Jewish problem very clear. He was determined that official German law ought to reflect his position on the matter. The *Reichstag* passed two mandates. The *First Law*, meant to protect German blood and honor, prohibited marriage and intercourse between Jews and Germans. The *Second Law*, intended to clarify who was a true German within the Third Reich, gave citizenship and other basic rights to only those of pure Aryan blood and excluded Jews and all other sub-human groups.

As Franz read the new laws, he was quite pleased by the description of a true Aryan German. He and Klára qualified as persons of pure Aryan blood because they each had four German/Austrian grandparents. The law clarified who was Jewish and who was a *Mischling*, one of mixed blood. A Jew had three or four Jewish grandparents and a *Mischling* had one or two Jewish grandparents. Either way, neither was an acceptable German citizen.

The two laws imposed harsh restrictions. A Jew could no longer find employment as a civil servant in Germany, could not be a lawyer or a doctor or a journalist. Jewish people were barred from hospitals and education beyond the age of fourteen. *J* for *Juden* would be stamped across all Jewish identification papers. The First and Second Laws made legal and encouraged racial discrimination against the Jewish people of Germany.

Budapest

Tamás heard of an underground fascist movement in Hungary and wondered if he should share the information with Leopold. In recent months Tamás and Elizabeth were guarded in the information they shared with Leopold, because he became so agitated whenever he heard about radical politics in his beloved Hungary.

When Tamás entered the library with afternoon coffee for Leopold and himself, he found Leopold reading a letter from a friend in the Hungarian parliament.

"Listen to this bit of interesting information, Tamás." Leopold read aloud from the letter...

> *Inspired by the fascist movements in Germany and Italy, Ferenc Szálasi has founded the Hungarian fascist party, called the Party of the National Will. Szálasi's ideology reflects that of Hitler, also placing great importance on ideals of nationalism. Szálasi, like Hitler, is an anti-communist, anti-capitalist and a militant anti-Semite.*

"My friend writes that Szálasi, however, runs into conflict with Hitler on one point...'Szálasi believes that Hitler's Master Race must also include the Magyar who are, in his opinion, also a powerful and strong race.'"

Leopold looked up at Tamás and sighed, "Well, I agree that the Magyar were a strong and powerful people, but this Master Race business is insanity! Evidently Szálasi also has a few goals that reflect Hungarian rather than German values and he is determined, foremost, to accomplish land redemption for Hungary. Well, I agree with that, but not at the expense of selling out Hungary to the Germans and Hitler. And, of course, I deny all fascist goals and their means to accomplish them."

Tamás was relieved by Leopold's calm response to Szálasi and his fascist ideas.

Berlin

In the early evening Klára sat at her dressing table. She wore a luxurious Vionnet, emerald-green satin evening dress. The full-length, bias-cut fabric clung to her slender figure in sensual drapery. Her black hair fell in straight shafts onto her shoulders. "Gita, you're the only one who could ever do anything with this hair of mine," Klára sighed. "I have no luck on my own to end up with any style close to elegant."

Gita did have a way of mastering Klára's difficult-to-manage hair by simply sweeping the hair upward on each side, sliding in diamond clips and swirling it into a rather glamorous chignon in the back.

Klára looked at herself in the mirror, recognizing she would never match her mother's beauty, but thought, *I'm definitely improving with age.* "Not too bad," she said as she peered at her reflection, "my eyes are definitely my best feature, so what if I have terrible hair."

"Madam, you are lovely, beautiful!" Gita laughed, "The emerald color of your dress complements your eyes perfectly."

Klára took her emerald necklace from its velvet box and Gita fastened it around her neck.

At that moment, Franz entered Klára's room. A large closet and lavatory separated her bedroom from his. Gita immediately slipped from the room, her head down, making no eye contact with Franz. Franz rarely came into Klára's room for any reason, but tonight he appeared and paced back and forth.

"What are you wearing?" A very unusual question for him. "That's a good choice. Green flatters you. Can't you do something with your hair?"

Klára touched one of the diamond clips and it instantly slipped from her hair. With great frustration she struggled to replace it. Franz seemed agitated, compelling her to ask, "Why are you so nervous?"

"Tonight is very important, Klára, the Führer will be there and I want you to make a very good impression."

"You aren't wearing your tuxedo?"

"No, no from now on our dress uniform is expected at all public occasions."

Franz stood in full gray uniform with a chest of medals, including the S.S. insignia. Klára said nothing, but she felt a cold shiver up her spine.

The von Werner couple arrived at the Berlin Opera House early and went to their private box joining other Nazi officers. Franz stood at the railing observing the seats below as they began to fill. Many in the room looked up to greet him with a nod or a salute. It was obvious to Klára her husband had become a powerful man. Just as Franz and Klára took their seats the Führer entered his own box, greeted the audience below, and then motioned for the orchestra to begin the music.

The curtain rose on the opera *Die Walküre,* The Valkyrie, the second of four operas in Wagner's *The Ring* cycle. Spectacular voices sang the story—a conundrum of secrets, hidden identities, doomed lovers, and disgruntled gods all based upon Nordic mythology—set to a dramatic score as varied as the plot with exuberant militaristic marches and lyrical romantic melodies.

When the intermission arrived, Franz took Klára's arm and together they walked briskly from their box to the top of the elegant grand stair leading down into the great lobby. At that point Franz saw someone he wanted to talk to, so he told Klára to wait at the top of the stair, he would return. On Franz's way down the staircase, he asked a waiter to take a sparkling wine to her. Klára stood at the top of the stair, surveying the crowd below and sipping her wine. She looked down upon the elegant lobby, jammed with people, talking and laughing in a very noisy atmosphere.

Suddenly Klára's eyes met another who stared back at her...Dolf...and he was walking through the crowd toward her. She met him half way down the grand staircase. He kissed her hand and continued to hold both of her hands in his. Again, her tears began to flow, "Dolf, you always make me cry."

"I'm sorry, I don't mean to," he responded. "Do you always wear that necklace?"

Klára's hand went to her throat, touching the tiny stones, "It reminds me of happier times...of you."

Knowing this meeting would pass too quickly, Klára felt an urgency to see Rudolf again and asked, "Where are you staying, can we meet tomorrow? I need your help."

"The Adlon. Come for a coffee. In the afternoon?"

"I'll be there at three."

They continued to stand together on the steps, simply looking at each other in silence within the whirl of chatter that surrounded them. Franz came up the stairs, stopped just behind Rudolf and cleared his throat to get their attention. Rudolf, still holding Klára's hands, turned toward Franz.

"Dolf, this is my husband," Klára said calmly, "the Baron Franz von Werner." She turned toward Franz, "My old friend, Count Rudolf von Házy...Dolf."

"I've heard of the great Dolf for years. I understand you've been like a brother to Klára." The two shook hands. "So, we meet at last. Handsome tuxedo." Franz complimented the count, but with a tone of contempt in his voice. Franz was thinking...*this man will never wear the uniform of the Reich. He's a degenerate, a cripple, an artist.* "What brings you to Berlin?"

"I'm here on the business of salt," Rudolf answered.

When the house lights dimmed, Franz took Klára's arm, and bid good evening to Count von Házy. Once returned to their box, Franz muttered, "Your Dolf is taller than I expected him to be. His limp is so noticeable. He must feel great shame about his deformity. What can he do for his country? Has he never married?"

Klára absentmindedly answered, "No."

"He's probably homosexual."

Klára looked at Franz, but decided to say nothing.

The luxurious Hotel Adlon on Pariser Platz stood within walking distance of Klára's home. The day was sunny with a brisk wind as Klára left her front door and hurried along the sidewalk to the hotel. She wore a handsome emerald green suit and green felt hat with a veil and pheasant feather. The Adlon lobby clock struck three times just as Klára entered through the revolving door. She crossed the lobby to the lift and went up to the mezzanine restaurant.

Sitting at a table by the railing, Rudolf watched her from the time she entered the hotel. As Klára entered the restaurant and walked toward him, he stood. They shared a kiss of greeting as the waiter pulled out her chair. Once they were seated and ordered coffee, the two old friends engaged in quiet conversation.

"Did Franz say anything about our meeting last night?"

"Very little, actually."

"Good. It's good to see you again, Klára. How is András?"

"He's wonderful, the joy of my life."

"You said you needed my help? I'm here to help you, tell me how."

Klára looked at Rudolf for a long time, searching his eyes. He frowned, "What is it?"

"Who can I trust?" She pleaded. "The world is changing so quickly. I see and hear things that I cannot believe. Franz has become someone I do not know or even care to know. I'm sometimes terrified in my own home."

"You ought to leave. Go back to Budapest."

"Franz won't let me take András, because he says it's unsafe to travel beyond Berlin." She reached out to Rudolf and held his hand, "Can I trust you, Dolf?"

"You need never ask that question, Klára, I'm yours forever. Ask me anything."

"Oh, Dolf, why did you leave me that day so long ago? Everything has gone so wrong since that day. I've made terrible mistakes."

"But you have András. He must give you great happiness."

"He does, but he's surrounded by such horror."

"You want me to help you go home?"

"No, it's harder than that. It's my housekeeper, Gita." Rudolf looked puzzled as Klára continued, "She's Jewish. Oh, Dolf, you wouldn't believe the plans I've heard spoken by Franz and his wicked friends. Gita, too, has overheard terrible hatred and evilness directed at Jews. We are both terrified for her future. I must find a way to help her. Gita's son-in-law has already disappeared from his home, leaving her daughter and grandson alone. No one knows where her son-in-law has gone. Gita's terrible situation makes me think of our dear friend Rózsa and her family. If Rózsa ever found her family in such a dilemma, I would hope someone would help her. I must do something to help Gita and her family escape this country. She has a brother in The Netherlands who will take her and her family. But I don't know how to help her get there."

"A difficult problem, Klára, but I can help Gita." Rudolf looked so calm.

"I'll contact you tomorrow, perhaps another walk in the park? And then Klára, you and András, too, must leave Germany as soon as possible. These are very dark times, Klára."

The next day after making arrangements for Marta to take András to a children's puppet play, Klára met Rudolf in the Tiergarten. Even though Marta could not spy on them, Klára remained terribly nervous. "Relax, keep smiling," he reassured her, as they sat down on a park bench. "You must give Gita these instructions exactly as I say them to you. You can put nothing in writing, so concentrate on all the details. Gita, her daughter and the boy must go to the Shillingmeyer Bakery on Rosenstrasse just after eleven on Thursday morning. They are to bring nothing with them, except perhaps what would fit in their shopping baskets. On Wednesday, the day before, you must fire Gita from your employ so that she will not be missed on Thursday. Let it be known by the household staff that you have fired her. You may give her some severance pay, if you wish. As soon as possible, you must prepare her for what is going to happen. Repeat to me what I have told you."

Klára repeated all of it and they parted.

Klára returned home to a very quiet house—Marta and András still at the play, the cook and maid shopping, and Hedy outside in the garden. Klára found Gita in the linen closet folding freshly laundered sheets. Klára stood in the pantry door with an ear to all entrances and began to inform Gita of the plan to help her and her family, repeating Rudolf's instructions carefully. Klára's concern and risk so completely overwhelmed Gita, she could hardly respond. Klára repeated the details, "Do you understand?"

"I know the street and the bakery," Gita said with confidence. "We can do this. But how can I ever thank you, Baroness, you are too kind, too good. What will happen to you? It's an unthinkable time for Jews, but it's a danger-ous time for people like you, too. You and little András must go from here. Terrible things are happening."

"Yes, Gita, I, too, want to leave," lamented Klára. "Tomorrow will be a dif-ficult day for us. You'll need to be an actress, Gita. Please don't forget that you have been dear to me since we met at Aunt Eugenia's home. You have helped me create a well-run home and taught me how to be a good mother. I'm grate-ful for all that you have done for me these past years. I wanted so much to do something for you and your family."

They embraced each other and Klára left the pantry.

On Wednesday morning Klára asked Marta to send Gita to the morning room. Klára sat at her lace-covered breakfast table and poured another cup of tea. She looked through the window into the garden. The leaves were turning color. Some had fallen already and a cold wind sent them into swirls of amber and red against the pewter-gray sky. Gita opened the door and slipped quietly into the room, leaving the door slightly ajar.

"Gita, the Baron does not want a Jew working in our home any longer," Klára took a deep breath, "therefore your service here is no longer needed. You must pack your things today and leave immediately."

"But Baroness," Gita sobbed, "what will I do? Where will I go?"

Cry, Gita, cry, because I cannot, Klára thought. "Here are your wages through the month, the rest of your worries are of no concern to me."

Klára reached across the table with a generous amount of money. When Gita reached out for the money, she and Klára briefly locked fingers. Gita's tears were very real as were those that filled Klára's eyes. Gita turned away and left the room quickly. Klára dabbed her tears away and returned to her breakfast as though nothing had happened.

Marta hurried into the room immediately and asked incredulously, "You let Gita go?"

"Yes, I did." Klára made direct eye contact with Marta, "Why do you ask, Marta?"

"I just thought that you liked her…even if she is a Jew."

"Gita was an employee, Marta, just like you. Bundle András for the park, it's much colder today than yesterday. I think I'll walk with you today. I enjoy brisk weather like this."

Marta left the room. Klára sank down into her chair, lowered her head and prayed silently—*make Gita strong and brave and me as well.* Klára thought about her meeting with Rudolf and wondered when she would ever see him again, wishing that she, too, was going with Gita away from the horror of these days.

—⚬⚬⚬—

Gita, her daughter, Bela, and her grandson, Lars, filled with fear, bravely made their way on the cobbled stones of Rosenstrasse. They turned the corner on that cold, windy morning and saw the little bakery that represented freedom from their fears. They walked as normally as possible to the shop, looked at the pastries in the window and entered. A bell over the door made a cheerful ring. Gita hesitantly approached the counter.

"I'm here to pick up a chocolate torte for my grandfather."

"The torte is right back here," the baker answered and led the three through a curtained doorway into a back room.

A tall man Gita did not know met them and led them downstairs to the cellar. Gita, Bela, and Lars sat down at the only table. The stranger gave each one of them new identification papers, took their old papers and put them into the stove that burned brightly, heating the room. Gita, watching their papers burn, had a moment of regret mixed with fear. *Who is this man? Why do we trust him? Who are we now?* She felt a surging panic rise in her chest.

The tall stranger, sensing her anxiety, reached out to touch her hand and said with a smile, "We have a mutual friend who cares deeply for all of us." The man spoke to Gita for a few moments more and then left them alone.

At mid-afternoon the baker brought a meal to them. "You'll be alone for tonight. There are cots with blankets along the wall, so settle in. You'll be leaving early in the morning."

Truly, at a very early hour the three were awakened by sounds from the bakery above. Eventually the baker brought coffee and warm rolls down to them. He also brought a change of clothes for each of them and announced they would be leaving within the hour.

Gita, her daughter and grandson dressed in the clothes given to them. Clothes more stylish, much finer than their own. They folded their old clothes and placed them on the table. Then they sat down and waited. After almost an hour, the baker appeared at the top of the cellar stairs and called down to them, "Time to go."

They climbed the stairs, thanked the baker, and left the bakery. A large car waiting for them at the curb took them away from Rosenstrasse. After an extended journey they arrived in the busy Baltic port city, Lübeck, where the tall stranger reappeared with tickets for ship passage to Amsterdam. He told the little group to board the ship, go straight to their cabin; the passage would be over night. Gita's little family left the car and walked nervously to the ship. Their new papers in order, they had no problem boarding. A steward helped the group find their cabin which turned out to be quite luxurious with a sitting room, bedroom, and private bath.

"If anyone comes to the door, we are to say that the child is ill and that we won't be leaving our room until we dock in Amsterdam," Gita told Bela. "Lars, you should go into the bedroom and get into bed." She kissed Lars on the forehead, "You can take a long nap."

In the evening after the ship had left port, there was a light rapping at the cabin door. Gita opened the door slightly and peered out into the hall. On the floor by the door was a covered tray. She took it inside and removed the cover, "Oh, it's a lovely supper for all of us—a pot of tea, a roasted chicken, carrots, potatoes, bread and butter, and three little cakes. God bless the wonderful Baroness and the mysterious man."

Lars was awakened and all, with big smiles, dined on the delicious feast. Gita thought about the man who was their savior and remembered his last words to her. She told them, "Our mysterious friend gave me a warning. He implored me to encourage my brother and our families to leave Holland for the west as soon as possible."

While Gita's family enjoyed their supper, the tall stranger struggled with a blanket as he tried to cover his feet and pull it up to his chin at the same time. The deck chair was not very comfortable, but the stars were bright and the sound of the ship cutting through the sea was peaceful. Rudolf didn't mind at all giving up his soft, warm cabin bed, knowing that Gita's family was worth any discomfort on his part. He also imagined that if his actions brought Klára happiness, he was willing to make any sacrifice, great or as small as this one. He smiled at the moon, remembering the many times he and Stefan and Klára had looked at the moon together, and thought of Klára's little note sent to him about looking at the same moon although they were far apart. He slept contentedly.

The next day Rudolf stood at the ship railing and watched Gita and her family walk down the ramp. Making eye contact with a man in the crowd, Rudolf nodded toward the family. The plump little man walked to Gita, greeted her and ushered the family into a waiting car that disappeared into the traffic.

Rudolf left the deck and went up the grand staircase toward his cabin as the steward passed and greeted him, "Count von Házy, will you be sailing with us this afternoon?"

"Not this trip, Hans."

Within the hour Rudolf disembarked from the ship, walked across the pier to another, boarded it, and sailed to Sweden where he visited the Swedish Red Cross.

December

By the end of the year, just as MI6 suspected, Hitler's secret plans were fully underway to proceed with rearmament in direct opposition to the Treaty of Versailles. Hitler began to rebuild Germany's military strength in all areas— U-boats, ships, new machinery and training for thousands of troops. Hitler's intention to prepare for military aggression against his European neighbors became clear to Britain and her allies. Time was the only unknown factor, before Hitler and his military would begin their aggressive acts.

Berlin

One winter evening Franz welcomed an old acquaintance, Rike Friedrich, a fellow S.S. officer from Cologne who was passing through Berlin on his way to Munich. Klára served the men brandy in the reception room and then excused herself. She had no desire to stay in their company. As the two men shared memories of old times, she could hear their loud laughter. Despite the impropriety Klára felt about listening to others' conversations, she convinced herself it was important to know what Franz was saying and doing whenever possible. She positioned herself outside the study and listened.

Rike took a magazine from his briefcase, "Have you read the most recent issue of von Liebenfely's *Ostara* magazine, Franz?"

When Franz shook his head in the negative, Rike responded, "I think you would find this article interesting." Rike handed the opened magazine to Franz.

Franz read the headline aloud, "Are you blond? Peril awaits you."

"I hope that the German people take to heart Rosenberg's warnings about the threats to our Aryan purity from non-normal people. We Germans must recognize the importance of breeding, the importance of blood." Rike's voice was quite serious, "Our Aryan blood carries the soul of our race. Our blood is sacred. The dark races, especially the Jew, are a threat to us, we who are blond and blue-eyed. We must address this threat to our purity."

"*Lebensborn*, Wellspring of life," Franz scanned the article, "Himmler advocates this program?"

"Yes, he does, Franz," answered Rike enthusiastically, "and we are perfect for it with our blond hair and light eyes. Himmler tells us it's our sacred duty as S.S. officers, married or single, to father as many Aryan children as possible for our country and for our Führer. Young Aryan women, too, are encouraged by Himmler to participate in *Lebensborn*. He says the same, it is their duty, he tells them, to experience the joy of carrying babies for the Third Reich."

Rike took a breath, the idea of *Lebensborn* excited him so, and he wanted Franz to feel the same. "All of the women must prove they are from racially pure stock with Aryan grandparents. Himmler assures all of us, emphatically, that there is no shame for an S.S. officer in mating out of wedlock with Aryan women, Aryan women who are very fair, blonde and blue-eyed. All *Lebensborn* children are declared legitimate by the Reich. As babies they are raised in S.S. nurseries or some babies might be adopted by good Aryan families."

"A guarantee that the children will be Aryan and look like it," Franz laughed, "This is an excellent plan, pure genius! We can repopulate Europe with *Ubermensch!* A race of superhumans!"

"Currently *Lebensborn* is located in a village near Munich, but soon there will be others. In particular, Hitler wants to encourage Nordic women of Norway and Denmark to participate." Rike laughed joyously, "Soon you and I can travel from place to place making Aryan babies."

Klára could hardly believe what she was hearing. Yet another hideously twisted idea somehow made to sound probable, right and justifiable to the Nazi mind. How could these men become so manipulated and corruptible? In Franz, she had come to realize, it was hatred and insecurity mixed with cruelty and insanity. Klára knew she was living in a nightmare, a nightmare shared by thousands. Tears rolled down her cheeks, she was horribly sad, but she was also angry.

1936
January, Budapest

A most unpleasant cold wind blew light swirls of snow along the sidewalk as Leopold walked toward Gerbeaud's. Concerned about his friend, Dr. Klein, Leopold looked forward to their meeting over coffee. Leopold sat by a window and watched through the frosted pane. When he recognized Jakov Klein approaching the restaurant, wrapped in wool coat, muffler, and hat, Leopold could see that the doctor walked as one much older and resigned, without his usual energy. A cold gust of wind came in the door with Dr. Klein, making Leopold shiver as he stood to greet his old friend.

"Jakov, it is good to see you! Thank you for coming on such a cold day."

"I've been looking forward to it, Leopold. How's your family?"

"Everyone is well, as far as I know. Of course, Klára is in Berlin still, but we hear that she and her boy are well," answered Leopold. "Tamás sends his regards. How is your family?"

"Ah, that's a good question, Leopold. Samuel is concerned as to his employment at the pharmacy." Dr. Klein looked at Leopold quite seriously, "as am I at the Institute, yet again. Ferenc and Abram can't find work, but they seem to stay busy. Rózsa is our only contented one. But now with the possibility of these new laws inspired by Germany, who knows what will happen, even with Rózsa."

Both men were well aware of the Nuremburg Laws passed by the German *Reichstag* in the fall and enacted on the third of January. Hitler encouraged all nations friendly with Germany to pass similar laws of their own to handle what Hitler conceived to be the *Jewish problem* within all populations.

"Horthy and Premier Gömbös have been more than accommodating to Hitler." Leopold looked at his friend with compassion, "I fear it is only a matter of time before Hungary passes similar anti-Semite laws. This terrible injustice breaks my heart for you, Jakov."

Leopold felt heaviness in his whole being when he looked at a man whom he had known for more than thirty years. How his beloved Hungary could act with such pure hatred toward its own good, contributing citizens completely mystified Leopold.

"Jakov, know that I will help you and your family in any way that I can." Leopold spoke with great firmness, "Tell your sons to come to the wine company and I'll find work for them and for you as well, if it comes to that. Neither you nor your family deserve any of this persecution. I beg your forgiveness for these unfair actions that have happened. Our country is led by men who cannot recognize evil even though it has surrounded them."

"I'm grateful to have such a fine friend as you, Leopold. I know our Hungary is a good country and that not everyone hates the Jew, but, now, everyone seems so afraid. Of what they are not sure, but they must blame someone and this far-right propaganda that's sweeping across our land makes it easy to blame the Jew. I fear we are in for difficult times. We'll endure as we have through the centuries, but it's good friends like you who give us hope for a better future."

The two old friends sipped their coffee and half-heartedly ate their chocolate torta.

—⚏—

Hungary did adopt many of the same policies restricting Jews from certain employment and professions. The laws of 1936 were much worse than those of 1921. As Jakov had predicted, a severe propaganda campaign was launched to convince Hungarians that Jews were to blame for the economic hardship suffered by Hungarians, despite the actual fact that Jews were heavily taxed and many were jobless. Just as in Germany, the government condoned and encouraged brutality and violence against Jews in Budapest and throughout Hungary. Times became quite desperate for the Jews.

Many young Hungarian Jews, for purposes of self-preservation, turned to old assimilation ways, Magyarization, using dress and culture to aid their disappearance into the non-Jewish population. Others renounced their faith, ceasing to practice Judaism altogether, while an increasing number of Jews entered into mixed marriages with the Jewish partner converting to Christianity...anything to save themselves.

Early March

Professor Klein walked up the stairs of the university and down the hallway as he had done for nearly forty years. He carried his briefcase filled with student papers for return and his lecture notes on "Methods for the Purification of Organic Compounds." He also carried his hat and umbrella as he shuffled along the hallway. Professor Klein entered the lecture hall, greeted the waiting students with a nod, hung his hat, coat, and umbrella on hooks by the doorway and walked to the podium. More students entered the hall and took their seats as Professor Klein opened his case, took out stacks of papers, placing one small stack on the dais and the larger on the desk.

He turned toward the blackboard and with chalk wrote the lecture title across the board. He continued to write a list of terms and equations when suddenly something struck the back of his head. Professor Klein was quite astonished...an eraser, he saw it as it fell to the floor. It had only hurt a little, but he couldn't understand where it had come from. As he turned from the blackboard toward the classroom expecting to see curious, interested students, he was bombarded with more erasers and books. Papers flew into the air as he fell onto his desk and then onto the floor.

Suddenly Ottó Barna was kicking him and then he recognized Vida Kuruc screaming "Jude" in his face. Ottó and Vida dragged Professor Klein from the lecture hall out into the hallway and toward the balcony railing. They would have thrown their teacher over the railing, but when he passed out, Ottó and Vida thought he was dead, so they left Klein slumped on the floor.

When Professor Klein came back to consciousness, the hallway was empty of people, but filled with debris from his and other classrooms. Klein used all the effort he had to make his bruised body stand and then dragged himself back into the classroom to get his briefcase, coat, and hat. The old battered man could only find his hat. Klein looked at the blackboard...*Jude* in large letters written across his own writings.

Tears filled Professor Klein's eyes. He could not understand; he had always been a favorite professor. *Vida and Ottó were good chemistry students who talked with me regularly.* Klein remembered seeing some students flee from the room as he was beaten, in fear for themselves he imagined. Klein began to mutter to himself, *"Why?"* over and over again. As he stood staring at the blackboard, Klein felt dizzy and when he touched his forehead, he realized there was blood. He reeled, reaching for the desk to steady himself before falling to the floor.

At that moment Professor Donát Földi and a chemistry student, Erzsi Révész, came into the room. They helped Dr. Klein into a chair and made him sit for a moment. He was obviously severely injured, but Földi knew no hospital was allowed to take him. So Professor Földi and Erzsi decided it would be best to take him home. They helped Professor Klein down the stairs and into Földi's car and drove him to Dohány Street.

Mrs. Klein opened the door and instantly shouted for Magda. They all helped Jakov to the parlor where Magda and the maid hurriedly made a bed for him. Erzsi and Professor Földi tried to explain to Mrs. Klein as best they could what had happened to her husband, but since none of it was in the least rational, Éva could never grasp what had happened to her beloved Jakov. Magda called Dr. Weisz to come immediately; when he arrived he went into the parlor and began his examination of Jakov.

"There seems to be severe bruising, possibly a concussion, cuts and abrasions, certainly a terrible beating for a man in his seventies." The doctor looked seriously at Éva, "Despite these physical injuries, I'm more concerned about his mental attitude. It may pass, but Jakov is disoriented, confused, and extremely distressed."

Éva knew that his heart was broken. Jakov spoke in a quiet, resigned voice, "No one helped me. They ran away. I gave extra time to help Ottó Barna just a day or two ago. Ottó is a good student who loves chemistry. There was such hatred in their eyes. No one stopped them. Everyone ran away."

A few days later, Jakov suffered a severe stroke. His paralyzed body did not recover. He remained in a kind of catatonic state, sitting in his chair staring and muttering words that no one could understand.

Éva turned her attention to his hobby of researching Hungarian Jewish history, family trees, and old names. She hoped talking about his work would help him recover. For so many years, most evenings he worked on his research while he listened to her play the piano. Even now the only thing that brought him some happiness was hearing Éva play beautiful Hungarian melodies. She sat with him throughout the days, talking to him, reading the newspaper and letters from Rósza and Eszter. But one cold, snowy day in late March Jakov Klein died. Éva Klein instinctively gathered together all of Jakov's research papers, rose from his side and put them inside her spinet piano.

April, Berlin

Three-year-old András laughed as he sat in the center of the nursery floor with his mother while she pulled a little wooden train along the grooves of a braided rug. Marta was away on her day off. Liesel entered the room.

"There's a telephone call for you, Madam."

"Stay with András, please, Liesel. I'll be right back."

Klára went down the staircase to the telephone, "Hello?"

"Klára, it's Hannelore. How are you? It's been so long since we've talked."

"Oh, Hannelore, it's so good to hear your voice." Klára smiled, very pleased. "Are you here in Berlin?"

"Yes, I am and I would love to see you. Could we meet? This afternoon?"

"Why, yes. Please come here to my home on Ebertstrasse."

"Will Franz be there?"

"No, he's in Munich." Hannelore's question did not surprise Klára.

"Yes, I'll come. When should I arrive?"

"Any time will be fine. We'll have tea and something to eat. You can meet my András."

"Wonderful! I'll be there within the hour."

As Klára replaced the receiver, she thought of all her old friends in Cologne, especially all her Jewish friends. Klára frowned, as she thought to herself, *this visit may have a purpose other than a simple reunion. Something terrible no doubt…something caused by the wickedness that is swallowing all of us.* Tears came to her eyes when she thought of the good times she and Hannelore had in Cologne and how Franz had put such a miserable stop to it all.

Klára dressed András in a little blue sweater and told him that he was going to meet Mommy's pretty friend from Cologne. They went downstairs to wait. Hedy brewed the tea and Inge made trays of sandwiches and sweets. By the time Hannelore arrived, Klára felt quite anxious. They greeted each other warmly and introductions were made. Hannelore gave András much attention, talked to him in his own language, and made him laugh. They all laughed, relieving Klára's anxiety.

"You're so fortunate, Klára, to have such an adorable little boy," Hannelore said.

The two young women sat in Klára's morning room, enjoying the warm sunshine while Klára poured tea and offered sandwiches. András took several little sweets before Liesel arrived to take him to the nursery for his nap. Klára and Hannelore settled back into the chintz-covered sofas; a shaft of sunlight fell across the room. They both felt the comfort of conversation between old friends.

Klára confessed to Hannelore how much she missed the old gang, lamenting that she had made few new friendships since her arrival in Berlin.

"We have missed you very much as well, Klára," Hannelore told her and added, "I wanted to see you one more time before I left Germany."

"You're leaving?" Klára asked with definite sadness in her voice. Even though it had been nearly three years since they'd seen each other, Klára felt a sense of loss, knowing she would have one less friend in Germany. Aunt Eugenia, Gita, Dolf…all gone from Germany, now Hannelore, too. Klára's expression revealed her concern.

"I'm sorry to have upset you, Klára, but, you see I must go." Hannelore's tone was compassionate. Then, while studying Klára's face, she added "Max and I must go."

"Ah," Klára diverted her eyes from Hannelore, "Max. Yes, he must leave Germany," she bit her lip, feeling very tense. Her voice broke as she spoke, "as soon as he can."

"And how is Franz?" Hannelore asked with a slight hesitation, "Staying busy?"

Klára looked directly at Hannelore. "I suppose that he is well. We don't see him very often, because he's so busy."

"Klára, I understand that you have particular sensibilities not always in agreement with your husband's."

Klára's heart pounded in her throat as panic rose to brighten her cheeks with heat. The same gripping fear she had felt the day she *fired* Gita. Klára tried to compose herself, "Tell me about our old friends…Mose and Ruthie…Oskar. What's happened to them?" and held her breath while Hannelore spoke.

"I'm hesitant to tell you what has happened, Klára, it's all so unbelievable," Hannelore sipped her tea, set her cup back on the table, and sighed deeply before continuing, "Mose went to America again last year. None of us could understand why he came back to Cologne, but he did. He began to play with a jazz band again in various cabarets and then one night the Gestapo came into the club. They rounded up everyone they thought to be Jews or Gypsies, arrested them and they were gone. The next day Lars went to the Gestapo headquarters to inquire about Mose, but he never found out anything and none of us have seen or heard from Mose since that night.

"Freddy was stopped on the street in broad daylight by the S.S. a few weeks ago." Hannelore took a breath, "He had his papers, but there was no 'J' stamp and the soldiers were certain he was Jewish, so they ripped his pants down in front of hundreds of people, you know, to see if he was circumcised. When they saw he was a Jew, they beat him and shot him dead right there on the sidewalk. Max witnessed everything."

Hannelore took a handkerchief from her bag and dabbed at her eyes, "And then just over a week ago Oskar was waiting for Ruthie on Fischmarkt when he was accosted by the Gestapo. They stopped him on the street randomly, because, we supposed, they suspected him of being a homosexual. Who knows why? Oskar had papers, but the Gestapo threw them on the sidewalk and began to beat him brutally. Of course no one did anything to stop them. Just as they were dragging him toward a waiting truck, Ruthie arrived and ran hysterically toward the soldiers; she tried to intervene, but they beat her, too, and ended up arresting them both.

"By the time Max and I left Cologne no one had heard anything about them or seen them." Hannelore's anguish was clear to Klára. "We only know that the S.S. is deporting Jews to labor camps and once that happens, no one ever hears from anyone again."

Hannelore looked so distraught that Klára reached out to hold her hand as she continued, "Then we heard that Max and others had been reported to the Nazis and that arrest warrants were issued, so we left Cologne and now we will escape Germany."

Klára felt nauseous; horrible thoughts and images filled her mind. Her dear friends tortured, murdered, disappeared and she knew it was all true, because she had heard the plans discussed in her own home. Klára felt terrible waves of guilt; she should have done more to warn them, but her focus had been only on Gita and her family. Klára had not realized her friends in Cologne were in such terrible danger. She could only express deep remorse, "I'm so sorry, Hannelore, I should have warned you... all of you."

"Klára, I don't mean to distress you." Hannelore squeezed Klára's hand, "I know your heart, Klára. You could never embrace fascism. I know that I can speak freely to you." Hannelore took a shallow breath, "Max and I and many other good German people are part of the Resistance, the underground, fighting against the Nazi government. But we had to leave behind our Resistance work when we received word that the Gestapo had orders to arrest Max. It was imperative for us to leave Cologne at once."

"Oh, Hannelore, I would help you if I could, but I don't know how...."

"No, no, Klára, we don't need your help, but we want you to meet someone, because we think that you can be of help to her. She has a flat near here and you share some things in common; her brother is an S.S. officer." Hannelore smiled, "But like you, she does not share Nazi beliefs. Her name is Countess Maria Maltzan, Dr. Maltzan, a veterinarian. She's a very brave woman who acts on her beliefs. She would like to meet you."

"What can I do? I'm willing to help if I can," Klára frowned and breathed in slowly. "I have heard such horrible things spoken by people in this very house. I know these same people have done horrible things to so many innocents. I'll do whatever I can." Klára sounded determined. "I'm very glad that you have asked me."

Hannelore rose from the sofa, "I must go now, Klára. Thank you for tea. You're very dear to me and Max. We'll let you know when we're settled...far, far from here."

"Please, give my love to Max and be careful, be safe."

Klára watched Hannelore walk down the stairs and hurry across the street toward the tram stop on the corner. Klára went to the telephone and dialed the number Hannelore had given to her. After just one ring, the Countess answered. The two women made arrangements to meet at the mutually convenient Hotel Adlon the following day.

—ʍ—

Hannelore took the tram from Klára's street to the Zoologischer Garten at the far western end of the Tiergarten. As the tram pulled to a stop, Hannelore hopped from the lowest step and walked leisurely toward the Elephant Gate entrance, purchased her ticket, and mixed in with the crowd of people. Filled with children and families and happy couples, it was a good day for a trip to the zoo. Hannelore followed the meandering walkway into the garden, passed the Grottenteich, the zebra and the seals, on toward the Penguin House and beyond to the Aviary.

She scanned the crowd, looking for Max, finally spotting him standing by a group of children who were holding the strings of several brightly colored balloons. Max appeared to be with the children, rather than alone. She walked past him into the Aviary; he followed her. Within moments they were joined by a nondescript older couple. The woman approached Hannelore, smiled and uttered a few words..."Damner Millinery Shop at Zalleestrasse and Jebenstrasse." The woman raised her eyebrows and asked Hannelore to repeat the words to her. When Hannelore had repeated the words, the couple disappeared into the crowd of children moving through the Aviary.

Max and Hannelore walked out of the Aviary, past the beaver exhibit, Brown Bear Rock, the hippopotami and finally out the Lion Gate exit. Both were breathing heavily, but acting nonchalant. They made their way to the corner of Zalleestrasse across from the Damner Millinery Shop. They crossed the busy street and entered the shop. The shopkeeper took them up the stairs to his private apartment on the second floor.

Later in the afternoon two ordinary German men entered the shop. The milliner greeted them as friends and ushered them upstairs. Once inside the parlor he introduced them, not by name, but by position to Hannelore and Max. The men were proud members of the Swedish Protestant Church of Berlin, active in the moral resistance to Nazi policies. They gave Max and Hannelore visas for entry into Sweden, Swedish citizenship papers, and two tickets for a late evening train and ship to Värtahamnen. After a small supper of *Linsensuppe mit Bratwurst*, Hannelore and Max prepared to leave. They had no luggage; they would take nothing from their lives in Germany. The shopkeeper pulled his car from the garage at the rear of the building and drove them, breathless and terrified, all the way to the station without uttering one word.

At the station, Max and Hannelore got out of the car, expressed their gratitude and said farewell. They hurried to the platform where a steaming train awaited them. A waiting conductor led the pair to a particular car where he sequestered them in a compartment that would not be checked during their long journey.

—m—

The next afternoon as Klára walked along Ebertstrasse toward Unter den Linden to the Hotel Adlon she noticed the new German flag displayed everywhere, from street poles to shop windows. As she entered the hotel an enormous flag was being draped from the hotel balcony. Franz had told Klára all about the new flag, personally designed by Hitler as a symbol for his Nazi Party and that the new flag would fly everywhere throughout Germany.

Klára stared at the banner—a bright red field with a white circle at its center that contained a black *hakenkreuz*. Hitler chose the *hakenkreuz* or swastika because it was an old sacred symbol representing good fortune. Klára remembered seeing the same symbol on some of the collectibles in Aunt Eugenia's home—both Hindi and Buddhist sculptures and clay vessels from India where the symbol represented a positive sign for hope and security. In Hitler's writings he referred to the *hakenkreuz* as an emblem of encouragement for Aryans in their struggle for victory. Klára wondered... *victory? Over whom? Over what?*

She entered the elevator and rode up to the mezzanine, walked into the restaurant, and took the same table near the potted palms where Dolf had waited for her almost six months ago. From her vantage point, she could clearly observe the revolving door into the hotel lobby and wondered whenever a woman entered if it could be the Countess Maltzan. As Klára sat at her table within the palms, an old memory swept into her mind—the memory of playfully spying on Stefan and Dolf from the cherry tree at the Balaton villa—and she shivered with the thrill of intrigue, but she also felt the seriousness of the moment.

Now, perhaps, she could help someone else, continue the kindness Dolf had shown for Gita and her family. Klára imagined that the countess needed her help to leave the country, although she had no idea how she could help to accomplish that task without Dolf's presence. Klára was lost in her thoughts when suddenly a handsome young woman stood before her, "Baroness von Werner?"

"Yes...Countess Maltzan?"

As the countess took her seat, she spoke, "It seems that we have a few mutual friends...Hannelore and the Count von Házy."

"The Count?" Klára was surprised, "You know Rudolf von Házy?"

"Oh, yes, for some time now. Count von Házy is a good friend, such a delightful man and a fine artist."

"Yes, indeed."

The two women ordered coffees and *Berliners*. Klára studied the woman who sat across from her. She assumed they were very close in age—in their late twenties. Countess Maltzan also had coal black hair and Klára wondered if it was as difficult to manage as her own. The Countess wore hers pinned up under a black felt hat with a black netting that fell across her large brown eyes. The Countess looked at Klára with compassion, an expression Klára would come to know never left the face of Maria Maltzan. She addressed Klára, "I understand you have an adorable little boy," she smiled. "You are very fortunate."

"Yes, I am," Klára answered as she sipped her coffee. "Hannelore told me that you needed my help. What can I do?"

"Hannelore believes in you, trusts you completely. She assures us that because you are so highly placed by your husband's position in the Reich you may be able to serve the Resistance as a courier while attracting very little notice or suspicion."

"A courier?" Klára was quite astonished, "Of what?"

"Papers, packages...you need never know what they contain. Packages will be delivered to you at various times in various places and then you'll transfer them to me or to others, always in very public places, perhaps here or in the park or even in your church," the Countess paused. "You understand there is an inherent danger involved in whatever we ask you to do? You must protect yourself and be prepared for the worst...keep as much money on hand as you can and a suitcase packed. What do you think?"

Klára's heart pounded in her throat. She knew it was terribly dangerous, but Franz was never home and he knew nothing of her daily routine. András was her primary concern, so it would be Marta whom she would have to watch.

"I will do it." Klára smiled at the Countess.

Only a few days had passed when Hedy brought a message to Klára as she was in the garden cutting winter's dead spikes from the roses. Klára read the message... *your embroidered linens are ready for inspection... Wilhelm Fine Linen Shop... on Seydelstrasse.* She was only puzzled for a moment, since she had ordered no such linens... *this has to be a courier assignment of some sort.*

Klára responded with a smile, rose from her chore, and asked Hedy to let the chauffeur know she would be going out soon. Within the hour her car arrived in front of the linen shop on Seydelstrasse. When Klára entered the shop, only one young saleswoman was present behind the counter.

"I'm the Baroness von Werner, come to inspect some embroidered linens."

"Ah, yes, good day Baroness," smiled the woman. "They are over here."

She guided Klára to another counter and from underneath she brought out a large box and removed the lid. Inside were beautifully embroidered pillowcases and sheets. The needlework was executed with delicate perfection. The woman showed Klára the items in the box and then asked quite innocently, "Would you mind delivering another box to St. Veronika Catholic Church on Luisenstrasse to the priest, Father Matthaüs?"

Of course, Klára agreed to the errand. The young woman took an ornately embroidered chasuble from its hanger and folded it carefully within another large box. Klára summoned her chauffeur to carry the two boxes from the shop to the car, thanked the young woman, and left the shop.

When the car arrived at St. Veronika Church, Klára asked the chauffeur to carry the heavy box inside for her. She announced to one of the sisters that she had come to see Father Matthaüs. Within moments a young energetic priest appeared. He opened the box immediately, removed the chasuble and put it on, appearing very pleased. The long heavy coat hung handsomely from his shoulders. Father Matthaüs made intentional eye contact with Klára, looking at her with sincerity, he said, "Thank you for taking your time to deliver this to me. I'm very grateful to you."

Klára and her chauffeur left the church and made their way home. Klára thought to herself, *that was very easy... I wonder how many documents were hidden in the lining of that coat?* She stared out the window of the car as it sped down Unter den Linden. Suddenly she caught a glimpse of the small red flag attached at the front of her car as it whipped in the wind. *How ironic it is that I am using an official Nazi car to transport documents for the Resistance.* Her thoughts filled her with satisfaction.

Once at home with her embroidered linens, she carefully unfolded each pillow case and sheet to find several envelopes that she tucked into a safe place to await further instructions.

Klára did not have to wait very long before she received a call from the Countess Maltzan asking her to meet again for coffee at the Hotel Adlon. Klára put all the papers in a Fassbender and Rausch chocolate bag along with a box of chocolates and walked to the hotel. The May day was bright and warm;

birds twittered away in the trees above her head. This time Klára found the Countess waiting for her in the restaurant. Transferring the documents to the Countess seemed an easy enough task; giving her the box of chocolates was not at all difficult, but the next task requested by the Countess was not so easy.

"Only a few days ago members of the Nazi Party met to discuss private German companies," Countess Maltzan informed Klára. "You know that the party demands all German businesses to be in complete compliance with Nazi government goals."

After Klára nodded, the Countess continued, "Two lists of owners were made—one listing those who are loyal to the party and the other listing those who should be arrested and their companies seized by the government. Obviously, the second list places many people in imminent danger. The Resistance would find this information very useful. An informant has told us the Baron von Werner took notes at this meeting and that he placed the notes into a blue folder.

"A copy of those notes would be invaluable. The information could help us save lives. Do you think it possible for you to make a copy of those notes for us?"

Klára promised to try, but she left the meeting with the Countess feeling quite unsure about how she might accomplish the task. Even though Franz was absent much of the time, when he was at home, he spent all of his time in his study. There were piles of papers on his desk, files in drawers, but he kept his briefcase close and never left it behind when he was away from the house. Klára only hoped the blue folder was not in his briefcase.

When Klára arrived at home, Franz was not there. Neither Hedy nor Marta knew where he was or when he would return. Marta was just preparing to take András for his usual afternoon outing in the park, so Klára feigned a headache and took the opportunity to make a first investigation of the study. She decided that if anyone asked her why she was in the study, she would say that it was to look for Franz's copy of *Mein Kampf*. So, the first thing she did upon entering the study was to place the book in a hard-to-see spot on a shelf, in such a way that it would require a search to locate it. Klára began to go through the papers, scanning the words as she sorted through each stack.

She found that Franz kept track of the railcars needed to transport the arrested Jews and other undesirables to various labor camps. The number of arrested and relocated persons shocked her. Klára was amazed to find the blue folder in the second file drawer that she opened. The notes were handwritten and difficult to read, but she began immediately to copy them. After only a few moments she heard someone at the front door, perhaps Franz or Marta. She returned the folder at once, shoved the notes into her pocket, exited the study, and sat down in the parlor with a book, her heart pounding.

Copying the pages of handwritten notes turned out to be difficult and took Klára three visits to the study before she completed the task.

On the last visit Franz ran into her just as she was leaving the study. He was surprised, suspicious, even distraught to find her in his study. "What were you doing in there, Klára?"

"I was looking for your copy of *Mein Kampf.* I was certain that you had one...don't you?"

"Yes, I have a copy. It's right here." He frowned when the book was not where he thought it should be. "Someone has moved it." He scanned the shelves, "Here it is."

Franz handed the book to her, "I'm surprised, Klára, that you're interested in Hitler's thoughts."

Although she thanked him, took the book, and left the study, Franz remained skeptical as he watched her walk away. He closed the study door and locked it.

June

"I have to travel to Munich next week for an official inspection of facilities at Dachau," Franz announced to Klára. By now Dachau was in full operation and served as a model for other camps. Franz, a major in the S.S., was to attend the inspection with Heydrich and other officers. "You and the boy will go with me. You can visit my mother in Fürstenfeldbruck while I attend to business. We'll be there only for a week or so."

Klára was surprised he wanted her to accompany him, but she was happy to leave Berlin. When they arrived at the manor house, Baroness Renate von Werner began at once smothering András with kisses, overjoyed to see her grandson. Marta frowned upon the over-indulgence of the child, but she held little influence over the Baroness. And after all, this woman was the mother of her much admired employer, so Marta decided to stay quietly in the background.

Within a few days, Franz telephoned to say he had been called back to Berlin, but that Klára could stay longer. During lunch that afternoon on the veranda, Renate happily suggested, "We must travel to Vienna for a shopping trip and on the way we can detour to Linz to see your grandparents."

This was a most agreeable idea to Klára. They left on the train early the next morning, only planning to stop in Linz long enough to have lunch at the von Schrader home before continuing to Vienna. Klára's grandparents met the group of women at the station. Elation at meeting András was short, because Emmencht von Schrader seemed terribly agitated, not at all his usual jovial self. Béate, Klára's grandmother tried to calm him, but all the way from the station to the house on the Promenade, the Baron continued to make snide remarks about the *government* involving itself in his business and how appalled he was that Austria seemed to be going along with idiotic German ideas *once again*!

"Your Hitler has great disdain for a capitalist like me. He thinks business has but one reason to exist...to serve him and his Nazis...*community* he calls it!" Emmencht was steaming, "Of course, he wants the profits. Business is not so beneath him that he won't take the profits!"

Emmencht did not stop his tirade during their lunch. Klára was very relieved that Marta was far away with András in the nursery, very much out of earshot, because Klára knew Marta would not hesitate to repeat to Franz every word uttered by the Baron. Every time her grandfather said the word *government*, he glared at Klára.

"I cannot believe that a granddaughter of mine is married to a Nazi!" Emmencht looked directly into Klára's eyes and shook his fork at her, "Well, I won't serve them...never!" He tore at his roast beef with his teeth, "My business is no concern of theirs!"

"Oh, Baron, please do not upset yourself so," Renate laughed loudly.

Emmencht's face was red and his breathing short and deep.

"Calm down, Emmencht," cautioned Béate as she patted his hand, "You'll give yourself a heart attack. Remember, my love, these ladies are our guests."

Klára reminded them all in a soft, steady voice, "Franz was not a Nazi when we married."

"Well, I think he looks very handsome in his uniform. I'm very proud of him," stated Renate.

The Baron looked at Renate incredulously, "You have always been a silly woman with little sense."

"Emmencht! You should be ashamed. Renate is our guest."

The Baron turned to his wife, "She has no idea what the Nazis are up to, not even in her own neighborhood." At that he rose from the table and retired from the dining room.

Not fazed in the least, Renate responded, "Oh, I'm not insulted. The Baron has always teased me, ever since Elizabeth and I were girls. He always admonished me for my lack of interest in books," she assured them. "Poor Baron, he looks so tired. Age has not been kind to his appearance."

Klára excused herself from the table to find her grandfather. She found him walking in his garden of roses. "I'm devastated that my coming here has upset you so profoundly, Grandfather. It was never my intention."

"I'm too gruff, Klára." He turned from the roses and embraced Klára, "It is I who should apologize. Béate is right; I let my emotions get the better of me."

Her grandfather could see the unhappiness in her eyes, "You and András should leave Berlin for good, Klára, as soon as possible. Another war is on the horizon and Berlin will be at the center of it. You'll not be safe there."

Klára only studied her grandfather's strong hands as he held hers. She looked into his kind eyes and remembered Franz's list of *disloyal business owners* that she had copied.

"Perhaps, it is you and Grandmother who should be alert and careful. Your views do not sit well with Nazi ideas. I'm equally concerned for your safety."

Within the hour, the three women and András were on the train to Vienna. They checked into the Hotel Kaiserin Elizabeth. Once Marta and András were settled, Renate and Klára took a taxi to the Restaurant Griechenbeis on Fleischmarkt for dinner. Renate was terribly excited to be in Vienna and talked on and on about where she wanted to shop, but Klára's mind was elsewhere.

"You're very quiet tonight, Klára. Aren't you excited about our shopping trip?"

"I'm thinking about my family. They're at Lake Balaton, so near. I haven't seen them for more than a year." Klára looked at the Baroness, "Would you mind, Mother Renate, if András and I took the train to Lake Balaton tomorrow? We are so close. It's hard to imagine not seeing my parents."

"You would rather go to Balaton than shop?" The Baroness could hardly believe it.

"My family, I would love to see Mother and Papa," Klára could see the disappointment rising in Renate's eyes, "Of course, you can come with us. Mother would love to see you, too."

"Well, yes, I suppose I could go. I have always found Balaton so primitive but it would be nice to see Elizabeth. What a surprise it would be!"

"I'll send a telegram to let them know that we are coming. We can leave on the earliest morning train and be in Balatonfüred by early afternoon."

I will give Marta a holiday here in Vienna... Klára thought to herself... *I don't want her at the villa.*

Tamás was waiting for them when their train arrived in Balatonfüred. Klára gave him a heartfelt embrace despite Renate's frown at such familiarity. Klára, so glad to see him again, could not contain her excitement at being back at Lake Balaton after such a long absence, almost six years.

Everything looked the same to her and gave her a lovely, comfortable feeling. As the car pulled into the graveled driveway, the entire household stood on the veranda waiting to welcome them, Papa and Mother in front, with Silva close behind.

Klára embraced her parents. Her joy, deeper than simply seeing them again, came as a profound relief just to be in their loving and secure presence. It was a feeling she had not felt for a very long time.

Elizabeth and Leopold took turns passing little András back and forth until Silva demanded her turn. Formality did not exist between Klára and Silva who greeted each other warmly. Klára had not seen Tamás or Silva since her wedding in Cologne.

While Klára walked arm in arm with Leopold into his study, Elizabeth guided Renate to her guest room followed by Silva cradling András. Klára's conversation with her papa was fast and jovial, filled with news, both good and bad. Leopold asked light questions about Franz, avoiding any serious subjects, but the avoidance was noticeable.

Finally, with obvious concern, he asked, "Are you all right? What is Franz up to these days? Is there talk of war in Berlin?" Her papa appeared worried, "You must come home more often and stay longer. Berlin may not be a good place to be in the future."

Klára knew she should not dare tell him what she knew of Franz's activities, or what she knew of Nazi horrors, or of what her true feelings were for her husband and certainly not of her involvement in the Resistance. She knew her Papa would be both heartbroken for her miserable marriage and terrified for her safety. Instead, she asked about Mrs. Klein and how she and her family were dealing with the loss of Professor Klein.

"I'm glad that you attended his service, I should have come home to be with Rózsa."

"I believe that Rózsa comes often to Budapest to visit her mother." Leopold's thoughts drifted away, "It was a horrible occurrence, insanity really. So hard to imagine how human beings can become so indoctrinated with lies and evilness that they completely lose their humanity. Imagine beating an old man who never hurt anyone, but only contributed good to this world." Leopold sighed heavily, "There is evilness in this world, Klára, and I fear that it is very close to you and our precious András. You must bring your little one here if someday things go awry."

Klára stood on her toes to kiss her papa on his forehead, "I love you Papa. I love you for caring about us so much, but we must go back to Berlin, at least for a little while longer. But I will think about what you have said.

"I wonder if Rózsa might be in Budapest now? Wouldn't it be marvelous if she could come to visit for a day? I'm going to telephone on the chance that she may be there."

Two days later Rózsa arrived at the villa, more beautiful than ever, Klára thought. They had not seen each other since that summer in Eger, but they renewed their friendship as though only a day or two had passed. Klára expressed her regret for not having come for Dr. Klein's service and asked about Mrs. Klein.

"Your presence was not expected at all, Klára," Rózsa assured her, "but I was very grateful for your kind letter and your father's presence was very appreciated by our family.

"My mother misses father terribly. That's why I try to visit her whenever Pál has business in Budapest. Samuel and his family are just a few blocks away and my other brothers still live at home. Did you know they have jobs in your father's warehouse? I think the two of them give my mother something to do, feeding them and all the rest of it. I'm glad they're with her, so she's not alone, but still she's lonely without father."

Klára squeezed Rózsa's hand, "I know how much you loved your father, how much he meant to you. Tell me about Pál and your little ones."

Rózsa brought photographs of her children, "I wish you could have met my little girl on this visit. Here she is, little Vera, she has red hair, too. Only a few months younger than your András. And here is my big boy József, seven years old already." She smiled her beautiful smile, "I'm so happy that I've gotten to meet your lovely little boy and I'm amazed at how much he looks like your papa. Does he favor his father at all?"

"No, he does not. Not in any way." Klára realized her answer had a finality to it that sounded rather harsh. "And how is your darling Pál?"

"He's still darling as ever. I love him more every day." She looked at Klára, her expression turned serious. "You know Hungary could pass a law that makes my marriage to Pál illegal. I no longer go to synagogue. It's good that we live in the country, I think."

"Are you safe, Rózsa?" Klára had tears in her eyes. "Can Pál keep you safe? You should leave Hungary."

"We have thought about it, but we think it will be all right. We are surrounded by family in Eger and then there is Mother. We just can't leave. Where would we go?"

"What about Palestine to be with Eszter? Perhaps you should all go there."

"Well, she's the only Zionist in the family. None of the rest of us are political. If we just stay out of the argument, stay away from politics, we think we will be all right." Rózsa seemed confident, "Tell me about Franz. You rarely mention him in your letters. What's he like? I can't believe I have never met your husband after all these years!"

Klára thought about all the times she had wished for Rózsa to be there to share her true feelings, but now that the chance was here... *what could she possibly say?*

"What is it Klára? Is everything all right?"

"No, Rózsa, nothing is right," Klára was suddenly sobbing. She wanted to say, *Franz is a monster and I still love Dolf with all my heart,* but how could she say those words?

"Tell me... what's wrong?" Rózsa put her arms around Klára, "What has happened?"

Still Klára could not bring herself to tell Rózsa anything, "Berlin is just so far away from those I love and I miss all of you so much. I've wanted to talk with you so many times. I have no one to share my thoughts with... it's so lonely."

"And Franz? Can't you talk to Franz?"

"Franz is very busy. He has little time for András or for me." Klára looked away from Rózsa, "I'm certain that my relationship with Franz is opposite from yours with Pál."

"What do you mean Klára? What are you saying?"

"Franz and I are not in love, Rózsa. In fact, I made a terrible mistake. Except for András, I adore András. He is the only good to come of it."

"I can hardly believe this, Klára. I'm so sorry. So, will you stay here now and not go back to Berlin?"

"No, I must go back. At least for a while; I have work to do there."

"Work? What kind of work is so important?"

"I'm doing some little things for the Resistance…the resistance against the Nazis…Franz is a Nazi."

"Klára that is dangerous, terribly dangerous! You can't be involved in such things. You can't put yourself or András in such jeopardy! Please stay here with your parents. Please don't go back there!"

"I should not have told you, Rózsa. But I've wanted to tell you everything for so long. I don't mean to frighten you. It's just that I've heard too much and I know too much about the Nazis' plans. I can't just stand by and not try to help those they want to harm. It's what I must do."

"Oh, Klára, please come back as soon as you can." Then Rózsa thought of Dolf. "You've seen Dolf, haven't you? He was in Germany…I remember from your letters that he visited you."

"I've seen him a few times," Klára smiled. "I'm not sure where he is right now. Paris, I think."

"You still love him, Klára, don't you?"

"He's very dear to me, Rózsa, always, forever." Klára put her arm around Rózsa's waist, "Let's walk and not talk of these bad things anymore. Let's talk about all of our happiest memories. I want to laugh again."

The two young women walked together arm-in-arm along the water's edge. They did laugh over old memories and they made new ones when they spoke of their children. When it was time for Rózsa to go, Klára rode in the car, too, as Tamás drove to the station. Good-byes were difficult, but they promised to write and they promised each other to stay safe.

After another few days it was time for Klára and András and Renate to return to Vienna. The farewell was terribly wrenching for Klára and for everyone. Klára promised to return as soon as she could and that she would think about leaving Berlin for good. As the train sped from the station she watched her dear family standing on the platform waving farewell.

"Wave to them, András, say 'good-bye' until we see them again someday soon."

September, Berlin

Klára had never seen Franz so elated. After his return from the Nuremberg party rally, titled *Parteitage* this year, Franz enthusiastically began to tell Klára and Marta about what he had seen and heard, even though they had followed day by day the activities and speeches on the radio. Every word he uttered captivated Marta completely. She was obviously enraptured by his position, so near to Hitler himself she could swoon!

"*Party of Honor* was the theme this year," Franz spoke effusively. "Of course it was held in Zeppelin Airfield as usual. Speer's marble reviewing stand with its great flight of stairs and multiple columns made a grand background for Hitler. Hundreds of flags were waving, searchlights crisscrossed the night sky and thousands of Germans shouted 'Heil' as our Führer arrived at eight o'clock. His speech was so inspiring! Did you listen to it on the radio? Well, you could not possibly have felt the same emotions felt by all of us who were there!"

Franz told his story in excited spurts, "Hitler praised all of us for following his voice, his dreams, his words and his belief in the greatness of the German people. Hitler said, '*We have been poor and defeated, but now we are rich and brave and courageous! The German people have been demoralized and suppressed, but now we are a resurrected country, proud and manly because of our commitment to nationalism… to the memory of an ancient and powerful nation.*'

"Hitler made all of us, thousands of us, proud to be German! He encouraged us when he said, '*We are unified by one ideal to make Germany strong and whole again*' and he reminded us that *our* Germany and all of Europe must rid itself of our enemies… those who disagree with him or with Nazi policies. In particular, Hitler wants to rid Europe of the Bolshevist Jews and our Führer assured us when that task is complete—the cleansing of Germany of those *unacceptables*—the Reich is guaranteed peace to last for centuries! '*We Germans are superior, confident and strong!*' he shouted. Magnificent! Did you hear it? Did you listen to our Führer?"

"Oh, yes, Sir! We heard every word and we heard the crowd interrupt him many times with their huge roars of adulation," gushed Marta. "You're right, Major Werner, our Führer is magnificent!"

"Every day there were parades of workers, political leaders, the youth, the Wehrmacht, and the women of the party. All the speeches addressed the most important issues… the evils of Bolshevism, the Jewish problem, German independence from foreign resources and, of course, the return of all lands taken from us in the Treaty of Versailles." Franz sighed heavily, "A glorious week, but now it's good to be back in Berlin… there's much work to be done!"

November, Budapest

Leopold and Elizabeth sat in the library near the large fireplace with its roaring fire one cold November evening. Leopold, reading the evening newspaper while Elizabeth sewed on her needlepoint, shook his head at Regent Horthy's newest appointment of prime minister. Leopold read aloud from the editorial, "Horthy has chosen Kálmán Darányi as Prime Minister because he will act in a conciliatory manner toward the German Nazi Party and will eagerly support Hungarian anti-Semites."

Leopold puffed in an agitated manner on his cigar. "It's obvious that Horthy has made a deal with Hitler," Leopold said with a heavy sigh, "the devils...it's the same old story...Germany will promise restoration of Hungarian territories lost in the Treaty of Trianon and give Hungary financial support...and in return Hungary will lose its soul to the Third Reich!" Then he added, "And in the end there will be war and Hungary will be on the wrong side and lose everything once again."

Elizabeth tried to calm him, "Perhaps none of these terrible things you dread will come to pass, dear. Perhaps Germany will be satisfied within its own borders. How can Germany possibly want another war?"

"These new laws passed by our parliament deeply concern me! The First Jewish Law," lamented Leopold, "restricting employment opportunities for Jews. Irrational! To penalize our own citizens because of their faith...stifle their abilities that serve their own country well! They pay taxes and contribute economically."

The two sat in silence for a time before Leopold spoke again. In a low, calm voice he addressed his wife. "Elizabeth, I must express my opinion about our son-in-law. I know that you still have faith in him. You're unwilling to judge him or his choices, but I am not. Franz is a part of this...this Nazi propaganda of pure Aryan Master Race nonsense! These evil ideas have become law! The whole thing is spinning out of control...where will it end once it's under way?"

Leopold leaned toward Elizabeth, "I'm concerned for Klára and little András."

Elizabeth remained quiet, pretending to focus on her stitches, but she shared Leopold's fears. She wanted to believe that Franz was caught up in events not of his making...that he had no choice. After all, Hitler was dictator and no one could disagree with him. Elizabeth assured herself that Franz was still the charming person she had known long ago...that in his personal life and in his relationship with Klára he was not a *Nazi*. Elizabeth was certain she had not misread him so completely.

And, yet, she remembered how Stefan had not liked Franz as a little boy. Stefan's words haunted her memory... *Franz shows you and his mother one side and then another side to the children... he is cunning... a deceiver... he is very clever... his bad behavior only happens behind his mother's back. I do not trust him... I will keep my eye on him when he is around Klára.* Elizabeth shook Stefan's words from her head. She determined to continue believing in Franz as a good husband, father, and businessman.

"Perhaps you should not let your opinion of despicable Nazi behavior inform your opinion of Franz, Leopold. Surely, things are not as bad as you suspect, my dear."

1937
February, Linz

In February the Austrian Chancellor Schuschnigg agreed under pressure to admit politicians of the National Socialist Party into his government. Those new far-right members immediately demanded that Austria become a part of Germany. In disgust, Schuschnigg resigned. The National Socialist activist, Arthur Seyss-Inquart, an avid member of the German Brotherhood, who loved all things German, became the new chancellor and immediately advocated for annexation of Austria by Germany.

Soon after the far right took over the Austrian government, government agents paid a visit to the von Schrader home in Linz. Knowing a visit by these agents would be a disaster for the Baron, who could not keep his thoughts to himself, the Baroness intervened. She told the agents at the door that her husband was in his bed with a fever. Nonetheless, the three men gave their demands to the Baroness in writing and promised they would return for his answer within the week.

Béate read their demands... *Baron von Schrader must swear allegiance to the National Socialist Party, commit his entrepreneurial expertise to the party, and contribute his financial assets for the good of the Nazi Party.*

Fanatics, Béate thought, but she knew she had to let Emmencht know what they wanted. After he read their demands, Emmencht looked up from the paper; his face was growing quite red.

"Be calm, Emmencht. What can we do?"

"We must leave our home, Béate, as soon as possible."

The very next day the Baron and Baroness packed several small cases with a variety of items including gold and other valuables, deeds and other important papers. They set aside envelopes with severance pay for each of their staff and left their home with their chauffeur, the baron's valet, and Béate's personal maid.

The group of five drove to a small rail station on the outskirts of Linz, boarded the train and traveled across the snow-covered landscape all the way to Rorschach, Switzerland. Once they had arrived safely, the Baron and Baroness moved into an old villa in the small lakeside village, a house that had been in their family for centuries. The Baron sat down and wrote a letter to his daughter.

Budapest

Elizabeth opened the letter from her father. She read his words several times and then walked to the library, opening the door slowly. "Leopold, may I come in? I have news."

Leopold walked to the door, opened it widely, and escorted her into the room. He noticed the paper in her hand and guided her to a chair. "What is it, my dearest?"

"A letter from my father and mother. They've left Austria for Switzerland...to live. Father says they left everything behind, because agents from Austria's new Nazi Party harassed them and because they expect an imminent German invasion. Father implores us to follow them as soon as possible," Elizabeth was shaking and began to sob, "Oh, Leopold, what should we do?"

Leopold read Emmencht's letter. "I admire your father's decision to leave Austria. I'm certain Emmencht is well aware the Nazis would coerce his expertise and influence for their purposes. Your father is a man of integrity. He has refused to finance their ridiculous war."

Leopold's thoughts wandered back several months to a group of friends who contacted him. The group had recently become associated with the German Colonel Metzger, a highly placed officer in Hitler's Nazi Party and they wanted Leopold to meet him. Metzger, a loyal German who loved his country, did not want to see Germany destroyed by the fanatical Hitler.

Metzger, an agent of Canaris's *Abwehr*, on a mission to undermine Hitler's efforts, pressured the group of Hungarian financiers to disengage their support for Hitler's government and military machine. Quite aware that Hitler's goals would eventually lead Hungary into war, Leopold and his friends saw the wisdom in Metzger's mission and agreed to cease all financial support of companies that endorsed Hitler's war efforts.

In the last few months, Leopold had been active, in a very low key way, in influencing fellow elite Hungarians to withdraw from the prime minister's move toward an alliance with Germany. Leopold also subtly warned financiers and industrialists to protect their funds against a possible invasion by Germany. Many of his friends had already left Budapest for their remote country homes or even for other countries.

Leopold turned his attention back to Elizabeth. Should they leave Budapest for Lake Balaton or should he take everyone to Switzerland or was it already too late? And what about Klára? She was still in Berlin in the heart of evil. Leopold spoke to Elizabeth, "We'll wait a bit to see what happens, my dearest Betka," as he gently put his hand atop hers. She smiled at him through her tears, trusting his decision completely.

Spring, Budapest

As soon as Rudolf arrived in Budapest from London by way of Vienna, he hurried straight to the von Esté home. He had not visited there since the day Elizabeth had sent him from the house, devastated in his quest to marry Klára, but now, driven by a sense of urgency, Rudolf was willing to walk into a place where he felt there would be no welcome.

Rudolf had learned from an MI6 peer that Klára had been contacted by the Berlin Resistance and was instrumental in several attempts to gain important inside information. He was infuriated at his Berlin contacts for putting Klára in harm's way, but what could he do? She had agreed and was already an active part of the underground movement by the time he heard of her involvement.

Still it terrified him to think of Klára participating in espionage. He could only imagine the danger surrounding her and he was certain Franz would not protect her. Klára's husband was far too close to Hitler to ever go against him.

Tamás opened the front door and greeted Rudolf warmly, "Welcome back, Sir. I'm happy to see you again. It's been a long time, too long."

Rudolf returned his warm greeting. "Is the Duke at home? I would like to visit with him."

"He's working in the library. I'll tell him you're here." Tamás rapped gently on the great oak door, opened it, and walked in. After only a moment he reappeared, followed by Leopold and Fejedelem.

"Dolf!" Leopold exclaimed as he walked toward Rudolf with open arms. "How good it is to see you! You look well! I have missed your visits. It has been too long. Welcome, welcome!"

Leopold embraced Rudolf wholeheartedly and guided him toward the library, "Come in, come in," he continued, "Please, Tamás, join us."

The three men entered the library, closing the door behind them. Tamás poured from a deep-green bottle, three glasses of *Zwack Unicum*, one for each of them. He passed out the glasses and lifted his own, "*Hoz-a Egészség!* To your health" and then took his seat in the intimate circle of chairs with Leopold and Rudolf. Fejedelem nestled at Leopold's feet. Each man sipped the bittersweet liqueur and smiled to himself as the liquid slipped down his throat. But their smiles quickly disappeared as they leaned forward and listened to Rudolf.

"I'm certain you both must know the winds of war are stirring. I fear Germany is once again rushing into war and I believe Hungary seems to be joining with the German side," Rudolf paused, "the wrong side once again." He looked Leopold in the eye, "I strongly encourage you to call Klára home."

"Klára is a married woman, Dolf. I can't order her to come home. I do agree with you, but I have no authority over Klára."

"Still, I hope that you'll try and also, you should think about leaving Budapest as soon as possible."

"Where should we go?"

"Perhaps Britain or even America."

"Oh, Dolf," Leopold laughed. "We're not going to leave our home for such a distant place. You are too pessimistic."

Leopold rose from his chair and stood by his desk. He looked at the large globe on its stand and spun it as he spoke, "Men of reason must sit together and put an end to this nonsense. We've all suffered too much from the Great War…from all wars."

"No one is interested in going through that again," Tamás offered.

"You're both too optimistic," insisted Rudolf. "There's no way to reason with fascism, with fanatics who are blinded by hate and prejudice and ambition."

"There have always been evil men in this world, Dolf, from the beginning of time, but God willing there will always be some who are aware and willing to disagree with them."

Rudolf changed the subject, "Have you received word from Admiral Canaris?"

"I have." Leopold sat down, rather surprised. "The Admiral informed me that someone would be asking for something. I now surmise that 'someone' is you."

"I do represent an interested party. Our role is to undermine Hitler's goals. We must divert as much money as possible from the Nazis' war machine. We know that some industrialists see this monstrous endeavor as a way to become even wealthier. We must divest of any investments that support this war effort."

Leopold and Tamás nodded their heads thoughtfully. "This is about ending a war before it begins," Leopold agreed, "about saving our country, our people before the destruction and devastation can harm them. I'm proud of you, Dolf, for being a part of this noble effort." Leopold seemed to look away at some distant place, "I believe that Stefan would be with you…don't you?"

"Of course he would be!" Rudolf declared with a smile, "We all know what a Monarchist he was! One of the Reich's ultimate goals is to destroy the royal families of Europe. Definitely! Stefan would be right here fighting them in whatever way he could."

Leopold wiped the tears from his eyes. Tamás patted Leopold's hand.

Rudolf studied his two old friends. He had always admired them and he thought about the impact they had made on his life.

"Now, back to Klára and her son," Rudolf stated emphatically, "I'm certain if they remain in Berlin, they will be in mortal danger. Not only from the course of war, but from her own husband. Von Werner is very much a part of Hitler's inner circle. He is not to be trusted. To be quite honest, I can hardly stand the thought of Klára and András living in his house."

"Well, I'm certain you're right, Dolf," Leopold laid his hand on Rudolf's shoulder, "I respect your opinions and I will do my best to bring Klára home. We'll see what we can do."

Then Leopold held Rudolf's attention, eye to eye, "I always imagined she would be here with me and her mother... in Budapest." He added with a touch of scolding in his voice, "I thought that she would be your wife."

Rudolf looked stunned. He frowned and for the first time since that day he met with the Duchess in this very room, he reconsidered her words and realized they may not have been the words of the Duke.

"I always thought so, too, Sir," Rudolf bowed his head and spoke softly, almost reverently, "I have loved Klára since she was sixteen, but this is my sin to love Klára who is married to another. I cannot even ask God for forgiveness, because I cannot repent or deny my heart."

Tamás and Leopold were equally taken aback by Rudolf's confession. Neither had believed he still loved Klára, since he had disappeared from their lives when she longed for him so desperately before leaving for Cologne. They could think of nothing to say, but only looked at him with a depth of shared sorrow. After moments of silence, the three men stood and heartily embraced each other.

"Stay safe, my dear friends. I'll return to Budapest as soon as I can." Rudolf managed a smile.

"Go through the kitchen, Dolf," Tamás commanded, "give Silva a kiss and then, I'm sure, she'll give you a big piece of *diós torta* before you walk home."

"Let's all go to the kitchen for a piece of torta," Leopold said and they walked out of the library together.

Late Summer

After Rudolf's visit, Leopold was determined to speak with Klára in person. "Betka, I want to go to Berlin to see Klára and András. I so hoped they would come to Balaton this summer." Leopold had a faraway look in his eye, "We must see how she is doing and then encourage her to come home with us to Budapest."

Three days later Leopold and Elizabeth were on a train to Germany. Klára and her chauffeur met them at the *Potsdamer Bahnhof*, only a very short drive from Klára's home.

"We had to come," Leopold huffed, "since you will not come home to us."

"Oh, Papa, I miss you both terribly. I'm thrilled you have come. András is so excited."

Klára had planned to go back to Budapest and Lake Balaton, but...her thoughts wandered back over the summer months...*she was so busy, delivering falsified visas, ration cards and identification papers*. Klára had even begun to meet with Germans willing to hide Jews and other "undesirables" in their homes while awaiting papers that would allow safe passage out of Germany.

"We can't understand what keeps you so occupied in Berlin," her mother fretted, "everyone misses you when you are not with us."

"I'm so happy to be with you again." Klára smiled. "We'll have a wonderful time. We shall take András sightseeing and to the zoo and to Wannsee...the weather is very good for sightseeing." Klára's elation was convincing. Leopold thought to himself that Klára seemed genuinely happy when she announced joyously, "We are here," as the chauffeur pulled the long black car with its Nazi flags along the curb.

While Klára ran up the front steps, Leopold helped Elizabeth out of the car. They were all met at the front entrance by András and Nanny Marta. Hedy took their things as they entered the reception hall. András was not at all shy with his grandparents, greeting them with "How do you do?" and firm handshakes. Leopold and Elizabeth were quite impressed by his mature manners.

"You may thank Nanny Marta for that...her standard for good manners is very high. Franz is in Munich this weekend and then he travels to Czechoslovakia," Klára informed them. "I don't think you'll see him this trip."

Klára invited András to sit with them at the dining room table for an early supper. He felt very grown up as he sat on an extra high cushion beside his grandfather. Inge made a special supper of *Schwartenbraten*, roasted pork with bread dumplings and sauerkraut.

"Inge made *Schwarzwälder Kirschtorte*, Black Forest Cake, for dessert!" András announced in his own mix of German and Hungarian, "It's very nice. You'll like it, Grandmother."

After finishing their delicious supper, the three adults took András upstairs to his room. Once prepared for bed, he snuggled under the covers while Leopold told him stories and Elizabeth sang an old Hungarian folk song to him. András said his prayers, yawned and closed his eyes. Leopold, Elizabeth, and Klára whispered good night and left his room.

Downstairs in the first-floor parlor they settled into comfortable over-stuffed sofas while Hedy served glasses of *Weizen Doppel Korn*. Leopold stared at the portrait of Franz hanging over the fireplace.

"What is the meaning of that?" Leopold pointed toward the painting, knowing full well the symbolic message.

"It's Franz, of course. Painted by the German artist, Peiner, meant to inspire Aryans."

Leopold let the *Doppel Korn* slip down his throat, but its thick sweetness could not relieve the bitter taste in his mouth. He understood the implications of the painting—the perfect Aryan specimen looking upward toward a lofty landscape. He found the image deplorable. Leopold had come to Berlin for a reason and had no intention of waiting for "just the right moment." Now was the right moment.

"Klára, we received a letter from your grandfather. Did you know that he and your grandmother have left Linz?"

Klára shook her head in the negative. She was not surprised, but asked, "Why?"

"You don't know? Can't you guess?" Leopold's face was turning pink.

"Leopold," Elizabeth patted his hand. "Remain calm, dear."

"Emmencht is convinced that Austria's days of independence are numbered...that the Nazis are on the verge of invading his country. Your grandfather knows very well what kind of people these Nazis are. He knew they would try to force him into some despicable collusion, so he chose to leave everything behind rather than chance being compelled to submit to their devious demands."

"Where did they go?"

"To an old villa in Rorschach, Switzerland, on Lake Constance," answered Elizabeth. "We went there many times when I was a girl."

"I'm not concerned about *where* they went," Leopold practically shouted, "I'm concerned about *why* they went! *Nazis*! And, Klára, you are married to one!"

Klára jumped from her chair and ran to the parlor door which she closed immediately. "Papa, lower your voice. It isn't safe to express your opinions here!"

"That is exactly why your mother and I have come. You cannot stay here with your son! You are both in danger!" Leopold looked at Klára with as much conviction as he could muster.

"Papa, I do have friends here. Not all Germans are Nazis! In fact, recently I've been greatly encouraged by the good will and concern exhibited by many German people. Over the last few months I've met good German people who are diametrically opposed to Hitler and his government. They're fully aware of the brutality that has overtaken their country."

Klára paced across the room and spoke with adamant animation, "Of course, I'm not blind to the fact there are many more Germans steadfastly supportive of Hitler...they think he's the messiah. Some Germans trust him implicitly to guide them into *'a bright future and salvation!'* " Klára hesitated, stopped talking altogether; she knew she'd already said far too much.

Leopold and Elizabeth just stared at her.

"What have you been up to, Klára? Who are you befriending? You live in the home of a Nazi…one who is particularly close to Hitler. If you are engaged in any kind of activity against their policies…will he protect you if you are found out?" Leopold was standing by this point. "And now you tell us that private opinions cannot be expressed here in your own home! Can you trust anyone here? Who is the spy?"

"Marta." Klára had a terrified look in her eye, "Marta is the Nazi. She adores Franz and watches my every move. She's a *Zellenleiter*."

"A *Zellenleiter*? What is that?" asked Elizabeth.

"She's the 'street cell leader,' the one who reports any suspicious anti-Nazi behavior she sees or hears to the *Ortsgruppenleiter*. That's the local area leader who reports to the *Kreisleiter*, who is the circuit leader who then reports to the *Gauleiter*. The *Gauleiter* is the district leader, who is Doctor Goebbels and he's the leader in charge of Berlin."

Leopold collapsed into his chair, "Good God, Klára, this is too much to bear. Your situation is worse than I imagined. I dreaded finding you ensnared in your husband's clutches and now I suppose that you are in some way actively opposing him." Leopold looked up at his daughter, his eyes filled with tears. "Does Dolf know what you are doing? I know that he's seen you here in Berlin. When last I saw him, he begged me to bring you home."

For the first time in her life, Klára lied to her father, "Papa, you are letting your imagination get the better of you. I oppose the Nazis in my heart, but I'm not engaged in any such activities as you are imagining. Please, stop upsetting yourself. András and I are perfectly safe here. We'll come home as soon as we can."

After the traumatic discussion with her parents, Klára tried to keep the conversation turned to lighter things—however difficult it might be. Everywhere they went in Berlin, red Nazi banners hung from windows and flagpoles, billowing in the wind. Soldiers strutted along the sidewalks as Berliners made way for them. Leopold took note of the soldiers' arrogance and forceful dominance. He saw the posters of Franz plastered to walls and lamp posts and he heard the blaring loudspeakers spewing ridiculous propaganda…*Aryans are the Master Race…the Jewish-Bolshevik conspiracy feeds on the good German worker…anyone who denies our Führer is an enemy of the Reich*…and on and on. But little András was oblivious to it all, thoroughly enjoying his grandparents' visit and heartbroken when it was time for them to go.

All packed and ready to go, Elizabeth stood at the window of the guest room and looked out into Klára's small garden surrounded by a tall brick wall and sighed heavily.

Klára knocked on the slightly ajar door, "Mother, are you all ready to go? I'm so sad for you and Papa to go. I'll miss you terribly."

"Klára, in all the days we have been here, you have not mentioned your husband once, not even his name, not even to András." Elizabeth looked away from her daughter. "Is he so unbearable, Klára?" She hesitated, "Franz *is* kind to you, isn't he? And to András? He isn't cruel to you, is he?"

Klára could see the agony in her mother's eyes. "Franz is not cruel to András, Mother. Don't worry about that. It's just that he's gone most of the time. We see him very little, even when he is in Berlin, he is very busy. I know it sounds strange, but András doesn't know his father very well."

"I don't know him very well either, Mother." Klára hesitated, "Franz and I are quite the opposites. Our conversations do not go very well, but I'm not telling you this to upset you. I simply want you to understand that I keep very busy with András, my friends and with St. Veronika's. I'm perfectly content and you're not to worry about me." Klára laughed, "I'm quite grown up!"

Elizabeth smiled at her beautiful daughter, kissed her and the two of them walked downstairs to meet Leopold who was standing with András. They went together to the station so András could see the big engines and say their farewells there. Klára suffered a great sadness as the train steamed away into the distance.

August

Klára sensed Franz had grown suspicious of her from the day he discovered her coming out of his study. Fortunately, there had been no reason for Klára to return to the study, but another problem had arisen of which she was certain—Marta had been assigned by Franz to spy on her. When Klára received assignments, she tried to act as naturally as possible, particularly careful not to arouse Marta's attention and so far, things had gone well. Klára's assignments fit easily into her regular day of shopping or going to mass or visiting a friend. *Perhaps too easy*, she thought and cautioned herself against carelessness.

One afternoon in late August, Klára stood in her garden and took a paper note from her pocket; it had been handed to her earlier that morning in the Tiergarten by a young man riding a bicycle. Marta had been sitting near the wading pool, watching András splash around happily, when she saw the boy on the bicycle give something to Klára. Now Marta watched from the window of the morning room as Klára opened the paper. Marta hurried out into the garden and confronted Klára at once.

"What have you got there?"

"Marta…" Klára, quite startled, was speechless. She frowned at Marta, regained her composure and spoke, "What do you mean?"

"I think Major von Werner will want to know what you are doing getting messages from strangers."

"You should not address me in such a manner, Marta. Are you spying on me?"

"Perhaps you are the spy or do you have a lover?"

"This conservation is ridiculous. I have a mind to inform Franz that you have severely overstepped your place."

"You may tell the Baron whatever you want, but he'll disagree with you, certainly when I tell him that I have caught you in an intrigue."

At that moment Hedy came into the garden, walked straight to Klára and took the paper from her hand, "Thank you, Madam." She turned to Marta and said, "This note was meant for me, Marta," and walked back into the house.

Klára glared at Marta and went straight to the nursery to sit with András. She was terrified. She had barely glanced at the words written on the paper...*An address? A few words? Why did Hedy take the note?* Klára was angry with herself for being so nonchalant, so careless. *Everything has gone so smoothly until now...and the work is so important...how could I have been so careless?* It was hard to breathe. *What did Hedy do with the note? Where was Marta now? What would she say to Franz?* Klára thought, *At least he's in Munich, maybe things will be calm again by the time he returns.*

After supper when András was tucked into his bed and Marta was in her room, Klára went downstairs to find Hedy. They stood together in the parlor. Klára was breathless...Hedy spoke first.

"Here's your note, Baroness."

"Thank you, Hedy." Klára bit her lip nervously. "Why did you take it? Did you read it?"

"Marta is unbearable, Madam." Hedy took a breath. "You are not alone in this house. You may have thought you, alone, are resisting the Nazis," Hedy's eyes were lowered, "but there are many German people who do what they can to help those who've been singled out by prejudice."

"What are you saying, Hedy? What have you done?"

"Inge and I have been helping to feed a family with *your* food. They're hidden in the cellar of a house near here—the Pfieffer house. Their cook is Jewish and the Pfieffers have been hiding her family in their cellar for several months now." Hedy hesitated, "It's been difficult for the Pfieffers to feed them on ration cards."

"Yes, Hedy, that's good...we must share...I'm proud of you and Inge." Klára felt overwhelmed and embraced Hedy, "And you've known that I was involved in such efforts, too?"

"Yes, we've known, since the days you spent in the master's study going through his papers. Inge and I made sure Marta was occupied away from the study."

Klára suddenly realized the assignments she thought so easily accomplished had only been easy because her household was watching out for her. Klára felt humbled by their involvement.

"Thank you, Hedy. Please let Inge know how grateful I am." Klára felt a surge of panic, "We're all in peril, if Marta should tell Franz about the note. He will not believe any story we make up. He's suspicious of me already. I know he's asked Marta to spy on me."

"I've written another note to take the place of this one. If the Baron asks, I'll show him the one I have, so you can destroy your note."

Klára opened the note and read it, nothing more than an address. Tomorrow she would deliver the packet she had received from her most recent visit to a pastry shop on Friedrichstrasse to the address.

"We must be very careful. I've become too cavalier, too indiscreet. I promise to be more careful from now on. Marta will be more alert to all of us, now that she's seen you come to my aid."

"Inge and I watch Marta, too, very closely."

"And Liesel? Is she aware of all of this?"

"No, Liesel is oblivious to these things and it's best to keep it that way," answered Hedy. "She's a bit slow-witted and terrified of Marta. She can say nothing in Marta's presence, she only stammers and I'm certain she would only faint if Marta pressed her. Inge and I are very careful that Liesel knows nothing."

The two women parted, bidding each other a good-night.

The next afternoon while Marta watched over András as he napped, Klára took the tram the distance across the Spree River to the address on Grunerstrasse and she knocked on the door. When the door opened, a charming young blonde woman with a large smile greeted her. Klára handed over the packet, unaware of its contents, but believing it could be identification papers or travel passes or, perhaps, ration books. The woman thanked her profusely and squeezed her hand.

"God bless you and keep you safe," she said to Klára as she closed the door.

When Klára turned from the door to descend the steps to the sidewalk, she noticed a man standing by a fenced oak tree at the sidewalk's edge. A tall, well-dressed man holding an ornate cane, his face hidden by a tilted hat, but she recognized his form instantly.

"Dolf!" She hurried down the steps to embrace him, "Dolf, you're here! It's wonderful to see you."

Crowds of people passed by the two as they stood together on the busy street. Rudolf held Klára's hand, "It's good to see you again, Klára." He embraced her warmly and smiled as he stared into her emerald eyes. "I've come to persuade you to leave Berlin. Your father wants you to come home. Everyone was terribly disappointed when you didn't return to Lake Balaton this summer."

"I've been so busy, Dolf." She looked at him knowingly, "I've been doing important work."

"Yes, I know, Klára. Let's walk together, perhaps we can stop for lunch. There's a place near here on Waisenstrasse."

They walked arm in arm, she leaned against him feeling wonderful to be near him after such a long time, "I miss you, Dolf, more than you can ever imagine."

"I've missed you, too, Klára. You look lovely—just as I always remember you."

They ducked into an old baroque building that housed the restaurant, Zur Letzten Instanz. The host greeted them and led them to a circular staircase spiraling up to a small wood-paneled room where Rudolf and Klára were seated at a table for two. He ordered a bottle of *Spätburgunder* from the Rheingau region of Germany. The waiter poured the wine, descended the stair, and left them alone in the little room. The two clicked their glasses, "*Egészségedre!*"

The rich red wine warmed their throats, relaxing the tension that gripped both of them. They smiled at each other as they reached across the table to hold hands. The touch brought a shiver of electricity to Klára and she lowered her eyes. His touch was all too much for her...forbidden desire swept over her...to sink into his arms and kiss him as she had so long ago.

"I do know what you've been up to and I want to forbid it. I do not want you to be involved in such dangerous undertakings. I fear that Franz would not protect you if he should discover you are acting against his party."

"No, he would not. I know that," Klára looked at Rudolf with such sincerity, "but I cannot do nothing. So many innocent people have already been hurt, because I did nothing to warn them...my friends in Cologne...arrested and disappeared. You never met any of them. They were so wonderful, so full of life."

"Klára, you can't take on this mission because you think you may have had anything to do with the arrests of your friends. None of this is your fault."

"I do know that, Dolf, but they were so dear to me. Even Franz liked them in the beginning, before he became a Nazi." She looked wistful, "He sang with us and played the piano with the little band we had formed." She bit her lip and winced. "Then after he put on that hideous uniform, he hated everyone, even the music, jazz. He forbid me to ever see my friends again or to play jazz music again."

Klára looked into Rudolf's deep brown eyes, so sensitive and attentive. "When my friend, Hannelore, came to visit me here in Berlin, she told me about the horrors faced by our Jewish friends and others who the Nazis decided were unacceptable. I knew about the horrors perpetrated upon innocents, because I had heard Franz and his friends discuss their hatred for Jews and *non-normal* people they deemed to be *unfit to live*. I heard these men discuss their deplorable reasons and the unspeakable tortures they planned for these human beings," Her eyes filled with tears, "And I did not warn them! How can I do nothing?"

Rudolf held her hands in his and loved her more than ever. He tried to console her, "I'm filled with regret that you've had to endure the unbearable." Rudolf raised her hands to his lips, "It's entirely my doing that you find yourself in this terrible predicament. I want to help you leave this danger and sadness behind. I want to take you and András home."

"And you, Dolf, aren't you in danger, too?" She smiled at him while wiping tears from her eyes, "I have no idea what you're doing here or what you've done in the past, but I know that you're involved in dangerous endeavors. Would you stop, if I forbid it?"

"I would consider it," he smiled at her, "but you're right, now is not the time." Rudolf cleared his throat and sat up straighter in his chair. "I'm planning to move back to Budapest. I've taken a position at the Hungarian Academy of Drawing."

"Oh, Dolf, I'm thrilled to hear that! You've always wanted to teach there. I'm so happy for you."

"I'll continue to do some traveling, but I fear too soon there will be plenty of my kind of work to do in Hungary. I want to be there, when I'm needed. Perhaps, if you come home, there will be times we can work together." He looked thoughtful, reconsidering his offer, and added, "As long as I can assure your safety...only then."

"It would be good to be in Budapest again. I dream of it." She held his hands in hers, "I'm able to do what I have done here, because Franz is rarely at home, rarely in Berlin. He's in Munich now." Klára spoke matter-of-factly, "When he's in town I try not to take assignments. I usually don't get any assignments. I assume *they* must know when Franz is away."

"Do you know what Franz is doing in Munich?" Dolf did know, but would never have told her what he knew.

"I do. He's visiting the *Lebensborn Institute* and, yes, I know what he's doing there."

"You know!" Rudolf was astonished. "What do you think of it?"

"I'm repulsed by all of it, but Franz is repulsed by me and by his own son. We are not blonde or blue-eyed. Franz is devastated that his child is dark. In his opinion, poor András does not look like the ideal Aryan, instead he looks like me." She sighed. "Franz can make all the Aryan babies he wants. I'm glad when Franz leaves Berlin, I can get my work done, work I believe very important."

Rudolf peered into her beautiful face, "I'm so sorry, Klára, for the part I played that has brought you so much misery."

"I've never blamed you, Dolf. I've only dreamt of how it could have been."

They lingered as long as they could in the little room until the hour was late. They parted with regret, promised to think of each other and to stay safe. Rudolf walked away in one direction; Klára walked in another.

—〰—

Within a few days Franz returned to Berlin. Because his assignments for the party had increased greatly, he had rarely been home since mid-summer.

After a brief cursory greeting to Klára and András, Franz went into his study followed by Marta. She closed the door behind them. Klára sat at her morning room table writing letters, a place from which she could see the study door. She waited. Her heart pounded in her throat...*what would Marta say to him...what had she observed...what would he do?*

After twenty minutes or so Marta emerged from the study, she smiled at Klára as she passed on her way upstairs, but said nothing. Finally, Franz stepped out of his study and walked toward her.

"Marta tells me that you are in and out of the house on many errands. She does not know where you are going or where you have been."

"Am I expected to give reports of my activities to the nanny?"

"What are you up to, Klára?"

"I have my regular routine every week, Franz," Klára determined to look him in the eye and control her breath as she said, "Marta is welcome to go with me, if you think she should, but then we will need to find another nanny for András."

"Why are you accepting notes from strangers, Klára?"

"Marta's imagination has confused her. Where there is nothing she sees intrigue. The note was for Hedy regarding news of a relative, nothing of interest to Marta or to me."

"These times demand loyalty and trust. Marta exhibits loyalty and she has my trust. Marta has eyes and ears for the party. She informs me of those who are disloyal and those who are not to be trusted."

"Of what are you accusing me, Franz? I shop, I go to mass, I play with András and I help the Carmelite nuns at Sacred Heart. We help the poor orphaned German children."

"There's nothing specific, Klára, but Marta does not trust you and she's warned me that you are not what you seem to be...a quiet, timid, little mouse."

"How dare she say such things about me to my husband! I don't want her in my home any longer, Franz."

"Marta is here to stay, Klára, and she's watching you."

1938
Winter, Berlin

Determined to rise above Marta's suspicions, Klára insisted that Marta accompany her on every mundane excursion—whether it be shopping for lingerie, sausages or chocolate, mass at St. Veronika's, visits to the children's orphanage, or the return of library books—Marta was present for every errand.

Klára remained as cautious as possible after her confrontation with Marta and Franz, but she continued to accept clandestine assignments. They came to her in various ways—inside her psalter or a library book, within the folds of lingerie or layers of chocolates, or wrapped up with her bratwurst—while others were whispered within the blessings of Father Matthäus or the Mother Superior.

For Klára an added feeling of satisfaction came when the passing of important information or papers occurred right under Marta's nose. Klára often felt a smile creep across her lips when she thought of herself as a cat rather than a mouse, but she took care and made sure that Marta saw nothing.

One cold winter's evening while Klára was in the privacy of her own room, she opened a message given to her earlier that day by Father Matthäus. The encrypted message was from the Countess. She wrote…

> *Our friends have word that Hitler recently met with his inner circle… important plans were discussed… notes were taken… could you make a search?. . . the topic to look for… Living Space or Military Force… any information will be invaluable.*

Klára reread the message, crumpled it, opened the door of her bedroom's ceramic stove and tossed the paper into the glowing fire. Franz was away on business, Klára had lost track of where exactly, so the next morning seemed a good time to begin a search for the needed information.

"Hedy, I need to go into Franz's study again, but it's locked."

"Inge has an old ring of keys in the cellar. Maybe one of the keys will fit the door."

"We must find something important for Marta to do."

After several ideas were rejected, it was decided that Klára and András would take Marta with them to shop for a new winter coat for András; he had grown so tall. While they were away Inge and Hedy would go into Franz's office and go through the papers.

Klára gave Hedy the information needed for the search.

After Klára and Marta left the house with András, Inge tried each old key until the study door clicked open. Inge returned to the kitchen to keep watch while Hedy went straight to the desk. After carefully moving each stack and replacing it as exactly as possible, Hedy found a folder with the words "November Conference" written across the top. She opened it and scribbled down every word as quickly as possible. She put everything back as it was, walked out of the study, and locked the door behind her. She took her scribbles to the kitchen table and began to recopy them, knowing every word was terribly important.

November Conference... the ultimate goal is to conquer European ter-
ritories that can provide raw materials and space for agriculture for
the Reich... Force may be necessary against resisters... Hitler expressed
concern about the importance to make the greatest gain for the Reich at
the lowest risk... Germany intends to annex Austria and Czechoslovakia
at the earliest opportunity... whether by military or by politics remains
undecided... German military strength must rebuild to two hundred forty
thousand troops... all goals must be accomplished 1943 to 1945....

When Hedy finished writing, she folded the paper, placed it in her apron pocket, threw her original scribbles into the fire and eagerly awaited Klára's return. While Marta was busy giving András a bath, Hedy passed her notes to Klára at her supper. Klára thanked Hedy and Inge profusely for their efforts and for their bravery.

The next afternoon while Marta held András's hand outside the Gottlieb flower shop next to the Adlon Hotel, Klára stood inside the shop looking at branches of holly berries and tannenbaum. Klára casually greeted the Countess Maltzan and at the same time furtively passed on to her the important information written down by Hedy. The Countess purchased a small potted fir, left the shop and smiled at the handsome little boy standing proudly in his new navy coat as she walked past Marta and András.

A few moments later Klára emerged from the shop with an armful of holly branches. She seemed quite happy, "These should brighten the dreary days. Let's all go to the hotel for hot chocolate."

As Klára took András's hand, the chauffeur took her branches and then followed in the car behind the threesome. Klára, András, and Marta walked the short distance to the Adlon along the snow-covered sidewalk.

Budapest

Rudolf got out of the taxi, stepping into the deeply piled snow which covered the drive of his grandmother's house. Apparently no one had used the front entrance for weeks. Rudolf studied the old familiar house and breathed a deep sign of relief... *home again to stay, at least for a while.* His warm breath fogged the air and dissipated as he reached back into the cab to retrieve his bags. In addition to his new teaching duties at the Hungarian Academy of Drawing, he imagined there would be much to do in Budapest. Rudolf hoped this was the beginning of what he had always dreamed would be his life.

He climbed the stairs, opened the door and entered the dark house. The ancient László greeted him with a sincere, but feeble handshake and led him into the parlor. His still elegant grandmother, the Countess Alexandra, was waiting for him in the dimly lit room, seated by the fireplace. Dressed in her usual black, the diamond brooch holding her shawl in place reflected the fire brilliantly.

Alexandra smiled at her grandson, "We are so delighted that you've come back home to us, Rudolf." She wiped away her tears with a lace handkerchief, "Your trunks arrived before you, so we knew that this time you were really coming home."

Rudolf bent down to kiss her cheeks, her skin scented with lavender, "I had to be here for your birthday, grandmother. We must celebrate. Eighty-five is a very special number. I'm happy to see you looking so well."

"I don't want you or anyone to make a fuss." Alexandra looked away shyly, "I've had enough birthdays. This one certainly is not so special. I'm simply old, very old."

He laughed, kissed her again and took a seat beside her. They began to talk of times past and of things to come. When Alexandra tired, he went upstairs to his old room, opened the draperies and looked into the moonlit garden and beyond into the von Esté garden and house. He thought, *I must find a way to bring Klára back to Budapest, but for now there are more pressing matters.*

Upon Rudolf's return to Budapest, his first MI6 assignment was to gather information regarding the current political climate in Hungary and to analyze the intentions of Horthy's government. He began his report with a background explanation...

> *Unlike other former Austro-Hungarian countries, Hungary never became a republic, but instead chose to remain a kingdom with the Regent Horthy in power until the return of a king which has somehow never materialized. The upper echelon of Hungarian society remains the aristocracy who retain their lands and significant power within the parliamentary government.*
>
> *The aristocrats are not uniform in their political preferences...some are far-right conservatives and some are progressively democratic. Hungarians of German and Jewish origin dominate the middle class in which a large percentage of professional positions and industrial ownership has been held by Jews, a situation now in jeopardy. By far the majority of the Hungarian population is made up of a post-feudal peasant class.*
>
> *As this new year begins, Hungary is struggling with severe social and economic stress that has increased since the Great War, in particular among the young educated and peasants. Vast numbers of these Hungarian youth and peasants are unemployed and angry, they are looking for someone to blame. As two seemingly unrelated, disenfranchised elements they have become fertile ground for an active national socialist movement with strong anti-Semitic beliefs. The Hungarian far right, specifically Ferenc Szálasi's*

*National Party of Will, eagerly embraces the Jew as the one to blame for all
of Hungary's problems, just as the Germans have been led to do. I believe
that Hungary is on the brink of crisis. No doubt a move by the Hungarian
far right toward German Nazism is inevitable.*

*Next month a conference will be held in Budapest to discuss Hungary's
territorial claims… territories lost to Hungary with the signing of the 1920
Treaty of Trianon, long a contentious issue for Hungarians. Since neither
England nor France has any interest in renegotiating the conditions of this
treaty, Hungary is, and has been, looking to Germany for help to reacquire
these lost territories. The Italians encourage Hungary to improve relations
with Romania, Czechoslovakia and Yugoslavia, the countries that hold
large pieces of the former Hungarian territories. Both the Germans and
Italians appear to sympathize with Hungary and both have promised to
help Hungary regain these lands.*

*Although Hungary highly values its independence, a chance to regain
lost territories is a strong enticement, regardless of the obligations such
a favor might incur. The Regent, Admiral Horthy, is planning a trip to
Poland to discuss with the Poles their mutual distrust and dislike of the
Soviets. Both Poles and Hungarians are friendly with the Germans and
Italians.*

Rudolf hoped his report would stir the *Entente* to act in some significant way to
head off the German-Italian alliances with Hungary he suspected were forming, but he also assumed nothing would be done. He was fully aware that
Prime Minister Neville Chamberlain of the United Kingdom was determined
to avoid any confrontation with Hitler, to avoid war at any cost.

March

The *Anschluss* of Austria began at eight o'clock in the morning on the thirteenth of March when German forces marched across the frontier into Austria
while German planes flew overhead. Hitler's annexation of Austria into the
Third Reich met little opposition from the Austrian population. In fact, the
German soldiers were welcomed by Austrians waving flags and strewing flowers in the path of their "invasion." Most Austrians seemed pleased, even proud,
to become part of the German Reich. Many enthusiastically embraced fascism
and Hitler's ideals of Aryan superiority.

By the fifteenth of March, Adolf Hitler, an Austrian himself, stood on
the balcony of the *Neue Berg*, a part of the Hofburg Palace, and looked out
onto the *Heldenplatz*, Heroes' Square. He had successfully added Austria to

his realm without the slightest battle and felt great delight. Once Hitler had savored his Austrian success, his eyes turned to Czechoslovakia.

April, Budapest

Leopold and Tamás read in their newspaper that the national socialist government of Austria *invited* the Germans into Austria, at least according to the German account.

"This is just the beginning of German expansion, I fear," Leopold lamented and then he read about the actions of his own government.

"This month, the Hungarian Parliament, encouraged by Prime Minister Darányi, ratified the 'First Jewish Law.' Once again this law restricts the number of Jews allowed to participate in professions, act as administrators, or engage in commercial or industrial enterprises. The law specifically defines the term JEW as any person born to even one Jewish parent and includes as a Jew anyone who has practiced the religion of Judaism...even an apostate, one who had renounced Judaism, is still considered a Jew and subject to the restrictions.

"Insanity! What is the meaning of this law? What is its purpose?" Leopold was incensed; his face reddened, "What do they want these people to do? They are productive, intelligent citizens contributing for the good of Budapest and all of Hungary! Do they want to rid the country of her own people?"

"The policies of the Reich seem to have spread all the way to Budapest," stated Tamás, "I am amazed to see how powerful their fear-mongering campaign against our Jewish people has been and how quickly it has spread throughout Austria and Hungary."

"Worst of all, to my horror, this far-right government is using the noble ideals of Magyarization as a reason...a tool...to discriminate against our Jewish people," complained Leopold. "The national socialists corrupt everything they touch! I'm destroyed to think of poor Jakov Klein and the despicable events that ended his illustrious life. What are we coming to? I fear hell on earth is about to overwhelm us."

Then Leopold raised his eyes to Tamás, "We must bring Klára home!"

May

In May the Regent Horthy appointed Béla Imrédy as prime minister to replace the radical Darányi. Imrédy proudly proclaimed himself Hungarian, a Magyar! He had no use for German intervention in Hungarian affairs. Convinced that a Magyar was certainly as superior a race of men as an Aryan, Imrédy immediately prohibited all fascist group activities in Hungary, including Szálasi's Party of the National Will.

Imrédy did, however, agree with the Germans on one thing…they shared a "Jewish problem." Imrédy believed that the Jew was the source of all Hungary's troubles and as soon as he became the new prime minister he drafted the "Second Jewish Law." This law placed further restrictions on the Jewish people of Hungary, expanding bans on employment and specifically defining Jews by blood to include even those persons with one distant grandparent. The law further stipulated any attempt to convert from Judaism to the Christian faith would be held irrelevant by the Imrédy government. *Born a Jew, always a Jew!* The new prime minister's beliefs were quite abhorrent to Leopold, in particular, his use of Magyarization to explain his anti-Semitic policies.

As Leopold, Elizabeth, and Tamás sat on the terrace of the Lake Balaton villa sipping last year's wine, Leopold spoke his thoughts aloud, "They have completely corrupted the glorious ideal of Magyarization! This terrible law completely reverses the 1867 laws that gave every Jew equal citizenship in Austria and Hungary!"

"Don't let your anger get the better of you, Leopold," cautioned Elizabeth. "Here, let me wrap this shawl around your shoulders. The afternoon air is cool and I don't want you getting chilled."

"Imrédy's government makes me very upset, Betka!" responded Leopold. "How can we not be upset! They've taken the ideal of unity…to bring all the different peoples of Hungary working together under one language to make Hungary a great nation and, instead, this government uses Magyarization to divide us. For Imrédy it is *us* against *them*. *They* are not Magyars! We will not let them be Magyars, if they have even one drop of Jewish blood. *They* are not *us,* even if they have lived here for centuries."

"Imrédy does not understand that his policies make Hungary weak and vulnerable to the fascists," lamented Tamás. "Imrédy gives the fascists a cause, a reason. Now they can use Magyarization against our Jewish citizens. Imrédy places Hungary a step closer to fascism; a step closer to allying with Hitler's Germany."

"Imrédy claims to deplore fascists, but he is a fascist."

Despite Imrédy's edict to rid Hungary of fascist elements, Nazis grew in number, especially among the young, the military and the unemployed. In Vienna, Adolf Eichmann established the Gestapo office of Jewish Emigration and organized a plan of safe passage from Austria for Jewish citizens who could pay the price—an exorbitant price—for space on a train that would take them to a safe haven. If a Jew had the money, jewels, deeds, or another valuable commodity to exchange for passage, he could take advantage of the emigration plan. Through this exchange, freedom for money, Eichmann's office gained significant wealth.

When news reached Budapest of an opportunity for Jews to leave Austria safely, word spread rapidly. A way to escape the intolerable situation in Hungary was of particular interest to wealthy Hungarian Jews with Austrian connections.

Budapest

"Mama, we've come with a serious matter to discuss with you, may we come in?" Samuel and Rachael stood at Éva Klein's front door. Samuel held his hat in his hand and looked at his mother with great compassion. She frowned at his formality.

"Of course you can come in. When could you not come in?"

Éva led her son and daughter-in-law to the parlor. They all sat down. "What is it, Samuel? What has happened now?"

"I've lost my position at the apothecary, because I'm a Jew."

Samuel had a look in his eye that Éva recognized as righteous indignation. She had seen it before whenever Samuel's argument or opinion was proven right after he had suffered defeat.

"Papa was too trusting, even though I warned him long ago that we should leave Hungary. Now we have no choice. Delay is not possible. We cannot stay in Budapest any longer. None of us can stay here, Mama."

Éva wrung her hands in her apron. She looked around the room at the pictures of her family. She thought of Jakov's tomb and Sándor's name incised in stone at the synagogue.

"I'm taking Rachael and our children to Vienna. I have a friend who has arranged for us to take a train out of Austria. The Germans are charging an exorbitant price, but I can pay it. You must come with us, Mother. I'll pay for you and for Ferenc and Abram. We leave in two days."

Éva sighed deeply as she raised her head to look at Samuel and Rachael. They both had a frantic look in their eyes.

"We must leave for the sake of the children, Mother," Rachael said. "We want their grandmother to come with us, please."

"What about Rózsa and her children?"

Samuel shook his head, "We don't know what to do about Rózsa, Mother. Since she is not practicing her faith in Eger and her husband and his family are gentile, perhaps there will be no interest in Rózsa, certainly none in her children.

"We don't have the time to go to Eger to convince her to leave with us. We cannot hesitate; we must go now, the day after tomorrow."

"I don't know, Samuel. I'm not certain what we should do. I'll speak with Ferenc and Abram, when I see them." Éva stood up, "Will you stay for supper? Magda has made *shlishkes*. You like *shlishkes* don't you, Rachael?"

"We'll say hello to Magda, but we can't stay for supper, Mama. We must leave; there's much to do at home to prepare for our journey."

"Please, Mother, let us know your decision by tomorrow." Samuel and Rachael rose and began to walk toward the kitchen.

After Samuel and Rachael left, Éva and Magda sat at the kitchen table eating the delicious little potatoes tossed in sugar, breadcrumbs, and butter. For a while they did not speak, but at last Éva broke the silence, "I don't know what to do, Magda. You must make decisions, too. Evidently, things are going to become very hard for Jews in Budapest. You will want to be together with your family. They'll need you."

"Don't worry about me. My family has not practiced Judaism for generations. I love your family as my own," Magda spoke defiantly. "I'll stay with you as long as you need me."

"I hope Ferenc and Abram will show up tonight." Éva rubbed her eyes, "They worry me so. What can they be doing every day and night? It's become difficult for them to make their way to work at von Estés' and they can't be in school. Trouble! I know they're making trouble."

Late that night Éva, hearing steps on the stair, rose from her bed, put on her robe and walked into the hallway just as Abram came to the top stair and Ferenc stood by his bedroom door.

"What have you boys been up to? Have you had any supper?"

Lace curtains at the end of the hall allowed moonlight to filter into the dark hallway, slightly illuminating each of the three figures as they stood apart, but together.

"We've been with friends, Mama, nothing special," Abram said casually, "just coffee."

"Samuel and Rachael were here tonight. They're leaving Budapest for Austria. They paid passage to leave Austria by train. They want all of us to go with them. They will pay our passage, too."

"No, Mother, we can't go!" Ferenc protested fervently, "Neither Abram nor I can leave. We have work to do." He hesitated, "But you should go, Mother. You *must* go."

"What work do you and Abram have to do, Ferenc?"

"That's not for you to know, Mother." He was glad for the darkness that made it easier to speak furtively to the mother who knew him well. "There are things under way in Budapest that must be stopped or at least disrupted."

"I knew the two of you were making trouble, endangering yourselves. I demand that you stop! We must go with Samuel. I've made my decision!"

"Mama, we're doing good work," Abram put his arms around Éva, "not just for ourselves, Mama, but for our people. Someone has to fight them for the Jews' sake. Our leaders are old; they want *to wait and see what happens*, but Ferenc and I have seen and heard what is happening and we can't just sit and wait."

"Stop, Abram, you'll frighten Mother," warned Ferenc. "It's true, Mother, we do have obligations that we can't leave, but you must go—go now with Samuel. We'll come to you wherever you are after this government has been overthrown."

"How did my children become so political? So involved in these matters?" Éva sat down on the settee in the hallway and rubbed her forehead.

"I won't go either. The least I can do is feed you and take care of your needs while you engage in these dangerous things. Magda and I...we'll be here for you."

The boys protested, but Éva wouldn't hear it, so they both kissed her tenderly and went to their beds. Éva went back to hers as well, but sleep did not come until the early hours of morning.

July, Switzerland

Rudolf traveled to Lake Geneva for an international conference in Evian les Bains on the French side of the lake to provide a report on the rising persecution of Jews in Germany, Austria, Hungary and other like-minded countries. As unidentified clandestine agents, Rudolf, his British counterpart, Clive Jeffreys, and other agents attended the conference as non-speaking observers with contrived reasons for their attendance. The conference delegates represented more than thirty countries and were there to consider the fate of the Jewish people in Germany.

Written reports, some prepared by the secret agents, were intended to inform the delegates' understanding of the Jewish plight in Germany. In their debate, the delegates openly expressed sympathy for the Jewish people and rejected the harsh discrimination being used against them. But by the conference's end, every country participating declared they would not accept any Jewish immigrants because the Jewish refugees would have no financial assets or means to support themselves in foreign lands.

Rudolf and Jeffreys rowed out onto Lake Geneva where they could air their opinions and not be heard. The delegates' lack of will to intervene greatly disturbed both men, but neither was surprised by the lack of action.

"The Jews are caught in an impossible dilemma. They are forbidden by the Nazis to take their financial assets out of Germany and now no one is willing to give them refuge because they have no financial assets!"

"What can be done for them?" Jeffreys asked, "How can they save themselves?"

In the end, the conference agreed to form a committee to study the Jewish problem. A discussion on *International Humanitarian Law* ensued. A number of reports, compiled by the agents, contained pertinent information gathered from their network of covert contacts. Each report described the dire situation developing in Germany for certain unwanted populations. The numbers of persecuted Jews, Gypsies, and other "undesirables" were unclear in the reports, but the arrests and deportations to labor camps throughout Germany were suspected to be in the thousands.

Members of the conference believed the reports they heard and declared their compassion for those caught in this horrible situation. But, once again, in the end, even though some advocates implored the nations to act and act quickly, the delegates decided the current *International Humanitarian Law*, as it was written, could not be used to intervene in German internal affairs.

The conundrum for the conference was that Germany seemed to be arresting and imprisoning their own citizens whom they declared to be enemies of the German state and German people. International law was written specifically to protect prisoners held in foreign lands by that land's government. The law was not written to protect a government's own political adversaries who were being held within their own country.

When Rudolf and Jeffreys listened to these discussions between the nations' delegates, their frustration grew and their patience became exhausted. They found it almost impossible to believe the delegates could remain unmoved by the detail of what they had read from the reliable sources presented.

With great passion, the agents, including Rudolf, became the only advocates for the oppressed. "The Nazis intend to incarcerate all those they deem to be socially and racially *undesirable* in Germany." Rudolf whispered to Jeffreys, "*Undesirables*, all of them—Jews and Gypsies, homosexuals, the unemployed, the disabled and deformed, alcoholics and anyone else who opposes them, including Catholic and Protestant clergy!"

Clive shook his head in despair as he and Rudolf walked from the conference, "The Nazi plan is to rid Germany and its allies of all those they have designated as a threat to the Reich. Even though this threat to humanity is well under way, it must be stopped!"

"Thousands of Jews and Gypsies have already fled Germany for safety. You know that many Jews have landed in Britain and a great number of them joined the British army," stated Jeffreys. "They've sworn allegiance to King George to join the fight against the Nazis, a battle they're determined to win! The world ought to do something for them before it's too late!"

As a compromise, the International Red Cross agreed to make a formal request to the Reich for permission to visit the labor camps. But the Red Cross stipulated that if the Reich refused, the Red Cross would make no further attempt to visit the German camps or intervene in Germany's business. Rudolf left Switzerland disappointed by the nations' inept response, but determined to never stop gathering information for MI6 on Nazi actions and influences in Hungary.

Unfortunately, the results of the conference, its failure to act on the plight of Jews, emboldened the German Nazis to push ahead with their heinous plans for the Jews and other undesirables of Europe. The Nazis reveled in Europe's lack of interest in the Jewish problem and were elated to see that all of Europe had isolated the Jews and would not intervene in the Nazis' plans. The Nazis had freedom to proceed as they desired.

Summer, Lake Balaton

Leopold and Tamás spent their weekends at Lake Balaton and their week days in Budapest at the wine company, but their minds were on the events surrounding Hungary that summer. They heard about the results of the international conference on humanitarian law and were, as Rudolf had been, disgusted by the nations' inability to act. Leopold could not shake his ominous feelings about the future. Leopold told Tamás that he was going for a walk in the vineyard and would return in time for supper.

Leopold left the cool shade of the gazebo and walked with Fejedelem past the press and into the dusty rows of vines. *The harvest at least will be hearty this year*, he thought as he passed by the clusters of plump green grapes. He walked a distance all the while thinking of Hungary... *Horthy has created an intolerable situation. Imrédy will destroy Hungary with his prejudice and cruel policies. How can they envision Hungary without thinking of her whole peoples? There is no such being as a pure Magyar. We are all mixed up together for a thousand years. They are leading Hungary straight into the grasp of Germany.*

Leopold stopped to catch his breath. It was difficult, his chest ached. He felt so tired that he let himself slip to the ground. Fejedelem lay down by Leopold's side and put his head on Leopold's knee. Leopold patted his companion's head and whispered, *"Klára."* He could see her as a child running through the vines laughing and calling to him, *"Find me, Papa, catch me, Papa."* Oh, how he longed to have her near to him again, away from Berlin and away from her husband, the Nazi.

Tamás stood on the veranda looking toward the vineyards rubbing his jaw. Silva laid out the supper for the maid to serve and called to him, "Has the Duke returned? Supper is ready."

Elizabeth came out onto the veranda, "He's been gone too long, Tamás. Please go find him."

Tamás called to two of the gardeners to accompany him and the three men began walking through the rows of vines. Finally, they found Leopold leaning against a trellised vine in the shade of its leafy canopy. His eyes were closed.

Tamás could hardly speak, "Leopold, Leopold, are you all right?"

He breathed a great sigh of relief when Leopold stirred and opened his eyes, "Yes, yes, I'm all right, just tired."

"You nearly scared the life out of me, Leopold." Tamás sat down beside him.

"Here you are being 'the nanny' again," Leopold laughed. "You've always been there for me, Tamás, through all these years. You are my dearest friend." Leopold patted Tamás's arm and looked at him with a serious expression, "I didn't feel well, Tamás. I had to stop walking and rest. I must be getting very old."

"You're younger than I am, Leopold," scolded Tamás. "Perhaps, you're simply hungry or thirsty. Elizabeth sent me to fetch you. Silva has supper ready."

Tamás and the gardeners helped Leopold to his feet and Tamás was surprised at how shaky Leopold seemed. They helped him all the way back to the villa. Elizabeth and Silva were quite concerned to see him unable to walk on his own, but Leopold was not one to be fussed over, so they said very little. Instead, Silva suggested that Leopold and Elizabeth have dinner on the veranda where they could both sit on chaise lounges and have their supper served on lap trays.

"Well, Betka, this is the life!" smiled Leopold. "I feel like an ancient Etruscan lounging around on cushions. This *csirkeleves*, chicken soup, is very good, but I can't eat it all."

The two sat together on the veranda until Tamás came to get them. Tamás helped Leopold upstairs to his bedroom where he stayed for a few days resting while Elizabeth and Silva pampered him.

For the remainder of summer Elizabeth and Tamás avoided politics in conversations with Leopold. They encouraged him to think of less disturbing topics and to find more pleasing subjects. Leopold obeyed their demands to rest and build his strength, at least until their return to Budapest.

September, Berlin

As he had every September, Franz returned home after the annual Nuremberg Party Rally exhilarated by the experience. He was in the best of moods as he related the details of speeches by Hitler and Rosenberg and described the crowds of thousands at the spectacular event. "The theme this year was 'Rally for Greater Germany' in honor of all the new territories acquired by the Reich. Hitler was especially joyous in his praises for the S.S. and our accomplishments on his behalf."

Obviously enthusiastic about the Hitler Youth organization, Franz seemed exhuberant. "Their marching and athletic abilities, their wholesomeness and dedication to the Führer and to Germany! I will be very proud of András the day he becomes old enough to be part of such a noble group of young boys! Boys who know the importance of blood and country and loyalty to the Führer," Franz spoke in a firm voice filled with pride. "They were such handsome, well-disciplined boys."

He pulled a tissue-wrapped package from his briefcase, "Some of us had special uniforms made for our little boys. Boys too young to be real members of the *Deutsches Jungvolk* but we wanted them to know that same sense of pride, so here's a very special little present for András."

"Go dress him, Marta. I want to see how he'll look."

Marta was ecstatic at the idea and left the room immediately, headed for the nursery. Klára remained by the doorway watching Franz empty his briefcase of folders and papers, wondering what grievous plans they contained. She forced herself to say something, lest Franz would question her attention to the papers he held in his hands.

"I had lunch at the Adlon with Mitzi Müller and Astrid Brenner yesterday. Their husbands were at the rally, too. Did you see them there?"

"Of course, I did," Franz seemed annoyed. "Since when have you been interested in those two? I thought they weren't your type, non-musical...loyal Nazis. I thought they bored you."

"They do," Klára answered matter-of-factly, "but I thought it might please you if I took an interest in fellow officers' wives."

Franz smiled, "What did you talk about?"

"Oh, the important things...the best shops for a permanent wave, for chocolates and lingerie."

"How would you know about permanent waves?"

"I don't, personally," Klára admitted, "but I suggested a salon anyway."

Just at that moment András marched into the study. With prompting from Marta, the little boy stood very straight, stretched out his arm toward his father and, in the strongest five-year-old voice he could muster, shouted "Heil Hitler."

Franz had never been more thrilled by his son than at that moment. "Bravo! Well done, András! You are growing up to be a very fine lad! Look how handsome he is. The uniform looks very nice.

"There seems to be some room for growing." Franz studied the little brown shirt and black lederhosen. "This was a very good idea of mine."

Marta shared Franz's enthusiasm and showered András with compliments.

Klára was aghast, but concealed her feelings as best she could. Seeing her little boy in such a uniform, his little upper right arm encircled by a red armband with its white stripe and swastika made her feel ill. András paraded around the study in the uniform that represented so many things she knew to be evil, despicable, terrifying.

"Well, what do you think of our little soldier, Klára?" Franz asked the question already knowing exactly what she thought, but he wanted to watch her struggle to find an acceptable answer.

"He is a handsome boy," she smiled at András, "who likes parades and pretending as all boys do."

Early October, Budapest

Tamás entered the library with coffee and freshly made *fánk*, "Silva thought you might enjoy a mid-morning treat after our late night." Tamás knelt to gather the still scattered photographs and memorabilia from the carpet. "How are you feeling this morning?"

"Ah, yes, that would be very nice, Tamás. Thank you and thank Silva for us. Her *fánk* is the best in Hungary," Leopold said as he reached for another sugary doughnut, "I do feel content, but a bit tired."

"Leopold told me about the two of you reminiscing into the wee hours last night," smiled Elizabeth, "it seems to have been a lovely adventure in the past, according to Leopold"

"Yes, it was good…to remember when we were so young…so many adventures."

"At least, I slept without nightmares when I went back to bed," Leopold stated flatly, "but the nightmare of Klára and András in Berlin still torments me by the light of day."

Since the von Estés return after their summer at the lake, Elizabeth and Tamás continued to shield Leopold from political news, especially news coming from Germany, but current events once again caught Leopold's interests. Neither Elizabeth nor Tamás could deny him his newspapers or the radio or discussions with his friends and, so, his stress began to rise again, especially when he read of recent developments between Germany and Czechoslovakia, Hungary's neighbor.

According to reports in the newspaper, Leopold read…*Hitler is making strong demands on Czechoslovakia. Hitler demands independence for the Germans living in the Sudetenland, territory that Hitler ultimately wants surrendered to Germany.* Leopold could not help but wonder what Hitler was up to. The Sudetenland portion of Czechoslovakia was part of the disputed territories Austria-Hungary lost through the 1920 *Treaty of Trianon*. Leopold was surprised to read…*Hitler's goal to acquire the Sudetenland seems to be supported by both Britain and France.* Again, Leopold wondered why.

After a summer of negotiations, Czechoslovakia finally realized the futility of their efforts to resist invasion by the Third Reich. For the government of Czechoslovakia, it was painfully clear that no one would come to their aid against Hitler. The British and the French were determined to avoid war. In late September, representatives of France, Italy and Britain, including Prime Minister Chamberlain, met with the Germans, Poles, and Czechs in Munich. In their presence, the President of Czechoslovakia signed *The Munich Agreement* that officially gave the Sudetenland territory to Germany. By early October, the German Wehrmacht moved into Czechoslovakia without a shot fired, moving ever closer to Hungary.

Late October, Budapest

Leopold sat in his Budapest office; he looked up from the stack of papers on his desk and let his eyes move slowly around the room. It was a fine office. Fejedelem stood up, stretched, yawned, and licked his master's hand. Leopold rose from his desk, walked to the window, pushed it up and leaned out. The air was fresh and brisk; he loved fall best of all; he breathed in the fresh breeze. He waved at the concertina player who stood across the street, the music drifting sweetly up to him. He loved Gypsy melodies. Leopold shut the window. He felt tired. He would quit for the day. He put on his coat and hat, left his office with Fejedelem at his side, said good-bye to Judit, took the lift down to the ground floor, and left the building.

He had only walked to the corner when he fell to the sidewalk. The Gypsy concertina player saw him fall, as did the owner of the tailor shop, and the *maître d'* of the café across the street. They all ran to help him.

"I know this man," said the *maître d'*, "it's Duke von Esté. We must call an ambulance for him."

Fejedelem lay by Leopold's side protectively, sensing that his beloved master needed help. The three men found Leopold short of breath, red-faced, and very disoriented, but conscious.

By the time the ambulance arrived, Leopold was feeling a bit better and demanded that he be taken home rather than to the hospital. He thanked the men who had come to his aid, but insisted he was merely tired and needed to rest at home. When the ambulance delivered him to his front door, Elizabeth and Tamás and the entire household went into a state of panic.

"What were you thinking, Leopold?" scolded Elizabeth. "Why didn't you call Tamás or Auguste to come early to fetch you? Were you thinking of walking all the way home?"

"Leopold, I would have been there for you in minutes," exclaimed Tamás.

"Stop fussing over me, you two," protested Leopold. "It's my favorite kind of day, sunny but cool. Fejedelem and I wanted to walk. A walk is good for me. I just simply suddenly felt tired and a bit dizzy, that's all."

"Come into the library. Ana, please fix a bed for the duke on the sofa. Come Leopold, lie down," Elizabeth's voice had resolve. Leopold's protestations did nothing to relieve her anxiety as she gave directions, "Tamás, please call Doctor Kovács to come right away."

"Oh, Elizabeth, that is not necessary," Leopold argued, even though he was still short of breath and his face was very flushed.

"I insist. Humor me, please," said Elizabeth as she and Ana tucked the sheet over the leather sofa and fluffed the pillows. The two women helped Leopold down onto the sofa. He seemed frail and somewhat shaky.

Elizabeth's heart beat in her throat; she felt a rise of anxiety in her chest. "Please, my darling, rest quietly. I will sit here by your side until the doctor arrives."

Silva brought a pot of herbal tea and cups into the library. "I made a blend of chamomile, marjoram and rosemary with a bit of lemon verbena for you, Sir. A cup of this should help your circulation and let you get some rest." She placed a cool cloth scented with lavender on his brow.

"You're so good to us all, Silva." Leopold touched Silva's hand and smiled at her, "Tamás did a very good thing when he brought you into our lives."

"Yes, he did, Leopold," Elizabeth agreed as she thanked Silva and held the cup to Leopold's lips. "Now drink this good remedy Silva has made for you."

Leopold sipped the tea and settled back into the pillows. He closed his eyes. Elizabeth, Tamás and Silva remained silent as they watched him sleep. Leopold had grown thin and older over the last few years. Worry over politics had brought much stress into his life, as did his fears for Klára and little András.

Within the hour, Doctor Kovács arrived. Ana brought him directly into the library. He spoke quietly with Elizabeth and Tamás, then gently awakened Leopold. After his cursory examination, Doctor Kovács reported that Leopold had surely suffered a heart attack and seemed severely weakened by it. He needed bed rest and no stress. Doctor Kovács also suggested the family send for Klára to return home as soon as possible. He held Elizabeth's hand and calmly told her that he believed Leopold's heart was quite damaged.

That evening Tamás directed Auguste and one of the gardeners to help carry Leopold upstairs to his bed. Fejedelem followed them faithfully and curled up on the floor beside his master. Leopold felt more comfortable in his own room and finally drifted off to sleep, until he was awakened by Father Nikola. They spoke quietly for a while, then the priest gave him communion and they prayed together. Father Nikola blessed his old friend and promised to return in the morning.

On his way out Father Nikola passed Silva at the doorway as she brought in a serving tray for Leopold with another bowl of *csirkeleves* and more tea.

While Silva helped Leopold with his supper, he requested that Elizabeth play the piano for a bit and leaned back against the pillows to listen as the music drifted up the stairs and into his room. He opened his eyes now and then just to look around at the familiar objects in the room. His gaze remained on images of Stefan and Klára and András in gilded frames on the dresser. Tamás sat nearby and asked if there was anything he wanted.

Leopold slept for a while, he was unsure of how long, but when he opened his eyes again he saw Cili in an aura of light standing at the foot of his bed. He was quite surprised. Evening had come and his room was dark except for the table lamp on the bedside table. He stared at her image and a smile came to his lips.

"Tamás, did you see Cili standing there?" Leopold lifted his hand toward the foot of the bed, his voice only a weak whisper.

Tamás moved closer to Leopold, "Cili? Do you mean Elizabeth?"

"No...no...oh...I...I remember Cili has been gone for many years, but she has come back, Tamás. I think for me. I saw her in the vineyard, too, last summer."

"Sleep, Leopold, you'll feel better tomorrow," but for the first time, Tamás doubted his own words.

Elizabeth entered the darkened room and took a seat very near Leopold. "How is he Tamás? He seems so weak, so unlike my strong Leopold."

"He enjoyed your music. I think it calmed him. He fell asleep smiling."

Neither Elizabeth nor Tamás left his side. Silva and Ana sat nearby. Just past midnight Leopold motioned to Tamás and whispered in a faint voice, *"my dearest friend..."* Leopold's breath was very short, as though he was gasping for air. His eyes opened wide, he whispered, *"Klára...Tamás...our Rudolf must bring her home."* Then he became very agitated and tried to rise from his bed.

"I promise, Leopold, we have already sent for her," Tamás assured him.

"We have sent for her. Klára will be here soon. Be calm, my sweet," implored Elizabeth, as she wiped the perspiration from his brow. Silva brought fresh cool cloths to her.

Leopold's eyes were closed, but his lips continued to move. Tamás leaned down to hear what he was saying. He realized Leopold was whispering the names of those he loved, those who had passed before him... *Cili...Stefan... Christián...Gabriele...Mama...Papa.* Tamás wondered if it was as Leopold had said, his loved ones had come for him. Grief overwhelmed Tamás. He had never imagined his life without Leopold. Tamás turned to Silva, "Please summon Father Nikola and Doctor Kovács to come again, quickly."

In the earliest hours of morning Father Nikola and Doctor Kovács sat in Leopold's room; he was terribly weak. Just as the first morning light sifted through the lace curtains, Leopold opened his eyes, grasped Elizabeth's hand and in a raspy voice murmured, *"My sweet Betka..."* He brought her hand to his lips as she laid her head beside his chest. Tears ran down her cheeks onto the blanket. She tried to stifle the moans that were rising in her throat. How could she go on without her Leopold?

Leopold did fall asleep again, holding Elizabeth's hand with a slight smile on his lips. With a contented expression, Leopold slipped peacefully away from them.

Leopold's death seemed so sudden to those who loved him, who surrounded him in that room. Both Elizabeth and Tamás sat by his bedside through the morning and into the afternoon. It was difficult to accept that he had left them. At the urging of Doctor Kovács and Silva, they rose at last from his side. Elizabeth and Tamás embraced each other and offered kind words of consolation. They shared a great love for Leopold.

Silva, though heartbroken, found solace in keeping busy, beginning her duties immediately. She strewed dried rose petals and lavender over Leopold as he lay on his death bed. Throughout the house she turned the mirrors to the wall and draped them with black cloth, prepared the blackened cedar wreaths for the front doors and began cooking foods for the family and the guests who would come to pay their respects to the great gentleman, Duke Leopold von Esté. Tamás returned to the kitchen to help Silva and to direct Ana and her staff of maids to prepare the rooms for guests. He also sent a second telegram to Klára.

Berlin

A spectacular autumn morning found Klára seated comfortably on a sunny park bench watching András play with other children while the ever-vigilant Marta stood talking with other nannies in the shade of the linden trees turned golden against a bright blue, cloudless sky. Klára saw Hedy crossing the street, entering the park and coming toward her. She had such an urgent look about her that Klára walked to meet her.

"You have a telegram from Budapest, Baroness. I thought that I should bring it to you at once."

Klára opened the yellow envelope and read the words... *Klára... Return to Budapest... Your father is very ill... Tamás*

"Come, we must go!" Klára called to Marta and András, "Come now, András!"

András ran toward her, he could tell by his mother's tone that something serious had happened, "Mommy, what's wrong? Mommy?"

"My beloved Papa, your sweet grandpapa, is very ill, András," she answered him. "We must travel to Budapest right away."

Along with Marta they hurried out of the park, across the street and into their home. Klára knocked on the study door where Franz was working, entered and informed him of her news. She told Franz she wanted to leave as soon as possible. Franz offered no words of concern for her father or compassion for her, but instead simply insisted that she take the train to Budapest. "The train will be safer than flying," he told her, "and take Marta with you."

Proud of these caveats, Franz enjoyed placing stipulations, limitations on his permissions for Klára and of course, he wanted Marta to keep an eye on things. "You must take Marta with you, if Marta does not go, then András must stay here in Berlin with her."

Franz barely looked at Klára as he packed his briefcase, "I'm leaving for Poland tonight," he told her, "I expect you to be back in Berlin by the time I have returned in three weeks." He stood up from his desk, "I have appointments now. You may be gone by the time I return." Then he added, "Have a safe trip. Give my regards to your mother."

Just as Franz opened the front door to leave, a second telegram arrived. He took it and handed it to Klára, "Another wire for you." Without the least curiosity, he hurried down the stairs to his waiting car and sped away. Klára opened the envelope. She gasped and sank down onto the velvet bench just inside the doorway.

Hedy came to her side, "What is it, Madam? More bad news?"

"Oh, Hedy, my dear Papa has died. I was not there by his side. I loved him so. I should have gone home last summer to be with him."

Klára wiped away the tears that streamed from her eyes, "Please help me pack some things for András and for me. We must leave for Budapest as soon as possible."

BOOK III

1938 – 1945

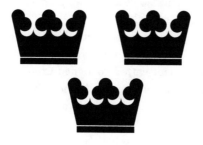

1938
October, Budapest

Billowing puffs of steam rose as the train lurched against some unseen weight holding its giant wheels immovable. *This train is as anxious to leave Berlin as I am,* thought Klára as she rubbed vapor from the glass and peered out into the almost empty Friedrichstrasse station. Only a few people stood by huge concrete pillars waving good-byes to passengers in other cars. Finally, with a great surge of energy, the train broke free into the night. Metal grinding against metal accompanied by whistles echoing through the hollow depot were sounds at once soothing and unnerving to Klára. Darkness enveloped the train as it left the station.

Klára settled back into the tufted velvet cushions and took a deep breath knowing they would not arrive in Budapest until late the next day. Her compartment private, she sat alone with András as he slept in the narrow bed beside her. Great mental anxiety seized her as thoughts of her beloved father came to mind and made her lips tremble. How much she loved him and how strange it would be to arrive home and he would not be there; thoughts, too, of Rudolf, wondering if he would be there.

With a gloved hand Klára rubbed her aching forehead as she absentmindedly took off her hat and ran her fingers through her dark hair. She looked down at András as he slept with a contented expression, making her smile, but then thoughts of Franz came to mind. *Franz.* She sighed. She was glad his work had called him away. *His work*... Klára shuddered... *how much our lives have changed since such an innocent beginning in Cologne.* She thought of their wedding in the *Marienkapelle* and her Papa's words that day, "Are you certain this is the young man you want?"

Certainly he is not, should have been my answer.

A light tapping at the compartment door interrupted Klára's thoughts; a soft voice spoke from the passageway, "It's Marta."

Klára opened the door for Marta as she brought in a tray with a plate of biscuits, a tea service for two and a flask of milk for András. Marta, still wrapped in her gray wool coat and felt hat, set the tray down, took off her things and sat down.

As she watched Marta sip her tea, Klára thought to herself... *I was forced to bring you with us, Marta, but you will have no influence in Budapest. I do not trust you at all and I have plans that will leave you out of András's life forever.*

The two women settled in for the journey with their cups of hot tea and biscuits, but with no conversation. The sound of bells coming closer, then fading away made Klára keenly aware that the speeding train carried her and

András farther away from Berlin with every mile. She sighed with some relief. Eventually, Klára excused herself to the adjoining sleeping compartment while Marta made her bed in the compartment with András. The rhythm of the train's movement kept him sleeping through the evening.

Klára had fallen asleep quickly, but was awakened by the train's change of rhythm, a slowed syncopated sound of wheels on the track. Still very dark, she knew it was far too soon to have arrived in Budapest. Klára sat up in her bed, pulled the window shade away from the glass and strained to see out into the darkness. At first she was not certain of what she was seeing. Her train continued to move, but slowly, as it passed a group of cars sitting on a side track—dark gray boxcars sitting still, illuminated only by flashes of light from her own train. Klára saw *them*—their eyes, their hands and arms sticking out from between the slats, and she knew who they were.

By late afternoon the train pulled into Budapest's Nyugati Station. Klára peered through the window searching for Tamás. At last she saw him standing rather stiffly on the platform, so formal, so familiar, in his finely tailored gray wool suit. Klára continued to wave her hand until at last he spotted her and tipped his hat to her. She smiled widely; it was good to see Tamás again. The train came to an abrupt stop with a forward jerk, steam rising all around the outside. Klára wrapped her woolen scarf around her neck, the weather looked very cold. Marta had dressed András, but Klára checked his muffler, making sure it wrapped around his ears and gave him a kiss on the nose, "Grandmother will be so pleased to see you. She'll be very surprised to see how you've grown. And now you'll get to see Tamás again, he'll be so happy to see you, too."

Only a few moments passed before Tamás entered the compartment with two porters. Klára took his extended hand and held it in hers. "I'm so sorry for your loss, Tamás." She noticed how grayed his dark hair had turned, how furrowed his brow since they last met. "I know how much my father meant to you and you to him."

Tamás, his eyes lowered, bowed to her and kissed her hand. He raised his eyes to hers, they were welled with tears, and answered, "You are very kind, Baroness, it is true that I miss the Duke, he was my life-long friend." Tamás regained his composure and added, "But it is I who should be offering my condolences to you, Madam. I know how close you were to your papa."

"Tamás, here's my big boy, almost six," Klára held András's shoulders as he stood in front of her, "Do you remember Tamás, András? You've not seen him in a very long time, since we were last at Lake Balaton. I know that you and Tamás will become very good friends."

"A pleasure to see you again at last, Master András," Tamás bowed to the child's level and shook his hand. "It is true. We shall become the best of friends, just as your grandfather and I were for many years."

"I'm very happy to see you again, Tamás," András replied. "My mother likes you very much."

"He looks just as your Papa looked at his age," Tamás said aloud as he took his handkerchief from his pocket once again to wipe the tears from his eyes. With formal authority Tamás organized their departure from the train to a large touring car.

Being home again brought Klára joy beyond her expectations. A year and a half had passed since she was in Hungary and seven since she had been at her home in Budapest. Klára greeted the chauffeur, Auguste, as the car left the station and entered Teréz körut. The porters loaded their trunks onto a small truck and followed the car through the streets of Budapest. Every architectural feature, every street, even the people hurrying along icy sidewalks, looked familiar to Klára. She rolled down the window and breathed in the aromas of her beloved Budapest. The car turned left onto the broad avenue—her street, Andrássy Avenue—lined with great mansions, private gardens and huge sycamore trees, their leafless branches now covered with frost.

As they rode down the avenue, Tamás turned in his seat and spoke to her, "The young count has returned home to honor your father. He has inquired as to your arrival."

Klára smiled discreetly; she would be happy to see Rudolf again. *Tamás still refers to him as the young count,* she thought, *even though he is now well past thirty.*

And then there it was. Her family home. She saw the campanile first as its height rose above the trees. The stately Italianate mansion stood far enough back from the avenue to allow a semi-circular drive in the front where Auguste parked near the entrance. Snow-dusted topiary marked the splayed front steps that led up to great double doors draped with black ribbons and cedar wreaths. Tamás held open the front door as Klára, holding András' hand, stepped into the reception hall.

Tamás whispered to her, "Your mother is waiting for you in the library."

Klára knelt down to unwrap András from his outer clothing, "Now you will go to see Silva. She makes the most delicious desserts. Remember?" András nodded and smiled broadly. "And we know how much you love desserts. If you give Silva a big hug, she may give you two helpings."

Klára tousled his black hair and gave directions to Marta, "Take András to the kitchen. Tamás will show you the way. András can see Mother tomorrow when he's rested. Go have your supper now."

Klára took off her coat as she slowly surveyed the hall. It was exactly as she remembered it. She noticed the heavy wood paneling that smelled of wax, the medieval tapestries brought from their family castle that hung from the ceiling against the paneling, and the Mucha stained glass windows on the landing of the great staircase. From where Klára stood she could see into the dining room to the far wall, on which hung a large sepia photograph in an ornate, gilded frame—the photograph of her Hapsburg family, taken at a wedding, the date *"October 21, 1911"* in white printing across the corner. The handsome groom and bride, Duke Karl and Duchess Zita, were surrounded by the Emperor, Franz József, and dozens of Klára's family members. *It's so good to be home*, she thought, *but it will never be the same wonderful place without dear Papa.*

Klára entered the library to find her mother sitting behind her husband's desk. Elizabeth stood and Klára fell into her arms, both of them let all their grief spill out onto each other. Still as beautiful as ever, Elizabeth, dressed in black, seemed so distraught and devastated that Klára felt alarmed by her mother's expression and posture. They spoke quietly about Leopold and his last words. Elizabeth consoled her daughter, assuring her, "Your papa thought of you and spoke of his love for you and András even as he passed from this earth. He died peacefully, in his bed with Tamás and me and Father Nikola at his side."

At last their conversation turned.

"Mother, I want to leave András here in Budapest with you. Marta will return to Berlin with me."

"Although I understand you may have good reason to do such a thing, Klára, it is never right to separate a boy from his father." Elizabeth's words sounded hollow to Klára, without her mother's usual conviction.

"Franz is not in Berlin, Mother, he's in Poland. I'm not sure at all when he'll return. Actually, I'm seriously considering closing up the house and coming back here before Christmas."

"Are you thinking of leaving your husband, Klára?" Elizabeth appeared to be quite distressed as she wrung her hands and avoided looking into Klára's eyes. "That would be a difficult choice. You must accept that you are bound together by God."

"No, I'm not thinking of leaving Franz, but you cannot know how he has changed. He has become so dark, Mother." Klára did not want to reveal too much, "Franz has taken such an opposite direction from my sensibilities."

"Well, dear, perhaps you can help him change his direction." Elizabeth took a small gasp of air, "I...I regret..." Then Elizabeth looked up at Klára, "Perhaps your expectations are too rigid, Klára. Every young marriage has problems. It takes work and understanding, more on your part than his. You know that."

"Yes, I do know that, Mother, but that isn't it." Klára studied her mother who seemed suddenly distant, lost in thought. Klára tried to explain more fully, "In Berlin the talk is all about war and the Nazis have fooled the people into wanting it! Franz and his friends do not fear war, instead they arrogantly desire it. It's maddening! They dismiss all reason and speak of their goals as glorious, as though something divine—in the name of Christ they find their authority, but it's all lies, Mother, very dark and wrong." Klára rose from her chair, "The Nazis encourage young children to march around in uniforms with sticks pretending they're soldiers. I will not see András caught up in this evil game Franz and his friends are planning."

As Klára paced in front of the book shelves, she continued, "I was too young during the *Great War* to have real memories of it, Mother, but I do certainly remember more recent battles and the tragedies, the losses they caused. I have looked into yours and Papa's faces and I have seen the sadness in your eyes that never goes away and I know the empty place in your hearts and in mine. Stefan's loss has never been fully understood nor the sacrifice accepted. Now, this great sorrow for you, Mommy, losing Papa." Klára tenderly touched her mother's hand, "Papa would be against another war. I know he would."

Elizabeth nodded her head slowly in agreement, "Yes, he warned against war. You may leave András with me, Klára; certainly, if you feel that he would be in danger in Berlin. The rest we can speak of later. It is all too much for me now. I know that Silva is longing to see you and to feed you. Go now. Come to my room later for a goodnight kiss. I am so glad that you are home, but now I am very tired."

Truly, Silva was waiting for Klára in her cozy kitchen with its delicious aromas coming from cooking pots and a warm oven. The ever-affectionate Silva warmly embraced Klára and expressed her sympathies, "Your great father will be missed by all. He was the finest of gentlemen. Your András is a darling boy. He favors your papa very much, just like a little Leopold. András and Marta have already retired to the nursery." Silva continued, her bright blue eyes smiling, "We are all so happy you're home, Miss Klára. Are you starving? Sit down. I've made all your favorites."

Klára patted the head of Fejedelem, her papa's beloved Vizsla hound while Silva shook her head, "Poor old Fejedelem. He hardly knows what to do with himself. He so misses the Duke."

Klára took her old place at the big wooden table in the center of the kitchen. Her place since she was a child. Silva's kitchen held many of her dearest memories, especially of times when the extraordinary Slovak cook let her help create scrumptious delights. Klára breathed in the tempting aromas, "So, Silva, what do you have for me? I'm afraid I'll leave here twice as big as I've come."

After an hour or so of pleasant conversation with Silva, including Klára's news of her intent to return permanently to Budapest as soon as possible and a second helping of *gulyásleves*, Klára said good night. "I feel exhausted. I think I'll go up to bed now. Thank you, Silva. Your *gulyásleves* is more delicious than I remembered. It's so good to be home again. I must give Mother a kiss before she falls asleep," Klára embraced Silva once more.

"Here, Miss Klára, take this cup of chamomile tea and *szalonnásrántotát*, eggs and bacon scramble, up to your mother. She's had no supper."

Klára took the small tray and walked down the darkened hall to the stair, passing by a large baroque mirror turned toward the wall, draped with a black cloth. Upstairs, she knocked softly at her mother's door, entered, crossed the room and set the tray on her mother's bedside table. Elizabeth sat propped up in bed against a bevy of overstuffed pillows. The large room, lit only by one lamp, seemed oppressively dark and heavy, befitting her mother's despair. Klára kissed her mother's cheek and poured a cup of tea. "Silva sent this tea, so you can get a good sleep and *szalonnásrántotát*, because she said you've had no supper." Klára patted her mother's hand and kissed her again, "I'll leave you now. Good night, Mommy."

At the opposite end of the hall was the nursery. Klára gently opened the door and tiptoed into the room, dark except for a shaft of light that fell across the floor. The light came from the slightly ajar door of Nanny Marta's adjoining room. Klára leaned over András's bed. Her eyes, once adjusted to the dim light, could just make out his face, asleep against his pillow. *How precious he is...he will be happy here.* She kissed his forehead, tucked him in, and tiptoed out of the room. Klára sensed Marta standing in her doorway, but chose not to acknowledge her.

Klára crossed the hall to her own room...*her room*, of so many years. She turned on the bedside lamp only, wanting to keep the room as dark as her mother's had been. Ana, her mother's maid, had unpacked Klára's cases and put everything away. Pulling out a drawer to find her nightgown, sitting at *her dresser* and brushing her hair gave Klára the feelings of home she had missed. Klára walked to the window and pulled back the drapery. Several inches of snow covered the garden, lit only by moonlight. The trees stood like black skeletons, leafless, against a silvery sky. She allowed her eyes to wander beyond the shared garden wall to the back of the von Házy house to Rudolf's window. From her angle, she could only see the lighted window, but not beyond the window into the house. *There is a light...he must be there.* Her breath grew short; her heart beat faster.

Rudolf was there. He stood at his window, daring to look toward Klára's window. Suddenly the slightest hint of light... *the draperies must have parted...she must be there.* His breath grew short; his heart beat faster.

Klára's bed had been turned down for her; she slipped into it, nestled down and closed her eyes. For the first time in a very long time, she felt safe, incredibly and completely safe. How she longed to stay in Budapest and never leave again. Tears filled her eyes, but finally, she fell into a peaceful, much needed sleep.

—⁓—

Ana drew open the draperies allowing sunlight to fill the room. Klára yawned and stretched in her bed. Still, how good she felt to be home again.

"Good morning, Ana."

"Good morning, Miss...Baroness."

"Is András awake?"

"Oh, yes, he and your mother had breakfast together about an hour ago." Ana smiled at Klára. "He is such a handsome little boy; he looks so much like your father."

"Yes, he does, Ana."

"Would you like me to draw your bath first or to bring your breakfast?"

"Bath, please," Klára answered as she snuggled deeper into the down comforter. "Thank you, Ana. I'll go down for breakfast. It's wonderful to be home again, even though it will never be the same without Papa."

Ana nodded her head as she left the room. Both women felt the heavy weight of sadness.

Klára entered the library to find her mother sitting once again at Papa's desk, "Good morning, Mommy. Ana said you and András had breakfast together."

"Oh, yes, we did. He is a darling little boy, Klára. I look forward to his staying with us, but I dread your leaving." Elizabeth had a soulful look, "Can't you simply stay and send Marta back alone? Your Papa was so distressed about your living so far away…in Germany…with…" she turned her face away from Klára; she could not speak another word.

"I so regret that I didn't come back to Balaton last summer." Klára hurried to her mother's side and embraced her. "The thought that I caused Papa any anxiety is very painful to me," Klára held her mother close, "and now I'm upsetting you. I'm so sorry, Mommy."

"Then stay, Klára. I need you here and András will miss you terribly."

"I must go back to Berlin, Mommy, but I'll return to Budapest before Christmas. There are loose ends that need tying in Berlin, but I promise by Christmas I'll be back here with you and András."

"I will be very pleased to have you here with me, Klára. You have been missed by all of us," Elizabeth said as she held Klára's hand. "Now we must ready ourselves for Leopold's memorial service and for the people who will come to pay their respects. I expect many to visit since your Papa was so admired, so loved."

Extra staff had been hired to help Silva in the kitchen and Ana with the house. With all the new activity and busy people scurrying here and there, the once somber, quiet house became more tolerable for the family and staff who greatly missed the duke. By noon tempting aromas from Silva's kitchen filled the entire house.

Shortly after noon, Klára directed Marta to take the rest of the day as a holiday, "Explore Budapest, Marta. I'll take András with me to the service. There's no need for you to go with us to St. István's."

By one o'clock Tamás stood at the foot of the staircase prepared to escort Elizabeth and Klára to the car waiting for them in the drive. Silva and Ana would follow in a second car to the basilica.

Elizabeth appeared at the top of the stair, dressed in black from head to toe in a woolen suit and a black, veiled felt hat with black feathers. Klára and András joined her on the landing. Klára in a black velvet coatdress and black homburg hat decorated with satin ribbons and netting and András in a little dark blue suit with short pants and long socks. The three made their way together down the stairs and Tamás guided them out of the house and into the car. Elizabeth sighed deeply, but remained composed, careful to conceal her devastation. This was a day she had not expected to come so soon. Klára patted her hand while András became distracted by the unfamiliar sights of Budapest as the car passed quickly through the streets of the city.

The car turned from Andrássy Avenue into Erzsébet Square and then onto Hercegprímás Street. Long before the car stopped in front of the church, András had seen from a distance the landmark copper-covered dome that towered over *Szent István Bazilika*. András stepped from the car and stared at the great flight of stone steps leading to the impressive neo-classical church with its Greek temple-like entrance. He leaned back to look at the tops of the twin towers rising high above the pediment.

Tamás offered his arm to Elizabeth as she emerged from the car and they all began to climb the steps toward the massive golden doors decorated with sculpted busts of the twelve Apostles. Klára and András along with Silva and Ana followed Elizabeth and Tamás into the narthex. The enormous church was cool and quiet inside, except for the sound of their footsteps on the stone floor. As the little group passed into the nave, they were amazed, but not surprised, by the great number of mourners who had come to share their memories of the grand Duke von Esté.

They made their way up the aisle toward the high altar and sat in chairs at the front of the church. András could not take his eyes from the enormous dome that rose above his head. Sunlight streamed in through the clerestory illuminating the mosaics that lined the dome's interior, making them sparkle like gold.

"Look, Mama, the sky is golden here!" he exclaimed.

"Yes, dear," she shushed him, "you must not talk now, András," as she put her finger to her lips, "you must only listen for a while."

András had so much to look at in the beautiful church... massive piers and columns and arches, colored glass, gilded altar paintings, ornate reliquaries, and numerous sculptures in marble and bronze, and gold everywhere. András slid off of his chair, tugged on his mother's sleeve and leaned toward her ear. "Is that man God?" he whispered as he pointed toward the marble statue standing in the center of the apse high altar.

"No, András, that's Hungary's first Christian King... Saint Stephen," Klára whispered. "Sit still now and think of your grandfather."

"What should I think, Mama?" András truly wondered, because he was very small when he saw his grandfather, only a few times in his young life.

"If you're quiet, you'll hear wonderful things about your grandfather. You'll come to know him through what others say."

When the service began there were many who came to speak of Duke Leopold von Esté. As hard as they tried neither Elizabeth nor Klára nor Tamás nor anyone else could stifle their tears as they heard each man speak of their beloved Leopold.

The Regent Horthy spoke of his "admiration for the Duke von Este's concern for all of Hungary's people, his sense of fairness and his relentless efforts to persuade all of us in power to be thoughtful in our actions to keep Hungary secure and prosperous."

Prime Minister Imrédy reminisced about Leopold's "compassion for the poor and disenfranchised and how he personally reached out to those unfortunates."

General Gömbös lauded "the Duke's involvement in many crises and how he brought calm and reason to all discussions. His presence as a great gentleman gave a sense of authenticity to any gathering."

Count Teleki wiped tears from his eyes when he spoke of "Leopold's beloved son, Stefan, who was lost in an effort to bring peace and equality to Hungary." Teleki looked down at Leopold's family and told them, "Hungary has lost another one of her greatest sons."

In their hearts, Elizabeth and Tamás were grateful for the kind words spoken by these men, but they were skeptical of those who offered them. They knew that although these men highly respected Leopold, they had not heeded his words of warning or caution over the years. So many times when Leopold's vision of unity, fairness and tolerance had proven to be the correct direction, many of these same men had chosen a different path for their own reasons.

Now, even today as these men had risen to honor him, Elizabeth and Tamás could remember Leopold's words... "Horthy and Imrédy are leading Hungary into perhaps her darkest time despite my pleas for them to reconsider their direction. I have warned Horthy of Szálasi's Arrow Cross and of Bethlen's overtures with Hitler and of Imrédy's anti-Semitism. Neither Horthy nor any of them were moved by my pleas. They seem determined to join with Germany against the world. Once again our dear Hungary will be on the wrong side."

Elizabeth and Tamás were more impressed by the sincerity of the many others who rose to say kind and admiring words in remembrance of Leopold. The stories of fellow vintners and businessmen and those who worked for Leopold were more personal and meaningful than those of the government leaders. Klára listened to each man speak of her papa with a deep sense of pride for the great man she knew him to be. She looked down at András who seemed to be listening to the long eulogies and smiled at him. András looked up at her with mint-green eyes... the color of her dear papa's eyes.

After the priests administered the Eucharist to the mourners, the service was over. Klára took András's hand as they rose from their chairs and turned toward the aisle. Instantly her eyes engaged Rudolf who stood across from her. Klára was relieved to see him there and gave him a warm smile. Elizabeth, too, saw Rudolf; she entered into the aisle first, took a step toward him and reached for his hand which he extended to her with a bow.

"My grandmother and I offer our sincere condolences, Duchess."

Elizabeth, her eyes lowered, implored him, "Dolf, please join us for supper this evening." She raised her eyes to his, "I wish to speak with you."

"I would be honored, Madam," he answered as their eyes met.

Elizabeth managed a slight smile before she and Tamás continued down the aisle.

Rudolf stepped forward, embraced Klára, offered her his arm and walked with her and András as they made their way toward the narthex. In the narthex, Rudolf bent over to shake András's hand and to tousle his hair, "You've grown since we last met. What a big boy you've become!"

"This is my dear friend, Dolf, Count von Házy. You won't remember meeting him, András, because you were only a baby then."

András smiled at Rudolf. He liked his mother's friend, so tall with kind brown eyes.

"Ride back to the house with us, Dolf, and stay for a while."

"Thank you, Klára, but I have a car waiting. I will see you later. I've been invited for supper. Your mother invited me."

At the von Esté home the staff had spread the feast prepared by Silva on the huge dining room table as a buffet for the guests who came to honor the duke and pay their respects to his family. Standing in the reception hall to greet everyone, Elizabeth and Klára were most gracious hostesses for the long line of guests that came through the front door into their home. For hours they stood in the foyer and ate nothing all evening. Finally, as the line began to dwindle, Silva brought plates of food for them, "I insist that you eat, eat to keep up your strength," she said forcefully, "and you should rest a bit. Sit here on this bench and eat your supper."

"I cannot eat all of this, Silva," protested Elizabeth as she sat down, sighing deeply. She was tired.

"Eat what you can, but eat. Eat, Madam, or you will have no strength for the days ahead."

Fearing they might miss greeting a guest or thanking a departing one for coming, Klára and her mother remained on the bench near the entrance. By eight o'clock in the evening there were very few guests left, most were bidding their hostesses farewell. Both women were exhausted.

Rudolf approached them to say, "Ladies, you have both served the duke honorably today, but you must be very tired and no one will fault you for retiring at this late hour."

Klára took his hand as she rose from the bench, "Come, Mother, we should go upstairs now."

Elizabeth was emotionally spent and physically exhausted, but she replied, "Rudolf, please come into the library with me. Excuse us, Klára, please go to bed. I'll see you in the morning."

Rudolf followed the Duchess into the library, half fearing what she might say to him. They entered the dark room. Elizabeth turned on a lamp near the desk.

"Please shut the door, Rudolf." She sat down in one of the big leather chairs and motioned for him to pull another chair close to hers. Although still elegantly beautiful, she looked small and much older than her fifty-two years. She seemed terribly sad; Rudolf felt drawn to console her, but was reluctant to do so.

"I did a wicked thing, Rudolf, and I must beg your forgiveness."

He reached for her hand, "Whatever it is that concerns you, let it wait. Your heart is too heavy."

"My treatment of you has added to that heaviness." Tears began to stream from her eyes. "Leopold loved you as a son and I led you to believe that he did not."

Elizabeth was determined to say everything that had filled her with guilt for so long. "I deprived my sweet Leopold of your presence for years, because you believed that he no longer loved you," She wiped her eyes and continued her confession, "And my precious Klára who has always loved you... I manipulated your lives for my own personal desire... to see Klára marry the son of my childhood friend."

Elizabeth broke into sobs, but when Rudolf tried to console her again, she shook her head. "Nothing but tragedy could come from such intervention into what should have been. Leopold became so distraught over Klára's situation, being so far away, married to a *Nazi*. He could hardly stand it, his troubled thoughts of her added so much stress to his last months. I am certain his worries injured his heart." Elizabeth bit back her tears, "How can I ask your forgiveness when I find it impossible to forgive myself?"

"Elizabeth, it's true that the words you said to me in this very room, so many years ago, were devastating to me. I'd thought always of you and Leopold as parents who loved me. I had anticipated your enthusiasm about marriage between Klára and me. I was crushed by your rejection, but..."

Elizabeth whispered through her tears, "I regret..."

"No, Elizabeth, it's not altogether your fault. I stayed away too long. I became involved in matters that focused my attention away from Klára. I let her leave me. I hurt her." Rudolf held Elizabeth's hands in his, "I have loved Klára all her life, I should have gone to Cologne and brought her back to Budapest regardless of what I thought to be your opinion. The truth would have become known... I regret, too, Elizabeth."

"If you could forgive me and come back into our family... Leopold missed you so, as I have. Your being with us again would mean everything to me."

"I'm grateful for your honesty, Elizabeth," Rudolf managed a smile for her, "and I do forgive you. We'll speak of this matter no more. For you to consider me part of your family is my honor. You can depend on me always to help you in any way I can."

"Thank you, my dear Dolf." Elizabeth stood and kissed his hands, "Thank you for your generous spirit and kindness. You must help me watch over Klára and András."

"Of course, I will," promised Rudolf. He added thoughtfully, "And there is the good that came from all of this...András."

"Ah, yes, and Leopold adored him."

The two walked from the library and stopped at the foot of the stair. Rudolf and Elizabeth shared kisses on both cheeks and then she ascended the stair as Rudolf watched. He turned toward the door to go, but Tamás called to him, "Come to the kitchen, Count, and have a cup of tea."

As Rudolf walked with Tamás through the dining room, Tamás spoke, "I hope you and the Duchess have worked out your differences."

"You don't miss much, do you, Tamás?" Rudolf laughed, "And to answer you...yes, we have. I'm back in the family."

"I never knew you to be out." Tamás slapped Rudolf on the back and laughed, "Good, good!"

When the two men entered the kitchen, Rudolf was surprised to see Klára sitting with Silva at the table sipping one of Silva's tea concoctions.

"We're trying to convince the Baroness to stay," said Silva as she poured a cup for Rudolf. "You know that she's leaving András here, but *she* insists on going back to Berlin in just a few days."

"No, I didn't know that András is staying. That's very good news!" Rudolf turned toward Klára as he thanked Silva for the tea and sat down at the table, "and I think very wise of you, Klára, to leave him here, but I think you should stay as well."

"We have warned her that war is coming and that Berlin will surely be in the center of it," said Tamás. "Perhaps you can convince her."

"Tamás is right Klára, I'm sure you know as well as we that war is on the horizon."

Klára stirred her tea thoughtfully, then looked up at the three people she knew loved her and were truly concerned for her safety, "I must go back to take care of my house, gather some things and give my staff, who have been very faithful, their severance." She smiled sincerely at them, "I promised Mother that I would return to Budapest before Christmas."

"What if you're there when war breaks out?" Silva asked. "You could be caught behind the lines."

"Don't worry, Silva, I'll stay alert to events and make sure that won't happen."

"You'd be safer if you do not go back." Rudolf sounded worried. "Couldn't Franz or Marta do those chores for you? Look after the house, pay the staff, send your things?"

Klára looked at Rudolf knowingly, "Dolf, I have obligations that I cannot quit...commitments...matters in Berlin that are important."

Her words made Rudolf smile. There was a haunting familiarity about them, but he also knew the truth, her words meant danger for Klára. He winced, "We want your safety, Klára, and we want you here with us."

She reached across the table and squeezed his hand, "And I love all of you for your concern. I'll come back as soon as I can. Watch over my little boy while I'm gone."

The following day the family, accompanied by Rudolf, went by train to Sopron. Leopold's body was interred between the tombs of Cili and Stefan. The new caretakers did a good job of warming the drafty rooms and preparing a comforting supper, but nothing was the same since the passing of Gáspár and Ilonka. Tamás and Silva placed wreaths of cedar on the tomb shared by Tamás's parents at the corner of the castle cemetery, near an old oak tree.

Klára had only visited the castle a few times since the death of Stefan; the castle had never held the same fascination for her that it had for Stefan, but she and Rudolf did show András much of the castle and its ruins and vineyards. They also gave him a tour of Sopron sights, but their time was very short because Elizabeth wanted to return to Budapest after only a three-day stay. Elizabeth had never felt comfortable in the castle. The train trip back to Budapest was a somber one.

Berlin

A week later Klára and Marta left Budapest by train for Berlin. Klára waved good-byes to András who stood between Elizabeth and Rudolf while Tamás stood nearby. Klára was determined to return to Berlin, even though it was terribly difficult to leave all of them. She had unfinished business in Berlin and she wondered what might be waiting there for her.

Marta, quite perturbed about leaving András in Budapest, reacted with as much hostility as possible in every conversation with Klára. Marta finished every exchange with either *"the Major will not be happy with your decision"* or *"I will tell the Major that I objected vehemently to your leaving the boy."* Klára slept most of the way to Berlin, in part to avoid conversation with Marta.

When they arrived in Berlin the two women traveled by taxi straight to the von Werner house. Franz had not returned from Poland and would not return for two more weeks. Klára expected to use the time to pack and to tend to her household, but was also ready to receive new assignments from the Resistance. Concerned that matters had grown more dreadful for those oppressed by the Nazis, Klára was certain new courier assignments awaited her. She could hardly stand the thought of innocents being harmed when she might possibly be able to help them.

Two weeks later, Franz returned from Poland. He proudly announced his promotion to Lieutenant Colonel and went straight to his study. Leaving the door ajar, he immediately telephoned some unknown person. Klára could easily overhear his side of the conversation... *"Things are going very well militarily for Germany...Yes, Heydrich and I have been directed by Hitler to form Einsatzgruppen...it is an ingenious way to exterminate Poland's Jews...nothing can save them...we will eliminate all of them regardless of class or financial status or any other reason...our plans will go into effect as soon as possible."*

Franz hung up the telephone and began rifling through a stack of papers. Klára stood in the doorway of his study, "My papa's memorial service was very nice, well attended...many wonderful things were said about my father...about his sense of fairness and equality."

Quite suddenly Marta joined Klára at the doorway and interjected, "She left your son in Budapest."

"What?" Franz put down the papers he was looking at and turned toward Klára and Marta, "What did you say?"

"She left András in Budapest. I strongly objected. I told her that you would not approve."

Franz glared at Klára, his eyes the color of ice, his jaw tight, his anger obvious. "What does this mean, Klára? What was your purpose in that act? What is your plan? To return to Budapest?"

"My mother was heartbroken to see me leave. András gives her great comfort, so I thought it best to leave him there until Christmas when I plan to go back for him."

Franz stared at her for an extended time before he spoke, "I doubt I can spare you at Christmas time this year. There will be social events for us to attend. You may not see the boy again for a long time."

Marta smiled and left the room. Klára stood in the doorway staring at Franz, wondering how he had become so cruel. She said nothing to him and he did not look at her. As she turned to go, he called to her, "Klára! I will be coming to your bed tonight...."

Klára walked from the study, not waiting to hear the rest of his odious words.

There was never any discussion about Marta retaining her nanny position. Franz assumed that András would return and until that day Marta would remain in the house and simply continue her *Zellenleiter* duties while she waited for the boy's return.

November, Berlin

Klára walked briskly along the sidewalk, her head bowed against the cold wind that chilled her to the bone. Franz left that morning for Munich, giving her a sense of freedom, real or not, to go about her personal acts of resistance that defied Franz's authority and the Nazis' goals. On this day, Marta had a bad cold and had chosen not to accompany Klára on her errands; Marta, in fact, found Klára's routine boring. Klára stopped in a small pastry shop on Behrenstrasse to pick up two packages of strudel, one tied with string and the other without string. *Such a little act of defiance*, she thought.

She planned to walk north as usual along Wilhelmstrasse, across the Spree Bridge and then several blocks on Luisenstrasse to St. Veronika's. But when she left the pastry shop and turned the corner, she and other pedestrians were abruptly stopped by a skirmish on the sidewalk that spilled out into the street. Several S.S. soldiers were violently harassing an elderly man. They shoved him back and forth between each other and punched him several times calling him "Jude" and other vile names. No one among the observers said a word of protest or stepped in to stop the brutal treatment of the old man. In fact, the pedestrians simply averted their eyes and hurried on their way.

Klára hated herself and everyone else who refused to interfere, but she thought of her packages and walked faster. She had gone only one block past the Adlon Hotel when she realized acts of harassment were happening along every street. *What has happened*, she wondered, *to bring about such open hostilities against the Jews*? The remainder of her walk to St. Veronika's was just as disturbing.

Once inside the cool, dark interior of St. Veronika's, Klára felt safe and sighed with relief. She walked straight to a side chapel, knelt at the altar and lit a candle. The interior remained very dark, but she could see there was no one else in the chapel; in fact, there were only a few worshippers in the large nave. A narrow wooden panel by the altar concealed a doorway; it clicked open and Father Matthäus stepped into the chapel.

"Hello, how have you been? It has been a while since I've seen you here."

"Yes, Father, I've been away from Berlin for a while." Klára offered no details, the less information exchanged the better. She didn't know if Father Matthäus even knew her name. Klára placed the package of strudel without string on the altar, rose from the altar, glanced at the young priest and left.

The walk back to Ebertstrasse was just as traumatic. S.S soldiers and Gestapo were engaged in violent acts on almost every block. She hurried up her front stairs and into the reception hall; she could hardly breathe. The images she had witnessed plagued her mind as she slowly hung up her coat, unwrapped her scarf and took off her hat; she took a deep breath and walked into the kitchen where Inge and Hedy were busy with supper. Klára put the strudel box on the table without a word. The three made a habit of speaking in whispers to make sure Marta could not hear their words.

"Something has happened. There are S.S. soldiers everywhere attacking Jews. Have you heard anything?"

"On the wireless," answered Hedy. "They say that on Monday last a German diplomat in Paris was shot by a Polish Jew."

"The Jew and his family are refugees living in Paris," added Inge. "They say the assassin was just a teenager."

"Now the Nazis are calling for revenge on all Jews," said Hedy. "*Gauleiters* throughout Germany are calling for a pogrom in each of their cities against the Jews and their businesses. Goebbels has forbidden looting, saying that looters will be shot. The pogrom begins tonight."

"From what I saw this afternoon, it's already begun," answered Klára. She thought... *no looting... only because the Nazis want to do the looting themselves!*

Marta interrupted them when she came into the kitchen to get her supper tray. She had a very red nose and sounded miserable as she thanked Inge and left the kitchen preferring to eat alone in her room. Liesel joined Inge, Hedy and Klára in the kitchen where they ate their supper without speaking while listening to the wireless. Sounds of sirens filled the night.

Not until Friday morning did Klára leave her home and she was shocked by the destruction she saw everywhere. Smashed windows of Jewish shops left the sidewalks littered in glass; symbols—the Star of David, the Menorah and the word "Jude"—were splashed across doors and walls, the paint dried in careless splatters and runs. She had heard on the wireless that synagogues were severely damaged, including the great Berlin synagogue on Oranienburgerstrasse.

As she did every Friday morning, Klára walked to Reichstagufer beside the Spree to the fishmonger's to pick up two packages, one tied with string and one without. From there she walked on to St. Veronika's, but stopped across the street when she saw two black cars idling in front of the church. Within moments several Gestapo came out with Father Matthäus; they pushed him into the back seat of one of the cars. Klára fell back against the stone wall of the building behind her and watched the two cars speed away. Terror struck at her heart. She turned and walked home as quickly as she could, not remembering any of her steps.

Once inside, Klára went straight to the kitchen, the only room where she felt some safety. She sat down at the table as Inge poured a cup of tea for her. Klára was visibly shaken. "It's devastating out there, Inge. So much destruction." Klára felt drained by fear.

What would she do with the contents of the package without string? She believed whatever the contents, it meant the difference between life and death for someone, "I brought the fish. I'll take care of it," she said as she slid off her stool and took the two packages of fish to the sink.

Inge watched with curiosity, since Klára had never done such a thing before. Klára opened the package without string and pulled out the whole trout. Inside the trout she found a metal tube; she held it in her hand staring at it. She knew it held something important. Klára washed her hands and the tube, dried her hands and the tube, and said to Inge, "You can take over on the fish, I'm going upstairs."

Upstairs in her room, she opened the metal tube; a rolled paper fell out. The paper was covered in some kind of code. None of it made sense to her. She rerolled the paper and inserted it back into the tube. *What should I do with it?* She'd had no contact with the Countess Maltzan for months, but decided to telephone her.

"Hello Countess, it's been a while since we've had a visit. Could we meet for coffee? Perhaps at our old place? This afternoon, at four?"

At four Klára met the countess at the Adlon, at their same table in the palms. Klára discretely passed the metal tube across the table. "You know that Father Matthaüs was taken by the Gestapo? I was unsure as to what I should do. I opened the tube, but of course I couldn't read the code. I had no idea of what to do with this, I thought of you."

Klára realized she was so nervous she had been talking non-stop, "I'm sorry, Countess, I'm talking too much, but I am so worried about everything."

Countess Maltzan reached across the table and patted her hand, "I did hear about Father Matthaüs. His arrest will be a great loss to us. We know that the Gestapo will use every manner of persuasion to prevail upon him to reveal his contacts. They will torture him, but he was never given anyone's name, never knew who his contacts were." The countess looked as sincere as possible to reassure Klára. "You did the right thing to call me. This is vital information for the Resistance."

Klára did feel some relief and managed a smile. The countess looked down at her coffee cup and stirred, then lifted her eyes to Klára, "Have you heard your husband use the term *Einsatzgruppen?*"

Klára nodded in the affirmative. The countess continued, "Colonel Heydrich is in charge of *Einsatzgruppen* and, of course, your husband is one of his most valued aides. Keep your ears open, Klára, if you should hear anything that the Resistance should know, do not hesitate to call me."

"I will."

"The Nazis believe they have found the solution to their 'Jewish problem,'" stated the countess, then added, "first they persecuted to the point of driving the Jews out of Germany, then they confiscated their property. The S.S. and Gestapo have carried out all of these monstrous acts. Many Jews have been arrested and jailed in the last few days. Some will be able to buy their way out;

some will be taken to the labor camps and some we'll never know what happened to them. Now they will simply eliminate the Jews, all of them, by death. Already it has begun and it will get much worse."

"I know," Klára agreed, "it's an unbearable situation. I'll stay in Berlin as long as I can, to help you as much as I'm able, but you should know that I'll be going home to Budapest as soon as possible. My son is there now."

"We're grateful for whatever you are able to do for us. Your particular position has been invaluable to the Resistance."

They parted, going in opposite directions. Klára walked home, observing the street cleaners who were trying still to sweep up the glass and other debris that covered the sidewalks. The newspaper reported that the Jews would be charged for the clean-up and for all necessary repairs to damaged properties. Klára sighed with relief that Franz had not been in Berlin during this event, because she would not be able to hide her true feelings and she knew he would only ridicule those feelings and admonish her sympathies. Klára thought about what she would say to him.

How can you treat these people so brutally? And he would answer her, *People? These Jews are not people, Klára. They are parasites, vermin to be exterminated.* She decided that when Franz returned she would say nothing to him about the *"night of broken glass."* As she walked quickly along the street she said a prayer for the well-being and courage of Father Matthäus. A cold wind whipped through the streets, forcing her to pull her coat tighter and tuck her chin into the muffler wrapped around her neck. Snowflakes began to fall.

December, Budapest

A quiet, solemn András sat at the bottom of the great staircase watching Silva direct the housemaids as they hung golden ribbons and boughs of red-berried holly over the doorways. He watched the maids standing on ladders, stretching to hang the branches as Ana handed shiny ribbons and golden balls of glass up to them. His grandmother sat at the grand piano playing cheerful holiday songs, music familiar to him, music his mother had played for him at their house. Although the flurry of preparations for Christmas in the von Esté house attempted to provide ample distraction for him, András missed his mother very much. His sad little eyes followed the maids' every move until Tamás entered the reception hall.

Tamás asked András if he would like to help set up the crèche. The little boy was happy to take Tamás's hand as they went into the dining room where a large box was sitting on the table. Tamás opened the box and began to take out the figures, carefully unwrapping each one—a shepherd, an angel. He encouraged András to help. András took out the figures, one by one, a camel, a wise man with a pot of gold, a lamb. Soon András was smiling widely and called to his grandmother and Silva, "*Come see ... come see!*"

He and Tamás set all the figures around the rustic wooden stable placed on the sideboard and then put the Holy Family in their proper places. András looked up at Tamás, "It's very pretty. My mother will like it very much. We have one at our house, but this one is much bigger."

Elizabeth and Silva both exclaimed joyfully over the good job the *men* had done and then Silva called them all into the kitchen where she had a kettle of warm apple cider on the stove and a plate of *ischler.* In no time chocolate from the shortbread spread around András's mouth and on every finger. Elizabeth laughed as she took a damp warm cloth to his face and hands, "You're covered ear to ear!"

Elizabeth was having a difficult time with the approaching holiday, so soon after Leopold's death, so much like the holiday season had been after Stefan's death so many years before. They had both died in October. She took a deep breath and looked at the beautiful little boy who stood before her. András brought all of them such unexpected joy. She and Tamás and Silva had agreed they would make the most wonderful Christmas possible for him. They would do all they could to keep him happy and occupied, knowing how much he missed his beloved mother; they all missed her.

"Here, András, have another *ischler.*"

Just as András took another cookie from the plate, Rudolf entered the kitchen through the garden door. He brushed snow from his shoulders and hat as Tamás took his things. András slid off his chair and greeted Rudolf with a vigorous hug around the knees. András suspected his new friend had treats in his pockets because he visited often and always brought some surprise. This time it was Turkish taffy wrapped in silver paper.

"Cookies, now candy," scolded Silva. "Your appetite for supper will be ruined!"

"Stay for supper, Dolf," implored Elizabeth, "We would love to have your company and you can tell us about your students at the Academy."

Silva also tried to entice Rudolf, "I'm serving *nyulpörkölt*, stewed rabbit, tonight and *ischler* for dessert."

"All of your Uncle Stefan's favorites," smiled Rudolf as he tousled the little boy's hair. "Of course, I'll stay. What have you been up to today, András?"

"Tamás and I set up the crèche today and Ana and the servants decorated the hall. Do you want to see?"

Rudolf and András left the kitchen hand in hand. Tamás had a packet of mail for the Duchess, "Where would you like to have your mail, Madam?"

"I'll take it in the library, thank you."

Elizabeth took the stack of letters to her desk. Among the business correspondence she found letters from Klára and from her sister-in-law, Eugenia. She opened Klára's letter first.

Dear Mommy, I regret to tell you that I will not return to Budapest before Christmas. Franz has many social obligations during the season and he insists that I be present to attend with him. I am heartbroken to be apart from my precious András and from you at this time. I know this season must be bittersweet for you and for all the household. Christmas without Papa is unimaginable. I do hope that having András will cheer you in some way. Please shower him with kisses and hugs from me. Please tell him that I love him with all my heart and would be there with him for Christmas, if only I could. Please give my love to Tamás and Silva and Dolf. I miss everyone deeply and love you all. I will try to telephone soon.

    Your adoring daughter, Klára

Elizabeth shook her head sadly and dabbed her eyes with her lace handkerchief as she refolded Klára's letter and replaced it in its envelope. She would let the others read Klára's words for themselves. When Elizabeth took Eugenia's letter from the stack, she noticed the ornate stamp with the word "Mexico." She opened the envelope.

Dearest Sister, Konrad and I were devastated by your news that finally arrived today in Acapulco. My dear, sweet brother's passing is such a shock! He was my beloved little brother! It is so difficult to believe, so unexpected. We are destroyed.

    I regret deeply that we are at such a great distance we cannot be there to comfort you or to attend our Leopold's service at Szent István Bazilika. We are overcome with grief.

    Konrad and I are in Mexico for the winter. We plan to return to Canada in the spring, although we have been disappointed by the current atmosphere in Canada. Certainly not all, but a good number of Canadians in high places are Anti-Semites and Xenophobians, suspicious of Jews and afraid of all foreigners. Their response to pleas from desperate Jews of Germany for sanctuary has been less than charitable.

    Konrad and I are thinking of moving to far western Canada, to Victoria or Vancouver. We understand that the Westerners are more progressive in their thinking. We have decided that we will not return to Germany until the Germans come to their senses and shoot all the Nazis.

    We have heard, of course, that the Nazis have taken hold of our Austria. I also have heard from your dear mother that she and your father left Linz and are living in Rorschach. If things begin to turn sour for Hungary, you must leave, too, please. I am certain that your parents want your

family to be there with them. Konrad and I have great concern for Klára
and her baby. We imagine that they have come to Budapest for Leopold.
We pray they do not return to Berlin since at the present time it is a place of
great evil.

Our hearts are with you now and our prayers, too, are for you and for
the soul of my dear brother, Leopold.

Until we meet again, your faithful sister, Eugenia

1939
January, Budapest

Soon after Epiphany, the holiday decorations were taken down; Christmas came and passed without Klára's return. Once everything was put back in order the quiet routine of winter settled over the von Esté household. Outside a freezing blizzard had dropped heavy drifts of snow covering all of Budapest while inside the von Esté home Tamás kept the house warm with glowing fires in the enormous fireplaces. Several times a day he had the gardeners go around the upper floors of the house to stoke the smoldering embers in every ceramic stove standing majestically in the corner of each room.

While Fejedelem lay at her feet, Elizabeth sat at Leopold's great library desk studying the accounts for the von Esté Fine Wine Company. She had a good mind for figures and for years had kept the accounts for Leopold's company. András lay stretched out on the library's thick carpet, just as his mother had done as a child, looking at the oversized Atlas with its hand-colored plates of exotic peoples and places among the maps. Lying near Fejedelem, András turned the pages carefully and dreamt of strange and distant places.

Tamás entered the library. "Master András," he smiled a knowing smile at Elizabeth, "Count Rudolf is here to see you."

Elizabeth rose from her desk and joined Tamás at the doorway, "Come, András, you know the count will have a nice surprise for you."

They walked together to the kitchen where Silva and Ana were speaking softly to the count. When András entered the kitchen, Silva and Ana parted in front of Rudolf to reveal a silky reddish-brown bundle in his arms. Everyone was smiling broadly.

"Come see what the count has brought you, Master András."

András ran forward to Rudolf who leaned over to expose a young puppy in his arms.

"This little fellow is for you, András. We know that old Fejedelem is not such a good playmate for you and we all thought you needed a puppy closer to your age, now that you are nearly six years old. This puppy can grow up with you."

András took the gangly little animal in his own arms and dropped to the floor. The puppy eagerly licked his face and jumped all over him while András rolled around with laughter. The puppy instantly knew he was meant for András and kept his eyes locked upon his new young master who loved him immediately.

"What are you going to name him?"

András thought for a moment and then shouted, *"Hóvihar, Blizzard, Hóvi* for short."

"Ah, very good choice. We like Hóvi...it fits him well," Rudolf said approvingly.

Rudolf had traveled through the blizzard to Balatonfüred to visit Fábián Vadas, who like his father raised Vizsla hounds and had a litter of puppies born in mid-November.

"Hóvihar is an early birthday present for you, András, because I'm leaving Budapest tomorrow. I've taken a leave from the Academy and I'll be gone for a few months and I wanted you to have a special friend while I'm gone."

"Will you bring my mother back with you, please?" András looked at Rudolf with all the earnestness of a nearly six-year-old.

Elizabeth agreed with her grandson, "Oh, yes, please Rudolf, if Klára has not returned before you come back, will you visit her in Berlin and insist that she come home with you? We would be so grateful."

Rudolf promised that he would do just that for all of them.

England

Early the next frosty morning Rudolf left Budapest by train for the long trip to Calais, France. From there he took the ferry to Dover, England, and then the train to London where he met his MI6 mentor, Clive Jeffreys. Together they drove north from London into Buckinghamshire to Bletchley Park, the new secluded site for MI6 headquarters. Rudolf found the increased number of intelligence agents working for the British Secret Service at Bletchley quite impressive. There were literally thousands—cryptologists, analysts, technicians, and espionage agents, both military and civilian. Jeffreys guided him around the facility of cottages and workshops, explaining their current and future projects. Rudolf took the time to tell Jeffreys what he had on his mind.

"I believe it would be prudent for Britain to ally with Hungary as soon as possible before it is too late to stop the development of an alliance that I see forming between Hungary and Nazi Germany. Britain could breach Germany's plan to take Hungary and all of the Balkans, Greece, and Romania. The Allies could stop the Germans where they are now, in Austria and Czechoslovakia. With the Russians to the east, Germany could expand no further."

"Well, certainly that advice should be passed along. Everyone is dedicated to the defeat of the Jerrys," proclaimed Jeffreys in answer to Rudolf's assertion, "but our main goal here is to break into the Germans' encrypted communications. Specifically, our mission now is to discover the keys that will allow the decoding of the Germans' Enigma and Lorenz encryption machines. We are very good at the interception of German communications. We have plenty of communications between the Abwehr, S.S., Gestapo, and Wehrmacht, but we can't decode them yet. Progress on decryption has not gone as well or as quickly as we'd hoped."

"Fascinating work, Clive," responded Rudolf. "With the number of cryptologists I see here, perhaps success is near. What do you have in mind for me?"

"We want you to become an agent within the new MI6 Special Liaison Unit, the SLU," confided Jeffreys. "Your connections all over Europe are invaluable to MI6. Certainly, you may remain headquartered in Budapest, if that is your wish, but we'll be calling upon you to travel, perhaps with short notice on occasion."

After several weeks of preparation for his new role as an SLU agent, Rudolf learned vital information he would share with resistance groups in France, Germany and Hungary. He was invited to attend a meeting with Ewald von Kleist-Schmenzin, an emissary to Britain from Admiral Wilhelm Canaris, one of Rudolf's old contacts. Kleist brought a message of warning to the Brits.

"Canaris and I are convinced that Hitler is engaged in a disastrous course of expansion that will lead to war and ultimately to Germany's own destruction." Kleist chose his words carefully, "I must state that the Admiral and I were more than disappointed by the British Prime Minister's participation in the Munich Agreement. Chamberlain's choice of appeasement gave Hitler legitimacy on the world stage that he should never have had and led to the sacrifice of Czechoslovakia to the Reich.

"Can you not see what is happening?" Kleist had a stricken expression. He paused to allow the weight of his words to penetrate beyond the Brits' stoic expressions, "Canaris and I recently attended a briefing with Hitler and his upper echelon of S.S. officers and Gestapo where plans for the invasion of Poland were laid out. Quite matter-of-factly, the Nazis also discussed plans for the complete annihilation of Poland's Jewish population, a plan called *Einsatzgruppen.*"

Kleist looked around the table at the faces of his audience. He wanted them to take seriously his words and their ramification for the entire world.

"Providing this information to you does not mean that Canaris and I are traitors to our beloved fatherland." Kleist's words rang with a controlled passion, "I come here as a representative of Canaris because we see Hitler as an insane fanatic who is leading Germany into an impossible position. His Nazi policies are despicable and will only lead the world to isolate and despise our country and citizens. Hitler must be stopped before untold suffering spreads as a plague across all of Europe."

Rudolf knew Kleist's words were true. If Hitler was allowed free rein, consequences awaited all of Europe, including his own Hungary. Rudolf, like Kleist, wanted the Allies to act, but he knew the Allies would proceed with great caution, allowing too much time for Hitler to have his way. Fear of another *great war* was too strong in the West. The Allies convinced themselves they had to find some other way than war to stop Hitler...the reason why these Brits were working so diligently to decode Hitler's communications.

February, Budapest

Tamás sat at Silva's kitchen table, stirring his coffee and perusing *Új Magyarsag*, his Budapest newspaper. He read aloud to Silva as she stood over a bubbling pot on the stove.

"Ah...the Regent Horthy has appointed the nationalistic Count Pál Teleki of the Hungarian Life Party as the new Prime Minister, replacing the fascist-leaning Imrédy."

"Well, that is no surprise," Silva stated.

"Apparently, Horthy, as well as many other Hungarian leaders, has grown anxious about Prime Minister Imrédy." Tamás spoke his thoughts aloud, "Imrédy's open embrace of the far-right National Socialist movement in Hungary was becoming a problem for Horthy. Especially when Imrédy welcomed Ferenc Szálasi's Arrow Cross Party into his government." Tamás looked up from the paper and addressed Silva, "We should have nothing to do with the Arrow Cross. It's Hungary's equivalent to Germany's Nazi Party. The paper says right here...'*Imrédy lifted the previous ban on the far-right Arrow Cross Party, allowing it to grow freely and gain political power.*' "

Tamás continued to read from the article, "Imrédy led Hungary out of the peace-loving League of Nations and into the *Anti-Communist Pact* with Germany, Italy and Japan. These are the facts that alerted Horthy to the dangerous potential of a fascist alliance with Germany," Tamás shook his head in disbelief. "Imrédy's obvious goal is to join Hungary with the German Axis. I know that Horthy is vehemently opposed to that alliance, but on the other hand," he pondered, "it's no wonder Horthy is nervous about Imrédy's overtures to Germany since Horthy, himself, has acquiesced to Germany's enticements."

Silva was fully aware of Hungary's history and she knew the facts, but Tamás was passionate and he wanted to state aloud the absurdity of the situation. "I'm certain that Horthy rationalized to himself if he went along with Hitler's invasion of Czechoslovakia, then Hungary would receive its former territories at last, through a revision of the *1920 Treaty*. How naïve can Horthy be? He acts as though the whole transaction is the culmination of some great Magyar myth! Horthy has obligated Hungary to Germany once again!"

"Tamás, you're getting too emotional," cautioned Silva. "Hungarian politics has always been complicated from the beginning of time and forever. It's best to pay no attention to it."

"But we must, Silva. We must be alert always to the shifts of power. It does matter to each one of us."

Quite suddenly András and an exuberant Hóvi burst into the kitchen through a servant's door from the concealed passageway.

"Surprise!" András yelled to the startled pair in the kitchen. "Hóvi and I came up from the cellar. We've opened every door on this passage—one into the dining room and one into a bedroom upstairs and one on the top floor. Now we're going back down to the cellar and up another staircase to see where it goes!"

As he turned to go, Silva called to him, "Perhaps you and Hóvi should take a rest. Come sit at the table with Tamás for some hot cocoa and *burgonya lángos*."

András slid onto a chair with a big smile on his face; he loved *burgonya lángos*, the crispy, fried potato cakes Silva served with sour cream. "Are you having *burgonya lángos*, too, Tamás?"

"Of course, Young Man, who could turn down Silva's potato cakes?"

András filled his winter days exploring his new von Esté home. Hóvi faithfully followed András everywhere as he climbed the hidden staircases and passageways concealed within the walls of the massive house from the depths of the cellar up to the servants' quarters on the third floor. The staircases and passageways were designed for the convenience of the servants, allowing them to go quickly from top to bottom of the great house and have access into every room. In some of the rooms the doorways were not at all obvious to the delight of András who loved to seemingly disappear right before the eyes of the maids or even his grandmother. But his most favorite place in the whole house was the open campanile at the top of the house, only accessible from the servants' quarters on the third floor.

Bitter, icy winter winds stung András's cheeks and turned his nose bright pink when he stood in the campanile's outside balcony. His view from the campanile fascinated him.

He could see a good distance in all directions—to the southwest, he had a view far up Andrássy Avenue and to the northeast he could see the snow-covered Városliget city park, and from the back of the balcony, András could look toward Count Rudolf's house and down into his garden.

It was definitely his favorite place, even though his grandmother scolded him for going into the servant's quarters, telling him... *"You must respect their privacy, András."* So, he always asked Ana, *"Would it be all right for me to stand on your balcony in the campanile?"* And she always said, *"Yes, it will be all right, but be careful, don't fall."* András wasn't worried about that, because the walls of the balcony came just under his chin.

The winter passed slowly for András, despite the adventures he shared with Hóvi or the efforts made to keep him busy. Elizabeth gave him basic piano lessons, although he much preferred to listen to her beautiful melodies; Silva invited him to help her with the baking, just as his mother had done; and Tamás told him stories, hundreds of wonderful stories about his own family, about the adventures of Tamás and Leopold in America, about his grandfather when he was young, about his amazing Uncle Stefan, about his beautiful mother and grandmother, and about the dashing Count Rudolf, even the story about how the count got his wooden leg... a story that completely enthralled András.

March

From London, Rudolf returned to France by ferry and then took a train to Paris. He had not been in Paris for months, but he still paid the rent for his flat and wondered if Yvette might still use the flat now and then. He had not seen her in a long time. As the taxi wound its way from the Gare du Nord along the wet and icy streets of Le Marais, through the Place de la Bastille and across the Pont de Sully, Rudolf began to feel a sense of familiarity. He had always loved Paris and hoped someday to return in happier circumstances with Klára by his side. When the taxi turned from Boulevard Saint Germain onto Saint Michel and neared the Jardin du Luxembourg, he felt a wave of excitement to be back in the heart of such creative energy. When the taxi stopped at the entrance to the little alley, he got out with his bags and looked up toward his balcony.

The flat was dark. Rudolf climbed the spiral stone staircase, reached up to the lintel above the doorway, found the key and opened the door. It was obvious from the thick layer of dust that no one had been living there for a long while. He managed to light a fire in the tiny iron stove and to shake the dust from the bed covers before deciding to go out for dinner. He ran into Mme. Deverau on his way down the stairs. She welcomed him back and when he asked if she had seen Yvette, she answered that she had not, not for a long time. Rudolf used the telephone at the foot of the stairs to call his friend, János Géza, who agreed to meet him at a nearby café for supper. The night air chilled Rudolf as he walked quickly the few blocks to the *vin rouge café*.

The two old friends caught up on all the news of Paris and Budapest that had passed in the last half year. Rudolf gave a casual warning to János, "There could be a German occupation of France… Paris. Perhaps you should think of leaving, going back to Budapest. There will be much work to do on behalf of Hungary, if war should come."

János took Rudolf's warning seriously, but answered, "If occupation does occur here in Paris, there will be work to do here. You know where to find me when you come again."

They parted that evening, each wishing the other, *"Jó szerencse! Amíg mi találkozik újra!"* "Good Luck! Until we meet again!"

As soon as Germany occupied Austria, proud and courageous French men and women began to form various resistance groups throughout France. There were those who took the signs of Hitler's obsession for expansion seriously and they wanted to be prepared. Because János was a member of the French underground, Rudolf, as an MI6 SLU agent, knew they would surely be in contact again.

Late March, Berlin

When Klára returned to her house after a rather long walk to the library and back, she entered the kitchen to find Hedy and Inge very upset. A terrified Hedy tried to stop crying, while Inge stood by wringing her hands in her apron, unable to give any comfort to Hedy.

"What has happened now?" Klára asked.

"The Pfieffer home was raided this morning by the Gestapo," whispered Hedy. "Everyone was arrested, all of the Pfieffers and the Jewish family hiding in their cellar."

"God have mercy," repeated Inge over and over, barely audible.

"How did you find out?"

"Marta told us," answered Inge. "She was so proud that as a *Zellenleiter* in her street cell she was able to turn the Pfieffers in for their anti-government activities. She bragged to us about the reward she will receive from Doctor Goebbels, himself."

"Someone informed Marta about the Pfieffers," lamented Hedy. "We don't know who, but we wonder if they might have seen me take food to their house. If I was seen then the S.S. or Gestapo will come for us. They could come at any moment."

Both women were distraught, almost beyond control. Klára tried to offer reassuring words, but she knew their stress had good reason.

"You're right." Klára verified their fear. "If the Gestapo finds out that we were supporting the Pfieffers with food, we are doomed. We must act quickly. Both of you must leave Berlin as soon as possible. I'll help you."

"You are kind and good, Baroness." Hedy left her chair, took Klára's hand and kissed it, "We'll do whatever you think best."

"Both of you should return to your homes. I'll give you money for train tickets and a good severance for your living expenses."

"I'll take Liesel with me to Rügen," offered Inge. "She doesn't need to know why or what has happened. I'll tell her it's for a holiday."

"Hedy, we'll tell Marta some story about your family and that you had to leave immediately."

"The house will need replacements for us, Baroness," stated Inge. "We can't leave you here without a cook or maids to run the house. I'll find the replacements for you."

"Thank you, Inge. That's a good idea. Perhaps you should go first, Hedy, this evening or tomorrow morning and then you and Liesel the next day. We need to plan a story for Marta. A good story that will not alarm her."

When all the details were worked out, Klára went upstairs. She, too, had to make a plan for leaving, as soon as she could get away. She took a small bag from her closet and thoughtfully began to fill it with only a few things that were dear to her—pictures, letters, papers, jewelry. She folded a few dresses on top of the treasures and replaced the bag in the closet. Klára would be ready to leave whenever the right moment appeared.

Later that same day, in mid-afternoon, Marta left for her *Ortsgruppen* district meeting, providing a good time for Hedy to leave the house without any questions. She was packed and ready to go. Klára gave her an envelope containing a generous severance pay and extra money for tickets. They embraced as friends who had shared acts of courage and conviction.

"Gott sin mit Sie," Hedy whispered as she kissed Klára's cheeks. And then she was gone down the steps to the waiting taxi. She would take the train to Cologne and then an omnibus to the Eifel village of Monschau, her home in the Ruhr River valley. Klára breathed a sigh of relief. It would be unlikely for Marta to notice that Hedy was gone before the next morning's breakfast.

Within an hour Liesel announced to Klára the presence of two women, Ilse and Frieda, waiting for her in the parlor. Klára greeted them, both were eager to begin work. Klára gave them a cursory interview and then took them to the kitchen where she left Frieda with Inge to learn necessary procedures while she guided Ilse through the rest of the house, explaining her chores and expectations.

Both Ilse and Frieda were gone from the house before Marta's return, but Klára was so unnerved by the whole experience, she decided to go for a walk in the Tiergarten and then on to the Adlon Hotel where she entered a telephone booth and called the Countess Maltzan. Without identifying herself, Klára simply said, "Do you have time for a walk in the park?"

The countess immediately answered, "I will meet you in half an hour."

The two women met outside the hotel's entrance, but instead of going inside they turned toward the Tiergarten and walked together.

"I'm certain *they* are listening to my phone calls. It's good that you didn't give your name and only spoke in vague terms."

"I must leave Berlin as soon as possible. A family in our neighborhood was hiding the Jewish family of their cook in their cellar. They were all arrested this morning. My cook and housekeeper have been giving them food for months. I've sent my housekeeper away from Berlin already and the cook and maid will go tomorrow."

The countess assured Klára that her haste in their removal was not ill-conceived and added that Klára should also leave Berlin as soon as possible.

"Yes, I must leave as soon as I can. I feel that time is running out. I'm so afraid. How can *you* not be afraid?"

"I'm terrified every minute, Klára, for myself and for those I love and for all those I don't even know," the countess answered. "I suspect that I will be caught one day, but what else can I do? I have nothing but myself to lose."

"I think of my son and my family, I have so much to lose, Countess. I should be as brave as you are and continue, but I cannot. I must go home. Will you help me?"

"Of course I will. I have no plan at the moment, but something will present itself. You may have very short notice, be prepared to go at any time."

"Franz is away from Berlin at the moment. I've no idea when he will return, but whenever he does, I hope that he will spend long hours at S.S. headquarters. He replaced my chauffeur with an S.S. driver. It's becoming more difficult to go and come without someone watching my every move."

Very conscious of the burdens borne by the countess, Klára held her hand, "I know that I'm asking much of you with little notice, but I'm growing desperate and I fear that I could make a terrible mistake."

The countess understood and promised to help. Klára thanked her and said good-bye. Feeling somewhat better, Klára walked home, had a light supper and went to her room early.

The next morning when Liesel, instead of Hedy, served Marta breakfast, she asked Liesel, "What's wrong with Hedy today?"

Liesel, always terrified of Marta, lowered her head and murmured an answer so softly that Marta could not understand it. Instead Klára answered, "Hedy received news from her mother that her father is gravely ill and that she should come home to Dusseldorf right away. I felt she should go, so I gave her two weeks. She left this morning."

"Hmm, I didn't know Hedy came from Dusseldorf. That's so very far away. I doubt she'll ever come back."

Inge spent the entire day preparing a big pot of *Pichelsteiner*, a stew of meat and vegetables, and an apple strudel. She spoke to Klára tenderly, "I can't leave you without good food to eat. I have no idea if Frieda will cook the things you like."

"I'll miss you, Inge." Klára embraced her and gave her an envelope with two months wages and enough money for two train tickets.

After supper was served and Marta had retired to her room, Inge and Liesel left. Klára watched their taxi speed away down Ebertstrasse until it was out of sight. Now she was all alone. Even though Frieda and Ilse would arrive before dawn in the morning, they were strangers and really of no comfort to Klára. She hardly slept at all. Before the sun had risen, Klára was waiting at the door to meet Frieda and Ilse. She took them to the kitchen where Frieda immediately began to prepare breakfast.

When Ilse served breakfast to Marta, she was very pleasant and Marta liked her. "I think this young woman is an improvement. She seems quite cheerful. Hedy was always so morose."

When Marta finished her coffee, she went into the kitchen where she was quite startled to find Frieda. "Who are you?"

"Good morning, I'm Frieda, the temporary cook. For two weeks I'll be here, Madam."

Marta went back into the morning room and addressed Klára with little decorum, "Where did Inge go? When?"

"Well, I let her go for a holiday. With Hedy gone to see her family, Inge felt anxious. She's not seen her family in a long time. It seemed only fair to let her go home, too, so I gave her a holiday."

Klára tried to keep her voice calm and her demeanor cool. She didn't want Marta to hear or see the fear that gripped her heart. Thinking of Hedy and Inge going home helped calm her fears. She thought, *Hedy should be almost there by now.* "Of course, Liesel went with Inge. She can do nothing without Inge's direction."

"Too many changes with no warning, Baroness." Marta felt uneasy. "The Colonel will not like it."

"Marta, everyone senses that war is in the wind," answered Klára. "It makes everyone a bit on edge. People need to be with their families when they feel insecure."

"The Führer has promised no bombs will fall on the Fatherland, ever," Marta emphatically reminded her. "Why should anyone be nervous? The Führer is determined to take back all of Germany's territories without any violence. There will be no war, Madam. Germany and the Führer are too strong. No one will dare go to war against us."

"Well, nonetheless, we're all feeling the need to be with our families. Where is your family, Marta? Wouldn't you like to take a holiday to see your family?"

"It's far too cold for a holiday. March is not holiday weather," she retorted, "and my family is non-existent." She studied Klára, "You aren't planning to leave, are you? The Colonel won't allow it."

"No, no... I will be here until the summer; then I will go back to Budapest to bring András home." Klára excused herself from the table and went to her room, leaned against the closed door and tried to catch her breath.

Franz returned to Berlin three days later and, like Marta, felt the departures of Inge and Hedy very strange. He was suspicious. "It all seems too convenient, Klára. On your own whim, you give everyone holidays, in March? And you organize replacements so quickly?"

"Frieda and Ilse were suggested by Inge. She didn't want to leave us for a day without help," explained Klára. "I really don't see what is so strange. Hedy had to go, her father is dying. I certainly understood that, having just lost my father. That circumstance affected Inge. She became very anxious and felt a great need to be with her family."

Franz studied Klára's face until she turned away, then with no inflection in his voice, he said, "Send for András, Klára. Have your mother bring him here or she can take him to Fürstenfeldbruck. Marta can go there to fetch him."

"That's an excellent idea, Franz, thank you."

Klára realized she was becoming a prisoner and she *had* to leave within the next two weeks. After that Franz would know Inge and Hedy were not coming back and that fact would make him tighten even more his control over her.

Mid-afternoon, only two days later, while Klára was sitting in the sunny morning room reading, Ilse approached her with a telegram. Franz was not at home and Marta had been gone from the house for less than twenty minutes. Klára opened the envelope. The words she read were shocking to her... *"András has pneumonia. Return to Budapest at once."*

Klára crumpled the telegram, left it on the table and hurried to her room, changed her clothes and took out her packed bag. She sat down and looked around the room. There was nothing else there she wanted, but now how was she going to leave? Her thoughts were interrupted by a soft knock on her bedroom door.

Ilse looked into the room, "Your taxi is here, Madam."

Klára thanked her, but wondered who had called a car for her. She made her way down the stairs, said good-bye to Ilse and left her house with no regrets.

The car waiting for her, not a usual taxi, was an ordinary black car with a driver. The driver took her bag, opened the rear door and as she ducked into the back seat she realized someone was seated inside.

"Dolf! I can't believe you are here. I've longed for you to come and now here you are!... Here to save me from all this." She fell into his arms with joyous relief and kissed his cheeks, "Did you come from Budapest? Have you seen András?"

"András is fine, Klára," he answered as he gently held her hands while the car sped away from the curb. "I'm sorry that you were frightened, but we had to create a reason for you to leave."

Klára thanked him again and kissed his cheeks and his hands. She couldn't take her eyes from his face, his kind brown eyes. She felt his strong arms around her and she felt safe, "I've been so worried that I would never go home again, never see András or you. Dearest Dolf, I love you so," she confessed. "You can't imagine how happy I am to be with you again."

"I couldn't wait another day to take you away from here, Klára." Rudolf kissed her forehead, "I promised András and your mother I would bring you home."

He tried to keep his breathing controlled, but he was rapt with emotion, seeing her again, having her in his arms, taking her away from this place, taking her home. "I'll never let you live in such danger again. You and I are flying from Berlin to Budapest tonight. Have you ever flown before?"

She shook her head *no* and smiled at him, tears welling in her eyes, "You always make me cry, Dolf...with happiness."

"I have new papers for you. There should be no trace of your travels. We'll be home by morning."

As dusk arrived they were sitting together looking down on Berlin as the plane banked steeply over the city and took them far away. One stop in Prague to refuel and then on to Budapest where Tamás stood waiting for them at an airfield west of the city. Klára was thrilled to see him again. The chauffeur, Auguste, with Tamás beside him in the front seat, drove the couple back to Andrássy Avenue where everyone was waiting for them.

András stood in the campanile watching for the car and when he saw it, he and Hóvi ran down the stairs all the way to the front entrance where he joined his grandmother and Silva, eagerly waiting to greet his mother.

Berlin

When Franz returned home from S.S. headquarters late in the night, the house was quiet; everyone had retired to their private rooms hours ago. He worked in his office for a brief time and then went upstairs to his bedroom. He rarely went into Klára's bedroom or even spoke to her at night when he returned from wherever he had been and this night was no different. He did not even think of her as he prepared for bed.

Marta had returned from her meeting early in the evening; she had gone to the kitchen to get her meal from Frieda, the new cook. They had spoken briefly with no reports of consequence to Marta. She took her tray upstairs to her room and left the empty tray outside her door as usual. The tray was gone in the morning when she opened the door to go downstairs for breakfast. She took her seat at the morning room table and opened her *Der Stürmer* paper. After a few moments she realized she heard no one in the kitchen, nor did she smell anything cooking. She left her place and walked into the kitchen. There was no one there. Only a plate of strudel covered by a white napkin in the center of the table.

Where have they gone? Marta sucked in a deep breath and stood without any words. Walking back into the morning room, she noticed a crumpled paper on the table. She read the telegram and then suddenly the thought—*she has left*— came into her mind. Marta quickly made her way upstairs and opened Klára's door without knocking. Klára's bed had not been slept in; nothing seemed to be missing, everything was in its place, but Marta knew—*Klára was gone.*

Marta went back downstairs, made a pot of coffee and waited for Franz to make his appearance. Marta had mixed feelings. She knew the baron's fury would be roused and she feared him, but she was also elated that Klára was gone. *Klára has never been one of us,* Marta thought, *never loyal to the Führer, never a believer in the cause. Good riddance in my opinion!*

At last Franz came into the morning room in his full dress uniform, looking so handsome and superior, Marta thought. She poured a cup of coffee for him and casually said, "They've all gone, Colonel von Werner—the new cook, the new maid, and your wife."

She kept her eyes lowered on the coffee cups and her voice as soft and controlled as she could, "The cook was here when I came home last evening, but I didn't see the others. I've no idea when they left. Perhaps you knew they were all going away?" She took a quick step toward him, handing the telegram to him, "I found this on the table."

Franz scanned the words, but said nothing. He reached down for the coffee cup. Marta dared to glance up at him. He stood with the cup to his lips. She was startled by the look in his eyes, seemingly drained of all color, icy white, staring far away with a look that made even Marta shudder. She wondered if it was concern for the boy or disdain for his absent wife. He replaced the cup onto the table without the slightest sound.

"I'm far too occupied to bother with Klára or the boy for now, but in time…" Franz placed his hat on his head, put on his gloves—all the while his jaw clenched tightly. "Hire a new staff for the house, Marta. They must be party members. Klára was never of any importance here. She will not be missed."

April, Budapest

A rhythmic April rain splattered gently on the glass panes of the conservatory, while from inside the greenhouse Klára watched streams of water run in random patterns across the glass. She breathed in the rich, earthy air that filled the warm interior and sighed, thinking to herself, *for a long while I never thought it would be possible to feel so safe or content again.* Klára smiled as she watched András and Hóvi weave in and out of the jungle-like palms and ferns as if they were on some exotic adventure. To see her beloved son happy in his new home far away from the madness of Berlin brought her great relief. Her thoughts drifted to Rudolf. Soon after their return home, Rudolf had left Budapest for destinations unknown. She knew his clandestine involvements likely meant he was in some kind of danger and she said a silent prayer for his safety.

Spain

On his way from Budapest to London, Rudolf first stopped in Spain where the Spanish Civil War had just ended and General Franco, a fascist, had gained control. Rudolf had traveled there to meet Wilhelm Canaris. Canaris, still the head of Abwehr, the German intelligence organization equivalent to MI6, was in Spain to influence Franco on behalf of the Nazis. Rudolf and Canaris met at the Sobrino de Botín Restaurant on Calle Cuchilleros where they dined on *cordero asada*, roasted lamb, and drank *fino sherry*.

In the old wine cellar of the Botín, Rudolf and Canaris spoke openly to each other. Canaris trusted the young man who sat across from him. From the beginning of their covert relationship, Canaris saw von Házy as a man much like himself, a true genteel human being of proper good breeding with human-itarian sensibilities and an uncompromised sense of integrity. Canaris believed that von Házy desired as much as he to stop the Nazis before they could bring catastrophe upon Germany and all of Europe. Canaris also felt assured that the good count neither hated nor blamed the noble German people for the atrocities planned by Hitler and his Nazis.

"I arrived in Spain as an agent of Hitler," Canaris confessed. "My assign-ment—to convince Franco that it would be in Spain's interest to grant Germany certain concessions." Canaris smiled slyly, "Instead, of course, I advised Franco to take the opposite position—to remain neutral in the coming war."

"In support of your advice for neutrality, Britain has dangled an attractive incentive before Franco...a fortunate alliance created for all of us."

"Yes, most definitely, the money deposited in Swiss bank accounts for Franco and his generals was a very welcome enticement from the Brits. I must say, much appreciated by Franco," affirmed Canaris. He leaned forward toward Rudolf, "Personally, I'm grateful for Britain's decision to join with me and my associates to interfere with Hitler's plans."

Canaris willingly shared more information with British intelligence by passing an envelope across the table to Rudolf, "I took these notes myself at a recent meeting with Hitler. You must pass them on to MI6 immediately," he cautioned. "The Polish invasion is imminent. My notes also include information divulged about the S.S. *Einsatzgruppen* plan for mass extermination of Polish Jews. Knowledge of that possible atrocity should be exposed as soon as possible.

"I know that von Kleist previously passed on similar information to the Brits. We wonder how this information was received, because we have seen very little reaction from the West."

"Sadly, it's true." Rudolf shook his head, "The West seems to drag its feet when action is so necessary. But I only deliver information, Admiral. I have no influence on how it's received nor do I have any influence on the action or non-action taken. Certainly, I offer my own point of view and sometimes implore them to take action, but I feel that my voice is rather small. I'm sorry I can't offer more."

"I understand. These things tend to move quite slowly, even while the terror seems to grow at rapid speed." Canaris looked at Rudolf seriously, "That's why, at times we must take action into our own hands. Within the Abwehr and Wehrmacht there are officers who can no longer tolerate the direction Hitler is taking our beloved Germany and, at this moment, those officers are devising plans for the assassination of Hitler."

"The Brits would be supportive of assassination plans, but they would maintain a hands-off attitude concerning such action." Rudolf sat back in his chair, "Our agents would be grateful for the Germans to take care of the Nazi problem from the inside. Such a plan could bring an end to the threat of war, allowing the West to do nothing, to remain openly inactive." Rudolf assured Canaris, "I will help, if you need my help."

The two men shook hands and parted.

London

After leaving Spain, Rudolf arrived in London. That evening he met Olivia Allen-Gainsborough for drinks in the elegant Rivoli Bar at the Ritz Hotel on Piccadilly; it had been a long time since he had seen Olivia. The attractive young woman was waiting for him in the bar. Dressed in a gold lamé evening gown with diamond clips holding back her chestnut hair, she reminded Rudolf of the American actress in "The Thin Man." *Nora Charles? What was her name?* He tried to remember.

Olivia stirred her Pimm's Cup as he walked toward her. At one time, ten years ago when they first met, the two had had an intimate relationship, but Olivia had never held his interest. No one ever held his interest for long, except for Klára. However, Olivia seemed quite delighted to see him again.

Rudolf walked to her side and kissed her hand as he greeted her.

"I'm looking forward to sharing this mission with you, Rudolf," she cooed. Olivia hoped for another chance at a personal liaison. He was so smashingly handsome and such a refined gentleman. Olivia had been terribly disappointed when he left England ending their intimate liaison and then, ever since, seemed disinterested in renewing any romantic relationship with her. *Oh, well,* she thought, *perhaps the war will bring me new chances.*

"It's very good to see you again, Rudolf. How are things in Budapest?"

"So far, much the same turmoil as usual," he answered. "Still holding off the Nazis with one arm while embracing them with the other. We shall see where it takes us—to disaster, no doubt."

"Well, it's our hope to divert disaster," Olivia responded. "What news do you have for us?"

"For Sinclair, ASAP." Rudolf removed the envelope from his vest pocket, "Let's hope the information spurs action from the West."

Olivia raised her glass to click against his dry martini. "You know they will study every aspect first, don't you?"

"Of course, *Ez az élet*, Such is life."

"Are you sure Budapest is where you should be, Rudolf?" She paused, "When war comes to Europe? Perhaps you should stay here with us."

"Possibly you're right, Olivia. The day may come when London will be a safer place than Budapest, but I can't leave those who rely on my protection. And if war should come to Budapest, my help will be needed there." He sighed, "We shall see."

Rudolf remained in London and Bletchley Park for almost a month. From England he and Olivia traveled to France.

Summer, Lake Balaton

During the summer of 1939 rumors of imminent war spread across Europe. Despite their fears, the von Esté family left their Andrássy home, as they did every May, to spend summer at Lake Balaton. András could hardly wait, because he had heard all his life of the wonderful summers at the lake. And he found it every bit as exciting and wonderful as he had imagined it to be. Against the background of a loud cicada serenade, András and Hóvi shared every adventure throughout the hot summer days.

Klára and Tamás introduced András to all the customary activities at the lake, swimming at the Kisfaludy Strand or at Hévíz, sailing in the regattas, hiking and exploring all the fantastic geological sites, in particular those on Tihany, where they also visited Rudolf's grandmother. Tamás and András spent much time walking through the vineyards while the old gentleman taught András everything he knew about the grapes and the vines. Silva's contribution to András's entertainment was to make *meggyleves* along with all the other typical summer recipes for him to taste. András loved all of it.

"You have an empty tummy like your Uncle Stefan," Silva teased him. "It takes a lot of good cooking to fill you up!"

András liked to hear that he favored his Uncle Stefan. András knew not in appearance, because he looked like his grandfather, but *in his ways* as Silva put it. "András, you have *ways* like your Uncle Stefan—that smile and sweetness of yours—like him. And just as mischievous, just like Stefan! Everyone smiles when they see your smile. Everyone wants to make you happy, because you bring such happiness to all of us."

Sometimes, on a rainy day or on a day just too hot to be outside, András and Hóvi tiptoed into his uncle's old room. On this particular day, a breeze blew through the open windows sending the lace curtains fluttering into the cool, dim, quiet interior. András walked reverently around Stefan's room looking at the model biplane hanging from the ceiling, the intriguing music box that he dared not touch, the framed photographs on the dressing table, the books in the bookshelf, and the wooden oars and hiking sticks standing against the wall. András always had the feeling that Uncle Stefan might walk into the room at any moment. Everything seemed to be waiting for him just as he had left it.

András took the photograph of Stefan from the dresser and studied it...a young man, very fair, with a broad smile. Replacing the framed photo on the dresser, he gazed at the other images—one of his grandmother standing at the shoulder of his grandfather, another large colored photograph of a young woman in a sky-blue dress with a halo of blonde curls around her beautiful face, one of his uncle, as a boy, standing arm and arm with another young boy who looked very much like the Count Rudolf, and finally, a colored photograph in an ornate silver frame of a lovely little girl with black hair and shining eyes who he recognized as his mother.

András pulled one of the books from the shelf, it was about sailing and had many pictures of riggings, different kinds of sails and instructions for tying knots. He lay across the bed and began to turn the pages. His uncle loved to sail and, so he, too, would love to sail.

At that moment Ana came into the room in a great rush, "Oh, Master András, you're here! The rain is coming in a gale off the lake. Help me, please, get these windows closed before everything is drenched!"

July

Rudolf spent the summer traveling with stops in Balatonfüred as often as possible. In July he appeared at the lake just in time to go with the von Esté household to the Anna Ball. They all sat outside on the terrace with a good view of the dancers.

The boys in their uniforms and jingling spurs impressed András. Their lively performances of intricate Hungarian folk dances thrilled him. His own dreams began that night of an Anna Ball when he could wear the gold buttons and spurs.

Soon András was dancing around the terrace, too, along with Count Rudolf who waltzed with Klára and then Elizabeth. Even Tamás twirled Silva over the pavements. The Anna Ball transported all of them to a night of fantasy and reminded the grown-ups of times past, happier times so distant from the horrors that loomed over them that summer. They stayed out late into the evening, well past András's bedtime. That night became his favorite night of the entire summer.

Another warm July evening Rudolf and Klára drove into Balatonfüred and walked along the strand to the Veranda. They sat at a table on the deck and gazed at the spectacular view of the lake and the distant southern shore where lights flickered on as dusk began to fall. Rudolf reached across the table and took Klára's hands in his. Neither spoke, but the moment was poignant for both of them.

Klára broke the silence, "This is all that we can ever do, Dolf. Hold hands and, really, we shouldn't even do that. I fear we are hopeless."

Rudolf looked down and breathed in the summer air—*what could he say?* He looked up into her eyes, "I will never dishonor you, Klára, or your marriage, but never ask me to leave you. I will never leave you."

He smiled at her, "I'll always be near you, just promise me you'll never return to Berlin."

"That's an easy promise for me to make, Dolf, but what does the future bring for us? What will happen after the war? Will I be able to stay in Hungary? It terrifies me to think of the future. I can't bear to think of what may happen to my András if he should ever again come under the influence of Franz."

"Don't worry about that now, Klára. I can assure you that Franz is quite occupied making war plans and I suspect the war will keep him away from András and from you for a long while." He raised her hands to his lips and kissed them tenderly.

Germany and Poland

In August, Reinhard Heydrich, Franz von Werner, and two other S.S. officers passed by the colossal stone *Reichsottenführer* standing guard by the iron gate entry into Lichterfelde Kaserne, headquarters of the S.S. in Berlin. As they got out of their car and climbed the stairs into the building, Heydrich smiled wickedly as he said, "The Führer has signed a non-aggression pact with Stalin and the Soviet Union in preparation for our invasion of Poland. Hitler promised the Soviets that we Germans will not extend our invasion into Russia."

An S.S. lieutenant laughed, "Well, Hitler had to appease the Russians so Stalin won't get in the way of our tanks."

"As September nears, Hitler grows impatient for a reason to begin his invasion of Poland," Franz stated.

"That's why we're here," answered Heydrich. "Colonel Himmler has evidently devised a plan of action to speed up the invasion."

Once the men settled into the posh green leather chairs around a large table in the conference room, Colonel Himmler entered and began to reveal the details of what he called *Operation Himmler*. "My plan will give Hitler the reason he needs to begin his invasion of Poland. It's quite simple, but, I must say, devious."

Himmler smiled. "My plan will cast the blame for the invasion of Poland upon the Poles themselves!"

Himmler had definitely piqued their interest; the S.S. officers leaned forward, arms on the table, as they peered at Himmler. "The site I have chosen for the ruse is Gleiwitz, a small village on the German-Polish border, the location of an unimportant, non-descript German outpost and site of a German radio station."

On August thirty-first in the early morning hours, a unit of German soldiers dressed in civilian clothing engaged in a vicious attack against the Gleiwitz radio station, killing all German workers. Shortly after the raid Heydrich and his S.S. officers arrived in full military uniform to investigate the "massacre." They found the body of a dead Polish soldier in uniform near the site, providing the evidence they needed to claim the Poles launched the pre-emptive attack.

Feigning righteous indignation, Hitler immediately ordered his troops to march into Poland. In the pre-dawn hours of September first, a massive invasion of troops, tanks and air power stormed across the Polish border. Soon afterwards the Soviets crossed into Poland from the east to defend their borders and met the Germans in the middle of the country. At that point Germany and the Soviet Union divided Poland, each country taking half for their own. A harsh period of brutal enslavement of the Polish people began under the boot of both Germans and Soviets. Hitler gave Heydrich's *Einsatzgruppen* free rein to deal with Poland's Jews.

By late September the Polish armies and air defenses had been completely overwhelmed. The German forces stood at the gates of Warsaw, Poland's capital and within ten days Warsaw surrendered.

Shortly after the initial invasion of Poland, the governments of France and Britain issued an ultimatum to Hitler to cease his act of aggression. Their ultimatum was ignored. France and the British Commonwealth declared war on Germany. A second *Great War* began.

Berlin

Rudolf traveled to Berlin once again on the business of salt. *"Every army must have its salt"* was written on his business card. Rudolf sat in an old café on Wilhelmstrasse, only a few blocks from the Adlon Hotel, waiting for Wilhelm Canaris. When Canaris arrived the two men greeted each other and began their discussion over tankards of Schultheiss beer.

"Shortly after the invasion of Poland," Canaris began, "my Abwehr agents returned to Berlin to inform me of the S.S. *Einsatzgruppen* atrocities they witnessed. Of course, I wanted to see for myself the severity of the S.S. actions, so I spent several days touring Poland, including the village of Będzin where the Jewish synagogue was set ablaze with all of Będzin's Jewish citizens inside." Canaris leaned toward Rudolf, "They were all burnt alive. What I saw in Poland disgusted me. I'm convinced the S.S. has committed despicable war crimes. When those crimes are revealed, great shame will befall Germany."

Canaris took a deep breath.

"I reiterate that my purpose in giving this information to British intelligence is to overthrow Hitler and his Nazi Party," Canaris stated convincingly and then added with great stress, "The Resistance to Hitler within Germany is growing, Count von Házy. We are placing our trust in Britain to do the right thing. We have faith in the new Prime Minister, Mr. Churchill, to deal sternly with Hitler and his criminal entourage."

Meanwhile on the German-Polish border, Reinhard Heydrich spoke to Franz von Werner, "Well, Canaris has returned to Berlin after his tour of our great Polish conquest. He continues to pose as a loyal German, but I watch him closely. I still do not trust Canaris, even though it appears Hitler continues to have faith in him. Canaris has never joined the Nazi Party nor has he ever sworn an oath of allegiance to our Führer. How can he be trusted?"

Franz agreed.

Heydrich continued to speak of Canaris, "He is not as loyal as he would like for us to believe. Even if Hitler trusts him, I do not. We must keep our eye on Canaris, Franz."

Late September, Ḫungary

At the end of September Rudolf and Klára decided to take András to Eger to visit Rózsa and Pál and their children. The Szabós met the train and took everyone in their truck back to their place in the country. Rudolf rode in the back of the truck with András and the Szabós' children, József, nine years old, and Vera, six like András. Klára rode in the front cab with Pál and Rózsa and their little baby, Sárika, who was almost a year old. When the truck pulled into the Szabó complex, József jumped out of the back and called for András to follow him as he ran toward the sawmill. Vera hurried to follow the two boys.

"József has been excited to take András on a tour of the barrel making," said Pál. "They'll be busy all morning."

"Let's go into the house and have some refreshment," invited Rózsa. "I have *kávé* and *strudli* for us. It is wonderful that both of you are back in Hungary to stay. . . at last! "

Happy to be together once again after so many years apart, the adults sat around the Szabó dining table catching up on all the news of their families and politics. Klára held the tiny Sárika in her arms, "It looks like she may have gotten your beautiful red hair, Rózsa. I'm so glad. Sárika is a lovely baby."

"Yes, she is," agreed Pál. "I'm a fortunate man to have two redheaded daughters as beautiful as my Rózsa."

After an hour or so of small talk, the conversation turned serious when Pál stated, "We were very glad to hear that Hungary has declared *neutrality* in Germany's new war. We've had our concerns about Prime Minister Teleki."

"It's wise for you to be apprehensive of Teleki," said Rudolf. "He seems to be against any alliance with Germany, in particular one that would draw Hungary into the war. But we can't forget that at the same time Teleki remains an active anti-Semite."

"Last spring we were terribly disappointed when he decided to support the passing of the Second Jewish Law by the Hungarian Parliament," fretted Rózsa. "Such a terrible law! It frightens me. We were surprised that Teleki embraced a law written by Imrédy, his rival. The law is so harsh, restricting Hungarian Jews even further. Jews aren't allowed participation in any area of Hungary's cultural or economic life." Rózsa shook her head in despair, "and it defines a *Jew* as anyone with Jewish ancestors no matter how distant. Christian conversion no longer counts. It's a deplorable situation."

"To be honest, Rózsa, I'm deeply concerned for you and for your family," Klára said as she reached across the table to take Rózsa's hand. "The Germans have already marched into Austria, Czechoslovakia, and Poland. I'm concerned for all of us. I've seen with my own eyes how the Nazis treat their own citizens. They will have no mercy for ours."

"Our parliament is loaded with elected far-right Arrow Cross members. They worry me as much or more than the Germans," said Pál. "Fortunately, powerful Hungarians have subtly controlled and checked the Arrow Cross for years. I suspect the Arrow Cross party will lose popularity as soon as Hungarians realize they are Nazis in disguise. I believe all this anti-Semitism is a temporary trend," Pál avowed as he tried to reassure Rózsa. "Perhaps, it's a way to appease the Germans—to create the illusion that Teleki's government is in line with German thinking, even though Hungary declared neutrality and has no plan to participate in Germany's war."

Pál added another positive note to calm Rózsa, "We've experienced these kinds of policies before, they're bad, but they seem to fade away and then everything returns to normal again."

"What you observe is true, Pál, but Rózsa's concerns are legitimate," cautioned Rudolf as he spoke seriously to Pál, "Have you considered leaving Hungary, at least for a while?"

"No, I have not, Rudolf," answered a stunned Pál. "Where would we go? Why? Do you think things are that serious?"

"Not at the moment, Pál, but to be blunt, yes, the situation could become very bad."

"I stopped going to synagogue years ago. Only a very few people in Eger know that I'm Jewish," Rózsa answered. "None of the children know that I... or that they are Jewish. Pál's family is so well-respected here in Eger. We aren't afraid, but I do fear what might happen in the future," Rózsa confessed. "I think having to leave Eger, emigrating from Hungary, leaving our families would be a greater fear. I couldn't bear to take my children from their grandparents, from their aunts and uncles, from their family."

"Let's hope all this anti-Semitism is just propaganda," stated Pál. "Horthy remains the real power and he's primarily anti-Hitler. He doesn't want Hitler's influence in Hungary. Horthy speaks with pride about being a *Magyar*! We Szabós are patriotic Hungarians; we embrace Magyarization, we speak Hungarian. My oldest brother fought in the *Great War* and Rózsa's brothers did the same. We hold sacred everything Hungarian! We are *Magyars!*"

"My dearest father said those very words, Pál, and they killed him." Rózsa looked off into space as tears welled in her eyes, "They beat a gentle old man to death for no reason other than his faith."

Pál rose from his chair and knelt beside her, "We'll stay alert and if things seem to be getting worse, we'll leave Hungary. I promise to keep you and the children safe, Rózsa. We'll make a plan of protection for the worst possible situation."

Rudolf could see that Pál was convinced he and his family could protect Rózsa and their children, but Rudolf was just as certain the Szabós should be alarmed and seriously consider leaving Hungary while possible exits still existed. Equally concerned, Klára knew from experience the cruel, inhumane nature of the Nazis. *If the Germans should invade Hungary, Rózsa and her children would be in grave danger.*

"Rózsa, if you ever need me, I will help you in any way that I can," Klára was emphatic.

"As will I," Rudolf assured the worried couple. "If the Arrow Cross or Nazis...if either one should become more problematic...if we should find out anything...we'll contact you. If you need help, contact us as soon as possible. We'll help you in whatever way we can."

The four sat silently for a few moments, contemplating the severity of their conversation and the dire possibilities that loomed ahead in a future that seemed very dark. Rózsa broke the silence, "Let's find the children and go into Eger to see the sights. András must see the minaret and the castle! We can have supper in town before you take the last train back to Budapest."

After a long afternoon of sightseeing the families decided to go down into *Szepasszony-volgy*, the Valley of Beautiful Women, to have supper in one of the little cellars. The children had a glorious time getting to know each other and visiting all the interesting places of Eger. András regretted leaving his new friends when he and Klára and Rudolf boarded the evening train for Budapest. András stood at the end of the last car waving good-bye to the Szabó family until darkness surrounded them.

Late November, Budapest

A big storm pelted Budapest with several feet of snow, covering the von Esté garden and creating a winter wonderland for András and Hóvi. András plodded through the mounds of snow while Hóvi bounded over them. He built a snow fort and made stacks of snow balls. Hóvi wrecked everything, but András didn't care, they were having the best time.

Inside the von Esté house, Elizabeth, Klára, Tamás, Silva, and Rudolf sat around the dining table discussing their future plans. The threat of war loomed over them.

"I think that we should consider spending Christmas at the Lake Balaton villa," Elizabeth sighed. "We need to find out what winter is like at the lake. Who knows what the new year will bring us? We may not want to stay in Budapest."

"It's a good idea, Duchess," agreed Rudolf, "to have a contingency plan in case we find ourselves in an impossible situation. But I think you should keep Switzerland in mind as well. As a place of refuge, a place where your family would find safety."

"I would rather stay in Balatonfüred than go so far from Budapest, if possible."

"It will be cold at the lake, more snow than here and the lake will be frozen," Tamás informed them. "The villa was built to benefit from the cooling lake breezes. The window arrangements are intended to maximize those breezes through every room in the hot summer, so the villa will be much colder than this Andrássy house."

"Well, we can wear layers of sweaters and leggings. We can put woolen caps on our heads and gloves on our hands," suggested Silva, "and I'll keep the kitchen's ovens and fireplace glowing. Everyone can take their meals in the kitchen. We can close off the bigger rooms. Ana and I will pack up the downy comforters and woolen blankets. We won't freeze."

"I'll bring the crèche and Ana the decorations," said Tamás. "We can make a warm and wonderful Christmas with everyone together at the lake in winter."

Rudolf's grandmother, the Countess Alexandra, stayed in Budapest, but Rudolf made his way to the lake several times to see how the von Estés were weathering the winter's chill. He found them making the best of a cold situation. Silva's baked Christmas goodies filled the villa with scrumptious aromas of cinnamon, ginger and nutmeg. Ana decorated the rooms festively and Tamás constantly stoked the fires to keep the rooms cozy. Elizabeth played traditional noëls that drifted through the house while outside András and Hóvi romped through great piles of snow.

Even though the wind was cold Klára had never been happier. Rudolf joined in their fun, making snow angels, helping to build snowmen and a snow fort with plenty of snowballs they hurled at each other. The von Estés filled the villa with laughter and good cheer, even though it remained a very cold place.

1940
January, Berlin

Shortly after Swedish attaché, Per Anger, took possession of his new office in Berlin's embassy, he received a visitor, the Austrian Count Rudolf von Házy. Anger rose from his desk, greeted von Házy and invited him to sit. Anger viewed his visitor as a gentleman, an impressive figure of a man, tall and elegant, only a few years older than himself.

In very guarded language, Rudolf explained that he, too, was a visitor in Berlin. "I hope you'll find Berlin hospitable, despite the current chill hanging over the city." Rudolf continued by telling Per Anger a story, "My friend is interested in reconnecting with his Scandinavian relatives in Norway. He's unable to speak with you in person, but he hopes you will deliver this message to his relatives." Rudolf added rather forcefully, "Winter brings wolves to the gates. We have seen them. They are there, the threat looms at Norway's wall."

Sliding his hand across Per Anger's desk, Rudolf left a small piece of paper as he withdrew his hand. Per Anger took it. Rudolf stood up, thanked the attaché for his time and said he hoped they would meet again.

As Rudolf left the office, Per Anger noticed for the first time that the count walked with the slightest limp. Per Anger unfolded the piece of paper; only a telephone number was written on the paper. Although inexperienced in coded conversation, Per Anger recognized that von Házy had come to his office because he wanted to share important information with the Swedish Embassy.

Taking a deep breath, Per Anger dialed the number written on the paper. The phone rang only one time before it was answered at the other end. A deep, rather gruff voice spoke, "I am a contact with the German Resistance. We will keep you informed on the movements of the Nazi army. Warn your friends in Norway and Denmark that invasion is imminent; the Nazis are already in country."

Per Anger composed an encrypted message to send to the Swedish Foreign Department in Stockholm... *I am now in contact with the German underground resistance who has brought the following message.* Anger sent the warnings he had received, including the count's strange message exactly as it was spoken to him, but he had great concern about the message. He worried that it might not be understood.

Unfortunately, his message was understood, but the Swedish Foreign Office chose to disregard it, partly because Anger was a young and inexperienced attaché.

A few days later, an anonymous contact, one of Canaris's Abwehr agents, passed another cryptic message to Per Anger citing specific details about the forthcoming Nazi invasion of Norway. This time Per Anger decided to send the warning directly to the Norwegian Foreign Minister. Anger's warning so stunned the doubtful Minister, he decided to contact directly the German authority in Oslo and ask him if there was truth in the warning that Germans were planning to invade Norway. The German officer innocently denied any such plan existed, but, in fact, the very next day Norway and the city of Oslo were occupied by the Nazi Army.

Despite the Norwegian Minister's disregard for Anger's warning and the German occupation of Norway, Rudolf was pleased to hear that the reputation of the young attaché Anger increased. After all, Anger's interpretation of the underground's encrypted information had been proven correct. Anger's quick action in forwarding the information to the proper places made him a highly valued attaché in the Swedish embassy. Rudolf sensed that Anger was someone to trust and Rudolf ascertained that he and Anger could work together in the future. Per Anger stayed in the Berlin office for another year and a half where he continued to receive beneficial information regarding the operations of Hitler and the Nazis from both Abwehr and British agents.

ffiarch, Paris

In his role as an SLU agent, Rudolf traveled to Paris where he and his old friend, János Géza met once again at the *vin rouge café* for supper. After their meal of *estouffade de boeuf* the two men traveled in János's car out of Paris heading south into the twilight. Before dawn they arrived in the forested, rocky hills of Limousin. János pulled from the paved road onto a graveled lane and drove another mile before stopping in front of an old farm compound. A single light shone from an upstairs window of the main farm house.

"We are here, Dolf, but it looks like there's no welcoming party."

They got out of the car and walked in the darkness toward the house. The walled complex of buildings appeared pale silver in the moonlight disallowing Rudolf any judgment of the property's condition. As János raised his hand to knock on the door, it opened and Yvette emerged.

"I thought you would never get here! I knew it would be you coming, Rudolf! I could hardly wait to see you again!" She squealed as she jumped up into his arms, "It's been years!"

"Yvette, what are you doing here?" Rudolf was completely surprised.

"I'm a patriot! What do you think? My Joël Graund is here, too. Now you can meet him at last. He's a sharpshooter."

As effervescent as ever, Yvette led Rudolf and János into the dark house. While talking non-stop she lit a lantern on the table and offered the two men bottles of wine, bread and cheese.

"I was so happy to hear that you were coming tonight, Rudolf. Of course, no one said your name, but I knew it had to be you with János. Another Hungarian! One with a cane! It had to be you."

"How've you been, Yvette? How is your daughter?"

"Belle-Marie is still with my sister. I don't see her very often," Yvette looked away wistfully. "She calls Monique *'Mama.'* " And then Yvette was all smiles again as she sliced the bread. "What about that girl…what's her name? Do you ever see her?"

"Klára? Yes, I see her sometimes." Rudolf's eyes met Yvette's for a moment before she turned away. He thought about a time when Klára had seen Yvette in Paris and had so tragically misunderstood what she had seen, but all that seemed so long ago.

Rudolf was anxious to meet the rest of these *Resisters* who called themselves *La Croix-de-Liberté*, but introductions would have to wait until morning. After their fill of wine and cheese, Rudolf and János were led to an attic loft where they made their beds on fresh straw with down comforters.

The next morning Rudolf and János were welcomed to a breakfast table filled with fresh eggs and pitchers of milk. A scruffy looking man stood at the black iron stove cracking eggs into a big skillet. He turned toward them, "I'm Jacques-Pierre, leader of *La Croix-de-Liberté*. We're ready to work with you. We want to be ready for the Germans, because we know they're coming! Unlike most Frenchmen we are not so trusting of Pétain."

After breakfast, Rudolf and Jacques-Pierre sat alone together discussing the part *La Croix-de-Liberté* would play in France's growing network of resistance fighters.

"So, you know our little Yvette? She is a bundle of energy…no?" leered Jacques-Pierre, in a manner suggesting that he imagined a carnal relationship between the two of them. "We only have a few women in our ranks. Women are better left at home to raise the children…umm, but some like Yvette can be helpful at times," and again, he smiled the same wicked smile.

Rudolf gave Jacques-Pierre the codes he would need to decipher the messages coming across the wireless from Britain. He also provided information on safe houses and on ways to contact other Resisters. Only Émile, son of Jacques-Pierre, would share this important intelligence.

—ᴍ—

By spring Germany had already conquered Poland to the east and Czechoslovakia and Austria to the south. Now Hitler's focus turned to the west. By April both Denmark and Norway had fallen and by early May the German invasion of Belgium, the Netherlands, Luxembourg and France had begun. The German tanks had no problem breaking through a very weak French line of defense cutting off French and British divisions in the north, forcing the Brits to make a frantic evacuation across the Channel to England.

The threat of Germans approaching Paris was a terrifying idea for Parisians. Hundreds of citizens began to pack their belongings, load their cars and leave the city. In the first weeks of June the German armored columns crossed the Somme and pushed south toward Paris. The French army disintegrated, leaving the Parisians in a panic. All roads leading from Paris became clogged with fleeing refugees. The situation became so difficult many Parisians gave up and returned home, stocked up on supplies and locked their shutters. Yvette and Joël Graund settled into Rudolf's old flat and waited.

Their wait was not long. On the fourteenth of June the Nazis occupied Paris and within days the Nazis controlled two-thirds of France. At Compiégne the Germans and the French Marshall Philippe Pétain signed an armistice that allowed the French to establish an independent government in the unoccupied one-third of France.

Yvette and Joël, holed up in the tiny flat for more than a week, discretely watched the occupation from their balcony. One afternoon Joël climbed from the balcony up onto the roof where he had a better view of the Boulevard Saint Germaine. From his perch along the cresting he could see the masses of German soldiers marching through the streets, but at the same time he observed many Parisians going in and out of their flats to shop or to their jobs. Glad to hear Joël's news, Yvette had felt claustrophobic in the confined flat and wanted to escape it for normal life.

It was a Friday, a beautiful sunny June day, when the two of them left the flat and went for a walk in the nearby Jardin de Luxembourg and then on to the quay along the Seine. Suddenly several cars streamed by, causing much excitement. One of the cars was an open Mercedes with two uniformed men seated in back. Several German soldiers standing near Yvette and Joël stopped at the curb, stood erect, extended their right arms and shouted "*Heil Hitler!*"

In the Mercedes, Hitler himself with the architect Albert Speer was on a whirlwind tour of Paris for only a few hours before flying back to Berlin. Yvette and Joël looked at each other. *He's such a little man, not so scary. La Croix-de-Liberté can certainly wage a good fight against him and his illegal occupiers.*

By the next week, Joël and János were sitting around a wireless in the cellar of a small café listening to a speech by Charles de Gaulle. De Gaulle was one of the French generals cut off in the north by the German invasion. He had fled to London where he set up a kind of government-in-exile. With help from the Brits, De Gaulle established contact with the French Resistance and made a passionate appeal to all French people, soldiers, and sailors to join him in continuing the war as allies of Britain against the Germans. Joël and János and the others in the cellar were moved to tears. As proud Frenchmen they all stood in place and sang together "La Marseillaise," in whispered voices.

By the end of June János prepared his report for MI6. He wrote…

All military hostilities in France, other than the occasional acts of sabotage, have ceased. The official French Senate and Chamber of Deputies met in the town of Vichy in central France to draft a new constitution creating the Vichy government. The officials also voted to give full governing powers to Marshall Petáin as he governs the unoccupied part of France. Petáin's Vichy government is made up of ultra-conservative men who have always opposed the French Republic. These conservatives, known to be stubbornly patriotic, have fought the Republic for decades. Their goal is to create a more nationalistic France, a France exclusive of all foreigners and Jews. Petáin and his Vichy government have already drafted a series of anti-Semitic policies, an obvious concession to the Germans.

Berlin

The Führer promoted Wilhelm Canaris to the rank of full Admiral, despite Heydrich's expressed apprehension. Heydrich sat in his own office looking at the box of personal file cards. He took the Canaris card from the file and read the last entry... *"Canaris speaks openly against the perfectly legitimate S.S. actions in Będzin, Poland."* Now, Heydrich added another negative notation to the card... *"Canaris, now Admiral, will have complete access to Third Reich classified information. Canaris must be watched. Canaris is not to be trusted."* Heydrich was convinced that Canaris had goals counter to Nazi purposes. He thought, *Canaris is too soft, too liberal in his sensibilities.*

After Hitler's occupation of Poland, Admiral Canaris became more certain than ever that Hitler had to be stopped. Canaris and other Wehrmacht officers had formed a highly secret group of Resistance within the official Abwehr intelligence wing of the Third Reich and now these like-minded gentlemen were in complete agreement. Adolf Hitler was a madman leading Germany to disaster and he had to be stopped. Based upon their shared anti-Nazi feelings, they used their positions in the Abwehr to plan various scenarios to rid Germany of Hitler. The tight circle of Abwehr Resistance members remained in close contact with British MI6 and SLU agents, in particular Count von Házy.

By the end of summer, the fears of Canaris and his friends were realized. Despite Hermann Göring's promise, *"Bombs will never fall on the Fatherland, certainly never on Berlin,"* in August the British RAF bombed the Tempelhof Airport and armament factories in Berlin. Even though not particularly successful, the British had demonstrated Germans were not impervious to attack. Neither Hitler nor Göring could make such promises any longer. And, more importantly, the nighttime air raids emboldened the Abwehr Resistance in their clandestine opposition to Hitler.

Fall, Budapest

Tamás and Elizabeth sat together in the library on a September morning reading the newspapers, shaking their heads and discussing how Leopold would be so distraught over the news. Hitler's Third Reich had issued the *Second Vienna Award* taking Northern Transylvania from Romania and returning it to Hungary, a gesture gratefully accepted by the Regent Horthy. *"Finally, our lands lost so long ago in the 1920 Treaty are returned!"* stated Horthy. But Tamás declared, "Of course there will be a price to pay. We shall find out what it is soon enough."

By November that price became clear. Germany pressured Hungary to sign the *Tripartite Pact* aligning Hungary with the Axis Powers—Germany, Italy, and Japan. Neutrality was no longer an option for Hungary. Hungary once again found itself on the German side in the second *Great War* against the world.

In an independent act of good faith, Hungary's Prime Minister Teleki signed the *Treaty of Eternal Friendship* with Yugoslavia promising that Hungarian troops would never participate in an invasion of Yugoslavia.

Although Teleki was determined to keep Hungary independent of Germany, he did align with the far-right conservatives in Hungary's Parliament. His intent was to appease the German-leaning members of parliament by increasing anti-Jewish legislation. New laws further excluded Jews from many occupations, including military service, and from all cultural activities. At the same time the government encouraged Jewish communities in every Hungarian city to organize social aid projects to assist their own people with the hardship issues of unemployment. All Jews were required to register with their community officials in order to receive any available help.

—⁂—

Whenever Pál had business in the city, Rózsa and her children went with him to visit her mother. Éva loved having her grandchildren in the house. Their presence reminded her of the days when the house was filled with her own six children...noisy with constant voices, music, and laughter. She took her three grandchildren into the music room where she played lively tunes as the children danced and sang. Vera joined her grandmother on the piano bench to proudly show her what she had learned to play since their last visit. Rózsa stood nearby, happy to be in her mother's lovely home again.

Pál sat at the kitchen table with Rózsa's brothers, Ferenc and Abram while Magda poured cups of steaming tea for them.

"We're non-Jews," Ferenc told his brother-in-law. "Neither I nor Abram have registered with our Jewish community council and we haven't let Mother register either. You haven't registered Rózsa have you?"

"No, we haven't registered. I haven't thought too much about it. I don't suspect we'll need any aid from the council," he answered.

"It isn't about receiving aid, Pál," argued Abram. "It's about collecting a list of our names. The list is about knowing who we are and where we are."

"Why would the council want such a list?"

"It isn't the council really, you know," said Ferenc. "It's the government, the ultra-right. Their goals are similar to the German Nazis. They want to rid Hungary of all Jews."

Pál shook his head; such an idea was just too inconceivable for him.

"The problem for us, Ferenc and I," Abram said, "is that we are excluded from the military, from joining the Hungarian Army. So, we stand out. We're both strong, healthy men who aren't in the army. People wonder why not? Well, it's an easy answer. We must be Jews. It's getting dangerous for us to go out in the daytime, even to go to work at the von Esté building. Most Jewish workers who work there simply sleep there."

"If we can, we go to work, but some days it's impossible. There's so much harassment to get there." Ferenc smiled, "But at night we go out with friends like us."

"What are you doing at night?" Pál asked.

"Mostly we talk about what we would like to do to turn things around. We have no resources or connections, but we want to be ready if a serious resistance against these ultra-conservatives should rise up. We'll be ready to join the fight."

"There's so much danger for all of you," lamented Pál, "for all of us."

Pál's thoughts moved to Count von Házy—to his warnings and his offers of help if they should ever need him.

"You should contact Count von Házy. He's offered to help us in any way that we should need his help. My sense is that his offer is not a hollow one. I'm convinced he has ways to actually accomplish his offer. Von Házy is a man who moves in rather mysterious ways, but I trust him completely."

1941
April, Hungary

A blustery day, more like March than April, blew branches of yellow forsythia in Rudolf's way as he passed through the gate into the von Esté garden. The cherry trees were loaded with buds ready to burst into flower. He entered through the kitchen door and greeted Silva who was busy making loaves of bread. Rudolf breathed in the delicious scents of yeast and olive oil and baking bread.

"We've not seen you for a while." Silva gave him a big smile. "How is the Countess feeling today?"

"Grandmother is quite anxious about returning to the lake. She wants to go as soon as the weather allows, but she can hardly imagine going anywhere without László," answered Rudolf. "His passing has shaken her severely."

"Dear László was her faithful companion for so many years."

"Thank you for looking in on her." Rudolf laid his hand on Silva's shoulder, "She greatly appreciates the attention, as do I."

"The Duchess and Tamás are in the library. It seems to be a busy time for them. Go on, join them and I'll bring in coffee and torta soon."

When Rudolf entered the library, Elizabeth and Tamás stood up, leaving stacks of papers on the desk, to welcome him warmly.

"I have very bad news," Rudolf had a grave expression. "Teleki is dead! He committed suicide."

Tamás leaned back in his chair, "That is terrible news!"

"What drove Teleki to such an extreme act?" asked Elizabeth.

"So much has happened so quickly," began Rudolf. "In March Hitler thought he had Yugoslavia's commitment to the Reich, but when the Yugoslavian delegation returned home and announced their agreements with the Reich, a coup erupted. The Yugoslavian government was overthrown and replaced with an anti-German king."

"The account of those events alarmed no one," Tamás declared, having read only sketchy reports of these events in Hungarian newspapers, "but, in fact, it's these seemingly small events that have great ramifications for Hungary."

"Hitler saw the Yugoslavian coup as a betrayal; he was enraged. He ordered an immediate invasion of Yugoslavia," Rudolf continued. "Hitler demanded that Prime Minister Teleki send Hungarian troops to participate in the invasion, but Teleki refused. After all Teleki had given his word to the Yugoslavian delegation that Hungary would never participate in any invasion of Yugoslavia. Knowing that his honor was at stake, Teleki took his own life this morning rather than go back on his word."

Rudolf added, "Horthy has already appointed the pro-German Bárdossy as the new prime minister."

"Why would Horthy chose such a right-wing member of the cabinet?" voiced Tamás. "One so obviously pro-German?"

"Well, Bárdossy will have no such qualms as Teleki about sending Hungarian troops into Yugoslavia. He has made no such promises to anyone."

"The fact is that Hitler dangled territories lost in the *Treaty of Trianon* in front of Teleki, but the bribe did not sway him. However, the bribe did appeal to Horthy and Bárdossy. They see the occupation of Yugoslavia as an opportunity to reclaim more lost territories. Hungarians will be marching alongside Germans into Yugoslavia within days."

"It's always about that treaty," lamented Elizabeth. "If the West had not been so severe in their redistribution of lands from the Austro-Hungarian Empire, perhaps... Well, it's far too late to even dream things could be different.

"Dolf, you remember that lovely old Perlmutter family home, the one at the corner of Andrássy and Csengery Streets?" Elizabeth asked, "Ferenc Szálasi has made it the headquarters for the Arrow Cross Party. He calls it the 'House of Loyalty.' I wonder what Bárdossy will do about that?"

"I think Bárdossy will allow Szálasi and his Arrow Cross free rein," sighed Rudolf.

When Rudolf left the von Esté house, he ran into Klára who was waiting for him in the garden. She spoke to him softly as she stood in the shadow of the vine-covered trellis, "It's good to see you, Dolf. It's been a long time."

Rudolf embraced her, he couldn't stop himself. He missed her. *He stayed away from her for so long waiting for her to grow up and now he stayed away because he couldn't have her.* She looked up at him and they kissed each other, but it was agony they felt rather than pleasure, so he let her go.

"I must leave again soon, but then I'll come back to stay." There was resolve in Rudolf's words, "I plan to reasume my position at the Drawing Academy and travel less, but now there is just too much work to be done." He sighed heavily, "As you've seen, my grandmother is very frail and tired. She seems ready to close her eyes and welcome eternal sleep at any moment." Rudolf remained quite formal. "I'm determined to be by her side when she takes her last breath. You and your mother and Silva have been very attentive. I know that you've spent many afternoons with the Countess reading to her or playing the piano for her. She finds those afternoons peaceful. I'm most grateful to the von Estés for bringing such comfort to a precious old lady in her last days."

Rudolf couldn't bring himself to look into Klára's eyes; it was too difficult. But she forced him to look at her. She held his hand to her lips, he could feel her tears. He put his arms around her once again, "Do you cry for my grandmother, Klára... or for us?"

"For her... for us... I miss you."

"I must go, Klára, but when I return we'll talk again. Perhaps there's something we can do."

The April War

Just as Rudolf left Budapest for a rather long trip, Hitler began his campaign of retribution on Yugoslavia. The *April War* or invasion of Yugoslavia began on the sixth of April. The Budapest newspapers reported that Horthy and Bárdossy fully cooperated with the Germans, allowing Hungarian troops to join with the Germans as they marched across Hungary into Yugoslavia. By the twelfth of April the air bombardment of Belgrade by the German Luftwaffe, called *Operation Punishment*, brought about the complete surrender of the Serbs. The Axis annexed Yugoslavia.

The sudden, unexpected need to invade Yugoslavia meant the plan most dear to Hitler, the invasion of the Soviet Union, had to be postponed. Now, with Yugoslavia taken care of, Hitler could turn his full attention to the Soviets and their Red Army.

Late June, Neutral Sweden

One bright Nordic summer day, Rudolf left the opulent Grand Hôtel in Stockholm and walked along the wide Södra Blasieholmshamnen as he watched swans gliding by on the Riddarfjärden; he crossed the Strömbron Bridge onto Gamia Stan where he made his way through the narrow, cobbled streets of Old Town to the office of Per Anger. Anger had been recalled to Sweden as an official diplomat of the Foreign Trade Department. Part of his duties included trade relations between Sweden and Hungary, specifically the exchange of Swedish steel for Hungarian food stuffs.

Rudolf entered Anger's light and airy office to find the pleasant Anger standing ready to greet him warmly, "It's very good to see you again, my friend, and how goes the price of salt these days?"

"Very steady, thank you for asking," Rudolf responded, "and congratulations to you on your new position in foreign trade. I assume you are pleased to be home again?"

"Ah, yes, it's good to be back where one can savor *surstromming*, fermented herring, and *kottbullar*, meatballs!" laughed Anger. "Let me pour shots of *branvia* for us before we begin our serious discussions." Then Anger added, "I'm grateful for all of the valuable information you and the British have given us over the past year. It's been very helpful."

Anger had the sweetest smile and pure blue eyes that always made his words ring with sincerity. "Although Sweden retains its neutrality, the government continues to make concessions to the Germans, concessions that call into question our objectivity. Like Hungary, Sweden walks a tightrope—anti-Soviet, anti-Nazi—wanting to remain independent, but constantly squeezed between two evils."

"Speaking of Hungary, I've come to encourage you to commit to a move to the Swedish Embassy in Budapest." Rudolf leaned forward in his chair. "It's my belief that in the near future your presence may make a valuable difference in the lives of Hungarian citizens. The future of Hungary appears precarious. Hungary needs friends in neutral places. I think we can work well together toward a common good."

The two men decided to meet again. They shook hands. Per Anger promised he would come to Budapest... *"as soon as arrangements can be made."*

Berlin

After Sweden, Rudolf had other important stops to make before returning home. He walked into Berlin's Tiergarten to see Admiral Canaris sitting on a bench throwing nuts to gray squirrels as they scurried from the linden trees to his feet and back to the trees again. Canaris looked up to see the tall, dark Count von Házy advancing toward him across the pavement. He noticed that Rudolf spun an elegant cane in his hand as he walked making Canaris wonder if he ever really needed the cane; his limp was barely detectable. Canaris stood to greet Rudolf. Canaris put into his pocket the small metal tube that Rudolf passed to him during their handshake. The two men walked together along the pathway casually engaged in conversation.

"The Brits are happy that *Operation Barbarossa* is finally under way," Rudolf announced to Canaris. "The Yugoslavian coup certainly must have made the impatient Hitler very anxious."

"Hitler has been obsessed by plans for the invasion of the Soviet Union for months," agreed Canaris. "His ambitions for the complete destruction of the Soviet state and its Red Army have nearly consumed him. In a speech I attended, Hitler explained to his armies how the success of *Operation Barbarossa* will affect the Reich. Of course, we all want the defeat and demise of communism, but Hitler became completely carried away by his corrupted idealism. He spoke little of communism while emphasizing the importance of a symbolic victory of the superior Aryan race over the inferior racial diversities of the Soviet states. Then finally, back to the point, Hitler added, *'Our success will destroy the false ideologies of communism....forever.'*"

"On that one point Britain and the Western Allies agree with Hitler," stated Rudolf who was charged by the strongly anti-Communist MI6 Director, Stewart Menzies, to deliver information to Canaris. "It's for that reason alone the West is eager to support the Nazis in their war against the Communists. And, now you have in your possession some valuable information that will no doubt help the Germans in their attack on Russia."

Canaris felt the metal tube in his pocket and took a deep breath of the sweet summer air, bit his lip and lamented, "Unfortunately, Hitler has other beliefs that affect his agenda.... the conspiracy theory of an evil Bolshevik-Jewish union conspiring to control the world's economies and governments."

"When Hitler spoke to the Wehrmacht, it was with passionate fervor as he encouraged the German soldiers...no, demanded them...to forget their noble ideals of knighthood and attack the Jew and the communist with aggression, without mercy." Canaris seemed angry as he walked alongside Rudolf. "In fact, Hitler has ordered ruthless severity against all who oppose the Reich—Jews, Slavs, the clergy, the academics and philosophers, the nobility. Who will be left?"

Canaris stopped walking and looked at Rudolf with a kind of desperation, "Hitler equates his battle to heroic battles fought by mythical Nordic gods of legend."

Rudolf thought about the profound nature of Canaris's words and of their terrible consequences.

"It will be Heydrich's *Einsatzgruppen* leading the way in Russia as they did in Poland," Canaris's voice had a terrible wretchedness in it. Rudolf heard his sadness and felt it, too, as Canaris continued, "They have their orders to search out and execute, with no arrest, no trial, anyone with ties to the communists. They will be shot on the spot. Then the *Einsatzgruppen* will turn their focus on the Jews and mass murder will begin as it did in Poland. The *Einsatzgruppen* have monstrous goals, unspeakable aims! The sole purpose for that organization is murder and the men who serve in that murder squad are the S.S., the Gestapo and special police forces. All of them willing to slaughter the innocent without mercy."

Suddenly a cloud passed over the sun casting a dark shadow in the park. Rudolf felt his throat tighten, tears welled in his eyes and dread gripped his heart. Dread for the future and for the people he loved. Rudolf bowed to Admiral Canaris and they parted, each knowing that the fate of many lay in whatever action they would take to stop the horrors conjured up by the madmen all around them.

After Canaris returned to his office, he sat alone at his desk and pulled the small tube from his pocket, unscrewed the lid and emptied the rolled paper onto the desk. He flattened the paper and read the coded message. A detailed report of all strategic military positions in Russia mapped out on the paper. Information held only by Britain at that time.

Operation Barbarossa, the invasion of Russia by German forces, began soon after the city of Kassa, Hungary, was bombed, perhaps by the Soviets, perhaps by the Germans. The facts were never clear, but the affront to Hungarian sovereignty brought Hungary to declare war on the Soviet Union and to become a full Axis partner with Germany and Italy. Hitler accomplished his goals one by one.

August

After several months traveling from city to city on MI6 missions, Rudolf was back in Hungary at last. He hoped that he would not be called away again. Since his return he spent most of August going back and forth from Budapest to the Tihany villa. But now Rudolf was back in Budapest where important matters demanded his attention.

A coded message arrived from Berlin one morning. "On 31 July, Field Marshall Hermann Göring issued a mandate to S.S. Gruppenführer Reinhard Heydrich." Rudolf read the mandate with apprehension...

> *In addition to your previous orders to address the Jewish Question through emigration and evacuation, you are now charged to make a plan that includes all necessary arrangements... the administration, finance, operation and physical facilities needed for the Endlösung der Judenfrage, Final Solution of the Jewish Question, a question that plagues all of Europe within the German sphere of influence. You are to use all at your disposal... the S.S., the Gestapo, the S.D. Security Service, local police forces... to accomplish the Führer's ultimate goal for the Third Reich.*

Endlösung... the Final Solution... Rudolf held the message in his hand... an ominous term, its meaning sent chills. He knew counter plans must be made as soon as possible to oppose the horrific actions that would be part of Heydrich's *Endlösung.*

Certainly, Rudolf knew Hungary's Jews would not escape Heydrich's Final Solution. Prime Minister Bárdossy, using the anti-Communist excuse, had allowed the Hungarian Arrow Cross Party to re-emerge from Teleki's imposed exile. Ferenc Szálasi and his party had an immediate influence on the government's pro-Nazi, anti-Semitic policies. Bárdossy, in his efforts to please both Hitler and Szálasi, encouraged the parliament to pass a harsh Third Jewish Law, based upon the Nuremberg Laws of Germany. The law prohibited marriage and sexual intercourse between Jews and non-Jews and nullified any pre-existing intermarriage between a Jew and non-Jew. The law also made further strict prohibitions against Jewish participation in Hungarian political, economic, cultural or social activities.

Bárdossy and Hitler have tied Hungary to Berlin so firmly now, Rudolf thought. *It's only a matter of time before Heydrich brings* Endlösung *to Budapest. German soldiers are already walking freely within the city and Arrow Cross is nothing more than* Nyilas, *Hungarian Nazis.*

Budapest, Late Summer

All the von Estés were at the lake, except for Klára who returned by train to the city for a very specific purpose. As her taxi traveled from the station she noticed a few German soldiers on the streets and her thoughts turned instantly to Franz. He, too, would come one day to Budapest; he could come at any moment. Klára's trip to town had a purpose, to visit Father Nikola at the parish church in her Andrássy neighborhood. She had serious questions to ask the priest; she needed to know what she had to do to end her marriage to Franz.

"Nothing, nothing can be done, Madam," the old priest was obviously agitated. "Marriage is an institution established by God. No man can put it asunder. Marriage is a Holy Sacrament. Say nothing more on the subject."

"But surely there is something, Father, something that can be done?" Klára pleaded, "I'm married to a man who does not love me. He has changed into someone I cannot love. The marriage is intolerable."

"God has joined you to him. It is up to you to help him become a better man."

"Father, my husband believes so differently from me on grave, moral issues."

"Saint Paul declared that the relationship between husband and wife should be a reflection of the relationship between Christ and His Church. Paul said, 'Let women be subject to their husbands, as to the Lord, because the husband is the head of the wife, as Christ is the head of the Church. Therefore as the Church is subject to Christ, so also let the wives be subject to their husbands in all things.'"

"But Christ also told husbands to love their wives and my husband has told me that he does not love me."

The priest looked at Klára thoughtfully, but seemed uncomfortable with the conversation. Klára realized that Father Nikola had no intention of helping her in this endeavor. She thanked him and moved away from him. She sat down in a pew and knelt to pray. Once again Klára felt helpless, but she also knew, there was no question, she could never live with Franz again, certainly never *be* his wife again. Nor would she ever again let András fall under his influence. Tears began to stream down her cheeks as she made her solemn supplication.

"Baroness," a quiet voice startled Klára. "I'm sorry to interrupt your prayers, but I may be able to help you."

Klára looked up to see the compassionate young parish priest, Father Mihály, leaning toward her from the pew in front of her, "I didn't mean to eavesdrop on your conversation with Father Nikola, but I heard what he said and I feel obligated to tell you that there are ways sanctioned by the Church to nullify a marriage. I'll be happy to speak with you."

Father Mihály led Klára from the dark interior of the nave out into the sunlit cloister. They sat down on a bench near the herb garden; its pungent mix of scents drifted in the air.

"Tell me about your marriage, Baroness."

Klára confessed everything to Father Mihály. The good times in Cologne, their mothers' influence on their relationship, her disappointment and misunderstanding about Rudolf, her feelings for Rudolf, that she entered the marriage in love with another man. Then she explained about Franz and his transformation into a Nazi, espousing monstrous beliefs completely in opposition to her own and, finally, her fears for András. Klára told Father Mihály that Franz had told her he never loved her and had only married her to please to his mother. "My marriage to Franz is untenable, Father. What can be done?"

"Certainly you must obtain a civil divorce first, Klára. If you wish to marry again, in particular, a Catholic, then here is where the Church stands on the matter." Father Mihály became quite serious, "It's impossible to invalidate a valid marriage. Marriage is considered a binding union that makes a second marriage impossible. You must prove there were *impediments* present, concealed at the time of the marriage that would have disallowed the marriage to take place. If such an impediment did exist then your marriage would be invalid; not binding from its beginning. A tribunal will consider if the impediments you present do, in fact, invalidate the union according to teachings of the Church."

"Must Franz be a part of this process?"

"Yes, Baroness, even though he is not here in Hungary. Even though he may be difficult to work with, he must be part of both the civil and tribunal processes. Your husband must answer the tribunal's questions; he can answer those questions in writing, but both sides must be heard. Remember the impediments you claim must have been present before the marriage took place. Go home and think about what these conditions may be and come back. I will help you."

Klára thanked Father Mihály and left the cloister. She knew it would not be easy, but she was determined to sever all ties, especially sacred ones, to Franz. First of all she would pursue a civil divorce.

Berlin

Franz stood in his study perusing his *Der Stürmer* newspaper. The publisher Julius Streicher had written, *"When Germany's noble war draws to a victorious close the Jews will be erased from the earth."* Franz smiled. He and Heydrich were heavily involved in working out the details for Hitler's mandate, *Endlösung*.

Heydrich sent out invitations for a conference to be held on the Final Solution. Franz felt a great sense of pride to be so close to Heydrich, such an important man with such an important mission for the Reich. Franz was thrilled to be an integral part of it.

A statement in *Der Stürmer* by Nazi Propaganda Minister Joseph Goebbels intrigued Franz. Goebbels asserted... *"Hitler prophesied that the Jews would cause another world war and that their annihilation would be a necessary consequence.* Hitler believed the actions of the Reich were guided by the avenging hand of God to rid the world of vermin." Franz had personally heard Hitler say, *"The Third Reich and I are doing God's work."* Franz smiled to himself and thought, *but the benevolent Hitler also demands the extermination of these Jews and other undesirables be done humanely.*

Personally, Franz believed this kindness of his Führer was unnecessary, but he admired Hitler's thoughtfulness. One of the topics for discussion at Heydrich's conference would be the methods, humane methods to be used to accomplish *Endlösung*.

As Franz mulled over the enormity of these words, he was interrupted by Marta, who brought in a tray with hot coffee, cognac and a plate of *Berliners*. "Excuse me, Sir, but I thought you might desire some refreshments and I have mail for you. One envelope from Budapest is marked *URGENT.*"

"You take such good care of me, Marta," Franz responded as he took the thick envelope from the stack of mail, "Thank you."

Franz used a letter opener to rip the envelope and removed the papers, documents indicating they were official applications of divorce from a Budapest attorney. A second folded document was from the Church. He turned from page to page in both documents scanning the words. His smile grew wider. He laughed, tore the papers in half and said, "Take this garbage to the kitchen and burn it in the oven, Marta."

"I may need to plan a trip to Budapest one day soon, Marta." Franz poured the cognac into a cut crystal glass and threw it down his throat, "there are matters left undone."

Franz poured himself a second glass, sat down in his leather chair, sipped the liquor slowly and stared off into space.

September

Hitler desired to reward Reinhard Heydrich for what the Reich believed to be excellent results of *Einsatzgruppen* projects in Poland and more recently in the Soviet Union. He gave Heydrich a new title and a new position, *Reichsprotektor of Bohemia and Moravia* with headquarters in Prague.

Before Heydrich left for Prague he met with Himmler and asked him, "How do you think the Wehrmacht found out about the many secret Russian positions held by the Red Army? From where did such clandestine information originate?"

When Himmler answered that it was an intriguing question, Heydrich shared his secret thoughts, "Von Werner and I have been watching Admiral Canaris for years. You know that he is not a member of the Nazi Party, never has been. Despite Hitler's faith in Canaris, I hold no such faith. I'm of the opinion that Canaris is an agent for the British. I believe it was Canaris who supplied the tactical information on the Soviet positions to the Wehrmacht, information he obtained from the British. The purpose of his treachery eludes me, but I have no doubt that Canaris is a traitor to the Führer."

Himmler rubbed his chin, the idea was incredibly dangerous, to accuse one so near Hitler, but it was certainly possible. Himmler began to think of other bits of information involving Canaris, "Perhaps we should begin an investigation of Canaris. His comings and goings, his contacts."

"Now that von Werner and I are off to Prague, we will no longer be able to keep our eye on Canaris. It will be up to you to watch him. The stakes are high. We have no idea as to his goal or purpose."

September, Prague, Czechoslovakia

From the moment he arrived in Prague, the extraordinary capital city of Czechoslovakia, Heydrich was determined to make an immediate impression upon the Czechs. *Authority with a strong dose of fear* was Heydrich's method to accomplish an understanding with the Czechs. He never wanted the Czechs to doubt for a moment the awesome power of the Reich, nor should they doubt his authority over them, authority to do as he saw fit.

Informed that an active Resistance movement existed in Prague, Heydrich immediately ordered two hundred Czech civilians, possible Resistance members, hanged in a public square without trial or protest. Following that execution, Heydrich turned his focus to the Jewish ghetto, Theresienstadt, being created in northwest Bohemia. The Gestapo, already responsible for administration of Theresienstadt, was ordered by Heydrich to begin arrests and executions of Jews within the ghetto. Heydrich's desired reputation as *The Butcher of Prague* spread quickly.

Heydrich increased deportations of Bohemian-Moravian Jews to various concentration camps in the East and intensified the numbers of possible Resistance members executed. He was infamous for his brutal treatment of both Jews and Czech Resisters.

Franz admired Heydrich for his dichotomy of character. On the one hand Heydrich approached the Jewish problem in a vicious, dispassionate manner that brought thorough results, but on the other hand Heydrich was a sensitive artist who could charm anyone into a friendly, non-threatening relationship. Heydrich's knowledge of the arts and culture impressed Franz; he especially admired Heydrich's vision to make Prague the cultural center of the Reich. Franz often accompanied Heydrich and other officers to the Opera House for special performances, some commissioned by Heydrich himself!

Despite Heydrich's many obligations as Reichsprotektor of Bohemia and Moravia, his primary focus remained the Jewish problem. His busy agenda always included orders for arrests and executions, all conducted by the terrifying Gestapo. Heydrich used a reward and punishment policy. Special privileges rewarded those Czechs who showed loyalty to the Reich, in particular, monetary rewards given to those who turned in Jews to the Gestapo. Instant punishment—consisting of harsh, brutal consequences—awaited the slightest protest or resistance against the Nazis.

In defiance of Heydrich's harsh policies, the Czech government-in-exile encouraged the underground to fight on with courage. With assistance from British Intelligence, MI6, the Czech Resistance responded against Heydrich's intolerable oppression with sabotage and printed propaganda.

Ḫungary

By the end of 1941 Hungary was a fully engaged ally of Germany, a member of the Axis, and completely involved in the war. Whether by bribery, force, or fear the Regent Horthy had capitulated to the desires of Hitler and the Third Reich. Hungarian soldiers entered southern Russia by the first of July and defeated the Soviets in horrific battle. Thousands of Jews from sub-Carpathian Russia were deported to Galicia in German-occupied Ukraine, where they were all shot to death by the S.S. *Einsatzgruppe*.

1942
Berlin

In late January while in Berlin on business, Rudolf met with one of Canaris's officers who passed to him detailed notes recorded during the Wannsee Conference, recently held to discuss the Final Solution, *Endlösung*. Rudolf returned to the Adlon Hotel, anxious to read the notes. As he crossed the lobby, the memory of meeting Klára in the mezzanine restaurant, so long ago, bombarded his thoughts. He felt relief that Klára no longer lived in Berlin and was no longer engaged in dangerous activities. Rudolf entered his room, locked the door, sat down at his desk and began to read...

Reinhard Heydrich convened the long-awaited conference on Endlösung, *Final Solution for the Jewish Question that plagues the Reich. Fifteen Nazi officials, including Adolf Eichmann, were present at the meeting. The delegates affirmed the supreme authority of Heydrich as chair of the conference and as director of the Final Solution.*

Heydrich presented Hitler's previous preferences for the forced emigration or evacuation of Jews and other undesirables to labor camps and announced those preferences were no longer practical. There are several reasons for this, Heydrich said. Since the war began, we can no longer negotiate with American Jewish organizations to exchange monetary funds for Jewish lives; most European countries are now closed to Jews who have no financial means of support; and all labor camps are at near capacity.

"Therefore," he announced to the delegates, "The Führer has reached a decision on the fate of European Jewry. They are to be eliminated from all of Europe. Elimination is the most practical option for the Reich to use against the Jewish problem. This conference is convened to decide on the methods by which this mandate will be accomplished."

Heydrich reiterated the identity of the superior Aryan Race as people of German, Nordic, Celtic, Slavic, Greek, or Italian origin. All others are considered undesirables, including the disabled, homosexuals, communists, and any dissenter against Hitler and his policies. Endlösung, *the Final Solution, will be their fate, their complete annihilation from Europe.*

Conference delegates discussed the implementation of Endlösung, *including ways to move masses of people from the ghettos to the camps, methods for converting the labor camps into death camps, and how to end Jewish emigration from Germany. That particular dilemma was solved by agreement to simply close Germany's borders. The other two questions required more discussion. At first the delegates wanted the Jews to march on foot from their ghettos to the Eastern death camps, but that method would be too inefficient. The transportation of Jews by rail, by boxcar, would be a more efficient method. Baron Franz von Werner assured the delegates that the rails and boxcars were available and ready. The delegates decided the most efficient means of extermination would be gas chambers and ovens for disposal.*

Heydrich reported most towns and ghettos were encouraged to establish their own Jewish Councils. He explained that the most respected and trusted Jewish citizens—rabbis, professors, doctors, attorneys—served on the councils.

Each council is charged to keep lists of all Jews in their area. The lists must include addresses, numbers in households, occupations and assets for every Jew. Many Jews are already registered in their local communities; soon every Jew will be listed. In the end we will force these councils to help organize, administer, and finance the Final Solution.

As Rudolf refolded the ominous report, he shuddered; he was sickened by what he had read. No doubt of the horror in the report, such inhumane proposals discussed so matter-of-factly. Rudolf breathed in heavily, knowing that the S.S. *Einsatzgruppen* had already begun mass gassing of Jews in Poland and that the Hungarian army had participated along with Nazis in the massacre of Jews and Serbs in Novi Sad, Yugoslavia. *Endlösung* was well under way. Rudolf encrypted the report and forwarded it to MI6; he wanted to leave Berlin as soon as he could, to go home and stay there. Rudolf was convinced the shadow of Nazi evil would spread quickly and would soon cast Hungary in darkness. He wanted to be in Budapest, close to those he loved.

Spring, Budapest

By early spring Rudolf was home again. He walked over to the von Esté house where he found Tamás and Elizabeth busy sorting papers, packing them into file boxes. A roaring fire in the fireplace helped to take the chill off the cool spring morning.

"We want to be ready, Dolf, just in case we decide to leave Budapest for the villa."

"Probably a good plan, Duchess, the situation may become untenable here in our own Budapest." He shook his head, "I hesitate to tell you and Tamás of what might be looming ahead of us." Then Rudolf added, "I've heard that the Regent Horthy has replaced Bárdossy with yet another new prime minister. We now have the so-called moderate, conservative Miklós Kállay."

Both Elizabeth and Tamás looked resigned. Elizabeth raised her eyebrow, "Good riddance!" she said. "Bárdossy allied Hungary too closely with the Germans, taking us into another war! He brought such suffering to the Jews of Hungary. But this change is a surprise; we thought Horthy supported the actions of Bárdossy. Why the change?"

"Horthy, it seems, was becoming anxious about Bárdossy's growing alliance with Germany. Horthy feared Bárdossy's obvious willingness to allow the Nazis to have authority over Hungary's Jews. Horthy believed Bárdossy's extreme feelings against Jews threaten the very independence of Hungary," stated Rudolf. "I understand Horthy told Bárdossy, *'Hungary is quite capable of handling its own Jewish problem without any help from the Germans.'"*

"Horthy, himself, has made despicable alliances with the Reich, Novi Sad for one," asserted Tamás. "He tries to appease the Germans and at the same time keep them at bay. Kállay is just as anti-Semitic as Bárdossy. The Jews will fare no better under Kállay."

Only a few weeks after their conversation in the library, Kállay announced Hungary's intention to continue its support of Germany's fight against the Soviet Red Army. Kállay wanted to prove to the Nazis that Hungary was still on their side. He also encouraged Hungary's parliament to pass a law that confiscated all Jewish property. Even though Kállay loudly proclaimed Hungary's ultimate goal was to clear the entire country of Jews Rudolf was aware of Kállay's secret negotiations with the West to find ways to extricate Hungary from the Axis.

By April Horthy and Kállay experienced severe problems walking their narrow path between appeasement and national integrity. Their words and speeches expressed severe anti-Communist and anti-Semite opinions, enough to stay in German favor, but at the same time both men resisted pressure from Hitler to deliver thousands of Hungarian Jews into German custody.

These people have citizenship papers!. . . Horthy formally protested to the Germans... *We have no right to require them to relocate in Germany.* Finally, to satisfy the Nazis, Kállay promised Berlin... *We will deliver all Hungarian Jews to Germany for resettlement at the end of the war. We need the Jews' labor here in Hungary to support our economic well-being.*

Far-right Arrow Cross members of parliament argued against Kállay and demanded the immediate deportation of Jews from Hungary, but Kállay's decision prevailed. Rudolf received information that the Reich was well aware of the Arrow Cross challenge to the stance of Horthy and Kállay against Jewish deportations. The Arrow Cross strength of opposition revealed a weak link in Horthy's authority and Rudolf knew the Nazis would find a way to take advantage of that weakness.

Madrid

Lost in thought, Rudolf stared at a pair of parrots sitting on a perch preening their feathers. His shoulders felt warmed by the April sun as he sat on a bench in Madrid's Parque del Retiro. He remembered his meeting with Admiral Canaris in the same place so many years ago and all that had happened since that meeting. Canaris arrived taking a place on a bench next to Rudolf's bench. The two men took no notice of each other, but simply sat in silence for several minutes before Canaris opened a small brown sack and began to toss seeds onto the paving stones for the wrens and doves that instantly flocked to his feet.

"I'm sure you've heard about my confrontation with Heydrich," Canaris began. "Ever since he left Berlin for Prague he's had spies watching my every move. Heydrich and Himmler have been suspicious of me since *Operation Barbarossa*. They're certain I have British contacts. When the S.S. arrested Paul Thümmel I had to intervene."

Rudolf did know about the events of which Canaris spoke. He had been notified immediately by MI6 of Thümmel's arrest. Thümmel, a Czech, was, in fact, an agent for the British and had been one of many Canaris contacts.

"I told Heydrich that Thümmel was a double agent, working for Abwehr as well as the British. I tried to convince Himmler that Thümmel's true loyalties were with the Fatherland," stated Canaris, "and that Thümmel's service to the Reich was invaluable. But my intervention only convinced Heydrich that his suspicions were correct, that I am a British spy and Thümmel was my contact."

"It's ironic that Heydrich stumbled on the truth." Canaris laughed, "I'm certain he'll pursue it to the end. He's already informed Hitler of his suspicions and formally appealed for my arrest and worst of all Heydrich has requested that Hitler place Abwehr under the S.D." Canaris threw another handful of seed onto the pavement. "So far Hitler has not complied, but it may only be a matter of time."

These were the reasons Rudolf had traveled to Madrid. Canaris was worth saving. Extraordinary measures would be taken to insure his safety. Not only had Canaris provided valuable information to the West, he had also made great efforts to save hundreds of Jews and other undesirables by bringing them into the Abwehr. Some Jews he made employees of Abwehr, others he gave falsified papers, many he helped leave Germany. Canaris personally saved hundreds from extermination. Rudolf admired Canaris as a courageous human being who acted upon his beliefs regardless of personal risk.

"MI6 will act on your behalf, Admiral. Your service to humanity is greatly appreciated in the West."

Czechoslovakia

As early as the winter of 1941 British intelligence had made contact with the Czech Resistance in Prague. A group of underground fighters were smuggled into Britain for training with MI6. In April of 1942 this endeavor focused on a plan to handle the Canaris situation. In May, two of those Czech partisans trained in Britain, Jan Kubiš and Josef Gabčík, parachuted back into

Czechoslovakia. With help from local resistance, Kubiš and Gabčik devised plans to end the reign of terror perpetrated on the Czech people by *The Butcher of Prague*.

In May Reinhard Heydrich was called to Berlin for a meeting with Hitler. Heydrich still brooded over his confrontation with Canaris and remained incensed that Hitler had not shared his negative conclusions regarding Canaris. On May twenty-seventh Heydrich prepared to travel back to Berlin for his meeting with Hitler where he planned to reiterate his case against Canaris. It was a lovely, warm spring day.

Perhaps this conference with Hitler in Berlin will net a different result, Heydrich imagined, *a result ending Canaris once and for all as I have long desired.* He stood self-absorbed before his bedroom mirror tying his tie. Heydrich was proud of his accomplishments as the Reichsprotektor of Bohemia and Moravia. He smiled at his own reflection, arrogantly believing himself to be all-powerful, invincible. After all he had cowed the Czech people into submission through a vile mix of reward and punishment and he maintained complete control over the region and its people.

A staff soldier entered the bedroom to collect Heydrich's bags and carried them to the car as Heydrich followed. Franz admired Heydrich as he passed by. In Franz's opinion Heydrich was incredibly handsome in his perfectly fitted light gray uniform with the proud German eagle on the armband. Heydrich's crisp white shirt and black tie were visible under the open black collar of the jacket; he looked sharp and elegant. Franz desired to emulate Heydrich's sense of style in every way that he could. Heydrich's manner of walking, his erect posture and his meticulous attention to detail of dress, all were copied exactly by Franz.

"Sir, you should be more careful," warned Franz, knowing that Heydrich often traveled through the Czech villages and countryside in his convertible Mercedes. "Riding around in that open car of yours, especially without an armed escort, may be putting your life in jeopardy."

"No one would dare approach me, Franz," Heydrich proclaimed with his usual conceit. "You shouldn't worry yourself," he laughed. "The Czech people are terrified of me. They're quite aware of my power to end their lives and all happiness. I'm perfectly safe, I assure you. I'll return next week."

Heydrich walked briskly from the house and jumped into the back seat of his dark-green open convertible, demanding that the driver speed away. Franz saluted as the car made its way down the drive, watched until it turned onto the highway, and then returned to his work within the house. Franz had a report to finish on the deportation of Bohemian-Moravian Jews to the Riga and Belzac camps.

As the Mercedes sped over winding country roads on its way toward the German border, Heydrich laughed off Franz's suggestion of an armed escort.

He sincerely believed he had nothing to fear from these peasants. *They have been completely subdued by the might of the Reich*, he thought, as he observed the landscape. But when the speeding car drew near the Troja Bridge, the driver slowed only for a moment to make the sharp hairpin turn.

At that very spot, Kubiš and Gabčik stepped into the road. At first the revolver they carried misfired, but the bomb they threw exploded near the rear of the car causing it to careen and crash. Heydrich and his driver jumped from the car, waving their guns and firing at their attackers. Kubiš and Gabčik fled from the road immediately, uncertain of their success or failure.

Heydrich survived the attack and the car crash, but he was severely wounded by shrapnel from the explosion. He was taken to the nearest hospital where the local Czech medical staff did their best to treat his injuries. As soon as Franz heard of the assassination attempt he wired the tragic news to headquarters in Berlin and then hurried to Heydrich's bedside. When Himmler learned of the murderous act he sent his own doctors from Berlin to attend Heydrich.

Franz faithfully remained day after day by Heydrich's side witnessing Heydrich's intense suffering. The shrapnel and attached debris trapped within Heydrich's body caused severe blood poisoning and his condition worsened. There was nothing that could be done to save him. After nine days of agonizing pain, Heydrich was dead.

The site of Heydrich's assassination was near the small mining village of Lidice, only a short distance from Prague. The S.S. believed the people of Lidice guilty of collaboration with the assassins. The assault so incensed Hitler that he commanded the S.S. and Gestapo to severely retaliate against the people of Lidice.

On the tenth of June the Nazis descended upon the village. All men and boys sixteen and older were rounded up and shot, the women and children were either killed or sent to labor camps while some of the youngest children were taken for adoption by German parents. Finally, the entire village of Lidice was obliterated, burned and wiped from the earth, its name erased from all documents.

Following the Lidice massacre, a thousand Jews from the Prague ghetto, including men, women, and children were deported to concentration camps in the East. From that day forward, in honor of Heydrich, the extermination of European Jews was code-named *Operation Reinhard*.

Franz returned to Berlin to attend the elaborate funeral for Heydrich where more than a thousand German soldiers stood in rapt mourning for the martyred Nazi. Hitler and Himmler eulogized Heydrich with speeches of glorification for the fallen Aryan warrior. Soon after the funeral, Franz learned that Heydrich's position as S.S. Intelligence Chief would be given to Ernst Kaltenbrunner, who would remain in Berlin. Franz's knowledge of Heydrich's system of gathering information was recognized with a new assignment in the special *Protektorate* office in Prague. Franz's new position gave him more responsibility and prestige than his previous assignment as aide to Heydrich.

Summer, Hungary

Klára climbed the Metro steps up to Andrássy Avenue and walked toward her house, suddenly coming to a stop when she saw the black car with its Nazi flags parked in the drive by the front steps. A young German soldier leaned against the driver's side. She swallowed and took a deep breath; she walked with determination into the drive. Klára nodded to the driver as she ascended the splayed steps and opened the front door. Leona, the maid, met her at the door and took her valise, "You have a guest. He's waiting in the conservatory."

When Klára walked into the conservatory she found Franz standing near the fountain. He had watched her enter through the glass doors.

"So, what's this?" he asked as he indicated her dress.

"Red Cross. My Red Cross uniform," she answered. "I volunteer several hours a week. There are so many injured soldiers coming back from the Russian front."

"Your maid told me that the family is at the villa in Balatonfüred." He held a palm frond in his hand and absentmindedly stripped it of its leaves, "so the boy is there, too?"

"Yes, he enjoys the lake very much in the summer."

"Well, as soon as this war concludes I'll have him back in Berlin; you as well, Klára. I would insist upon your return now, but at the moment, I'm assigned to Prague."

Klára took a quiet breath, "I don't understand why you've refused to sign divorce papers. You care nothing for me or András. Our marriage is a sham."

"Poor Klára." Franz smiled a sinister smirk and walked toward her. She instinctively backed up toward the door. "Why did you include the annulment papers for me to sign, Klára? Are you thinking of marrying someone else? Some nice Catholic who can't marry a *divorced* woman? Did you really think I would ever declare our marriage invalid from the start?" He laughed as he drew near her face, brushed her lips with his and whispered in a mocking tone, "You know I loved you, Klára, on our wedding day. Remember how I begged you to marry me?"

Even though tears filled her eyes, Klára was determined not to cry. Suddenly, she pushed him away as hard as she could, catching him by surprise. He fell back from her a few steps, but only laughed and sneered, "There's nothing you can do, Klára. You're mine for as long as I want you and that boy of yours, too."

"Well, I'm off now." Franz clicked his heels, "Only in town for a few hours on business, I'm flying back to Prague this evening."

Franz walked straight back to her, grabbed her shoulders and kissed her hard until she tasted blood in her mouth, *"Auf Wiedersehen, Meine Liebe,* until we meet again."

Franz left the conservatory and the house. Klára sank to the slate floor and did not move from her place against the glass door for a long time. *Oh Papa, I miss you so, and Dolf, where are you now!*

July, Paris

Outside the *vin rouge café* Rudolf and János Géza sat together on metal chairs sharing a bottle of claret and watching the Parisians hurry past them on the sidewalk. Jews were mixed in with the crowds of people, easy to identify because they wore the yellow Star of David badges. Before the two men had finished their bottle of claret, Yvette and Joël joined them.

"The World Jewish Congress just issued a report through the Swiss Consul, the Germans have devised an official policy to exterminate all European Jews," announced Joël. "The policy is called *Endlösung.*"

"Yes, it's true. *Endlösung* is already under way in labor camps in the East," confirmed Rudolf.

"The Resistance here in France is focused on undermining the Nazis through sabotage and counter-intelligence. There's no organized effort to save France's Jews." János made a clicking noise as he settled back into his chair and let out a long breath as though considering the horrors to come. "The fact is some of the Resistance groups are as anti-Jew as the Nazis."

"But some are not," objected Joël. "We've got Jews in *La Croix-de-Liberté* and we've made contact with a Zionist resistance group. *La Croix-de-Liberté* is working with Jewish Resistance in Vichy France…the Resistance is a militant force in the area with a goal to safely conduct Jews across the Pyrenees into Spain. We're told the Americans are funding their efforts."

Rudolf and János traveled with Joël a few miles outside of Paris for a meeting with Jacques-Pierre and other leaders from various resistance groups. The three men arrived at an old dilapidated chateau, went into the once elegant dining hall, and joined several other men seated at an antique gilded table large enough for fifty. Crowded around one end of the table, Rudolf shared codes to be used to decipher radio messages from Britain. When the day of Liberation from their Nazi occupiers arrived, these brave Frenchmen would be prepared.

Within days after Rudolf left France, he learned that thousands of Jews were deported by the Germans from Paris, as well as another thousand arrested in Vichy France.

September, Budapest

After Paris, Rudolf was once again home. He had been away most of the summer. As soon as he had settled in and looked in on his grandmother, he went round to the von Esté front door. Leona greeted him saying that Klára had not returned from the hospital as yet, but was expected by supper time. Rudolf learned from Leona that the family remained at Lake Balaton, while Klára returned to Budapest during the week to work for the Red Cross at the soldiers' hospital.

"Is the Baroness dining alone tonight?" Rudolf asked Leona. When Leona answered in the affirmative, he added, "Then I'll invite myself to join her."

Klára eagerly awaited Rudolf's return and welcomed him to join her at the dining table. "The house is so quiet and lonely with everyone still at the lake, just me and Leona and the cook. You must come every night for supper, Dolf, whenever you can."

"I will." Rudolf leaned close to Klára and took her hand, "Now tell me about this job you've taken."

"It's only volunteer, but I think it's very important. So many men damaged terribly by the war, some physically, all mentally. There's so much to do, more than my skills are capable of." She smiled at him. *He's so beautiful and kind*, she thought.

"I'm glad you've chosen to do this work, Klára."

"Yes, but you know, I miss the courier job I had in Berlin. As dangerous as it was, I would do it again, if there was a need here. You would tell me, if I could help, wouldn't you?"

Rudolf simply smiled at her enthusiasm, but said nothing about his activities, perhaps he would tell her at a later time.

Klára fell silent for a long moment and then she told him about Franz's brief visit, "I knew he'd come some day, but I was far more frightened of him than I thought I would be. He threatened me that at the war's end he would take András and me back to Berlin."

Again Rudolf reached for her hand, "That will not happen, Klára. I won't allow that to ever happen."

"I have done something," she hesitated to tell him. "I want you to know."

His brow furrowed as he listened to her.

"I asked my attorney to prepare divorce papers and the priest to prepare annulment documents. The papers were sent to Franz in Berlin, but he refused to sign them. He told me he would never sign them."

"You included annulment papers with the divorce papers? What did he say about that?"

"Oh, he knew right away that I must want to marry someone else. He didn't ask who. He just implied that no Catholic would ever marry a divorced woman."

"Klára, you know that I'm waiting for you." Rudolf considered his words carefully, "I will go on waiting, but I'm not waiting for a paper to tell me the wait is over. I'm only waiting for you to tell me. We can keep trying to get Franz to sign your papers." Rudolf held her hand. "We will wear him down. Keep sending the divorce papers to him, but we should not worry about an annulment for now."

October

Only a few weeks after the von Estés returned to the city from Lake Balaton they invited Rudolf for dinner. As they sat around the table the conversation turned to serious current affairs in Budapest.

"The atmosphere in Budapest had changed. It's grown so still," said Elizabeth. "When Tamás and I went to the office on Hercegprimas Street today, we could hardly believe what we saw. On the streets there were so few gypsies playing music and even in our own office, the Jews were wearing yellow badges on their clothes."

"Kállay has made this order for Jews to wear badges just to prove he's as evil as the Germans," stated Tamás. "I think of Leopold and how devastated he would be to know how Kállay has distorted the ideal of Magyarization! Now the parliament uses the ideals of Magyarization to separate those undesirables from descendents of the Magyars. They say those undesirables—including Jews—must be separated from us, to keep us pure! The audacity of the pure Magyars! There is no such thing!"

"Leopold would have raised his voice, but now no one speaks out," lamented Elizabeth. "We all live in fear. When the government openly oppresses one group, we all become oppressed. The government takes away our voices to oppose; none of us can speak against their oppression. No one feels safe from their own government!"

"Kállay is making a show for the Germans, but he still denies Hitler what he wants most—the complete evacuation of all Jews from Hungary," avowed Rudolf. "He's told Hitler mass deportation of Jewish laborers will harm Hungary's economy."

Klára sat silently through the disturbing conversation, but now she spoke, "I'm concerned about Rózsa, Dolf. We should make another visit as soon as we can."

Rudolf and Klára took András on the train to Eger, just for the day. The early morning train sped toward the rising sun through a snow-covered countryside. Pál met them at the station and after a quick drive through the forest of beech trees they were in Rózsa's kitchen for bowls of *csirkeleves* and slices of *Dobos torta*. After their meal András ran off to play in the snow with József and Vera while Rózsa and Klára sat together talking in the parlor. Rudolf remained in the kitchen with Pál.

"Klára and I came today because we are concerned about all of you." Rudolf's words had serious tone, "Klára wanted to see for herself that you are safe."

"We, too, are concerned, but we feel safe at the moment. It's grown more difficult to communicate with Rózsa's mother. Phone lines into the Jewish Quarter are no longer reliable and mail delivery in and out of the Quarter seems inconsistent. Rózsa is far more worried about her mother and brothers than she is for herself."

"We'll visit Mrs. Klein soon to let her know Rózsa is thinking of her." Rudolf tried to be reassuring, "And, Pál, remember to let us help your family in any way we can."

That evening they caught the train back to Budapest and settled into their compartment. András waved vigorously to József and Vera as the train pulled out of the station. Rudolf and Klára watched as steam and mist rose to obscure Pál, Rózsa and their children. Both Rudolf and Klára felt just as apprehensive on leaving Eger as they had felt on their arrival.

Winter, Budapest

On the twenty-sixth day of November, Per Anger arrived in Budapest to serve as the new Swedish Legation Second Secretary along with Sweden's Ambassador Carl Danielsson and the Swedish Red Cross representative, Valdemar Langlet. Trade issues between Hungary and Sweden would be the focus of Anger's job.

Although the war raged throughout Europe, when the Swedes arrived in Budapest, they found no evidence of the conflict within Hungary's borders. Except for a large number of wounded Hungarian soldiers, the war seemed very distant from Hungary. War-related hardships existed, such as some goods in short supply, but nothing else appeared severe. Shops and markets remained busy with shoppers, restaurants stayed open, a few gypsies still entertained, and the people continued to enjoy themselves at parks and bath houses. Overall, life in Budapest and most of Hungary remained relatively normal for most people.

One snowy December evening Rudolf met his old friend, Per Anger at

Gerbeaud's for coffee. They sat at one of the more secluded tables and shared glasses of hot steaming coffee spiked with *körtepálinka*, pear brandy.

"You've heard the rumors coming from the few who have escaped the labor camps in Poland?" asked Anger. "The tales of death and torture are despicable, terrifying."

"Yes, I've heard," answered Rudolf as he stirred the hot liquid. "Descriptions of boxcars crammed with human beings. Labor camps really death camps of starvation, disease, exposure and mass extermination in gas chambers. The stories have made their way to Budapest, whispered on the streets, but no one can believe them. The horrors are too incredible, but you and I know the tales told are true."

"Yes, indeed they're true," Anger shook his head. "From my experience in Berlin I'm quite aware that Hitler and his Nazis are more than capable of committing such atrocities." He sighed deeply. "The question now for you and me is what should be done? What must we do?"

"Everything we can do must be done! And as quickly as possible to save whomever we can before this evilness makes its way to Hungary."

1943
January

The new year began with Hitler's first defeat—his armies overpowered by the Soviets at the Battle of Stalingrad. Hitler bragged about the success of bombing Stalingrad into submission; he was particularly proud of taking the city named for Stalin. But less than fourteen days after Hitler made his boast the Soviets crossed the Volga, broke through the German lines and surrounded the German forces. Hitler ordered his armies to stay in place promising that the Luftwaffe would keep them supplied with food and munitions, a promise that turned out to be impossible.

By February thousands of German soldiers were dead from starvation, wounds or had frozen to death. Along with the Germans the Second Hungarian Army and the Hungarian Labor Force, primarily Jews, also suffered defeat, losing more than one hundred thousand men to capture or death. When word of the Stalingrad defeat and terrible loss of Hungarian lives reached Budapest, a grim sense of loss and foreboding seized the people.

In the current atmosphere of Budapest both Jews and non-Jews shared a sense of anger and terror, in part due to their own government's policies. Of course, some continued to blame the Jew for every problem, but there were many who did not and those persons searched out ways to support Hungary's disenfranchised Jewish citizens. Ferenc and Abram Klein had been waiting for the right time to join an active Resistance organization. The time seemed right to react boldly against the pro-German policies of Hungary's government. The two brothers joined with their Zionist friends to form a militant reactionary unit within Budapest's larger Resistance organization that also included Jews.

On a cold February afternoon while Ferenc and Abram sat at their mother's kitchen table with friends, there was a knock at the door. The small group fell instantly silent. Before Magda opened the front door, the brothers' three guests disappeared from the kitchen into the cellar. Both Ferenc and Abram held their breath until they heard Magda greet the familiar visitor, "Good-day Count von Házy. It's been a while since we've seen you. I'm sorry Mrs. Klein is not at home this afternoon."

"Yes, I'm sorry to have missed her, but my visit is unexpected. I simply wanted to say hello and to see if she needs anything. Please tell her that I stopped by, will you?"

"Of course, Sir," answered Magda, but before she closed the door, Ferenc joined her at the entrance.

"Count von Házy, will you stay for a while? My brother and I have friends we would like you to meet. Please come in, join us for tea."

Magda took Rudolf's coat and hat and led him to the kitchen. She was quite uncertain if Ferenc had made a wise decision to involve the count. *The Klein boys are immersed in very radical matters that may seem too extreme to the count*, she thought just as the three Zionists, all near the age of Rudolf, emerged from the cellar.

Abram introduced Zsuzsanna, a tall, rather plain woman with black hair piled atop her head, "Zsuzsanna is a journalist."

Next came Theodore who did not look Jewish at all; he was fair-haired with pale, small eyes behind very thick glasses. "Theodore is our intellectual, we call him *the detonator.*"

Theodore did have the stereotypical look of an intellectual, unruly hair and an unkempt, non-caring appearance to his dress.

And finally, there was Armin, a handsome, dark, Eastern-looking Jewish man who considered Rudolf with an irritated sneer. "Armin is our perpetually angry skeptic, but almost always right in his perception of what is really happening."

Ferenc explained why he had asked Rudolf to join them, "Our family has known Count von Házy for many years. He knew Eszter quite well." Ferenc turned toward Rudolf, "They were all friends of Eszter's, too."

Although the confident recommendation for the count had been given by their brother-in-law some time ago, the brothers had never forgotten. "We know Count von Házy's sympathies. He is well-connected and we know he can be trusted," stated Ferenc.

"We are but one Zionist unit within the larger Resistance group." Ferenc spoke with fervor. "We are ready to act, but we need connections to information and resources. We don't want to act independently because we know there's strength in a unified effort."

"We've heard the rumors about the death camps," Zsuzsanna informed Rudolf, "about the gas chambers in Auschwitz. We're realistic; we believe the rumors to be true."

"What is unbelievable is that our Jewish leaders have been told," ranted Armin, "and yet, they say 'We cannot believe such evil is possible.' They are old men who trust Horthy and Kállay. 'We trust our government to take care of their people,' they say, as though we are their people!

"I've known all my life that becoming a Magyar would get the Jew nothing," a seething Armin murmured. "It was always a farce thinking that being a Magyar would save us!"

Listening to each member of the group speak, Rudolf could hear the passion, the anger, in their voices. "I can certainly help you with information and I know others who are able to help you with resources," stated Rudolf, but he added, "I admire your passion. I respect your desire to act against this tyranny, but you must proceed with caution. You must curb your impulses to act without care. You cannot act rashly without considering the risks. If any of you are discovered it would endanger the entire network of resistance. Those who are willing to risk their own well-being to help you must stay in your consciousness at all times. You must never put the organization in jeopardy with reckless acts. You have a concern about trusting me. I have a concern about trusting you."

"Your group may not act independently of the greater Zionist Resistance fight against this enemy." Rudolf stated firmly, "Do you understand?"

"We understand, Count," promised Abram. "We know the risks. For ourselves, none of us has anything to lose, but we realize that we must be careful for the sake of others. We have already acted with other Zionists in acts of sabotage, but we have done nothing entirely on our own."

"I've worked with a group of Zionist women in attacks against the Arrow Cross," stated Zsuzsanna. "We've slashed tires and stolen *Nyilas* uniforms, uniforms of the Hungarian Nazis. Sometimes it's easier for Jewish women to strike the enemy than for Jewish men. I'm ready to do more and I know many other women who want to stand against this terrible oppression."

Their desire to do *something*, rather than simply wait to see what might happen, impressed Rudolf. He promised that he would do what he could and would send word to Ferenc soon. When Rudolf left the house and walked past the Dohány Synagogue he noticed how many houses on the street had been painted with nasty slurs against Jews and how many aimless people, even children, sat outside in the cold.

April, Budapest

"Hitler is growing impatient with what he believes to be my failure to address the Jewish Question," lamented Horthy. "He continues to demand deportations. He says that I'm ineffective!"

"Well, we've issued a new *numerous clauses*," protested Kállay. "Perhaps that will satisfy them for a while. This latest policy should completely eliminate Jewish participation in all areas, professional, commercial and in education. We've already moved all Jews off Hungary's farmlands and most provincial Jews are living in detention camps. What more can we do! We've separated the Jew from the Magyar race!"

In response to these new harsh Kállay measures, the Zionists organized a relief and rescue mission. Many provincial Jews were brought secretly into Budapest to live with relatives or to *safehouses* willing to accommodate them. Some Jews were smuggled out of Hungary altogether and sent to Palestine. Diplomatic Zionists attempted to negotiate with Kállay's government to rescind the harsh laws or for leniency, but to no avail.

When all else failed, the Resistance turned to clandestine acts and espionage. Printing illegal newspapers and pamphlets and raids on the Budapest Birth Registry to falsify records brought the Resistance some success. Most Resistance acts were random and quick, such as mining bridges and tunnels, cutting telegraph and telephone lines, or blowing up automobiles. In time more effective acts of Resistance transpired, including assassinations and destruction of major properties throughout Budapest.

Summer, Budapest

With her family at the lake, as usual, Klára waited for Rudolf to join her for supper as he had every evening since his return home, but this evening he never arrived. Klára decided to take her supper into the garden. The heavy scent of roses filled the air as a large moon and millions of stars illuminated the hot summer night. Sitting under the vine-covered pergola, she noticed lights at Rudolf's house, a light in his bedroom window. Without hesitation she put down her plate and walked straight to the garden gate, opened it, went to the von Házy's kitchen door and knocked. A surprised housekeeper, Zela, opened the door to find Klára.

"Come in, Baroness. The Countess has retired for the night. She had a good day today."

"I'm glad to hear that news, but I've come to see the Count, if he's home."

Zela hesitated, "He, too, has retired for the evening, but I can announce you, if you wish."

"No, no. I'll just go up," Klára said as she swept past the housekeeper.

Zela frowned, uncertain that Klára's proposal to go up to the count's bedroom was proper, but what could she do, except go about her business in the kitchen?

Klára hurried up the stairs to Rudolf's bedroom door. She stopped, took a deep breath and knocked. When he answered, she entered. He was sitting at his desk by the window. He was surprised to see her, stood and walked toward her.

"I apologize that I didn't let you know I was detained. I...I have a very important task to accomplish. I planned to speak with you later tonight or in the morning. I'm sorry, Klára. Believe me, this is of the utmost importance, otherwise I would have never missed our supper together."

"Can I help?" She knew he was involved in clandestine matters and that interested her, "I would like to help, Dolf, really."

"I don't want to put you in danger, Klára."

"I know, but if I can help, I choose to help, dangerous or not."

"Late this afternoon I was called upon to provide new identification for a Jewish family. The papers are needed by morning. I hurried home to get started on the task and the hours passed so quickly, it grew dark and then here you are."

"I don't want to disturb you, Dolf, but can't you show me what you do?"

Rudolf considered saying no to her, but decided to give in, *no more secrets from Klára*. He guided her to the valet closet that connected his room to another bedroom meant to be a valet's room, which was never used since Rudolf never had a valet. Rudolf reached up to the dark wood paneling of the ceiling and pulled the panel open. A small, narrow stair descended to the closet floor.

"Up." He motioned for Klára to climb the stair. He followed her up into the concealed, windowless attic room. He pulled up the stair, closing the panel and then turned on a light. Klára looked around the small room, a well-organized workshop. There were stacks of Hungarian identification books, a shelf with engraved and clear copper plates of all sizes, reams of papers, a hand-turned press, and etching supplies—inks, wax, stylus and acid.

"I have many official plates for birth and marriage documents and I can make very convincing identification books. That's what I was working on tonight. I just finished making four new books using the family's old books and inserting new pages."

"These are very good." She studied other identification books he showed her. "I can tell no difference."

Klára was proud of his work and of him. She looked around the small space again. It had been as dark as a cave before he turned on the light. "It's rather claustrophobic in here. Do you ever feel trapped? How do you know what's happening outside? What if it isn't safe to come out? It's all terribly frightening, Dolf."

"Yes, it is, a bit, Klára, but I also find it exhilarating, the possibility of saving lives." He smiled at her, but his thoughts fell back into the darkness of *the cave*. The terror of that childhood experience still haunted his dreams. An involuntary shiver swept over him as he felt the damp coldness of the dark and the loss of time. *This place is different, of course,* he thought, *I have purpose here.*

"For me, Klára, the darkness out there is by far more terrifying than the darkness of this small space. I want to believe what I do in here pierces the dark evilness with a small bit of light." He laughed at himself, "Was that poetic? Sometimes I think I'm speaking Stefan's thoughts. That sounded like something he would say."

"Stefan would be so proud of you, Dolf, using your talent in this way. Of course, he would insist that you involve him in your work!"

"True. He would have been the first to fight against this evil." Rudolf started to lower the stairs, but stopped, "Before we descend the stairs, so you won't worry about me, look at this." He revealed several small peepholes with devices that allowed him to see into the closet, his bedroom, even into the hallway. There was also a camera that when turned on showed both the front and rear of the house. He also revealed to her a concealed second door and explained, "beyond this exit there are a few steps leading to the outside and up to the parapet that encircles the house."

Klára did feel much better about his circumstance; he did have means of warning and an escape route, "It seems you've thought of everything, Dolf."

"Probably not," he humbly replied as the two descended the stair back into his bedroom.

"So, what can I do? Can I be a courier, again?" She was relentless.

Dolf crossed to the buffet in his room, poured two glasses of a red wine, and handed the first to Klára, "A perfect *von Esté* Merlot from Tihany. I suppose you could do some courier work again, but you must do exactly as I say. Take no chances, listen to your instincts alerting danger and never put yourself in jeopardy! When it feels perilous, get out. Promise!"

She promised, they clinked glasses and took sips of the rich, woody red wine.

"I'll deliver this assignment, but I'm sure there will be more for you to do soon enough. I need to alert our contacts."

The next week Klára had her first assignment to deliver a package. Just as in Berlin she had no idea of its contents. She took the Metro to Erzsébet Square and then walked out of the square toward Bárczy Street to a little corner bakery, Édesbolt-Péküzlet. A bell jingled as she entered the shop and the two ladies standing behind the counter greeted her.

"I hear your baker makes the best *szilvás bukta*, plum-jam-filled sweet roll, in town," Klára said with a cheerful expression.

"Yes, you're in the right place," the older gray-haired lady answered. "Our Déki makes the best in all of Hungary. I'll take care of you, Madam."

"I'll take a dozen, please."

As Klára paid for the rolls she also discreetly passed the small package she carried to the saleslady, took her pastry box, bid farewell and left the shop. It seemed such a small effort, but Klára felt exhilarated. It was good to be doing something she knew had importance and would make a difference in the life of someone.

Summer, Lake Balaton

Klára and Rudolf made time in their busy schedules to be at Lake Balaton for the *Anna Ball* and the sailing regatta. András was quite thrilled to dance with his mother on the terrace outside the ball and to sail at top speeds with Rudolf and Tamás across the milky lake. Just as in the past, Lake Balaton served as a place of escape from war and social turmoil. Every summer seemed to be just as the summer before and the summer before that. A good place…good to be all together again.

One afternoon, Tamás approached Rudolf, "Fábián Vadas has asked us to come to the caves. Since we're supporting this effort, he thinks we should see what he's doing up there. Vadas said we could bring András with us."

"I think András is old enough to go," Rudolf agreed. "He's a mature ten-year-old who can grasp the magnitude of what he sees and he must learn how to keep secrets. Of course, we'll need Klára's approval."

Just after lunch the two men and András rode off on horseback toward the Bakony Hills and Köves Só Barlang. They left their horses tied in the quarry below the mouth of the cave and walked up the hill to meet Vadas. As they walked Rudolf told András, "This is the cave where I left my leg when I was twelve. It's still in there, crushed under some big boulder."

András looked back to Rudolf, his eyes wide in astonishment, "Aren't you afraid to go in there again?"

"No, András, not at all," Rudolf laughed. "My father brought me back here to the cave as soon as I was able to walk. He made me sit in the depths of the cave alone in the dark to face my fears. After a long time my father came back, turned on his flashlight, and told me… *'Now you can face life. There is really nothing inside this cave more terrifying for you than the world outside. Nothing that requires more bravery than walking out of this cave into life, into living a full life!'*"

"I don't understand. I'm not afraid of life." András was bothered by Rudolf's papa's words. "Do you think life is scary…terrifying?"

"What I do know, András, is that life is beautiful most of the time and that's the easy part, but it can turn dark and scary and you must know how to survive the terrifying. Life is worth living only if you are not afraid to live it, even the worst of it. Do you understand?"

"I think so," András answered very seriously.

Fábián Vadas, a big rugged man with a broad smile, met them at the cave's entrance and led them inside. He patted András on the head, "You know we've placed our trust in you to keep what you see here a secret. You may not tell anyone what you see."

"We've made a kind of medieval arrangement with Vadas," explained Tamás. "We've promised to supply financing for food and munitions and in return Vadas and his men will protect us, if necessary, as best he can."

As the men and András climbed over the boulders at the entrance, Rudolf remembered well his experiences in Köves Só. The piled boulders led to an iron gate that had been recently installed across the tunnel. Vadas unlocked the gate, allowing them to pass onto a wide, smooth pathway cleared of its natural debris. A string of electric lights stretched ahead, lighting the tunnel's pathway. The tunnel led to a large natural open space filled with boxes of munitions and guns of all sorts. Several men and women were obviously involved in specific chores.

They descended deeper into a second natural cavernous space where András saw cots for sleeping and tables with chairs near a pit fire and cooking facility. When they sat down at the table, a man brought them coffee, bread, and cheese.

"We've discovered two additional entrances into the cave; there are probably more, but we have several escape routes. There's an opening near the top of the hill that requires descending several ladders and another follows a stream that comes into the cave as a waterfall. That's also our source of fresh water. Certainly a few locals know we're here, but we feel secure. We think we can do much damage when the need arises."

As they rode back to the villa, Rudolf and Tamás felt safer, while András felt proud of being included with the *men* to see the important work of the Resistance.

October

By early October, Hungarian police, influenced by the Arrow Cross, began a vigorous drive to empty countryside villages of their Jewish population. Jews in mass were trucked to detention camps under the false pretense of resupplying Hungary's labor force, severely diminished from war losses. Provincial Jews continued to flee to Budapest, because the city was thought to be the final refuge in all of Hungary. The population of the Jewish Quarter grew at a disastrous rate. Police with Arrow Cross connections, authorized by the government to maintain order within the Quarter, used brutal methods, including beatings and murder. The Arrow Cross Nyilas created a harsh, unbearable environment for Budapest's Jewish community.

Both Rudolf and Klára along with many other Hungarians worked to help Jews escape their dire circumstances. On occasion Klára drove a Red Cross truck or an ambulance to secretly transport food and medicine to *safehouses*, while Rudolf used his skill to create falsified papers, often the only way for Jews to conceal their Jewish identity. The fall months became very busy for both of them.

November, Budapest

In the midst of a terrible blizzard Rudolf returned home after being away for several days on MI6 business. He had asked Elizabeth and Klára to look in on his grandmother in his absence. As he shook the snow from his hat and coat, Zela whispered to him, "Your grandmother suffered a bad spell in your absence. The von Estés called for the doctor, he suggested that the priest be called. It's good you've returned, Sir."

Rudolf hurried upstairs to his grandmother's room. Countess Alexandra looked so small lying in her huge bed. Rudolf could see that she was failing. Klára sat beside the Countess as Rudolf knelt beside the bed.

"I'm glad you've come back, Dolf," Klára said.

The doctor leaned close to Rudolf, "She's resting comfortably now, I think she's been waiting for you."

"Grandmother, it's Rudolf." He spoke softly as he took Alexandra's hand, "I'm here. Can you give me a smile?"

The countess looked so weak lying within the mound of bed covers. She opened her eyes and managed to turn her head toward his voice. In the softest whisper she murmured, "Oh my sweet Rudolf, you've come home at last. I'm leaving soon to be with my Francis and Christián and László, too. I miss them so."

She closed her eyes, her breath shallow. Father Nikola entered the room and walked to her side; he said prayers and offered the final unction. Some time during these rites Alexandra passed away.

Expected, but still a staggering loss for Rudolf, he moved to the window and looked down into the garden. Threatening clouds still hung over Budapest; the afternoon had grown dark. Klára moved behind him and put her hand on his arm. "I'm so sorry, Dolf, but I'm glad you were here."

"Yes, it was good to be here to say good-bye. I'm all alone now. I have no one left."

"You have all of us, Dolf. You have me."

Rudolf turned and embraced her, he closed his eyes and in an instant felt the strong emotional connection they had for each other. He let go of her, moved apart from her and stared into her emerald eyes. He couldn't breathe. Rudolf walked from his grandmother's room to his own, went inside and shut the door.

Three days later the von Estés accompanied Rudolf and his grandmother's body to the Eisenstadt estate. Rudolf had not been to the house or property since the deaths of his parents. A caretaker managed the old manor house and lands. For Rudolf the house represented great sorrow; it was a place about which he cared little.

In the late afternoon of their arrival, after a brief service in the manor's chapel, Rudolf's grandmother's body was interred between her beloved husband and son. László rested nearby. The Budapest group and a few local guests gathered for supper in the great hall.

Afterwards the party retired for brandy in the parlor. Rudolf walked around the room amazed and somewhat horrified; it was preserved exactly as it had been since the day of his parent's car crash, since their funeral service. A stunning portrait of Gabriele, his beautiful mother, hung over one of the many sofas in the room. He found framed photographs of himself and Stefan and Klára as children. Rudolf held the images in his hands and thought of his happy childhood, his idyllic past. Nothing in the room had changed and yet, everything had changed completely. Rudolf seemed terribly sad; his life had not turned out as he, as a child, had imagined it would. He bid everyone good night and retired to his rooms upstairs.

Sleep eluded Rudolf, he felt restless and tormented. Instead of bed, he resigned himself to a big, overstuffed chair before the fireplace. It was late, he stared at the blazing fire, but sleep would not come. Rudolf thought that, perhaps, he should drink himself to oblivion, but there was nothing to drink in his room. He went downstairs to the wine cellar and chose two bottles, opening one of them. One bottle he carried and the other he drank in gulps as he left the cellar. Walking aimlessly into the long hall lined with glass doors overlooking the lawn, Rudolf stopped to gaze outside. The night looked cold and desolate as the moonlight shone on the snow-covered lawn. He leaned against the windowed door staring into the night, drinking from the second bottle, when the slightest of sounds disturbed his sorrow-filled thoughts, Rudolf turned toward the far end of the hall where he saw a form dressed in white. He thought he was seeing a ghost, but when the form swept closer to him, he realized it was Klára. Rudolf let out his breath, dropped the bottle he was holding and closed his eyes.

"Do you love me still, Dolf?" she whispered close to his lips.

He held her face in his hands and without any hesitation began to kiss her with abandoned passion. This time Rudolf would not, could not stop himself nor would she ask him to stop. They had waited long enough and the need for each other had grown to a crescendo of emotion. Klára sank into his embrace, responding to him as though in a dream.

There was no floor, no doors, no walls as they moved as one into the study. All reservation, all denials, all impediments disappeared at last as the two lovers answered every desire in each other.

Before dawn the two went back to Rudolf's room and slept entwined in perfect rapture until the first light of morning streamed through a crack in the heavy draperies. Klára slipped out from between the covers and back into her robe.

"You're leaving me?" Rudolf asked her.

"I should be in my own room, if András should wake up first," Klára said.

"There's no going back, Klára," Rudolf flashed a handsomely wicked grin at her. "You are mine at last after way too long. The waiting is over."

"Don't think for a minute I'm some random one-night stand, Dolfie," she teased him as she leaned over to kiss him once again. "We are together now as we should have been for the last ten years. By now we should be thinking of ourselves as an old married couple."

"I prefer newlyweds," he said as he pulled her back to him and kissed her so passionately she stayed in his embrace once again.

"I must go now, Dolf. I don't want to explain this glorious night to anyone. I want it to be ours alone, at least for a little while longer."

She looked into his dark, brooding eyes and thought to herself... *I've wondered what making love with you would be like. This night with you has been everything and much, much more than I ever imagined making love could be...* "Never leave me, Dolfie."

"I never have. I never will, Klára," he promised and kissed her again.

"Stop kissing me," she begged. "Make me go before we're discovered."

"Go. I'll see you at breakfast."

Several hours later, after successfully getting back into her own room and napping blissfully, Klára sat at the dining table with András and Elizabeth. Several other overnight guests were seated at the table as well. Elizabeth conversed with them while Klára and András spoke quietly to each other about their return trip to Budapest. Rudolf entered the dining room with warm, rather exuberant greetings for everyone, his mood noticeably changed from the previous evening.

"I hope everyone had a good night in the old house. I certainly did, the best I've had in years!" he boasted, "I hope the breakfast has been satisfactory, it appears to be a feast! I'm famished."

Rudolf filled his plate with pastries, dried fruits, a great slab of ham and boiled eggs.

"I'm glad that you're feeling more cheerful today, Rudolf," Elizabeth commented. "We thank you for your hospitality. The old manor house has been maintained very well by the staff; it's quite lovely."

The other guests agreed and made similar complimentary comments to Rudolf. He sat down at the table across from Klára, daring her to look at him. She took the dare and tried her best to be nonchalant, but could not stop the far-too-broad smile that spread across her face, nor could she stifle the little laughs that seemed to have no reason. Elizabeth frowned at her and asked if she was all right. Klára assured her mother that she was fine... *just remembering the dream I had last night.*

That afternoon on the train back to Budapest, Klára sat down by her mother in the dining car. Elizabeth remained engrossed in the menu.

"Mother, I want you to know that I have seen an attorney in Budapest about divorcing Franz. So far, Franz has refused to sign the papers, but I intend to pursue divorce. I will never be his wife again. I know that divorce is not acceptable, but I believe it is the right thing to do in my case. I have also spoken with Father Mihály about an annulment. He supports my report of impediments."

"Impediments?" Elizabeth looked up with a startled expression, "from before the wedding?"

"Yes, from the beginning, Mother." Klára kept her head lowered; she did not look into her mother's eyes, "I would rather not speak of the details."

"No, please, I'm so sorry for you, Klára."

"There's something else, Mother," Klára hesitated. "I love Dolf and he loves me. When I'm divorced and the marriage is annulled, Dolf and I will marry. Dolf will be a good father to András. He adores András and András adores him. I intend to be happy and to make Dolf as happy as I can. I love you and I won't bring shame to you, Mother. I promise to be discreet. I hope that you understand."

The constant metallic rhythm of the train's movement along the track could not soothe the pounding in Elizabeth's head. *Impediments,* she thought, *Renate and I, we were the impediments. We connived to separate two people who loved each other, were destined for each other. Two whom God had put together, Klára and Rudolf, Renate and I, we separated them! We put them asunder! We designed the marriage of my sweet Klára to Franz. Stefan warned me of his nature, his character, but I was determined.* Tears streamed down her cheeks. *I am the impediment!*

"Mother? Mother, I'm so sorry to disappoint you, but...."

"No. No, you're not a disappointment, Klára." Elizabeth reached across the small table and took Klára's hand, "I accept the love between you and Rudolf. I will not judge you. We'll pray that Franz will be reasonable and give you the divorce, until then you and Rudolf must take the time together that you have. I love you both."

The two women wept as the train sped back to Budapest. Klára feeling relief and Elizabeth riven with guilt as she thought to herself... *I will go to see Father Mihály. There is a confession that I must make. He must know that I was the impediment.*

Once they were all back in Budapest, Rudolf and Klára went back to their activities, Klára to the soldiers' hospital and driving the Red Cross truck, Rudolf to his meetings and forgeries. Together they listened to the BBC on the radio in his secret room. They heard about the successful bombing raids by the British RAF on Berlin and German industrial sites. They kept track of the Soviet's Red Army movements, particularly noting their closeness to Hungary's borders. They also heard that the Regent Horthy had given approval for a Military Court procedure against those Hungarians involved in the 1942 January Massacre of Jews at Novi Sad, Yugoslavia.

"That won't go over well with Hitler," Rudolf frowned and said aloud, "he'll wonder why Horthy thinks the massacre of Jews is a crime, a war crime. We shall see what comes of this."

1944
January, Budapest

By January a severe rift between Budapest and Berlin occurred just as Rudolf assumed it would. Regent Horthy's approval of a military trial for the perpetrators of the Novi Sad Massacre was only one of many reasons Hitler became convinced neither Kállay nor Horthy could be trusted by the Reich. Hitler suspected the two Hungarians were engaged in talks with the Western Allies, or even possibly with the Soviets. Making overtures to the West for a break with the Axis would be bad enough, but the possibility that Horthy might align with the Soviets was Hitler's worst fear. Hitler's suspicions brought about a serious Nazi response, placing Hungary in a perilous situation.

The Klein brothers contacted Rudolf to meet with them again. This time the meeting took place in an obscure cellar restaurant located within the Jewish Quarter. Armin Stein and Zsuzsanna Weisz were there along with Abram and Ferenc. A tense, agitated discussion ensued as they shared their concerns with Rudolf.

"So many Jewish people throughout Hungary have been driven from their homes into detention camps or, if they're lucky, into the Quarter!" said Armin. "Of course, added to those already hiding in the Quarter it's become seriously overcrowded."

"Kállay has ordered some of the larger houses, like the Kleins', to take in whole families of Jews from country villages." Zsuzsanna sighed as her fingers tried to smooth her furrowed brow. "They've moved Jews off their own farms into the city."

"Our Jewish leaders say nothing in opposition. The old men remain quiet, obedient; they are brilliant, but they're naïve and they allow no young voices, no opposing opinions. The elders are blind to what is *really* happening." Ferenc spoke in a hushed voice, "it's only a matter of time until the Nazis begin forced deportations to the East."

"Rumors are spreading everywhere! We've heard about a report written by escapees from a place called Auschwitz. Supposedly it describes atrocities committed by Nazis against Jews, atrocities too abhorrent to speak aloud," offered Abram. "How can we be expected to sit silently by and wait?

"Now Kállay has all the Jews wearing the yellow Star of David, just as Hitler did in Germany! Our Jewish leaders say nothing against this policy. They just put the yellow badge on their coats and go on as though it is normal," protested Abram. "Well, Ferenc and I will never wear it on our coats! None of the Zionists will wear it!"

"It's so ironic that Hitler chose our sacred symbol to mock us! We're proud to be Jews; proud of our heritage," said Armin, "but we refuse to degrade the Star of David to a symbol that marks us for harassment and death. We won't cower before them and easily identify ourselves to strangers who want to ridicule and destroy us."

"We're part of the Aliyah group that works to help Jews emigrate to Palestine. We've increased our efforts, but it's such a slow process and terribly dangerous. Only a few can be saved by that route," explained Zsuzsanna. "We must find something better, faster, that will help all of us. Germany has closed its borders, barring all Jewish departure. It's only a matter of time before Hungarian Jews find themselves in an impasse. Hostile forces surround Hungary. Emigration is already practically impossible without the right papers."

"The right papers are possible," Rudolf assured them, "there are sources."

"Even with the right papers, there's no place to go. There are so few options, so few ways out of Hungary and every one of them perilous."

Late February

Tamás found Elizabeth in the conservatory tending her orchids. He handed an envelope to her, "A boy just brought this to you from Mrs. Klein. He's waiting for a response."

Elizabeth reached for the letter wondering why Mrs. Klein would write to her. She opened it.

My Dear Duchess, Please come to pick up your piano at your convenience. Thank you for its use these many years. In gratitude, Mrs. Klein

Elizabeth read the letter again. The meaning of it mystified her. She gave the letter to Tamás, "What do you make of this?"

He read the note, "The piano isn't yours?"

"No, but I think she means for me to have it, don't you?" Elizabeth sighed, "I think we must respond quickly. I feel there's some kind of urgency to this note."

Elizabeth held the note in her hand; she studied the handwriting, thinking about all the years of sitting in Mrs. Klein's parlor while Klára had her lessons. Elizabeth remembered Rózsa's wedding reception, the music. "Tell Mrs. Klein we'll come this afternoon."

"I'll make arrangements for a van." He paused, "Do you want me to inform Klára?"

"No, we'll take care of this. Klára seems to be very occupied these days."

"I'll tell the boy to let Mrs. Klein know we'll be there soon." He hurried from the conservatory.

Within the hour, Tamás had engaged a van. Tamás, rather than Auguste, drove the car with Elizabeth inside while the van followed them to the Klein's address on Dohány Street. She and Tamás noticed so many people on the streets wearing bright yellow stars on their coats and walking quickly with their heads down, intent on going about their business. The numbers of Hungarian Nyilas in the neighborhood surprised both of them. Both were also stunned at how obviously the police stood in the path of those with yellow stars and deliberately harassed them.

The once vigorous and cheerful atmosphere of the Jewish sector was very different from the years of Klára's piano lessons. Sidewalks littered with broken glass, the word *Jude* and obscenities scrawled across many buildings shocked and sickened Elizabeth; she felt an ominous fear grip at her throat. Suddenly she and Tamás realized they were in a very dangerous place, but Elizabeth felt more determined than ever to find out the reason Mrs. Klein had sent her cryptic note.

The car and van pulled close to the curb. Elizabeth and Tamás climbed the stairs to the front door that had a large Star of David carelessly painted on it. Before they could knock, Mrs. Klein opened the door. She thanked them profusely for coming; tears trickled from her eyes. She twisted and untwisted the lace handkerchief that she held with both hands and dabbed at her eyes.

The house was in disarray. Partially packed boxes, stacks of books and framed portraits filled the entry way. Mrs. Klein apologized for the untidiness, "I'm trying to move my things and make room for other families who are coming here."

She was so distraught, twisting her handkerchief. Suddenly she thought of a different time, a more genteel time, "Oh, may I take your coats? Please sit down. May I get tea for you?"

Her shoulders began to shake; she steadied herself against the door frame, "I no longer have servants. My dear Magda left yesterday. She didn't want to go, but her family needed her. They... all the servants have left to be with their families. There's so much harassment, just too dangerous for anyone to go out or come and go. Everyone is just hovering together, waiting."

"Don't concern yourself with us." Elizabeth moved to Éva's side, embraced her and guided her toward a chair in the music room. "Where's your family? Where's Rózsa?"

Mrs. Klein composed herself, took a deep breath and answered, "Rózsa is still in Eger. Travel to and from Eger is so dangerous now. Samuel and his family left Budapest years ago, intending to make their way to Palestine to be with Eszter, but, instead, they ended up in England. Ferenc and Abram are here, but I haven't seen either of them for days." She looked devastated, "I'm worried sick about all of them to the point of distraction."

Passing by two grand pianos Mrs. Klein walked to a small spinet. "I would be so grateful if you would take this piano. I'm so sorry to ask you, but I didn't know where to turn. Our husbands were very close and it's because of my Jakov that I even dare ask you to do this kindness for me." She stroked the wood and added, "There's much danger in my request. I've hidden Jakov's papers in the piano, his university papers and his personal research. I can't bear to think of his life's work destroyed."

Éva looked up from the piano; her expression one of desperation, "If the papers are discovered, it could be terrible for you. If you chose not to do this, I will understand."

"I'll take the piano," Elizabeth said with conviction. "I want to do this for you and for Professor Klein. He and Leopold were very close. Tamás and I can take care of this."

Tamás left the room to fetch the men from the van. The three men returned and began to push the piano from the room. Elizabeth and Mrs. Klein moved to the window to watch the street. As the men moved the piano down the ramp placed over the stairs, two Arrow Cross soldiers stopped them and demanded their papers and their intent.

While producing their papers, Tamás intervened, "The Duchess von Esté has reclaimed her piano loaned to this house for many years. She has exercised her right to remove it from these premises."

The soldiers held the papers while they looked over the piano. They made loud, disparaging remarks as they handed the papers back to Tamás. "The Duchess will have to fumigate to get rid it of Jew bugs." Another said, "How could she loan it to a Jew? Is there anything else she wants to take from this house?"

"No, no. This is all she wants." Tamás motioned to the truck, "We're paying these men by the hour." He was dismissive of the soldiers, as he nudged the movers to continue, "Good day to you, sirs."

Elizabeth and Mrs. Klein watched the exchange without moving the lace curtains. They both held their breath until the soldiers moved away. Their hearts beat rapidly while the piano was rolled up into the van and the doors were shut. Mrs. Klein sighed deeply, "Thank you. Thank you so much. You must go now, quickly, away from here."

Elizabeth held her hand as they walked to the front door. She gave Mrs. Klein a final embrace and descended the stairs to the car. Tamás opened the door for her and then got into the driver's side. Elizabeth looked back at Mrs. Klein who stood at the door for only a moment longer, motioned farewell with her hand and shut the door. Tamás and Elizabeth drove away with the van following behind.

Once they reached their home on Andrássy, Tamás directed the men to move the piano into the dining room. Elizabeth went to her room feeling completely exhausted. After less than an hour, she returned downstairs to find Tamás. "We must go back. We can't leave her there alone."

By the time Elizabeth and Tamás drove back to Dohány Street it was early evening. Mrs. Klein was very surprised to see Elizabeth standing at her door again. She ushered Elizabeth into the hallway, looking at her curiously.

"You can't stay here by yourself," Elizabeth said firmly. "You must come to stay with me. Pack your treasures, don't worry about clothing. Come with me now before it becomes too late."

"Oh, Duchess, this is too much." Mrs. Klein was incredulous, and at the same time overwhelmed by gratitude. " I could never place you in such danger."

"No argument. We'll find a way to keep you safe through this perilous time. Now hurry."

Mrs. Klein hurried upstairs. She was gone for less than fifteen minutes when she returned with two suitcases and a violin case. "I've been going through all of my memories in this house ever since I was told to make room for others, so I had already gathered my most precious pictures and letters and heirlooms."

She moved quickly through the parlor, dining and music rooms picking up more pictures, linens, books, music that she placed into the suitcases, "That's it…that's my life."

Then she frowned, "I'm concerned about Abram and Ferenc. When they come back, they won't know where I've gone and I certainly can't tell them."

"You could leave a note someplace, a simple explanation. Just to say you're well and that you've left of your own will and hope to see them again."

"Yes, I'll do that." She wrote the note and placed it in the kitchen on a board by the stove where the family had always left messages for each other.

With that final act, the two women left the house. Mrs. Klein locked the door and placed the key under the window ledge nearby, wondering if she would ever unlock that door again. Tamás drove the two women away from Dohány Street and out of the Jewish sector. None of them felt safe or easy until the car was back on Andrássy and parked in the driveway.

At that very moment, Elizabeth realized she had to invent a story for Mrs. Klein to explain her sudden presence to the servants. "We have to tell the servants something. First, rip that star off your coat. We'll say that you are an old friend who has come to Pest because your husband has died and you're all alone." Elizabeth took a deep breath, "After all these years, we have never called each other by our first names. Call me Elizabeth from now on."

"And I am Éva, dear friend." She squeezed Elizabeth's hand.

Tamás opened the car door for the two ladies and led them to the front door. He escorted Mrs. Klein to one of the guest rooms upstairs. Then he went straight to the kitchen to tell Silva all the details of his harrowing day.

Silva gladly accepted the task of sharing Mrs. Klein's story with the staff. Éva from this day forward would be called Mrs. Pap, a long-time friend of the Duchess. She was mourning the loss of her husband and was not to be bothered with chit chat from the staff. Silva had prepared *paprikas csirke* for supper and set the dining table for four. That evening Elizabeth and Éva sat at the table together while Tamás stood nearby; he filled their wine glasses and joined in the discussion regarding their next move.

Soon after seven o'clock, Klára and András arrived home. They walked into the dining room to discover the little group of brave resistance. Elizabeth spoke, "Klára, you remember my dear friend, Mrs. Éva Pap? Since her husband's death, she is all alone, so she's come to stay with us for a bit."

"Ah, yes, I remember you well, Mrs. Pap." Klára smiled as she and András took their places at the table. "It's very good to see you again."

Later, after András was in bed, Klára sat with her mother, Mrs. Pap and Tamás. "You realize this is very dangerous, Mother? Running a *safehouse*? You need to reduce the staff. Tell them that you're closing parts of the house due to rationing of fuel and that we'll help them find other places of employ.

"Who knows when this war and the Nazis will finally come to Budapest?" Klára wondered. "We know it's inevitable. And we must make plans."

They all agreed with her. "I think it's time to seriously think about leaving the city and moving to the villa until the war is over."

Again there was agreement. Elizabeth seemed to have already given the move some thought, "We should remove all the valuables from the house, Tamás. The art, the vases, Leopold's books, the tapestries, perhaps the carpets, too. We could store some of them in the cellar. The rest we can take with us to the villa."

"There's a false wall in the wine cellar that conceals a large cave-like room within the foundations," offered Tamás. "I believe that hidden space would be a perfect storage place until we return." He added, "Perhaps we should board up the Mucha windows as well."

Preparations moved quickly over the next week. Elizabeth let go all the Andrássy house staff, except for Silva and Ana, and Auguste and Leona who always stayed with the house while the family spent their summers at Lake Balaton. Tamás oversaw the packing of all household valuables and then he, together with Auguste and Rudolf, carried them down to the concealed cave in the cellar. Silva saw to the covering of furnishings with muslin sheets, while Elizabeth and Ana packed clothing and goods needed for the villa. Lastly, Elizabeth and Éva Klein/Mrs. Pap packed all of their important records, including wine company documents, property deeds, contracts, certificates and their husbands' papers, including those of Professor Klein concealed within the piano. Klára took responsibility for packing her papa's library. Some treasures would go into the cellar cave, but the more precious things would go with the family to the villa. She packed books with András in mind; books her papa had encouraged her and her brother, Stefan, to read and study. Among them the *Atlas*, the big oversized picture book of flora and fauna, books about philosophy, especially Stefan's favorite, Plato's *The Republic*. Classics and histories of the world and of Hungary, in particular, Gardonyi's *Egri Csillagok*. She packed Leopold's old albums of photographs and his memorabilia box and her thoughts turned to her papa's stories. *Tamás and I must find time to share these family stories with András.*

Klára decided she would stay in Budapest to continue her Red Cross work.

Everyone agreed the upper floors of the house should be closed. Klára and Leona would move into rooms near the kitchen. Leona would use the empty cook's room while Klára would occupy the apartment of Tamás and Silva, just down the hall from the kitchen. Tamás and Silva emptied the apartment of their personal things, including Tamás's chair, his desk, and Silva's bed, the one she had brought with her to the von Esté house when she was first hired.

After two busy weeks, the family was ready to leave Budapest for Lake Balaton. Klára promised to visit the villa regularly. She stood at the door, waving good-bye and watching the car followed by a van as they turned onto Andrássy Avenue and sped away. Back inside the house Klára looked around at the strangeness of it all, quiet and dark. The colorful Mucha window, always a brilliant light illuminating the reception hall, now boarded up. The house seemed empty of life now; even the potted plants were gone, except for those in the darkened conservatory where most of the glass panels were painted black. She walked around the rooms touching the shrouded forms, every piece of furniture holding memories of her beloved family, the joys and tragedies they had shared.

Now, all alone Klára went into her new apartment and closed the door behind her. *The Tóth apartment will make a cozy accommodation for me*, Klára thought. *Its warm ceramic stove and bright windows opening onto a private garden are quite charming.*

Suddenly feeling very tired, Klára stretched and yawned as she walked into her new bedroom. She went to the garden door and opened it. Winter still chilled the breeze that surrounded her; she shivered, but breathed in the cold, crisp air. It was invigorating.

"They've gone already?" Rudolf's deep voice startled her. "I wanted to say good-bye."

He walked close to her and enfolded her in his arms. Rudolf loved holding her, she was tall and fit against his own form perfectly; he only had to look down slightly to her beautiful mouth.

"You missed them. Everyone's gone." She melted into him, "I was thinking of taking a nap in my new bed," she whispered as she pulled him into her new apartment.

He closed the door behind them; they were both quite pleased by their new circumstance.

March

By March Hitler decided he had had enough of Regent Horthy's devious behavior toward the Reich. He had received definite affirmation of his suspicions that Horthy was trying to forge an alliance with the Allies. Hitler invited Horthy to attend a conference at Klessheim Castle in Austria. When Horthy arrived, Hitler did not conceal his anger, denouncing the regent with accusations of disloyalty and betrayal. Hitler demanded that Horthy make a statement to be aired over the radio to the Hungarian people. Horthy was forced to be convincing in his announcement... *the people of Hungary willingly invite the Germans into our country.* By the time Horthy returned to his beloved Hungary on the twentieth of March, *Operation Margarethe* was complete.

Operation Margarethe began on the nineteenth of March when the German Wehrmacht marched into Hungary and within a day occupied the entire country. Hitler allowed Horthy to remain as regent of the Hungarian kingdom—as a puppet—but appointed Edmund Veesenmayer as the Nazi military governor. Hitler also required Horthy to replace Kállay with a new prime minister, Döme Sztójay, a Hitler supporter. Sztójay immediately legalized the Arrow Cross and gave its leader Ferenc Szálasi greater powers.

Soon after the German occupation, S.S. Colonel Adolf Eichmann arrived in Budapest with a mandate from Himmler to expel all Jews from Hungary. Eichmann was ordered to oversee the mass deportation of Hungarian Jews to death camps in the East as soon as possible. On his way to Budapest, Eichmann stopped at Mauthausen, a death camp in Austria, to make sure it would be ready for Hungarian Jews, even though most of them would be going to Auschwitz. Eichmann established the Budapest *Sondereinsatz-Kommandos* as a special task force to direct the deportation and extermination of Hungarian Jews.

Eichmann immediately began searches for Jews across the country, especially for those who had gone into hiding. Monetary rewards were offered by the Nazi *Kommandos* for information on Jews and their abettors. Highest rewards were given for discoveries of hidden Jews. No one could be trusted from the postman to the chimney sweep, from teacher to clergy, maid to grocer. An atmosphere of terror swept the entire country. Jews began to realize the threat was real; it had arrived, and they were, every one of them, in peril!

The new Veesenmayer-Sztójay government insisted that a formal Jewish Council be established for the Jewish Quarter in Budapest; a council of eight well-respected elders taking orders from Eichmann and reporting directly to him. Eichmann informed the Jewish leaders...*your purpose will be to announce and enforce German policies. In addition, your council will be responsible to keep your people calm, to assure your people that the Germans have no plans for deportation and to encourage your people to go about their lives as normally as possible despite the inconveniences of war-time life.* Eichmann further promised...*there will be no brutal treatment of the Budapest Jewry, if the Jews are obedient and follow the rules.*

When the Jewish Council took him at his word, Eichmann was pleased and smugly told his staff, "Everything seems to be going as planned to accomplish the Final Solution in Hungary."

—m—

"When the Germans marched into Hungary," Per Anger said as he and Rudolf sat in his office, "I knew exactly what to expect, the same reign of terror I witnessed in Berlin."

"I was somewhat surprised that the Nazis began such severe persecution of Jews so soon after their arrival."

"I'm not surprised, Rudolf. The Nazis know they are running out of time and they don't want to waste a moment putting in place their plans for the Final Solution and now, that includes Hungary's Jews."

"So, what is your plan for us?"

"I have permission from the Swedish Legation to issue provisional certificates of citizenship for Jews. Each certificate will identify its holder as a Swedish citizen with rights of travel and, hopefully will protect the holder from arrest."

Rudolf nodded his head, approving the plan, "Certainly I'll do what I can to help with the manufacture of the papers."

"The situation for Jews in Hungary will only grow more desperate. In the meantime, Minister Danielsson is willing for the legation to do all that it can to accommodate the Jewish community."

Within the week long lines of people stood every day at the Glass House on Vadasz Street to apply for the Swedish certificates; demand was very high. Anger and the Swedish Legation were able to convince the Veesenmayer-Sztójay government, as well as both German and Hungarian authorities, that the documents were legitimate and should be accepted, even though the Swedes knew the certificates had no actual legality whatsoever.

April

By April, thousands of displaced provincial Jews arrived at the Budapest railway station and found themselves surrounded by S.S. and Wehrmacht soldiers carrying machine guns. The Jews were marched off to the Kistarcsa Detention Camp for internment to await the unknown. Sztójay's Hungarian government promised Hitler the delivery of one hundred thousand able-bodied Jews for German factories without knowing the Germans, in fact, had no interest in Jewish workers at all. The Hungarian Jews were simply destined for annihilation.

Beginning in mid-April, Eichmann arranged for one hundred forty-seven trains with boxcars to begin arriving at Budapest train stations. The final destination for each train would be the death camp at Auschwitz. A single boxcar was built to carry no more than forty, but the Nazis crammed a hundred Jews into each car. Men, women, children, the young, the old, the infirm, all without food or water, filled each boxcar for the three-day journey from Budapest. Two or three trains left the station each day holding three thousand Jews per train.

Formal grievances were registered by the Red Cross protesting against Eichmann's inhumane treatment, but he answered all complaints with derogatory obscenities. "Jews have a preference for large families crowded together in small apartments, so the trains are of no inconvenience to them." And Eichmann promised, "I'll speed up the deportations to relieve their suffering." Jews who escaped capture continued to flee to Budapest, go into hiding in the city, and spread their stories of horror.

—⁂—

Fábián Vadas rode his horse up to the herb garden at the von Esté villa; he dismounted and tied the reins to the iron trellis. Tamás came out of the kitchen into the garden.

"Fábián! Welcome! What brings you here?"

Vadas walked toward Tamás, greeting him warmly, "It appears circumstances are changing quickly, Tamás. The Soviets are amassing along Hungary's southeastern borders. If they cross into Hungary, the Germans will surely be pushed this way. You must consider leaving the villa. Move up into the forest, perhaps into the shepherds' old cottages. My men will keep an eye on the neighborhood for you."

"Come in, Fábián. Have something to drink." Tamás dreaded informing the household of this news; he didn't want to convey his deep concern to the women in the house. At the moment, only he and Silva, Elizabeth, Éva Pap and Ana were at the villa. Klára, András and Rudolf were still in the city.

Vadas greeted Silva and sat down at the big oak table, "It's only a matter of time until they're here. One or the other, Nazis or Soviets, one is as bad as the other. I'm suggesting that you should take refuge in the forest."

Silva left the kitchen returning shortly with Elizabeth and Éva. They all sat down together at the table. Vadas repeated his proposal that the family should leave the villa and move up into the cottages. The women agreed with him and as soon as he had gone they began to prepare for the move. The villa had to be closed, furnishings covered with dust sheets, and valuables packed or stowed away. Since there was no way of knowing how long they would be at the cottages, Silva packed clothing and bedding for all seasons. She filled baskets and boxes with dried meats and fruits, honey, bottles of wine, a barrel of cabbage, strings of onions and paprikas, various medicinal herbs, and sacks of seeds. They would still have the gardens by the villa, but she decided while there was still time they should plant new ones on the hill.

Once again Elizabeth and Mrs. Pap gathered their important papers. Elizabeth insisted on packing lace tablecloths, her Herend porcelain and silver, saying, "We must keep the elegant niceties that give our lives a civility above this offensive, barbaric war."

Elizabeth also insisted that comfortable chairs and mattresses, carpets and desks, tables and bookcases, paintings and books, especially Stefan's music box and Leopold's albums and memorabilia box, all be moved up to the shepherds' cottages. "I refuse to let the Nazis make us live miserably."

While the women packed, Tamás walked up the hill to the stone cottages. The shepherds had been gone for several years and the cottages stood in neglected condition. An overgrown briar hedge stood along the edge of the hillside and helped to conceal the cottages from the road. In fact, Tamás could barely see the villa from his vantage point atop the hill.

There were three cottages in fairly good condition and a fourth in need of some work and a small barn. Vadas sent several men to help repair the thatched roofs, strengthen the shutters and doors, and replace the glass windows. The cottages were primitive, lacking electricity or running water, but they would be warm and comfortable. Each cottage had a black potbelly stove for cooking and a fireplace for warmth. A spring-fed well stood just outside the cottage grouping. Several trips by a horse-drawn wagon moved all the furnishings and packed boxes up the hill.

At the end of the week the family, plus several chickens and two dairy cows, and several horses moved from the villa up to the cottages. Everyone decided that Tamás and Silva, who would prepare the meals for everyone, should have the largest cottage with the biggest fireplace. The table in the Tóth cottage would be large enough for all to gather round and Ana would occupy the cottage's loft.

Elizabeth and Éva would share their cottage with Klára and András when they returned from Budapest. The smallest cottage would be used by Rudolf whenever he was at the lake and that left one unoccupied cottage.

The little group gathered for their first dinner at the Tóth's cottage and gave thanks for Silva's delicious goulash and honey cakes. After dinner Elizabeth and Éva went to their own cottage, lowered the heavy black draperies over the windows, lit their oil lamps for a few moments to prepare for bed and then thought about their strange situation before falling asleep in their new home.

May, Eger

Late in the night a loud knocking at their front door awakened Pál and Rózsa. Panic swept over them as they sat up in bed. Pál got up; Rózsa wrapped herself in a blanket and followed him to the door. When Pál opened the door, he was surprised to find old Dr. Kiss standing there. Kiss had been the Szabó's doctor since Pál was a young child; he had delivered all the Szabó babies.

"What's happened?" Pál asked, fear evident in his voice as he looked toward his parents' large house across the drive. "Come in, come in." He could see it was something serious by the doctor's expression.

Dr. Kiss and his son entered the house. "We've come to warn you, you and your family. All of you must leave here tonight." The doctor sat down, pulled a handkerchief from his pocket and wiped his face. "My son and I have come to your home first. I thought it would be easier for you to convince your father how serious the situation has become and that he must leave tonight as quickly as possible."

"What's happened?"

"There's talk in Eger. Too many people know that Rózsa is Jewish. That's bad enough for Rózsa and your children, but now there's a rumor your whole family is Jewish. The old widow Madách claims to have knowledge of some ancient history she says proves it."

Dr. Kiss took Pál's arm, "You know the Nazis pay informants for every Jew they turn in. This rumor about your parents, your family is convincing. Widow Madách says that her great-grandfather knew your family to be Jews from the Ukraine. That information is enough to condemn your family. We've heard that more Nazi soldiers and trucks will be arriving in Eger by noon tomorrow. We believe they will come here soon after, sometime tomorrow or tomorrow night."

"You should gather only your necessities, valuables and go while it's still dark." The good doctor breathed heavily.

Rózsa gave the two men cups of tea and thanked them for their warning.

"We must return to Eger before light," said the doctor, "and you must go now as soon as you can."

Dr. Kiss and his son were gone as quickly as they had come. Rózsa and Pál stared at each other for a moment. They embraced each other, then parted to begin their exit from a life they both treasured.

"Get dressed, pack as light as you can while I go tell father." Pál breathed heavily, "I'll hurry back to help with the children."

Rózsa dressed while making lists of important things in her head. She woke fourteen-year-old József and explained to him what was happening. They got three cases and began to pack photographs, some linens and silver spoons along with a few items of clothing. She and József awakened eleven-year-old Vera and five-year-old Sárika and by the time Pál returned they were dressed and ready to go. Rózsa wondered where Pál would want to go. She knew she wanted to go to Budapest to be with her mother.

Within an hour of Dr. Kiss's visit, Pál was putting the cases into his truck. "Father is taking everyone to the Ukraine. There's family there, non-Jewish family, but I'm concerned about the border. Father thinks they can get through, because their papers only indicate they are Magyar Hungarians, nothing about being Jewish. It's less than a hundred miles to the border, so they'll try to make it before morning."

"And where will we go, Pál?"

"I'm thinking we should go to Budapest to be with your mother. There should be some safety in numbers in the city." He smiled at Rózsa to reassure her, "At least Budapest can be the first stop; then we'll decide what to do next."

While Pál's brothers packed their car and the company truck, Miklós and Borbála stood bewildered outside their home. In all there were ten of them, Pál's parents, his two brothers, one sister-in-law and five children, one of them Pál's little sister.

Miklós wanted to take a stand and protect his barrel factory and sawmill. He resisted leaving his family's life work. Miklós wanted to protest, demand that the Nazis prove their accusations, but Pál's mother was too afraid.

"But Miklós, they know!" She pleaded, "They know and we know what is said is true. They will shoot us all. Please, Miklós, we must hurry."

The family members embraced, knowing it could be the last time any of them might ever see each other. Each one promised to hold the faces of their loved ones in their memories forever.

"We must keep them safe, Pál, our children," his father admonished him.

"God be with us all."

Pál helped Rózsa and the two little girls climb up into the truck bed. The children were sleepy and snuggled beside Rózsa under blankets and pillows in the back of the truck. Vera and Sárika held on to their favorite rag dolls made by their dear grandmother, Borbála. Pál threw a black tarp over all of them. József sat in the front seat with his father and stayed awake as the truck wound its way on back roads around the town of Eger and through the Bükk Hills. József wanted to help his father keep an eye on the winding road with its many difficult curves.

The night was moonless and dark; a light misty rain was falling. Pál had blacked out much of his headlights and traveled with very dim shafts of light on the road. József watched ahead for approaching car lights. Only once were there lights ahead; Pál pulled off onto the side of the road into the brush until the car had passed. They had to refill the tank one time on the way with the gasoline they carried with them. Eger was only sixty miles from Budapest, but it was a grueling journey.

When Pál drove into Budapest it was still dark. They entered the city north of Városliget City Park and wound their way through the narrow streets until they neared the Jewish section. Pál parked on Vas Street, a side street around the corner from the Klein house on Dohány Street. He and József got out of the truck while Rózsa climbed from the back. There was very little activity on the dark wet streets. In fact, it seemed eerily calm. They decided it would be best to get into the Klein house as quickly as possible. Pál and József each carried a sleeping child and a bag while Rózsa led the way, carrying other baggage.

They saw no one along the way, but terror surged with every pounding heartbeat. They stopped in front of the Klein home. While the little group hid in the shadows, Pál ran up the stairs. He knocked on the door and rang the bell, but no one came. The door was locked. He whispered down to Rósza, "No one seems to be home. Do you have a key?"

"No, but mother often left a key under the window sill to the left of the door. There's a little ledge."

"Yes, here it is." Pál opened the door and they all hurried inside. It was evident at once no one was there or had been there in some time.

"They've taken her." Rózsa was completely distraught, "Where could she be?"

Then suddenly they heard someone upstairs and froze in their places. Pál called out, "Who's there? Come out. Show yourself."

"Oh, Pál…Rózsa," suddenly Abram appeared on the stairs, "I'm glad to see you!"

Rózsa was elated to see him; she fell upon his shoulders and cried uncontrollably.

"Where's your mother, Abram?" Pál asked.

"She left here in February. We didn't know where she was at first, but then discovered she was living with the von Estés." He yawned before continuing a long narrative, "I thought you might be Ferenc, but you were too noisy for him. Then I thought maybe you were the country Jews, the ones the government expects to cram into houses of the Quarter. Why are you here? You should've left Hungary a long time ago. Rumors are that the Nazis are going to build a wall around the Jewish sector. You don't want to get caught in here."

Abram stopped talking for a moment, but then added, "I think you should contact Count von Házy. He might be able to help you. You should talk to him, but you'll have to do it in person. Mother's telephone hasn't worked for a long time."

"Is there anything to eat here?" Rózsa frowned, "The children will be hungry in the morning."

"Nothing fresh, just some farina, crackers. Ferenc and I only come here to sleep some nights."

"Stay here. Settle in," Pál spoke gently to Rósza, "I'll find some food for us."

"I'll go with you," said Abram. "I know where to go and how to get you there. We won't need ration books."

József wanted to go, too, but Pál said no. "Stay here, Son, protect your mother and sisters. Perhaps next time."

Pál noticed that Abram didn't have a yellow star on his coat. Abram confessed to Pál that he and Ferenc were involved in the Resistance. None of us wear the star. We won't make it easy for them."

"Where is Ferenc?" Pál asked.

"I don't really know," Abram answered. "I saw him yesterday, but not since then. I think he might have a girlfriend. He'll probably show up tomorrow."

"Aren't you concerned about him?"

"Not yet."

Just as the sun was rising, Pál returned to the Klein house. His absence had been relatively short, but it seemed very long to Rózsa. Abram did not return with him; he had found Ferenc and they had work to do. Pál brought a few root vegetables, a loaf of stale bread and a small flask of milk. Rózsa made the farina with a bit of the milk. When the children awoke in the early morning, they sat at the kitchen table. József ate in silence while Vera and Sárika, sensing the tension in their parents, began to cry. Rózsa and Pál tried to calm them, but knew something had to be done to make this dire situation tolerable.

After the children ate their breakfast, Rózsa took them up to the attic to play. She told them they must play quietly together. The children understood there was danger and they promised to be very good. József sat in a corner by a small window reading while Vera and Sárika played with Rózsa's old doll house. Rózsa sat on the stair and listened to them play. She remembered the music that used to drift up the stairs from the music room below and all the happy times in this house. *Her wedding... her father and her mother... Magda in the kitchen... Eszter and her brothers.* Tears filled her eyes, her heart ached for times past.

Very early the next morning Rózsa and Pál decided that he should go to see Rudolf von Házy and then to Klára's to let Éva know they were in Budapest. Pál drove onto Andrássy Avenue and then to von Házy's street. He parked in the drive, went to the front door and knocked. After a few moments, Zela answered the door. She told Pál that she had not seen the count that morning, but that he might be having breakfast at the von Esté's. Pál drove around the corner, parked at the von Esté's and knocked on the front door. Klára answered.

"Pál, come in!" She was elated to see him and embraced him heartily. "Oh, it's wonderful to see you! We have wondered about you every day. How are Rózsa and the children?"

"We're all here in Budapest in the Klein house. We had to escape Eger in the middle of the night. We just arrived here yesterday. We saw Abram and he told us that Mrs. Klein was here."

"She was here, but she went with my mother to Lake Balaton months ago." Klára kept talking as she led Pál through the house. "Pál, you must realize it's no longer safe here in Budapest for Jews. András and I just arrived for the weekend. Only Leona and Auguste live here now. Of course, Dolf still lives in town."

As Pál followed Klára to the kitchen, he noticed the wooden panels covering the stained glass windows on the landing, the furniture covered with sheets, and paintings gone from the walls.

"I'll have Leona gather some food for you to take back to Rózsa," Klára said, "but it's not safe there, Pál. You must speak with Dolf right away. He was just here for breakfast. He'll help you."

After a cup of coffee in the kitchen, Klára and Pál walked across the von Esté garden. As they walked, Klára implored him, "You must bring Rózsa and the children to Lake Balaton."

The garden, no longer well-kept, concealed the old doorway in the wall; it stood behind an overgrowth of hedge and honeysuckle. "We like it this way, hard to see, but we know it's here." Klára held back the shrubbery while Pál pushed open the door. There was just as much growth on Rudolf's side of the wall. Pál and Klára walked to the rear of Rudolf's house and knocked on the kitchen door. "Zela, it's Klára."

Once inside Rudolf and Pál embraced and spoke of old times. Rudolf became very serious, "Rózsa and your children need new papers right away. I have a contact at the Swedish Embassy. I'll arrange for them as soon as possible, as soon as I have their old papers. You'll need a new certificate of marriage, too. Rózsa and the children should stay out of sight until they have new papers."

"I'll be back with the papers as soon as I can." Pál was very anxious. He wanted to get back to Rózsa and the children to start the process of new papers as quickly as he could.

Even though Rózsa had never registered as a Jew with the Eger Jewish Council or worn a yellow badge, her papers indicated her Jewish origin by maiden name, location of birth, and previous address. If she could be identified as a Jew, then her children were automatically Jewish, too.

Pál drove back to Dohány Street, parked on Vas Street again and hurried to the Klein house. Rósza was elated to get the bag of food from Klára, but even more thrilled to hear the news of her mother and Rudolf's promise to help. Rósza took the bread, tea, milk, some vegetables and a piece of dried beef from the bag and began to think how she could ration the food to last. Pál took their papers and left again. He drove back to von Házy's and gave them to Rudolf.

"I will work on these immediately," Rudolf said. "Meet me at eight tomorrow morning at Gerbeaud's in Vörösmarty tér. I'll have the papers ready for you then."

After a fearful night of little sleep, Pál arose early, kissed Rózsa good-bye and hurried off to Vörösmarty tér. Rudolf was already there; he ordered coffees for them. Pál gulped down his coffee and glanced at the papers, very official-looking Swedish certificates. He was anxious to get back to his family. Pál thanked Rudolf and they parted going in opposite directions.

Pál hurried back to his truck and sped away into the Jewish sector and onto Dohány Street and then he saw them…two large trucks parked in the middle of the street. Pál stopped his truck immediately; he could not believe his eyes. He turned around the corner and parked on Nagy Diófa Street. He got out of the truck and walked to the corner of Dohány Street.

To witness what he saw happening took all his strength. He had arrived at Dohány with the life-saving papers, so hopeful, until he saw the big canvas-covered trucks parked in the street. Nazi soldiers were directing people from the houses up into the trucks. There was Rózsa holding Sárika in her arms as she walked toward the truck followed by József holding Vera's hand. They carried stuffed bags with them.

People seemed to be everywhere…men, women, children, and soldiers and, yet, it was as though Pál could hear nothing. Perfect quiet except for the random barks of dogs. Pál fell back against the stone wall of the corner building and watched. He felt as though his heart would stop; he could not get a breath. The soldiers slammed the truck's back gate closed, the engine started and Pál watched as the truck made its way down Dohány Street with its cargo of people standing together in the truck in silence.

Pál knew he could have done nothing to save them. He sat in his truck for only a moment, taking deep breaths, the memory of the horrific sight burned forever in his mind. Pál started his truck and drove to Rudolf's house. He parked in the drive, bounded up the stairs to the front door hoping that Rudolf would be there. In a few moments Rudolf did answer the panicked knocking. Pál immediately related what he had seen, pleading with Rudolf for help.

"We must hurry, Count. I don't know where the Nazis have taken them."

"Probably to Déli station. We must hurry. Zela, please inform the Baroness where we've gone and to expect guests."

Rudolf grabbed his suit coat, rushed out to Pál's truck and directed him to the Swedish Embassy. Rudolf and Pál pushed through the crowd of people around the embassy and hurried up the stairs into the building. Per Anger met the two distraught men.

"There are people to rescue, Per, personal friends of mine," stated Rudolf. "We must hurry. They were taken in trucks from their homes on Dohány Street less than an hour ago. Probably destined for Déli station."

"There's no time for papers to be forged," worried Anger. "We'll give the Swedish certificates a try."

With three large trucks Per Anger followed Pál and Rudolf in Pál's truck through the winding streets of town, across Margit Bridge, around Castle Hill and into Déli Station. There were hundreds of people, some still crowded onto trucks, others clinging to small bundles while they stood in lines, and many more already in boxcars waiting on tracks by the station. Pál felt overwhelmed by the mass of miserable people. Waves of insanity began to take possession of his rational thoughts. Pál gripped Rudolf's arm as they walked toward the station with Per Anger.

Anger spoke with a Hungarian policeman named Batizfalvy. Rudolf recognized him from other Swedish forays with Anger into Nazi territory within the city. Batizfalvy was one of a very few Hungarian policemen with Jewish sympathies. He led the men toward the tracks.

"Batizfalvy thinks they may already be on the train," Anger told Rudolf. "Either way it's better for us to start there and work our way back."

Anger walked straight to the Nazi officer who seemed to be in charge of loading the boxcars. "Sir, I'm Per Anger, Second Secretary of the Swedish Embassy. I must tell you in the name of King Gustav V that your soldiers have made a serious error this day. Many of those who have been arrested today hold Swedish papers. These persons must be released!" Anger stood firmly on both feet and stretched himself as tall as possible to face the German in authority and demanded, "They must be released immediately!"

The German captain looked skeptically at Anger and started to speak, but Anger did not hesitate, he responded firmly to the German's skepticism. "If you do not let me find my people and release them immediately, I will inform Herr Edmund Veesenmayer."

Mere mention of the feared Veesenmayer's name jolted the German captain into action; he responded to Anger's threat, "Go ahead; look for your people."

Anger and Batizfalvy ran beside the cars, calling out "What is your name?" The people inside the cars began to respond with shouts, calling out their names and thrusting out their hands between the slats. Anger handed out the certificates and repeated the names he heard to Batizfalvy who directed S.S. guards to open each designated car and let out the captives.

"Rózsa Szabó! József Szabó!" shouted Rudolf and Pál as they walked quickly alongside the boxcars.

Pál was frantic as he ran along the track shouting their names. At last he heard her voice, "Pál, we're here! We're here!"

"Open that car!" Batizfalvy motioned to the S.S. guard.

Pál could not believe his eyes when he saw Rózsa standing above him in the opened car. She had the look of a woman completely mad, near hysteria; her red hair wildly framed her pale face while her eyes, opened wide as plates, stared at him with a kind of fury he had never seen.

As Rózsa was helped out of the crowded car Pál realized she had used her scarf and coat belt to tie Sárika to her body. A terrified Vera clung to her mother's coat by one hand while she tightly gripped a bag with the other. Rózsa spoke in frantic sobs, "Pál, I lost József! József is lost! I don't know where he is."

"We'll find him," Pál promised her, but his heart was breaking, too.

Rudolf and Batizfalvy continued to run along the track calling "József Szabó!" as they passed the boxcars, but József never answered.

"We must go!" Per Anger called to Rudolf and Pál, "We've tested their patience as long as we can."

"But we haven't found József, yet," Pál pleaded.

"We can't leave him!" Rózsa clung to Pál, sobbing, "We can't."

"We must go now, Pál," demanded Anger. "We have rescued many this day."

In defiance of the S.S. guards that day, one hundred and fifty Jews, including Rózsa and her daughters walked with Per Anger from the station. Anger loaded one hundred and forty-seven Jews onto his trucks and drove away while Rudolf and Pál took the remaining three with them. As Rudolf drove the truck away from the station, Pál tried to console the inconsolable Rózsa. She stared from the truck bed into the mass of desperate people, her eyes searching the crowd for her beloved son, but they had to leave the station. It was far too dangerous to stay any longer. Their success was gravely tempered by their failure to find József.

Once back at the Swedish Embassy, Anger sent each of the rescued Jews to safehouses in and around Budapest. Rudolf drove Pál's diminished little family to the von Esté house. Klára and András were there to meet the Szabós at the door with welcoming embraces. Leona had *paprikas csirke* ready for them in the kitchen, but Rózsa was too distraught to eat. Klára took Rózsa into the garden while András sat at the table with Vera and Sárika.

Rózsa could not stop grieving for József or saying his name over and over. Finally, Klára convinced her to drink some lavender and lemon balm tea and then to take a bath. Klára gave Rózsa new clothing to wear and guided her to the table where Leona gave her a bowl of soup. The little girls had left the table hours earlier with András, who was giving them a tour of the house.

András led Vera and Sárika from the kitchen into the maze of hidden staircases in the walls of the mansion; they climbed from cellar to attic and out into the open campanile. Sárika did not like the darkness of the stairs or the long climb up to the attic. She was happy to be outside and begged András to hold her up so that she could see the panoramic view. Then she didn't like being up so high and wanted to go back to the kitchen, but Vera and András began talking and didn't pay much attention to her.

"You could hide many people here in your house," Vera said. The enormity of the house and its secret staircases greatly impressed Vera; she felt some sense of safety in the von Esté house. "The Nazis could never find us here."

Images from her family's harrowing experience suffered just hours earlier haunted her thoughts. "Will you hide Jews here?"

András responded that he didn't know. Then he looked at Vera with a worried expression, "Are you a Jew?"

"I guess so," Vera sighed as she looked off into the distance. "The soldiers called us Jews and said very bad words to us, but we didn't know we were Jews." Vera sounded very confused. "What is a Jew anyway? Something very bad I think."

"I don't know," András answered, "but I don't think Jews are bad, because Dolf and my mother are your friends. They wouldn't be your friends, if Jews were bad."

"We lost my brother." Tears filled Vera's eyes, "We couldn't find him and he's with those soldiers. They don't like Jews and they think he is one. What will happen to him? What might they do to him?"

András felt terrible, he wanted to help Vera. He touched her shoulder, "Don't worry, Vera, Dolf and your father will find him. The Nazis will let József go. Why would they keep him from his family? He's just a boy."

Vera managed a smile. András's words did make her feel better. After all, his words were reasonable. Of course they will let József go. Why would they keep him? She took Sárika's hand. "Thank you, András. You must be right. Let's go back down to the kitchen now. I'm sure mother needs us with her and father, too."

The children emerged from the maids' staircase into the kitchen to find everyone sitting around the big oak table. Papers with blue and yellow colors were scattered over the table. Klára gathered them into a pile.

"Please take the girls into the garden to play for a while, András," Klára said. "Leona has made some sweet water for you, take the glasses with you."

When the children had gone, the adults continued their conversation.

They decided Klára should take Rózsa and the children to Lake Balaton while Pál would stay in Budapest with Rudolf to make another search for József.

The next morning Rózsa and the children, with their new Swedish papers in hand, got into Klára's French-built *Avions Vorsin* and began their journey to Lake Balaton. Both women were purposely well-dressed, appearing to be well-connected, important. Rózsa wore a dark-green dress of Klára's, her red hair piled on top of her head and Klára had on a gray serge suit with a white blouse. The children were dressed in proper play clothes provided by András.

On their way out of town, passing by soldiers at every corner, Klára and Rózsa became extremely nervous, but no one seemed to pay any attention to the *Avions*. Klára drove across the Erzsébet Bridge over the Danube, then west of Castle Hill toward the highway to Balaton, less than seventy miles away. For several miles the highway followed the rail tracks causing Rózsa great discomfort as she strained to see any sign of boxcars traveling on the track, but none were there.

Just outside the ancient Hungarian town of Székesfehérvár, the *Avions's* right front tire suddenly went flat and Klára had to pull over to the side of the highway. Everyone got out of the car. The children ran into a nearby field of sunflowers while Klára and Rózsa studied the spare tire. Within moments three young German soldiers on motorcycles pulled alongside the *Avions* and inquired if the women needed help. Vera was instantly terrified, but András convinced her that the three of them should stay among the sunflowers and pretend to play as though nothing bothered them. Klára showered platitudes and gratitude on the soldiers for stopping.

While two of the soldiers changed the tire, the third asked to see the women's papers. The young, very polite lieutenant treated both Klára and Rózsa with great respect, especially when he saw that Klára was a baroness and wife of an S.S. officer. The lieutenant only took a cursory look at Rózsa's Swedish papers without any suspicions. Klára could see that the young Nazi was impressed by the decorative nature of the document. From the colors and ornate seals he seemed to assume Rózsa was someone of importance, too. He handed the papers back to the ladies and tipped his cap to them, never asking to see the children's papers.

After some small talk, the soldiers said good-bye as the women and children piled back into the car and drove away. The soldiers followed them for a while and then passed in front of the *Avions* seemingly to escort them into Székesfehérvár. The motorcyclists continued in front of the *Avions* as Klára wound her way through the streets of Székesfehérvár. She and Rózsa breathed a huge sigh of relief when the three soldiers turned off at last and disappeared onto a side street. Klára drove on confidently along the north side of Lake Balaton, through Balatonfüred and on to the villa, finally stopping in the front drive. Tamás had seen the approaching car from the hillside and walked down to meet them with Hóvi at his heels. Klára drove the car into the garage and then everyone walked together up the hill toward the cottages.

Éva met them halfway. She greeted her daughter and grandchildren with pure elation and overwhelming relief, then guided them the rest of the way up to the little cottages nestled in the trees. It was decided that Éva would move with the Szabós into the empty cottage. More mattresses and furnishings were needed from the villa, but that could wait for Vadas's men to help.

András, excited to show Vera and Sárika around, was cautioned by Elizabeth, "You are forbidden to ever go down the hillside or to the villa. You must stay up here in the forest, out of sight!"

"New kittens were born while you were in town," Silva informed András.

András and Hóvi took Vera and Sárika to see the new litter nestled in a shed. Klára smiled as she watched the children try to corral Hóvi's enthusiasm while they spied on the sleeping kittens. The mother cat seemed oblivious to the observers as she licked the tangled mound of kittens around her. Klára felt content here on the hilltop. *As always, the world seems so far away from the tranquility of Balaton.* She hoped that Dolf and Pál would arrive soon.

June

Everyone sat around the wireless in Tamás's cottage, listening to a BBC report. "On the sixth of June the Allies landed on the beaches of Normandy in France bringing hope to all of Europe." They all cheered when they heard the news and then cheered again when the reporter announced that Allied air raids had hit Budapest industrial sites and railways.

Rózsa sighed and thought to herself, *Perhaps the bombing will stop deportations from Budapest. Perhaps the Germans have been weakened. Perhaps the war will end soon.*

July, Budapest

When Per Anger learned that the Swedish diplomatic office finally recognized the need to expand rescue efforts in Budapest on behalf of Hungarian Jews, he was elated. A new attaché, Raoul Wallenberg, arrived at the legation on the ninth of July.

"It's good to have you here in Budapest, Raoul." Anger warmly welcomed him. "Our rescue mission in Budapest is in desperate need of more help and fresh ideas."

Anger explained to Wallenberg the current office activities and proudly showed him the *fake* Swedish certificates of citizenship currently being distributed to Jews. Anger complained, "The distribution is much too slow and the number too small, but, regardless the certificates have saved lives."

"You've created the perfect ruse, Anger," Wallenberg complimented his new associate. "Color and style appeal to the Germans. They like the *official look*, but I think we should make them even more elaborate and print as many as possible!"

Wallenberg appreciated the valiant efforts of Anger and Danielsson and was eager to offer his own more brash and unconventional ideas. "I want to help the Jews with passes and immigration papers, but there are other ways to confront this evilness, at its root. We must use every method available to save lives—bribery, extortion, threats, harassment—whatever means it takes to stop these Nazis. At this point it's becoming clear the Germans are losing the war; the end is near. My goal is to convince the Nazis and their co-conspirators that they will face harsh retribution as war criminals if they continue their heinous acts."

"We must encourage non-military Hungarians to become involved in the protection of their Jewish citizens, the innocent victims of this horror!" Wallenberg's passion for the mission became obvious to Anger. "Hungarian citizens must be told, if they turn away from their chance to help their fellow citizens, they will suffer terrible guilt after these crimes come to light."

Per Anger smiled at Wallenberg's enthusiasm, "You must meet Count Rudolf von Házy; he will welcome your enthusiastic point of view and ideas."

Shortly after Wallenberg's arrival, the Swedish Legation had a social gathering to introduce the newcomer to the Hungarian diplomatic circle, including Gabor Kemény, the Hungarian Foreign Minister, and his wife, the Baroness Liesel Kemény. Anger knew that the Baroness was sympathetic to the cause of saving Jewish lives. Count Rudolf von Házy and the Baroness Klára von Werner were also among the guests. At the end of the evening when most of the guests had gone, Rudolf and Klára stayed behind to speak with Anger and Wallenberg.

Anger reintroduced Rudolf to Wallenberg as a printmaker and active in Nazi resistance.

"This is the *Schutzpasse!*" Wallenberg was eager to show all of them the new elaborate protective pass he had designed, "A Swedish guarantee of immigration status to every holder of the pass. It's based on the Provisional Passport that Sweden issues to her own citizens who lose their passports."

"I like the design," Rudolf studied the prototype, "It's quite official looking." He smiled as he looked up at Wallenberg, "The Germans will believe it, I'm sure."

"The Swedish *Tre Kronor* seal," Anger interjected as he pointed to the symbol of three crowns, "is a nice touch, as are the stamps and ornate signature of the Minister."

"The high quality of paper adds to its legitimate appearance," commented Rudolf.

"The blue and yellow colors were the convincing element of Anger's Swedish certificates," Klára offered, remembering her own experience. "The color and ornate flourishes make the document more authentic."

"Yes, I agree. Those flourishes will help to convince the Hungarian government as well. They must be persuaded to accept it as a legal document," stated Anger as he added, "the Foreign Office only authorized fifteen hundred passes."

"I'm thinking thousands," Wallenberg smiled. "I can't see why we should limit our humane endeavor to so few when there are so many suffering this evil oppression."

"I offer my services to manufacture the documents," Rudolf said. "I assume you want to start immediately."

"Yes, we're grateful for your help, Rudolf. I have plans to expand every effort undertaken by the Relief Office, so we'll need more workers and I want to hire as many Jews as possible to fill those jobs." Wallenberg shared his plans, "We need more trusted *distributors* to hand out the passes; we need to establish more *safehouses*, hospitals, and soup kitchens; and we need to develop new methods for distributing medicine, food and clothing."

Wallenberg's enthusiasm was infectious and invigorated Anger, Rudolf, and Klára to face the difficult and dangerous work ahead. A shared spirit for the work bound them together as great co-conspirators in their efforts to undermine the Nazis. Rudolf continued his work with the British MI6 and, under Wallenberg's direction, added a second layer of intrigue. When information needed to be shared, Rudolf's varied alliances were helpful. By late summer Klára was a volunteer driver for both the Red Cross and Save the Children foundation, distributing food, medicine and clothing.

August

By August, more than three hundred Jews worked and lived at the legation on Vadasz Street. But Wallenberg was never satisfied; he wanted to engage more Jews and sympathizers against their Nazi oppressors. He enlisted many Aryan-looking Jews to help with clandestine activities. Rudolf recommended Theodore Rubin, the tall, fair-haired Jewish man who looked more German than Jew and also Pál Szabó who wanted desperately to join in their campaign against the Nazis. The Resistance had stolen plenty of uniforms from the S.S., the Wehrmacht and the Arrow Cross to give the volunteers a choice of uniform appropriate for the mission. Both Pál and Theodore could carry off their transformations as German soldiers or Arrow Cross quite convincingly.

In or out of uniform, Pál and Theodore worked in the Legation Office with Rudolf delivering the *Schutzpasse* to Jews throughout the city. Without the *passe* Jewish citizens of Budapest lived in constant fear of arrest and deportation. Eichmann sent trainloads of Jews out of Hungary every day and the Regent Horthy was powerless to stop him. Jews depended on the continued efforts of Wallenberg and his team to save as many Jews from the trains as possible.

One August evening, as Wallenberg sat in his office, he received word of a train loaded with Jews ready to leave the station. He called out to Anger, "We must go, immediately! We have very little time."

Wallenberg grabbed his hat, met Anger on the stairs together with Rudolf, Pál and Theodore, and arrived at the station followed by several Swedish Legation trucks. Batizfalvy met the five men in front of the station house and led them to the train.

Later that night, Rudolf and Klára sat at the big oak kitchen table in the Andrássy house eating Leona's *töltött paprika*, a stuffed peppers dish. Rudolf was quite animated as he described what he had seen.

"I was in Wallenberg's office when he received word of a train, loaded and ready to leave Budapest for Auschwitz. Wallenberg shouted, 'Drop everything! We must get to Déli Rail Station before the train leaves!' He acted as a man obsessed when we arrived at the station; he climbed to the top of the boxcars and began to drop bundles of Swedish passes down into the cars. Jumping from car to car, all the while yelling orders to the guards, 'Open these cars! Let the people out who hold Swedish passes!' It was unbelievable! We guided many women and children to the waiting trucks."

"Nazi officers ordered their subordinates to shoot him, but they shot over his head, certainly because they admired his courage. It was truly a grand sight to see. Wallenberg saved more than a hundred tonight," Rudolf said, "but of course, that number is small in comparison to the filled cars. Wallenberg said, 'Not nearly enough...we must do more.'"

Rudolf stared at his bowl as he stirred the paprikas seemingly lost in thought. Klára reached across the table and touched his hand. "But some were saved. That's a good thing. We can be glad for that."

"Yes, we must be grateful for the bits of good. I received a message yesterday, bad news about an old friend. The German Admiral Canaris was arrested for his part in a failed assassination attempt on Hitler's life at the end of July. Many co-conspirators were immediately executed, but so far Canaris has been saved. The Brits speculate Himmler wants to use Canaris as a pawn to negotiate amnesty for himself when Germany surrenders to the Allies. Whatever the reason, I hope the war will end quickly enough to save Canaris. He's a good man."

"Well, the Soviets are at our borders to the east and south," said Klára. "They'll drive the Germans out of Hungary soon enough, but I really doubt the Soviets will be much better, do you?"

"With the liberation of Paris, the Allies are coming closer and closer. Perhaps, we'll get lucky and it will be the Americans who occupy us instead of the Soviets."

They laughed, agreeing that dream, although a perfect one, was probably too optimistic.

September, Budapest

The Regent Horthy sat in his opulent office on Castle Hill behind his enormous desk. He was greatly disturbed by the letters he had received from many world leaders, among them Pope Pius XII and the American President Roosevelt. Horthy rose from his desk and paced before the windows that overlooked the Danube far below. Stopping to look out toward Pest, Horthy could not see the Jewish Quarter from his vantage point, but he thought about the sector and its people. He held in his hands the written pleas that begged or threatened him to stop the deportation of Hungarian Jews on humane grounds.

In particular, the personal letter sent by Sweden's King Gustav V bothered Horthy. The king's words implored him to stop the deportations, stating that, *"You must consider the reputation of Hungary."* Horthy decided he would respond to the king's letter and thought about the words he would write... *I have done all that I can do to give Hungary's Jewish people justice. I have kept Hungary's strong principles of humane treatment for all.*

Horthy, in fact, agreed with the writers of the protest letters; he did not desire the deportation of Hungary's Jews to Germany. Horthy did, however, recognize that many Hungarian citizens blamed the Jews for Hungary's economic problems and Horthy agreed that Jewish activities had to be controlled, but he disagreed with deportations, as too extreme.

Compelled by the letters and his own sensibilities, Horthy decided to end the Nazis' deportation plans on humanitarian grounds. He sat down at his desk to write a proclamation when his secretary entered the office with a letter marked *urgent*. Horthy ripped open the envelope. The letter was from leaders of the Budapest Jewish Council. Horthy read the words with dread, "Eichmann has sent several truckloads of Jews— including women and children—from the Kistarcsa detention camp to the station for deportation. Please stop the train. Please save these innocent people!"

An order issued by Horthy demanded that Prime Minister Sztójay immediately stop all deportations, in particular, the train newly loaded with fifteen hundred Jews from Kistarcsa. As Horthy signed the order, he knew his actions interrupted both the Nazi and Arrow Cross plans to evacuate all Jews from Budapest. Horthy realized he would be in direct conflict with the S.S. officer Eichmann, but Horthy proceeded to do as his conscience guided him. By the time Horthy had received the urgent message, the train had already left the station and was speeding toward Austria. But later that afternoon, Horthy received confirmation his order had stopped the train just before it crossed the border. The train returned to Budapest with its cargo of Jews who were sent back to the Kistarcsa detention camp.

Horthy's interference so infuriated Eichmann that he left Budapest and Hungary with his unit of men. Within the lull of Eichmann's absence and the halt of deportations, efforts were stepped up by the many organizations to save as many Jews as possible. Certificates of citizenship and protective passes from Sweden and other countries, including Spain, were distributed. The Vatican reissued baptismal certificates to Jews in detention centers whose earlier conversions had been nullified by the state. Swiss agents arranged immigration permits to Palestine, and Valdemar Langlet, director of the Swedish Red Cross purchased properties to increase the number of *safehouses* throughout Budapest. Langlet gave the houses Swedish flags and official titles with signs, such as *The Swedish Library* or *The Swedish Research Institute.*

A few weeks later when Eichmann returned with his troops to Budapest, he was more determined than ever to speed up the purge of all Jews from Hungary. *Entjudung*, ridding the Jews, became another step toward the desired Final Solution. Once back in Budapest, Eichmann's first act was to reissue his previous order for the delivery of fifteen hundred Jews from the Kistarcsa detention camp for deportation and he made certain they were the *same* fifteen hundred saved by Horthy only weeks before.

This time Eichmann devised a clever plan to prevent any warning of Jewish deportations getting to Horthy. All Jewish leaders who had previously warned Horthy were called to Eichmann's office for a meeting. While the leaders sat in Eichmann's office waiting for the meeting to begin, S.S. soldiers brutally loaded the Kistarcsa Jews onto trucks and took them to the railway station where they were loaded into boxcars and sent to Auschwitz. Eichmann did not release the Jewish leaders from the bogus meeting until the train had crossed the Austrian border.

Pleased by his cleverness, Eichmann continued to demand more deportations, but once again Horthy stood in the way. Horthy officially declared, "Jews cannot be deported to Germany! By my order Hungarian gendarmes will prevent any Hungarian citizen from being arrested for the purpose of deportation. The gendarmes have orders to protect the Jews from Eichmann's henchmen. The Hungarian government officially prohibits further evacuation of Jews from Budapest."

Again, Eichmann was enraged by Horthy's interference and requested that his German commanders transfer his unit out of Budapest. Within days after Eichmann's departure Horthy dismissed the pro-Nazi Prime Minister Döme Sztójay and appointed a loyal Hungarian, General Géza Lakatos, as the new prime minister. Lakatos formed a new anti-German government and approached Horthy with a proposal.

"I want to ask permission to make contact with the Allies in order to prepare an armistice between Hungary and the West. The war is ending with an apparent German defeat and already we have seen Romania break with the Axis and align with the Soviets. I believe it would be in Hungary's interests to join with the West, either Britain or America."

Horthy, agreeing with Lakatos, gave his approval for the contact and then addressed another serious problem, "Let us issue orders for the arrest of Ferenc Szálasi and officially abolish the Arrow Cross."

"It's a good idea, but it will be a difficult task," Lakatos lamented, "because even though Eichmann is gone, the Nazis still protect Szálasi."

The Jewish community welcomed the changes made by Horthy and Lakatos, but the hopes of Horthy and Lakatos were dashed when the English and Americans decided to place the fate of post-war Hungary into the hands of the Soviets.

September, Lake Balaton

Rudolf, Pál and Klára were at the Lake Balaton cottages when they heard the news on Tamás's wireless. The BBC reported, "The Red Army of the Soviet Union has crossed the border into Hungary and now occupies eastern and southern territories." Those who gathered around Silva's table received the news with dread. No one believed the Soviets to be any better than the Nazis and now it was apparent to everyone that very soon the Soviets would replace the Nazis in Hungary. One tyranny for another.

Just at the moment despair and pessimism spread unabated through those in the Tóth cottage, András and Vera with little Sárika entered the cottage with wide smiles. András and the girls had gone to his cottage to fetch Stefan's music box. András had taken the box carefully from its shelf, carried it to Silva's cottage where everyone was gathered and now he placed the box on the big table.

"What a good idea, András!" Elizabeth exclaimed as she clapped her hands, "We need some gaiety! To hear some beautiful music again will lift our spirits."

Tamás turned the crystal crank and the waltz music began. András and

Vera held hands with Sárika and began to twirl around the room. All the adults felt cheered by the children's innocent abandon as they laughed and kicked up their heels.

When the music stopped, András took a turn at the crank, but this time it was difficult to turn. Something seemed to be jamming the works. András looked into the smoky little window to see the mechanism inside, "I think something is in the way, stopping the cylinder from turning."

Tamás bent over to look through the window and then turned the box on its side to look for the tiny latch.

"Here it is," cried András as he moved the tiny concealed hook. The door popped open and he reached inside with his smaller fingers to pull out a piece of paper. Everyone gathered close to him as he unrolled it and smoothed it out on the table. A lovely drawing of a young girl...

"It's Eszter," gasped Éva Klein. "What's written there on the corner?"

"For Stefan," András read aloud the words, *"I will love you forever, Eszter."*

There was silence, only for a moment.

"You drew this, Dolf?" asked Rózsa.

"Yes, I did; a very long time ago."

"I don't understand," said Éva as she sat down. "Eszter loved Stefan?...and did Stefan...what does this mean?"

"Yes, Mrs. Klein, Stefan did love Eszter," interjected Klára. "He told me that he did. They loved each other."

Everyone turned toward Klára trying to make sense of a story never told.

"And you knew of this, Rudolf?"

"Yes," he admitted to Éva Klein as he stood very close to Klára.

Everyone looked from Mrs. Klein to Elizabeth. Éva sat motionless, she had a puzzled look and then she uttered one word..."*Stefania.*" Éva looked up at Elizabeth who stood by the table staring down at her, just as puzzled.

Both women suspected they knew the meaning of the name of the girl in Palestine. Éva reached out to hold Elizabeth's hand. The two women turned to Klára, imploring her to confirm what they suspected. Klára bit her lip, remembering perfectly that December night so long ago. "Yes," she whispered, "Eszter told me the night before she left for Palestine."

"You never told me, Klára." Rózsa was astonished.

"She made me promise not to tell anyone. I wanted to, but I promised her. I hated having this secret between us for so long. I'm so sorry."

Éva took the drawing from the table, held it to her breast and stood. She patted Klára's hand and spoke in her lovely soft voice, "Don't worry about this, Klára. You were only a child. It was a difficult secret for Eszter to share with a child. There was nothing anyone could have done to change her choices. You have no blame in this matter."

The drama unfolded around the three children as they watched without saying a word. They knew some great secret had been revealed about the fabled Uncle Stefan and an Aunt Eszter who lived in Palestine. They also knew they dare not ask anyone to explain the secret.

Tamás stood by the open cottage door, his thoughts racing back through all the years. He could still hear Leopold's voice agonizing over Stefan's death...agonizing all the rest of his life. *Why? Why, Tamás, did Stefan involve himself in politics? When did he become so adamant about the king's return? What made him want to enter a battle for the king? What cause possessed him to give his life for such a futile endeavor?* Tamás lit his pipe and stared out into space. After all these years the answers became very clear to him...*for love.*

———⚬———

By mid-September, with the advance of the Red Army toward Budapest, the Horthy-Lakatos idea to make an alliance with the Allies gained importance and urgency. Lakatos convinced Horthy that a compromise had to be found with the Soviets for the preservation of Hungary. Horthy sent a team to Moscow, led by Professor Count Teleki, the son of former Prime Minister Teleki, to negotiate an armistice with the Soviets. In return for Hungary's agreement to cease all military action, Hungary wanted assurances from the Soviets that at the war's end, the Soviets would not occupy Hungary. Horthy and Lakatos were determined to maintain their strong anti-Communist position.

October, Ꜧitler's Bunker

Despite the July assassination attempt on Hitler's life at Wolfsschanze, he continued to live at the heavily fortified bunker compound, because he still felt safer there than anywhere else. On a particular October morning Hitler took his usual morning walk with his dog, Blondi. As they strolled through the golden aspen trees of the Masurian forest, Hitler's thoughts were focused on Hungary. *I have had enough of this Regent Horthy...he is a traitor to the Reich!*

Hitler smiled and spoke aloud to the beautiful German Shepherd that walked elegantly by his side. "I know what Horthy's been up to. Every café crowd in Budapest knows what he's trying to do. Does Horthy really think the Reich will allow his surrender to the Soviets? Well, Blondi, I have the answer. We will not! I have plans for Horthy and Hungary!"

Just before his noon meeting with *Kommando* Colonel Otto Skorzeny, Hitler and Blondi returned to the bunker. Hitler greeted the Colonel warmly, "Are you ready to launch my new Operation?" Hitler laughed heartily, "I'm calling this one *Miki Mouse.*"

The two men sat down with other officers to discuss the details of *Operation Miki Mouse.*

Budapest

On the eleventh of October, Horthy and the Soviets had a preliminary agreement on the terms of surrender that included the Soviet's post-war guarantee of Hungary's independence. Horthy felt relieved; he believed he had averted disaster and secured the future for Hungary. Even when on the nights of October thirteen and fourteen the Allies heavily bombed the rails and rail-yards of Budapest, Horthy knew the bombs fell against the Nazis rather than the Hungarians. Finally, the Allies determined the time had come to stop deportations of Jews from Hungary.

Using spotlights and radio signals, the Hungarian Resistance, including Armin, Theodore, Abram and Ferenc, guided the Allies' planes to their targets those dark October nights. Allied bombs also fell on the heavily Nazi-populated town of Székesfehérvár. Despite massive destruction of the town's transportation system, a single Székesfehérvár highway remained as the only undamaged way of transport into or out of Budapest.

On Sunday, the fifteenth of October, Horthy sent his son Miklós Horthy, Jr. as Hungary's official representative to a secret meeting in Pest with Soviet agents arranged by Yugoslavian envoys. The Soviets expressed very cordial greetings to Miklós upon his arrival and invited him to the table. In the best of spirits the optimistic Hungarian and Soviet representatives began their serious discussions to finalize the armistice. Suddenly the Nazi Colonel Skorzeny's armed Kommandos rushed into the room and held everyone at gunpoint. Two Kommandos yanked Miklós from his chair, shoved the furniture aside, and rolled him up in the room's carpet. They carried him from the building to a waiting car, drove to the airport and immediately flew him to Vienna. Once there Miklós was taken to Mauthausen concentration camp. His father, the Regent Horthy, had no idea that his son, *Miki*, had been kidnapped.

That same Sunday afternoon, at two o'clock, Horthy spoke with great confidence to his countrymen in a radio address from Buda's Castle Hill. "In Hungary's best interest, I have agreed to an armistice with the Soviet Union, thereby officially withdrawing from the Axis. It is clear that the German Reich has lost the war. A war that Hungary never wanted with our neighbors. A war forced upon us by Germany. Hungary desires peace with the Soviets and the Allies. In return the Soviets have agreed that post-war Hungary will have an autonomous government."

As Horthy delivered his last word across the radio waves, Kommandos seized the radio station in Pest and pronounced Horthy's proclamation null and void. Meanwhile Colonel Skorzeny with several German tanks and troops made their way to Buda Castle. Once there Skorzeny stood arrogantly at the castle gates and threatened destruction if Horthy did not surrender to him at once. Realizing that the castle did not have the military strength to resist Skorzeny, Horthy ordered his Hungarian troops to "Stand down, do not resist." The Germans took control of Castle Hill and Edmund Veesenmayer arrested Horthy.

On the following Monday morning Horthy's old friend, Prime Minister Lakatos, presented a document for Horthy's signature. Horthy's eyes filled with tears as he read the document. It had three parts: Lakatos to be replaced with yet another new prime minister, the fascist, Ferenc Szálasi; the Arrow Cross Party to be legalized; and Horthy to abdicate as regent.

"Why do you bring such a document to me?" Horthy asked Lakatos in disbelief.

"You must sign, dear friend," Lakatos implored him. "They have kidnapped your son. Miki is being held in Germany. Hitler demands your signature in exchange for his life."

Horthy signed the document bringing an end to twenty-three years of service as regent for Hungary. Hitler's *Operation Miki Mouse* succeeded completely.

On Tuesday, the seventeenth, Skorzeny escorted Horthy by train from Budapest to Hirschberg Castle in Bavaria. Hitler *"invited"* Horthy to remain at the castle as a *"guest of honor under guard for his own protection."* Miki's time in custody at Mauthausen remained undetermined.

Also on the seventeenth, Adolf Eichmann returned to Budapest and that same evening Szálasi 's Arrow Cross began a new reign of terror against the remaining Jewish population in Budapest. German Nazis and the Hungarian Nyilas were seen as one in the same, equally terrifying. With his new power as prime minister, the fascist Ferenc Szálasi promised Hungarians "greatness and prosperity for all as allies of Germany and victory in the war!"

Arrow Cross Party ideology mirrored that of the Nazi Party in that both subscribed to the ideal of a master race (Szálasi included the Magyars), shared a strong sense of nationalism and an abhorrence for capitalism, communism and Jews. Szálasi made clear his distain for the Jews and all others he deemed undesirable living in Hungary... "We must seek out every Jew and separate them from *us*, the Magyars. We must end the corruption Jews bring to our Magyar race. Stop the Jews' infiltration that dilutes our Magyar culture and end their insidious control of Hungarian wealth."

When Tamás heard such statements on his wireless at Balaton, he thought to himself... *I'm glad Leopold can't hear the Prime Minister of Hungary so deliberately distort the Duke's ideal of Magyarization, an ideal the Duke advocated all his life.*

While eating supper in the Andrássy kitchen, Rudolf and Klára heard the same radio report and reacted to Szálasi's odious statements exactly as Tamás.

"Papa would be sick with shame that the leadership of his beloved Hungary has sunk so low into hatred and fear of its own people."

"The Nazis and the Nyilas have silenced all voices that oppose them. There's no one strong enough to alter their direction. Add in the factor of desperation in the face of a lost war and we're all in a state of peril, not only Jews, but all of us. No one is immune from the horror the Nazis can inflict." Rudolf added, "That includes us, Klára. Neither of us is safe from exposure, arrest. That's why I think it's time for you to leave Budapest for Balaton. Get away from here now."

"I don't want to leave you, Dolf. Being here with you these last few weeks has been the happiest time of my life. I don't want to give this up. When we leave here, it will be impossible for us to be together as we have been," she sighed and bit her lip. "How will we bear that separation?"

"We'll find a way to be together, Klára." Rudolf reached for her hand and stared into the beautiful eyes that still entranced him after all the years of loving her. "I promise. Now I want you to prepare to leave and, in the meantime, promise me you'll do nothing to put yourself in danger."

"I still have some medical deliveries to make; they're counting on me. I still have government permission to drive Red Cross vehicles, so far it seems safe enough, but I promise to go soon."

Within days of Szálasi's rise to authority, he and Eichmann, as part of their anti-Semitic obsession, declared the *Schutzpasse* invalid and ordered the arrests of all Jews holding such passes, just as Wallenberg feared. Wallenberg responded in haste to call upon his friend, the Baroness Liesel Kemény, the wife of the Hungarian foreign minister, to use her influence to make sure the passes would remain valid. At her urging, the Baron Gabor Kemény, in defiance of Szálasi's order, reinstated all passes as legal protection for their holders.

Late October

Late one October afternoon Klára received a note from Zsuzsanna Weisz of the Aliyah group, the underground organization that helped Jews immigrate to Palestine. "Urgent" was written across the fold. She opened it. "We have a delivery for Rózsadomb Hospital—typhus. Please pick up—Szabó Library on Baross út." Klára refolded the note thinking about the coded words she had just read and spoke to Leona.

"Please tell the Count I'll be late for supper. I've an errand to run for the Red Cross."

Klára got into her Red Cross van and drove onto Andrássy toward the city.

Darkness came early and cast the city streets in dark shadows as she made her way along Károlyi, entered Kalvin tér and turned onto Baross Street which ran alongside the elegant rococo Szabó Library. Klára stopped the van along the curb, rolled the window down and peered out at the shadowed niches around the library. Then she saw them…two women, one of them dressed as a nurse, a man and three children huddled together. They emerged from behind the wrought-iron gate and stepped onto the cobblestone street. They walked quickly to the rear of the van where Klára and the second woman, who turned out to be Zsuzsanna, helped them climb up into the van. Klára returned quickly to the driver's seat.

"Safe journey," said Zsuzsanna, as she stood close to Klára's window. "I know that you did not expect to transport people, but we are so grateful to you for taking them. Sorry the notice was so short. Our plan was to take the family just after lunch, but our truck broke down and then we thought of you. They all have passes, so there should be no problem. Oh, and remember they have typhus. The Germans won't dare touch them!"

"Make sure you make it back before curfew and use the Chain Bridge," warned Zsuzsanna. "At sundown all the other bridges are closed."

Klára said good-bye, drove around the block and back onto Károlyi. Just as she turned onto József Street, three Arrow Cross police stepped in front of the van and motioned for her to stop. The policemen approached both sides of the van and demanded to see her papers. Klára showed her Hungarian and German identification papers and her Red Cross permit for driving the van.

"The Baroness von Werner?" The young policeman sounded skeptical, "Your husband is an S.S. officer?"

"Yes," she affirmed.

"Why are you driving a Red Cross truck?" He asked in a disdainful tone as though he hated the Red Cross. "Oh, I understand; you're some kind of humanitarian," he said with scorn. "Have you got Jews back there? Open it."

Klára got out of the van, her heart pounding in her throat. She only hoped the people inside would remain calm. As she walked to the back, she said as calmly as she could, "I'm taking children to Rózsadomb Hospital. They have typhus. There's a nurse with them."

The policeman drew back from her, slowing his step. When they reached the back of the van, he motioned for her to open it. Klára held her breath. The policeman shined his flashlight in the back. The three children were all in the beds attached to the interior walls. The man was nowhere to be seen and the nurse had on a face mask; she offered identification papers to the policeman, but he waved her off.

It was as Zsuzsanna said, the policeman would not touch them; he feared typhus. Klára breathed a sigh of relief. Without any comment, the policeman motioned for Klára to close the van's door.

"Rózsadomb? You're driving all the way to Rózsadomb? You'll barely get there by curfew." He sneered at her, "Stay off my street. I don't want to see you again tonight. I'll make a report of this."

Klára had only driven a few blocks when the nurse moved from the back of the van into the cab, taking the front seat next to Klára. Klára thought the woman looked vaguely familiar.

"Aren't you the Duke von Este's daughter?" the nurse asked.

"Yes," Klára answered as she shifted the truck into gear and drove onto *Széchényi Lánchíd,* the Chain Bridge, heading toward Buda.

"I'm Jolán Löwy. My father owned the lace shop next to your father's wine business on Hercegprimás Street."

"Oh, yes, I thought you looked familiar. I remember you selling lace to my mother. How is your father? Your family?"

"That's my father in the back with his grandchildren. We're all that's left of our family." Jolán spoke with a resilient tone to her voice. "My father recognized you. He said 'Go up front with Miss Esté. Tell her thank you.' He said to tell you 'We admired your father. He was a great voice for all people of Hungary. He would be very proud of what his daughter is doing for Hungary's people.' My father said to tell you 'We're not surprised that you would be involved in this heroic act.'"

"Oh, it's not so heroic," Klára answered, embarrassed. "I usually just deliver food and medicine."

"It is heroic," argued Jolán resolutely. "We're in such a desperate situation. Those who help Jews in any way are blessed, brave human beings, people like you and Zsuzsanna."

"Zsuzsanna was a friend of my brother's, Stefan. He knew your brother Imre, too."

"Oh? I didn't know they knew each other. Actually, that's where we're going...to be with Imre in Palestine. Zsuzsanna arranged Swiss immigration papers for us."

Klára's thoughts raced back to Stefan and Eszter...*so long ago*...and then so recently to Stefan's music box when Elizabeth and Mrs. Klein learned the truth for the first time. Klára asked, "Imre married Eszter Klein, didn't he?"

"Yes. Did you know Eszter?"

"I know her sister Rózsa. We've been friends for a long time."

"The Kleins should go to Palestine, too. I know Eszter would love to see her mother again. We're excited to meet Imre's children. They have a girl and two younger boys; the girl is grown; she's over twenty, I think."

While Jolán spoke of plans for their future and their lives in Palestine, Klára drove along the Danube onto Fő Boulevard toward Batthyány Street, lost in thought of what could have been.

"There it is," Jolán startled Klára from her thoughts, "on the left. See, the one with the sign."

Their destination had never been the Rózsadomb Hospital, but rather a Swedish *safehouse* in Buda on Batthyány Street. A wooden panel painted with red crosses and the words, *Roten Kreuzes Schutzpasse*, marked the house. Klára parked the van at the curb and the Löwy children got out and ran up the stairs of the townhouse where an elderly couple stood at the open door. Both Mr. Löwy and Jolán embraced Klára and thanked her for her help.

"Please give my regards to your lovely mother. Tell her that I think often of her husband's acts of kindness through our years of trial. He was the best of men."

Mr. Löwy and Jolán hurried up the stairs, turning once to wave a final farewell and then disappeared into the house.

Klára felt very alone in the van. The sun had set, the night was moonless and dark and she had a long distance to go. She retraced her travels back across Chain Bridge toward Erzsébet tér. As she got close to the square there was some kind of demonstration going on, a large bonfire blazed in its center. Klára could see a mass of people in the square surrounded by German soldiers. She slowed the van realizing the street was blocked. Her only alternative was to turn into a narrower cobblestone street, but it, too, became blocked by the crowd that spilled over from the square.

Panic began to rise in her chest. Klára tried to still her racing heart, telling herself to remain calm. She had no choice but to abandon the van and begin walking through the dark street out into the square. Staying close to the shadowed walls of the buildings, Klára crossed the tér hoping she had gone unnoticed. She felt greatly relieved as she entered another dark cobblestoned street that led away from the square.

However, within a few steps Klára realized someone followed her. Her own footsteps were echoed on the cobblestones by another. Klára felt rooted to the stones, unable to quicken her steps as though walking in slow motion. She was frozen by fear as though in a nightmare. Klára tried to catch her breath and stopped to glance behind her. Then she saw him, the silhouette of a man backlit by the blaze of fire in the square behind him. He was coming steadily, relentlessly toward her until his shadow overcame her own.

Suddenly a second man stepped from the shadows a short distance in front of her. He stood firmly on both feet and lit a cigarette. She could see he wore a black leather coat...he was Gestapo. Klára stopped walking, between the two men and stood very still. The man behind her closed in, took her arm and pushed her toward the Gestapo while speaking firmly, "You've missed curfew. Show Herr Körtig your papers."

Klára fumbled in her bag, pulled out her identification and Red Cross permit and handed them to the German.

"Ah." He shined a flashlight on the papers, "So, you are the Baroness von Werner who drives Red Cross trucks. We know about your deliveries. Sometimes more than medicine, perhaps? You were driving earlier this evening? We heard a report about the S.S. wife driving to Rózsadomb Hospital."

Klára's breath was very shallow; she bit her lip, but said nothing.

"So, did you make it to Rózsadomb Hospital?"

Klára still said nothing.

"No? I think not. So where did you go? Who did you deliver? Who are your contacts?" He spoke very softly, very close to her face. "Well, these are not questions for the street. Don't you agree, Madam?"

She could see his sinister sneer by the flickering firelight. "No, no, no. These questions will get much better answers at the Margit Prison, don't you agree, Baroness?"

He looked past her to the man holding her arm, "Take her to the car, Engle."

Klára walked between the two men down the dark, cobblestone street toward the brightly lit square. She felt limp between them, but they held her up, propelling her toward the light.

As Klára and her captors walked toward the fire-lit square, a group of Wehrmacht soldiers approached the threesome. Klára closed her eyes in fear as she listened to their German words, "Heil Hitler! Can we be of assistance?"

Körtig and Engle hesitated for a moment to return the *Heil Hitler* and in that instant two of the soldiers rushed forward as if to take Klára, but instead plunged knives into the chests of Körtig and Engle. Klára felt her head spin and she began to fall to the street, but one of the soldiers caught her just before she hit the cobblestones. Klára opened her eyes to see a familiar face, Abram Klein, dressed as a German soldier. She felt faint.

"Are you all right?" Abram asked as he held her at arms' length studying her from head to foot, but before she could answer he began giving orders. "Move quickly. Walk behind us, Klára."

As if from a dream Klára watched as two of the *German* soldiers picked up the limp, dead body of Körtig and supported him between them. She swallowed and tried to shake herself back to reality and then suddenly she recognized Pál. He, too, was dressed in a German uniform and then she realized the other *Germans* looked familiar, too.

Abram and the other soldier pulled Engle up by the arms and draped the dead man's arms over their shoulders; Engle appeared much heavier than Körtig. The *German soldiers* walked with their burdens as quickly as they could on the cobblestones in the opposite direction, away from the square, away from the fiery light into the darkness. Klára followed closely behind them. Their destination was a black Bentley, parked on a side street. While Klára climbed into the back seat, Pal and the other *soldiers* put the two bodies in the trunk, got in the car and the driver Theodore Rubin, also dressed as a German soldier, went south toward the Danube.

Just past the Erzsébet Bridge, Theodore pulled alongside the river. As the car idled, the four men got out, opened the trunk, stripped the bodies of clothes and identification and threw the nude bodies into the fast-moving Danube.

Theodore drove Klára to the von Esté house. Pál accompanied Klára up the steps to the front door where they were met by Rudolf. After Pál spoke with Rudolf for a moment, he returned to the car and Theodore drove away with the Resistance fighters inside.

"Klára, I'm angry with you." Rudolf began as they entered the hall and he looked at her, eye to eye, with a rare angry expression. "What were you thinking, Klára! You were only to deliver medicine and food. That's dangerous enough! What possessed you to do this dangerous act? What if they had taken you to prison? They would have tortured you to get names! Not only would you have been harmed, but the whole Resistance could have been exposed!"

"I'm so sorry, Dolf," Klára sobbed.

Rudolf knew by morning the two Gestapo men would be missed and when the Germans realized they were gone, a hundred innocents would be murdered in retribution. He chose not to discuss that detail with Klára.

"You promised me you wouldn't put yourself in jeopardy," Rudolf shook his head and sighed. "Pál and the Resistance had an assignment tonight to follow Körtig. Körtig had plans to send the bonfire mob into a frenzied murderous rampage into the central ghetto. The Resistance had Körtig in their sights when Pál saw you cross the square. They followed you and, not according to their plan, but fortunately Körtig's plot for the ghetto was ended. God was with us tonight! I can't imagine what might have happened if Pál had not seen you. It was a miracle, but it could have been a disaster, Klára."

So much trouble on her behalf, Klára was devastated. "I'm so sorry, Dolf."

Klára did sincerely regret causing Rudolf concern, but she was also grateful that she had taken the chance and finally she spoke, her tone filled with chagrin, "The family...they were the Löwy family, Dolf. What's left of them. Imre Löwy? They have immigration papers for Palestine to be with Eszter."

Rudolf put his arms around Klára and drew her close to him. When he realized how upset she was, he immediately softened his tone, "I'm sorry to be angry with you," he held her close, and kissed her, "but the thought of you in danger drives me insane with worry. You can never frighten me so terribly again." He kissed her forehead and held her very close, "I am proud of you though. You remind me of Stefan. He would have done what you did without a thought for his own safety. Your father instilled a strong sense of care for others in both of you."

"Papa would be very proud of you, too, Dolf."

"Please go to Balaton, Klára. Leave all this behind. It's only going to get worse as the Germans become more desperate in the face of defeat."

"I'll go, if you and Pál come with me." She looked deeply into his kind, brown eyes. "We worry about you, too, and we need you with us to protect us there."

"We'll come as soon as we can, but there are some important matters we must accomplish before we can leave," he said firmly. "Very important matters, Klára, but I promise we will come as soon as we can. But you should leave here tomorrow."

Klára did leave the following morning; she drove the Red Cross van. Two Red Cross nurses accompanied Klára as far as Székesfehérvár where she left the nurses at the hospital and continued on alone to the villa. Klára drove the van into the garage and parked it alongside her *Avions* and Tamás's Mercedes Royal Coupe.

November, Budapest

For many years when the von Esté family went to Lake Balaton, it was Leona who stayed at the Andrássy house looking after things. She had been in charge of summer at the house in town for more than thirty years. Leopold always thought of her as a formidable woman, valuable to the family, responsible, but without a hint of humor. Her normal pose was a square stance with her arms folded over a large bosom. In the summer at the Andrássy house, she definitely had the last word. Since Klára left Budapest, Leona remained alone in the house while Auguste lived in the rooms above the carriage house.

Leona and Auguste were sitting in the kitchen eating a bite of supper when they heard a loud knocking at the front door followed by the constant ring of the kitchen bell indicating the front door. Leona got up and walked to the reception hall hearing the loud knocking all the way. She was quite irritated by the rude behavior of whoever it was doing the pounding and ringing. When she opened the door it was an S.S. officer who stood there. Even though Leona thought she recognized him, she did not greet him, but gave him a stern expression instead.

He was taken aback by the woman who blocked the doorway. "Is the Baroness von Werner at home?"

"No, she is not."

"When do you expect her?"

"I do not expect her."

"Well, where is she?" he asked in frustration.

"Well, who are you to ask about the whereabouts of the Baroness?"

"I am her husband, the Baron von Werner, Madam, and I demand to know where she is." He cleared his throat, "May I come in?"

Leona stood aside and let him pass, "The Baroness is at the lake with her family."

Franz looked around at the dimly lit interior and noticed that the furnishings were covered by sheets and the windows on the landing were covered with wooden planks. Leona did not like his arrogant attitude or smug expression. And from what she had observed over the last years and especially over the last few months, she didn't think Miss Klára liked him either.

"It's too dark in here," he commented with authority. "Turn on the lights."

"It's against the law to turn on lights after dusk."

"The draperies are drawn. The windows are boarded up. Turn them on!"

Franz walked around the reception hall pulling the cloths from the furnishings and piano. He marched into the dining room where he noticed the obvious empty space on the wall and demanded, "What was removed from there?"

"A photograph of the family."

"Where is it?" he asked. He walked toward her, "Where is everyone?"

"I told you. They're at Lake Balaton."

"Is the Baroness still driving a Red Cross truck?"

"I couldn't say what the Baroness has done or will be doing."

He turned his attention to the rooms and walked back toward the parlor. Leona followed him, watching his every move.

"Why is everything covered?" he asked. "Boarded up? It seems more than necessary for a normal excursion to the lake. Perhaps they've left Hungary altogether? I would say this appearance of abandonment seems quite disloyal to the Hungarian government, as though they have given up on the future."

"There would never be anything disloyal to Hungary in the actions of the von Esté family. They simply decided to stay at the lake a bit longer this year. They have stayed through the winter before. When the family returns to Budapest, everything will be as it was," she stated without any emotion.

"I have just arrived in Budapest for my new assignment," Franz announced. "I expected to see the Baroness here. I suppose that I will be forced to go to Lake Balaton to see her."

Just as Leona was about to encourage the departure of Franz von Werner, she heard very distinctive footsteps approaching from the reception hall. She and von Werner turned toward the parlor entrance as Rudolf emerged. Auguste stood behind him.

"Ah, it's Count von Házy," Franz said. "What a surprise to see you here."

"As it is to see you, Sir," responded Rudolf. "You are new to Budapest?"

"I've just arrived," Franz replied, "I'd hoped to settle in here with my wife, but since she is not in town, I may as well make my residence in the Palace. The distance makes this house too inconvenient anyway."

Franz studied the count who stood leaning on his cane, "What brings you to this house?"

"I look in on Leona occasionally to see if she might need something."

"That seems exceptional, but, then you've always been a kind of von Esté family member, a brother to Klára. Is that right?" But before Rudolf could answer, Franz asked, "Now what is it that you do? Since you're unable to fight for your country, how do you compensate for that flaw?"

"I work for the Hungarian Trade Commission. I'm just a simple bureaucrat. Certainly no comparison to those brave, patriotic men who wear the uniform, but I do what I can."

Franz considered the look of Rudolf von Házy. Very tall, slender and dark, black hair with a slight streak of silver rising from the left temple and dark piercing eyes, if one liked the dark appearance, Franz thought, some may consider him a handsome man.

"Have you seen Klára recently? Have you been to Lake Balaton?"

"The answer to both questions is no," Rudolf answered and then turned to Leona. "I left a package for you in the kitchen." He turned back to Franz, "I must take my leave now."

Leona was pleased when Franz also left. She and Auguste returned to their cold dinners sitting next to the package of bacon left by Rudolf. Leona smiled as she remembered Franz's comments to Rudolf and said aloud to Auguste with a twinkle in her eye, "That Nazi knows nothing of the Baroness or the Count."

Late November

Outside a heavy snowfall covered the streets of Budapest in a frigid shroud while inside the Swedish Legation, Rudolf and Per Anger, dressed in their coats, mufflers and fingerless gloves, worked as part of a production line to create more certificates of Swedish citizenship. There were never enough it seemed. Rudolf turned the wheel of the press while Anger applied the stamp of authenticity to each paper.

Anger worried with the worn rubber stamp trying to print a clear image, "We need a whole new set of stamps. I thought this nightmare was coming to an end with the rails destroyed. I thought Eichmann would give up his insidious goal to rid Hungary of all Jews, but now he decides to make the Jews walk all the way to Austria!"

The legation had just learned that Eichmann and the Arrow Cross would force thousands of Jews—men, women, children, the old and infirm—to march the one hundred and twenty-five miles through bitter winter weather to the Austrian border.

At that moment Wallenberg entered the office; he seemed exhausted as he flopped into a chair, his face red with cold. "They've begun to move people from the Quarter to the Ujlaki brickyard in Obuda. Thousands of them huddled together without food or shelter; they wear very little clothing against the cold. The march begins tomorrow."

The next day Pál drove the car for Anger and Wallenberg as they traveled alongside the procession of miserable human beings. The two men rolled down the windows of the car and handed out certificates and bread to as many as they could. Rudolf followed behind in one of three Swedish Red Cross trucks. After going about a mile, Pál turned the car around, backtracked, and then Wallenberg got out of the car and ran beside the marchers, physically pulling out those with papers and pushing them toward the Red Cross trucks. A few fortunate souls without papers also managed to scramble into the trucks.

The death march continued toward Austria day after day and Wallenberg's crew returned every day to travel alongside the marchers, saving those they could. Despite their efforts, many succumbed to exposure, starvation, and pure exhaustion. Those marchers who faltered along the way were shot or tortured by the guards. Regardless of the numbers pulled from the march each day by Wallenberg, he always lamented how few they had saved.

All of November's days and nights were busy. Rudolf spent his days with Wallenberg or the Resistance in rescue efforts and his evenings in the Swedish Legation helping produce documents. All the while concern grew within Budapest as the Soviets drew closer and closer. Time seemed to be running out. Questions haunted their thoughts. What will happen to the Jews and to the Resistance when the Soviets drive out the Germans?

—⁂—

Two ghettos formed in Pest—the *International Ghetto*, a group of *safehouses* that stood along Pozsonyi Street parallel to the Danube and Margit Island where various countries provided protective documents for the Jews who lived there and the *Central Ghetto*, a much larger area encompassing the old Jewish Quarter. Near the end of November Szálasi's government ordered a forced labor crew of Jews to construct a high fence around the Central Ghetto.

The fence ringed the ghetto from Károlyi körút to Király utca to Erzsébet körút to Dohány utca. Only four gates, all guarded by Hungarian policemen, gave access to the ghetto. The Arrow Cross / Nyilas death squads made regular forays into both ghettos, arresting and murdering Jews at will. None of the relief organizations were allowed inside the ghetto, not even the Red Cross.

Food rations were reduced to below minimum standards and within a brief time starvation, freezing temperatures, and lack of sanitation led to disease and death; typhus and tuberculosis were rampant. The Zionist Halutz rescue movement was the only group able to penetrate the ghetto sucessfully, but the aid they brought was very small. Halutz's major contribution was helping a few Jews escape the ghetto.

—ᵚ—

Rudolf watched the flag thrash about in the cold wind. *The Blood Banner,* the red field with its black swastika within a white circle, like an open eye never sleeping. The banner whipped noisily back and forth, furling and unfurling, waving over the Pest side of the Margit Bridge. Rudolf stared at the flag and remembered another obnoxious thing that mesmerized him one night long ago in Paris. Back and forth it ticked, *The Object to be Destroyed,* the metronome with its menacing eye. Man Ray's object d'art that even the artist wanted to destroy. It had seemed so sinister. One day Rudolf imagined he would drag down that horrid flag and all that it symbolized and destroy it.

A sudden tapping on the car's window startled him back to the moment. He rolled down the glass to see Pál and Theodore, both dressed in S.S. uniforms, standing close to the car. "It's time. We're ready."

Rudolf got out of the car and the three men walked quickly through the snow toward the Danube. They were joined by Molnár, a pro-Jewish Hungarian policeman and Abram Klein. The Resistance had learned only that afternoon there would be another Arrow Cross execution of Jews on the banks of the Danube by the bridge just across from Margit Island. Since the Arrow Cross had come to power, their reign of terror had raged through all of Budapest. The Nyilas committed murders every day and every night. No Jew felt safe anywhere in hiding, in a *safehouse* or in the ghettos. The men trudged on, hoping they would not be too late.

Once the men arrived at the river they moved forward more slowly. Rudolf forced Abram to the back of the group. Abram had not worn any disguise and everyone agreed he should not have come with Molnár. They had warned Abram of the horror he might witness. His brother Ferenc was among the captives. The scene at the river sickened them all. There were two groups of men and women; each group bound together as one with ropes. Arrow Cross soldiers with guns guarded the prisoners.

Just as Molnár, walking between the two *German soldiers,* Pál and Theodore, appeared from behind a building, the Nyilas thugs pushed one bound group of perhaps ten or more young men and women toward the river bank. They were all Jewish—university age and members of the Resistance. Ferenc Klein and Armin Stein were among them. Before Molnár could intervene, the Nyilas pushed the whole bound group into the icy river. They all tumbled into the freezing water, some of them broke free from the rest and tried to swim, but most quickly sank from view, then bobbed upward covered in frost.

When Ferenc fell into the river, Abram recognized him at once and instinctively wanted to rush forward to save him, but Rudolf stopped Abram by holding him against the stone wall of the bridge abutment. Together they watched in horror as the Nyilas stood on the bank shooting at the poor, struggling human beings and laughing when they hit their targets as if they were in some macabre arcade game. Abram watched as the limp bodies were caught up in the ice floes of the fast-flowing Danube.

Rudolf held him tightly. "Wait here, Abram." Abram tried to stifle his sobs of anguish.

When the Nyilas reached for the second bundle of horrified individuals and pushed them toward the river, Molnár, escorted by Pál and Theodore, boldly approached the Nyilas and in a commanding voice asked, "What is going on here?"

"We're executing Jewish criminals," answered the Nyilas who seemed to be in charge.

"Well, that's enough for tonight," boomed Molnár. "We'll take charge of them from here on. You're needed at Teleki Tér to help put down a labor demonstration."

The Nyilas seemed disappointed to have their fun interrupted, but they gave over their prisoners to the hands of those they thought to be S.S. soldiers and left the river bank.

Once the Nyilas were out of sight, Pál and Theodore untied the captives and allowed them to go their own way. Rudolf and Abram hurried along the river bank searching for any survivors. Miraculously a few had made it to the bank, two who dragged themselves up the bank arm in arm, one already too frozen to be helped, another dying of his wounds and then finally, they discovered Armin, wounded but alive. Rudolf and Abram pulled him up the bank. Their small cadre of Resistance felt great satisfaction that Armin had survived, but they stood with Abram in profound sorrow at the edge of the Danube and watched the ice floes carry the frozen bodies away from them, knowing that one of them was Ferenc. The following day Pál took Abram to Lake Balaton.

December

All Jews who did not hold protective passes were ordered to enter the Central Ghetto where conditions were deplorable. Eichmann planned more marches, but time was running out. As the Soviets approached the outskirts of Budapest, Eichmann and Szálasi decided their only choice to rid Budapest of the Jews was to blow up the Central Ghetto with its entire population imprisoned within the fence. They made plans to plant explosives around and within the ghetto.

Lake Balaton

In the final days before the Soviets' arrival, Rudolf bid farewell to his friends at the Swedish Legation and wished them well. He went back to his home, packed up his certificate-making equipment and supplies, said good-bye to Zela, and drove around the corner to the von Esté house. Elizabeth had implored Rudolf to bring Leona and Auguste with him when he returned to Balaton.

Leona met Rudolf at the door and insisted he go with her to the warm kitchen. The rooms of the house were freezing and covered with frost. Leona gave him a bowl of soup and listened to his proposal.

"The Duchess insists that I bring you and Auguste to Lake Balaton. Very soon Budapest will be a very dangerous place for everyone,"

"Sir, I have lived here for thirty-five years," she argued. "Please thank the Duchess for her concern, but I have no desire to leave. I feel responsible for the things in this house. This is the home I know and I prefer to stay. I could never leave."

"The Duchess is concerned for your safety as the war draws near to Budapest."

"I would prefer to stay here, Count. If the bombs start to fall, Auguste and I will go to the cellar. And after it's all over we will be here when everyone comes back."

Rudolf spooned up the last sip of soup. He thought about what she said. "There's a chance, Leona, that the family may not come back to Budapest. If the Soviets are in charge it may not be in the family's best interest."

"In that case, it may even be more important for me to stay here," she said emphatically and asked, "Is Zela going with you?"

"No," he smiled. "Zela feels the same way you do. She became a bit cross with me for suggesting that she leave the von Házy home." He laughed, "So, I suppose I have failed with all of you. Please take care, Leona," Rudolf said sincerely as he left the house and drove his Bugatti to Balaton.

Winter was even colder at the lake. When Rudolf arrived at the villa, it was almost buried in snow. Snowdrifts as high as the first floor windows and piled on the gables made the house appear fantastical. There was no hint of human presence anywhere, the driveway uncleared, no trails leading away from the house in any direction. Rudolf drove past the villa to the edge of the woods, pulled off the roadway through the drifted snow into the woods and parked the car, making sure it was out of sight. He walked through the trees to the top of the hill and then back down toward the cottages, almost obscured by the snow on their rooftops.

Shoveled trails led from the woods, connecting cottage to cottage, to the well and to the outbuildings. Rudolf walked down to Tamás's cottage, opened the door, and completely surprised everyone. They were thrilled to see him, rising from their occupations and hurrying to bring him in from the cold. They took his snow-covered coat and hat and removed his wet boots, all the while asking questions about their dearly missed Budapest. Rudolf answered honestly that things were grim. He assured them they had made the right decision to leave the city and huddle in the forest. With heavy thoughts of home, each person in the cottage returned to their own activities.

Silva and Ana moved back to their preparations of yet another soup. The two women were grateful for their supply of vegetables, farina, dried and salted meats. They had far more resources than any Budapest citizen where food shortages were pushing the majority of people toward starvation.

Klára and Rózsa sat with the children at the large table, keeping them occupied making decorations and gifts for the Hanukkah and Christmas seasons. On the table were woven wreaths of cedar strung with red berries to hang around the cottages. Klára and Rózsa guided Vera and Sárika with embroidery of old handkerchiefs while Tamás taught András how to carve soft pine wood into little figures. The crèche had been left behind at the villa, so András was determined to make a new one for the big cottage.

By now the Szabó/Klein cottage had become quite crowded with four adults and two children. Changes were made—Rudolf moved into Tamás's cottage loft and Ana moved from Tamás's cottage into the cottage of Elizabeth and Klára. Éva and Abram moved into the smallest cottage.

As the days went by, Rudolf and Klára found few moments to be alone together. Walks into the cold, snowy forest seemed to be the only place where they could share intimate moments. They followed the shoveled paths into the forest.

"This is horribly frustrating, Dolf. We can never hope for more than this. We can never show openly our affection for each other. Only in secret can we be together."

"Those months on Andrássy were wonderful, Klára. We'll have them again," he tried to be reassuring. "It's difficult for me, too. Me in the loft and you next door."

"I still have those papers for Franz to sign, if only I could make him sign them." She looked so dejected. "I don't even know where he is."

Rudolf studied her mittened hand holding his; he took a breath, "I saw Franz a few weeks ago."

Klára stopped walking, "Where?"

"At your house on Andrássy," he answered. "He's in Budapest at the Palace."

Klára shivered, her brow furrowed, "I knew he would come back. When the war is over he'll come for András and for me."

"That will not happen, Klára," Rudolf held her close to him. "I will never allow that to happen. After the Soviets have taken control of Budapest, we'll find Franz and force him to sign your papers," he said the words confidently, "and, if we don't find him or if he won't sign, then we will simply disregard Franz. We'll live together in the open legally or not."

Klára believed Dolf, but she knew without doubt as long as she was married to Franz, he would not allow her to have happiness with Rudolf or to have her son, András.

When they went back to the cottage, Fábián Vadas and several of his men were there with the most recent news of Soviet movement, " The Soviets are drawing ever closer to the outskirts of Pest."

Those hearing the news felt both relief and anxiety. Relief to rid their country of the Nazis, but great anxiety at the thought of Soviets in control. Everyone had questions.

"If only the Americans or British had opted to enter Hungary instead of the Soviets, but that was not to be," they lamented. "When do you think the battle will begin?" "Will the Germans be driven this way?" "Have you seen the Red Army in our area?"

Vadas could not answer their questions, except to say, "Soon" and "Without a doubt we will see foreign troops in Balaton by spring."

Since early December each evening all the adults at the cottages gathered around the big table to listen to Tamás's wireless. The voices they heard through the static were often breathless as they described the Red Army's invasion of Budapest.

On Christmas Eve they listened intently to the report...

It had been expected the Soviets would begin their invasion through Pest, but the Soviets surprised the Germans by sending a small force into the northeastern boundaries of Buda...A probe that got as far as Szent János Hospital on Diós Árok Street before they were seen by a group of university students who sounded the alarm...the Russians are here!

The main Wehrmacht forces were in the midst of Christmas parties miles away from Buda when they got the urgent call to return to duty... Within hours trucks filled with S.S. and Wehrmacht troops crossed the bridges from Pest back into Buda while the Soviets secured positions in the forested Schwabian Hills to the east of Budapest.

The reporter continued his description...

German-Hungarian forces reinforced a semi-circular defense of Buda...that includes Margit Island along the Danube to Gellert Hill, the

Palace and Castle Hill, to Farkasrét Cemetery and around to the base of the Schwabian Hills and back to the Danube.

*   In Pest the German-Hungarian forces have pulled their eastern defenses back to a tighter line along a raised railway embankment south to Csepel Island. Sporadic forays of Red Army units have infiltrated Budapest neighborhoods on both sides of the Danube and have engaged in hand-to-hand combat. Inhabitants of the city are huddled together in cellars and in churches, even in the depths of the great Opera House on Andrássy Avenue. . . all awaiting the onslaught with dread.*

Tamás turned off the radio at the end of the report. Everyone sat in silence around the table lost in their own thoughts. *What would become of their beloved Budapest and country at the hands of the Soviets? How will the Jews be treated under Soviet occupation? What will happen to all the people in the ghettos? What will become of the Hungarian landholders and aristocracy in light of Soviet communist ideology?*

Although Klára heard the same radio reports, her thoughts focused on a vision of Franz trapped inside the Budapest Palace. She thought, *if only I could take the papers to him and convince him to sign them before he escapes the Soviets and flees back to Germany where I'll have no way of finding him.*

That night Klára became obsessed by the notion of meeting with Franz in Budapest—*before it's too late.*

Klára had paid close attention to the information Fábián Vadas supplied about the local activities of the Nazis. "German forces continue to hold the town of Székesfehérvár and its connecting highway with Budapest, the only open road into or out of the city."

Budapest

In Budapest that night and every night since Christmas Eve, Leona and Auguste, and old Zela, the von Házy's housekeeper, sat in the cellars of their respective houses listening to rumblings of artillery fire and explosions so fierce the thick walls of the great mansions shook. The only light in their dark surroundings came from the candles they lit. The time, day or night, passed unknown to them, they remained in the cellars so long.

Outside the sky glowed red every night from exploding bombs dropped from low-flying aircraft. Fear of what they might find when they emerged from their safe havens, kept the two women and Auguste underground. As long as they could still hear the thud of bombs hitting the ground and feel the walls vibrate they stayed in their cellars.

Germany

Hitler, rabid over the turn of events in Hungary, remained determined to save Hungary and its oil reserves for Germany. And he was still determined to defeat the Communist Soviets! Against the advice of his staff, Hitler turned to the Eastern front in Poland and ordered the Fourth S.S. Panzer tanks deployed from that front to Hungary. Then he turned to his Western front and deployed S.S. and Wehrmacht divisions from there to Hungary. Hitler's Wehrmacht commanders vehemently disagreed with all of Hitler's decisions, reminding Hitler that the advancing Allies from the west and Soviets from the east remained imminent threats to the German homeland.

Budapest

The Germans maintained their stronghold on Castle Hill while the Soviets relentlessly inched closer each day. On the twenty-eighth of December in a gesture meant to appease the Soviets and Allies, Bela Miklós, speaking for Hungarians, formed a new provisional government and disavowed any alliance with the German Reich.

Hoping to avoid a complete Soviet take-over, Miklós prepared a document of surrender to the Soviets that included a favorable outcome for Hungary. Miklós also ousted Ferenc Szálasi and the Arrow Cross.

Despite the declarations made by Miklós, the Germans and Arrow Cross maintained a stranglehold on Budapest and the Hungarian people. By December twenty-ninth the Soviets had completely encircled Budapest and the *Siege of Budapest* began.

1945
January

Budapest was surrounded, except for the western route to Székesfehérvár—the highway Klára would chose to take. Just after breakfast Rudolf and Tamás left with András to collect wood from their stock in the forest. Everyone else seemed busy that morning in their own cottages. As Silva cleared away the breakfast, Klára reappeared in the large cottage very well dressed in her best emerald green wool suit with black boots, black muffler and a hat with a black plume. Klára informed Silva of her plan to drive into Székesfehérvár to shop for a birthday surprise for András and to be back before supper.

Silva protested, reminding Klára of every possible danger. "Székesfehérvár! Why would you go so far? You should not leave the forest, Baroness, it is far too dangerous! Wait for the count to come back. He could go with you, if you insist! Go to Balatonfüred instead, it's much closer. Please, Klára, don't go today."

"Don't worry about me, Silva, I have all the proper papers, Hungarian and German," Klára argued. "Remember, Silva, I'm the wife of an S.S. officer, I won't be in danger."

Her words, so filled with distain, surprised Silva. She watched with a deep sense of dread as Klára walked quickly from the cottage.

Klára skirted the edge of the forest where the snow had receded from the base of the trees. The sky was bright blue and the melting snow glistened. She walked to the garage, went inside, hoping that her *Avions* would start easily, that she would have enough gas to get to Budapest, and that the *Avions* would not get stuck in the snow. Klára thought she'd worry later about getting back to the villa.

The highway from Székesfehérvár to Budapest was much worse than Klára had imagined. Heavy traffic going to and coming from Budapest made moving forward very slow. The good thing, she thought, was that no one paid any attention to her, except to yell directions and wave their arms at her to *keep moving*! As she neared Budapest she saw smoke rising from all directions. She decided to park her car on Palota Street and walk the rest of the way up the hill to the palace.

The sun was already low in the sky; it had taken much longer to get there than she anticipated. Thoughts that had plagued her sleep the night before once again came into her head... *What if Franz is no longer in Budapest? What if he has been killed? What if I can't find him?* She shook the thoughts from her head... *I have come to find him and if he is here I will find him.*

When Klára reached the top of Castle Hill and got a view of the city, she was shocked. The entire city was under siege. Even in the fading afternoon light, flames and smoldering ruins were evident all over the city and, most shocking of all, large sections of the palace were on fire. As she approached the palace she walked against the push of people fleeing from her destination. She entered through a side entrance of the nearest wing and met with chaos inside, soldiers hurrying in all directions. Klára stopped several S.S. officers and asked the way to Colonel von Werner's office. Finally, one soldier pointed to the stairs, shouted "second floor," and hurried away. Klára made her way up the stairs again against a surge of people coming toward her. At the top of the stair she asked a young woman who looked quite terrified as she tried to control a stack of loose papers in her arms. The woman stopped for only a moment to point down the great hallway, "down there toward the fire," she said.

Klára walked on the shiny marble floor without fear, only determination. Smoke began to seep into the hallway. Suddenly one of the great wooden doors opened and an S.S. officer rushed out into the hall followed by clouds of smoke. "Colonel von Werner?" she asked.

He nodded while coughing into his hand and ran toward the stairs. Klára caught the door before it closed and entered the room—a room that had obviously been a great banquet hall in times past. The interior was dark except for the roaring fire in the massive fireplace at the opposite end of the room, which struck Klára as very strange. She thought, *Why go to the trouble of lighting a great fire in the fireplace when the whole city and the palace are burning around you?*

Heavy velvet draperies were pulled across the windows. Her eyes adjusted to the darkness, she saw Franz, illuminated by the firelight, standing next to a great mahogany desk. Papers were piled in disorder all over the desktop. File drawers were pulled from their cabinets and many papers lay scattered on the floor. Wild-eyed and waving his pistol, Franz shouted orders. Other soldiers in the room gathered papers frantically and threw them into the raging fire.

Klára cautiously walked further into the room and called to him, *"Franz,"* but no one could hear her. She said his name again, louder in a low, but firm voice.

He turned, "For God's sake, Klára, why are you here?"

"Franz, I have brought the papers for you to sign. You must sign them now. The Russians have surrounded the city!"

Franz stared at her with madness in his eyes. The other men stopped what they were doing and stared at the two of them. Franz waved his pistol at them and screamed, "Don't stop! Burn! Burn! Go away, Klára, I'm busy here. I'll never sign your ridiculous papers! You're mad to be here!"

"Franz, it's finished. There is no more for you to do. This insanity is over! Go back to Germany while you can. Forget about me and András."

"András? You know I will never let go of either of you!"

"Please, Franz...!"

"I have no time for you, Klára. Go away. You are not part of this," Franz turned his back to her and walked from the desk to the fireplace in a robotic fashion, throwing a stack of papers into the fire and screaming orders to the others.

Suddenly loud reverberations rattled the palace; bombs dropped very nearby. If not for the heavy draperies, shattered glass would have filled the room. The chandelier loosened from the ceiling and swayed precariously over their heads. Klára screamed his name once more just as another explosion shook the room causing the fireplace wall to crumble, sending flames into the room. Klára saw the flames envelop Franz where he stood. Fire erupted all around her just as a strong hand grabbed her shoulder and turned her from the terrible sight. A sheltering arm guided her quickly from the flames.

German soldiers ran in every direction. The palace walls and ceiling were coming apart. The deafening noise and fire everywhere forced Klára and her protector to move quickly. He opened another door along the hallway. They entered the room and Klára looked up into Rudolf's beautiful eyes. With little time for words, he simply said, "I know a way."

Behind a great tapestry he ran his hand along the paneling until there was a click and the panel swung inward. A light flickered from the labyrinth below. They followed the winding stair as it spiraled downward. "Remember?" he asked.

"Of course," she answered and squeezed his hand as he led her down the stairs into the labyrinth, "How did you get here, Dolf? How did you know that I had come here?"

"Vadas's men followed you all the way from the villa through Székesfehérvár to Castle Hill and from there to the palace. When I got back to the cottage and learned from Silva that you had gone, Tamás, Pál and I left immediately! We have been close behind you all the way. We would have stopped you, if we'd caught up with you. There was no need to guess where you were going! What am I going to do with you, Klára? Your promises to keep out of trouble mean nothing!"

"I'm sorry, Dolf, but I had to ask Franz to sign these papers," she still clutched them in her hand, "but he wouldn't and now he never will." She sobbed as they walked through the tunnels of the labyrinth.

Scores of people filled the passages—refugees from the city of Buda trying to avoid the crumbling buildings; nurses, doctors and patients huddled together listening for the next bomb to drop; German soldiers resting from battle waiting to go out again into the night's mêlée.

Rudolf and Klára walked well beyond the outer walls of the palace, past the strings of lights. Rudolf turned on a flashlight as they continued into the dark tunnel.

"You need not worry ever again about that, Klára. Franz won't ever bother you again." Rudolf spoke with confidence as they both envisioned the terrifying image of Franz engulfed in flames. "Tamás, Pál and Vadas's men are waiting for us. Let's hope they are still in one piece."

Even though they were deep underground, the shock of explosions rumbled through the labyrinth. For more than a mile the pair made their way through the passageways where many citizens of Budapest had taken up residence from the moment they heard the Russians were coming.

Eventually Rudolf and Klára came to the right wrought-iron staircase, its railings decorated with red devil statues. The stair led up into the wine cellar of *Vörös Ördög*, the Red Devil restaurant. Rudolf pushed open the black iron door into the damaged and deserted cellar. They made their way upstairs through broken and scattered furnishings to the entrance where the door hung by only one great medieval hinge. Rudolf pushed it away and they stepped out into the night.

Rubble and debris filled the cobblestone street. Several buildings had been reduced to ruin; some were on fire. Klára looked back toward the palace and saw the whole sky ablaze. As they hurried toward Uri Street, soldiers rushed by completely uninterested in them. Klára and Rudolf simply joined the throng pushing toward the streets leading down from Castle Hill.

As Klára and Rudolf reached the intersection, headlights flashed and the ignition sounded. Tamás waved to them. The couple got into the car and Pál pulled out into the street, honking to part the pedestrians. From Castle Hill the car passed Déli Station Square where crowds of people pushed toward the station, but with the rails destroyed, there would be no way for anyone to leave from there.

Pál followed as many back roads as he could until they reached Székesfehérvár. The hour was very late, well past curfew, although soldiers had no possibility of enforcing curfew on the thousands who poured out of Budapest. Once inside the city of Székesfehérvár, soldiers stopped their car telling Pál he could not drive in the city at night and to park immediately.

The four of them, Rudolf, Tamás, Pál and Klára decided to walk to the Magyar Király Hotel where they could sit in the restaurant until morning. The hotel was swarming with Nazi soldiers who were not so occupied with the urgency of the moment that they did not notice the small group sitting just beyond the lobby. Many times through the night soldiers asked to see their papers and about the situation in Budapest. *"Is it going well for the Germans?"* Or, *"Is it hopeless for us?"* The foursome noticed that the younger Germans expressed a more pessimistic outlook about the turn of the war.

Determined to stay awake and ready to leave the moment of daybreak, the four drank coffee all night. When the sun appeared they purchased some bread and cheese and left the hotel. Back in the car, Pál sped toward the villa.

When András saw Tamás's car coming on the road below, he shouted, "They're back!" and took off running down the hill. Relief spread over the cottage inhabitants. By the time Tamás, Pál, Rudolf and Klára made their way up the hill to the cottage Silva had soup ready for them. Everyone gathered around to hear their story. Klára told them what had happened at the palace and that Franz was killed in the fire. She reached out her hand to András and held his hand tightly in hers.

Klára looked into the eyes of her newly twelve-year-old son, "I'm sorry, András."

András only shrugged his shoulders, he had nothing to say. He kept his thoughts to himself...*I've never known my father, not in the slightest. I've not seen him since I was five or six. I do know he's a Nazi and that's nothing to be proud of. I'm glad I never knew him.* Even so, it did seem strange to have such a lack of feeling...*he was my father, but he never paid any attention to me. I have few memories of the man.*

Rudolf and Tamás, both large, imposing men sat at the table near young András. They were the men he knew; they had always been there for him and he knew they loved him. They were the men who had shaped his very being, taught him the important things of life. András held his mother's hand and offered consoling words to her, "It's all right, Mother. I'm all right."

Budapest

On the twentieth of January representatives of the Béla Miklós provisional government signed an armistice with the Soviets, formally ending Hungary's part in the Germans' war against the Soviets and the Allies. Signing the armistice, however, did not end the siege or misery for the people of Budapest. Availability of food and medical supplies within the city had come to a complete stop with the destruction of the airport and blockades of all major roads. Citizens and soldiers alike—German, Hungarian, and Soviet—were all starving.

February

After one hundred and two days under siege, on February thirteenth, Budapest fell to the Red Army. By the time the Germans surrendered their hold on Castle Hill, there was little left of the great palace that had once stood majestically on the crag above the Danube.

The last week of February, Rudolf drove Pál and Tamás in his Bugatti to Budapest. They left their car below Castle Hill and walked up the hill to Holy Trinity Square then across to the severely damaged Mátyás Church. The debris of Buda's great architectural structures lay all around the three men. As they stood at the edge of the hill near the ruin of Fishermen's Bastion, looking out across the Danube toward Pest, they were devastated by what they saw.

Every bridge that spanned the Danube had been destroyed, blown up by the Germans as their tanks and troops fled from Pest to Castle Hill. The great piers of the Chain Bridge, rising from the frozen river, were all that remained of the handsome landmark. The grand romantic-style parliament building was a pile of smoldering rubble. As far as they could see there was nothing but ruin. Hundreds of buildings destroyed, the airports and rail lines ruined, and thousands of people killed or injured. The scene of devastation that stretched out before them broke their hearts. Budapest once a most vibrant and beautiful city, now lay gray in ash and smoke, broken and depressed.

Rudolf was determined to cross the Danube, to go into Pest. The three men made their way down the hill from the bastion following what was left of the stone staircase. They walked through the rubble-filled streets to the bank of the Danube to a spot just under the former Chain Bridge. With a guide the three men crossed the frozen Danube following ropes that had been strung between the piers of the bridge. Great mounds of jagged ice made the way very treacherous.

They climbed up the Pest-side bank to the nearest square and stood in awe, surveying the damaged buildings, abandoned artillery, wrecked trucks and cars, evidence of the horrific battle that had destroyed their beloved city. Street-by-street fighting had taken place only days before their arrival. Litter and debris still lay in burning heaps. No motorized traffic at all, only people aimlessly wandering, searching for food or for those lost to them.

Their main objective was to visit the Swedish Legation. To get there they walked past Szent István Bazilika which miraculously had suffered little damage and continued on to Hercegprimás Street where many buildings, including the old Löwy lace shop were burned-out shells. Tamás shook his head when he viewed Leopold's von Esté Fine Wine Company building; it had sustained heavy damage to its upper floors, but remained standing. The once-colossal, crouching Atlas figures that held up the building's cornice lay strewn in broken chunks across the sidewalk.

Tamás found the company's brass plaque lying in the rubble and picked it up. He closed his eyes for a moment, remembering times past when Leopold insisted that the company always present a pristine appearance and sometimes polished the brass plaque himself. Tamás walked away from the building with tears in his eyes.

They finally arrived at the Swedish Legation on Vadasz Street. Rudolf was anxious to talk with Per Anger. Anger was elated to see them. He stopped packing boxes and immediately began to bring Rudolf up to date on legation news.

"The work has been relentless! Wallenberg worked tirelessly from the Buda office. He learned just after the New Year that since Eichmann could no longer deport the Jews from the central ghetto, he planned to blow it up. Wallenberg recognized that the only person who could stop the massacre was General Schmidthuber, in command of all German troops. So Wallenberg sent a message to Schmidthuber warning him that he would be held solely responsible for the massacre, that he would be named a war criminal and hanged in shame for war crimes after the war. As in the past, Wallenberg's threat was taken seriously and the ghetto was saved. Probably more than one hundred thousand Jews saved!"

But then Anger shook his head, "I'm exhausted and I'm beside myself with worry about Wallenberg. We were so optimistic when Miklós declared the Nazis' disintegration, but then Wallenberg disappeared several days ago and we've heard nothing from him, not a word. He went to speak with the Soviets about the post-war circumstances for Jews and no one has seen him since Wednesday, the day he left."

"I'll be returning to Sweden as soon as possible," Anger declared. "There's so much post-war work to do throughout Europe. We'll keep our eye on Budapest from afar. What are your plans, Rudolf?"

"We've come into Budapest to observe the situation. I think already we have seen enough to make the right decision. As soon as the Allies have ended this debacle we'll likely leave Hungary for a while."

Rudolf and Anger embraced as old friends and wished each other well. As Tamás and Pál were leaving the legation, they ran into Theodore Rubin. Rubin told them he was staying in Budapest.

"I'm eager to begin working with the Soviets. I believe the Communist point of view will benefit the Jews of Hungary," Rubin stated.

Tamás and Pál were skeptical, but Rubin was so optimistic, they hesitated to express their true opinions to him.

Rudolf arranged to borrow a Red Cross truck and drove to Andrássy Avenue. There was very little obvious damage on Andrássy; the Opera House appeared unscathed. The Perlmutter house, once the Arrow Cross headquarters, now seemed to be taken over by the Soviets. Finally Pál parked the truck in the von Esté driveway. They knocked, but there was no answer. Finally, they went round to the kitchen where they found Leona sitting at the table.

Overjoyed to see them, she related her story of surviving the siege. She and Auguste had stayed in the cellar for almost one hundred days, only coming out a few times to see if the house was still standing. Tamás thanked her for taking such good care of the property. He told her they were not going to return for a while, but that she and Auguste could stay, if they wished.

"I do have some bad news for you, Sir," Leona said to Rudolf. "When we heard of the armistice, Auguste and I came out of the cellar. The sunshine felt so good, even though there were still piles of snow and it was very cold. We went right away to your home, Count, to look after Zela. We knew she'd been all alone for so long."

"We asked her to stay with us, but she was very stubborn, you know. Anyway, we found her in the cellar, all wrapped up in a comforter lying in a little bed. She had died in her sleep. Auguste and I buried her in your garden, Count, near the arbor where the ground was not frozen."

Tamás stood at the kitchen door looking out into Silva's garden. The dried, dead herb bushes were covered in snow. A vision of the garden came to him when the house was brand new and Elizabeth laid out the first shrubs and trees. He remembered the day he brought Silva to the house and later when she made the kitchen garden her own. He recalled strolling in the garden with Leopold. Tamás spoke a whispered *good-bye* and turned from the window. He doubted in his heart that he would ever stand in the von Esté house again.

Pál drove Rudolf and Tamás back to the site of the former Chain Bridge. As the sun was setting behind Castle Hill they left the truck, climbed down the bank and crossed the frozen river. In darkness they made their way back to the Bugatti and spent an uncomfortable night trying to sleep in the car until early morning light when they set off for Székesfehérvár. German tanks still controlled the highway; the Germans were gearing up to hold their ground. Soldiers motioned to Rudolf several times to pull over for a check of their papers, but since Rudolf had attached special seals and signatures to their papers, the soldiers waved them on, believing they had important clearances from higher ups. The three men were relieved to arrive back at the villa and trek their way up into the forest.

That evening they sat at the big table relating to everyone what they had seen in Budapest. The children were most amazed to hear they had walked across the frozen Danube! But the rest shuddered at the thought of all the beautiful bridges spanning the Danube purposefully destroyed. And the palace and parliament gone, it was unthinkable.

Éva was glad to hear the ghetto had been saved along with her home as were Elizabeth, Klára and Silva who cried to hear that the von Esté house and Leona remained intact. The report, however, left an unclear vision of the future for each of them. *Should they return? Where should they go? Where will they be in the future? Are they safe now?*

Ϻarcʰ

In early March each family at the cottages began to hear reverberations of loud artillery fire coming from south of the lake and then from the north. They were anxious to hear what was happening from Vadas's men.

When Fábián arrived at last, he and his men had news, "The Germans have launched a new offensive to retake Budapest and the oil fields at Nagykanizsa. There are several tank units on the offensive to the north and to the south of Lake Balaton. We learned from a reliable source that this action is the fantasy of Hitler. He calls it *Fürhlingserwachen*, Spring Awakening; it's meant to be a counter-offensive against the Red Army to repossess Budapest and drive out the Soviets."

"We also heard that Hitler's Panzer commanders realized long before Hitler that this plan is completely unattainable, impractical!"

"Although they'll try, the Germans know fate is against them. The Soviets have already countered them," one of Vadas's men assured his listeners. "Fábián predicts that the German tanks will be stuck in the mud long before they can cause any trouble. The Germans look at the offensive as a last, valiant effort, but it will get them nowhere."

"The Germans and Soviets are so occupied with each other, they're not threatening to the rest of us," another of Vadas's men added, "at least not for the moment."

—⁂—

By the end of March the weather was still chilly, but this particular day was beautiful, spring-like. Only traces of snow remained while buttercups and wild violets bloomed in the forest and meadow. Klára stood leaning against the open cottage door in a shaft of bright sunlight; Dolf sat outside on a wooden bench across from her. She had on a shirtwaist dress and sweater; she looked fresh and young, still slender and lovely. He stood up and walked toward her; he took her in his arms and kissed her in front of whoever was there to see. It had been months since he had had the chance to kiss her in that way. "Marry me, Klára."

"I will."

Surprised, but happy to see the couple together at last, everyone was overjoyed. Rudolf and Klára decided to marry the next day, so wedding planning began immediately. Ana redesigned one of Klára's old summer dresses while Silva planned a wedding feast of rabbit stew and an extravagant torta.

Early in the morning of the next day, Rózsa, Vera and Sárika collected flowers to make garlands for decorations and a ringlet for Klára's hair and more for her bouquet. Rudolf and Abram moved the big table outside near the well while Tamás and Pál drove to Balatonfüred for the priest.

Klára and Elizabeth stood side by side in their cottage before the one small mirror available. Klára stood in the dress Ana had designed. It was a fine, softly woven batiste in a pale cream printed with green and yellow flowers. Ana added a lace flounce around the deep V-neckline and a wide cream sash that accentuated Klára's narrow waist; she shortened the sleeves and lengthened the skirt as long as possible.

"Thank you, Ana, I like it very much," Klára said as she stared at her reflection in the mirror, "but there's nothing I can do with this hair of mine."

She sounded slightly dejected as she flipped one side of her hair, a very plain style reflected back at her. A straight bang cut just above her dark eyebrows and straight on the sides, almost to her shoulders, "It's what it is."

"You look lovely, Klára," Elizabeth reassured her. "The dress is perfect and this will set it off just right," she said as she fastened the emerald necklace around Klára's long, slender neck. "Rudolf will be very pleased," her mother promised as she placed the ringlet of flowers on Klára's dark hair.

"Beautiful," she pronounced and kissed Klára on both cheeks.

Elizabeth could see the happiness in her daughter's eyes. *I've caused so much sorrow in my daughter's life.* Now, at last, Elizabeth felt the guilt lifting from her heart. *It's time for this good thing to happen for Klára and Rudolf at last.*

Just before noon all was ready. Fábián Vadas and three of his men arrived on horseback. Rózsa and the girls had decorated the trees and the well with garlands of spring flowers and strewn petals to make a pathway for Klára to walk along toward the altar—a small table in front of the well. Rudolf and András moved with the priest to the altar. Elizabeth turned the crystal handle of Stefan's music box and Abram played Sándor's violin. Vera and Sárika walked forward throwing more petals; Rósza walked behind them and stood on the other side of the priest.

Finally, Tamás escorted Klára toward the altar. Rudolf was overwhelmed by her beauty, tall and slender with flowers in her hair, her lovely dress, a bouquet of spring flowers in her hands, and the sweetest expression in her eyes and on her lips. Tamás wept with profound joy as he placed her hand in Rudolf's hand. Tamás moved to Silva's side and held her hands in his; she, too, shed tears of joy. In fact, everyone was weeping, but smiling, too, at the joyful sight. So many years, so many loved ones gone from their side, such a difficult time and, yet, here a glorious event filled with love and hope.

After the priest performed all the rites of marriage and everyone participated in communion, he pronounced Rudolf and Klára man and wife. András embraced them both instantly; he made it very clear that they were a family and that he fully accepted Rudolf as his father.

Silva called everyone to the table and the priest blessed the food and all who were present.

"The wedding supper is a humble one, only a root vegetable soup with stewed rabbit," Silva apologized, but no one was disappointed. It was delicious, and when Silva presented a torta made with honey and chesnuts, everyone gave a cheer and clapped their hands.

That night after songs and dancing, Rudolf and Klára disappeared from the festivities. For a while no one noticed their absence, when it was noticed, only smiles appeared, no one was worried about where they had gone.

The two had decided to take a risk and go to the villa. They went into the house through the kitchen door. The house was dark, cold and very quiet. They went up to Klára's old bedroom. Rudolf lit one candle and she gathered extra pillows and comforters to make a warm, cloud-like bed for the two of them. Rudolf poured glasses of wine and they both climbed into the warmth of the comforters.

"I have a toast," he said as his glass touched hers, "to us, who have always been, and will always be," he said. "I love you, Klára, forever."

Klára took a sip of wine, "And to you, my dearest Dolfie, my husband," and then she began to sob, "I was so afraid we would never be together, but you always knew we would be. I love you, Dolf."

"Don't cry any more, Klára, let the past go. We are together now."

They snuggled together under the downy comforter. Rudolf wiped away her tears and kissed her eyes and cheeks until she could think of nothing else but him and the moment.

—⁓—

Each cottage family began to think of what they should do, where they should go when the war would finally end. Although they had grown very close—as if a single family, the children said—they knew the time would come for them to part.

Rudolf spent much of his time preparing new papers for everyone. He meticulously created realistic documents with decorative borders, special seals and signatures. The Soviets, it turned out, were just as impressed with ornate documents as the Germans had been. He created letters and official Austrian papers declaring diplomatic offices for himself and Tamás. Their Austrian roots were made clear in birth and marriage certificates.

One afternoon, only a little more than a week after Rudolf and Klára's marriage, Rudolf came out of the big cottage into the sunshine. He stretched and squinted in the bright light; he made eye contact with Klára, they shared a smile and then Rudolf called to András, "Will you go for a walk with me, András?"

As they walked into the forest Rudolf spoke in a serious tone, "Your mother and I have a proposition for you. It requires your permission. It is entirely your decision to make."

András looked up at the tall man as they walked along the trail. Rudolf twirled his cane as they made their way into the woods.

"I'm creating new documents for all of us in preparation for the future, whatever that might be. Perhaps we will stay here in Hungary, perhaps we'll leave. Whatever we decide we must have identification that gives us protection. Your mother and I believe, in these circumstances, we must emphasize our Austrian heritage."

Rudolf stopped walking and turned to András, "We propose to give you Austrian birth documentation and to give you my von Házy name as our son, your mother's and mine, with your permission."

András understood the depth of meaning in taking on a new identity. He stared at Rudolf for a moment, unable to speak. He took a deep breath and smiled as he spoke, "You've offered a great honor to me...to be your son and have the von Házy name as my own...I accept gladly."

"Once we are in a safe place, if you wish, you can undo all that we will do and resume your birth name."

"No, Dolf, I will never want to go back. I will be proud to have you as my father from this day and forever."

The two embraced each other, both wiping tears from their eyes. Then broad smiles spread across their faces. Rudolf threw his arm over András's shoulders, "It is I who am so proud of you, András. From this day forward you are my son. I could not be happier. Thank you, from my heart."

Klára sat at the big oak table, nervously watching the pathway leading out of the forest. She was anxious to know how her son would answer Dolf's question. When she saw the two of them coming out of the woods, Dolf's arm over András's shoulders and both with glowing smiles, she rose from the table, rushed toward them and embraced them both.

That evening when everyone was gathered round the table, András announced to all of them, "From this day on I am András von Házy, son of Count Rudolf von Házy."

Cheers, clapping and kisses expressed the joy all around.

Tamás stood with a glass of wine in hand, "A toast... *Egészségére*... to the von Házy family... Rudolf, Klára and András! May they live long in happiness together!"

Early April

As Vadas predicted the German Panzer tanks did become bogged down in the wet marshy lands south of Lake Balaton and those German troops north of the lake were in no better situation. By early April the Red Army had soundly defeated the German counter-offensive on all fronts and on the fourth of April all Soviet operations in Hungary against the Germans ended in victory. The last of the German troops began to leave Hungary as quickly as possible as the Soviets marched in to take complete control of the country. The Soviets moved on to Vienna and on the thirteenth of April, liberated the city from the grasp of the Reich.

—⁂—

One April morning as the families went about their daily chores, biding time until the future became more clear to all of them, András and Vera came running from the edge of the hill shouting, "Someone has come to the villa!"

Everyone walked to their only vantage point and looked down at the house, asking questions. *Were they soldiers? Was it a truck or an automobile? How many?* Then they saw two figures come round the house from its front and begin to climb the hill, a man and a woman.

Abram squinted his eyes against the sun, "It's Zsuzsanna and Armin!" and then bolted down the hill. He met them halfway down the hillside and then walked back up the hill with Zsuzsanna Weisz and Armin Stein. They were greeted warmly with many questions about Budapest... *The war and the condition of the city?... The Soviets?... What was happening now?*

"Budapest is calm amid the destruction, at least at the moment," answered

Zsuzsanna. "People seem to be wandering about in a daze, searching for what they have lost; not knowing where to look or where to go."

"The Soviets are in charge. There's no way at this point to know what kind of rule they will exert on the people. Zsuzsanna and I suspect it won't be good, so we decided to leave while we can. We're on our way to Palestine, Abram," said Armin, "and we want you to go with us. We've got immigration papers and plans to meet with an underground movement that will help us get all the way to Palestine."

Abram studied his old friends; he wanted to go with them. His eyes fixed upon Zsuzsanna, he had long admired her courage and intelligence. Abram would willingly follow her anywhere.

"I would go with you, Zsuzsanna, but for my mother," and he turned toward Éva who sat at the big oak table listening to their discussion. "I must know that she is safe and taken care of, if I'm gone from here."

"Mrs. Klein, you must come with us, too," insisted Zsuzsanna. "We can accommodate your immigration as well as Abram's."

"Yes, Mother, you should go with Abram," agreed Rózsa. "You could see Eszter again and your grandchildren."

"But what about you and Pál and your children? What are you going to do?" Éva questioned.

"We have no choice. We must go back to Eger," answered Rózsa. "I couldn't bear the thought of József coming home to find no one there. We must be there when he comes home." Rózsa twisted her apron and looked toward Pál, "I know that Pál is hesitant to go back. He's worried about returning to a hostile environment, a place where we might be harassed, but I can't let that stop us. My concern is for József. After he returns home, then we, too, will leave Hungary for Palestine."

Zsuzsanna and Armin glanced at each other. They shared a different opinion from Rózsa's view of future possibilities... *if he comes home... if there is still a way into Palestine... if the Soviets allow you to leave...* but neither voiced their thoughts aloud.

Over the past several years Zsuzsanna and Armin had been working with Aliyah to arrange clandestine immigration for Jews from Hungary. Members of Aliyah were very aware of the dangers and intrigues involved in their illegal immigration activities. Not only the dangers involved in leaving Hungary, but also those perils that awaited the overland crossing through several countries and then by sea to the promised land of Palestine. The difficulties were monumental, but Zsuzsanna and Armin were convinced that now was the time to go, before more obstacles were put in place by new rising post-war governments.

The next morning as everyone sat around the big oak table, Éva stood up at her place and announced, "I have decided to go with Abram and his friends to Palestine. I never in my wildest dreams thought that I would ever do such a thing. *Palestine!* My Jakov would not believe that I have made such a decision. But I have made this decision only because Rózsa and Pál have promised that they, too, will leave Hungary when József can come to Palestine with them."

"Thank you to our dear, dear friends... Elizabeth... Rudolf... Tamás, Silva, Ana... Klára and András. You have all risked everything to save me and my family from the horrors that surrounded us." Éva wiped tears from her eyes, "We will be grateful to you forever, our dear, dear friends. We will never forget any of you. I look to the day when we will meet again."

That afternoon Éva and Abram Klein left their family and friends and began their journey with Zsuzsanna and Armin, taking with them Sándor's violin and all they owned in two suitcases.

The cottage families left behind felt a sense of melancholy. They suffered the loss of Éva and Abram profoundly. Their hilltop seemed quieter, more spacious, and less secure. They felt restless, anxious to make their own decisions about where they would go and when.

"What should we do, Dolf?" Klára looked worried, but managed a smile for him. "Should we move into the villa or perhaps go home to Budapest? What do you think we ought to do?"

"It would be lovely to go back, Klára, to the life we had." Rudolf put his arms around her. "Even if we had to rebuild Budapest into the city it was, the city we loved, we could do that," he kissed her, "but neither Tamás nor I believe we should stay in Hungary. At least not now, not for a while."

"Are you certain we should leave? Could we go back to Budapest to see our Andrássy house just one last time?"

"I don't think we should take the risk. Remember, Klára, the Soviets are Bolsheviks at heart. What they did to the Romanovs, I fear they will do to all aristocrats."

"Where should we go... Switzerland?"

"That would be my choice," answered Rudolf, "Fábián has suggested a route and his men will escort us when the war is over. When it's safe for us to travel."

Late April

A crack in the curtains allowed a shaft of sparkling sunlight to stream from the window and fall across Klára's closed eyes. It was early morning, but Klára stretched happily under the down comforter and snuggled closer to Rudolf. She loved these moments alone with Rudolf in the loft of the shepherd's cottage. Knowing that every sound could be easily heard within the cottage, Klára and Rudolf had mastered love-making with the quiet art of whispers and slow movements, but this morning they listened for Elizabeth and András to leave the cottage for breakfast. When everyone else had left, Klára and Rudolf took great pleasure in their morning alone together.

András sat at the table in the Tóth cottage stirring his steaming farina and asked Silva, "Can you make *meggyleves*, sour cherry soup, for us, Silva? We haven't had *meggyleves* for months."

"Oh, I'm sorry, András, but I have no dried cherries left. We haven't had any cherries for a month or so," she ruffled his hair. "We've run out of all that I brought from the villa. I could make honeycakes."

"That's all we ever have...honeycakes."

"And lucky to have them, András," interjected Tamás. "These are hard and dangerous times."

Looking rather dejected, András finished his cereal and then he and Vera and Hóvi went outside together. They walked off toward the edge of the forest and stood in the shadow of the trees looking down at the villa.

"I wonder if there are any dried apples or cherries down there," pondered András as he viewed the villa below. "Somewhere in the pantry or cellar? Maybe Silva missed a sack? I think I'll go down and have a look."

"No, András, we're not supposed to go down there. It's too dangerous." Vera took hold of his sleeve, "There are still Germans and now Russians, too, who would kill us."

"You don't have to go with me. You stay here. Hóvi stay with Vera! I'm not afraid."

And he was gone, down the hill. Vera watched him dart across the hillside, keeping to the shadows. She looked beyond the hillside to the road. She could see to the east and to the west; there was not a single car in any direction, just an old horse-drawn cart with a single driver, the only sign of movement. Vera looked back to see András, but he was completely out of view. She sat down on a big rock and waited for him to return, hopefully with bags of dried fruit and she thought about Silva baking something delicious.

When Klára walked out of her cottage into the warm April sun it was almost noon. Vera saw her go into Silva's cottage. András had been gone for a long time and Vera was worried about him. She wished he would hurry back, but still he was nowhere in sight.

A few moments later Klára came out of Silva's cottage and called, "András, Silva needs some wood for the oven. András."

Vera heard Klára's call; she bit her lip knowing that András was going to be in big trouble if he didn't return soon. She heard Klára call again and Vera stood up to see if she could see András running up the hill, but again he was nowhere in sight. Then she did notice a car coming from the east along the road and she held her breath. The car turned into the driveway leading to the villa and disappeared as it pulled up to the front of the house. Vera jumped up from the rock and ran toward Klára.

"What's wrong, Vera?" Klára asked as she looked into Vera's ashen face. "Has something happened to András?"

All the women came out of the cottage, "What is it, Vera?" implored Rózsa.

"András went down to the villa to find dried fruit," she bit her lip again. "He hasn't come back yet and now there's a car that just arrived."

Klára gasped, her eyes widened, she ran to the forest edge and then ran down the hill before anyone could stop her. Tamás started to go after her, but it was too difficult for him. He commanded, "Vera, go find the men...hurry!"

Without caution Klára made her way as quickly as she could to the back of the house. Just as she got to the kitchen garden door, she could hear voices from inside, arguing. One voice she recognized as András. Her heart beat in her throat as she entered the house, realizing she had no protection with her, nothing to defend András or herself. Klára walked with as much strength as she could muster into the dining room where András stood next to the table with a German dressed in an S.S. officer's uniform.

"András, come here," she demanded.

As András ran to her, the man turned. Klára felt faint, not with fear, but with astonishment. Even though the man was terribly disfigured, there was no doubt *who* it was.

"Klára," he said.

"Franz! You're alive!" She held András close.

"The boy has grown." Franz leaned against the table and laughed. "He didn't recognize me."

Franz flung his arm in the air as a gesture of futility; the arm was obviously of little use to him.

"I...I thought you were dead...the fire...what happened?" Klára spoke as if in a trance.

"Well, you can see I did burn alive, but something kept me living." He spoke with distain in his voice, "Maybe it was to see you again."

Bandages on his face and neck concealed some of the injuries, but the exposed parts of Franz's face had a bright-red scalded appearance with terrible folds of scarred flesh. Even Klára had feelings of compassion for the once beautiful face she had known.

"Don't pity me, Klára." He walked toward her. "I'm here for you and the boy. We're leaving Hungary today."

Franz approached Klára and grabbed András by the arm, "Come with me, boy."

"No, Franz, he isn't going anywhere with you; neither am I."

"Out! To the car...now!" Franz pushed András toward the hallway and then grabbed Klára, shoving her after András, causing her to fall. Franz kicked her with his boot, "Get up! There's not much time!" By now Franz had pulled a revolver from his coat, "Walk, boy, to the car or I'll shoot your mother here and now."

András walked backwards from the dining room while helping Klára to her feet. The two of them clung to each other as they walked to the front door.

"Franz, this is insane. You can't make us go with you. This is our home."

"Quiet! Out the door!"

Franz had kicked in the door when he arrived, so it hung by broken hinges. András had to push hard to open it further to allow their passage through to the veranda. The three walked toward Franz's car while Franz continued to gesture after Klára and András, waving the gun in the air.

The three were so engrossed in each other they did not notice the five Soviets running toward them up the driveway until the soldiers fired their guns. András pushed Klára down and both of them slid under Franz's car. Instantly Franz fell to the gravel, his dead eyes staring at them, blood streaming from his limp body. Klára screamed just as the Soviets grabbed at her arms and pulled her from beneath the car. They yanked the struggling András away from Klára as he tried to protect her.

"Leave him…he's only a boy," Klára begged.

Two Soviets held each of them by their arms while the fifth leered at Klára and made obscene gestures. The Soviets laughed loudly. Klára was terrified for her precious son, even more than for herself.

Suddenly more shots rang out. The Russians let go of Klára and András who immediately fell to their knees and covered their heads. András pulled his mother toward the car once again as they heard loud shouts and gunfire.

Completely terrifying and then eerily quiet…Klára and András could see bodies lying all around them in the gravel. Neither Klára nor András could move or take a deep breath; they clung to each other crouched by the car, waiting.

Fábián Vadas and several of his men, along with Rudolf and Pál—and Hóvi barking at their heels—ran from the corner of the house onto the gravel drive. Rudolf ran to Klára's side to help her and András to their feet. Klára collapsed into Rudolf's arms. András embraced his mother and Rudolf while Pál stood beside them.

When they had composed themselves, the men began to consider the carnage that lay around them. Rudolf was surprised to see Franz among the dead. Vadas's men put all of the bodies into Franz's car. They treated Franz with slightly more deference by placing him in the front seat while the Russians were piled in the back. Fábián Vadas drove the car from the driveway around the house and out beyond the vineyards toward the old pastures. Klára went back into the villa alone.

Rudolf, Pál, and András used branches to rake away the blood and tire tracks from the gravel and then they tried to reposition the front door as best they could. Klára walked back through the dining room toward the kitchen where she met Rudolf and András at the garden door. Klára held Rudolf's hand without speaking as they walked back up the hill toward the meadow.

Klára continued on to the cottage while the men and András walked toward the pond. Vadas's men dug a mass grave for the Russians and a separate single grave for Franz. Fábián drove Franz's car to the edge of the pond where all the men pushed it into the water and watched until it had fully submerged.

When they had finished their gruesome chore, the men, including András, who was one of them now, walked up to the cottages, each one lost in his own thoughts. Hóvi trotted proudly by his young master. Fábián and his men waved good-bye and disappeared into the forest.

—᠁—

Silva had a hearty *gulyásleves* for supper that evening. The von Estés, the von Házys, and the Szabós sat outside around the big wooden table as a family. They held hands when they said grace. Tamás thanked God for saving them that day. Rózsa asked a special blessing for József wherever he might be and she remembered her beloved mother and father and her brothers and sister— Eszter and Abram and Samuel, Sándor and Ferenc. They all sat in silence, still holding hands. Many around the table thought of Leopold and Stefan and how they were still missed after all these years. Then András broke the silence, praying that God would have mercy on Franz's soul.

The group around the table ate with a kind of reverence for the blessings of their lives. The day had been a difficult day, a horrible day, with death, but with life, too. They had experienced the dichotomy of war that afternoon in their little piece of Hungary. The horror of violent, bloody death and the elation of surviving, escaping the imminent grip of death, all in the same moment.

After their fill of stew, Klára brought out a surprise, Silva's *csokoládé torta*. Silva followed behind with a large bowl in her hands.

"I saved a piece of dark chocolate all this time to celebrate the end of the war," smiled Silva happily, "and here we have *meggyleves*, too, special for András!"

András was truly surprised, "I found the cherries in the pantry, but I forgot all about them."

In some ways having something so special as *meggyleves* and chocolate torta would seem frivolous after such a horrific day, but this group of people, each one of them, felt a sense of survival in the midst of terrible times. The cake and cherry soup tasted better than they remembered. They knew that the war was drawing to a close and that they had managed to live, to survive. An accomplishment they recognized and they embraced it with a kind of blessed joy.

EPILOGUE

—⟋⟍—

1945

On the fourth of April all German offensive operations in Hungary came to an end. The Red Army had soundly defeated the Germans and driven them out of Hungary. The Soviets moved into Austria and on the thirteenth of April, liberated Vienna from the grasp of the Reich. On the seventh of May the Germans signed an unconditional surrender of all forces, bringing the war to an end.

On the twentieth of May, Pál and Rózsa announced to everyone living in the shepherd cottages, "The time has come for us to leave Lake Balaton, to go home to Eger."

Klára and Rudolf voiced protests immediately, noting every danger, but Rózsa insisted, "We must go back to Eger, Klára. We've got to be there when József comes home. He has no idea where we are. He could never find us, if we don't return home."

Only a few days later, as the Szabó family prepared to leave, Rózsa embraced Klára, "My dearest friend, how can we ever thank you enough for all you and your family have done for my family? You have saved our lives. We will be forever grateful."

Pál and Rózsa, along with Vera and Sárika, left the hilltop. They turned back for one last look at their dear friends... *we promise to write... until we meet again... stay safe*! And then they were gone in Pal's old truck, escorted by some of Vadas's men, down the roadway toward the east.

—⟋⟍—

Those left behind, Klára and Rudolf, Elizabeth and András, Tamás, Silva and Ana, sat outside around the big oak table silently considering their own thoughts and memories of the months spent on their hilltop. The Esté family felt great admiration and love for the Szabó family, who had become far more than just friends. András missed his playmates intensely. The Szabó's parting filled everyone with profound sadness and created a concern about their own futures. Uncertainty about when and where they should go and what they would find when they finally chose added to the anxiety they felt.

Once again Klára and her mother voiced their desires to return to their Andrássy home, but Rudolf, fully supported by Tamás, denied any possibility of going that direction. He and Tamás were convinced they must go west, out of Hungary and argued, "We cannot presume the Soviets... those Bolsheviks... to be trustworthy occupiers of Hungary."

Rudolf and Tamás considered returning to Eisenstadt, but by late July occupied Austria had been divided into quarters among the Soviets, the French, the British and the Americans. For those living on the hilltop, Eisenstadt was no longer a possible destination because it, unfortunately, ended up in the Soviet-controlled quarter of Austria.

Clearly, their only choice was Rorschach, Switzerland. Within a few days they were packed and ready to go. Rudolf drove his Bugatti with Klára, András and Hóvi away from their beloved villa toward the Hungarian border while Tamás and Silva with Elizabeth and Ana followed closely behind in the Mercedes coupe. The family's most valued treasures, among them Stefan's music box and Leopold's albums and memorabilia box, crammed both cars.

Because Sopron had suffered severe bombing and bordered the Soviet sector, Rudolf and Tamás avoided the shorter route to Austria, instead choosing a longer, safer route leading them to the border of the British sector of Austria. The roads, so crowded with refugees and fleeing soldiers, made their trip to reach the border much longer than they had expected. Luckily, Rudolf's elaborate, *official* Swedish diplomatic documents, allowed their little group to enter Austria at Bad Radkersburg across the Mura River without any trouble.

Once safely in the British sector the family could breathe much easier. Within a day they had traveled to the village of Maria Wörth on the southern shore of the Wörthersee; a place so like Lake Balaton it almost seemed they had found home again. They lingered there until late summer, waiting for the best time to cross the high mountains into Switzerland where at last they took residence in Rorschach in a grand villa near the home of Elizabeth's parents.

—〰—

1992

A long, black limousine crossed the border from Austria into Hungary near the town of Sopron and wound its way through the Lövér Hills, through neglected vineyards to the remains of a once-fine house among castle ruins. The car stopped in front of what had been the grand entrance. A chauffeur stood by the car as the passengers got out. There were three of them—a tall man almost sixty, a woman in her forties and an elegant silver-haired woman in her eighties. The three spent more than an hour walking around the abandonded house, spending time in the castle cemetery, and surveying the property. After making some notations in a notebook, they re-entered the car and drove away.

Several hours later the same car traveled along the north shore of Lake Balaton and turned into the gravel driveway of a faded green villa, now a hotel. The three passengers once again exited the limousine. They had come home. They were András, his sister Gabriele and their mother Klára. The chauffeur offered his arm to the Countess von Házy and led her up the stairs to the hotel's entrance. The *proprietor* of the hotel greeted her, opening wide the front doors.

Klára and her son and daughter stayed at the villa for several days. Together the trio walked the grounds, evaluated the vineyards and visited the old dilapidated cottages on the hilltop. Both Klára and András were filled with memories of their lives at Lake Balaton so long ago. On their way back down the hill they stopped by the pond and wondered if *the car* had been discovered. One afternoon they took a boat to see the old von Házy Villa on Tihany, also turned into a hotel. András and Klára immensely enjoyed introducing Gabriele to their beloved Lake Balaton.

—⁂—

And then, finally, it was time to leave the lake and return to Budapest. As the car entered the Castle Hill area of Buda, they were amazed at the reconstruction and renovation projects taking place. They found the same renaissance throughout Buda and Pest, once again connected by the Chain Bridge, reconstructed to its original grandeur. An obvious effort was under way to recreate the glory and beauty of Budapest, *Pearl of the Danube*.

At last the limousine entered Andrássy Avenue where the old sycamore trees stood beautifully in full leaf. Many grand mansions still proudly lined both sides of the avenue, although some of the houses were in dire need of attention to bring back their splendor. Klára and András sighed with relief when in the distance above the trees they caught sight of their home's campanile. *Our house still stands!* As soon as the car pulled into the drive, Klára and her family got out and eagerly climbed the stairs.

Milán Nagy, the family's solicitor, stood at the open door to welcome them home. Earlier a von Esté family representative had presented official deeds laying claim to their Andrássy house, as well as the von Házy property around the corner. Klára and András entered the great reception hall with shared feelings of elation, relief, and sadness. A familiarity still existed for them, but the lack of tapestries and furnishings and the severely damaged Mucha window created a strangeness that momentarily overwhelmed them.

Followed by András and Gabriele, Klára turned from the hall and walked around her house from room to room, finding each one empty of the furnishings that had once graced the interior with unique beauty and history. Lastly, she entered her father's library. The sight of it startled her. His desk, too heavy and cumbersome to move, still stood in the room, but the chairs, tables, lamps, globe and all the books the family had left behind were gone.

Next the three went into the conservatory where they found a shambles of broken glass and pavers, overgrown and long-dead plants. From there they walked down the hall toward the kitchen, stopping for a moment at the little apartment where Klára had lived during those last days in Budapest. She opened the door and walked inside. Some scattered furnishings remained; she opened the bedroom door and gasped to see her bed still standing in a shaft of bright sunlight streaming through the garden door. Tears came to her eyes; she bit her lip as memories of her beloved Dolf filled her heart. She lingered for a moment, then left the room, closing the door behind her. Klára and her children continued into the kitchen to happily discover Silva's great oak table still standing in the center of the room. Klára sat down on the bench beside the table and closed her eyes. She could imagine hearing Silva's wonderful, laughing voice and remember the taste of her delicious *ishler* and then Klára imagined her dear Tamás sitting across from her. *Oh, how I miss them...all of them.*

András took his sister, Gabriele, who had never been in the house, on a tour of the hidden staircases, from the cellar all the way up to the open campanile. They stood in the warm summer air and surveyed the city. He pointed out all the sights, including their father's house—the von Házy mansion—just to the side of their own terribly overgrown garden. They made their way back down the stairs to the *secret* kitchen door where they burst in on Klára still sitting at the kitchen table.

Klára wanted András and Gabriele to accompany her on an exploration of the cellar, in particular, the wine cellar. Once inside the cellar, Klára pointed out to András the hidden entrance into the wall and instructed him how to open it. It took a moment for András to find the latch, but with some effort he opened the panel that allowed them to look into the dark, cave-like room within the foundations of the great house. The beam of his flashlight scanned across vases, carpets, paintings, books and stacked boxes. Klára pointed to one corner where a dust-covered object leaned against the wall. She asked András to bring it out of the darkness.

The three left the cellar with the object. András and Gabriele carried it to the dining room, laid it on the floor and unwrapped it to reveal the large sepia photograph of their family. Klára pointed out the various members to her children—their father, the blurred figure in the corner next to another boy, their uncle Stefan. She indicated Leopold and then smiled at András, who now with streaks of silver in his hair, looked even more like his grandfather. Seeing the image again brought a deep contented sigh from Klára, "I hope to have it back in its frame and hanging on the wall as soon as possible."

At that moment Milán Nagy entered the dining room followed by a group of people who he introduced to the family as their new temporary cooks, maids, gardeners and butler. Nagy also announced that painters would begin arriving that afternoon; furnishings and other household goods to come within the week. In the meantime, he had arranged for Klára and her children to live at the Corinthia Grand Hotel Royal on Erzsébet körut until the von Esté house could be made ready for reoccupation by the family.

—⁄∕∖∖—

The following day Klára waited anxiously in the hotel's atrium restaurant for the arrival of her dear friend, Rózsa Szabó. Klára had just turned eighty-two and Rózsa would turn the same in September. Klára wondered if she would recognize Rózsa or if Rózsa would recognize her. After all, it had been forty-seven years since they had parted on that Lake Balaton hilltop. Over the years they shared their lives through letters, but in those Soviet years letters were slow and at times never arrived at all.

Klára recognized Rózsa as soon as she entered the restaurant; even though Rózsa's red hair had turned as white as her own. The two women embraced each other warmly and studied each other's faces for a long moment before taking their seats at the table. Over cups of tea and Diós Torta they spent the next three hours remembering the past and discovering the present.

Years ago Rózsa had written...

We left Lake Balaton that day with a mix of sadness... leaving all of you behind. Two of Vadas's men went with us, all the way to Eger, and stayed for several months. We had such hopeful hearts our József would be waiting for us there. Pál and I and the girls moved back into our home and began our wait for his return. We also waited for Pál's family to come back from the Ukraine.

Even now as Klára sat across from Rózsa, after all these years, Rózsa had such a wistful look as she dabbed at her eyes with a handkerchief, "I had such belief that József would come home, but he never came."

Klára knew that in the early years after the war, Pál had reopened the sawmill and had gotten the barrel business going again. Life progressed somewhat normally while they continued to wait. After a year had passed only Pál's brother returned, the unmarried one, but Pál's parents and the rest of his family decided to stay with relatives in the Ukraine.

Rózsa began to speak again, but her voice trembled so badly Klára reached out to hold her hand, encouraging her to continue. "Things seemed normal for a while, but within a short time we felt the strong hand of the Soviets. The government changed and our family as all others in Hungary began a life of little freedom. Our sawmill and barrel-making businesses were no longer our own, but a kind of co-operative, community business—unprofitable and inefficient. By then, of course, it was too late to think about leaving for Palestine...uh, Israel. We were forbidden to leave Hungary.

"Even so with all our hardships, we were convinced that life for us in the country was far less difficult than in the city. At least we had our small gardens and basic necessities for survival," Rózsa managed a smile, a familiar smile, as she took a deep breath. "Now, Klára, tell me of your life."

From letters long ago, Rózsa already knew that the von Estés left Lake Balaton soon after her family had left the lake. The von Estés left Hungary for Switzerland where they settled near the von Schraders and had a baby daughter they named Gabriele in honor of Dolf's mother. They spent the next ten years re-establishing their wine business. In 1955, after Austria regained independence, Klára and Dolf, along with their children, and Elizabeth, Tamás, Silva, and Ana, moved back to the von Házy's manor house in Eisenstadt. From Eisenstadt their businesses in viticulture and salt became quite successful.

"After university András married a lovely girl, Alise," Klára told Rózsa, "they have four children, three boys and a girl. The oldest two are married and have children, my great-grandchildren. Gabriele married a charming young man, Johann. They were married for almost twenty years when he was killed in a terrible skiing accident. Gabriele has three children, two in university. And what of your children, dear Vera and Sárika? Tell me about your children, Rózsa."

"All our children are married and have children of their own—Vera and Sári, and our son Mihály, and another daughter, Borbála. I have eleven grandchildren and five great-grandchildren, every one of them lives near me in Eger."

"My Gabriele plans to move with me to Budapest to share the Andrássy house. For the moment András and Alise will stay in Eisenstadt, but plan to relocate to Budapest within the year, as soon as András can move into Papa's office on Hercegprimás Street. András has done a very good job with our wine business. He also plans to renovate the Lake Balaton villa and re-establish the vineyards there."

Klára sat quietly in thought for a moment and then spoke again, "During Hungary's national uprising against the Soviets, in 1956, Dolf came to Budapest to participate in the rebellion, but while here in the city the Soviets arrested him as a British spy. I heard nothing of him for twelve years."

"Count von Házy came to Eger one day during the Uprising," Rózsa interjected hesitantly, "a great surprise for us. He showed us pictures of your family. He told us that he would come again, but he never did. We never saw him again."

"Quite unexpectedly, in 1968, Dolf was part of an exchange of prisoners between the East and the West," Klára's expression changed as she spoke, "My beloved Dolf returned to Eisenstadt at last. By then at sixty-five years of age his health was broken, but not his robust spirit. We felt blessed to have him with us for another ten glorious years."

The two old ladies leaned forward to grasp each others' hands for comfort and support.

"We lost our Pál only a year ago to cancer," Rózsa shook her head in sorrow. "He was so happy to live long enough to see the end of Soviet rule!

Finally, we felt, we could breath freely again!" Rózsa proudly added, "The entire time Hungary struggled under the Soviets, Pál worked with an underground communication system using espionage skills he learned from the count."

"Tell me about your mother and Eszter," implored Klára.

"Mother passed away in 1963, but she and Abram made it all the way to Palestine and lived with Eszter and her family. Abram and Stefania's husband were both active Zionists in the wars before Israel became a state in 1948. Stefania had four children; one of her sons was killed in the Six-Day War. She and her husband have five grandchildren. Her husband is still active in the Israeli government and Abram is retired from the Israeli army. Samuel and Rachael eventually ended up in America...in Philadelphia."

Klára took a deep breath, "Amazing...amazing to think of a part of our family so far away—a child we never met and now she's a grandmother.

"Stefan lives on," Klára sighed. "My dear mother was my constant companion until her death in 1974. Our beloved Tamás died a few days before his ninetieth birthday. Silva died just last year, we never knew her age, but she was a delight to her very last breath. Tamás and Silva were part of our family through those many years. I miss them terribly still."

The two old friends agreed to see each other often. Klára invited Rózsa to spend a long holiday at the Lake Balaton villa in July.

—⚬—

After Rózsa left the hotel, Klára asked her chauffeur to take her on a drive around the city. "Please turn onto Hercegprímás Street and drive to the von Esté Fine Wine Company."

As the car pulled in front of the building, Klára's heart beat faster. Workmen had just finished sandblasting the façade and the stones glistened in the afternoon sunlight. She remembered from years ago Dolf's description of the building's destruction that he had seen on his last visit to Budapest. He had told her about the destroyed Atlas figures, how they had lain in huge chunks on the sidewalk. Now she could see those restored sculptures—the colossal, crouched Atlas figures—once again in their places holding up the cornice. She also noticed that András had replaced the brass plaque Tamás had saved from the rubble long ago.

"I want to go into the building," Klára told her chauffeur. He helped her up the stairs into the ground floor where he asked the workman polishing the brass stair railings if they could go up in the elevator. One of the workmen happily entered the cage, ushered them in and asked what floor they desired.

"The third, please," Klára answered and closed her eyes—it was as if old Zol stood once again in the gilded cage.

When the door parted on the third floor, Klára walked to her father's old office. Again there were workmen repairing the plaster ceiling, the wood paneling and the window sills. "Don't stop your work," she told them, "I'm only here to look around."

Like in the Andrássy house, Papa's desk still stood in the room, obviously damaged, even by fire, but still there, in a different place, but still there. Klára breathed in deeply, remembering her father's handsome face... *he had such joy in this place and in the people who worked for him. I still miss him so*, thought Klára.

Klára walked over to one of the tall windows and peered out onto the street below, as her Papa had done so many times. The window was open and she leaned out just a bit to breathe in the aromas of her beloved Budapest and then she heard the Gypsy music drifting up from the sidewalk below. She lifted her hand, waved and smiled at the concertina player. Klára closed her eyes. It was good... her return to Budapest.

CHRONOLOGY OF PRINCIPAL CHARACTERS AND EVENTS

Fictional Characters in Italic

1848 Franz József becomes Emperor of the Austrian Empire

1859 *Eugenia is born*

1867 Austro-Hungarian compromise establishes the Dual Monarchy

1872 *Tamás is born*

1873 Buda and Pest are united to create the city of Budapest

1874 *Leopold is born; Christián is born*

1886 *Christián's accident*

1896 Hungary celebrates one thousand years of history

1897 *Leopold and Tamás go to Paris; they meet Jakov Klein*

1898 Empress Elizabeth of Austria is assassinated

1899 *Leopold marries Cili; Christián marries Gabriele*

1900 *Leopold builds a villa at Lake Balaton*

1901 *Stefan is born*

1903 *Leopold and Tamás go to America; Rudolf is born*

1907 *Leopold marries Elizabeth and builds a new mansion in Budapest*

1910 *Klára is born; Tamás marries Silva; Rózsa is born*

1914 Archduke Ferdinand is assassinated; the Great War begins
Rudolf is injured

1916   Emperor Franz József dies; Karl becomes the new monarch

1918   The war ends; King Karl is forced to renounce his titles

1919   *Rudolf goes to Prague*

1920   Miklós Horthy becomes Regent; Treaty of Trianon,
Hungary loses much of its territory; anti-Semetic laws enacted

1921   Karl attempts to reclaim his throne; Battle of Budaörs
Eszter emigrates to Palestine

1924   *Rudolf goes to Paris*

1929   *Rózsa marries Pál*

1930   *Klára goes to Cologne*

1932   *Klára marries Franz; Franz joins the Nazi Party*

1933   Adolf Hitler becomes Chancellor of Germany
András is born; the von Werner family moves to Berlin

1935   Germany passes anti-Semetic laws

1936   Hungary also enacts anti-Semetic laws

1938   Germany annexes Austria
Rudolf returns to Budapest

1939   Germany invades Poland; World War II begins
Klára leaves Berlin

1940   Hungary joins the Axis Powers

1944   Swedish diplomat Raoul Wallenberg comes to Budapest;
the seige of Budapest begins
Franz comes to Budapest; the secret of Stefan and Eszter is revealed

1945   Budapest falls to the Red Army; occupied by Soviet troops,
Hungary comes under Soviet domination
*The von Házy and von Esté families leave Hungary;
the Szabó family remains*

1956   An uprising against the communist government is crushed by
Soviet troops

1991   All Soviet troops leave Hungary

1992   *The Return to Budapest*

AUTHOR'S NOTE

This is a work of fiction; however, the story of the three families—the von Estés, the von Házys, and the Kleins—is set in real places, among real events, and interwoven with appearances by real people. Members of the ruling Hapsburg dynasty of the Austro-Hungarian Empire—Emperor Franz József, Empress Elizabeth (Sisi) and her companion Countess Sztaray, Archduke Ferdinand, King Karl and Queen Zita—are all real persons, as are the two assassins, Luccheni and Princip. More information on the Hapsburgs can be found in *Kings and Queens of Hungary/Princes of Transylvania*, by István Gombás and on the Battle of Budaörs in *Imperial Twilight: The Story of Karl and Zita of Hungary*, by Bertita Harding.

The battles of Mount San Michele and Lutsk actually occurred during the Great War, World War I. A valuable source for much of this information was *The First World War: A Complete History*, by Gilbert Martin.

Regent Miklós Horthy and all prime ministers mentioned are real persons, as are other Hungarian figures such as Count István Széchenyi, Ferenc Deák, János Mikes, Colonel Antal Lehár, Count Gyula Ándrássy, Count József Cziráky, Pál Hegedüs, Stefan Rákovszky, Prince Ferenc Esterhazy, Dr. József Vass, and General Gömbös.

Good overviews of European politics and events during the period addressed in this novel, from the waning years of the Austro-Hungarian Empire through mid-1945, are *Europe Since 1815*, by Gordon A. Craig, *Great Problems in European Civilization*, by Kenneth M. Seaton and Henry R. Winkler. *A Concise History of Hungary*, by Miklós Molnár, *A History of Hungary*, by Peter F. Sugar and others, *A Brief History of Hungary*, by István Lázár, *Hungary*, by Steve Fallon and Neal Bedford, *Germany*, by Joanna Egert-Romanowska and Malgorzata Omilanowska, *Austria*, by Teresa Czerniewicz-Umer and others, *Budapest*, by Barbara and Thadeusz Olszánska, and *Paris*, by Teresa Fisher.

Real persons connected to the Nazi Party in Germany, besides Hitler, are Heinrich Himmler, Reinhard Heydrich, Ernest Röhm, and Herman Göring. Other factual persons include Edmund Veesenmayer and Colonel Otto Skorzeny, S.S. officer Adolf Eichmann, Intelligence officer Wilhelm Canaris, who shared information with British agents, and his agents Colonel Metzger and von Kleist-Schmenzin. Newspaper editor Julius Streicher is also a real person. Valuable sources for information on these men, Hitler and his rise in Germany, and Nazi influence in Hungary are John Toland's *Adolf Hitler, Vols. I and II; Hitler's Speeches, 1922-1939, Vols. I and II*, Norman Baynes, ed.; and on-line sites—Spartacus Educational and DEGOB, The Holocaust in Hungary.

Resistance figures including Jan Kubiš and Josef Gabčik in Czechoslovakia and Countess Maria Maltzan in Berlin, Swedish diplomats Per Anger and Raoul Wallenberg in Budapest, Budapest policemen Batizfalvy and Molnár, and Baron Gabor Kemény and his wife Liesel are all factual persons. There are several interesting books on the resisters—*Women Heroes of World War II*, by Kathryn Atwood; *Righteous Gentile: The Story of Raoul Wallenberg, Missing Hero of the Holocaust*, by John Bierman; *Wallenberg: Missing Hero*, by Kati Marton; and *A Quiet Courage: Per Anger, Wallenberg's Co-Liberator of Hungarian Jews*, by Elizabeth R. Skoglund.

Artists mentioned in the text, including Hauszmann, Lotz, Mucha, Kandinsky, Švakinsky, Čapek, Kupka, Teige, Balanchine, Diaghilev, Picasso, Stein, Man Ray, Móholy-Nagy, Gropius, Schmidt, and van der Rohe are all real persons. The actual premier of Diaghilev's "Train Blue" was June 1924. Several books used as sources: *Mucha: The Triumph of Art Nouveau*, by Arthur Ellridge; *Art and Ideas*, by William Fleming; *Art Since 1900: Modernism, Antimodernism, Postmodernism*, by Hal Foster and others; *Gardner's Art Through the Ages*, by Fred S. Kleiner and others; and *Pablo Ruiz Picasso: A Biography*, by Patrick O'Brian, and *The Shock of the New*, by Robert Hughes.

ACKNOWLEDGMENTS

Thank you to all those who encouraged me from the beginning of this endeavor, especially my husband Robert of forty-four years and my daughters—Wendy, Jessie and Kate. Thank you to those who wrote extensive critiques and gave valuable suggestions—Betsey and John Owen, Judy Boreham, Tammy Reid, and Denae Veselits. Thank you to my group of readers who were so supportive—Janet Bordovsky, Eileen McCloskey, Clara Woods, Dee Anna Christiansen, Betsy Ward, Gretchen McDevitt, Judy Machiando, Virginia Berg, Barbara Grigsby, and my dear sons-in-law, Tim Shelton and Jim Fitzgerald. Also thanks to those who read the manuscript and shared their opinions—Kathy Bohus, who with her family escaped from Eastern Europe in 1968, and Rabbi Michael Goldstein.

Thank you to Sherrill Carlson, my editor, who so meticulously caught inconsistencies, asked great questions and made excellent suggestions. Sherrill made the long process a real working pleasure. Thank you to Jennifer Shontz for her creative eye that captured the feeling of the book with a beautiful design. Jennifer's sense of humor and artistic expertise made the work a pure delight. And thank you to dear friend Elizabeth Ward for her extraordinary cover design, truly a work of art.

Thank you to Michael McCloskey and San Juan Books for taking a chance on historical fiction; your encouragement and positive attitude were greatly appreciated.

Finally, deep gratitude for those cherished friends and family in Eastern Europe who shared their stories and inspired the spirit—sense of family, courage, integrity, loyalty, and importance of friendship—found in the novel's fictional characters. Especially our beloved Josef and Stefani and their amazing family—Andrea, Milan and Zdena, Peter and Éva, Vladimir and Betka, Miro and Viera, Michaela, Lucia, Sasha and Martin; Jan and Melinda, Veronika and Kristina; and my dear friends—Zelmira, Barbara, Zsofia, Gita, Katarina, Lucia, and Silva. Thank you all.

ABOUT THE AUTHOR

Barbara Filo lives in Spokane with her husband, Robert. They have three daughters—now adults—and are grandparents of four. Barbara spent more than twenty years as art historian at Whitworth University in Spokane where she led the British Isles Study Abroad Program for many years, spent a sabbatical at *Galeria mesta Bratislavy*, Slovakia, and is now Emeritus faculty.

Rick Singer Photography

MORE BOOKS FROM SAN JUAN PUBLISHING

The Light on the Island, by Helene Glidden, $16.95. A classic story of
a young girl growing up on Patos Island in the San Juan Archipelago.

Once Upon an Island, by David Conover, $17.95.
The adventures of a young couple who did buy their dream island.

The Sport Parent's Manual, by Tom Doyle, $8.95.
A coach shares the lessons he has learned over the years.

True Coaching, by Tom Doyle, $16.95. Practical strategies for coaches.

Gloria's Miracle, by Jerry Brewer, $21.95.
The story of a young girl who changed lives because of her courage and faith.

Living High: An Unconventional Autobiography, by June Burn, $17.95.
The freedom of an adventurous life in the 1920s, 30s, and 40s.

Areté Again, by Tobin Wilson, $16.95. Meditations on religious life.

The Secret Code of the Monks, by Rev. Otto A. Koltzenburg, $16.95.
A history of monastic life and contemplative mysticism.

and for children

Andrew Henry's Meadow, by Doris Burn, $12.95.
One boy and his dreams. Illustrated.

Springer's Journey, by Naomi Black and Virginia Heaven, $16.95.
An orphaned young whale finds her way home. Illustrated.

Available from your local bookseller
or from San Juan Publishing,
P.O. Box 923, Woodinville, WA 98072,
425-485-2813
www.sanjuanbooks.com